THE CAROUSEL
OF DESIRE

Eric-Emmanuel Schmitt

THE CAROUSEL
OF DESIRE

*Translated from the French
by Howard Curtis and Katherine Gregor*

Europa
editions

Europa Editions
214 West 29th Street
New York, N.Y. 10001
www.europaeditions.com
info@europaeditions.com

Copyright © 2013 by Editions Albin Michel
First Publication 2016 by Europa Editions

Translation by Howard Curtis and Katherine Gregor
Original title: *Les perroquets de la place d'Arezzo*
Translation copyright © 2016 by Europa Editions

Library of Congress Cataloging in Publication Data is available
ISBN 978-1-60945-346-6

Schmitt, Eric-Emmanuel
The Carousel of Desire

Book design by Emanuele Ragnisco
www.mekkanografici.com

Cover illustration: Katerina Belkina, *For Lempicka*

Prepress by Grafica Punto Print – Rome

Printed in the USA

CONTENTS

THE CAROUSEL
OF DESIRE

PART ONE
ANNUNCIATION

PRELUDE

Anyone coming to Place d'Arezzo for the first time would experience a sense of strangeness. In spite of the opulent Versailles-style stone and brick houses lining the round square, where the shady lawn, the rhododendrons, and the plane trees suggested a Nordic kind of vegetation, there was a hint of the tropics about the place. Not that there was anything exotic in the well-balanced façades, the tall windows with their small panes, the wrought-iron balconies, or the fancy attics rented out at astronomical prices; nor was there anything exotic in the often gray, mournful sky, or the clouds skimming the slate roofs.

Even if you turned your head, you wouldn't necessarily grasp what was going on. You had to know where to look.

Those walking their dogs were the first to sense it; following their bloodhounds as the latter excitedly crisscrossed the terrain, snouts to the ground, they would notice the waste matter strewn on the lawn, small, dark pieces of excrement ringed with white rot; then their eyes would climb the tree trunks and they would notice the curious natural constructions that darkened the branches; then the flutter of a colored wing, chatter piercing the foliage, strident cries accompanying the birds' colorful flight, and the onlookers would realize that Place d'Arezzo concealed a host of parrots and parakeets.

How could such animals from faraway lands—India, the Amazon, Africa—live in Brussels, how could they live free and healthy in spite of the dismal climate? And what were they doing here, in the heart of the city's most exclusive neighborhood?

"A woman leaves you because she no longer sees in you the qualities you never had."

Economist Zachary Bidermann smiled as he said this. He was amused by the fact that his young colleague, a distinguished intellectual educated at an elite college, should be as naïve as a teenager.

"When she met you, your wife thought she'd found the father of her future children, although you didn't want any. She assumed she'd have a similar place in your life to your studies, and then to your work, but that wasn't the case. She hoped your many contacts would give her access to people who would be useful to her career, even though in the world of politics and finance, men like to fuck female opera singers rather than listen to them." This time, in spite of his thirty-year-old colleague's desolate expression, he laughed. "It wasn't a marriage, it was a misunderstanding."

"Are all marriages a mistake?"

Zachary Bidermann stood up and walked around his desk, fiddling with his new black resin pen with its platinum ring, on which his initials glittered.

"Marriage is a contract, ideally between two clear-sighted people who know what they're committing themselves to. Alas, these days we're too easily deceived by feelings, and most people don't enter into marriage in a lucid state. They're blinded, confused by passion, tormented by pleasure if they've consummated the act, or devoured with impatience if they haven't. It's sick people who get married, my young Henry, hardly ever people in full possession of their intellectual capacities."

"What you're actually saying is that you should on no account be in love if you want a good marriage, is that it?"

"Our ancestors knew that. They arranged marriages coldly, because they knew how important it was to settle down."

"Not exactly romantic."

"There's nothing romantic about marriage, you silly boy! Impulse, madness, grandiloquence, sacrifice, martyrdom, murder, suicide—those are romantic. Building your life on all that is tantamount to erecting your house on quicksand."

Behind Zachary Bidermann, on Place d'Arezzo, parrots and parakeets broke out in a disapproving clamor. Annoyed by these cries, he closed the windows on the glorious spring morning.

Henry looked around the soberly luxurious room, with its designer furniture, its silk rugs with their abstract patterns, its sandy oak paneling—workmanship so fine you didn't notice it. On the east and west walls, two sketches by Matisse faced each other, portraits of a man and a woman watching Zachary Bidermann in the middle. Henry couldn't bring himself to ask the question that was gnawing at him.

Zachary Bidermann leaned over him, mockingly. "I can hear your mind speculating, Henry."

"I beg your pardon?"

"You're wondering about my marriage to Rose, but since you're a somewhat inhibited young man you don't dare bring it up."

"I—"

"Be honest. Am I wrong?"

"No."

Zachary Bidermann pulled out a stool and sat down familiarly next to Henry. "It's my third marriage. It's Rose's third too. Believe me, neither of us had any intention of getting it wrong." He slapped his thigh. "You only learn from your mistakes. This time it's a healthy marriage, a good marriage. We're a perfect match. I don't think Rose and I have any regrets."

Henry thought about what Zachary Bidermann had gained from marrying Rose: wealth. At the same time, he thought, Zachary Bidermann fulfilled Rose's social and political ambitions: she had become the companion of a high-ranking dignitary, the European commissioner for competition, who knew and entertained heads of state.

As if reading Henry's thoughts, Zachary Bidermann continued, "A conjugal union is an association with such serious consequences that the interested parties should be relieved of all responsibility, which ought instead to be entrusted to reliable, objective, competent people, genuine professionals. If there are casting directors for a movie, why shouldn't they exist for couples too?" He sighed, and raised his famous blue eyes to the lacquered ceiling. "These days, we mix everything up. The ideas of parlor maids have drowned us in sentimental slush." Keeping a cautious eye on his watch, and aware that this private interlude had lasted long enough, he concluded, "Basically, my dear Henry, I'm glad you're getting a divorce. You're leaving the darkness to step into the light. Welcome to the club of the clear-sighted."

Henry nodded. Far from considering these words offensive, he received them gratefully, trusting in Zachary Bidermann's sincerity. For all the latter's apparent sarcasm and penchant for paradox, he wasn't a cynic, he loved life, but loved it with a clear head; whenever an illusion came crashing to the ground, he felt genuine pleasure, the pleasure of a crusader for truth.

Zachary Bidermann checked the time and sat down again, overwhelmed with guilt: he had taken six minutes of his break to discuss private matters. Even though he enjoyed these breaks, five minutes into them he would grow impatient and annoyed at wasting his time.

It was six minutes after nine in the morning, in his town house on Place d'Arezzo, and he had already been working half a day; up since five, he had analyzed several files, written ten pages of summary, and mapped out his priorities with Henry. Endowed with an iron constitution that required little sleep, this giant gave off an energy that provoked universal wonder and had allowed him, as a trained economist, to reach the highest positions of power in Europe.

Realizing the conversation was over, Henry stood up and said goodbye to Zachary Bidermann, who was annotating a report, already unaware of his presence.

As soon as Henry had gone, the secretary, Madame Singer, took the opportunity to come in. Thin, with a military stiffness, wearing a tight navy blue pantsuit, she came and stood behind the desk, to the right of her boss, and waited motionless for him to notice her.

"Yes, Singer?"

She presented him with the signature book.

"Thank you, Singer."

He called her Singer, like a soldier addressing his companion at arms, because as far as he was concerned Singer wasn't a woman. She was so shapeless, there was no risk of her distracting him from his task by showing him an attractive bosom as she leaned forward, displaying legs he would ogle, wiggling buttocks he would want to fondle. Her short, matte-gray hair, her sagging features, the bitter line of her lips, her dull skin, the absence of perfume, everything turned Singer into a functional creature who had been following him from post to post for twenty years. Whenever he talked about her, Zachary Bidermann would say, "Singer is perfect!" That he was right was proved by the fact that Rose would frequently say that too.

As soon as he had completed his signature marathon, he asked about his appointments.

"You're seeing five people this morning," Singer announced. "Mr. Moretti from the European Central Bank, Mr. Karopoulos, chief of staff of the Greek finance minister, Mr. Lazarevich from Lazarevich Finances, Harry Palmer from the *Financial Times*, and Madame Klügger from the Hope Foundation."

"Very good. We'll give them each half an hour. The last one's the least important, so I'll be quicker with her. But, Singer, under no circumstances am I to be disturbed during a meeting. You'll wait for me to call you."

"Of course, monsieur."

He rehashed these instructions every day, and people, especially Madame Singer, took it as an expression of the respect the great man extended to his visitors.

For two hours, he would display his intellectual prowess to those who came to see him. He would listen, like a motionless crocodile lying in wait for his prey, then shake himself and ask a few questions before presenting his thoughts in a brilliant, well-argued way, uninterrupted by his visitors, partly because Zachary Bidermann spoke quickly and softly, and partly because they were all aware of their own intellectual inferiority. The meeting would always conclude in the same way: Zachary Bidermann would seize a blank piece of paper and scribble some names on it, as well as telephone numbers which he knew by heart and could write without hesitation. He was like a doctor issuing a prescription after hearing a list of symptoms and making his diagnosis.

At five minutes to eleven, once the fourth visitor had left, he was suddenly seized with an uncontrollable sense of anxiety. Could it be hunger? Unable to concentrate, he looked into the anteroom where Madame Singer officiated behind her desk and told her he was going to see his wife.

An elevator concealed behind a piece of Chinese lacquerware took him to the floor above.

"Darling, what a lovely surprise!" Rose said.

Actually, it was hardly a surprise, since Zachary Bidermann burst into Rose's private quarters every morning at eleven o'clock sharp for a light meal with her. But they liked to give each other the impression that it was a sudden whim.

"I'm sorry to bother you out of the blue like this."

Nobody, not even Rose, ever walked into Zachary Bidermann's office without calling first, but he could turn up anywhere whenever he wished. Rose would accommodate him, considering it part of her role as a loving wife to be available, in the full knowledge that in any case his visits "out of the blue" always took place at eleven o'clock.

She served him tea and set before him plates of croissants and various sweetmeats. They chatted as they ate them—he would seize hold of them and stuff them in his mouth, while she, out of concern for her waistline, would take several minutes to nibble at a date that she held between two fingers.

They talked about current events, such as the tense situation in the Middle East. Having studied political science, Rose was very interested in international relations, so they engaged in trenchant analyses that demonstrated how well-informed they were, each trying to surprise the other with a little-known detail, an unexpected comment. They loved their chats, because they could compete with one another without feeling that they were rivals.

They always kept to general topics, and never touched on private matters; they never spoke of Rose's children from her previous husbands, for example, or of Zachary's offspring from his previous wives. They chose instead to converse like two political science students, relieved of the burden of family problems and domestic hostilities. This couple, young in spite of being in their sixties, owed their good health to selective amnesia regarding their past marriages and the ensuing consequences.

As they were discussing the Gaza Strip, Zachary remarked on the flavor of a macaron. "This is quite a treat."

"Which one? The black one? It's with licorice."

"Where are they from?"

"Ladurée's in Paris."

"What about these wafers?"

"Merck's in Lille."

"And these chocolates?"

"You must be joking, darling! They're from Sprüngli's in Zurich."

"Your table is like a customs haul."

Rose chuckled. There was nothing more eclectic than her world. Whether it was food, wine, furniture, clothes, or flowers, she purchased only the very best and didn't worry about the cost. Her address book contained only the top recommendations: the best upholsterer, the best picture framer, the best floor layer, the best tax expert, the best masseur, the best dentist, the best cardiologist, the best urologist, the best travel agent, the best clairvoyant. Aware that these people might not stay at the top for very long, she frequently updated her list, a task that absorbed her deeply. A rational woman, Rose might appear superficial, but her devotion to such trivial questions was a serious one; the only daughter of a wealthy industrialist, she put as much care into keeping up her home as she did into dissecting the unemployment figures or the tensions between Israel and Palestine.

"Your fair is still the best I've ever known," he said, stroking her cheek.

She understood the meaning of this remark and, without a second's hesitation, came and sat on Zachary's lap. He held her, his eyes moist, his nose rubbing against hers, and she sensed his desire to make love.

She wiggled her bottom on her husband's thighs to arouse him even more. "You bad boy," she breathed.

He pressed his lips to hers and they kissed, their tongues mingling at length, hungrily, their kisses enriched by the taste of butter licorice.

He pulled away. "I have a meeting," he murmured.

"That's a pity . . . '

"Well, it won't hurt you to wait."

"I know," she whispered, eyes closed. "You'd better calm down in the elevator, Zachary, or your visitor might be embarrassed."

They laughed conspiratorially, and Zachary Bidermann left.

Rose stretched voluptuously. With Zachary, she had become young again, or rather, she was young for the first time, given that when she was actually young she'd been a well-behaved and overly reserved girl. Now, at the age of sixty, she finally had a body, a body Zachary adored, a body he had such an appetite for that he made love to it every day, sometimes more than once. She knew that at seven in the evening, he would come back from the Commission and throw himself on her. He might even be violent—she bore a few bruises and scars she considered the trophies of her own attractiveness. They might do it again tonight. How many of her female friends could say as much? Who among them was possessed so often, and so ardently? Her previous two husbands hadn't desired her like this. Neither of them. No, she'd never been so radiant. She had the sensual glow of a happy woman.

By the time he returned to his office, Zachary Bidermann was no longer so on edge, given that his stomach was now full, but his heart was still racing, and he felt strangely anxious. He picked up the internal phone. "Who's next, Singer?"

"Madame Klügger of the Hope Foundation."

"Tell her I can only give her ten minutes. At eleven twenty-five, the driver's taking me to the Commission."

"Very well, monsieur. I'll let her know."

Zachary Bidermann went to the window and saw, out there

on Place d'Arezzo, some parakeets chasing one another in the nearest tree, beating their wings. Two males were fighting over a female, who was refusing to make up her mind and, although pretending to be alarmed, seemed to be waiting for them to decide for her.

"Little bitch," he mumbled so that only he could hear.

"Madame Klügger," Singer's solemn voice announced behind him.

Zachary Bidermann turned to see a tall woman in a well-fitting black suit—it made her look like a widow—standing by the door as Singer closed it.

He looked her up and down, smiled with his eyes, and said in a grave tone, "Come closer."

The woman approached on her very high heels, her swaying hips erasing her previous image as a widow. Zachary Bidermann sighed. "Did they tell you? I only have seven minutes."

"That's up to you," she replied.

"If you know your job, seven minutes are good enough for me."

He sat down and unfastened his zipper. The pretend widow kneeled and, being a consummate professional, applied herself to him with skill.

Six minutes later, Zachary Bidermann let out an ecstatic groan, straightened his clothes, and gave her a grateful wink.

"Thank you."

"At your service."

"Madame Simone will sort out the details."

"It's as agreed."

He walked her to the door and, just to pull the wool over Singer's eyes, bade her a respectful farewell, then went back behind his desk and sat down. His anxiety, his tiredness, his cramp had all disappeared. He felt in good shape, ready to go on the attack. Phew! Now he'd be able to carry on with his day at the expected pace.

"Three minutes, I have three minutes left," he sang to a cheerful tune. "Three minutes before I have to go to Berlaymont."

He grabbed his personal mail from the table and started looking through it. After two invitations, he opened an envelope that looked different from the others, because it was pale yellow. Inside was a folded sheet with two sentences on it:

Just a note to tell you I love you. Signed: You know who.

He took his head in his hands. He was furious. What kind of idiot was sending him this? Which of his mistresses could have written such a stupid message? Sinéad? Virginie? Oxana? Carmen? Enough! He didn't want any long-term affairs! Women always ended up getting attached, developing "feelings," falling into that awful, stinking, sentimental soppiness you couldn't escape from.

He picked up a lighter and burned the paper.

"Hooray for wives and hooray for hookers! They're the only women who control themselves."

He had made love to her so well that she hated him.

His long, muscular body, his prominent buttocks and shoulders, his firm, mixed-race skin that smelled of ripe figs, his narrow waist, his powerful thighs, his slender yet strong hands, his pure neck with the invisible joints, everything attracted her, everything teased her, everything set her belly on fire. Faustina wanted to throw herself on him, stop him from resting, beat him.

"I don't suppose you're asleep, are you?" she muttered, exasperated. After a night like that, she should have been feeling intense satisfaction, instead of which she was shaking with rage. It was as if he had reduced her to an ulcerated mucous membrane, excited, tense, wanting more. Was it possible that drinking didn't quench your thirst, only made it worse?

How many times did I come?

She'd lost count of how often she'd climaxed. She and he had plunged into one another endlessly, overflowing with contagious excitement, yielding to sleep only briefly, not to recover but rather to prolong the ecstasy. Without knowing why, she thought of her mother, her respectable mother she wouldn't be telling about her exploits, her sad mother who had never known such pleasure. *Poor Ma . . .*

Rubbing her shins, Faustina thought of herself as a sinner and drew pride from the thought. Yes, last night she had been nothing but a body, a woman's body penetrated by a man, a body that had reached the heights several times, and was still filled with longing.

This bastard has turned me into a slut. She stole a tender, fleeting glance at the sleeping man.

Faustina didn't like shades of gray. Whether thinking about her contemporaries or about herself, she swung from one extreme to the other. Depending on the moment, a female friend would be labeled an "angel of self-sacrifice" or a "depraved monster of selfishness," and her mother was either her "beloved Mommy dearest" or "that heartless middle-class bitch I was assigned to by an accident of birth." As for men, they were deemed handsome, adorable, hateful, generous, stingy, thoughtful, offhand, honest, sly, so timid they wouldn't say boo to a goose, psychopaths, worthy of "spending the rest of my days with" or "putting out of my mind." She herself, in her own eyes, would waver between two positions: the pure intellectual devoted to culture, and the slut who wallows in her base instincts.

A balanced opinion would have bored her. What she enjoyed wasn't thought but lively thought. In other words, feeling . . . At every second of the day, her ideas were guided by her moods, and her words were triggered by her emotions.

She understood the world in conflicting terms and felt divided: whenever she neglected her books to take refuge in her lover's arms, she would leave one of her personalities for the other; her behavior did not complement the way she had behaved before, but rather denied it; she would change. Faustina saw herself as not so much balanced as double.

"Stop pretending to be asleep," she repeated.

He didn't react.

Leaning over to see his face, she noticed that none of his features was moving; worse, his long black eyelashes, thick and curved, which drove girls mad, were motionless.

She felt humiliated by this indifference.

I can't stand him anymore.

Of course, she knew she was lying to herself; what rubbed

her the wrong way was that he wasn't paying attention to her anymore; what exasperated her was to find that she was so dependent on him after one night.

Male chauvinist!

A deep sigh burst from her, a sigh that meant, *Lousy creep*, and at the same time, *I'm so happy to be a woman.*

She hesitated. Perhaps it was better not to break this moment . . . And yet she needed to do something, to intervene, no matter how, because the wait was torture. What was she waiting for anyway? For Monsieur to finish resting? To fall asleep herself? Through the drawn curtains, she could see that the sun was rising; in the distance, the parrots and parakeets out on the square were proclaiming the start of the day to late sleepers.

Studying her lover, she decided to kick him out of bed. Then she stopped herself. Would he know why she was attacking him? Did she even know herself?

As soon as he stirs, I'll throw him out.

Dany rolled onto his back and, without opening his eyes, his hands searched for her, found her, and pulled her to him with a purr.

Soothed as soon as his palms slid down to her hips, she slipped docilely alongside him, pressed her back against his muscular stomach, and growled in the same way.

There was no need for verbiage. A few caresses and quivers relit the spark of sensuality, and desire burned them up. She felt Dany's desire for her against her buttocks and waggled them to show her acceptance.

Without a word, eyes closed, they started to make love again.

Even though they were both exhausted, the silence and the blindness added the necessary spice to their lovemaking: not being able to see forced them to recognize each other through fingers, chest, skin, genitals—they were both renewing and remembering one another; by expressing themselves through heavy breathing and noises deep in the throat, they renounced humanity, reduced themselves to animals, bodies, organs that obeyed instinct.

After this exceptional bout of lovemaking, Faustina made up her mind: she would stay in bed all day.

Dany got up, full of energy. "No more lounging around. I have meetings at the Palais today."

Surprised, she saw him—he looked magnificent—grab his watch and gather his scattered clothes.

"You should go like that."

"What do you mean?"

"Naked."

He turned to her, smiled, and fastened the strap of his watch.

"Naked, with your watch on," she continued. "I'm sure you'd be a big hit."

"With the criminals?"

Taking advantage of the proximity, she put her arms around his neck. "With the female ones, that's for sure." She forced a kiss on his mouth. He gave in, amused, but it was obvious to her that he wanted to get dressed. Disconcerted, she didn't insist. She wished she could come up with an unpleasant remark, but couldn't think of one.

He went into the bathroom and turned on the water.

"You wear your watch in the shower?"

"First of all, my watch is waterproof. Secondly, it reminds me I'm about to enter a different area of my life: my work."

The area where I'm not, Faustina thought. She immediately regretted it. How stupid! The reaction of a sentimental idiot. Anyone would think it was the resentment of a jealous woman in love. But she wasn't jealous. She wasn't in love either.

We fucked, that's all. It was great. OK, it was amazing. But that's all.

She got up and watched him in the shower. She loved seeing men when they were wet, drops of water on their skin, rubbing their bodies; it was a private moment she stole from them. Just then, in fact, Dany was lathering his genitals, firmly and meticulously.

Seeing her watching him, he showed off. "You see, I take care of them."

"You'd better."

She pictured the next night she would be with him, and felt impatience pressing on her chest. She looked him up and down. "You're just sex on legs."

Flattered, he laughed. "Are you talking about me or yourself?"

She disliked his comment so much, she grimaced.

Already, Faustina was metamorphosing, abandoning the sensual woman who had given herself to this man for hours, thinking now that what had happened last night was his fault: she blamed him for the fact that she had behaved like some kind of sex-crazed bacchante. Of course, she hadn't been abused . . . but he had led her to perform acts she wouldn't have performed of her own volition.

Faustina moved away and thought of the tasks awaiting her. She had several novels to read—or at least the summaries. There were journalists to call. And a number of Parisian publishers. She had to look through her accounts.

Within a second, the literary publicist was reborn. Wrapped in her dressing gown, she hesitated. Should she start on her chores right away, or make them something to eat? A tray of steaming coffee, toast, creamy butter, jam, hard-boiled eggs: that might have been a bit too much like the awestruck woman in love, the clingy woman who wants the man to come back. *Let him sort himself out. He'll get a terrible espresso at the Palais de Justice, very black and very bitter. Too bad.* At the same time, she realized she was hungry herself, and that she'd love the delicious coffee she knew how to make. *Well, I'll make one for myself but not for him.* Dismissing her scruples, she busied herself in the kitchen and set the table, apparently unaware that she was laying it for two.

Dany appeared, fresh-looking in a silk suit, white shirt, and tie. "Mmm . . . smells good," he said. He looked approvingly at the mouthwatering spread on the table. "The perfect house-wife on top of everything else!"

"One more stupid comment, and you're out of here on an empty stomach."

He sat down and did full justice to her breakfast.

While he ate, she couldn't help staring at his fingers and putting herself in the place of everything he touched. She saw his mouth and became the croissant he was chewing, watched his Adam's apple swallowing and imagined herself as the coffee he was drinking.

Scared by her wild thoughts, she drew back in her chair and asked him about his work as a lawyer. He was happy to discuss it, especially the case of Mehdi Martin, the sex maniac who had made him famous, but he had talked about it so often he had nothing new to add.

How irritating he is! Apart from his skills in bed, there's nothing at all interesting about him. She felt reassured by this observation.

Dany looked at his watch. Thinking he might miss his first appointment, he darted to the door.

She gave a sigh of relief at the prospect of being rid of him, and decided to remain seated and calmly finish her breakfast.

"Shall we see each other again soon?" he said, coming back to give her a kiss.

"Oh, are we seeing each other again?" she replied, pulling away as she did so.

He was confused. "Well, yes . . . Don't you want to? I certainly want to."

"Really?"

"Don't you?"

"I don't know."

"Faustina, last night, you and me, it was . . . "

"It was what?

"It was incredible, stupendous, amazing, awesome."

"Oh, let's not exaggerate . . . " Her tone was stiff, like that of a modest office clerk whose talents are finally acknowledged.

He pressed his warm lips to hers and gave her a long, intrusive kiss. She trembled, realizing that she was losing control once again.

He tore himself away, breathless. "I'll call you later."

"All right," she whispered.

He left, slamming the door.

As soon as she was alone, Faustina switched on the radio. She knew how it would be with Dany: the same as with the others. They would see each other again, try to rekindle the magic of that first night, fail, then succeed, but only after a lot of exhausting weekends, and one day, they would stop seeing each other, using work as an excuse. How much longer would this go on? Two months? Three if it dragged on? *You know, my girl, you've just had the best. It's good now, but sometimes it'll be less good, and soon it'll be boring.*

She crossed the apartment and saw an envelope by the door. She picked it up and opened it. The unsigned letter contained a short message:

Just a note to tell you I love you. Signed: You know who.

She was shaken. It was like a sudden explosion. Leaning back against the wall, she cried, "What an idiot I am! He loves me and I'm stopping him from telling me. He loves me and I treat him like a dildo. My poor Dany, too bad for you you've wound up with a nutcase like me. Oh, Dany . . . "

And in a dumb show she would have found ridiculous a few minutes earlier, she got down on her knees, lifted the note to her lips, and kissed it passionately, several times.

T he two bodies lay together on their sides in the middle of the bed, as symmetrical as two forks in a silverware drawer.

She was asleep, he wasn't.

Lying there with his eyes open, soothed by the warmth emanating from Joséphine's body, Baptiste allowed his mind to drift from fantasy to fantasy.

Uncontrolled, he zigzagged between several worlds; at times, he knew perfectly well that he was at home, pressed up against his wife; at other times, he was walking up and down a beach of blinding sand, where menacing characters hid in the bushes, waiting to ambush him; and at other times still, he found himself in his office chair, writing the text he had to hand in . . . Like a car changing lanes, his mind transported him from one world to the other, sometimes by the water, sometimes suspended above the page he had to write, sometimes between the sheets; he moved between them so quickly that the landscapes lost their airtight boundaries: now his enemies were in the room, now Joséphine was tearing his article away and making fun of him.

Baptiste sat up. Shaking his head to dismiss these thoughts, he was annoyed that he had so many anxieties inside him: every day, all he had to do was lower his guard and fear would rear its ugly head.

Joséphine's soft contours, her high-set hips and delicate shoulders, rested on watered cotton. Her face expressed nothing and her long eyelashes were perfectly still. She must be enjoying the stage of sleep where you've stopped dreaming. So lucky . . .

Baptiste yawned.

He envied Joséphine's peace and quiet. Even though everyone who knew him saw him as a model of serenity, even though he thought he had achieved a balanced wisdom, his dreams always awakened stubborn demons, and anxiety filled his skull. Was his feigned calm nothing but appearance? Had he achieved merely superficial peace?

He extricated himself from the bed without disturbing Joséphine, looked down admiringly at her relaxed body, and felt pleased to be living with such a woman. Then he quickly washed, put on a pair of boxers and a shirt, and sat down at his desk. It might have verged on the ridiculous, but he was incapable of working when he was dirty or naked. Even though he had no one to obey, no boss to tell him what to do, and could work the hours that suited him, a gnawing necessity drove him to get washed and dressed, and sometimes even scented, before sitting down in his armchair like an employee clocking in at an office.

He switched on his computer and opened the file called *Fidelity*, which so far contained only three meager, uninspired, enigmatic sentences.

He was embarrassed by the topic, *Fidelity*, because it required merely a binary comment: either you were in favor of fidelity or you weren't. Sad, wasn't it? Either you supported the classic marriage vows, the religious and social ideology, in other words, the established order; or you challenged it in the name of freedom. Both thesis and antithesis were a prison. He couldn't find his own space between conformism and anti-conformism.

He turned to the square, where the chatter of tropical birds rang out. Did those feathered creatures ask themselves such questions?

To his bewilderment, Baptiste realized that he knew nothing about the behavior of parrots and parakeets. What did fidelity mean to animals? Did the male stick to one female or did he start relationships on impulse, according to chance or the seasons? Might there be a way of filling the pages with this information?

He started doing some research for a while, then gave up. Who cared? Whether or not fidelity was biological, animal behavior couldn't act as a model, since humans no longer lived in a natural world regulated by instinct.

Fidelity . . . He pushed back his chair. What about him? Was he faithful?

He'd become faithful. Even though, fifteen years earlier, he had declared to Joséphine that he would never respect such a stupid commandment, that he wouldn't castrate himself, and that he would remain free to satisfy his passing desires, he'd stopped having affairs. Joséphine was the only woman he kissed, the only woman he slept with, the only woman he made love to, and he was happy about it.

Why?

Because I'm lazy!

He burst out laughing, then remembered he had just quoted himself. In one of his plays, a character exclaimed, "Fifteen years! That's not love, that's laziness." During the performances, he had noticed with dismay that nobody found the line funny, except him—he hated noticing that kind of thing because, determined as he was to write for an audience, he had caught himself red-handed being selfish.

Yes, there was an element of laziness in his fidelity. Being a seducer required time and energy; as soon as he glimpsed the possibility of a flirtation with a woman, he was immediately aware of the enormous number of obligations involved: coming up with splendid turns of phrase, phoning, booking hotel rooms, devoting meals and outings to the mistress of the moment, making up plausible excuses for Joséphine; yes, you had to charm, coax, conceal, fantasize. What bothered him was not so much that lying was dishonest, but that it was tiring.

Why go to such lengths, and for what? A little fleeting pleasure. A convoluted affair that would end because he loved Joséphine and would never leave her. The truth was, he abstained because he'd lost the craving. It had been a long time since he'd last had the energy to alter his behavior because he liked the look of some gorgeous woman. He might fancy her briefly, but it would never lead to anything.

In all, he had cheated on Joséphine only three times. Three adulterous episodes, all concentrated in the first two years they were living together. In the ensuing thirteen years, he hadn't tried again. At the time, he'd been striving to show that he was superior to the choice he had made: monogamous by contract, the newlywed wanted to convince himself that he was still independent. No doubt because he'd kept the habits of his previous, very debauched lifestyle. Having now become the perfect husband, the only woman he touched was Joséphine.

He stretched until he shook. The twenty-year-old Baptiste wouldn't have wanted to meet the forty-year-old: he would have found him lackluster and conventional. On the other hand, the forty-year-old Baptiste would have explained to the twenty-year-old that he no longer needed to go to bed with the whole city because he, at least, was capable of creating something.

On his computer, after complex manoeuvres aimed at preventing all access, he opened the file containing his diary. In these secret pages, he liked to reflect on the basis of his vocation. Two clicks later, he found the relevant text:

I've had two existences in my life, one sexual, the other literary. However, both have served the selfsame purpose: to discover my contemporaries. Each time, I would embark on a novelistic exploration: a sexual one with my body, and a literary one with my pen.

My youthful existence was sexual. When I came of age, even though my ambition was to write, I would fail, barely able to get to the bottom of a page; in addition, when I reread myself, I found the results to be shallow. I would have started to believe that I ought to give up this vocation if a few promising bits of text here and there hadn't stopped me, and especially if I hadn't read À la recherche du temps perdu, *that successful book that encourages failed writers: in it, Marcel Proust presents a narrator who aspires to a literary career but doesn't achieve it, and yet everybody accepts the seven volumes of the book as a great work that finally came into being after all that fruitless trial and error.*

If I couldn't write, I used sexuality as a means of novelistic investigation. I would follow a woman whose eyes I'd liked; intrigued by a scarf or a handbag, I would start tailing a passing woman in order to discover her personality. I loved to wake up in a strange room, an artist's loft, a lawyer's apartment, and let my eyes wander over the accessories— photographs, books, posters, ornaments, furniture—that would draw out the story, and then imagine what I couldn't see, or ask questions over breakfast or during the days that followed.

I had a reputation as a heartbreaker, but a kind one. I must have been "kind" because I was interested in the women I picked up. I was also a "breaker" because I didn't want the relationship to last once I'd satisfied my curiosity. As for a "heart," I didn't have one. I was seduced, charmed, interested; but in love—never.

I didn't waste my time; firstly, because I had fun, got a lot of pleasure out of it, and—I hope—gave some as well, but mainly because I stored in my memory the details that now allow me to write.

The moment I met Joséphine, everything changed: I loved her, and I started writing. She revolutionized me. A new life began, my life as a writer and a husband. Nowadays, if I sometimes escape our apartment or our relationship, it's a function of our apartment and our relationship; it's here, at this desk, that I invent lives. If I flirt with women virtually, then as soon as I switch off my computer I join Joséphine and give her a kiss.

And Joséphine will read these novelistic escapades.

When it comes down to it, writing suits marriage.

Baptiste approved of the page he had typed two years earlier. And yet a kind of sadness colored his judgement. Was it not too irremediable? Would all the adventures he experienced from now on spring only from his mind? Would he never again be surprised by reality? By other people? By one person in particular?

Of course, he enjoyed some enviable advantages: the blossoming of his vocation, the germination of his talent, the fertility, the accolades, the repeated successes. Yet beneath all the gilding, wasn't something being stifled?

He decided to add a new paragraph to his text:

Success depresses me. Sometimes I miss the inconsistency, the energy, the fire, the impatience that led to it. In achievement lies concealed the bereavement of desire.

Overcome with nostalgia, he continued:

Must one choose between living and writing? In my own way, albeit without his genius, I am reproducing Proust's journey: to live and then to write. Why should the second activity banish the first? If I wasn't able to create while exploring the world through sexuality, what is stopping me, now that the artist is born, from picking up the torch again? I sometimes wonder if I haven't cleaned myself up too much, become too settled. I have put the unexpected, the imagination aside in order to dedicate myself, like a bureaucrat, to my work as a scribe.

He stopped, disappointed by what he sensed about himself between the lines. Ten minutes earlier, he had thought of himself as a happy man, and now he was allowing melancholy to spread through him like a cancer.

Resolutely, he closed his diary and returned to his chore, the article on *Fidelity*. As soon as the title appeared at the top of the page, he fled. *No, not today! Why did I accept this stupid project? An encyclopedia of love!*

He picked up the brush that was on his desk, not to brush his hair—which was short and thin—but to rub the palms of his hands and calm his anger.

He'd always refused commissions, and now an enthusiastic, skillful Parisian publisher had suggested he compile a subjective, personal encyclopedia all about love. The haphazard aspect of the task—articles organized alphabetically—had struck him as providing a respite from his novels and plays, which he always constructed with meticulous precision. *It'll give me a break*, he had thought presumptuously. And yet this damned book had proved to be really tough work! He found it hard not to have his usual plot and characters to carry him through; the absence of likable or dislikable people, and of a narrative structure, terrified Baptiste.

Joséphine came lightly toward him and leaned over his shoulders. "I'm so hungry I could eat a whole cow," she murmured into his ear.

It was her way of telling him she had enjoyed making love to him that morning.

"A cow or a bull?" he replied, pretending to be offended.

"Ooh, isn't Monsieur touchy!"

"I love you."

He spun around, grabbed hold of her, sat her down naked on his lap, and kissed her at length. Having not yet left the land of sleep and its sense of abandon, she collapsed in his arms, and her mouth offered no resistance.

After a kiss accompanied by much purring, she sprang to her feet. "Right, while you scribble away, I'll make us a substantial snack. OK?"

She left without waiting for an answer. Baptiste watched her walk away into the depths of the apartment, her slight figure unchanged after fifteen years, just as white as ever, a cross between those of a fairy and an elf, almost androgynous, which some considered too thin but he adored.

"Pâté, ham, sausage!" she shouted from the kitchen.

Joséphine always announced what they would do together, although with no intention of imposing it. She reigned naturally, never imagining that Baptiste might wish for a different kind of daily life. If anyone had demonstrated to her that she was being a tyrant, deciding the timetable, the meals, the decor, the invitations, the time and place of their holidays, she would have stared in disbelief. Living with an artist, she considered it her duty to save him from chaos, keep him away from all that was humdrum, organize his material life; besides, Baptiste had never raised the least objection.

He tried to focus on his new article. *Fidelity* . . . What if he were to write a poem about Joséphine? A poem in praise of a happy relationship that replaces and surpasses all others? A poem about passionate love . . .

He was interrupted by a coughing fit. No, the lyrical muse wasn't suited to his dry pen. He would get lost in the absurdity of hyperbole.

Idly, he grabbed the stack of envelopes in front of him. Apart from official mail, there were four fan letters to boost his ego.

The last envelope, which was eggshell yellow, looked different. Inside, there was a brief message:

Just a note to tell you I love you. Signed: You know who.

Baptiste examined both sides of the sheet, then reread the two sentences.

His heart began to throb, and he was overwhelmed with emotion: something was happening in his life.

His temples on fire, he felt like dancing around the table, shouting out loud, opening a bottle of whiskey, celebrating this dramatic turn of events.

Feverishly, he examined the envelope, trying to determine where it came from: it had been posted the day before, in the neighborhood. No other information.

Suddenly, he felt a chill: his eyes had just reread the handwritten address. It might have been his, but the letter wasn't for him. He had inadvertently opened Josephine's mail.

4

Who's a lovely boy, then?"

Ève was talking to the parakeet that had landed on her window. Plump in its yellow-green plumage, a little shy, the bird had delicate black lines that formed a mask around its beak and its dark eyes.

"Oh, look, you've put some makeup on. How lovely you are!"

The parakeet puffed out its throat, quivered, and danced from foot to foot, clearly sensitive to flattery. It had no idea that Ève would have paid the same compliment to a sparrow, a swallow, a butterfly, a ladybug, a stray tomcat, or any other creature that ventured onto the window boxes on her balcony, because Ève thought everything was lovely: Brussels, her neighborhood, her building, the square with its birds, her apartment, her furniture, her cat Barbouille, her various lovers.

She never saw life's unpleasant features. For instance, she hadn't noticed that there was no elevator in her building, or that the exotic birds were soiling Place d'Arezzo. Nor had she noticed that Barbouille was an unhinged, hysterical, tyrannical feline who tore the upholstery and stained the furniture with her urine when Ève was out—she would merely ask Mabel to clean up and regularly change the curtains, cushions, bed-spreads, and armchairs. Nor had she conceptualized the fact that what she called her love affairs could be given a more derogatory word: in fact, all the gentlemen who adored her were elderly, well-off, and gave her a lot of money . . . The thought that she might be a high-class prostitute never even crossed her mind. Once, though, when this reproach had reached her ears, she had tossed her splendid blonde curls in astonishment, concluded that the woman who had insulted her must be deeply unhappy, and almost felt sorry for an unfortunate creature so depressed as to make her odious and vulgar.

Ève couldn't fathom nastiness. And since anything that threw her had to be the result of nastiness, she would shrug, turn a deaf ear to criticism, and continue down her path of wonder. Why should she waste her time trying to know what couldn't be known? After all, she wasn't stupid!

The sun was warming the trees on the square and the birds were murmuring like gurgling water.

"What a lovely morning!"

She had made up her mind. To celebrate this lovely morning, she would go to the lovely market, then have lunch on a lovely café terrace with a lovely female friend.

Even though she shopped every day, Ève never ate at home, in keeping with two imperatives: the first was that an honest woman must fill her fridge and cupboards; the second was that an elegant woman must eat out, with a female friend at lunchtime, and in the company of a man in the evening. Even though these were mutually exclusive, Ève would have felt she had failed if she hadn't accomplished both these duties. This contradiction was fortunate for Mabel, her Filipino cleaning woman, who would end up taking away, just before its expiration date, the food Ève had bought and not used.

"Who shall I call?"

Throughout her life, no matter which city she had lived in, Ève had gathered a flock of female friends around her. What was a female friend? A lovely girl not quite as lovely as Ève, made up since dawn, fashionably dressed, not too taken up with work, delighted to go out, available at lunchtime even though she had the appetite of a sparrow, a kind of occasional sister with whom you could chat about clothes or boys. A notch above the female friend was the good female friend, the one you could have a drink with in the bar at around seven, all the while letting men try their luck. Above that, there was the great female friend, the one you could tell your romantic and sexual adventures in detail, the comforter who, at no matter what hour, would come and sleep over whenever your lovers hurt you, let you down, or deserted you. As for the best friend, that was a temporary model, the one you could tell absolutely everything for a moment, then never tell anything again.

The telephone rang. "Hello? Sandrine here. What are you up to?"

"I'm doing the housework," Ève replied, immediately moving three empty ashtrays.

"Shall we have lunch together?"

"I was just about to suggest that."

"At Bambou's?"

"Great! Bambou's at half past twelve. Big hug, darling."

"Big hug."

Overjoyed at having made a start on filling her schedule, Ève went to the bathroom, hoping Hubert Boulardin had finished his ablutions. "Are you ready, dear heart?"

"Come in, I'm doing up my tie."

"I'll wait."

She hated coming in on a man while he was getting ready, which was such a mundane, unerotic situation, a true passion killer. So she stuck to a rule: they had to wash and dress out of her sight. Perhaps unconsciously, in her eagerness to lend poetry to her life, she wanted to avoid seeing her more mature lovers in the cold light of day, while in her bedroom, with a few candles and lace curtains, she could imagine they were better-looking than they were.

Hubert, who was sixty, opened the door with an affable

expression on his face, cleanly shaven and dressed in a made-to-measure three-piece pin-striped suit.

"You look so handsome."

Flattered, he thanked her with a quick kiss.

She stepped into the marble bathroom, slipped off her silk dressing gown, and appeared naked before him. It took his breath away.

She looked down at her perfect, smooth, suntanned body, stuck her bottom out, and shoved her breasts forward. "Do you like my new polish?"

Overwhelmed, Hubert didn't understand what she was talking about.

Raising her right foot onto the tips of her toes, so as to show off her slender ankle and rounded calf, and arching her back even more, she pointed at her golden toenails. At that moment, she knew she was the replica of a pinup, the kind of fantastical Venus whose picture men used to display in their trucks or their lockers in the 1950s.

Hubert looked at the tiny mother-of-pearl marks on her flesh. "Very nice . . . original."

"So you like it?"

"Yes, I love it."

"I'm glad."

He tried to come closer. She immediately exclaimed in a husky, frustrated voice, "I'm so miserable! My breasts are far too large." She cupped them in her hands, her mouth curling into a sullen pout.

He almost fainted. "Your breasts are magnificent."

"No, they're too big, too round . . . "

Each adjective excited her lover even more.

" . . . too firm . . . " she went on, "too pointed . . . "

He was growing increasingly red.

"See, I look ridiculous," she insisted, turning to him.

"You're crazy! I must be seeing things!"

"You know, Hubert, I only like flat women. Totally flat. I'd have loved to look like that catwalk model . . . what's her name again? . . . Nora Slim."

She had deliberately mentioned the name of a certain professional anorexic, an elegant ghost with rings under her eyes and bones that showed through, loved only by a few teenage girls, fought over by fashion designers because they liked to create a stir, but repellent to men who considered women sexually tempting creatures.

As expected, Hubert protested. "What? That walking skeleton! Even if I were on a desert island, I wouldn't . . . You're a thousand times better than she is. It's absurd to think such nonsense. Why put yourself down? Look at these little love melons I'm so fond of . . . "

She let him caress her. When she sensed that he soon wouldn't be able to break free of her, she moaned, "Oh, darling, you're going to get me all hot and bothered, then abandon me and go to your board meeting."

He forced himself to stop.

She put her robe back on, heaved a sigh, and walked him to the door. "See you on Monday."

"See you on Monday," he echoed, appalled at the prospect of having to endure the company of his wife.

She had succeeded: he left relaxed but frustrated, filled with the urge to see her again.

Alone now in the bathroom, standing in front of the mirror, she felt the weight of her breasts with pride. The fact was, she adored them and was happy for men to be crazy about them. After a cold shower to tone her skin, she rubbed in expensive creams designed to firm up her flesh. For the time being, she didn't look her age—thirty-eight—but she was already considering cosmetic surgery and noting down the names and addresses of reputable doctors.

The telephone rang. Ève blushed with pleasure. Frequent calls were proof that she was loved.

"Hello, Ève, it's your Roudoudou," said a very deep voice.

"Hello, Philippe."

"Am I disturbing you?"

"I'm naked in front of the mirror, looking at my breasts."

"Bad girl, saying that to me, you know I love your breasts."

"You love them, really? I don't believe you . . . "

"And, naturally, I imagine you find fault with them."

"Oh, you know me . . . "

"I'm kissing your breasts now, kneading them with my hands. I'm really aroused . . . "

"Be careful, Roudoudou, don't get too excited. Your wife will arrive and wonder what's going on."

His voice grew hoarse, and he started breathing more quickly. "When can we all get together, your breasts, you, and me?"

"What a question! It's not up to me. I'm not the one who's married. I just sit here all day waiting, getting bored, getting all dried up."

She had to say this to Philippe Dentremont because he paid for the bulk of her lifestyle, the apartment, the car, the furniture. The head of an industrial empire, he had left Lyons for Brussels, moved to Avenue Molière with his wife and children, and found a home for his mistress a hundred yards away.

"Er . . . I can make it . . . at around six."

She already knew that, because they almost never met at any other time; she also knew she would agree, so she spiced up the game by exclaiming, "What about tonight?"

"Tonight?"

"Yes, tonight. I'd like nothing better than a long evening with you."

"Bad girl . . . "

"So tonight, then, my Roudoudou?"

"No, not tonight. It's my eldest son's birthday."

She was fully aware that Philippe's three children shared the strange characteristic of each having about ten birthdays a year;

not flagging up this absurdity, she got her own back in a differ-ent way, "Oh, yes, Quentin! The really handsome one . . . "

"A little shit who can't seem to do well at school!"

"Well, he has his father's looks, even if he didn't inherit his intelligence. That's already something . . . Especially as he's going to be a multimillionaire."

"Also thanks to his father! But that won't be for a while yet. I have no intention of stepping down."

"How old will he be tonight?"

"Seventeen, the idiot. So, your Roudoudou will come over at around six?"

"Let's meet at Bois d'Ébène first, you know, the furniture shop on Avenue Louise? I found the couch I wanted and you did promise."

"Of course, my sweetheart, I'll buy you your couch . . . except that—"

"It'll only take five minutes. And it's so close to home."

She assumed he would be so horny, he wouldn't argue about the price of the couch.

"All right."

"I'll make you some tea," she added in a honeyed voice.

"I don't give a shit about your tea! See you later!"

He hung up. Ève burst out laughing: she loved to hear men express their desire for her so fiercely.

What would she do tonight?

She looked in her diary. Nobody had as many season tick-ets to the theater, the opera, or concerts as she did. Judging by her schedule, anyone would have thought there was no woman in Brussels more in love with the arts. In truth, given that all her evenings were free—since Philippe had a family life—she often went out, just to substantiate her fidelity by telling him about the many shows she went to see in his absence. Of course, she did sometimes spend evenings with other men, but rarely, with a mixture of moderation and caution.

The telephone rang. She recognized the number and grimaced. "Yes?"

It was the real estate agency she was managing. They were asking if she could show a mansion to Rose Bidermann, her famous neighbor. Glad to add this acquaintance to her address book, she grunted a yes, just so that she could seem like an unpleasant boss.

Suddenly, her thoughts coalesced on a scene: she imagined the birthday of Philippe's eldest, Quentin.

"Seventeen! My God, he could be my son . . . "

She blushed. Last Monday, when she had passed him in the street, he hadn't looked at her as if she could have been his mother. Far from it. He had given her an indecent wink. The incident had upset her: firstly because Quentin wasn't aware of the intimate relationship between her and his father; secondly because she had seen Philippe in him, but a Philippe who was slimmer, lighter, purer, stronger, better toned, smoother; and finally because she saw in his eyes the same urgent appetite, the same hungry virility. For five seconds, she had felt like the woman par excellence, the absolute woman, the universal woman, the one all men lust after, whatever generation they belong to. This feeling had filled her with pride and she had breathed in vigorously. The young man had taken her emotion as a sign of consent and had followed her. She had loved the fact that he trailed her as far as her building, and that he had then stood gallantly on the square, his feet planted firmly on the ground, looking up at the façade, eager to find out which floor she lived on. And she hadn't hidden it from him, but had appeared at her window, pretending to feed the birds, acting as if she didn't see him, taking her time to breathe in the fresh air then, at the very last second, disappearing with the hint of a smile.

Ève noticed a letter under the door.

"Oh, look, what could that be?"

She was surprised, since she received very little mail: the address she generally gave out was that of her agency. Nobody except her gentlemen callers or her female friends ever sent her messages here.

She unsealed the canary-colored envelope.

Just a note to tell you I love you. Signed: You know who.

She immediately pressed the paper to her breasts.

"At last!"

She had no doubt that the sender was the very person she had been trying not to think about: Quentin, the son of her protector Philippe.

5

I want a dog."

"Now you're being pathetic."

Albane looked harshly at her mother Patricia, who lay slumped, or rather, sprawled on the couch, wrapped in an oversized robe, looking more like a heap of dirty laundry than a human form.

This morning, a cushion under her back, feet crossed over the armrest, hands on her belly, Patricia was rather enjoying complaining; she groused at just about everything, and wallowed in it. But glancing at Albane's young, tense, hostile body, she sensed the pent-up aggressiveness in it, and didn't insist.

For a minute, they listened to the parrots and parakeets cackling fiercely out on the square.

Patricia wished she could cry out that she missed tender loving care. Nobody caressed her anymore. Not a man, not even her daughter. On the pretext that, for some time now, she had been seeing boys, Albane shunned physical contact with her mother. Did one love banish another? . . . When your hormones change, do you also relinquish any filial urges? Where did it say that you can't think about your boyfriends and still kiss your mother on the cheek? Who'd written that rule?

Old age begins when people don't touch you anymore, Patricia decided. She shrugged. *No, that's an understatement. It's actually more serious than that: not only does nobody touch me anymore, nobody looks at me with love.*

"A dog . . . "

The word stuck in her throat. Yes, a dog would show her affection. A dog would love her unconditionally. A dog never stared at its mistress the way Albane looked her mother up and down.

"A dog's not going to make you more beautiful," Albane said.

"Nothing can make me more beautiful, my darling."

These words scared Albane, and brought relief to her mother. Albane protested irritably against this fatalism. "Beauty has nothing to do with youth."

"Only a young person would say that."

"Mom, I have friends whose mothers don't show their age."

Patricia perked up, delighted that she could contradict her daughter. "Listen to what you've just said. You're admitting that beauty is about being young, or giving the illusion of being young."

"I could list dozens of actresses who are forty-five and still turn on my male friends."

"That's their job, my darling. It's the professional activity of actresses to seduce. Don't be naïve. You sound just like your father. Every summer, he got upset that the champions of the Tour de France could pedal faster than him."

Albane turned crimson. With all the energy of her fifteen years, she hated the idea of giving up and needed to believe that she would be attractive her whole life. Although devoid of malice, Patricia enjoyed tormenting her by taking away her illusions.

"Mom, what color is your hair?"

"What? Come on, my darling, you know that."

"What color is your hair?"

"Auburn."

"Really?"

"It's always been auburn."

"Really?"

"And my hairdresser gets that auburn exactly right. She's finally discovered the right formula."

"Oh, really?" Albane grabbed a mirror from the chest of drawers and held it out to her mother. "You find me anything that's auburn on your head."

Offended, Patricia took the mirror with an authority that said to her daughter, *You'll see.* She held the mirror above her and thought at first there must be a mistake: limp, anemic white, gray and black hairs wound over her pale skin, their tips soiled with a kind of redness that looked more the result of a burn than of coloring. No, that minefield couldn't be her . . . She shook the mirror, as though that would reset it, then looked again. Nothing had changed. *When did I last go to Maryse's? It was recently, in November . . . It's April now, so it's been . . . Oh, my God, it's been six months!*

She lowered the mirror, discouraged, angry, seething with bad faith, still hoping that what she had just seen was incorrect.

At her side, her chin jutting triumphantly, her eyes cold, Albane was like a judge; no, worse, like the statue of a judge. "Mom, you're neglecting yourself."

Patricia nearly answered, "Since everybody else is neglecting me, why shouldn't I?" just to carry on complaining, but then retreated, aware that such a riposte would have been pointless, just words responding to words but doing nothing to alter the facts.

"What do you suggest I do, darling?"

The question threw Albane, who, expecting a denial, had been hoping for a yelling match and was preparing to trade insults.

"That's right," Patricia went on. "What should I do?"

Albane sat down and let out a sullen sigh. "Go to your hairdresser."

"I'll definitely go tomorrow."

"Then start a diet."

"All right."

"A real diet."

"I understand. How many pounds?"

"Start by losing twenty. Then we can tweak it."

"All right, my darling," Patricia said meekly. "What else?"

"Well, we'll go buy you some new clothes, avoiding baggy dresses that look like sails."

"Really? You'll come with me to the shops and help me choose?"

Patricia was begging for love like a child. The scene was taking an unpleasant turn: having become her mother's mother, Albane was forced to be kind even though she wanted to lash out.

"Yes, I'll help you. But lose some weight first."

Patricia nodded in agreement, and as her flesh rubbed her neck she realized she had a double chin.

Desolate, crushed, the two women listened to the parakeets on the square and wondered what those silly birds could possibly be talking about.

Patricia was drained. Now that she had capitulated to her daughter, she felt ready to give up on something else: what was the point of forcing herself to change? If time had already started destroying her body, didn't wisdom suggest she should just accept it? If not wisdom, then at least laziness. *It's horrible, how tempted I am to do nothing.*

"Why should I start doing all that?" she said aloud.

"You're joking, right?"

"There's nothing more trying than a diet. It's hard to break your habits. And what's the point anyway?"

"It's for your own sake."

"My sake? I don't give a damn. In fact, I choose not to give a damn."

"Are you serious? Neglecting yourself is like having no self-respect. Besides, you'll also be making the effort for me."

"Are you ashamed of me?"

Of course Albane was ashamed of her mother, but knew it would be too cruel to admit it.

"I'm not ashamed of you. But if you get a grip on yourself, I might actually be proud of you. All right?" Relaxing her jaw, Albane congratulated herself on her performance. Drunk on her success, she went on, "And this way, who knows, you might even meet a man."

The words triggered no reaction in Patricia.

Failing to decipher her impassive expression, Albane drove the point home. "But it's true! Why should your life be over?"

"My life?"

"Your romantic life . . . Your love life . . . "

She didn't dare add, "Your sex life," because she hated speaking crudely, and the only way she knew to speak about sex was crudely.

So that's my daughter's definition of happiness: clinging to a man! Patricia thought. *What conformity! What terrible lack of ambition! Tormenting yourself, tying yourself in knots, forcing yourself to make sacrifices, all in order to throw yourself into the arms of a man. Pitiful . . .*

But she merely muttered plaintively, "Oh, a man . . . at my age . . . "

Albane flared up, suddenly convinced she was right. "There are plenty of people who change their lives after the age of forty-five. You wouldn't be the first widow who remarries."

This time, Patricia gave her daughter a disapproving look.

Noticing it, Albane stammered, "Well, I don't mean you have to get married . . . The important thing is not to be on your own anymore, to be happy . . . "

Amazing . . . To think she plays at being a rebel, and assumes she's being original . . . Unless what she means about being happy is marrying her mother off so that she doesn't have to deal with her anymore. Yes, that must be it.

"Don't you have school this morning, darling?"

Albane hesitated, wondering if her mother was just putting on a veneer of friendliness in order to kick her out. But seeing her downcast expression, her victimlike humility, she dismissed her suspicions and admitted that she was going to be late. "See you later, Mom. I'm glad we had this chat."

"Me, too," Patricia replied in a faint voice. It had been quite a useful conversation.

Albane stood before her mother, squirming in embarrassment in her ballet shoes. Patricia realized she wanted to kiss her. *No way! First she lays into me and then she demands a kiss! Get lost!* Pretending to be despondent, she settled comfortably against the back of the couch and turned away from Albane to avoid any display of emotion.

"Hurry up, darling. Your old mom's going to think about how she can be young again."

Her eyes closed, her senses alert, Patricia waited until Albane had walked away, left the room, and slammed the apartment door.

Then she leaped off the couch, rushed to her bedroom, took out the dresses hanging in her wardrobe, and pushed away the armchair so that she could stand at the right distance from the stand-up mirror.

The mirror reflected the image of a person who had nothing whatsoever to do with her. This reflection told a different story than the one she was living. She might feel impetuous and impish, but what she saw was a solemn-looking middle-aged woman. Her body had changed volume, making her face much smaller. Even though she'd always had a short, round chin, in the past the regal manner in which she held her head used to guarantee a certain bearing; now, she had become so chunky that her jaw rested on a stump.

For a few seconds, she pummeled her stomach, waist, and chest with her hands, trying to mold them back into their old shape. But in vain. Only her breasts seemed more graceful, because they were rounder and softer. But who saw that, apart from her?

She went closer to the mirror, avoided looking at the disastrous state of her hair, and examined her skin. The texture struck her as looser and coarser, and there were red splotches on her cheeks. Yes, she looked like what she was, a depressed woman of forty-five who neglects herself.

A surprisingly virulent sigh escaped from her rib cage.

"What's the point?"

A sense of relief overwhelmed her. Yes, what was the point? Why not just accept this new Patricia? Why fight her, wage war on her with diets, deprivation, sport, constraints, until she disappeared? What if, instead, she were to welcome this stranger . . . After all, this Patricia was her . . .

She collapsed on the bed.

It's over! Enough of trying to please! Enough of grinning to get attention! Enough of being scared of turning into a whale! Enough of shopping for clothes and wondering what people will think of me! It's all over! I'm checking out of the love market. I claim back my life.

She gave a rippling little laugh. "What bliss!"

A minute earlier, she had felt desperate; now she was exultant.

She was free! Her decision had liberated her. She would no longer be the woman other people wanted her to be, or the woman her daughter wanted her to be, but the woman she was. Delighted, she got up and walked through her apartment like a queen. She grabbed a yogurt from the refrigerator, switched on the TV, and sat down in front of it, ready to stuff herself.

The first thing that came up on the screen was a long, repetitive, nagging commercial about a device intended to shrink your belly and help you acquire abs. Sporty American types, badly dubbed in French, appeared one after another to praise the merits of the device with fake enthusiasm.

What a charade!

The women all had orange complexions, and the men had skin the color of caramel. Their tan was like a uniform: they all looked alike.

Incredible how sport attacks your skin! Patricia thought. *As soon as human beings start messing about with weights and machines, their color starts to look weird.*

And the teeth! Bodybuilding had strange dental consequences: whenever they smiled—which was all the time—these sporty Californian types showed perfectly white canines, incisors, and molars, like a display in a prosthodontist's cabinet.

A new breed!

Patricia wasn't looking at ordinary men and women but at mutants. There was Jim the coach: had anyone ever seen a thorax like that, with muscles writhing like snakes beneath his tanned skin? Or what about Carrie, the journalist won over to this fabulous bum and tum device, who looked as bony as a hungry gazelle but still had a bosom and ass so firm and well-rounded they seemed ready to burst? Dipping her vanilla-covered finger into the bottom of the yogurt pot, Patricia concluded that aliens had already landed on Earth and, without arousing suspicion, had invaded the shopping channels.

The credit card payment details flashed up on the screen. Patricia felt a pang, but then calmed down. Once upon a time, she would have ordered this item to appease her conscience—giving her card number over the phone gave her the illusion that she had just done a session at the gym—and a little while later would have received the magical object, which would have joined its cousins, stacked up under her large bed; but today, she had broken her chains. Not only did she switch off the television without giving in to the sirens of market conformism, but she was about to eat the tiramisu she had been saving for her daughter.

Equipped with plate and spoon, her taste buds drunk on

the blend of cream, coffee and amaretto, she strolled about her apartment, singing to herself.

Leaning on the windowsill, she saw a figure down there in the middle of the square and quivered.

An almost naked man was tending to the lawn on Place d'Arezzo.

Nobody has the right to be that handsome.

Breaking off her nibbling, she stared at the gardener, his attire of shorts and hiking boots, his slim waist, his chiseled chest with its few well-placed hairs, his fleshy shoulders, his powerful thighs. *And that neck . . . so white . . . so pure.* The man had a straight neck that just begged to be kissed.

She blushed and bit her lip. Ever since that young man had been hired by the municipal council, he had been getting under her skin. Every day, she would search the street with her eyes, and as soon as he arrived with his tools, she would hide behind the blinds and watch him in secret. Inside her, everything would tense up when he appeared. The desire he aroused in her was overwhelming. She would start breathing heavily, and her body would spiral out of control. It made no sense! She had to go back to when she was thirteen to remember such a strong feeling—in those days, it was her cousin, Denis, a redhead with broad, milky-white arms, who had taken her breath away whenever she watched him playing tennis.

She had found out that the gardener's name was Hippolyte, a rare name befitting an exceptional individual. Every so often, in order to be near him, she would go down on the pretext that she had an errand to run. As she passed him, he would greet her cheerfully, which touched her so deeply that she struggled to stammer an elementary polite response, and then she would escape by walking faster. Several times, she had thought to take him a cold beer, but that seemed like a trial that was beyond her strength. She liked him so much that he completely disrupted her day: as soon as she sensed his presence, she would lose all composure.

He never changes . . . Nothing affects him . . . Oh, wait, he's not as tanned as he was last year . . .

She laughed at her own foolishness. Of course he would be less tanned. Winter had only just ended! Maybe it was only now that the weather had allowed him to take off his shirt. She looked at him languishingly: convinced that he had undressed for the first time this season, she was touched at the thought of all that white flesh, protected from the cold by woolen garments for so many months, being exposed to the sun's rays. The scene took on the sacred nature of an initiation. Hippolyte became an apprehensive virgin dedicating herself to a new life, while Patricia was the sun passing through the windows to strike that timid skin, and she was also the air enveloping his torso, tickling it, making it quiver.

Hippolyte tore out a dandelion, then stood up, his back arched, to examine it in the light.

Look at those buttocks!

She trembled, shocked at having uttered these words in her head.

A voice inside her insisted, *No, really, what beautiful buttocks! . . . Patricia! . . . It's true. Women look at men's buttocks. I can say it since I'm no longer in the market.*

She sighed contentedly: she had just acquired two qualities, audacity and immunity. From now on, she would express herself freely. Yes, she had the right to think anything she liked, since she was acting without self-interest. She didn't have to worry about seeming ridiculous anymore, because she was on the outside now, a mere spectator. Before, she'd had to display the restraint of a widow, the dignity of a bourgeoise woman who doesn't just give herself to the first little savage she encounters; worse, she'd had to conceal just how much Hippolyte fascinated her, or she would have exposed herself to being reminded—by others and especially by herself—that she couldn't expect to attract him, so alien to one another were they in terms of age, social class, and physical perfection. In other words, for as long as she had hoped to seduce him, her hunger for Hippolyte had made her ridiculous. But if she gave up on the idea, she could admire him to her heart's content and make any comments she liked. What a pleasure it was!

Grabbing his wheelbarrow and lifting it with a heave of his shoulders, Hippolyte plunged into the trees, a part of the square that was hidden from Patricia's sight.

She shrugged and went back to the kitchen. As she passed through the hallway, she noticed an envelope the color of fresh butter, looking odd among the bills Albane had placed on the table. She opened it and read the contents:

Just a note to tell you I love you. Signed: You know who.

She reread the message four times, then collapsed into the nearest wing chair.

"No! No!"

The letter horrified her.

"I don't want this anymore. I really don't."

Tears welled up in her eyes.

"Love is over for me! Over, you understand? Over! Do you hear me?"

She screamed.

She didn't know who had written her this note, or who she was talking to, but one thing she was certain of: never again would she open her door to love.

6

C ome on, kids, hurry up!"
Sitting behind the wheel of his SUV, François-Maxime de Couvigny leaned out of the window and turned his head to Number 6, where the front door was still open; others would have sounded their horn, but the young banker considered it somewhat vulgar to use his horn except in extreme situations.

Four blond children came out of the town house, hurtled down the front steps, and dived into the car. The three girls sat in the back, while the boy, although the youngest, heaved himself up next to his father with the pride of someone who, in spite of being seven, having long hair, a slight profile, and a very high-pitched voice, shared the status of being a male.

Séverine appeared in the white stone doorway, dressed all in beige, her hair held in place by a celadon band; with the sun on her face, she leaned against the door frame to watch her family leave.

"What about Mommy?" François-Maxime exclaimed.

The children immediately turned toward their mother and started making big, highly exaggerated gestures at her, as if shouting in sign language.

As he was about to pull out, François-Maxime de Couvigny noticed the gardener, bare-chested and in shorts, cleaning the lawn on Place d'Arezzo. The apparition made him frown and his eyes clouded over.

A high-pitched voice on his right interrupted him. "You're right to tell him off, Daddy."

"What?"

"It's not nice, Hippolyte is wrong."

François-Maxime looked at his son. "Who are you talking about, Guillaume?"

"Hippolyte the gardener over there! He shouldn't go around like that in a city. You should always wear clothes on the street. That's what Grandma said in Saint-Tropez this summer."

His eldest sister, Gwendoline, added her contribution from the backseat. "I seem to remember she said it when you wanted to go to the market in your swimming trunks."

Displeased, Guillaume turned on his sister. "She only had to tell me once, but some people behaved badly all summer."

"Well done, Guillaume," François-Maxime de Couvigny said. "It's good to understand the first time around."

Once again, he glanced at Hippolyte, who was displaying his chest and thighs in an unseemly manner, then shrugged, started the car, slowly passed the double-parked official limousine with black, reinforced windows into which Zachary Bidermann, one of the glories of the neighborhood, was disappearing, and drove up Avenue Molière.

"So, girls, what classes do you have today?"

In order of age, the girls replied by itemizing the subjects awaiting them.

François-Maxime de Couvigny barely listened to them, just enough to spur them on and relaunch their private discussions. With delight, he felt as much a spectator as an actor in the scene he was experiencing. In the rearview mirror, he watched his daughters, fair-skinned, with perfect teeth, dressed in a manner that suggested the family's affluence without proclaiming it too boldly; they spoke a fluid, elaborate language, made up of appropriate, carefully-chosen words, with impeccable syntax; even their pronunciation was careful, precise, proof of good upbringing. Above all, their physical resemblance was striking: although aged twelve, fourteen, and sixteen, they had the same shape face, the same brown hair, fine nose, long neck, and narrow body. They seemed to have come from the same mold, a demonstration of their solid lineage. In François-Maxime de Couvigny's opinion, nothing was more disturbing than dissimilar siblings. When that occurred, he either suspected weak genes or feared the mother had conceived these disparate individuals with several husbands. When you saw the Couvigny children, you knew their parents hadn't failed in their conjugal duties: they were an advertisement for marital fidelity. Only Guillaume had features different than those of his sisters, but that was all to the good, since he was a boy.

As he stopped at the red traffic light, an identical black SUV—the vehicle of the Ixelles upper middle classes—drew level with his, on his left.

"Oh, look, it's the Morin-Duponts!" Gwendoline exclaimed.

The Couvigny children called out to the Morin-Dupont children, another tribe with identical features, this one made up, in an exactly reverse symmetry, of three boys and a girl.

François-Maxime de Couvigny greeted the driver of the car, Pascaline Morin-Dupont. She responded with a gracious expression.

A quiver went down the back of François-Maxime's neck. She liked him and he knew it. His eyes glistened as he watched her, because he was eager to show her that he liked her too.

The result was that their pupils grew misty and they stared at each other a little too long, a little too intensely.

"It's green, Dad!" Guillaume cried as if this were a major occurrence.

François-Maxime's lips formed a disappointed smile for the benefit of Pascaline, a pout that meant: "What a shame it's not possible between us."

She agreed in her own way, by lowering her shoulders.

They drove off again.

Without saying a word, without the children noticing their complicity, François-Maxime de Couvigny and Pascaline Morin-Dupont had lived through a few delectable seconds, seconds in which a man and a woman admit they like each other but at the same time give up on the idea of an affair. They had just told each other that they were beautiful but would remain faithful.

The two cars took different directions. The Morin-Dupont children studied at the French lycée in Brussels, while the Couvignys attended École Decroly.

François-Maxime thought of his wife: how cute she'd looked earlier, leaning against the door frame, blinded by the sun. Cute and sad . . . Over the past few months, he had caught Séverine on several occasions when she was unaware of being watched, and noticed a morbid sadness, a kind of withdrawal into some unknown sorrow. Was it age? The fact that she was pushing forty? Maybe he should fork out for a gift . . . What if he bought her the marron glacé leather handbag over which she had gone into raptures on Saturday? He had wanted to buy it for her on the spot, but she had resisted, considering it ridiculous that her husband should grant her slightest whim. He had given in on that point, especially since the item cost as much as a piece of jewelry. Money was no object for either of them—she had inherited her wealth, while he had made his through his work—but they did judge prices in moral terms: was the cost exorbitant or not?

At the next red light, while Gwendoline was telling her younger sisters what she was learning in her drama class, a couple of young men in their thirties crossed the street, holding hands.

How ugly they look! How dare they go out on the street when they're so unpleasant-looking?

He looked at their muddy complexions, their flaccid figures, wide hips, short legs, bloated beer bellies beneath black T-shirts, the green and blue patterns on their arms, their earrings.

Look at those tattoos! And those rings in their ears and nostrils! Like cattle! Branded as if they belonged to a herd of cows! How wretched . . .

Obviously he himself, with his wiry body set off by his severe made-to-measure suits, that purebred body with its precise, economical movements, evoked another world, the world of high finance, of ice-cold predators who, even when they kill, remain refined and courteous.

And I don't understand the need to parade like that. Do we really have to know that those two sleep together? Why force other people to picture two sperm whales screwing? Have some pity!

He raised an eyebrow and gave a disapproving huff.

When he saw Guillaume looking at him questioningly, he realized that he had once again forgotten to accelerate as soon as the lights turned green—which, in the boy's eyes, constituted the yardstick of good manners—and reacted.

The car continued on its way at a senatorial speed until it reached the school.

François-Maxime got out of the car, kissed his children, wished them a good day, watched until they reached the main door, and waited, proud of his family, for them to disappear into the building. Then he got back in the car and drove faster to the Bois de Cambre.

He parked on Rue du Vert-Chasseur, at the edge of the forest, got out his sports bag, and strode enthusiastically across the cobbled courtyard of the Selle Royale riding center. He loved the impatient cacophony of neighing, swishing, snorting, the sound of horseshoes tapping on the ground; even though he generally liked only subtle scents, he couldn't get enough of the dark smell of dung, with its promise of the pleasures to come.

He greeted the overworked staff and went into a room that

served as a changing room, cloakroom, and storeroom. There, he got undressed, changed his socks, and put on his jockey pants, a polo shirt, and a pair of bespoke boots.

While François-Maxime was looking for a coat hanger for his suit, Edmond Platters, another rider, came into the room.

"Hello, François-Maxime."

"Hello, Edmond."

"You're so funny with your bachelor ways."

François-Maxime's shoulders quivered. Not only did he hate camaraderie, he detested any joke of which he was the butt.

Edmond continued his mockery. "Why this habit of changing your clothes? Can't you come here in riding gear like everybody else?"

"First of all, after I finish riding, I don't go back home but to my bank, where I work until eight in the evening."

He took care to clearly say "my" bank, because he knew that Edmond was often in financial difficulty. Then he turned and added, calmly, "Tell me, Edmond, when you go to the swimming pool, do you leave home in swimming trunks?"

Having been put in his place, Edmond grunted something and walked out.

François-Maxime finished carefully putting away his suit, shoes, and socks, annoyed at the fact that no sooner did men meet in a dressing room than they took the liberty of becoming familiar.

He was about to leave the room when he noticed that he had dropped the envelope he had picked up from his letterbox half an hour earlier. He slipped it in his pocket, promising himself that he would open it on his ride.

He walked to the looseboxes, paid his respects to the owner of the stables, then went to Bella, his bay mare. The stable boy had already groomed and saddled her, and was in the process of sliding in the bit. He patted the mare's nose. She had a slender head and broad shoulders. She closed her eyes as he caressed her.

Finally, he mounted her; the animal's high-set tail whipped the air, and they left the riding center.

At this time of day, there were few people tramping up and down the forest paths. An old lady was pulling a paralyzed poodle at the end of a leash. Farther on, a cheerful young Arab was walking some unleashed dogs, mutts he would collect from their owners in the morning and take out as a pack.

After riding past the tennis courts and bypassing the old racetrack, he took a path on which horses were allowed, then, leaving the Bois de Cambre, that part of the forest enclosed within the city, he plunged into the vast Forêt de Soignes itself and set off at a sitting gallop.

His thighs quivered against the mass of muscles. Giving his commands without shouting, in an even, almost low voice, he managed to forget himself in the saddle and merge with Bella.

At the crossroads, after glancing around to make sure nobody saw him, he left the riding track and followed a path strictly reserved for pedestrians.

After three sharp turns, he made his way into the trees and glimpsed the figures of solitary men walking around with their hands behind their backs.

He carried on straight ahead, then, some hundred yards from the first walkers, dismounted and tied his horse to a tree. He took five or six steps into the forest and leaned nonchalantly against the trunk of a squat oak.

A minute later, a young man of twenty in a white T-shirt appeared. His fists stuffed into the pocket of his jeans, he admired the horse, noticed its master, and approached, shifting his balance from one leg to the other, hesitating to cross the last few yards.

François-Maxime gave him a brooding look.

The young man hesitated shyly, unsure whether or not to continue. Then François-Maxime slid his fingers under his polo shirt, sensually caressed his chest, and lifted his face ecstatically to the sunbeam piercing the foliage, as if the young man wasn't there.

The young man froze, stared at François-Maxime with lust, wet his lips several times, checked that nobody was coming in their direction, and took the last few steps toward him.

Their pelvises came together. Then the young man grabbed François-Maxime's fly and opened it.

Without a word, content with sighs that expressed their level of satisfaction, each tended to the other's organ.

François-Maxime kept his eyes on the path. Whether he was the one who desired or the one who was desired, he loved the fear that came with the tension: not only was he indulging in forbidden love, he was doing so in the open air, which added the pleasure of transgression. Such a contrast with the cozy bedroom where he would go to Séverine for more predictable embraces! Here, there was the fresh air of nature, the smell of humus and heather and spring and game, and the possibility that an intruder might appear. There was also the risk of a forest warden suddenly bursting in on him. Or even a police officer. There was no knowing.

François-Maxime indicated with a groan and more rapid breathing that he was about to come. The young man understood and reached his climax at the same time.

Their excitement subsided.

A blackbird flew across the undergrowth.

Sensing her master's return, Bella gave a long neigh, impatient to stretch her legs. François-Maxime was jubilant: he was going to have a good day. The young man got up, rearranged his clothes, and smiled. François-Maxime responded with a benevolent look. Then the young man murmured, "My name's Nikkos."

François-Maxime closed his eyes for a second; he loathed that stupid compulsion men had to introduce themselves. What was pleasant in these fleeting exchanges was the furtiveness, the fact that bodies could exult far from the social comedy.

The young man was staring at him with large, beseeching eyes, waiting for a reply.

"I'm Maxence," François-Maxime murmured.

The young man received the name as if it were a precious gift. Nikkos grabbed François-Maxime's hand and whispered, shyly, "Goodbye, Maxence."

"Ciao!"

François-Maxime went to Bella, stroked her muzzle, untied her, got in the saddle, and rode away; he hated postcoital tenderness; that kind of cloying sentiment could retrospectively spoil the pleasure he had experienced. As far as feelings went, he had an ample supply of them at home, with Séverine and the children. So it was best not to get his wires crossed.

Once he and his horse were back on the paths where riders were allowed, he relaxed, forgot about what he'd just done, and, pressing his long legs to the animal's sides, thought about his work. He worked out a few plans and strategies for the current transactions, delighted with his mental clarity. He was sure he was going to have a splendid day.

The stiff corner of the envelope dug into his pelvis, and he realized he hadn't opened the letter he had received that morning. He unsealed it and read it.

Just a note to tell you I love you. Signed: You know who.

He gave a gentle laugh. "Ah, Séverine . . . " Smiling at the horizon, he declared out loud to the trees lining the paths, "I love you too, my darling!"

Delighted, he put the note in his pocket and decided that he would devote twenty minutes of his work time to going and buying the overpriced handbag she had seen on Avenue Louise. She deserved it, after all.

7

Two hundred and forty-two euros! Can you imagine? I gave him two hundred and forty-two euros up front to build my night table!"

Pulling on the thread of her tapestry, Mademoiselle Beauvert was only half-listening to Marcelle's recriminations; careful not to ruin her embroidered rose, she lent only a casual ear because, whatever happened, the concierge's prattling never veered away from two main lines: complaining or talking about money.

"I really need that night table, Mademoiselle! Because I changed my mattress. Because of my Afghan. Two hundred and forty-two euros I gave my son. Two hundred and forty-two euros, that's quite a lot for a few pieces of wood!" Marcelle shook then spanked the heavy velvet folds, punishing them for attracting dust. "Two hundred and forty-two euros in his hand, and now he tells me he has other things to do."

"What other things, my dear Marcelle?"

"Getting married!"

Furiously, Marcelle put the curtains back in their place against the wall. Then she crossed the room like an angry buffalo.

Deciphering what Marcelle had just told her, Mademoiselle Beauvert gave a start. "Your son's getting married?"

"Yes, and because of that, the young gentleman isn't doing odd jobs anymore. I can forget about my night table . . . And I've lost two hundred and forty-two euros."

She said, "Two hundred and forty-two euros", one more time, and disappeared into the kitchen.

Mademoiselle Beauvert wanted to follow her but decided not to, choosing instead to finish her pink rose petal, and above all to wait for Marcelle to get over her moaning.

Mademoiselle Beauvert raised her eyes to heaven. How did Marcelle organize her priorities? Putting two hundred and forty-two euros and a night table above her son's wedding—that was just being stubborn! She could only see things from her standpoint, a short, heavyset woman with a low forehead.

"Sergio! Sergio!"

"Yes, my darling, you're right," Mademoiselle Beauvert sighed.

"Sergio!" the voice insisted.

Mademoiselle Beauvert went over to the flame-red parrot, opened his cage, and put her arm in, inviting him to come out.

The bird gripped Mademoiselle Beauvert's ring finger with his eight digits, let her release him from his prison, and rubbed himself on her angora pullover.

"Sergio!"

She increased her caresses; the parrot seemed insatiable, wriggling as if every stroke increased his craving.

"Yes, *you* understand me, Copernicus!"

Copernicus danced from one leg to the other.

At that moment, Marcelle reappeared, her fleshy lower lip drooping, her eyes bulging, her neck drawn down into her stout bust, displaying all the grace of a pit bull. "Yes, believe it or not, the little bastard's getting married. And without even asking my opinion."

"Aren't you happy?"

"About what?"

"I don't know . . . that he's in love . . . that he's finally found the right woman . . . ?"

"Well, he certainly looked for her. But whether or not he's found her . . . "

"Don't you like her?"

"I don't know. He hasn't introduced her to me."

"What?"

"That's right. He doesn't want it to happen at my place. He wants it to happen outside."

In Mademoiselle Beauvert's opinion, the son was right. Better not scare the girl off by bringing her to the lodge where Marcelle lived. A storage room that smelled of leeks and cabbage soup; the decoration was nothing but a heap of frightful trinkets, wooden roosters, porcelain spaniels, fluffy kittens, post office calendars, Vosges barometers, Swiss cuckoo clocks; armchairs, chest of drawers, and tables were decked out in crocheted doilies; as for the cleanliness of the place, it left a lot to be desired, even though Marcelle cleaned other people's homes extremely well. Even if the bride came from a deprived background, she might still have taste.

"Sergio!" the parrot cried, Mademoiselle Beauvert having neglected him for a moment. She resumed stroking his hard skull.

Marcelle started polishing the TV set with great vigor. She gave it priority, considering it an important centerpiece in a home. "He's obsessed, your Copernicus, isn't he?"

"I beg your pardon?"

"He keeps repeating, 'Sergio.'"

"Copernicus isn't obsessed, he's telepathic," Mademoiselle Beauvert said huffily.

"Pardon me?"

"Telepathic."

Marcelle looked blank, unable to catch the name of what she assumed was a medical condition.

"Look!" Pleased to demonstrate, Mademoiselle Beauvert set Copernicus down on the perch next to the TV. "He senses what I'm thinking."

She walked away, sat in the armchair, ten feet away from

him, and leafed through a magazine, staring down at it but hiding it from him. After a few seconds, the bird cried, "Oh, what a nice car!"

Radiant, Mademoiselle Beauvert stood up and showed Marcelle the magazine: one of the pages had an advertisement for a sports convertible.

"Amazing," Marcelle grunted, looking at the parrot suspiciously.

"And now he's going to guess what I'm about to do."

She walked around the room, hesitated twice, then froze, struck by an idea. Immediately, the parrot chattered, "Telephone. Ring. Ring. Telephone."

Simultaneously, Mademoiselle Beauvert showed Marcelle that she was already holding her cell phone in her right hand.

Marcelle scowled. She didn't doubt the animal's accomplishments but found them suspect.

Mademoiselle Beauvert advanced triumphantly. "I've calculated that he knows four hundred words."

"Four hundred words! I'm not sure *I* know four hundred words."

Mademoiselle Beauvert gave a high-pitched laugh bordering on hysteria. "Linguists claim that three hundred words are enough to get by in a language."

Tight-jawed and grim-eyed, Marcelle looked at the parrot. "Get by? In that case, my Afghan knows fewer words than your parrot."

Delighted by the triumph of her pet, Mademoiselle Beauvert decided to indulge herself even more and tapped Marcelle's arm. "Marcelle, why do you say 'my Afghan?' Anyone would think you're talking about a dog."

"So? I love dogs too. I've had two. A Pekingese and a Bernese Mountain Dog. Unfortunately, they both died poisoned. Never had any luck with animals."

Mademoiselle Beauvert bowed her head, eager to conceal

from Marcelle the reason for those deaths: some of the building's tenants had been unable to stand those noisy, flea-ridden mutts, so they had put rat poison in some meatballs and given them to the two wretched gluttons. Dismissing this thought, she said, "I insist, Marcelle: you shouldn't say 'my Afghan.' The young man has a name."

"Ghuncha Gul."

"How's that?"

"Ghuncha Gul. His first name is Ghuncha Gul."

"Oh, dear . . . "

"I won't tell you his surname because I still can't pronounce it."

"Yes, it can't be easy . . . And does it mean something?"

"Ghuncha Gul?"

"These names that are so exotic to our Western ears often express unexpectedly beautiful and poetic things."

"Apparently, it means 'bunch of flowers.'"

Mademoiselle Beauvert looked at her openmouthed: it was hard to connect a bunch of flowers with the hairy, broad-chested, dark-eyed fellow who shared the concierge's bed.

Marcelle shrugged. "That's why I prefer to call him my Afghan."

The conversation being over, she went back into the kitchen.

Mademoiselle Beauvert withdrew into her shell. *Too bad for her. Marcelle doesn't deserve to know . . .*

After her telepathy demonstration with Copernicus, she had expected Marcelle to ask: "Since the parrot says Sergio forty times a day, who is Sergio?" Yes, a minute ago, she would have divulged her secret, because there are times when you feel like disclosing something you've been hiding forever, mysteries you've kept under wraps for the longest time because they define you, because they are part of your identity, because they allow you to assert: This is me. Fortunately, the circumstances had prevented her from revealing her private truth.

At that moment, Marcelle reappeared, head forward, fists clenched. "Who's Sergio?"

"I beg your pardon?"

"Your parrot there, the psychopath who can read your thoughts, keeps saying Sergio. Does it mean you think about Sergio all day long?"

Mademoiselle Beauvert stood up, blushing as if she had been caught in the arms of a scoundrel, walked forward a few steps, making her skirt whirl around her, sat back down, arranged a couple of folds, made sure her hair had kept the shape she had fixed with spray, then murmured, her eyes sparkling, "Sergio was my first love."

"No, really?" Marcelle came closer, her curiosity aroused. "How does he know that?"

"Who?"

"The parrot."

Mademoiselle Beauvert studied the tips of her pumps, comfortable in her own embarrassment, delighted with the attention Marcelle was paying her. "When I was given Copernicus, I taught him the word."

"Did Sergio give you Copernicus?"

"Good Lord, no. Copernicus arrived years later."

"Phew . . . I wouldn't have liked my lover to give me a parrot that kept repeating his name after he left me."

Mademoiselle Beauvert got on her high horse. "What are you talking about, Marcelle? Sergio didn't leave me."

"Oh, I'm sorry."

"He died."

"He died?"

"Yes, obviously! Sergio drowned in the sea off the coast of Cyprus. His sailboat sank."

"Was he alone?"

"Unfortunately, I was never able to share his passion for sailing, because I get seasick. And now I'm sorry. I would have preferred us to die together."

A thousand times, Mademoiselle Beauvert had pictured that moment: the two of them standing side by side on the deck, the fatal wave sweeping them away . . . She would imagine their two bodies, lost in the storm, clinging to one another, then, aware that they were going to die, kissing for a long time before sinking. This way, they would not have died from drowning, but from a long slow kiss.

Overwhelmed with regret, she blinked. Marcelle grabbed her wrist in her callous palms. "Don't cry, Mademoiselle."

Liberated by these words, Mademoiselle Beauvert let tears flood her face. It was such a delight to display this suffering in public, yes, a delight, for once, not to sit and sob in a corner on her own.

Marcelle was saying affectionate words to her, accompanying them with rough little slaps. She seemed embarrassed.

At last, Mademoiselle Beauvert took a deep breath, a sign that she was determined to pull herself together.

Marcelle sighed. "Such a shame you didn't have time to get married or have children."

"Oh . . . Would it really have been a good idea to produce orphans?"

"Funny," Marcelle said, trying to distract her. "I never think about my first love. I remember it well, but it's in the past."

"Not for me."

"What stops me from thinking about it is the ones that came after."

"What do you think, Marcelle, that I've only had one man in my life?"

"Well . . . yes . . . I mean, the parrot keeps repeating his name . . . "

"I've known some extraordinary men, many extraordinary men."

"Of course, Mademoiselle. You're so pretty, so classy, so well turned out, I have no doubt men must find you attractive."

Mademoiselle Beauvert appreciated the fact that Marcelle was paying her this sincere compliment. She shared her opinion, thinking herself reasonably beautiful. And reasonably well preserved at the age of fifty-five.

Reassured about her charms, she resumed the course of her anxieties. "Well, men do sometimes find me attractive, but do I find them attractive? That's the question."

Marcelle made a knowing face. "Ah, you're a lesbian!"

Mademoiselle Beauvert shuddered. "No, not at all!"

Given her chronic spinsterhood, some did indeed assume she preferred women to men.

"Absolutely not! What a strange notion!"

"You've just admitted you don't find men attractive. So I assumed you're a lesbian."

"No, I'm not attracted to women."

Seeing that Mademoiselle Beauvert was bursting with indignation, her temples scarlet, her eyes cold, Marcelle looked away, glanced around the room, saw Copernicus scratching his neck, and almost said, "Only attracted to parrots." But coarse as she was, she knew that would hurt her.

"Actually, I'm suspicious of the men who get close to me," Mademoiselle Beauvert continued.

"Now that's something I find amazing."

"I can't help assuming they have an ulterior motive."

"What?"

"Money, of course!"

Mademoiselle Beauvert had whispered these words, as if they were dangerous.

Marcelle nodded. There was a legend in the neighborhood that Mademoiselle Beauvert was much wealthier than her apartment or lifestyle suggested, that she was a billionaire who took great care to appear merely well-off. This sudden confidence confirmed the rumor spread by those in the know.

Marcelle trembled with emotion. With those few words, her employer had grown in her eyes: of the two revelations, the one about her first love and the one about her fortune, it was the second that impressed her more.

"How can I tell if they want me for my money? If I were poor, I'd gladly trust them."

Marcelle nodded, then exclaimed, "If I had money, it wouldn't bother me that men were even more attracted to me."

Mademoiselle Beauvert gave her a sarcastic smile that meant: You don't really know what you're talking about.

Marcelle didn't insist. She went back to the kitchen where she diligently performed her morning chores.

When she brought Mademoiselle Beauvert her stack of letters, the parrot cawed, "Mail!"

Marcelle gave him a black look.

"All right then, I'll leave you, Mademoiselle. I'll come by again this afternoon."

"Very well, my dear Marcelle. See you later."

As soon as she crossed the room, Copernicus cawed, "Goodbye, my dear Marcelle, goodbye."

Marcelle untied her apron with an angry gesture and stopped at the door. "I wouldn't like to live with an animal that's more intelligent than we are."

Mademoiselle Beauvert looked up from her bills, delighted. "Copernicus isn't more intelligent than we are."

Marcelle shrugged. "Well, he is, isn't he?"

"No, he's not."

"Can you guess what other people are thinking?"

"No, but—"

"Well, then!"

And with that, Marcelle left the apartment.

She closed the door just as Mademoiselle Beauvert was

opening an envelope containing a sheet folded in half, on which two lines were written:

Just a note to tell you I love you. Signed: You know who.

She hated this kind of advertising, which created a mystery and maintained it just to attract people's attention: a number of messages would follow until they finally revealed the good they wanted you to buy. Irritably, she threw the letter into her waste drawer, so that she could reuse the paper. She shook herself and once again bent attentively over her accounts, a literature she much preferred.

Meanwhile, Marcelle was descending the stairs, a cloth in her hand, wiping the banister as she went.

Pushing open the glass door of her lodge, with its net curtains, she saw her Afghan slumped on the couch, listening to the news of his country on a tiny radio. For a second, she wondered if it wouldn't have been better if he'd been out looking for a job, but then, observing him, so manly that he looked closer to forty than thirty, she thought how lucky she was, at the age of fifty-five, to have attracted such a young, vigorous lover, and something inside her quivered: from her conversation with Mademoiselle Beauvert, she had concluded that her Afghan must love her, a penniless concierge, without any ulterior motives.

She opened the only letter she had received:

Just a note to tell you I love you. Signed: You know who.

Heavy and tired, Marcelle sat down and rubbed her forehead as she examined the envelope.

Who had written this message? Her son? Was he trying to beg forgiveness for the two hundred and forty-two euros and the night table she'd probably have a long wait for? Or was it a boyfriend? An old boyfriend? Paul? Rudy? The assistant at the pharmacy?

Never mind. Whoever it was, it made no difference.

It's over, she concluded. *No more room. Last year, yes, but now it's too late: I have my Afghan.*

She raised her head, looked at her lover, and affectionately yelled at him to take his feet off the cushions.

T his is outrageous!"

" . . . "

"Honestly, you should have warned me."

" . . . "

"I was worried."

" . . . "

"Very worried."

"You needn't have been."

"It's the way I am: I worry. We didn't see much of each other last week as it was, and on Saturday you go out without me."

"I can do what I like."

"Of course."

"We're not married!"

"No, but—"

"So I can go out with my friends on Saturday night if I like."

"All right, you're free. But you could still have warned me."

"Warned you about what?"

"That you were going out with your friends."

"And why is that?"

"Why?"

"That's right, why?"

"Because I was expecting to go out with you on Saturday."

"I didn't promise you. Did I promise? Did I say, 'Albane, I'm going out with you Saturday night'?"

"Er . . . no."

"There you go."

"You didn't tell me because it went without saying."

"What?"

"Well, yes, given what there is between us . . . "

"In what there is between us, is there an obligation that I devote all my Saturdays to you for the rest of my days?"

"Are you joking?"

"No."

"I'm unhappy when you're not here. I feel like jumping out of the window."

"Albane, may I remind you that until four weeks ago, we didn't even know each other."

"It was love at first sight! That does exist, you know!"

There was a sudden silence over Place d'Arezzo. Only the parrots and parakeets on the upper floors continued their rapid chatter, indifferent to human woes.

The two teenagers were sitting on a bench, slumped forward, avoiding each other's eyes, passionate and at the same time overwhelmed by the complications brought on by their recent relationship. Albane had shouted the final words of her declaration with more exasperation than love. As for Quentin, he had withdrawn into himself; his huge new body, not yet proportionate—his long, wide feet were an oversized base for such a narrow body—had curled into a hostile ball; all he needed were the spikes of a hedgehog.

Overcome with nervous tics, Albane vaguely understood that she was being unfair. "Anyway, I was expecting to go out on Saturday night . . . I hadn't made other plans. As a matter of course, I wouldn't make a commitment on a Saturday without telling you first."

"I can't believe this!"

"Yes, it's true. I'd never do that."

"Well, you're you and I'm me. All right?"

"Didn't you think our Saturday nights were nice, the other times?"

"Sure, but we don't have to do the same thing again."

"Why, are you getting bored with me?"

"Albane . . . "

"All right, say it. Say it. There: you've said it."

"I didn't say anything."

"Then say the opposite."

"How can I say the opposite of something I haven't said?"

"I'm fed up with guys! I'm ready to give everything, everything, and you just give a crumb."

"Guys? Who do you mean by guys? How many of us are there?"

"One."

"Oh, yes?"

"There's only you."

"Really?"

"Only you!"

"Are you sure?"

"I swear it on my mother. Oh, Quentin, I spent Saturday night crying. That's right, just crying."

"You shouldn't have . . . "

"Well, I did. Because I love you."

"Right away, the big words!"

"Exactly, I love you. Even if you don't give a damn, I love you. Whether you like it or not, I love you."

Above the bench, as an echo to the young girl's outburst, a parrot let out a hoarse, sharp, ugly croak.

Albane bit her lip. Once again, her love had assumed an angry tone. Why could she only ever express her feelings with exasperation, like a pan hissing steam?

"Who was there on Saturday night?"

"My friends."

"Which ones?"

"What do you care?"

"I care about everything that concerns you. Was Franck there?"

"Pierre, Rafaël, Thomas . . . the usual gang."

"Who else?"

" . . . "

"Girls?"

"Are you jealous?"

"No, I just want to know."

"You *are* jealous!"

"Tell me who was there and I'll see if I have any reason to be."

"There weren't any girls."

"Oh, really? Did you go to a gay club, then?"

"There weren't any girls you know."

"Whereas you know them very well!"

"Albane, we met four weeks ago, so yes, naturally, I ran into people I used to hang out with before you."

"Girls you see again! Girls you maybe never left!"

"Shit, you're such a pain in the ass!"

"Oh, I'm a pain in the ass, am I?"

"Yes. And clingy!"

"Clingy?"

"You're getting on my nerves with your questions. 'What did you do? Who with?' For fuck's sake, leave me alone. It's weird, you didn't talk so much before."

"Before when?"

"Before we were together."

Another silence.

Albane felt as if she was about to faint: Quentin had just spelled out something that was very important to her—they were "together"—but he had mixed this admission with a reproach. What should she answer? Should she say anything at all? She talked too much, she talked badly, uncontrollably. In a way, she didn't talk, she barked. He was right, she was a "pain in the ass." If she couldn't stand herself, how could others stand her? Albane decided that her life verged on disaster.

"Don't cry, Albane."

"I'll cry if I want to."

"Stop!"

"What do you care, if I'm such a clingy pain in the ass?"

"Albane . . . "

"What are you doing here, anyway? You don't care about a clingy pain in the ass."

"Stop crying, I didn't say that."

"Yes, you did."

"I said it because you wound me up. It's not what I meant to say."

Albane saw a gleam of hope: Quentin's voice had changed, and he was giving off placatory vibrations. Best to be quiet from now on. Let him come to her. Don't ruin everything with a caustic remark.

"Albane, we're together, you and I."

"Oh, yes?"

"Yes, we're together."

"Really?"

"We're together! Don't you think we're together?"

"Yes, we're together. So why do you go out without me, Quentin?"

"It's a habit . . . a habit from before . . . Nobody can change overnight . . . "

Albane was so unused to admitting her own faults that she immediately felt overwhelming admiration for Quentin. He certainly did have humility and courage.

"I love you, Quentin! Oh, yes, it's crazy how much I love you."

"OK"

"I love only you."

"OK"

"I'd do anything, defend you against anyone."

"It's OK, Albane, I don't need an assistant, I can fight my own fights."

He had said that mockingly, in the tone of a self-satisfied male. Albane thought he was being contemptuous of her, knowing she was hopeless at sports—a subject she hated. Instead of taking advantage of the respite, she responded with a touch of bile. "I meant I'd defend you against criticism."

"What criticism? Do people criticize me?"

"No, it's nothing."

"Who criticizes me? Who?"

"I'd best keep quiet, since you always tell me I talk too much."

"That's just it! You talk about stuff I don't care about and keep quiet when it's something that concerns me."

"I'm trying to protect you. If you heard what they say about you, you'd be hurt."

"Albane, who criticizes me? Tell me, so I can smash his face."

In his emotion, Quentin forgot that his voice had broken the previous year; it regressed, becoming inconsistent, hollow, jolting from high to low. Albane was delighted that she had this power over him.

"Nobody . . . Nobody in particular . . . It's just a general thing . . . Just a rumor . . . "

"A rumor?"

"They say you enjoy it when girls like you . . . and that they like you very much."

"That's not a criticism, that's a reputation. A nice reputation."

He stretched his long legs in front of him and crossed his arms over his chest, smug and triumphant. At that moment, he wished that the gardener, who was working nearby and whose presence bothered him when Albane was sniveling like this, could hear what she had just said.

"And they also say you seduce girls then dump them," Albane went on, "that you use them like paper handkerchiefs. Isn't that a criticism?"

"Not really . . . Among us boys, it shows character."

"Among us girls, it means you're a bastard."

"A bastard? What would you prefer? A hypocrite? A guy who says things without believing a word of them? A guy who cries, 'You're the love of my life,' and then goes and sleeps with another girl?"

"That's a horrible thing to say."

"No, it's honest. You seem to prefer a smoothtalker, not someone who tells the truth."

"And do you tell the truth?"

"Always."

"Really?"

"Always."

"Do you swear?"

"Yes, I swear."

"OK! So then you're going to tell me the truth?"

"Absolutely."

"Right now?"

"Absolutely."

"All right then, tell me the truth. Do you love me?"

"Why does it always have to be about you?"

"What concerns me is us. Answer me, since you swore to tell the truth. Do you love me?"

"You're so stubborn!"

"All right, I'm stubborn, but do you love me?"

"You're very, very, very stubborn!"

"Do you love me?"

"Shit, you really are stubborn!"

Once again, silence fell between them.

They had never felt so far apart since they had been glued to this bench. The conversation was taking unexpected turns,

turns they couldn't control. They had met to make out, to enjoy a shared moment together, and instead they were just bickering endlessly. They were both unwittingly awkward and tactless and blamed their muddled thinking on each other's behavior.

"Quentin, have you ever said it?"

"What?"

"Have you ever said 'I love you' to anyone?"

"No. It's not the kind of thing I say."

"Have you ever thought it?"

"Stop it. That's my business."

"Answer me, because you swore to tell the truth. Have you ever loved anyone?"

"Before you?"

"Yes."

"No."

"And since then?"

"Since when?"

"Since me, have you loved anyone?"

"Somebody else apart from you?"

"Yes."

"No."

"And me?"

Eyes lowered, temples bright red, he grabbed her wrist, asking his hands to say what his lips could not utter.

Albane, her body quivering, let herself be convinced. "I'm happy," she said.

"You were crying earlier on."

"Of course. For the same reason that I'm happy now."

"What's that?"

"Because of what you've just said. Or rather what you've just not said."

They laughed, he from embarrassment, she with satisfaction. He looked at her. "You girls are so complicated."

"No, we're not. You just have to understand us, that's all."

"And how do we do that?"

"You just have to listen to us."

There was a crackle above them. In a rustle of wings and raucous shrieks, two male parrots were fighting pitilessly over a female. Other birds, witnessing this, flew from branch to trunk, commenting on the struggle. The branches shook with wild energy.

"Albane, would you sleep with me?"

"What?"

"Since we're together, we could sleep together."

"Are you crazy? I'm too young."

"Excuse me?"

"I'm fifteen."

"And I turned sixteen ten days ago."

"I promised myself I wouldn't sleep with anyone until I'm sixteen and a half."

"Why sixteen and a half?"

"It's how old my cousin was when she did it for the first time."

"Albane, I'm getting nowhere fast. You're old enough to be with me, but too young to sleep with me. So what do you think 'being together' means?"

"It means we know it and other people know it."

"Know what?"

"That we're together."

"In my opinion, 'being together' is more than that. It means to be in love all the way."

"What do you mean, all the way?"

"All the way."

In the trees, the fight was growing more intense, and the warriors' cries of rage were becoming disturbingly cruel.

"Quentin, give me some time, please."

"If I have to wait till you're sixteen and a half . . . "

"I'm prepared to wait for you. Because I love you."

"OK"

Quentin stood up, made sure that his shirt was tucked into his jeans, ran his fingers through his curly hair to give it more body, then, like a phlegmatic globe-trotter, picked up his backpack.

"I'm going to catch my bus."

Albane gave a start. "Already? And you're just going to leave me all alone like this?"

"Who do you want me to leave you with?"

"Without saying anything else . . . "

"If it's in your power to change the public transit schedule, then I'll stay. Go ahead, Mary Poppins!"

"You're laughing, but I'm sad."

"I never asked you to be sad."

"I'm sad because I'm going to be without you."

"I'll see you at six o'clock this evening, OK?"

He walked quickly away, speeding up with every step.

She followed him with her eyes, hoping he would turn around, ready to blow him a kiss, but he vanished around the corner. She sighed.

Picking up her satchel, she noticed a yellow envelope on the bench. She immediately understood. The reason he'd run off so abruptly was because he'd scribbled her this message. Heart pounding, she unfolded the paper.

Just a note to tell you I love you. Signed: You know who.

She bounced up, stamped her feet, clapped her hands. Quentin had certainly fooled her: he'd acted indifferent, pretended he wasn't in love.

Bursting with joy, she danced around the bench, overexcited, not noticing the surprised looks she was getting from the gardener. Then she threw herself back down on the bench and, legs flailing with happiness, pulled out her phone to tell her best friend. With the dexterity of a professional typist, she wrote:

Gwen, I'm happy. Will tell you.

Since she had ten more minutes before taking the streetcar, she decided to act out a little scene: she would fold the letter, put it back on the bench, pretend she hadn't seen it, then pretend she had just discovered it. That way, she'd again experience the same ecstasy as the first time.

She put the object down by her side, crossed her legs, and indulged in the luxury of whistling as she watched the parrots flying through the spring air.

Just then, a hand came from behind and snatched away the paper.

"Phew! I thought I'd lost it."

It was Quentin, out of breath, picking up the envelope.

Albane gave a start. "But Quentin . . . "

He was already rushing away. "It's nothing, I'd just forgotten something. I'm off to the bus station. See you at six, Albane, without fail!"

He was already around the corner.

Albane sat there with her mouth open, incapable of gathering her thoughts. If the note wasn't meant for her, who was Quentin going to give it to?

After two minutes of terror, she sniffed, grabbed her telephone, and unhesitatingly tapped out another text:

Gwen, I think I'm going to kill myself.

9

T hank you for seeing us."

"You're most welcome. The honor is all mine. I'm always happy to open my door to true art lovers."

Jovially, eyes sparkling with delight, Wim bowed to the Vandenborens, distinguished collectors from Antwerp.

"Of course, you know my assistant . . . "

Meg stepped forward. "We met at the gallery."

She held out her hand, but in Wim's opinion, two seconds were quite sufficient for introducing an assistant, so he intervened and gallantly took Madame Vandenboren's arm; Meg had no choice but to flatten herself against the wall to let them pass, bowing to Monsieur Vandenboren as he trotted behind his wife, eager to see the paintings.

The hallway was narrow because, in keeping with Wim's instructions, the architect had created a setting intended to dazzle visitors. The loft, which was over 2,000 square feet, looked all the vaster when you came to it via a tight bottleneck.

The Vandenborens were suitably awestruck by its surface area, its breadth, its immaculate white walls, and its functional, minimalistic furnishings. Before they saw even a single one of the canvases, they marveled at the space that housed them.

Feigning indifference, Wim, whose pudgy face was reminiscent of a little trumpet-playing cherub, spoke with a mixture of elegance and forcefulness. "Paintings fade if people don't look at them. Just like women, they need to be taken out, shown off, complimented, desired. They languish if they're shut away. Solitude kills them. Do you think Matisse, Picasso, or Bacon produced their masterpieces for museum basements or the insides of safes? Whenever I'm fortunate enough to acquire a masterpiece, I hang it here, and every day I gaze at it, examine it, and speak to it. That's what maintaining a heritage means first and foremost: a lot of attention. Works created with the heart must be looked at with the heart. Don't you agree?"

The couple nodded. Meg admired Wim's introduction: aware that the Vandenborens were very much in love, he addressed their taste for collecting in romantic language.

"This is how I divide up my activities: temporary exhibitions dedicated to an artist at the gallery, and my permanent collection over here. I keep the best pieces, the ones dearest to me, at home. Which, naturally, are also the dearest, period!"

He laughed, carrying the Vandenborens with him in his brief burst of hilarity.

Meg noted that Wim was applying a particular method of communication: relaxing his customers, making them feel comfortable. She was amazed at the ease with which Wim, who was such a snob, pulled the strings like a good merchant. Was it calculated or instinctive on his part?

"May I leave you for a few minutes? I must show a painter out. I've been seeing him downstairs. You know what artists are like: they're easily offended."

Principle number two: once harmony has been established, make yourself needed. Wim would leave the Vandenborens alone in this luxurious hangar, and they wouldn't say a word, in awe of the place, the paintings, the silence, and would only feel comfortable again when he returned.

Wim motioned to Meg to follow him. Together, they took the inner staircase, made of brown wood, and rejoined not a painter, as he had made out, but a couple of potential French customers who had been looking at paintings for an hour.

Wim turned solemn, austere, almost morose. "Coming back to our conversation, nowadays the only sound investment is art."

"If you choose a good artist."

"Naturally. If you have lousy taste, then you might as well stay at home."

Once again, Meg applauded Wim's performance: he was adopting a mocking tone with a touch of vulgarity in order to conform to Parisian taste.

"A painting," he went on, "isn't just a good financial deal that's likely to increase substantially in value, it's also a useful tax break."

The French gave a painful sigh. No sooner did you utter the word "tax" to a Frenchman than you knew you had inflicted hurt but you had captured their attention.

"They don't tax works of art in France," Wim continued.

"Not yet!" the Frenchman cried skeptically.

"They never will."

"Oh, you never know with them. It's always best to expect the worst."

Meg was amused by the "they" and "them." Who did Wim and the French couple mean? Politicians? The Right? The Left? The tax authorities? The Ministry of Finance? This "they" contained a combination of irrational fears.

"Oh, no, they'll never do that," Wim insisted. "There have to be rich people so that the poor people can be provided for."

"There's no room for common sense in our country these days. It got swallowed up by ideology."

Wim assumed a sympathetic expression. He knew it was pointless to debate this any longer. The atmosphere darkened. All four of them were united in the thought that the world was heading for the apocalypse.

Meg knew from experience that this was a crucial moment: the French needed a dose of pessimism before proceeding.

And indeed, the man resumed, "Anyway, you'd let me have the Louise Bourgeois sculpture for . . . ?"

"Four hundred thousand."

"Is that negotiable?"

"It's already been negotiated. I offered it to you earlier at four hundred and fifty thousand."

"You could make a little effort."

"Why should I? Tomorrow, I'll be approached by a Dutchman, a Chinese, or a Russian who won't argue about the price. Remember it's a Louise Bourgeois, an undeniable asset to France."

The man grumbled and his wife elbowed him more or less discreetly. Everything would be decided in the next three seconds.

"Louise Bourgeois was French. Her work will remain in France!"

Wim and Meg exchanged a complicit glance: the sale had been concluded, and Wim had been right to appeal to national pride. Even though the French are constantly running France down, they nevertheless still have the pride of being citizens of a great nation; if you mention "a Dutchman, a Chinese, or a Russian" to them, you evoke people they consider barbarians, and they immediately want to save world civilization by bringing French property back to France.

"Congratulations!" Wim exclaimed. "A wonderful purchase. I'm delighted that this work—so fundamental to the sculptor's career—is going to your home in Paris, where Louise Bourgeois was born and where she studied. A genuine return to the roots."

The French nodded. Even though they were making a private purchase, they claimed a legitimacy that no foreigner ever could have.

Wim shook their hands warmly. "Well done! Let's go to my office and sort out the details. Meg, take a look downstairs, then at the mezzanine."

Meg understood. She rejoined the Vandenborens, who were standing frozen at the entrance to the loft, and apologized for Wim with the customary phrase. "Wim has been detained downstairs. He's sorry he left you alone with his darlings. But please do walk around and look at the works. He'll be back as soon as he can."

She walked a few yards with them, stimulated them with some brief comments, then left them to their contemplation and went to the mezzanine.

What they called "the mezzanine" was the truly private section of the place. Although Wim made it seem as if the triple loft was his apartment, it was actually a showroom, of which he inhabited only the third floor. The couches, the bar, and the kitchen had a degree of decoration, but the living space was again minimalistic.

Meg knocked at the bedroom door.

Twenty seconds later, the door was opened by a slim girl with a mass of blonde hair, wearing a T-shirt and leggings.

"Oh, hello, Meg."

She lifted a strand of hair, which immediately fell back over her eye.

"Hello, Oxana, Wim has sent me to ask if there's anything you'd like."

"Anything . . . ?" Oxana said, fighting off the strand of hair, which was impairing her vision. "I don't really know . . . "

Meg figured that Oxana's brain was like her hair: messy. "Yes, like breakfast, for instance?"

"Oh, no . . . That's all right . . . I had a kiwi."

This irritated Meg. How could a girl who was five foot ten be content with a kiwi when she, who was eight inches shorter, needed several slices of bread with butter and jam?

"Would you like me to order you a taxi?"

"A taxi?"

"Yes, for you appointment."

Oxana became confused and hopped around the room, knocking into the furniture because her hair prevented her from seeing obstacles. "My diary! Where's my diary?"

Meg watched in dismay as Oxana searched her bed, the armchair, the couch, holding her hair up on her head with her hand. Confronted with such distress, and trying her best to conceal her contempt, Meg suggested, "Perhaps it's in your suitcase?"

Finding this a brilliant idea, Oxana rummaged in it and clicked her fingers in triumph. "Here we are! Today . . . Photo shoot at Studio 66." She pushed back her hair and looked admiringly at Meg. "What a memory, Meg! I'm impressed."

Meg nearly replied, "I heard you mention that appointment at least three or four times."

Meg found Oxana quite annoying, but didn't show it because Oxana held the key to the mystery of seduction . . .

As far as Meg was concerned, Oxana belonged to a different species. How could anyone have such an endless body without an ounce of fat? How could anyone have such long legs? Such a high, narrow pelvis? How could anyone digest food with such a concave belly? Surely, there wasn't enough room in there for intestines! Oxana, Meg thought, didn't look like a woman but a model—which was what she was. A model, in other words, a hybrid race midway between a child and a giraffe. At that moment, leaning against the door frame, Meg was looking at a zoological environment, a cage where a mane on legs, obsessed with her falling strands of hair, was flitting from handbag to suitcase.

If the first mystery resided in this absurd body, the second was linked to the attraction produced by this absurd body: men were crazy about Oxana. That someone like Wim—intelligent, educated, canny, loquacious—should install a big animal like Oxana in his bedroom was something of a riddle. Because Oxana was neither stupid nor intelligent, neither kind nor nasty, neither interested nor disinterested, neither calculating nor nonchalant. No, Oxana was none of those things. At best, she was like lukewarm water. How did Wim not get bored with her? How could such a big talker, who loved intellectual sparring, converse with this decal, this woman for the deaf and dumb?

"Too bad, I don't have time to wash," Oxana decided, tiring of her own excitement. "I'll just put on a dress and go like this."

There lay the third mystery: Oxana never seemed to have time to wash and yet she always smelled good. Meg was beginning to suspect that there was some kind of subterfuge behind this miracle: who was to say that Oxana didn't get up much earlier, shower, wash her hair, pamper her skin, then grab an old T-shirt from the night before and go back to bed?

"I'll order you a taxi," Meg said. "In ten minutes. All right?"

Not waiting for a reply, which was likely to take at least a minute, Meg booked the cab and went back to the loft, where Wim was commenting passionately on his paintings to the Vandenborens.

Meg stood aside in a corner to watch them, aware that nobody was paying any attention to her anyway.

She stared at Wim. Why did some of her female friends find him ugly? One of them had nicknamed him Riquet with the Tuft . . . True, he didn't have the body of a Prince Charming, he was short, with wide hips and narrow shoulders; but he was a good mover, his legs were flexible, he had a broad chest, he carried himself well, he would wave his hands elegantly as soon as he became impassioned about something, and he acted quickly and precisely, without hesitation. As for his features, they were round: round eyes, a round nose, a round mouth, round cheeks, a round chin, and a round skull with bare temples ending in a short crest that looked like a baby's hair.

Actually, Wim resembled a character in a cartoon. And Meg had always loved cartoons.

He noticed her from a distance and motioned to her to go open the mail. She obeyed immediately. What a brilliant man! She liked his hyperactivity: while developing a theory about the hidden tenderness of the painter Bacon for the benefit of the Vandenborens, he had found the time to see her and assign her her tasks.

She put the mail in order, organizing the bills, putting professional proposals into a file, and throwing advertising in the wastepaper basket. She was disconcerted by the last letter:

Just a note to tell you I love you. Signed: You know who.

She didn't like this message. Who had written it? Not Oxana: she was Ukrainian, and didn't speak French well enough. Who, then?

Whoever the schemer was, for a moment Meg admired her audacity: she certainly knew how to take the initiative.

Oxana appeared in the loft, perched on heels that made her six inches taller. *That girl really does have a vocation to become a lamplighter*, Meg thought. Oxana waddled over to Wim, who greeted her warmly, slid a hand over her back, and introduced her to the Vandenborens.

Even though she was some distance away, Meg, observing the scene, suddenly understood her boss: with her fashionable body, Oxana added to Wim's reputation. Never mind the fact that Madame Vandenboren was looking daggers at her, or that Monsieur Vandenboren was standing there frozen in order not to alarm his wife. Both saw Oxana as a sign of wealth and success. Oxana enhanced the luxury surrounding Wim.

The taxi driver rang the doorbell.

Meg interrupted the quartet and reminded Oxana that she had to go. She lifted her strand of hair and ran to the exit.

"Three little coffees, please, Meg."

The sale was going to take a bit longer . . .

Meg got three tasty espressos from the coffee machine.

Leaving the Vandenborens in front of the Basquiat they liked, Wim joined her. "Anything new in the mail?"

She gave him a brief summary, which he mentally registered, then handed him the anonymous letter. "There was also this. Sorry I opened it."

He grabbed the note and read it. Taken aback, he looked at Meg, then read it again, grimaced, and left it on the marble kitchen counter.

"A woman would have to be fat and ugly to write a note like this. Throw it away."

Then he took the coffees and went to rejoin the Vandenborens.

Meg rushed to the toilet, not because she needed to, but because she liked to be alone when she felt overwhelmed by events.

Once locked in the charcoal-black space, she gave free rein to her thoughts. *Why doesn't he love me? Why doesn't he ever look at me the way you look at a woman who loves and is loved?*

The mirror answered her: in it, she saw a short, rather broad woman with low shoulders, blotchy skin, and an outmoded hairstyle. For a moment, she thought she recognized her mother's image. Not her mother at the age of twenty, but her mother now.

She looked away, threw the note in the toilet bowl, flushed, closed the lid, sat down, and allowed herself a few minutes to weep.

10

P leasant night owl, chatty, a smoker, a drinker, socially inept, hates to go out more than one evening a month and would rather stay at home, a snob, overdoses on music, which he talks about when not listening to it, seeks lady owl of similar nature, depressive, excessive—hysterics welcome—unskilled in the kitchen, housework-impaired, for passionate conversations. No sex maniacs or marriage candidates need apply. Sole condition: a pleasant and not too loud voice. Please send tape, which will be listened to. All applicants will be considered impartially.

Pencil in hand, Ludovic was going over his ad, trying to put himself in the shoes of the woman reading it. Satisfied, he also jotted down *Wealth irrelevant*, a detail that struck him as particularly appealing.

Tiffany, a new friend, came out of the kitchen with the croissants she had bought him on the way, and resumed their conversation.

"What? Come on, Ludo, you're not going to tell me that at the age of twenty-six you haven't had sex with a woman?"

"Did I say that?"

"That's what I understood."

"Strange . . . "

Tiffany laid the table, an inquisitive smile on her lips. Ludo pushed his notebook aside.

"Now stop playing cat and mouse. Once and for all, Ludo, have you ever had sex with a woman?"

"Good question. I wonder that myself."

"That's cheating. Just answer yes or no. Have you ever had sex with a woman?"

"Hmm . . . "

"Hmm?"

"'Hmm' is a word."

"And what does 'Hmm' mean?"

"Something between yes and no."

"Be more specific."

"There's been nothing specific in my rare sexual experiences."

"You're so discouraging!"

"That's what I think too."

Tiffany looked fondly at Ludo. On the short side, with the beginnings of a belly and a pleasant face thanks to his abundant black hair, pale gray eyes, and scarlet mouth, he made the perfect friend: funny, helpful, never forgetting a confidence. Dressed in jeans that were too large for him and baggy pullovers—often blue and worn—he looked quite ordinary. And yet compared with other young people his age, his behavior was unusual: he was single, passionate about classical music, owned thousands of CDs, and had just set up a specialist magazine, *La Clé des scènes*, available both in print and online, which provided highly pertinent and independent comments on cultural life.

Peculiar as he was, Ludo aroused feelings of affection in everyone he met. Not only did people become friends with him, they felt as if they'd been friends forever . . . Was it because he looked more like a boy trying to grow up than a man? There were still childlike elements in his appearance. His softness, his roundness, the clarity of his expression, the blatant absence of muscles suggested a boy who has just broken out of the small children's playground to the older children's one. Hormones and testosterone had almost forgotten to visit his body. Of course, he'd done enough growing to reach five foot seven, and for a few fine hairs to grow here and there on his chin, but he still had a prepubescent look. There was no erotic glow in his pupils; his movements didn't originate from his pelvis, and his center of gravity was above his navel; he kissed cheeks the way most people shook hands: out of politeness, automatically, without suggesting that he was crossing an intimate boundary by bringing his body closer. Was it this obvious lack of sexuality that made everybody call him Ludo instead of Ludovic? Although intended to be friendly, the diminutive was a reminder that this likable creature lacked something.

For weeks now, in her eagerness to help him, Tiffany had been striving to understand why he lived alone.

Far from finding her investigation intrusive, Ludo responded to it good-naturedly, happy to talk about himself and giving answers that dumbfounded her. Tiffany now resumed her interrogation, spelling it out clearly as if speaking to someone who was hard of hearing.

"'Sex,' Ludo, 'sex.' It's not as if I'm asking you anything technical."

"Is there something technical about sex?"

"I mean, I'm not asking you for physical details."

"You're right. When it comes to physical things, the devil is in the details."

"How far have you gone beyond . . . beyond flirtations?"

Ludo burst out laughing. "Flirtations! I'm honored by your use of the plural. I've only had one or two flirtations, as you call them. Or maybe three . . . "

"Maybe?"

"I only get then in very small slices . . . "

"Ludo, have you ever gone . . . beyond flirting?"

"My flirtations have gone beyond me."

Tiffany sighed.

Sensing that he was exasperating her, Ludo leaned forward obligingly and tried to express himself clearly. "Would you like me to tell you about my longest, most beautiful love affair? I was fifteen. A new family had moved in on my street. From my window, I could see Oriane, who was also fifteen, and was the eldest of the four Morin sisters. Oriane had curly, implausibly thick auburn hair. I fell so much in love with her that I had to repeat my school year."

"Repeat your school year?"

"That's right! If putting your feelings before your education isn't love, I don't know what is! In the evenings, instead of doing my homework, I used to watch her doing hers. Nothing else mattered. I spent a year and a half like that."

"What happened in the end?"

"Her parents moved to Spain."

"You must have both cried a lot when you parted."

"I did, yes, because I'd devoted a year and a half of my life to her. No idea about her."

"Oh, come on!"

"Did she even know I existed? We never spoke. I'd investigated and found out her name was Oriane, but she almost certainly didn't know my name."

"And what happened afterwards? You said you were going to tell me about your most beautiful love affair."

Ludo burst out laughing. "That was it! You see, Tiffany, when I have a crush on a girl, I turn stupider than an ass and show as much initiative as a mollusk. The girl I love becomes the girl I don't come near, the girl I don't speak to, the girl I look away from."

"So you wouldn't behave any differently toward a girl you didn't give a damn about or even hated?"

"Ah, I feel understood." Pleased, Ludo started rolling himself a cigarette.

Tiffany crossed her arms and looked at him.

The telephone rang. "Want to bet it's my mother?" Ludo said sardonically.

"How do you know?"

He picked up the phone. "Yes, Mom. Of course, Mom. I swear, Mom. See you later, Mom." He smiled playfully. "My mother has just pointed out that it's her birthday today and that I mustn't get her anything. She was quite insistent on that. 'No flowers, no books, no perfume.' So now I have her order, I know what to look for."

He seized the tobacco between his fingers, rolled the strip of paper, shook it, tamped down the contents, and glued it with a flick of the tongue.

"Well done!" Tiffany cried admiringly.

"If you only knew how many pouches of tobacco I used up before I succeeded. I have butterfingers."

"Can't you say anything nice about yourself?"

"It doesn't come easily. Probably the way I was brought up . . . "

"Are you suggesting you were brought up better than the rest of us?" Tiffany said indignantly, as Ludo lit an old lighter.

"I didn't grow up with compliments. My father was stingy with them; he never praised my sisters or me; all he dispensed was sarcasm, criticism, mockery, and insults. As for my mother . . . well, the poor thing had no idea. People often try to work out why she didn't do this or that; I think it's quite simply that it didn't occur to her."

"You're joking!"

"My mother's neither horrible nor manipulative: she just forgets to think."

"You're not very nice about her."

"On the contrary, there's no politer way to justify her short-comings. Anyway, for twenty-six years I've received about as much praise as the Sahel desert has had rain."

"Then it's time to change, Ludo. No point putting yourself down."

"I always get in first. Since my father dished out nastiness, I anticipate out of caution: I'd rather be the one to condemn myself than wait for my friends to do it. And sometimes, like you, they pleasantly surprise me . . . Thank you, by the way."

Tiffany didn't insist. She knew he wasn't one of those narcissists who denigrate themselves because they're fishing for compliments; far from seeking flattery by cynical means, Ludo was his own severest judge, convinced that he possessed no good qualities whatsoever.

"Seeing yourself that way, Ludo, hardly gives you wings. All that self-criticism makes you inhibited."

"You're not wrong there." He stared at the smoke slowly drifting up from his nostrils. "Spot-on, in fact."

Tiffany took advantage of this consent to say, "You don't dare come on to women because you're afraid of rejection."

"It isn't fear, it's memory: I've had nothing *but* rejection. Not surprising when you think about it. What do I have to offer? I'm not exactly handsome, I don't have much money, and nobody knows if I'd be any good in the sack, not even me. No wonder they aren't exactly lining up."

"A woman could take a chance on you."

"She'd have to be a gambler."

"I know guys who don't have a third of what you have and are still fixed up."

Ludo recoiled from the words "fixed up."

Regretting her choice of language, which rather moved the goalposts, Tiffany went on, "I have lots of female friends who think you're charming. Really. I also think you're charming, Ludo. If I wasn't already with Josh, who's to say I—"

He put his hand on her wrist, both to thank her and to interrupt her. "No point in continuing, Tiffany. I'm touched. The problem is, it's always girls who are 'fixed up,' who are in love and faithful to their lovers, who tell me that, in another life, they'd probably have considered me. The ones who are free and looking for a husband at all costs don't exactly throw themselves at me. That's what I am: the man you don't immediately think of, but who comes to mind once it's become impossible." He laughed. "They should invent a new expression. There are the 'has beens' and the 'wannabes.' I'm the 'would have been,' the faithful woman's regret . . . I'd rather be their remorse."

Ludo spoke with brio, intent on embroidering and varying his expressions, as if his failure didn't affect him. Surprised, Tiffany wondered if this detachment was a male characteristic or something specific to Ludo: a woman would never talk about such a painful subject without crying.

Ludo was wallowing in his own eloquence now. All at once, his lips looked fleshy, his eyes misted over, and he sank voluptuously into his armchair. Was this his only pleasure?

Tiffany found him bewildering: she genuinely liked him, but her friendship for him was full of surprises.

The telephone rang again.

"Yes, Mom," Ludo answered, without even looking at the number on the display screen. A voice crackled in the receiver for a minute, then Ludo hung up, saying, "Me too, Mom, me too."

He took another croissant.

"She's wondering if she left her Chanel body milk here, and since she's never taken a bath or a shower here, the order's even clearer."

"The order?"

"The order for what I mustn't buy her but will give her this evening."

He grabbed the notebook where he had scribbled his ad and gave it to Tiffany.

"Here. As a woman, how would you react to this? Be honest."

Tiffany read through the draft:

Pleasant night owl, chatty, a smoker, a drinker, socially inept, hates to go out more than one evening a month and would rather stay at home, a snob, overdoses on music, which he talks about when not listening to it, seeks lady owl of similar nature, depressive, excessive—hysterics welcome— unskilled in the kitchen, housework-impaired, for passionate conversations. Wealth irrelevant. No sex maniacs or marriage candidates need apply. Sole condition: a pleasant and not too loud voice. Please send tape, which will be listened to. All applicants will be considered impartially.

She swallowed. "How long did this take you?"

"Three minutes and a lifetime. How is it?"

"A disaster."

Ludovic perked up, genuinely delighted.

For her, this was another surprise. "Are you doing it on purpose? Do you want it to fail?"

"No, I want it to sound like me."

"You're hopeless."

"Once more, I agree with you."

Since it was time for her to go to work, Tiffany stood up, moaning, "My poor Ludo," several times.

Ludovic walked her down to the front door of the building in order to pick up his mail.

Longing to smoke outside, he took his letters, stood in the doorway, facing Place d'Arezzo, where the birds were singing, and opened the envelopes.

When he opened the one written on yellow paper—*Just a note to tell you I love you. Signed: You know who*—he gave a tender laugh and shrugged, muttering, "Mom, you're going too far . . ."

11

Victor had been really lighthearted when he came down to pick up his mail, but now he sat huddled at the foot of the stairs, his back against the ceramic tiles, panting in the dark hallway. His hands were shaking.

Once again, he read the handwritten words:

Just a note to tell you I love you. Signed: You know who.

No other message could have inflicted this amount of suffering on him. It didn't matter who had sent it to him, it really didn't: he didn't want to hear that kind of declaration.

Feeling suffocated, he knew he was unable to go back up to the attic apartment where his classmates from the university were waiting for him. Besides, the woman—or man—who had written the letter might be one of the group upstairs . . .

He shook his head in exasperation. *Why can't they leave me alone? Why does it always end up this way?*

He decided to walk. On the pretext of buying something to eat for breakfast, he broke out of his torpor, left the building, and felt the warmth of the sun on his face.

"Good morning, Victor," said Ludo, who was smoking a cigarette on the front steps.

He stammered a greeting and hurried along the sidewalk.

"Good morning, Victor!" shouted Ève from her oxblood coupé, her hair blowing in the wind.

"Good morning, Victor!" cried Hippolyte as Victor crossed the parrot-infested square.

"Good morning, Victor!" the florist called out, arranging orchids outside his window.

To each, he responded with an awkward gesture. Everybody looked fondly on him: people loved Victor at first sight.

He was the embodiment of the attractive young man who is unaware of being attractive, well-built but bewildered by his own body, often leaning forward to make people forget how tall he was, hiding under several layers of clothing. He usually walked with the quiet suppleness of a cat, like a wild tiger lost in the city jungle, until someone addressed him, at which point he become another person: open, forthcoming, delighted to exchange ideas, asking pertinent questions and sustaining the conversation with manifest joy.

He had moved to Place d'Arezzo a year earlier and had been greeted by the neighborhood like manna from heaven, since human beings always believe that beauty is a gift of the gods. His clear, luminous, almost mother-of-pearl skin, made to seem even paler by the contrast of his deep mahogany hair, gave the impression that it had been painted that very morning by some deity.

Although he was handsome, he avoided all the caricatures his beauty might suggest: although his mane of hair looked "romantic," he had neither the bearing nor the egocentricity of a "romantic"; although he dressed tastefully, it was not through choice but because he couldn't help himself. Although he had an androgynous charm, feminine in the eyes, mouth, hairstyle, and hands, masculine in the torso, hips, and nose, he didn't cultivate this ambiguity but was content to just be. In other words, all ages and sexes liked Victor. Even the word "liked" requires qualification: it wasn't sexual desire he aroused, but rather a deep feeling of warmth, as well as the pleasure of seeing such a harmonious creature. There was no smugness about him; on the contrary, there was a certain reserve, a vulnerability, a sense of anxiety, even a fragility. People thought they knew the reason for this ever since a little vixen of a girl at the university had spread the news that Victor was an orphan. The rumor was neither confirmed nor denied, since Victor's modesty demanded respect.

Absorbed in his thoughts, he reached the bakery. The assistant, an amateur bodybuilder wearing a T-shirt to emphasize his sculpted torso, scowled when he saw him. "Yes, Victor, what do you want?"

"A raisin loaf, please."

To this militant advocate for exercise, Victor was a dismaying case. Even though Victor wasn't muscular, everyone found him attractive, including the bodybuilder. He had often pictured Victor with broader shoulders, prominent pectorals, well-developed buttock and adductor muscles; sadly, though, he had to admit that this wouldn't have improved him but made him ordinary or, worse still, inconsistent. Victor was a contradiction to his religion of the biceps.

Unaware of the debate he triggered in the assistant, Victor returned to Place d'Arezzo with his raisin loaf.

The walk had done him good. There was no need to panic. Nobody was claiming authorship of the message—and that gave him time. If, eventually, an identity was revealed, he would be able to decline. After all, he'd always managed to avoid involvement so far.

He entered the Art Deco building, climbed the stairs, walked along the top corridor, heard his friends' loud chatter, took a deep breath, and opened the door.

"You certainly took your time!"

"Stop complaining and look what I brought."

A round of applause greeted the appearance of the raisin loaf.

Photocopies of coursework were pushed aside, law text-books stacked up, and the young people stopped revising in order to pay homage to the delicacy, also helping themselves to more coffee. While some of his companions evoked childhood memories, others gave their recipes for raisin loaf, and still others pointed out the difference between a raisin loaf and a sugar brioche—in the latter, the raisins are replaced with pieces of sugar—Victor watched them, wondering if the author of the note was among them.

Was it Régine or Pascal? Probably not, since they were going out together. Everybody knew that Louison was with David, a medical student. Coline had just started a relationship with Tristan. So the only ones left were Julie, Salomé, and Gildas.

However sharp his antennae, Victor was unable to sense anything. As far as he could see, there was an atmosphere of honest camaraderie in the room, uncontaminated by sex.

"Are you all right, Victor? Something on your mind?"

Régine was leaning toward him. What to do? Flush out the culprit?

"It's the mail."

Everyone stopped talking.

"What?"

"Bad news?"

"Come on, tell us."

Alarmed by the group's intense interest, Victor immediately backtracked. "No . . . I'm expecting a letter to tell me whether or not my scholarship's being renewed, and . . . it hasn't arrived yet."

"Don't worry about it," Gildas said. "I'm in the same boat, and I know it won't arrive for another two weeks. If you're already feeling down, you're going to have two weeks of hell."

"Oh, OK, thanks."

Everyone laughed with relief, and the chatter resumed.

Victor looked closely at his companions. Had anyone changed since he had mentioned the mail? Was any of the girls seeking him with her eyes?

He wondered if he should take the investigation a stage further by leaving the letter lying around where it could easily be seen.

Getting to his feet on the pretext of making more coffee, he took it out of his pocket and put it down next to the sink. That way, he was sure that when people came to wash their hands, they would see it.

They started revising again. The nine students asked each other questions, checking the extent and accuracy of their knowledge of International Law. Victor's anxiety slowly subsided. He was fond of his friends, enjoyed spending time with them, and was glad to know there was no ambiguity among them.

By around noon, they had assimilated the coursework and arranged to meet up again the following day.

Victor kissed everyone, opened the window to cool down the room, which had warmed up under the pressure of all those seething brains, and collected the mugs. As he put them in the sink, he noticed that the letter had disappeared.

He looked everywhere. The kitchen was no bigger than a cupboard and it took him five seconds to conclude that somebody had taken the letter away.

That must mean one of those present had sent it. She had meant to prove it by taking possession of it. What would follow was self-evident: she would reveal her identity, and the problems would start for Victor.

He was suddenly overcome with anger, and felt like smashing everything. But at the last moment he remembered that everything in this apartment had been a gift. Without hesitation, he grabbed his phone and called his uncle. "Baptiste, I think I'm going to leave."

"Again? What are you talking about?"

"I'm going to leave Brussels."

"Why?"

"Do I need a reason? I'm leaving Brussels."

"What are you disappointed in, Victor? Brussels or your university course?"

"I don't know."

"Only yesterday, you were telling Joséphine you loved living here."

"That was yesterday."

"So what happened today?"

"I want to leave."

12

For the third time, she reread the page of Nietzsche. Even when she got a foothold on the first sentence, her attention would falter at the second one, and tumble before the end of the paragraph; it was as if the text was a steep staircase she was trying to go down but which gave way beneath her, causing her to fall; each time, dejected, she became aware of her failure only after regaining consciousness, and realized she had to start all over again.

"What's the matter, Nietzsche, dear? You're not as entertaining as usual," she moaned, rubbing her lower abdomen under her kimono with her left hand to make sure her waxing was perfect.

Diane smiled at the spring, which she welcomed as if it were already summer. Lying on a deck chair in the middle of her roof terrace, facing the parrot-laden trees, shielded from the other residents' eyes by strategically placed flowerpots, she offered her face and her plunging neckline to the warm rays of the sun. Lifting her chin so that her neck would be as tanned as the rest, she raised the book—*Ecce Homo*—higher and carried on reading.

The preaching of chastity is a public incitement against nature. Contempt for sexuality, tainting it with any idea of impurity, is a veritable crime against life—the true sin against life's Holy Ghost.

Footsteps on the sidewalk! She sat up impatiently. "No cheating," she said out loud. "No looking. I promised."

It was tempting, though. All she had to do was lean over slightly to see the man. Quivering, she tensed her neck, tightened her grip on the armrests, and stopped herself.

The footsteps continued, entering the narrow passage leading to their house.

"No, not even a glance! Play the game properly."

She quivered with joy. She refrained not so much out of respect for her promise as out of the pleasure she got from it. Any other woman would have tried to make out the person she would probably be going to bed with in the next few minutes. Not Diane.

She held her breath, waiting for the intercom to ring.

Instead, she heard the heavy front door open and close. *A neighbor . . . Just as well I didn't look,* she thought, trying to conceal her disappointment.

Unable to carry on reading, she put down the Nietzsche and read again the incomprehensible message she had received—*Just a note to tell you I love you. Signed: You know who*—concluded that whoever was playing this stupid practical joke on her would soon reveal himself, and decided to keep the sheet of paper as a bookmark in *Ecce Homo.*

Then she half-opened her robe and studied her body. There was nothing feminine in her gesture or her gaze: she was like a man stripping a woman he is about to enjoy.

"Not bad . . . " was the verdict.

She always marveled at how smooth and firm her flesh was, in spite of her slender figure. *I actually have the advantage of a pudgy, even plump woman's skin, even though I don't weigh even one pound too much. I'm so lucky!* While so many people complained about their bodies, tolerating them or mistreating them, Diane loved hers. She thanked nature, her parents, or whoever else it was that had given her a supple, sensuous femininity that, apart from anything else, didn't show the ravages of time. At forty, she considered herself to be a gift to herself and to others. And now he, the stranger, was about to enjoy her.

"Not bad at all!" she confirmed, and closed her robe.

A bell rang through the apartment. She panicked. How could the stranger be ringing the bell without first being let in through the front door of the building? She ran to the door of the apartment. "Yes?"

"It's me," said a voice she didn't know, a deep, hot, rough voice, the voice of a horny-handed giant.

"You've come to the right place," Diane whispered.

"Have you got your mask on?"

"I'm putting it on now."

"Very good. Open the door."

Diane smiled: not only did she like the voice—it sounded as if it had been through a lot—but the harsh, commanding "Very good" seemed like a good omen, promising a strict master who would appreciate the docility of the woman who submitted to him.

She took out the black crepe blindfold she had ready in the pocket of her kimono and tied it over her eyes. Thus blinded, she unbolted the door.

"Welcome," she said into the void.

"Don't talk crap."

A hand took her chin and lifted it. Cold lips pressed against hers. A tongue bored into her mouth, filling it with an imperious, all-consuming need; there and then, Diane knew she was going to have a delightful time.

When she tried to cling to the man's shoulders, he broke away, pushed her into the middle of the hallway, and slammed the door behind him.

"I have my gear. Where are we going?"

"What gear?"

"I asked you a question!"

"We're going to my bedroom."

"Take me there."

She was annoyed with herself for not having had the fore-sight to practice the route with her eyes closed. She had to grope her way to her bedroom. Confirming that she must look stupid, the man heaved an irritable sigh.

As soon as she managed to make out the correct corridor, she moved more quickly, brushing her fingers along the wall to her door.

They went into the room. Before she had had time to do anything at all, she was standing naked before him, the stranger's fingers having slid her kimono off her as if by magic.

She felt a cool wind on her shoulders.

She thought to hide her private parts, but stopped herself. On the contrary, she boldly arched her back.

He said nothing.

Diane's breasts hardened. She loved this moment, the moment when she was on offer, like goods for sale, to a perfect stranger. And she liked this one because so far he had demon-strated a pleasant mixture of gentleness and roughness.

A minute passed, long, rich, and tense.

She knew he was admiring her, devouring her with his eyes. The silence was the measure of his growing desire. Above all, she mustn't ask him if he liked her, or come out with anything else equally inappropriate.

He still hadn't spoken. She savored her victory. The more silent he kept, the more he worshipped her.

If she were just any old piece of meat, he would already have given her an order. But nothing stirred in the room.

She quivered at the thought of being so beautiful and revered. Shivers ran up and down her skin as the stranger's eyes caressed her. Without there having been any contact, she was already on the way to climax.

As if the man had sensed this and feared that his partner's orgasm would diminish his power over her, he interrupted the scene with an order. "Get down on your knees. I'm going to see to you."

She knelt. She heard the sound of a metal briefcase opening near her. What was he up to?

A pair of rough hands grabbed hers and she felt something cold and rather unpleasant around her wrists, then the man pulled her to the bed and stretched her arms in front of her. She heard a click.

Handcuffs.

Diane giggled.

She loved role-playing, so this was right up her alley. She shuddered with pleasure . . . It was great to be so passive . . .

He went back to his briefcase and fiddled with a number of metal objects. What was he going to do to her now?

The sounds continued. Was he hesitating? That wasn't his style. So what was he preparing to do? There was no reason to delay . . .

Diane suddenly panicked. She had just recognized the sound of a knife blade! A knife with a long, wide blade . . . a butcher's knife . . . a knife for cutting meat! She was sure of it! He was sharpening the edge.

Her chest and temples grew hot with fear. A series of frightening, increasingly menacing thoughts ran through her mind. What if he was crazy? What if he had only pretended to appreciate erotic refinement in order to satisfy another impulse: murder? What if she had let in a psycho? Nobody knew he was here. She moaned. There was no way she could move, since she was handcuffed.

In a second, Diane was bathed in sweat. Her perspiration must have spread a sharp smell through the room because the man sneered, "Oh, scared all of a sudden, are we? Wondering what's going to happen? Well done, darling, you never can tell with me."

She would have liked to reassure herself by saying something cheeky in response, but didn't have time. A rubber ball was rammed into her mouth, attached to an elastic band.

"This way, if you suddenly feel like calling for help, you can't," the voice said smugly.

She moaned. Of course, gagging her like that was a traditional part of S&M games, but it might also mean that her partner wanted to stop her screaming for help so that he could butcher her.

"Stop fidgeting!"

She wasn't moving, she was shaking.

Something liquid and icy was suddenly placed on her back. Surprised, she wondered what it was. Strange . . . It went up and down. Slowly. Because of her terror, it took her a few seconds to work out that it was the blade of the knife.

She felt an intense sense of relief: so he was playing, after all! He was a partner, not a killer.

She focused on the sensations he was giving her. The blade was following the curves of her body, leaving the flat area of her back to explore the contours and crevasses. Things were turning dangerous again. It was imperative that she not move.

She followed the journey of the knife, shuddering at being explored in this way. She realized that the situation was now reversed: he was the one at her service, the master had become the slave's slave by doing his best to surprise her, intimidate her, make her quiver.

She was particularly aroused when the blade ran along her breasts and her neck.

Behind her, she felt the man's breathing growing both faster and heavier. Was he feeling pleasure?

Once again, as if he had read her thoughts, he drew away.

She grunted to let him know she wanted him to come back.

He deliberately didn't react. *He must be a real sadist, the kind who doesn't want to serve his victim.*

As for Diane, she was going from role to role, like a true

adventurer of her own pleasure. Regretting having expressed a demand, and afraid he would doubt her versatility, she transformed herself back into the submissive.

After several intolerable minutes, she felt a strange tickling sensation. She recognized a feather duster. So he had decided to give her a real hot and cold shower, following the blade with the feather! She shuddered, knowing there was nothing more irritating than being tickled, which could drive her to the verge of madness.

Clearly, he was good at this game.

Something new all of a sudden. What was it? The man's finger? A tool? His tongue? She didn't know. Whatever it was, it came between her legs and brought her to orgasm in thirty seconds.

She knelt there dazed for a moment.

Then she realized that the man was putting his gear back into his briefcase.

"Bye, beautiful. I'm leaving you the handcuffs as a memento."

She barely had time to whine and struggle. He was already crossing the apartment and closing the door behind him.

The bastard had left her there alone, naked, blind, dumb, on her knees, handcuffed to the bed.

How many hours would she have to wait before her husband got back?

13

Coaled amid lilies and gladioli, Xavière was arranging bunches of peonies in vases and, from her shop, keeping an eye on the door of Number 8, where Faustina Valette, the publicist, lived, just to see if that hussy had changed lovers again. At the sight of the dashing mixed-race man who came out, her lips curled.

"Oh, no."

She had recognized Maître Dany Davon, who had become famous in the media when he had defended Mehdi Martin, the sex maniac sadly legendary for his serial killing of little girls, the shame of Belgium.

"This is too much."

As far as Xavière was concerned, Faustina had crossed the line: going to bed with Mehdi Martin's defense lawyer was like going to bed with Mehdi Martin. Dany Davon was no longer the kind of person respectable people could associate with. Taking on Mehdi Martin, albeit for professional reasons, was enough to pick up some of his scandalous aura and become a criminal yourself.

"You didn't go away for the Easter holidays, Xavière?"

Annoyed at being disturbed, Xavière turned and glared at Mademoiselle Beauvert. "No, I can't afford it."

Her creased forehead, knitted eyebrows, and surly expression signaled to her well-to-do customer that there was no room for idleness in her life.

"Closing for a day is too expensive. Flowers don't understand that it's a public holiday. Instead of resting, they wilt."

Her tone meant: *I don't behave like a murderer but like a responsible human being.*

Out loud, she went on, "So no point dreaming about taking time off. In another life, maybe . . . Money's so hard to earn."

These words implied: *No, whatever people in the neighborhood might say, I don't charge much for my flowers. I'm not making a huge profit here. If I were, instead of being poor, I'd be rich as King Midas.*

Then, with the confidence of an expert who has consulted every item in a dossier, she added, "Especially nowadays."

She had been dishing out this kind of comment from the very start, but since the European financial crisis and the breakdown in the world economy, it had produced a particularly powerful effect.

"Congratulations, Xavière," Mademoiselle Beauvert stammered in embarrassment. "Even without time off, you still manage to look great."

She marveled at Xavière's smooth, golden complexion, which set off her quicksilver eyes.

Touched by the comment, Xavière thought of the pretty fisherman's cottage she had refurbished by the North Sea, where she stayed secretly every Sunday and Monday. But since she wanted to make sure people didn't know her true lifestyle, she shrugged. "It's just a bit of makeup. You do your best with what you've got."

"But you're lucky you have such beautiful skin."

Xavière liked the compliment, which had an unusual effect on her: it made her angry. Who did this Beauvert woman think she was? Such intolerable familiarity! Talking about her skin, trying to be nice . . . If the conversation carried on like this, she would have to smile and be gracious, and that was out of the question! She was not about to let people drag pleasantries out of her.

"So, have you made up your mind about your flowers, then?"

Not only did Xavière not like it when people felt comfortable with her, she could stand them only when she was able to bite and scratch.

Terrified, Mademoiselle Beauvert pointed to a vase. "A selection of peonies, maybe? Pink and ruby-red ones?"

"Excellent choice."

The words had come out of her mouth automatically, since she had gotten into the habit of giving grades to her customers' artistic choices, thus maintaining constant tension in her shop.

"Orion, a bouquet!" she bellowed toward the greenhouse in the backyard.

A tall, lanky old man appeared, skinny except around his stomach. His clothes were in disarray, his hair disheveled, his mouth open, and his eyes quizzical, as if he had just been awakened.

"A bouquet for Mademoiselle Beauvert, please, Orion, if you don't mind?"

He took away the flowers and went off to execute the order. But before going through the door, he spun around, seized by a sudden realization, and approached the customer in an affable manner. "How are you, dear Mademoiselle?" he exclaimed warmly.

"Very well, Orion, very well."

As he bent down to kiss her on the cheek, clearly driven by a genuine warmth, she shuddered in surprise.

Xavière was amused by Mademoiselle Beauvert's disgust, knowing she was such a prude she couldn't bear expressions of affection. Orion saw his gesture through to the end, and when the kiss hit her on her cheek, Mademoiselle Beauvert closed her eyes.

"Mademoiselle Beauvert, always so fresh and stylish," Orion said.

"Thank you, thank you, Orion," she replied, eager for the contact to end as soon as possible.

"I'm going to make you the most splendid bouquet ever, Mademoiselle. It can never be fully worthy of you, but I'll do my best."

Mademoiselle Beauvert grimaced and gave a brief, sharp giggle, embarrassed by both Orion's attentions and the look Xavière was giving her.

As soon as he had left, she shook herself and went up to Xavière. "How is he?"

"Oh . . . " Xavière raised her eyes to heaven, implying that her husband was deteriorating.

"I'm so sorry for you . . . "

"Come on, he's the one to feel sorry for . . . As for me . . . Well, at least for the moment he isn't aware of anything."

"Really? So much the better."

"Of course . . . but for how much longer?"

To make sure that Mademoiselle Beauvert grasped the fact that this painful subject ended here, Xavière gave all her attention to arranging some arum lilies.

Four months earlier, seized with a sudden inspiration when dealing with a customer who irritated her by listing the various cancers afflicting her family, she had claimed that Orion had the onset of Alzheimer's.

Her story made quite an impression. Not only had the customer been put in her place, but the whole neighborhood had subsequently paraded past to see the unfortunate man. Because, even though there wasn't an ounce of truth in the story, everybody found it plausible, given that the florist's husband had never behaved normally.

Orion overflowed with kindness and affection. Just like a dog, he would manifest joy to everybody he knew. No sooner did he spot a familiar face than the only thing that mattered was to run to that person. How many times had he crossed the street, ignoring the cars, stepped over a fence in a municipal park, and nearly lost the flowers he was out delivering, in order to give someone a warm greeting? If people let him get close, there would be an outpouring of exclamations and compliments. He would keep repeating how happy he was to see them, congratulate them on something wonderful about themselves—their tan, their hairdo, their scarf, their coat, their poodle. Cordial to the point of craziness, he would smile one more time then walk away, not even noticing that the person involved had barely responded.

Whenever someone asked him a favor, he would become enthused by the task requested of him and vow that he would do everything in his power to give satisfaction. Unfortunately, his abilities weren't at the level of his goodwill, and since, in addition to a kind of universal incompetence, he was also absentminded, he always failed to keep his promises.

It was hard to hold a conversation with him. Either his joy at seeing you made him repeat the same sentence ten times, or he would walk away from you because he had seen someone else to say hello to. Those who invited Orion and Xavière for dinner had observed that only she spoke while he kept silent, listening with wide-open, even awestruck eyes to those who were talking. He intervened only rarely, and never appropriately. All it took was one word to set his mind racing. For example, hearing a conversation about religion, he had interrupted the dinner guests with, "Jesus? Jesus is great! Always handsome, always young. Ever seen an ugly Jesus in a church or a painting? No. Nobody has ever seen him as ugly, artists show him as being sublime. What a success! Christianity is quite something, isn't it?" From what kind of soul did these words come? What thoughts drove his quirky brain? Orion defied comprehension.

Xavière had met him twenty-five years earlier, at a time when she had been a free agent who often went out. One night she had seen him in a nightclub, standing tipsily on a table, doing a striptease while singing "La Vie en rose"—badly, at that. An accountant at the time, and the daughter of an accountant, she had immediately been drawn to the slim, distinguished thirty-year-old, a real party animal as only a Belgian can be. She had found him crazy, different, romantic. In addition, he kept pulling banknotes out of his pockets, treating his friends, and buying extravagant rounds for strangers.

They had gotten close on Xavière's initiative alone.

One night, she had admitted to him that she found him strange. He had replied, opening his arms wide, as if it was something blatantly obvious, "Of course. I've been like this since my swan dive."

"Excuse me?"

"One night at midnight, when I was totally plastered, I went back to my parents' house with some friends—they'd seen me home because I wasn't in a fit state to drive. I took them into the garden and decided to leap from the diving board into the swimming pool. Except that I'd forgotten it had been drained the day before."

"Did you smash you head?"

"I really enjoyed my swan dive. I remember it very well. It was absolutely the most heavenly swan dive I've ever done in my life. Pure, neat, with an extraordinary momentum, every second of it perfectly controlled, almost hanging in the air. It was a wonder. Only it was tough, landing on the tiles ten feet below. I think I even passed out."

"What happened afterwards?"

"Oh, then it was all up to the doctors. To be honest, I had access to the best—my father knew everyone at the Saint-Luc hospital. They were sure they'd done a good repair job on me. They looked really pleased with themselves. But the truth is, nothing's been the same since."

With that, he had casually laughed and bought a round of whiskey for the patrons in the bar.

Orion and Xavière had become lovers, early morning

lovers, exhausted bodies that leave the nightclub at closing time, just before daybreak, lovers trying to escape the grip of loneliness. They didn't screw well, they screwed politely, indebted to each other for help in getting through the difficult hours of sobering up.

When, after many questions and enquiries, Xavière had realized that Orion had no plans for the future and was squandering his father's inheritance, she had hastened to get closer to him, suspecting that if Orion kept spending at that rate, there would soon be nothing left of the nest egg.

One Sunday, at about six o'clock in the morning, as the rain lashed the windowpanes, after a passionless but polite bout of intercourse, she had expressed the wish to marry him. In his eccentricity, he had liked the idea.

They had a lavish wedding. Orion hadn't skimped. Entrusting an idle old aristocratic lady with the task of making the event a success, he had managed to have the ceremony held at Sainte-Gudule Cathedral, with a choir, an orchestra, carriages, and the reception in a château, its vast grounds filled with fairground attractions.

Finally, the day after their wedding night—during which he and Xavière had been so drunk that no caress was exchanged—they had gone on honeymoon to Brazil, where they had drunk their way from one luxury hotel to another and gotten on intimate terms with local high society, to which the aristocratic lady had introduced them.

Upon their return, Xavière discovered that Orion's fortune had all been frittered away. All he had left was a rented-out apartment—they turfed out the tenant in order to move in themselves—and a shop near Place d'Arezzo.

She had stopped him from selling it, suspecting that as soon as he had the money in his hands, it would melt like butter in the sun. Since one of her aunts had a shop in Liège, she had gathered some information and suggested to Orion that they open a florist's. He had found the idea so ludicrous that he had agreed.

Much to their surprise, they had made a success of it, since the wealthy local population lacked such a shop. Not only had they discovered a taste for their skills, but Xavière had turned out to be a clever manager and Orion a tireless worker. The transformation was astonishing: the former amateur dandy would go to the Mabru wholesale market at dawn, bring back the flowers, open the metal shutter at nine o'clock, stay in the shop all day, then lock the doors at eight o'clock. This went on seven days a week.

Now the decadent thirty-year-old become an elderly man with blotchy skin—owing to the daily comings and goings in the cold rooms at the back of the shop—balding, with hair gathered at the sides, which made him look like a scarecrow in the fields.

Xavière was younger than him and had weathered the years better. Still slim—she hated cooking, and Orion ate as little as an alcoholic—and nicely dressed thanks to being an almost professional shopper at sales, she looked like her husband's younger sister. She didn't consider him a spouse but rather an aging child she was responsible for, a kind of family slave who had to work hard in order to justify all the effort he cost her.

"Is that bouquet coming, Orion?" Xavière bellowed, annoyed at having to wait so long.

An ecstatic voice came from the back of the shop. "Almost . . . The masterpiece is on its way."

Xavière resolved to resume her conversation with Mademoiselle Beauvert. "He does everything his own way. He's getting worse and worse."

"Is he losing his memory?"

"Sometimes . . . Yesterday, for instance, he couldn't find his way to the shop."

"Poor Xavière . . . What do the doctors say?"

"They won't make a prognosis. You know, Alzheimer's is an umbrella term for various different kinds of degenerative illness."

Just then, quick as a bullet, Orion suddenly reappeared. "Here you are, my dear Mademoiselle Beauvert, I've done my best."

He went down on one knee and, theatrically but sincerely, handed her the bouquet. Meanwhile, Xavière was counting the money.

Mademoiselle Beauvert thanked them, took her purchase, begged Orion to get up, and left, relieved that she had managed to get through the test—buying something in this shop was always a test—without encountering too many obstacles.

"That Mademoiselle Beauvert is so pretty!" Orion said ecstatically.

Xavière carried on working without replying. She never listened to him. Certain that most of the time his babbling contained nothing interesting, she paid no more attention to it than she would to the yapping of a dog.

Orion was returning to the back of the shop when he pointed at a yellow envelope on the counter. "Did you see you've got mail?"

Xavière didn't react, so he picked up the letter and brought it to her.

"Here."

Xavière frowned in a hostile manner. "Thanks, there's no rush. I'm not usually in any great hurry to read my mail."

"It might be good news."

"You really think so? In forty-five years, I've never known the mailman to bring me good news. Poor Orion . . . "

He bowed his head pathetically. Whenever she wanted to put an end to a discussion with her husband, she would let out an exasperated "Poor Orion." Hurt, he once again took refuge at the back of the shop.

Once he had disappeared, she opened the mail.

Just a note to tell you I love you. Signed: You know who.

Annoyed, Xavière swallowed, checked that nobody was watching her, stuffed the paper into her pocket, and left the shop.

When she got to Place d'Arezzo, she walked up the front steps of Number 6. Séverine de Couvigny smiled when she saw her.

In the hallway, once the door had been shut, Xavière stood facing Séverine, grunted some incomprehensible sounds, then, at the end of her tether, gave her a loud slap on the cheek.

Once the slap had been dispatched, she relaxed and recovered the power of speech. "Have you gone crazy, Séverine? Don't ever do that to me again. Orion nearly read your note."

14

As he walked across Place d'Arezzo, Tom stopped dead at the sight of the gardener, so stunned that he held his breath.

That perfect torso, those tapered legs, that chiseled, pure, virile face . . . Why was such magnificence being inflicted on him? And without prior warning? He took a furtive look around to make sure nobody had detected the emotion that had just stabbed him through the heart.

The beauty of men was torture to him, arousing him to such an extent that he didn't know if it was misery or bliss he felt— probably both, since desire both galvanizes and torments us.

Gasping for breath, Tom stood and gazed at Hippolyte. His heart was pounding as if he was running, and yet his legs were rooted to the ground. For a moment, in an attempt to overcome his emotion, he tried to erase the initial bedazzlement, to go against his own judgement, to criticize that athletic body, to downplay its perfection. But in vain. The more he searched for a repulsive element, the more he discovered that everything, from the ebony hair to the slender ankles and the powerful muscles bulging beneath his soft skin, made Hippolyte irresistible.

A question began going around and around in Tom's brain, a question he often asked: did this guy like girls or boys? Tom was wary of answers too easily prompted by his own appetites, which led him to see homosexuals everywhere. All the same, he exclaimed narcissistically, "Too handsome not to be gay."

He continued on his way, circling Hippolyte in slow motion, casting dark, passionate, feverish glances at him, his jaw tensing, his Adam's apple quivering from repeated swallowing, which seemed to suggest: *I could eat you up.*

The gardener looked up and beamed a wide smile at him. Tom was taken aback. The response was so warm, so unrestrained, that he staggered the next few steps: the man with the body of a decathlon athlete had practically offered himself.

Only a straight guy with no ulterior motives smiles like that.

Still, before leaving the square, Tom stopped and turned again, waited ostentatiously for Hippolyte to notice him, and gave him another seductive look. This time, Hippolyte's expression wavered, his smile vanished, crumbling before Tom's interrogation.

Much too handsome not to be straight, Tom concluded, forgetting that he was contradicting himself. He crossed the street and, as a consolation prize, took from his pocket the message he had received that morning.

Just a note to tell you I love you. Signed: You know who.

These reassuring words aroused an emotion in him that was different than the previous rapture, a wave of gentleness and certainty that brought confidence in the future.

Tom walked into Number 7, called Nathan on the entryphone, then went up to the sixth floor.

Nathan was waiting for him in the doorway, lips thrust forward like a catwalk model. He was thirty years old, and wore an anise-green T-shirt over a lanky body and super-tight, low-waisted jeans, with his navel fully exposed.

"Hello."

Nathan said hello the way people blow a kiss, with a lascivious pout, his lips spread.

They kissed and Nathan closed the door behind them.

"Do you want a coffee?"

"I already had three at school this morning."

Tom had just come back from the philosophy class he had given from eight to nine o'clock.

"I don't know how you manage to churn out intelligent stuff at eight in the morning," Nathan moaned wearily. "I could never do it. Mind you, I couldn't do a lesson on Kant or Plato at noon, either. Or at six in the evening, for that matter."

"What about eleven at night?"

"At eleven I can do anything, and at midnight, with a few drinks in me, I can even speak Chinese."

Tom went closer to him and nibbled his ear. Nathan let him, all the while emitting frightened shrieks.

"Well done," Tom whispered, amused, still continuing, "that giggling is really manly!"

"If you're after a hairy ass, then go someplace else. And if you're after a pair of boobs, then also go someplace else, you jerk!"

Tom put a stop to his diatribe by kissing him full on the mouth. As a game, Nathan pretended to object, pushed back Tom's tongue, shrieked again, then, just as Tom was giving up, he caught hold of him, pressed his lips to his, and abandoned himself to a kiss.

"Well, that's done," he sighed, getting up. "We can tick cuddling off the list. Now I can have my coffee."

Leaving Tom sprawled on the couch, he disappeared behind the counter of his open-plan kitchen and came back with a sparkling tea set, fuchsia with light green polka dots.

He saw Tom's eyes grow wide at his purchase. "Fab, isn't it?"

"Well . . ."

"David McLaren makes these. You know, the one who made dried tropical plants a must."

"Oh . . . yes."

Tom always fled from this kind of chatter. He wasn't interested enough in interior decoration to remember any details at all.

Nathan feigned indignation. "I guess you don't like it."

"I'm surprised . . . It's not exactly my taste."

"Your taste?" Nathan said, gulping down a spoonful of jam. "What taste? You don't have any."

Tom smiled. He would never have allowed anyone else to be so rude to him but, in Nathan's case, he not only forgave his constant taunts, but actually expected them, as proof of his affection.

The two men had nothing in common apart from the fact that they liked each other. Nathan was tall, thin as a rake, and always wore the latest fashions. His tone was affected, his opinions outrageous, and his body language totally camp. Tom, on the other hand, was well-built, economical with his words, and had an easygoing manner. While it was immediately obvious to everyone that Nathan liked men, nobody suspected that preference in Tom, who exuded the serene, classic masculinity of a pleasant thirtysomething about to be married and start a family,

What Tom found irritating in Nathan, he also found attractive. He both loved and hated his flutelike intonations, his colorful, frequently vulgar vocabulary, his slavery to fashion, his constant change of hairstyle—shape, length, color— his addiction to trendy bars, his obsession with frequenting the latest gay hotspots. Nathan's homosexuality wasn't just a question of his sexuality, it had invaded all aspects of his life. From morning to night, he lived as a homosexual, thought as a homosexual, talked as a homosexual, dressed as a homosexual, socialized as a homosexual, and traveled as a homosexual. Tom, on the other hand, was content just to have sex as a homosexual. And—much to his surprise—to love Nathan.

Tom joined his lover at the table, filled a cup with coffee, and had a second breakfast with him.

Seeing a pair of shoes on the floor, he nearly choked. "What the hell is that?"

"A rocket for Mars," Nathan said, shrugging.

"You're not going to wear those, are you? The heels are three and a half inches high. You'll look like a—"

"Like a shepherd out on the moors?"

"Like a drag queen in civilian clothes."

"Brilliant! That's exactly the effect I'm after."

"But I'm going to look like your bodyguard."

"That's the second effect I'm after."

With a lascivious smile, Tom grabbed Nathan's arm. "Swear you'll never wear them."

Nathan held on to his hand and stroked it. "Absolutely. I swear I'll wear them tonight."

"I'll be ashamed of you."

"Stop flattering me, I find it exciting."

Charmed and disconcerted, Tom kissed Nathan's fingers. "Don't you think you'll look like a caricature of yourself?"

Nathan pulled a face. "But you love me because I'm a screaming queen."

"No, I don't."

"Yes, you do. It turns you on."

Tom tried to protest but couldn't, because Nathan might have a point.

"OK," Nathan concluded. "Let's just say the proverb about 'birds of a feather' doesn't quite hit the nail on the head here. It's not a gay proverb, anyway."

Tom nodded: although he himself had no desire to be as eccentric as Nathan, he quite liked the fact that Nathan was.

"You can't get two people more different than we are," Nathan went on. "When people meet us, they see me as a raging fashion queen and you as a soccer fan."

They laughed. In actual fact, Nathan was an influential adman with lots of qualifications, and Tom a philosophy teacher with no interest in soccer at all.

Tom thought of something he had recently said to one of his classes. "You have to know nothing about homosexuality to believe that man loves only himself in another man, that he cultivates his own reflection. That's just a relic of Freudianism, to think of homosexuality as a kind of mirror eroticism."

Nathan tapped on the table with his enormous rings. "Since you're being serious, I'm going to say something, Tom. What worries me is that you're not just into blatant queens, you're also into the muscleman type."

"Excuse me?"

"Do you deny it?"

"I—"

"You should have seen yourself in the square, with the gardener. You were like a prospector unearthing a giant gold nugget."

"Oh, so you were at the window!"

"Of course: I was looking at the same thing you were."

"Quite something, don't you think?"

"Yes, but not for us."

"What do you mean?"

"I mean, hands off! He's as straight as they come. Straight through and through."

"How would you know? Have you tried?"

"He has a daughter."

"You're kidding."

"There's often a little girl with him on the square."

"Could be his niece."

"Yeah, sure, his niece who calls him 'daddy.'"

Tom lowered his eyes in frustration.

"I like your reaction," Nathan went on, ramping up his natural hysteria. "Sorry to disappoint you, my friend, but you just get to eye up the Spartacus of Brussels, you don't get to screw him."

"Nor do you."

"Nor do I. Still, I got worried there, with you looking like Bernadette contemplating the Virgin Mary in the cave. Would you be capable of going with that guy?"

"Going with him?"

"Sleeping with him!"

"Yes."

"Asshole!"

"And you wouldn't?"

"You asshole!"

"Answer me," Tom insisted. "You're standing there at the window all morning, ogling the gardener and finding out all about his family. Wouldn't you go to bed with him?"

"Sure I would. But for me it's normal."

"Why's that?"

"Because I'm just a slut who loves anything in pants. I'm turned on by masculinity. But you . . . I don't understand how you can screw me and eat him up with your eyes."

"I'm not narrow-minded."

"Imagine if my eyes popped out of their sockets when I spotted a shrimp like me! I swear it'd piss you off."

Tom rushed to him, enchanted by his constant theatricality. "I love *you*."

"Yeah, right . . . they all say that," Nathan muttered, his eyes closed, fighting him off for the sake of it.

They kissed, then smiled at each other, all the gray clouds dispersed.

Nathan stood up and, on his way to the kitchen, whispered in Tom's ear, "I loved your note."

"My note?"

"The letter you sent me."

"Me?"

"Don't go all mysterious on me. You don't have to sign for me to know it's from you."

Nathan took a letter on yellow paper out of his pocket and read out loud:

Just a note to tell you I love you. Signed: You know who.

Delighted, he said in a squeaky voice, 'I've unmasked you, Mister 'You know who.'"

"Nathan—"

"I hope you'll soon send me a note announcing that we're going to live together."

"You—"

"Because I find it absurd to live in the same place but not in the same apartment, and pay two rents!"

"Please—"

"I know, we don't keep the same hours because you like to get up early and I like lounging in bed and don't work until later. But precisely because we can't synchronize our schedules, cohabiting would allow us to be together more often."

Nathan was indulging in his favorite subject: ever since they had started seeing each other—two years ago now—he had wanted them to live together. Tom always resisted: he was set in his bachelor ways, feeling at home only amid the hundreds of books lining the walls of his studio apartment.

To halt the flood of recrimination that was sure to come, Tom stood up, took a sheet of yellow paper from his pocket, and brandished it. "Look, I received this. And I know it's from you."

Nathan came closer. They looked at their respective messages. Even though there were a few negligible differences in the handwriting and in the force with which the pen had been pressed on the paper, the downstrokes looked the same and the wording was identical.

Nathan smiled. "You're pulling my leg, right?"

Tom also smiled. "No, *you're* pulling *my* leg."

"You wrote both of them to make me believe it didn't come from you," Nathan whinnied.

Tom laughed and shook his head. "No, it's you who played this trick on me."

They looked at each other, each trying to prove that the other was lying.

"What an actor!" Nathan cried.

"You sly baboon," Tom said.

"Female baboon, please. Female baboons are a lot smarter than males."

They sat back down at the table.

"Now tell me the truth."

"No, *you* tell *me* the truth."

15

With the giddy cacophony of parrots and parakeets as a background, two municipal employees were mowing the lawn for the first time that season. The cut grass gave off a fresh smell, not as sharp and green as it would be later on, but heavier and wearier, the smell of a convalescing lawn that had made it through the winter.

Hippolyte and Germain worked in tandem, although the local residents only ever noticed one of them. There was a reason for that: Germain was a dwarf and Hippolyte an Apollo, who put his colleague in the shade not only with his height, but also with his beauty.

Germain didn't resent it. On the contrary. Ever since he had known Hippolyte, his life had taken on a triumphant dimension: short, disabled, and graceless as he was, a man women avoided looking at, so painfully ugly were his features, he was the friend of the handsomest man in Brussels. When he was with Hippolyte, he could temporarily forget his own hideousness, concealing it from himself and others, who paid less attention to him. Whenever Germain walked into a café or a bowling alley with him, he was moved by the fact that he provoked beaming smiles; he swooned with happiness as soon as he heard, "Hey, guys," an expression that presumed a common element between him and Hippolyte.

"You know, my daughter's a genius," Hippolyte said as he filled the wheelbarrow with garbage. "I had to sign her up for three libraries so she would have enough books to read for the week. Three libraries! At the age of ten! And sometimes she goes down to the neighbor, who's a teacher, to borrow one more. The girl's a miracle. I've no idea how she could have come from me."

Germain couldn't help but agree. There was no point in contradicting Hippolyte's natural modesty: he would only get angry. Because he had always been bottom of his class at school, Hippolyte saw himself as a dumb animal, with way below average intelligence. Unlike so many others, who blame their failures on their families or circumstances, he held himself solely responsible for his shortcomings. Anyone who contradicted the humility with which he lived his life threw him, made him feel sad.

Because Hippolyte was happy. Even though he earned little, even though he only rented a cramped apartment for himself and his daughter, even though the little girl's mother had run off to Latin America and left him holding the baby, he was always smiling. He felt fulfilled by his job as gardener and road mender: firstly because he was a "civil servant," which, for an orphan who'd grown up in care, represented a kind of ennoblement; and secondly, because he worked in the open air, doing a physical job that made him healthily tired, not in an office where he would have been bored and people would have noticed his rustic simplicity. In his stubborn, generous head, he had two bosses, the municipal council and nature, and he felt indebted to both, to the council for providing money and security, and to his beloved nature, who requested that he watch over her in a city where she was threatened by concrete, asphalt, and pollution.

And so that day, on Place d'Arezzo, he did not feel degraded picking up dog shit, gathering old beer cans, or getting fresh parrot droppings on his arms and shoulders before he mowed the lawn. It was with care that he made the square beautiful, like a woman he had to satisfy.

A young man appeared, head bowed, a worried expression on his face. "Good morning, Victor!" Hippolyte called out.

The young man walked past without really answering, deaf to his surroundings. Hippolyte took no offense, wondering what was on the student's mind, since he was usually so friendly.

Outside Number 12, a limousine stood waiting, double-parked. Hippolyte knew that the famous politician Zachary Bidermann lived there. Although intrigued, he only looked at the front steps through the trees, as if he had no right to look at them directly. To his way of thinking, there were only two kinds of people: the great and the humble. Zachary Bidermann played in the major league, Hippolyte didn't. He took no offense at that situation, nor did he want it to change. Although Zachary Bidermann was clearly able to mow a lawn, Hippolyte couldn't chair a board of economists.

Shielded by a crimson rhododendron, he saw Zachary Bidermann come down the steps in a three-piece pin-striped suit, a flowing coat over his large body, quickly greet his driver, who was holding the door open for him, and disappear into the car. Faced with this sartorial splendor, Hippolyte, who was wearing nothing but shorts, suddenly felt naked, vulnerable, socially powerless.

Rose Bidermann, round and pretty, stood on the balcony, waving her husband goodbye.

Poor woman. It's no joke to be married to a brain. The man probably never thinks about sex.

Hippolyte glanced at the house of the writer Baptiste Monier—another one who impressed him. Whenever he made out the top of Monier's head through the window, he thought about the thousands of pages, alive with stories and characters, that came out of that skull. How could he remain still for so long? That alone, Hippolyte thought, represented an achievement. As for his writing talent . . . Hippolyte struggled to form even a sentence without starting over several times and filling it with spelling and grammar mistakes.

He should have been my girl's father instead of me. She'd have a thousand things to say to a writer.

Bent over an embankment, he suddenly felt a presence. He straightened up and saw a man watching him. Hippolyte greeted him with a broad smile. The man did not respond, but carried on crossing the square, then stopped, turned, and stared at him with a look of hatred.

Hippolyte was concerned. You seldom saw that kind of aggressive character in this neighborhood. What did he have against him?

He bent over again, puzzled, more used to being transparent than to being eyed venomously. He knew he didn't exist for most of the people who lived on this square—those two teenagers, for example, who'd been sitting on a bench and squabbling for the last fifteen minutes. But he didn't resent those who were indifferent to him: why on earth would they be interested in a municipal employee—and not a very clever municipal employee at that? It was an indifference he felt was justified, but that passerby's furious glare had thrown him.

Just then, he became aware of yet more disapproval on his left. The aristocrat from Number 4, the one with perfect children, an SUV, the particle "de" in front of his surname, and a double-barreled first name, was also staring at him, looking fierce and sullen.

Worried, Hippolyte checked there was no trace of dirt or blood to provoke criticism or make his appearance indecent . . . No. What, then?

The mixed-race lawyer who had gotten so much TV coverage during the Mehdi Martin case crossed the square at a nimble pace. He didn't notice either Germain or Hippolyte.

This reassured Hippolyte. He decided that he had done nothing wrong and calmly started raking the paths.

A yellow envelope lay beneath the largest tree. He picked it up. His first name was written on it: *Hippolyte.*

Who's been thinking of me? His first thought was that one of the local residents had slipped him a note as a thank you, as sometimes happened.

He opened it and read the message:

Just a note to tell you I love you. Signed: You know who.

Hippolyte turned scarlet.

He knew who the letter was from. No doubt whatsoever. He looked up and caught the woman looking at him, partly hidden behind the curtain. The fact that she withdrew into the shadows when she noticed he had seen her was proof.

Hippolyte blushed a second time and took a deep breath of the spring air.

He had never hoped that such a thing might be possible, never believed that his feelings would be returned by her. What a wonderful morning! Life was really spoiling him.

"Germain, I have an errand to run, I'll be back."

The dwarf nodded.

Hippolyte grabbed a towel from his bag, wiped the sweat off his torso, then covered it with a spotlessly white T-shirt.

He walked resolutely to the florist's, bought a bunch of plump, pink peonies from Orion, then went into Number 13 and resolutely climbed the stairs until he reached the door of the woman he desired.

PART TWO
MAGNIFICAT

The presence of parrots on Place d'Arezzo was puzzling. How did these birds from hot countries come to be on our cold continent? Why had this tropical jungle taken root in the heart of the city? By what strange madness were savage cries, rutting screams, wild debaucheries, raw, honest, barbaric colors stirring the gloomy calm of the capital of Europe?

Only the children here thought the presence of parrots and parakeets was normal, but as is well known, the weakness—and strength—of young minds is that they accept everything.

Adults tried to explain this incongruity with a legend.

Five decades earlier, at Number 9, the town house then occupied by the Brazilian consul, a telegram informed the diplomat that he was to return to Rio urgently. Forced to travel by air rather than by sea, he had had to keep his baggage to a minimum and realized that it was impossible to take his bird collection. Unable to find someone to take in his precious specimens, he had therefore, with a heavy heart, on the morning of his departure, opened the cages and restored the birds to the sky from the high windows of his living room. Unaccustomed to long flights, the multicolored mass of parrots, cockatoos, conures, macaws, parakeets, lorikeets, cockatiels, and kakarikis had seen it as wasted effort to venture beyond the nearest trees, and had set up home on Place d'Arezzo.

And so as they trod the sidewalks, visitors felt as if they

were entering some kind of crazy movie, in which, through a bizarre superimposition, the images came from civilization, the soundtrack from nature.

When Patricia had opened the door and seen Hippolyte standing on the landing, tall and broad and smiling happily, a spray of peonies in his arms, she had been speechless.

He had proffered the bouquet. "For you."

She had looked at the flowers, unable to accept them, using them as a wall between them.

Seeing her reticence, he had suddenly turned shy. "Don't you want them?"

Guessing from the anxiety on his regular, handsome features that he might leave, Patricia had surprised herself by taking the gift. Touched, he had sighed, a little calmer now.

"Why?"

Patricia hadn't recognized her own voice in that stifled question.

"Because I love you," he had said, as if it was a self-evident fact.

Patricia had flailed her arms in the air and opened her eyes and mouth wide, wanting to run away . . . and yet to stay.

"I've loved you for three years," he had stammered.

Looking around her for help, Patricia had wondered when her daughter would be back, if she should call the police, why she was wearing this hostess gown that made her hips look wider, and when she would slam the door shut. In a panic, she had felt her legs give way.

But before she could swoon, she had heard a thump: the

colossus had fainted and fallen to the floor, and was now lying at her feet.

Ever since that day, Patricia had changed. Unable to stop thinking about Hippolyte, she led a triple life.

First, she regularly met him at five o'clock in a café in the Marolles, a working-class neighborhood where nobody would recognize her. They would chat, she would let herself be warmed by his caressing gaze, and their hands would sometimes brush against each other; she was ecstatic with happiness.

Second, she assumed her usual role of mother to the surly Albane, from whom she kept her flirtation a secret.

And third, she spent her remaining hours slimming. Since she knew that she would not be able to resist Hippolyte's advances for very long, her physical transformation had become almost an obsession: she had to do away with the obese cow she saw in the mirror. Now that a stunning man wanted her, she hated her body; if someone had opened the doors of an operating room to her, she would have rushed in to have her fat pumped out, her hip bones sawed off, and her stomach reduced to the size of a quail's egg by having several yards of intestine removed while her belly was surgically tightened. In the absence of such a radical solution, she mistreated herself. Instead of embarking on a diet, she starved herself, making do with two green apples and half a gallon of mineral water a day. Rather than gradually taking up a sport, she forced herself to walk for miles and pulled out from under her bed exercise gadgets she had ordered over the phone, shamelessly overrunning the apartment with her bum and tum appliances, her weights, her muscle-building kits, and various other instruments of torture.

Convinced that she was the cause of this revolution, Albane hadn't protested. She was delighted to have this power over her mother, whom she now only ever saw dressed in a sweat suit.

No sooner was she alone than Patricia would raise her pain threshold by one notch. She would plug electrodes to the parts that needed toning and give herself electric shocks, suffering until she screamed. Many times, panting with exhaustion, her eyes bloodshot, her face bathed in tears, she had gone to the bathroom and said to the mirror, which played the part of Hippolyte, "You see what I'm doing, my love, don't you?"

But by the time she got to the café, she had removed all trace of her efforts, kept silent about her self-inflicted martyrdom, and recovered her trademark confidence and lightheartedness. Besides—and this was a true miracle—all her aches and pains would disappear as soon as Hippolyte was there.

She liked everything about the man: his kindness, his gentleness, his easygoing conversation. Only his physical perfection threw her into a panic. Patricia regretted that she was no longer twenty; partly because at twenty, she had actually been twenty—curvy, supple, with ideal proportions—but especially because she would not have judged herself. What is damaged by time is not the body but our confidence in it; we have discovered that other people's feet, legs, shoulders, and buttocks can be different than ours; we have succumbed to the disease of making comparisons, and we have learned, through a series of brutal revelations, that we, too, have changed. Since the glory days of her twenties, Patricia had known nothing but failure. To now present her damaged, neglected body to the exemplary Hippolyte seemed to her an indecent aberration.

Still, a confrontation was imminent . . . Every day, he expressed his desire for her with greater fervor; every day, Patricia's defenses crumbled a little more; soon, they would kiss, then progress to bed, a prospect both attractive and terrifying.

She was bracing herself for it with this one obsession: she had to be prepared.

One afternoon, double-locked in the bathroom, she dyed her pubic hair auburn. It made her weep to have to resort to such deception: she would forever need to correct herself, disguise herself, misrepresent herself. Poor Hippolyte would be holding an impostor in his arms.

At about six, while sipping her tea, she nearly asked, "So what is it you see in me?" This question would have led to her pouring out her complexes, listing her defects, so she desisted. Let Hippolyte build his illusions, she wouldn't attempt to knock them down. *If he likes hippos, then it's not up to the queen of hippopotami to discourage him.*

And so she kept everything vague. When her suitor spoke to her as if she was a gorgeous woman, his eyes would glow with the flame of desire, and so she would lower hers and blush, like an odalisque accustomed to having such an effect. The other thing she kept vague about was the anonymous letters: when she had realized that he had plucked up the courage to approach her only after he thought the message was from her, she neither contradicted him nor established the truth, and she neglected to mention that she had received an identical note.

Hippolyte carried the note on him, his "most precious possession," he had admitted to her. Patricia, on the other hand, had concealed hers in Ovid's *Art of Love*, of which she owned an expensive edition with artist's prints. Some evenings, when Albane was in bed, she would look at the yellow sheet of paper, stroke it with a respect verging on the sacred, almost believing that it *had* been sent to her by Hippolyte. What did it matter? Whoever it came from, that message had brought them together.

She often recalled the moment when she had had to bring Hippolyte around after he had fainted on her doorstep: that scene, more than any other word or action, had conquered her. Because he lay there, inert, she had taken him in her arms, lifted his heavy head, stroked his bushy hair, felt the texture of his muscles under the T-shirt, and discovered—to her astonishment—the surprising softness of his skin. Life had given her a gift: she could touch the man she had long desired without his knowledge. For a fleeting moment, she'd had the feeling she was indulging in a forbidden act. Yet he had agreed to it, his body had abandoned itself to hers; in fact, his body had needed hers.

When he had opened his eyes again, he had smiled at first, before embarrassment had overwhelmed him.

"I'm sorry. I—"

"No problem. I'm here."

They had looked at each other. At that moment, Patricia had imagined that she could love a man like this for a long time, take care of him, and that one day he would die in her arms. In a second, she had accepted all that would come from him. Why distrust a lover who was sensitive to the point of swooning from emotion, at once a colossus and a child? She was seduced by both his frailty and his strength, and more still . . . It was during that minute that their common destiny was sealed: before, she had desired him; now, she loved him.

On the Thursday, Albane announced that she was planning to go to a party in Knokke-le-Zoute with Quentin on Saturday.

"Quentin?" Patricia asked.

"Yes, Quentin, I've mentioned him to you a hundred times. We've been together for four weeks."

She had a surly expression on her face as she reminded her of this essential truth. Much to her surprise, her mother rushed to her and kissed her.

"I'm so glad, my darling."

Touched, Albane didn't resist.

"Four weeks, that's wonderful," Patricia said. "Four weeks, that's . . . amazing!"

Patricia went back to her exercise bike, all the while hatching a plan: if Albane didn't come back on Saturday night, maybe she could invite Hippolyte? And maybe then . . .

Turning red, she beat her own speed record. This had to be handled carefully. The roles of mother and daughter had been reversed: the adult, like a teenager, was concealing her affairs of the heart and trying craftily to rid herself of an inhibiting presence.

"Albane," she said that very evening, "whose house is the party in on Saturday night?"

"It's at Zoë's, in Knokke-le-Zoute."

"That's a long way. Who'll bring you back?"

"Servane."

"What a shame you'll have to leave the party early. Why not sleep over at your Aunt Mathilde's?"

"Mathilde's?"

"Why not? You've done it many times before."

"Not after a party."

"An even better reason: you'll be drinking and dancing and by midnight you'll be tired. Not a good idea to sit in a car for an hour."

Albane gave it some thought, smiled, and said, with surprise in her voice, "You're a really cool mom . . . "

"I trust my little girl, and I want her to be happy. Shall I call Mathilde?"

"No, Mom, no sweat, I'll take care of it. I'll just tell her you're OK with it." Still somewhat disconcerted, she added, with a puckering of her nose, "Er . . . thanks."

So the following day, Patricia invited Hippolyte for dinner on the Saturday. He quivered, knowing where the evening might lead.

"I'm going to make a fool of myself again, Patricia."

"Excuse me?"

"I'm going to be so happy, I might pass out again."

She grabbed his hand, not daring to say that nothing would upset her more. That day, they found it hard to continue their conversation. Their thoughts were already on that momentous evening.

It will either be the beginning or the end, Patricia kept telling herself on her way home. *Either he'll realize I'm a monster, or luck is on my side and he won't.*

At dinner, Albane was concerned by the fact that her mother wasn't eating the food she had prepared. "Mom, if you don't eat you'll collapse."

"Hmm?"

"If you don't eat properly, you could lose your hair and your teeth."

Patricia dismissed the remark with a loud laugh, but that night she dreamed her teeth were coming loose as she smiled at Hippolyte, a nightmare that woke her up several times.

The Saturday was exhausting. She got rid of her daughter in the morning by giving her money to buy clothes and go to the movies with her friends before setting off for Knokke-le-Zoute, then tidied up her apartment as if the police were coming to search it. She went to the trouble of taking her gym equipment down to the basement. It would have been ridiculous to leave it on display, like showing him a photograph that emphasized all her flaws.

Then she prepared a special meal. She felt a lot more confident on that front, since she knew she was a good cook.

Finally, she disappeared into the bathroom, washed several times, dried herself, put cream on, did her hair, then undid it, started again, aware she was overdoing it yet unable to stop herself. Then she changed several times, horrified at the clothes available in her wardrobe, and decided on a crimson dress.

Red. Isn't that a bit much?

Never mind. The advantage of a bright color was that it dazzled the eye, so that the shape underneath wouldn't show.

In her room, she arranged three fragrant candles, and placed tulle cloths over the bedside lamps to soften the light and create a pleasant, intimate, almost clandestine atmosphere, which also had the advantage of preserving modesty.

She jumped when the doorbell rang.

Hippolyte was there at the door, holding a bunch of flowers, and looking very touching in a dark, simple but elegant suit.

"It's my birthday!" she exclaimed, comically.

"Really?"

"No, I'm joking . . . "

"I hope it'll be our anniversary someday."

He said this in such an earnest, intense tone that Patricia stood there rooted to the spot.

He slowly put the flowers on the small table in the hallway and then, without the slightest hesitation, came up to her, took her in his arms, and kissed her on the mouth.

The evening did not go quite as planned. Instead of going into the living room to chat, then eating the delicious food she had prepared, they went straight to the bedroom.

He undressed her slowly, kissing every inch of her skin as he uncovered her with his fingers. Patricia quivered, partly because his silky lips gave her pleasure, and partly because she knew that, as long as he held her so close, he couldn't see her.

Several times, she shook so much she almost brought everything to a halt. Each time, he reassured her with a long kiss, then carried on exploring, like the devout follower of a totemic cult.

When she had nothing on but her underwear, she suggested undressing him in turn, and did so, with a lump in her throat. When was the last time she had unbuttoned a man's shirt?

She worked quicker than he did, she was in a hurry to fuse with his warm body.

When he was down to his boxer shorts, she feared she might not to be able to go any further. Nothing scared her more than uncovering his penis. In spite of her lack of experience, she knew this could be a tricky moment. Would she like it? Would she find it too . . . or not quite . . . ? Or worse, would it remind her of someone else's? All of a sudden, their closeness was becoming too concrete, too genital, and risked shattering her dream.

As if reading her thoughts, Hippolyte lifted her in his arms, got into bed, covered their bodies with the sheets, and lay on top of her. Smothering her with kisses and undulating imperceptibly over her, he undressed her, and his penis entered her without her seeing it.

C oming out of the European meeting, Zachary Bidermann
was surrounded by ministers and their chiefs of staff
in a state of intense intellectual excitement. He was
congratulated in twenty-three languages, people claimed it
was an historic moment, there was an enthusiastic consensus.
His performance had been dazzling: this brilliant man had
broken the deadlock that ideological policies led to, and
drawn up a balance and development plan for the next fifteen
years. They had been right to invite him to this financing
round that preceded the Council of the European Union. His
intelligence was a blend of qualities usually distributed among
a number of individuals: sharpness of analysis, mastery of synthesis, rigor, imagination, the inventiveness to develop original
theories, the ability to define concrete tactics, and communication skills. He had several heads in one, like a kind of intellectual monster, a Hydra no difficulty can bring down but
which, on the contrary, regenerates and develops with every
blow it receives.

Slyly, Zachary Bidermann enjoyed the compliments, conscious of needing to savor them because they would only be
given to him today; the very next day, political bigwigs would
appropriate his theories, claim them as their own, and forget
where they had come from. Not that Zachary Bidermann
cared! All that mattered were the interests of nations and individuals. In fact, behind this wealthy man with a taste for luxury there lay a generous citizen, a republican devoted to the

general good. Since he hated populist rhetoric and was wary of pathos and sentimental exhibitionism, he kept the heart of his mission concealed. Nobody suspected his generosity, which suited him well; he could influence his contemporaries more by hiding behind a mask of purely technical intelligence.

After ten minutes of commotion, Léo Adolf, President of the Council of the European Union, took his old friend by the arm and drew him aside. "Zachary, you're far too important to us here and in the Liberal Party for me to conceal the truth from you."

"What is it?"

"We've received a complaint about you."

"Who from?"

"Elda Brugge."

His face twisted in an irritable grimace, Zachary immediately saw the danger. "A complaint about what?"

"Harassment."

"Again?"

"Again, as you say. She's the fifth female civil servant to lodge a complaint."

Zachary tried to change the subject. "Look, Léo, you can't even flirt with a woman nowadays without her thinking it's harassment. Just because I'm chivalrous, that doesn't make me a lout."

"So you don't deny it."

"Come on, it's a trifle."

"Maybe so, but it's going to cause you problems."

"In what way? I do what I want . . . If it gets out, Rose will see the difference—as she has in the past—and I won't allow anyone to dictate to me what's right and wrong in terms of morality. We're not in America, thank God. Europe knows how to reject the demon of puritanism. First of all, what does this Elda Brugge say?"

"That you followed her several times after meetings, that

you called her on her private phone, that you gave her an
assignment in order to see her alone in your office, and that
there you allegedly tried several times to—"

"Rape her?"

"No. To caress her. To kiss her."

"And is that a crime?"

"Yes, in her opinion, because she was meeting you strictly
on a professional basis and rejected your flirtation. That's
harassment. Do I have to remind you?"

"Is that all?"

"What do you mean, is that all?

"Does she have anything else against me?"

"No."

"No recordings? No photographs? No letters?"

"No, nothing."

"So it's her word against mine?"

"Yes."

Zachary burst out laughing.

Although he felt reassured, Léo Adolf was taken aback. "So
you're not the least bit worried?"

"Look, Léo, it'll be easy to show that this woman is being
spiteful because she hasn't climbed the ladder as she'd hoped.
I'll easily prove her professional shortcomings. People will think
she's retaliating out of resentment. Especially since . . . "—he
laughed before continuing—"especially since . . . Well, have
you seen her? She's ugly! Really ugly!"

Léo Adolf's eyes opened wide.

"Come on!" Zachary insisted. "If a disciplinary committee
or a board of directors or whatever sees that beanpole with her
big ass and her turkey neck, nobody will believe I wanted her.
Especially if I show them pictures of Rose. It'll seem prepos-
terous. Talk about sexual bait! She'll only make herself look
ridiculous."

Léo Adolf was so shocked by his friend's attitude that he

said nothing. Even though Zachary had just admitted flirting with this woman on several occasions, he seemed to be enjoying the idea that his desire for her would seem implausible.

"But . . . but . . . "

"What?" Zachary asked innocently.

"You're despicable. You tried to have sex with her and now you say she's ugly."

"Haven't you ever done that?"

Léo Adolf turned on his heel and walked away.

Zachary caught up with him. "Léo, don't pretend to be so naive: the best lovers are the partly-beautiful, or partly-ugly, depending on how you look at them. Unlike beautiful women, they give you the lot, they give themselves to you fully, they reject boundaries. It makes sense: half-beautiful women need to prove they're better than the beautiful ones."

"Shut up."

"You should know that only too well, Léo. You had an affair with Carlotta Vesperini."

Stunned, Léo Adolf turned back and looked Zachary up and down. He was pale, and his lips were trembling. "As it happens, I found Carlotta Vesperini very beautiful."

Zachary lowered his eyes, sensing that he had just committed an irreparable gaffe.

"Let's drop the subject," Léo Adolf concluded.

"Let's drop the subject," Zachary agreed.

The President of the Union pulled himself together, while Zachary, relieved that his accuser had put a stop to this idiotic conversation, went to the lunch organized in the corridors where the key members of the European project were assembled.

A nagging sense of anxiety led him to him drink three glasses of champagne. But then, in conversation with a group of senior administrators, he recovered, developed a few original ideas, and gradually felt more relaxed.

He went up to a female member of the Swedish delegation. Before he had even said a word, the gleam in his dilated eyes told her plainly enough that he thought she was stunning. She blushed, and they struck up a conversation. While keeping his thoughts within certain boundaries, he examined her with lust: her small waist, her pert breasts, her tiny ears . . . She felt as if there were two Zacharys speaking to her, one developing brilliant theories, the other sniffing her like a dog about to mount a bitch. Disquieted, she was unable to split herself down the middle in the same way; either she prioritized her mind and concentrated only on the intellectual exchange between them, or she became nothing but her desired body and wriggled nervously.

Zachary embarrassed her and that delighted him.

A blond man with glasses approached and gave a slight bow. "Monsieur, let me take advantage of the fact that you're talking with my fiancée to thank you for your presentation."

A profusion of compliments followed, but Zachary had stopped listening. The Swedish woman's prevarication had been halted by the presence of her fiancé; she had left her body and returned to being a politician conversing with a world-famous economist.

As soon as he could, Zachary said goodbye to them and went searching for prey elsewhere. During the seconds in which his attention vainly wandered over the gathering, he felt a lump of unease in his throat. Luckily, he noticed a forty-year-old woman whose eyes met his. He brazenly walked up to her, as if she had invited him.

Again, his body immediately sent her the signals of desire. He shifted from foot to foot, moved very close to her face, and smiled, making it clear to her that he found her attractive.

She understood, and all at once was troubled and uncertain, which gave Zachary leave to start a conversation.

Since his body language suggested the opposite of

detachment, the woman suddenly exclaimed, "Are you flirting with me?"

He gave a subtle smile. "What makes you say that?"

She stammered, embarrassed, suddenly blushing at the thought that she might be ridiculous. "I'm sorry, I don't know what came over me."

"Not at all. I, on the other hand, am quite ready to flirt with you, if you'll allow me."

"I'm not sure I understand."

"You're irresistible."

The woman, who was German, began shaking. She looked around, spotted the emergency exits, then clicked her fingers and said, "I forbid you to treat me like this."

"Like what?"

"Like a piece of sausage meat. I have a degree in Politics, a PhD in Sociology, I work over eighty hours a week for my country and for Europe: I think I deserve somewhat different behavior from you."

Zachary grasped the extent of his mistake: in flirting with this functionary, he took away her identity, annihilated the image she had built, denied her career path, and sent her back to being the body she was before all that work.

Without a word, he left her so abruptly that she would be sure to wonder if she had read the scene correctly; with a bit of luck, she might even come and apologize to him.

He went up to one of the hostesses, who was certainly was not going to be offended by being eyed lustfully.

At that moment, President Léo Adolf walked past him, and Zachary felt the weight of disapproval on the back of his neck.

Angrily, he abandoned the hostess and charged straight to the office they had made available to him. He double-locked himself in, opened the computer, and typed in the name of a porn website.

When the first images appeared—full breasts, mouths

pursed like anuses, buttocks divided by a G-string—he gave a sigh of relief, freed from the pressure of other people, at last able to experience pleasure.

He chose a particular category on the site—he knew and liked them all—unbuttoned his pants, stroked himself, and came.

Delighted, relaxed, smiling, ready to go back and change the world or move mountains, he noticed with amusement that according to the clock on the screen it had taken just seven minutes to rid him of his tension. Would he still be alive if he didn't have these pleasures? No, he would probably have died of boredom. Or of depression, because despair was always prowling around him, patient and tenacious.

That afternoon, Zachary Bidermann again dazzled, impressing everyone he met.

At six-thirty, as he was calling his chauffeur in order to leave the European Union buildings, Léo Adolf came into his office.

"Zachary, I want to make sure you understand. We have great hopes for you. Vanderbrock is too weak to run Belgium in this crisis. The people look down on him, the media revile him, the members of parliament heckle him. He's lost all support as prime minister. You know perfectly well there's talk of you as a replacement. So I won't ask where the rumor originated . . . "

Zachary chuckled.

Taking this laughter as confirmation, Léo Adolf continued, "But anyway, the rumor has taken root. That's all that matters. Everybody thinks you're the savior we need, Zachary, and with good reason. You're the most brilliant person we have. We in the Liberal Party will support you. All the same, your habits could have a negative effect on us."

"How dare you bring that up again?"

"It's all about protecting yourself, and protecting us."

"No, it's about protecting the country. What I do in private doesn't affect that."

"I disagree. You may be able to downplay or even cover up scandals, but the question remains, a question your supporters need an answer to."

"What question is that?"

"Is Zachary Bidermann able to control himself?"

Zachary looked at him openmouthed. It was a question he had never asked himself.

"Sometimes," Léo Adolf continued, "it's a small step from sexual appetite to sexual obsession."

"Is that so? Are you a specialist on the subject now?"

"There are a few questions I want to ask you. The answers will tell you whether or not you're an addict. Are you able to stop? Have you ever stopped? Do you sometimes lie to conceal your activities? Do you feel an overwhelming anxiety, a craving, at the times when you aren't indulging in these activities?" He raised his hand in farewell. "You don't have to answer me today. Answer yourself first."

And with that, he left.

Zachary Bidermann closed his office door in a foul mood. If he played Léo Adolf's game, he would have to consider himself a sick man, whereas in fact he was perfectly fine. Nobody had the right to judge how he handled his stress.

When he got into his limousine, which was parked at the Rond-Point Robert Schuman, he told the chauffeur to take him home. "Self-control," he muttered to himself. "Nobody controls himself like me. If only they knew . . . Poor fools. They've got nothing left in them but ideas. Bunch of idiots! Fuck you!" Angry but invigorated, he tapped on the chauffeur's shoulder. "Rue des Moulins, Georges. I'll go to Place d'Arezzo later."

When he walked into the Les Tropiques sauna, the place struck him as shabby, unworthy of him, and he sighed with relief. The fact was, he liked the basic decor, the rubber palm trees, the photographs of sunsets on the walls, the sharp smell of bleach. Not one of his colleagues could ever have imagined that someone as prominent as he was could set foot in a place like that; and a man like him was just what he no longer wanted to be.

After putting his clothes into a battered steel locker, he wrapped a threadbare towel around his waist and went down to the basement.

On the bottom steps, a powerful smell of decomposing undergrowth, sweat, and rotting mushrooms struck his nostrils, and he felt intoxicated. He walked along dark corridors, passing couples and a few solitary individuals. He was galvanized by the constant moans. He came to the Turkish bath, his ears and nostrils on the alert; as he advanced, the smell of thyme with which the steam was imbued put the finishing touch to his sense of delight: the aroma, which in his childhood he had associated with medical concoctions for clearing the lungs, had become an aphrodisiac for him, a promise of happiness. He pushed open the steamed-up door. Wrapped in an all-pervasive cloud, beneath a failing light, featureless bodies stirred: five shadowy male figures and two female. He went closer, took off his towel and, naked, without identity, restored to the state of a lecherous animal, threw himself into that mass of flesh.

An hour later, the elegant Zachary Bidermann got out at Number 10 Place d'Arezzo, dismissed his chauffeur, went through his bedroom to take his customary shower, in order to remove all suspicious smells, changed his suit, and appeared on the reception floor all spruced up, smiling at Rose, who was waiting for him impatiently.

"Not too tired, darling?"

"In top form!"

"You're truly amazing. How do you do it?"

Flattered by the idea of being a superman, Zachary Bidermann kissed her without replying.

W hat do you recommend?"
Joséphine looked up at the Italian waiter, who stood there ready to take her order. Discouraged by the richness of the menu, she was trying to save herself the effort of having to think.

"I don't know what you like, Madame."

"What would you choose?"

Baptiste concealed his derisive expression behind the tall menu because he already knew what came next: the waiter would point out to her what he liked, Joséphine would grimace, he would suggest a second option, she would nod gently, reproach him sullenly for "really" not having the same taste as her, then ask what the people at the next table were having, and demand that very same dish. After this little comedy, which could last four minutes, she would conclude, "Actually, I'm not hungry."

The waiter withdrew. Joséphine and Baptiste clinked glasses.

After taking a sip of her Brunello, Joséphine fixed her husband with an intent look. "I have something important to tell you."

"What?"

"I've fallen in love."

Baptiste blinked, a reaction that mixed surprise and relief. Ever since the unsigned message, the strange yellow letter, had arrived, he had guessed that a plot was being hatched without

his knowledge and outside his control. It didn't take exceptional observation skills to notice that Joséphine kept rushing
to the other end of the apartment to make phone calls, disappearing for a long time on the pretext of going shopping, and
daydreaming in front of the TV news. Although he had already
formulated a theory, he had been waiting for the explanation
to come from her. Another husband would have followed his
wife in secret, searched through her possessions, stolen her cell
phone, established an inventory of her calls, and probably
made a scene and demanded the truth. But Baptiste considered such behavior to be beneath him. The son of a couple
who tore each other apart in domestic arguments, he had had
such a hatred of jealousy since childhood that he had purged
himself of it, and was averse to playing the inquisitor; but the
true reason for his wait-and-see policy was trust: Joséphine
couldn't possibly be deceiving him.

She was looking at him, awaiting his reaction before carrying on.

"I suspected as much," Baptiste murmured.

"I guess I didn't exactly conceal it," she whispered.

He nodded. *Just as long as the conversation keeps to this
respectful honesty,* he thought. He leaned toward her and
smiled. "So you're in love . . . Is that good news or bad news?"

She took his hand solicitously. "I don't know yet. After all,
nothing's going to change for you. No matter what happens,
it's you I'll choose, Baptiste, and it's you I'll stay with. That's
the first thing I wanted to say to you. It's you, you, you, before
anything else in the whole wide world."

Baptiste felt relieved. A wave of delight made him sink back
in his chair. So he had been right to believe in Joséphine's loyalty. He didn't mind what she told him now, because she had
just confirmed that he was still the chosen one. "When did it
start?"

"Two weeks ago."

"What do you want to do?"

"Arrange a meeting."

"Excuse me?"

"I want to arrange a meeting between the two of you," she repeated cheerfully. "It's natural, after all. You're my two favorite people in the world. It would make me happy if you liked each other."

"Really?"

"And who knows?"

"Who knows what?"

"You and I have always had the same tastes. There's a good chance you might react the same way I did."

Baptiste was so flabbergasted, he burst out laughing. "You really are unique, Joséphine!"

"I should hope so. So are you."

To recover from the shock, he poured them more wine

He stared at the ruby-red liquid in his glass. "Sorry to ask for details, Joséphine . . . Have you . . . Have you already consummated?"

"Yes." Modestly, she lowered her eyes. "And if you want details, it was very good. Oh, nothing like you. Very good. Different. You know I could never do without you where such things are concerned."

Baptiste nodded, knowing she was being sincere: she adored making love with him, and he was surprised he didn't feel more humiliated at discovering that she had given herself to somebody else. "Strange . . . "

"What?"

"That I'm not angry with you. Your confession moves me, make me feel worried and vulnerable, but I don't feel any anger toward you."

"I should hope not! After all I'm being honest, I'm telling you everything, and I've already assured you that you're more important to me than anyone else!"

He shook his head. "Try to be more understanding, Joséphine. We've been living together for twenty years, and you've just told me that the worst possible thing that could have happened has happened."

"No."

"For normal people, yes."

"Oh, Baptiste, please don't start putting on the normal people act. Neither of us is normal, or has any intention of being normal." She seemed really upset by this.

He laughed with delight. "That's exactly what I was saying. You've taken me aback, but I can't bring myself to be angry with you."

Encouraged by this, she replied loudly, almost shouting, "Because you love me and I love you. You and I can't destroy each other."

Hearing these words, the other patrons turned toward them and smiled benevolently.

Baptiste squeezed her wrist to calm her down. "You're probably right."

They began on the antipasti.

Oddly, Baptiste felt more in love than ever.

There was something mysterious and miraculous in the understanding between them. Joséphine dazzled him. Simple, luminous, she viewed existence without brandishing taboos or casting ordinary judgements. Life had taken her by surprise, and she wanted to talk it over with him.

"You know, ever since this affair began, I've realized you're the love of my life. I'm not joking."

He kissed her hand.

"You're the love of my life," she went on, really excited now, "because you're more intelligent, more talented, and more attentive than anyone else."

"Go on, I can take compliments."

"You're the love of my life because I think you're handsome, because I've liked you for twenty years, because I want to kiss you whenever I see you, because I need you to hold me in your arms and make love to me."

"You'd better be careful or I might believe you."

"You're the love of my life because I want to grow old with you."

"Me too."

"You're the love of my life because you're head and shoulders above all others."

"Don't exaggerate, Joséphine: you've found yourself another man."

"No, I haven't."

"But—"

"I'm in love with a woman."

Baptiste shrank in his seat, turned to stone.

"Her name's Isabelle," Joséphine added, eyes sparkling with love.

That night, Joséphine and Baptiste made love differently. The subtleties of Italian cuisine, the amount of Brunello they had drunk, the intoxication of a totally new situation brought them closer between the sheets. Because they were aware that other lovers would have lost their tempers, and perhaps even broken up, after that kind of conversation, it was as if their love had been renewed by the presence of danger. Trembling with anxiety and joy, Baptiste felt as if it was the last time. Joséphine, the first. It had been a long time since they had last felt such apprehension when faced with each other's bodies, such a sense of the sacred, such a respect for the intimacy they were offering each other, such bedazzlement at the reward of pleasure. They didn't embrace so much as commune.

The following day, Baptiste locked himself in his study. It

didn't matter that he wasn't able to write, he needed these hours of solitude.

All he knew so far about Isabelle was that she was the same age as they were, about forty, that she had grown-up children who were completing their studies in the United States, that she still lived with her husband but that all she shared with him were possessions and a few habits.

"You'll see," Joséphine had assured him, "she'll charm the socks off you. When she's not looking at anyone, she looks quite ordinary, but as soon as she smiles, she has a glow about her."

Baptiste had to admit it: he found the fact that Joséphine was having an affair with a woman less shocking than if it had been with a man. At least in this case he wasn't, strictly speaking, in competition: he and Isabelle weren't operating on the same turf, so Joséphine wouldn't be distracted by comparisons. Even so, he was worried by the fact that she had a female lover . . . He couldn't compete on that unknown continent.

He opened the window and looked out at the birds on Place d'Arezzo pursuing one another from branch to branch, looking more like playful monkeys than gorgeous creatures of the air.

That Joséphine was drawn to a woman didn't surprise him. Not that she had ever shown such tendencies before, but he thought it was normal to be attracted to the fair sex. He found nothing more erotic than naked women entwined in a bed. *If I'd been a woman, I'd have been a lesbian.* For a long time, he had been unable to fathom how his gay friends could remain immune to that spell, until he had realized that they did appreciate the beauty of women—some even dressed them, designed their makeup, photographed them, or directed them like nobody else—even if they didn't desire them. The only way he could explain this contradiction was by analyzing himself: he was capable of admiring a man without wanting to

have sex with him. In Baptiste's eyes, nothing sensual constituted a problem. Since sex was the experience of desire, all
forms of it were natural, even minority ones. The group to
which an individual belonged had little to do with his or her
choices or history, but rather with a biological lottery: whatever your gender, you were endowed with genes that pushed
you toward the bodies of one or the other gender, and possibly
even both.

He closed the window.

Joséphine appeared. "Is tomorrow night okay for you?"

"What are you talking about?"

"Meeting Isabelle . . . "

Baptiste sighed. He had feared this moment. "Give me
time. I want to think."

"Think? Think about what?"

"I need to get used to the situation."

"Get used to what? What situation? You don't know her."
She snuggled up to him. "My dear Baptiste, you have no reason to be upset. The situation's in your hands. You'll decide
the future. As far as I'm concerned, my position is clear: I
refuse to lead a parallel life and I can't shut myself up in the
closet marked 'adultery.' If you can't stand Isabelle, if you tell
me you never want to see her again, I'll leave her. I'll suffer, but
she'll go. I swear it. She either comes into our lives, or vanishes
from them."

"Is it as simple as that?"

"Don't be scared. You have nothing to fear, my love."

Mechanically, he stroked her arm. "But what about her?
Does she want to see me?"

"She can't wait."

"Isn't she scared?"

"She's terrified!"

They laughed. This shared anxiety strangely drew Isabelle
and Baptiste closer, Baptiste feeling a twinge of solidarity

toward her. *I've got the good deal here. Much as I dread the encounter, I'll still come out on top.*

"I'll give you an hour to decide. Just time for me to finish my cake."

"What kind of cake?"

"Lemon cake."

"My favorite! That's harassment."

She ran away, bright, impish, lithe.

Was it possible to love someone this much? Joséphine inspired love in Baptiste every second of the day. The only thing that distracted him was his creative activity, but even then he told himself that he wrote first in order to seduce her, bewitch her, hold on to her.

From the very first day, he had fallen under the spell of her fiery, headstrong personality. Joséphine was quick: it took her one second to diagnose a problem or a character, while Baptiste had to think carefully to reach an identical result. She worked through intuition, he through thought. Whereas he would stack up arguments and references before coming up with a critical judgment, he would see her get to the point at the speed of lightning, as though touched by grace. While he was an intellectual, someone who'd always been top of the class, passed all the exams, gained all the qualifications, Joséphine, who had avoided taking her Baccalaureate, came across as more intelligent than he was. She owed her uniqueness to no strategy, no culture; aware of being different, she was herself, nothing but herself, intense, unable to do other than she did. She wasn't impressed with authority, reputation, consensus; you could take her to see the work of an author who had been revered for centuries, like William Shakespeare, and she would come out saying, "What an awful play!"; she would sit next to a head of state at dinner and, no matter how wonderful or friendly he was—we know that politicians are, first and foremost, professional charmers—she would prove to him, without upsetting him, that his policies were wrong. In her eyes, a millionaire was worth no more than a garbage collector: on the contrary, owning a fortune made an error of taste unforgivable and she would not fail to denounce it. Baptiste's friends had soon nicknamed her "Madame Sans-Gêne," a reference to the solid, bold, loudmouthed marshal's wife who behaved at Napoleon's court in the same way she had when she was a laundress. When they married, their friends had made up a new nickname for the young couple: "The street kid and the intellectual." Then they had distanced themselves from their fellow students, who judged them in accordance with their own narrow prejudices. These days, Baptiste and Joséphine no longer saw them. They were free, happy, independent, and those old friends attributed this estrangement to Baptiste's roaring success as a writer.

Baptiste was never bored with Joséphine because he never knew what she would do. Her power over him came from her unpredictability. Not only did she not react like other common mortals, she didn't even react like herself. No sooner did you get a grip on her tastes or obsessions than she contradicted this classification in every detail. That was why you could never anticipate what she would like or not like. You might think that just because she proclaimed her admiration for Maupassant or Stefan Zweig, she preferred direct, unpretentious art without literary flourishes, but then she would wallow in the endless curlicues of Proust or recite the over-ornate poems of Saint-John Perse. After attacking some obscure, woolly-minded, incomprehensible intellectual, she would copy out diamond-hard, multifaceted maxims by René Char that didn't convey a direct message but revealed a multiplicity of meanings over time.

As changeable as the sky over the ocean, she reigned over Baptiste's heart, at once cheeky and sophisticated, welcoming and demanding, attentive and uncompromising, emotional and intellectual, sad and cheerful, loving and mischievous. As changeable as the weather, she could replace all women because she was all of them. He would often tell her, "You're not a woman, you're a whole catalogue of women."

Baptiste knew Joséphine provoked conflicting reactions: people either loved her or hated her. Mostly, they hated her. But that didn't affect Baptiste. On the contrary. Their excluding her was a way of filtering out those with simplistic, conventional minds. Thanks to her, he got rid of lots of idiots. Of course, the inference from all this was that Joséphine was unbearable; and yet she was the only one he could bear; all the others bored him.

She came back into the room, brandishing a charred pound cake.

"All right, so my mind's elsewhere: the cake's burned to a crisp. I'll only give you some if you're sure you want to get cancer."

He pulled her to him and held her tight. "It's all right for tomorrow night."

Joséphine's face lit up. "Really? Oh, you make me so happy . . . "

The evening had come. It was eight o'clock. Baptiste remained in his study for a long as possible. He didn't know where to put himself: his desk reminded him that he couldn't write a single line, but if he stood by the window, he risked seeing Isabelle too soon.

Joséphine had prepared a meal and lit candles, which he found grotesque one minute and delightful the next.

At last, he heard the doorbell. He felt a pang in his heart.

"I'll go," Joséphine said.

He heard the door open, then the indistinct babbling of the two women. Were they kissing? Were they taking advantage of his absence to behave like lovers?

Impatiently, he checked his clothes in the mirror. He had prevaricated long enough. On the one hand, he didn't want to look ridiculous by being too elegant; on the other, he felt he needed to be worthy of Joséphine, and not inflict a scruffily dressed husband on her. Glimpsing his reflection, he thought himself so nondescript that he wondered why Joséphine was interested in him, with looks like that. Then, holding his breath, he walked down the corridor to the living room.

As soon as he walked in, Isabelle, blonde, luminous, turned to him, and her face lit up.

"Hello, pleased to meet you."

He reeled, dazzled by her charms. She was no taller than Joséphine, and looked like her blonde sister.

Without hesitation, he leaned toward her, took her by the shoulder, and gave her a kiss on the cheek.

She quivered at the contact. So did he.

She gave off a delicious perfume.

Again they smiled, standing motionless a few inches apart.

"You see," Joséphine said, "I knew you'd like each other."

Baptiste turned to look at his wife. His joy-filled eyes were saying, "I've just fallen in love too."

4

G uillaume, don't slump!"
At his father's command, the boy sat up straight at his
desk.

"You must imagine you're on horseback every moment of your life, Guillaume," François-Maxime de Couvigny went on softly. "You must look straight yet supple. Both at the same time. Self-control, but without stiffness."

Guillaume glanced at his father, noticing his splendid bearing, with his straight back and loose neck.

"Please remind him of that, if necessary," François-Maxime said in English to Mary, the young Irish au pair.

"Yes, sir, you can trust me," the girl replied.

"Leave us please, I'll stay with him."

Mary left the room and went upstairs, where the Couvigny girls' rooms were.

"So, my boy," François-Maxime said, "show me your exercise book. Have you made progress in handwriting?"

He examined the pages, covered in his son's clumsy lettering. The boy worked hard but encountered thousands of obstacles: the nib would catch on the paper, the ink would blot, the paper would tear. It was as if there was a conspiracy against him.

Sensing that his father's critique would be a harsh one, the boy attempted a diversion. "I nearly got into a fight at school today."

"Why?"

"Because Benjamin and Louis said Clément's father is a fag."

François-Maxime de Couvigny stopped in his tracks.

"I told them it wasn't nice to say that. I mean, it doesn't sound nice, does it? I'd punch them if they called my father a fag."

A wave of terror swept over François-Maxime. "Really?"

"Of course," the boy went on, "I don't really know what it means."

François-Maxime threw his head back and burst into a loud, guttural laugh. He realized he was overreacting, but it didn't matter: the sound of the bullet whistling past his head made him feel alive again.

Séverine popped her head around the door, surprised by such hilarity. "What's going on?"

François-Maxime told her what their son had said. Embarrassed, Séverine also laughed. Trapped between his parents, Guillaume was torn between the pleasure of having entertained them and the feeling that he had made a mistake.

"What did I say that's so funny?" he finally asked.

Suddenly required to explain a delicate point, his parents stopped laughing. Séverine made it clear to François-Maxime that the task of teaching their son fell to him, the father.

"Well, Guillaume, 'fag' is a naughty word for something naughty."

"What?"

"A man who doesn't live with a woman but a man is called a fag."

"I don't understand."

"Well, a man like that sleeps in the same bed as another man, they eat together and go on holiday together."

"So they're friends?"

"More than friends. They do what a mommy and daddy do: they caress each other and kiss on the mouth."

"Yuck!"

The child had jumped up in his chair with a grimace of disgust.

How satisfying it was for François-Maxime to register his son's spontaneous revulsion! Such reassuring normality! He gave Séverine a proud look. She seemed more puzzled than delighted by her son's reaction. He felt it wise to add an extra layer. "And a man like that, who doesn't marry a woman and have a family, isn't a good man. He's useless. Useless to society and the human race, possibly even a parasite."

The boy nodded gravely.

"So it really is better not to use that . . . that word," François-Maxime concluded.

He couldn't bring himself to utter the word again. Not only did it belong to a coarse register François-Maxime never resorted to, but even repeating it out loud would be a big risk, as if it were contagious, or might lead to a confession . . . He so much wanted to ignore that reality that he shunned the words that referred to it.

"So is Clément's father a fag?" his son went on.

"Maybe not, Guillaume. It's a common insult among rude boys. Think about it: when your sisters call each other silly fools, they're not telling the truth."

"All right." The boy took a deep breath. "Anyway, I won't be a fag."

François-Maxime felt emotional as he looked at Guillaume. Clearly, he hadn't passed on his own tendency to him, he'd given him clean genes. The curse would end there, and his son wouldn't be forced to lead a secret life. For a moment, the forty-year-old man, devoured by conflicting impulses, felt envious of the seven-year-old child's clear certainties. He abruptly put down the exercise book without being as demanding as he should have been. "Your letters are looking better, Guillaume. Keep up the good work."

Smiling radiantly, he left the room and joined Séverine. She took him by the hand and went down the stairs with him.

"I'm grateful to you, but I wonder . . . "

"Yes?"

Séverine blushed. She found it difficult to complete her sentence. "François-Maxime, aren't you exaggerating when you tell him that . . . being that way . . . isn't good?"

François-Maxime stiffened. "Excuse me?"

"He'll meet people like that."

"Precisely. So he'll be able to decide who's right and who's wrong."

The subject was closed, and François-Maxime went to see his daughters. Every evening, he was in the habit of talking to each of his children about the day that had just ended and the homework they had for the following day.

Séverine watched him walk away, erect, self-confident, and felt sad that, unlike him, she was unable to subscribe to certain "facts" without hesitation. *Who's right and who's wrong! . . .* Taking advantage of the fact that no one was watching her, she went into the living room, poured herself a glass of whiskey, and gulped it down.

For some days now she had been feeling very uneasy because of those damned letters, those identical pieces of paper François-Maxime and Xavière had received. Neither had hesitated. Both her husband and her lover had immediately assumed that it was she, Séverine, who had sent them. Xavière had expressed her certainty with a slap, and François-Maxime with an expensive handbag, in which he had put the original message—*Just a note to tell you I love you. Signed: You know who*—and added: *Me too.*

What tormented Séverine wasn't the sender's real identity, but that they should think she was responsible. If only they knew . . . Didn't they realize just how incapable she was of such an initiative? Weren't they aware of her absence of feeling, her chronic indifference? François-Maxime and Xavière must love her very much to attribute that thought to her! If Séverine had received that note, she wouldn't have felt anything definite. Or not much. She didn't think she was capable of any decisive gesture toward anyone, and was astonished that nobody had realized that about her. François-Maxime had become her husband because he had proposed: all she had done was accept. Xavière had initiated her into the pleasures of Sapphic love because it was she who had taken the initiative, and Séverine had allowed herself to be led. She felt no passion of her own accord, but merely provided an echo to the passions of others. She was quite happy to assume her role as a mother, doing her duty and meticulously delivering gestures of love. It wasn't just passivity, it was an inner emptiness.

As usual, when confronted with the two letters, she had allowed them to believe that she had written them. What did it matter? What was important wasn't truth—which, at least in her case, was too ugly to tell—but maintaining the illusion. After she had slapped her, Xavière had been so aroused she had pulled her onto the living room couch. After presenting her with her gift, François-Maxime had been in a more cheerful, more playful mood than usual. She herself might not be happy, but at least she made them happy.

She poured herself another glass of whiskey. This time, she filled it to the brim and downed it in one go. That was another extraordinary thing: nobody suspected that she was becoming an alcoholic. Of course, she did cover up her secret drinking by gargling with floral water in order to mask the smell of bourbon, but even so!

She went down to the servants' hall. "What have you made for us, Grete?"

The cordon bleu chef gave the names of the dishes and listed the main ingredients. *Here too, I'm incapable of doing my share.* Séverine had never made the meals. The daughter of a wealthy family, she had never learned to cook since the task seemed to her to be beyond her abilities: to spend hours on something a mouth could swallow in a second was simply absurd. Although she admired cooks, it was not for their skill but for this cult of the useless, this dedication to a silly task, to preparing a feast that would immediately be swallowed up. They were the heroes of uselessness!

The family gathered in the vast dining room. True to tradition, there were hand-painted hunting scenes on the paneled walls. On the table stood a plethora of plates, glasses, and flatware, as if every day a banquet was being held. A maid moved discreetly behind the diners and served them.

François-Maxime led the conversation. It was important for the children to know that a meal wasn't just feeding time, but a time to shine with the brilliance of one's conversation and take an interest in other people's activities.

He grew angry when Guillaume failed to answer a question quickly enough on the pretext that he was chewing a piece of cod. "Please learn to speak even when your mouth's full, Guillaume."

"But—"

"Making the other person wait with the excuse that you're chewing is nothing but monstrous rudeness. It's the way pigs behave."

"Daddy!"

"The physical must never take priority over the spiritual, my boy. You must get used to speaking with your mouth full without anybody noticing. Look."

He lifted a slice of zucchini to his mouth with his fork and continued talking with ease, so that nobody was aware of the food on his palate. "I don't have to swallow any more quickly. I have enough room in my oral cavity to hide the food and I take advantage of my jaws moving to grind it. In this way, I can take part in the conversation and at the same time do justice to the dish."

The girls looked at their brother with haughty commiseration: they had been practicing these social gymnastics for years, and were thinking, *Honestly, poor Guillaume, he has to be shown everything*, forgetting that they had also had to accustom themselves to it.

After dinner, Mary, the young au pair, came to fetch the children.

François-Maxime and Séverine sat in the living room. He searched through the TV shows they had recorded for one that would entertain them. Meanwhile, Séverine's eyes wandered over the walls: she couldn't decide whether she liked the decor or hated it. The overall impression was one of opulence, luxury, and abundance, since the fabrics—from the walls to the curtains, by way of the couches and armchairs—bore various paisley patterns, while the light from the many lamps was reflected off animal sculptures and mother-of-pearl and tortoiseshell boxes. Ten years earlier, an English female architect had concocted this decor for her. The result gave a feeling of comfort but she didn't feel at ease in it. Ever since she had discovered Xavière's cottage by the North Sea, so characteristic, so consistent, so pleasant, she had realized her own uselessness: her interior had been imposed from the outside by a British woman who was probably now dealing with an emir from Qatar. In other words, here too her behavior had been dictated to her.

What if she threw out all this chichi stuff in favor of a bare, Zen style? She liked the idea. She'd even written down the address of an excellent minimalist decorator. *Stupid woman, you're doing it again!* Once again, she was thinking of another person organizing her world for her . . . So she gave up on the idea and hoped François-Maxime would choose his show quickly, so that she could go get a glass of whiskey.

"There's a program on European politics! Is that all right by you, Séverine?"

"Perfect."

They watched a political talk show recorded the day before. François-Maxime followed the debates with passion and clear bias, while Séverine, more reserved, paid polite attention, taking advantage of heated moments to go and secretly knock back more alcohol.

When the closing credits started, there was obviously nothing left to do but go upstairs to their bedroom. The prospect terrified Séverine, and she heard herself saying to François-Maxime, "Did I tell you my father's secret?"

Taken aback, he stared at her. When he realized that she was eagerly awaiting an answer, he switched off the television and sat down opposite her.

"Your father's secret?"

François-Maxime hadn't known Séverine's father. By the time they met as students at the Paris law faculty, he had already been dead a year.

Séverine put the decanter and two glasses on a tray and carried it over to the coffee table. This way, if he later noticed that she smelled of single malt, there would be a reason for it. Moreover, if he drank with her, it would go unnoticed.

Sensing that what she was about to confide was likely to be serious, he accepted the glass she held out to him.

"My father had a secret. When my eldest brother discovered it, it was the beginning of the end."

"The end of what?"

"Of the family. In five years, everything changed. My father died, my mother got cancer, my brother went to India, where he caught a deadly ameba, and my sister married a black man—not that that was bad in itself, but it was the worst possible thing Ségolène could have inflicted on my parents as long as they were around. Didn't you ever wonder why there was such carnage in my family?"

François-Maxime shook his head. When he had started

courting Séverine, he had lived through these tragedies with her and, by the time they got engaged, had attended many funerals. In a way, he had encountered Séverine's family just as it was disappearing. The result was that, two years into their marriage, Séverine was sharing with her only remaining sister what was left of the monumental family fortune. Then, when her sister relinquished her share, Séverine had gotten the lot.

"My father had always inspired admiration and terror," she continued. "We thought he was the embodiment of perfection. Fair, cultivated, strict, hardworking, invariably successful: we were in awe of him. He didn't show much affection and didn't expect any. I wasn't really aware of it, it was my analyst who pointed it out. Only one day my father fell off his pedestal."

"He did?"

"It was summer. We were all staying at our house in Hossegor, by the ocean, except for him. He'd stayed in Paris. He never took vacations and preferred to work, which is why we always felt rather guilty and vaguely ashamed. One Thursday, my brother, who was twenty-two, went back to Paris because one of his best friends was getting engaged. He'd forgotten to let any of us, even Dad, know and only told us on the morning of his departure. Anyway, he arrived in Paris in the afternoon and, to avoid an endless chat with our concierge, who talked too much, he went up to the apartment by the back stairs. That's when he saw my father." She poured herself another whiskey before continuing. "Or rather, a horrible woman who looked like my father."

"I don't understand . . . "

"At first, he didn't understand either. Through the banisters, staircase, he first noticed a big, square, ungainly woman leaving our apartment. He was surprised. For a moment, he thought my father had hired a new cleaner. She clumped down the stairs on her pumps as she walked down. Then he made out the woman's face and, even with the wig, even with the makeup, he recognized our father."

"Your father was a transvestite?"

"At first, Pierre refused to believe what he had seen, so he rushed down the stairs and ran away, in a panic. An hour later, he took a terrible liberty: he rummaged through my father's suite—my parents had separate bedrooms. There, he discovered a hidden panel inside the wardrobe, a false bottom containing dresses, skirts, extra-large blouses, size 10½ pumps, a makeup bag. He decided not to mention it and went to stay with a friend. But every day, he came back at the same time, waited in a café, and saw my father leave by the back door, dressed as a woman."

"I guess he followed him?"

"Yes."

"And?"

"Our father walked around as a woman. He went to have coffee as a woman. He browsed around department stores as a woman, looking at dresses, lingerie, and makeup, and buying himself trinkets. He spent a whole hour as a woman."

"Did Pierre tell all of you?"

"That summer, Pierre didn't say anything. But the following year, he started doing badly in his studies. He'd stay out all night without telling us. We were worried he might be taking drugs. One Sunday, at breakfast, at the head of the table, where he held court like a patriarch, my father gave him a dressing down. So my brother turned pale, stood up, went out, came back a few minutes later with my father's female gear, and threw it on the table. Then he told us all what he'd seen."

At this point, Séverine had to stop her hands shaking.

"All of a sudden, the accuser turned into the defendant. Since my father was white as a sheet and couldn't say a word, my mother stood up, looking very indignant, and told my brother to leave and never set foot in our house again. Pierre obeyed. For a few hours, we chose to believe that our brother was a liar, an inventor of stories, a monster. But my father withdrew into himself. Within a week, we realized he'd been fooling us for years. Three months later, my sister announced that she was going to live in Niger with her boyfriend Boubakar. My mother disowned her. Pierre, who I was seeing in secret, flew off to India. A year later, my father, who hadn't said a dozen words since that fatal Sunday, crashed his car against a plane tree, an accident we interpreted as suicide, although we didn't say it. The rest, you know. We heard my brother had died in Bombay. My mother discovered she had breast cancer. I think it was a relief to her. She allowed herself to be taken away by the tumor after four months. And finally, Ségolène, all the way over there in Niamey, disowned our family by rejecting her share of the inheritance."

François-Maxime went to Séverine and put his arms around her, but she pulled free because she wanted to talk some more. He didn't take offense.

"So you're the one true survivor of the catastrophe," he said, kneeling beside her.

"To all appearances, yes."

"What do you mean?"

"Inside, I have my doubts." She looked deep into his eyes. "I doubt that people are what they really are. I doubt that the people close to me are what they appear to be. I keep expecting a horrible revelation."

François-Maxime instinctively drew back. What was she trying to say? Did she know he wasn't what he gave the impression of being? Was her story a way of telling him that she was aware of his moral failings?

"Imagine, François-Maxime, if one day our children find out we aren't what we claim to be."

This time, François-Maxime recoiled even more. There was no doubt about it, she knew! "What . . . what are you trying to say?"

"Nothing."

"Do you . . . have something specific to tell me?"

She stared at him for a long time, expressionless, weighed down by her own cowardice. She didn't have the guts to admit her relationship with Xavière. "No," she murmured contritely.

"No?"

"No."

Reassured, François-Maxime ran to her and clasped her to him. "I love you, Séverine. You have no idea how much I love you."

The vehemence with which he said this owed as much to his relief as to his sincerity. For a moment, he had been afraid of losing everything he held dear: his wife, his family, his success, and his secrets. Lyrical and intoxicated, he kept saying over and over that he loved her, dancing joyously on the edge of the abyss he had just avoided.

Séverine burst into tears.

He comforted her, then, gently, as if she were as fragile as a porcelain vase, he led her to their bedroom and laid her down on the bed.

It was incredible . . . Always that curious effect . . . Whenever his wife cried, he desired her. Was it an underlying sadism that he couldn't control? Or did he, like a true old-fashioned male, think that only his caresses could give her peace?

Sensing he would have to be patient, he held her tight, caressing her and whispering a thousand sweet nothings to her. As soon as she smiled, he playfully rubbed noses with her. Tamed by his gentleness, she purred and laid her head and arm on his chest.

When he was sure that if they made love he would be able to see it through to the end, he tried to look into her eyes: she had dozed off with exhaustion.

He held her in his arms until she was fast asleep then, certain that she wouldn't be awakened by a movement of his, he slipped out of bed and went back to the living room.

Without switching on the lights, he climbed on a stool and grabbed an art book from the top shelf of the bookcase, closed all the curtains and doors in the room, turned on a single standard lamp, and sat down beneath it.

It was a book of pictures by the great New York photographer Robert Mapplethorpe, showing the usual tortured Herculean bodies, swollen black penises, convoluted patterns of bonds and straps in which esthetic perfection was blended with erotic fantasy. François-Maxime thanked the creator for allowing him to bring home these stimulants in the form of art, and proceeded to appease the tension that was stopping him from sleeping.

5

W ere you out last night?"

"I beg your pardon?"

Mademoiselle Beauvert raised her head, the better to hear the question asked by Marcelle, who, armed with a cloth, was searching for an object to attack in the living room.

"Well, I picked up your laundry from the dry cleaner's and came by here to drop it off. I rang the bell several times. Same thing the previous evening, when I tried to return the magazines you'd lent me."

Marcelle loved magazines devoted to the lives of kings and princesses, and would spend many wonderful hours in her lodge, admiring dresses, trains, diadems, palaces decorated with gold leaf, all the things she only had access to through pictures.

"To be honest, you're out a lot!" she concluded.

Mademoiselle Beauvert turned red.

"What's it all about, Mr. Hook-Nose?" the parrot started shrieking. "What's it all about?"

Mademoiselle Beauvert glared at him. This gave the parrot leave to scream, "Help! Help, Sergio! Help!"

Taken aback, Marcelle stared at the bird. "Your Copernicus is a bit touched," she said, adding, to herself, *I prefer my Afghan*.

Mademoiselle Beauvert stood up, turned around, and, twisting her fingers nervously, walked up to Marcelle. "There's something I must tell you."

"Oh, yes?" Marcelle replied, her curiosity aroused.

"I've met someone."

Marcelle opened her eyes wide and slowly nodded.

Mademoiselle Beauvert expressed her delight with a short, sharp laugh. "He's a world-famous musician. A pianist. American."

"Is he black?"

"No, white. But he's very close to Obama."

Marcelle waved her hands in admiration. "How long have you been seeing him?"

"A year."

"Does he live here?"

"No, in Boston," Mademoiselle Beauvert said, lowering her head modestly, as if the name Boston described one of her boyfriend's more disturbing characteristics.

Marcelle was surprised. "How do you manage? With him in Boston and you here?"

"He's in Brussels right now. The rest of the time, we talk on the phone."

"Well, I must say, Mademoiselle, you've bowled me over."

Marcelle was astounded. She found it hard to fathom how anyone could have a love affair over the phone. How would she manage with her Afghan, seeing that he didn't speak a word of French and she didn't speak a word of Pashtun?

"What language do you speak in?"

"English . . . "

"Well done!"

" . . . although he speaks French very well. He attended a master class in Paris for two years. Anyway, French has become the language of love for him."

She blushed again, as though she had just confessed to a very intimate detail.

Marcelle nodded, then said, by way of conclusion, "I'm going to get my vacuum cleaner."

Mademoiselle Beauvert also nodded, judging that Marcelle had taken the correct initiative.

While Marcelle was struggling in the cupboard, trying to unjam the thing, Mademoiselle Beauvert returned to her desk and grabbed a piece of paper. On it she wrote a few words in pencil:

Pianist. American. Studied in Paris. We've known each other for a year.

Just then, Marcelle reappeared. "Very close to Obama, you say?"

"Yes, Marcelle, very close."

"And he's not black?"

"No, Marcelle."

Marcelle plugged in the vacuum cleaner. "Mind you, I've never been with a black man. I'd have liked to. Just out of curiosity."

"Curiosity about what?"

Marcelle looked at Mademoiselle Beauvert and hesitated to answer, realizing she might shock her. She shrugged and switched on the noisy vacuum.

"Anyway, he's not black, so . . . "

She started energetically going over the large rugs.

Mademoiselle Beauvert added the note: *Very close to Obama but not black.* Before slipping the strange yellow piece of paper into her secret drawer, she checked again what it had on the back: *Just a note to tell you I love you. Signed: You know who.*

It's odd. I'm still waiting for the follow-up. They've been good at stimulating curiosity, but now they shouldn't delay or people are going to forget.

Relieved, she assumed that Marcelle would now stop trying to find out where she went in the evening. On the other hand, it meant she would regularly ask after her lover—what else could she call him?

The noise of the vacuum cleaner stopped. With the lead in her hand and her foot on the machine, like a hunter posing with her prey, Marcelle looked at Mademoiselle Beauvert. "My son's getting married in three months."

"That's wonderful. Who to?"

"Christèle Peperdick."

Mademoiselle Beauvert wondered if her brain was falling to pieces. "Christèle Peperdick?"

"Yes."

"*The* Christèle Peperdick?"

"Why, are there two of them?"

Mademoiselle Beauvert stood up, displeased. "Marcelle, don't pretend you don't know. I'm talking about Christèle Peperdick of the Peperdick champagne family."

Marcelle scratched her head. "Yes, that's the one I'm talking about as well."

"Are you trying to tell me your son, *your* son, is marrying the heiress to the Peperdick fortune?"

"That's right."

"And you're saying it just like that?"

"How else should I say it?"

"Come on, now! The whole world would love to meet the Peperdicks. And Christèle Peperdick's the most eligible girl in Brussels. How did your son pull it off?"

"Like everybody else: he flirted with her."

"Where did he meet her? How? Why? You don't seem to realize just how . . . " she wanted to say "unexpected," but changed her mind at the last moment, " . . . wonderful this marriage is."

Marcelle raised her eyes to heaven. "You never know," she grunted. "Marriage is all fire and passion at the beginning, then everything turns to ashes. Let's see how long the little darlings stick it out."

"Marcelle, your son's going to be a rich man!"

"Good, because he owes me two hundred and forty-two euros. Did I tell you? I gave him two hundred and forty-two euros up front so he could make me a night table. Well, I don't have my bedside table, and I don't have my two hundred and forty-two euros, dammit!"

Grumpily, she took out her anger on a chair that was in her way, kicking it twice and shoving it up against a wall.

Mademoiselle Beauvert was holding her head in her hands. Here was a mother harping on about her two hundred and forty-two euros and her night table, when her son was about to make the match of the century!

Faced with the utter absurdity of it, she started having doubts. "Marcelle," she said, "where do your future daughter-in-law's parents live?"

"At the end of Avenue Louise, on Square du Bois."

Mademoiselle Beauvert quivered. Square du Bois was a private street protected by black and gold railings, housing patrician residences of between 7,500 and 10,000 square feet, and was a kind of elite village where money—old and new—lived. It had been known as Billionaires' Row in the days of the Belgian franc, and Millionaires' Row since the switch to euros.

"Have you met this young lady? Or her parents?"

"Not yet."

"Hasn't your son suggested you should?"

"He made an insinuation I didn't like, so I threw him out. And if he sets foot here again, my Afghan is instructed to kick him out."

"Marcelle, what happened?"

"He wanted to check on the way I dressed and what I was going to say."

There was no doubt about it, then! Everything Marcelle had said so far was the truth.

"That's right, Mademoiselle," Marcelle said. "Like he's ashamed of his own mother!"

She let go of the vacuum cleaner, punched herself in the forehead, and burst into tears. Mademoiselle Beauvert rushed to put her arm around her and murmur a few words of comfort. Deep inside, though, she really felt sorry for the young man, who, having struck gold, was justifiably afraid that his mother might sabotage his rise.

A wave of kindness swept over her. She sat Marcelle down in an armchair, placed a stool in front of her and, holding her hands, said slowly, "Marcelle, your son loves his mother and wants to make sure his in-laws will like her too. He wants to be certain you'll be able to establish a good relationship with that family. There's nothing bad about his request."

"You think so?"

"I'm sure of it. I can help you, if you like."

"To do what?"

"Prepare for your first meeting."

Marcelle stiffened. "Come on, Mademoiselle, it's just a girl and her parents who make booze. It's not like he's introducing me to the Queen of England!"

"I'm afraid you may be underestimating the Peperdicks, Marcelle. Next to the Queen of England, they're listed among the fifty wealthiest people in Europe."

Marcelle turned pale. "No!"

"Yes. Usually, a girl like Christèle Peperdick—and I say this with the greatest affection and respect—would marry a rich heir or a prince. Not your son."

"Oh, God, what kind of mess has he gotten himself mixed up in now?"

"Help him."

"All right. What do I have to do?"

Mademoiselle Beauvert stood up and examined the concierge's tubby figure. "Maybe a little dieting to start with?"

"Why?"

"The rich are skinny. They may have more money for food,

but they half-starve themselves. Once people reach a certain level of income, all their efforts go not into buying food but into refusing to eat it."

"My poor boy eats enough for four."

"He's young, so he doesn't retain fat. Whereas we, at our age . . . "

Marcelle looked at her thighs, belly and arms, and for the first time seemed to grow aware of her bulk.

"Once you've slimmed down, Marcelle, we'll buy you some new clothes."

"With what money?"

"Maybe your son will return your two hundred and thirty—"

"Two hundred and forty-two euros! He'd better. Oh, shit, it's time for me to drop by Madame Martel's. I must go, I'll finish tomorrow."

She left her cleaning unfinished and headed for the door. Mademoiselle Beauvert automatically followed her.

"Mind you, even if he does give me my two hundred and forty-two euros back, I'll still have the problem of the night table."

"Then ask your Afghan to build you one."

"My Afghan? He can't touch a dish without breaking it. Butterfingers. He's an intellectual, a doctor of linguistics!"

"Linguistics!" Mademoiselle exclaimed, surprised that Marcelle should know the word.

Once the door was shut, Mademoiselle Beauvert sank into deep despair. Chance was a fickle thing. This was so unfair! She wished she was twenty again, making different choices. She identified with the two characters in Marcelle's story: the rich young girl wary of men, and the poor young man who builds his life on making a good match. Mademoiselle Beauvert herself had never overcome her fear of insincere boyfriends and hadn't made marriage the foundation of her life. The conclusion being . . . ?

There was no conclusion.

If this carries on, I'm going to go back there!

A shriek tore through the gloom. "Sergio! Sergio!"

"Shut up, Copernicus!"

The parrot laughed. It was a sour, vicious laugh. Out of revenge, she spread a blanket over the cage. "Time to sleep."

Then she threw herself into an armchair, feeling a strong sense of unease. The day wasn't going as expected. She had planned to read and watch television, and, instead, she'd had to justify herself, invent a new suitor, and listen to the concierge telling her about her son's unbelievable marriage.

This is too much. I'm going to have to go back there.

Although she had so little experience of life, she was disillusioned. Withdrawn in her arid, charmless apartment, she felt nothing but emptiness, both inside and out. What was the use of continuing this aimless, pointless existence? This void didn't soothe her. A secret restlessness ate away at the boredom, a nagging sense of anxiety, which might be the only trace of life that remained in her.

What if I went now?

Her alter ego answered, *No. You've already been there several times this week. You must control your urges.*

All right.

For several hours, she struggled, like a beast pacing up and down its cage. The remote in her hand, she channel-hopped, hoping that some image might grab her attention. She began reorganizing her wardrobe. She checked the expiration dates of the food in the kitchen—once, twice, three times. She tried reading *The Woman by the Water*, a novel by her neighbor, the writer Baptiste Monier, but she judged the first chapter to be below par, finding it hard to memorize the names of the characters.

Finally, at nightfall, she could resist no longer. *Why not? Who'd know, except me?*

In a conspiratorial voice, she ordered a taxi.

When she sank into the cab and gave the driver the address, he responded with a knowing smile. Bristling with dignity, Mademoiselle Beauvert lifted her chin and looked so surprised, so taken aback, that the driver was sure he had made a mistake.

He dropped Mademoiselle Beauvert outside the casino.

She felt herself come back to life as she climbed the steps. Full of joy and enthusiasm, and quivering with desire, she walked into the main room, where every member of staff welcomed her by name.

Why did I try to stop myself? I feel better already.

Still, she was determined to punish herself for exceeding her usual dose—she had played several nights in a row this week. As penance, she decided to avoid the more expensive games and limit herself to the slot machines.

She sat in front of a brand-new chrome model, decorated with drawings of fruit, slid in a coin, and pulled on the lever. There was a frenetic succession of lemons, melons, strawberries, kiwis, and pineapples. For a fraction of a second, Mademoiselle Beauvert glimpsed three dollars side by side, saw one vanish, then another, and felt a surge of anger. Chaos resumed at a furious pace, until finally the images settled: two dollars and a pear.

I'm almost there. I just need one more.

She set the machine in motion again. This time, she closed her eyes, as if saying to it, *Don't make fun of me by giving me false hopes. You have to obey me, not the other way around.*

As soon as the buzzer went, signaling that the meter had fixed the symbols, she opened her eyes. Three dollars. Bingo!

The money fell out noisily in a metallic, liquid stream. Too many coins for the holder she was carrying.

She went eagerly to the cash desk, clutching her new wealth.

With luck like this, I'm hardly going to stick to slot machines. That'd be an insult to luck!

Nothing seemed more sensible to her than the thought she had just had. If luck was on her side, then she had to respect it. Resolutely, she walked to the green table, around which people crowded reverently. Spotting an empty seat, she elegantly slipped into it, greeted her partners, and gave the croupier a wink.

The sight of the baize, the chips, and the roulette wheel made her skull tingle pleasantly. Confidently, unhesitatingly, she pushed her stack onto three red.

The ball ran wildly around the wheel.

The suspense built. Her heart beat like a drum. She was intoxicated by this protracted fever. The slot machines were disappointing because they let you win too easily. Better the emotions provoked by a high-risk game. The lower the chances of winning, the more delectable the wait. What better container for your emotions than danger? With every game, she risked losing her money, her honor, her social standing. With a mere move of the hand, she put the fragile balance of her life at risk, but far from going to her head, this awareness of risk made her savor each pure emotion with greater intensity. For as long as the ball rolled, she was no longer fifty-five, she no longer lived alone, she no longer pined after lost loves, but was the center of the universe. The stakes became cosmic: her will on one side, chance on the other. She was sticking her tongue out at fate. She was going to prove, not that randomness didn't exist, but that her will, her intelligence, and her perseverance would triumph over blind forces. Sex would never make her feel like this. Making love was a paltry game, lower even than the slot machines.

"Rien de va plus!"

Everything was going swimmingly well. She was killing boredom, feeling more alive than she had all day. After a few somersaults, the ball fell into its final pocket.

"Five black!" the croupier announced.

Missed. Too bad. She would carry on. The difficulty lay not in betting, but in stopping.

6

Faustina edged her way between the cars, checked the license plate, took the oyster knife from her bag, glanced around to make sure nobody could see her, crouched, and plunged the blade into the back right-hand tire. Then she slid across and repeated her action on the left-hand tire. Finally, she stood up majestically, pretended that she had picked up an object from the blacktop, and stepped back onto the sidewalk.

Now Dany was stuck. He wouldn't be able to leave at ten o'clock like the other evening, and she would have him to herself all night. Calmer now, she went back up to her apartment.

When she heard his amber voice, she quivered with pleasure; in the living room, barefoot, his shirt sleeves rolled up, ear glued to his phone, Dany, who was originally from the West Indies, was dealing with a case before finishing his working day.

She looked at him affectionately. As long as he was at her place, she adored him. On the other hand, as soon as he was elsewhere, she dismissed his profession, criticized him for being obsessed with it, suspected him of making awful male chauvinist remarks about her to his colleagues, feared that he was seeing former mistresses, and, perhaps even worse, fumed at the thought that when he slept alone at his place he forgot all about her. In other words, when he walked out of her door, she felt no curiosity about the rest of his life, only hatred.

Once he had hung up, she sat down on his lap and wrapped

her arms around him. "Damsel in distress needs rescuing," she murmured.

He responded to her caresses. She increased her sensual pressure. Their lips searched for each other. The phone rang again.

"We're closed!" Faustina exclaimed comically, like a baker lowering a shutter.

Dany leaned over to see who was calling.

"No!" she commanded.

"Don't be a child."

"I said no!"

"Faustina, I have to answer this."

Since she was holding him tight, he used his strength to free himself, unceremoniously set her back on her feet, and irritably grabbed the phone.

She was furious. He hadn't just pushed her away, he had dominated her by force. Up until now, she had known the strength of his grip only in lovemaking; now this brute was using it against her. That was pure violence.

I hate him! Instantly, she had but a single aim: to make him suffer, now, right away.

For the moment, Dany was talking to a colleague about a current tricky case, avoiding Faustina's proximity, keenly aware of the hostile vibes she was sending out.

She went back to the kitchen, composed herself, prepared an aperitif, and came back calmly with a tray.

From the corner of her eye, she saw that Dany had noticed the change. When he hung up, he turned to her.

"Sometimes, in my job, there are emergencies. That was something I really needed to sort out."

"Oh, yes. Your job, your amazing job."

"Why are you being sarcastic?"

"Whenever you bring it up, it feels as if I don't have a job, and that the rest of us mortals who don't have the great honor of being Maître Dany Davon of the Brussels Bar are just wallowing in our own mediocrity."

"I was simply reminding you that I have certain responsibilities."

She snatched Dany's phone and held it over the vase of tulips. "And I don't?" With these words, she let the phone drop into the water.

Furious, Dany rushed to pull it out. "You're twisted!"

He retrieved his phone, wiped it with a place mat, and rushed to the bathroom to get the excess water out with the hair dryer. Faustina watched him with a smile that implied: *You've no idea how ridiculous you look.*

When he had finished, he tried, his whole body tense, to switch on the phone. Miraculously, it was working. Relieved, Dany sat down on the edge of the bathtub. "Don't ever do that again."

"Or else?"

He sighed. "What is it you want?"

Faustina was astonished. She had expected an escalation of violence, the kind of fight where she knew she could be formidable, where exasperation and bad faith provided her with a never-ending stream of responses, but his asking her so simply what it was she wanted threw her.

Since he was waiting calmly for her answer, she realized she had to provide one. She hesitated, then stammered, "You pushed me away."

"Only temporarily, Faustina. Just long enough to answer the phone."

"That's not how I took it."

"You should have. Why do you think I'm here? To push you away? To tell you I don't want to see you anymore?"

Faustina realized how illogical her behavior had been; as usual, she swapped personalities on the spot. She threw herself in his arms and whispered in an emotional voice, "You're important to me. I was shocked when you used force against me."

He was filled with pride, happy with the turn things were taking. "Did I hurt you?"

"No."

"So you see, that means I was controlling myself."

To prove he was right, he lifted her, and she not only let him, but did her best to seem as heavy as possible. He carried her into the sitting room, laid her gently on the couch, and started kissing her.

Faustina immediately forgot what had just happened, her anger, her resentment, and moved her body against his. They made love.

Two hours later, they were eating seafood from a narrow folding table that Faustina had slid out onto her balcony.

The royal-blue night sky gently bathed the trees on the square. The birdsong was soft now, sleepy, lulling, deeper and less shrill than during the day.

Dany was sensually swallowing oysters. Every time he sucked in their contents, he would stare at Faustina.

"Why are you making that face?" Faustina asked, laughing.

"There's something so female about oysters. Their texture, their fragrance, their feel. It's as though I'm eating you."

He sucked in the last oyster greedily.

Faustina quivered as if it was she who had just slipped through his lips.

He poured her more white wine. "Beware of sex, Faustina, it's a drug."

"What are you talking about?"

"A drug means pleasure, highs, lows, withdrawal pains, and then starting all over again. If we continue fucking as well as this, we'll become addicted."

Continue fucking, continue fucking . . . she thought. *What else does he expect us to do?*

"If we continue fucking like this," he went on, "we'll end up being hysterical on the days when we go without."

Faustina thought about her own sensations: on the few occasions when their professional lives had prevented them from being together, she had been unbearably high-strung, and felt true pain. She shook her head. "So the only solution would be to fuck badly."

"Obviously. Except that I couldn't do that with you."

"Neither could I."

They took deep breaths of the fragrant night air. They had both just achieved the highest peak of romanticism they could ever hope to reach; to avoid falling into silliness, they exchanged conspiratorial looks.

"Have you ever experienced this feeling of addiction before?" Faustina asked.

He smiled. "I'm thirty-eight years old, Faustina. I wasn't a virgin when we met."

"Oh, I think you were a virgin, because you'd never known me."

"Fair enough. But even though it's true that I've never known anything as powerful as I have with you, during my . . . shall we say . . . ordinary experiences, I have taken the drug before."

Faustina accepted the explanation, since it established her superiority. All of a sudden, she had no qualms about surprising him even more. "If the only harm the drug causes is dependency, then why not take it?"

He laughed, delighted. "I'm up for it."

They clinked glasses.

"I don't believe there should be any boundaries in sex," Faustina confessed.

"What do you mean, exactly?"

"Well, that sex was invented to break boundaries: modesty, decency, propriety."

He gazed at for a long time, then exclaimed fervently, "What you say is brilliant!" He hesitated, as if on the threshold of a powerful emotion. "This isn't all just words, is it?"

"Excuse me?" she said, taking offense.

"I've rarely met a woman who puts her money where her mouth is in a situation like this. You know, we men dream of a woman who'd see sex the way we do, as a perpetual celebration, pleasure at its purest, a joy shared with others, powerful and innocent."

"It's as if my words were coming out of your mouth."

"Really?"

"Really."

His eyelids flickered and his swollen lips trembled. "Faustina, I don't dare take you at your word."

"You can."

"And you would follow me in my sexual obsessions?"

"Of course!"

Faustina's heart was pounding. Never had she seen Dany so passionate, so vibrant, so wholly absorbed with her. There and then, she felt she was becoming the important woman, the essential woman in his life, the one who would give him what none of the fools before her had been able to give him.

"Well?" she insisted, encouraging him.

"Well, I'd like to show men how beautiful you are, how good, how far above everybody else. Can you understand that? I'd get a real kick from being proud of you. I want them to know that you're the empress."

She swallowed, delighted with this role. "I'm game."

"Great. Have you ever been to Mille Chandelles?"

"Mille Chandelles?"

"The best swingers' club in Europe."

He leaned toward her, his mouth open, his eyes glistening and attentive. For a moment, she imagined the two of them there, with Dany showing everyone how much he cared about her . . . She quivered. Then she wondered what her mother would say in a similar situation. "No, of course not." Poor thing . . . Her mother was no longer a woman, just a widow. Her thoughts whirling in her head, she wondered which of her friends would dare say yes to such a request. None. They were either stuck or they were possessive. So Faustina saw this as an opportunity to be unique. If she declined, she would prove to be as oafish as her predecessors; if she embraced the risk, she would secure Dany.

"I'm game."

7

How can you stand having a mother who's crazy?" Claudine asked her son.

"I didn't get to choose," Ludovic replied slowly.

Tired, hair disheveled, eyes bloodshot, weary from concentrating, Ludovic had just spent four hours on his mother's bills and accounts. Usually, Claudine was merely confused, impecunious, late with paying her bills, but this time she had made some serious errors. Discouraged, he massaged his forehead.

"Seriously, Mom, how could you sign that agreement to sell? Your little apartment building's worth a lot more! And its three rents gave you enough to live on!"

Claudine cheerfully raised her head. "It was a bit silly, wasn't it?"

"It was damned stupid. I can't make it right this time. That crook has well and truly tricked you."

"I'm just a woman on her own, you know, a poor woman with no support. When your father was around . . . "

Ludovic knew the rest . . . In the past, Claudine wouldn't have made a mistake because she hadn't been allowed to take any initiative. Her husband managed everything—the household, the family, money matters—like an absolute despot. At the time, she would complain about it, cry in her room, and dream of a different life. But now she sounded as though she missed that hell.

"The lawyer let you do it?"

"Yes."

"Maître Demeulemester?"

"No, his assistant. He's gone to Thailand for three months."

"I can't believe it! A lawyer who abandons his clients and goes off on vacation for three months!"

"He has cancer, Ludovic, and his chemo failed. All the treatment did was turn his skin the color of cardboard and make him lose the few hairs he still had on his head."

Ludovic looked at his mother, who had suddenly become eloquent and passionate, her eyes gleaming as she spoke of disasters. She had the terrible habit of loving misfortune, finding out everything she could about it, collecting every detail. She became more interested in people as soon as they got sick than when they were well. She would quibble about going out with a friend, but was immediately available if that friend was taken to the hospital. It was easier to invite her to a funeral than to a dinner party. Other people's vulnerability, even their death throes, made her feel stronger and more alive. She drew energy from it like a carrion bird. Ludovic took care to stop the inevitable monologue before it started. "Mom, why didn't you tell me before?"

"About Maître Demeulemester's cancer?"

"No, about the sale of your little apartment building!"

"I didn't get the chance. You're always so busy."

"You see me every day. You talk to me several times a day!"

"That's what you think."

"It's the truth!"

"I didn't want to bother you."

"Well done! Now I'm faced with a financial tragedy, and it's too late to do anything about it! You worry me, you know."

Claudine was delighted with that word. She loved to worry her son, it was a way of taking over his life; this way, she knew that when he left her to go home, his thoughts would be with her.

"I'm scared you're going to make more blunders, Mom."

Claudine assumed the expression of a guilty child. The important thing was not to object.

"I don't know what to do with you anymore," Ludovic muttered, to himself as much as to her.

Claudine's face lit up. "You could demand that I be placed under supervision."

Ludovic looked at her in alarm: it was the solution he didn't dare resort to, out of fear of offending her or depressing her, and here she was, asking for it herself. And cheerfully at that!

"Yes," Claudine went on. "That way, I wouldn't do anything without your signature. Wouldn't that be perfect?"

"But—"

"What?"

"You're only fifty-eight, Mom. People usually take that kind of step when—"

"People take measures like that when they're useful. You seem to be saying that I—that you—need them."

Ludovic nodded gravely and warily. He put the papers away in the files he had prepared, accepted a fresh cup of tea, chatted about trivial matters, then left the family home. Even though he had hated his late father, blaming him for abusing his power and treating his mother like a child, he was now reassessing his interpretation of the past: maybe his father hadn't been the only one at fault, maybe Claudine called for that kind of behavior. She required a force outside herself, she refused to act as an adult, almost asked to be treated like a child.

Ludovic cut across the square, where some young North Africans were playing soccer.

What Ludovic found confusing wasn't registering just how immature his mother was, but exonerating a father he had labeled a "bastard." This novelty disturbed the image of the family he had built up for himself. His father, a brute, a monster who beat his wife and two children, had never before been entitled to extenuating circumstances; not even his death had led to his being idealized. Yet now Ludovic was discovering in Claudine a tendency to trigger violence: she knowingly made blunders so that he would have to redefine her, she pushed his boundaries, forced him to fly off the handle and dominate her. The fact was, she drove those around her to be tyrannical toward her.

Ludovic was ill at ease. What if he was wrong? What if it wasn't his mother who generated harsh behavior but he who was reacting aggressively? Had he inherited his father's temperament? Was he, by some genetic predisposition, reproducing the attitudes of the man he had hated?

He stopped on Place Brugmann, walked into an American-style restaurant decorated like an old Cadillac, sat down on a turquoise imitation-leather banquette, and ordered a burger with cheddar and fries. The Coke helped clear his head. He had to admit that there was nothing more revolting than Coke—it looked like gasoline and tasted molecular—but what bliss! As a child, whenever he sneaked out of the house, he'd have lunch in an American fast-food joint, just like an adult; now he stuffed himself, feeling like a child.

A little calmer now, he paused on Place d'Arezzo. Parrots and parakeets were squawking, dropping excrement, and fluttering around as if nothing ever happened in this city. To think that they didn't have mood swings! Ludo watched them with a mixture of hatred and resentment: even though he thought they were stupid, he envied their constant vitality and wondered why their lives were so uncomplicated and his exactly the opposite.

Back in his apartment, he put the finishing touches to two articles for his cultural magazine, then, relieved that he had done his duty, switched on his personal computer.

There were four responses to his ad on the dating site he had joined. How disappointing! When he'd subscribed, the promise had been that he would get about fifty responses: either he'd been swindled, or his text hadn't attracted anyone. Only four women in a whole week?

The first insulted him: *It takes a real old fossil to write something like that. If I were on a desert island, I'd rather have tortoises for company than this idiot. When you're as bad as that, the only option is masturbation.*

The second demanded that he be removed from the list: *Dear Moderator, If you accept lunatics like this, decent people are going to unsubscribe.*

The third took a different tack: *Feel like a dirty-minded fat girl? Call Virginie.*

The fourth sounded different: *I'm very interested in your advertisement. I have all the faults you want: I'm antisocial, insomniac, a smoker, hysterical, not very sexual, and I've been depressed for years. I'll add even more to your list: I don't cook too well, I verge on the irrational, I know nothing about music but love it. Having said that, before I send you a tape, which would be an act of premature immodesty, I need to know more about you. What was your most recent meal? What was the most recent piece of music you listened to? What's your star sign? If it's Gemini or Scorpio, don't bother replying.*

The tone of the message made Ludo smile. Finally, someone who understood him . . . He looked at her name: Fiordiligi. Another point in her favor: she had chosen a character from Mozart, the heroine of *Così fan tutte*, as her handle.

His face felt hot. He was definitely going to contact her. Should he reply now or wait till tomorrow?

He walked around his apartment, then returned to his table. Better not try such a good woman's patience. His quick fingers tapped on the keyboard:

> Hello, Fiordiligi. From your description, you're the ideal woman. Are you sure you aren't making yourself

sound better by investing yourself with faults? Are you lying in order to attract me? Are you really the disaster you claim to be? I'm afraid I'll discover your qualities if I contact you. Signed: Alfonso. P.S. I'm a Sagittarius. I've eaten crap. I listen to Scriabin in order to cultivate my depression artistically.

No sooner had he pressed the *send* key than the doorbell rang. Blushing as if he had been caught mid-coitus, Ludo switched off his computer and opened the door. "Tiffany?"

"Weren't you expecting me?"

"Er . . . No."

"I knew it. I told the girls, 'He'll forget, you'll see.'"

"Forget what?"

"Your appointment."

"What appointment?"

"Your appointment at the See Me Institute."

He didn't understand.

She rolled her eyes angrily. "The massage we gave you as a birthday present!" she insisted.

Ludovic slapped his forehead in dismay: his female friends had clubbed together to buy him a massage, but since that was something he hated, he'd put the voucher away in a drawer. But the woman who owned See Me had told the girls that he hadn't shown up. So, three days ago, Tiffany had fixed an appointment, and was coming to get him. There was no backing down now.

"You'll see, it will do you a world of good," Tiffany said, seeing how upset he was.

"It's just that . . . I've told you so many times . . . I'm not sure I like massage."

"How do you know if you've never tried it? Come on, I can't make sure you get laid, but I can take care of this."

For a moment, Ludo considered setting his kitchen on fire

to create a diversion, but Tiffany was sticking close to his heels, so escape was no longer possible.

They walked together to Avenue Molière, where the See Me Institute flaunted its sober elegance.

They went in and Tiffany gave Ludo's name to the receptionist, who instructed him in a honeyed voice, "This is the key to Locker No. 6, on your left past the door. In it, you'll find towels, slippers, and a robe. Please hang up your clothes there and go to the indoor fountain to wait for the therapist."

Ludovic wished he could run away, but Tiffany dragged him to the frosted glass door. "Go on, Ludo, enjoy the massage."

He told himself he would hide in the changing room, then run out before the receptionist had time to stop him.

As if she had heard him hatch this plan, Tiffany said, "I'll stay here and look at their specialties, prices, and membership packages."

Damn! If Tiffany was going to stay in the lobby, he couldn't escape.

Shoulders slumped, he went into the changing room. The air smelled of amber, with soft lighting creating a comfortable atmosphere. *Come on, Ludo, be brave*, he said to himself as he started undressing. It was a good thing there was nobody else in the room, or he would have felt inhibited. He took off his clothes, keeping his boxers on, and put on the robe, which was so large, thick, and warm that he felt as if he was disguising himself as a polar bear. Then he tried to put on the slippers, which were two pieces of sponge sewn together, and that was the last straw: the sight of his white, hairy legs was painful. They were so ugly! And his feet were even worse. Through some perversion of nature, there were hairs growing on the joints of every toe. Where else could you find anything uglier than those thin tufts of hair? Why did they have to grow there, when he was practically hairless on other parts of his body? He looked like a monkey, the embryo of a monkey, a monkey in the process of being formed, an unfinished monkey. He should have shaved before coming here. He did shave when he went swimming, but he was afraid of doing it too often because he had been assured that if you shaved too often the hairs became stronger, thicker, and rougher, in other words, acquired the vigor of a beard. That was all he needed! A beard on his feet, when he didn't have one on his face!

"Hello, am I disturbing you?"

He gave a start.

A stunning young blonde had just looked into the changing room. "Sorry," she said in a soft voice. "I did knock several times but you didn't respond."

"I'm Ludovic."

"Please come with me, Ludovic. My name's Dorothea, and I'm your therapist."

Irritated, Ludovic wanted to shoot back, "Therapist?" How pretentious was that? Couldn't she just say, "Masseuse"? No stratum of society being spared linguistic inflation, nobody called professions by their names anymore. Here was a manipulator of flesh giving herself an academic title to convince you she'd been to medical school. He suppressed his indignation and simply followed her with short, clumsy steps, since the soft slippers rendered movement dangerous. This place felt so alien that the prospect of making a scene struck him as utopian.

Having descended to the floor below, Dorothea admitted him to a small room with a high couch.

"I'll let you lie down here."

She gave him a tiny plastic bag containing a piece of fabric with an elastic going through it.

"What's this?"

"It's a G-string. You can put it on if you like, but nudity doesn't bother me."

Ludo felt faint. "G-string," "nudity." They were going in a direction he hated . . . He was about to cry out that he wanted to leave, but she had already disappeared and closed the door behind her.

Furious, he put away his robe and lay on his stomach, keeping on his boxers and adjusting them to protect his modesty. Then he calmed down, thinking that he was about to inflict on that poor girl the worst ordeal of her life: never before could she have touched such an ugly body. She was about to massage a tubercle.

There was a gentle knock at the door, and the therapist came in and, in a mouselike voice, asked him about his health and medical history. Ludo assured her that he was in excellent health, a detail that made him want to cry.

At last, the therapist announced that she was starting her "treatment" and placed her hands on various parts of his body, applying a still, constant pressure.

Even though he didn't enjoy it, Ludovic had to admit that it wasn't unbearable. So he took the time to look around. It was a cellar! He was stuck in a cellar. Above him stood a five-story building that could come crashing down. If it did, nobody would find him or his "therapist." How stupid! And they were trying to persuade him that it was pleasant? What was pleasant about shutting yourself up in a windowless hole? What was pleasant about knowing you were occupying the space usually occupied by a boiler, even if the paint, the ceramic tiles, the sound of running water, and the Indian music were trying to conceal the fact by creating an atmosphere of luxury and relaxation?

The mouse asked him if he was all right. "Would you like more pressure? Or less?"

"It's perfect," Ludo murmured in order to dismiss the problem.

Should I admit to her that I can't stand being touched? She'll be offended. Or think I'm crazy. Which I probably am. But that's nobody's business but my own.

The mouse announced that she was about to use oil.

So now I'm going to get all sticky!

"Do you have to?"

"Of course. They're Ayurvedic oils. Their scents and properties enhance the treatment. Are you familiar with Indian medicine?"

"Yes, of course."

The mouse is totally into her delusion that she's a therapist. It's only natural she lives in a cellar. Mice have been living in them for thousands of years.

He almost laughed but at that very moment, something greasy landed on his back. He shuddered with disgust. The stickiness persevered and moved about. She was in the process of making him mucky from his shoulders down to his lower back. It was horrible!

Ludovic felt that if this carried on, he would go mad. The oil repelled him, being covered in it made him feel sick, and this fanatic was using him to give credibility to her nonsense. He tried to calm himself with humor. *She's preparing me like a roast. All I need is a clove of garlic up my ass and I'm ready for the oven.* He flushed because the word "oven" reminded him of his grandparents, the Zilbersteins, who had died in Nazi extermination camps, and that brought on a wave of remorse. He was truly pathetic! His ancestors had been slaughtered after endless suffering while he, who had everything, who lived in a peaceful world, who was being pampered in a luxury establishment, couldn't even be happy. Shame on him . . .

How could he ask the girl to stop? How could he avoid her increasingly broad and emphatic gestures? Ludo felt as if he was going to faint. His head was spinning. Should he say something?

Suddenly, he straightened, got up on all fours on the couch, and cried out.

Taken aback, the girl screamed and stepped back.

Ludovic threw up.

He threw up for a long time, in several spasms.

There in front of him, on the towel, appeared the cheese-burger, the fries, the chocolate melt, all in insufficiently chewed pieces and drowned in Coca-Cola.

Phew! He was breathing more easily. The massage was over, and he was spared.

Half an hour later, back home, Ludo felt like the happiest of men, returning to his apartment as if he had just spent six months in jail. The expedition had had the advantage of making him even more attached to his own den and his own habits.

Why was it that he couldn't stand being touched? He didn't know. But it was a fact that his skin didn't like coming in contact with a stranger's skin. In addition, he felt the need to be in control, and allowing yourself to be caressed or massaged meant letting go. No, thanks.

Automatically, Ludo switched on his computer. His heart beat faster when he noticed that there was a new message waiting for him. Fiordiligi had replied.

> Dear Alfonso, Sagittarius is my favorite sign. I stuff myself with chips. This morning, I listened to some Schumann, which, if you want to keep feeling sad, is as good a prescription as Scriabin, don't you think? I would very much like to correspond with you. A Fiordiligi used to bad luck and surprised to glimpse a lucky star.

Ludo began a long letter. He was enchanted with this Fiordiligi. He was particularly touched by her last confession: if, like him, she attracted problems, then they were made for each other.

8

Diane had been tied to her bed for eight hours, blind-folded and gagged, without food or drink. Cooler air was coming into the bedroom from the window, mottling her naked skin with shivers. Her knees, chafed by the floorboards, were starting to hurt from bearing her whole weight.

Shortly after her visitor had left, she had waited to see what he would do next to free her. After all, the stranger had behaved like a gentleman, giving her some rare sensations. In her fertile imagination, she had pictured several possibilities, two of which seemed exciting . . . In the first, the stranger called the firefighters, claiming there was a fire in the apartment. They kicked the door down and discovered her, naked and handcuffed—they might even be turned on by the sight. In the second, the crueler of the two, the stranger told the police that he had heard screams coming from the fourth floor. The police came, freed her, and, because she didn't answer their questions, took her into custody, where she finally told them everything: a delicious prospect, a refined twist on the kind of sado-masochistic situations she enjoyed.

Eight hours later, she decided that she had idealized her stranger. He had simply run away, period, without planning any second act for this scenario.

And now, with her joints inflamed, she was trying, in spite of her hands still being tied to the bed, to find a less painful position. This really was sadism! But boring, pointless sadism: she was just hurting, that's all, with no pleasure involved.

At seven in the evening, her husband Jean-Noël came back from work. After calling her from the hallway, he went from room to room and discovered her in the bedroom. He immediately tore off her mask and gag.

"Please hurry up and remove the handcuffs," Diane cried. "I can't wait any longer: I'm bursting to take a leak!"

Luckily, the visitor had put the keys in plain sight on the night table. Freed, Diane got stiffly to her feet, moaned a few times, and ran to the toilet.

By the time she came back into the living room, Jean-Noël had prepared two martinis. She slipped on her silk robe and sat down with a sigh. "What a day!"

Jean-Noël laughed and collapsed into an armchair. "I think you may have quite a story to tell me."

They clinked glasses and, rubbing her sore wrists, Diane recounted her experience of that morning. Aware that her husband was captivated, she went into increasing detail, analyzing her many sensations, turning the episode into an epic.

Jean-Noël listened, mouth ajar, eyes gleaming with fascination.

"Anyway," she concluded prosaically, "with all that, I didn't have time to buy or cook anything, so you're going to have to take me out to dinner."

Jean-Noël did as he was told. Aroused by the adventure, he felt desire for Diane, but knew only too well how she would react to him: with disdain. "What, like this? In bed, Ma-and-Pa style? Oh, no, for pity's sake, we've done that, it's boring."

Diane loved inventive sex. In truth, Jean-Noël wondered if she liked inventiveness more than actual sex, seeing how much pleasure she got out of coming up with novel situations and staging them. Going to bed with Jean-Noël in a legal, middle-class, repetitive way bored her, and she made no attempt to conceal it. He was sometimes surprised and had even complained. But Diane wouldn't listen. "Oh, no, don't start on that again, you'll make me depressed. I didn't marry you to have dreary sex but to try the impossible. What's marriage for if it doesn't allow you to try out hundreds of ways to come? For pity's sake! As far as I'm concerned, conjugal life should be a stimulant, not a sleeping pill."

She meant it. In her loose, hippieish youth, she had ended up with a baby whose father she despised, and had devoted herself to bringing it up while doing all kinds of insecure jobs and living through some extreme adventures. Once her daughter had settled in the United States—on the pretext of finishing her studies, although Diane proudly claimed that it was really to get away from her unstable mother—she had remembered that, although she was blessed with a superb body, time wasn't on her side and that she would eventually become less irresistible, and so she had chosen Jean-Noël—a recently divorced, high-flying engineer—attracted by his comfortable financial position and glistening eyes.

He was forty at the time and had expected this to be just one more affair, but Diane had forced him to follow her into a world of sexual escapades: she had taken him to swingers' clubs, invited him to unusual parties, had given herself to other men in front of him, and had involved him in various sado-masochistic scenarios.

To Jean-Noël, this voyage of exploration had been an eye-opener. Although he was wary of women, considering them cunning and self-interested, he put all his trust in Diane, who was so different. She had conquered him and her victory was all the more complete in that she hadn't used any of the weapons of her peers, such as modesty, fidelity, tenderness, moderation, security. On the contrary, she was crude, dominating, outrageous, crazy, a lover of the unexpected, hungry for danger, and had set free the anti-conformist he had kept imprisoned in order to achieve success.

When she proposed marriage, he didn't see it as a trap, but

as another fantasy. He congratulated himself on marrying the least marriageable woman in world, freethinking, unfaithful, transgressive, a woman who would never obey him, who would be responsible only for her own pleasures, who would forbid him from making love in bed, on the kitchen table, or even on the piano, who would always lead him into unlikely situations that would set his heart beating with a mixture of passion and fear.

That evening, they went to La Truffe Blanche, one of the best restaurants in Brussels. The maître d' did a double take when he saw them but then, as the professional he was, he bowed and took their coats. In a flash, he ordered the waiters to prepare the table at the far end, the one kept apart from the others in a kind of shell. He was determined to isolate this couple because the previous time he had received complaints from patrons about the outrageous obscenities they had heard the woman say. In two hours, she had managed to empty the restaurant. Since the husband, noticing what had happened, had left a very generous tip, the maître d' wouldn't think of turning them away this time but thought it wise to take precautions.

But Diane didn't even mention sex over dinner. Instead she launched into a subject that fascinated her: the early Church fathers. As a matter of fact, she had decided to write a thesis about Origen. How had she discovered Origen? Why had she become interested in him? Jean-Noël wondered if it was the name, Origen, that had attracted her . . . There was *origin* and *gene* in the name Origen, which, poetically, made him into a fundamental character, the man from whom everything springs . . .

So Diane talked to him about this third-century theologian from Alexandria who castrated himself in order to devote himself to God, which Diane considered a mistake but also proof of true character.

"Mark said, 'If thy hand offend thee, cut it off.' What Origen does is castrate himself in order to escape temptation. Also, as a young man, he saw his father beheaded right in front of him. He's not weak, or melancholy, or dull, no, he's a violent man in a violent world. I'm interested in what he thinks. It doesn't actually matter if he's right or wrong."

Here too, Jean-Noël found Diane fascinating. Who today, apart from a fossilized academic searching through dusty libraries for a career niche, would become so passionate about Origen, Ammonius Saccas, or Gregory Thaumaturgus? This woman—his wife—had a gift for avoiding the ordinary.

When they got back home, she grabbed her volume of Nietzsche, propped herself up with pillows, and resumed her reading, putting the yellow letter next to her.

Jean-Noël took it and read: *Just a note to tell you I love you. Signed: You know who.*

"What's this?"

"I don't know." She continued reading but, twenty seconds later, added, "And I don't care."

Jean-Noël agreed, but slipped the message into his own book: he had just had an excellent idea.

Two days later, Diane discovered another yellow letter in her mail, and this time she was more interested. *Meet me tonight, Thursday, at 11 PM, La Vistule, next to the high-voltage building, at the foot of the antenna. Be naked under your mink. Signed: You don't know who.*

She smiled and bit her lip. "Well, well, this is getting better and better." Remembering that Jean-Noël was having dinner with colleagues that night, she was glad she could go to this intriguing rendezvous.

At ten-thirty, she set off in her little Italian car. Until the last minute, she had thought to disobey and put on black under-wear or maybe just garters, but then she had decided that the writer of the letter must have his reasons to demand nudity, and that it was pointless to sacrifice lace that cost a fortune.

Guided by her GPS, she left Brussels, drove through a forest, then some sinister hamlets—just a few squat houses along the side of the road—and ventured up a steep path that led to a wire gate. A sign eaten away by rust, hanging lopsidedly by just one nail, said *LA VISTULE*.

Diane got out, felt the cold around her, pushed open the gate, which screeched, then got back in her Fiat and drove into this muddy terrain with its potholed paths. This must have once been an industrial area but all that was left now was crumbling vandalized buildings, probably inhabited by squatters. The authorities had cut off the electricity supply and the place was shrouded in irredeemable darkness. Diane drove in the direction of a shape that stood out against the flat sky, assuming it must be the antenna. As a matter of fact, as she drew nearer, her yellow headlights revealed beneath the metal structure a kind of concrete bunker covered in *Danger of Death* signs.

She switched off the ignition. She was trembling.

How could she be sure that it wouldn't be just the anonymous letter writer who appeared, but also others who weren't part of the scenario, people who lived outside the law amid the ruins?

She looked around at the grim landscape, the gutted tippers, the piles of rubble, the rolls of barbed wire. She immediately pictured the headlines: *Woman Raped at La Vistule*. Pictures flashed through her mind, images of herself lying dead in the mud, blood all over her face. She could guess the comments: *What was she doing in that danger zone? Who forced her to go there? A murder that looks like suicide.*

Should she get out of the car? No, better to turn and go back.

At that moment, headlights blinked in the darkness.

"It's him."

She did not know who "he" was, but his presence calmed her.

She did have an appointment, after all.

A man's voice, distorted by a loudspeaker, came from the distance. "Get out of the car!"

Swallowing, she made up her mind to leave her shelter.

The headlights blinded her. All the same, she walked bravely toward them.

"Open your coat."

She opened her fur coat wide, revealing her nakedness.

"Good. Now take the path on the right and keep moving straight ahead."

She saw a clay path that led into darkness and slowly started along it, her high heels unsuited to this irregular terrain, especially when she couldn't even see it.

Suddenly, she was able to see the obstacles more clearly, because a harsh light cast her shadow in front of her: the stranger's car, a station wagon, was following her.

"Don't turn!"

Anticipating her reaction, the voice commanded her to keep walking. The throbbing hood of the vehicle was coming closer and closer.

What if he suddenly speeds up? she wondered, nervously.

In response, the engine roared, and that reassured her. The fact that the driver had tried to scare her meant that it was a game he too was playing scrupulously, that she could be afraid in the same way as when you watch a horror movie and suspend disbelief.

She walked another fifty yards, until the voice ordered her to stop.

"Put your coat on the hood."

As she did so, she shivered, because the April night was getting colder. The lights went out. Three men in ski masks appeared and they threw themselves upon her. She fought back a little, they overpowered her, and she stopped struggling and abandoned herself to them on the car body.

Twenty minutes later, as she was coming to her senses, a hand helped her back on her feet and put the mink coat over her shoulders.

The station wagon began to reverse, taking away two of the masked men.

The one who'd been left behind waited for the car to disappear, and for their eyes to get used to the dark, then removed his mask. "Will you give me a lift back?" Jean-Noël asked.

"You've earned it."

When they got into her tiny Italian car, he sighed, contented. "I enjoyed that."

"Me too," Diane chuckled. She meant it. "Especially when I was walking in the dark and could have been run over."

"I thought you'd like that kind of detail."

She gave him a grateful pat on the cheek, then started the car.

"Do you want to know who the two—"

"Oh, no!" Diane replied, offended. "You're going to spoil my memories!"

They drove back quietly, listening to a Bruckner symphony in the background, Diane having decided that Bruckner was an orgiastic composer.

When they got to Place d'Arezzo, Jean-Noël came straight to the point. "Shall we go to Mille Chandelles on Saturday night?"

"An orgy? Won't that be boring?"

Jean-Noël congratulated himself on living with the only woman capable of uttering such words as "An orgy? Won't that be boring?"

"I don't think so. I've spoken to the owner, Denis. He's invited a French chef with three Michelin stars."

"So?"

"So he has a proposition for you."

On Saturday night, at Mille Chandelles, Diane enjoyed herself as she never had before.

They prepared her in the kitchen for three hours. The prestigious chef, accompanied by four apprentices, had wonderful fingers. She might have lost patience, but, instead, she put up no resistance and joked with them as they worked.

When midnight was about to strike, the four cooks lifted the huge serving dish the size of a stretcher, music from the court of Louis XIV started playing, the doors were opened, and they walked in, majestically, carrying on their shoulders a truly choice morsel: Diane, naked and stuffed with two hundred exquisite appetizers.

For Diane, being served as a royal dish by a three-star chef represented the apotheosis of her licentious life. Was it because of that pride, the pomp of the music, the applause of the guests, or the intoxication produced by the fragrances and flavors with which she was garnished? Whatever it was, she felt tears well up in her eyes.

She was placed on the table and offered to the guests.

If her eyes had not been filled with tears of emotion, she would have recognized the man busy picking shrimps from her toes as the famous Zachary Bidermann, who had come stag.

9

Hello, Albane."

" . . . "

"Aren't you in a good mood?"

" . . . "

"Are you angry?"

" . . . "

"Have . . . have I done something to upset you?"

"Guess!"

"What?"

"You've no idea?"

"No."

"Your conscience is clear?"

"Yes."

"In that case, we have nothing to say to each other. Besides, I don't even know what I'm doing here."

Her eyes half closed, Albane looked around as if about to leap on the first horse to cross the square.

Sitting beside her, Quentin sighed, which made him sink further into the bench, then stretch out his endless legs.

The silence grew denser, camouflaged by the shrill cacophony of parrots and parakeets.

"Albane?"

" . . . "

"Aren't we speaking anymore?"

"No."

"Aren't we together anymore?"

"Absolutely not."

"OK"

Quentin leaped to his feet and walked away, his satchel on his back.

An imploring cry tore through the tropical din. "Quentin! Don't leave me!"

He stopped dead, and stood there hesitantly. He suddenly felt strong, equipped with the power to drive Albane to despair, and delighted with his own ascendancy over her. He turned, feeling like a magnanimous lord. "Yes?"

"Come here."

"But I thought—"

"Please . . . Come . . . "

Albane was tapping on the empty space next to her, beseeching him to sit back down.

She was so pretty this morning . . . Quentin thought girls were tiresome, yet fascinating: inventive and inexhaustible, they made a spectacle of everything. Whenever you were with them, every moment was an event. Even though Albane irritated him, he was never bored with her. First of all, she was always cute, whatever the circumstances, whether she was laughing, getting carried away, or crying—he loved to see her sobbing, it gave her a vulnerable air that he found very attractive—and second, she expected so much of him that she assured him of his own importance. She exalted his manhood with every outburst. At this moment, for instance, he saw himself as one of the Hollywood actors he admired. He could now play adult, manly roles, and that made him quiver with pleasure.

He went back and sat down next to her.

"Quentin, who was that letter for—the one you left on the bench?"

"For me."

"I'm sorry?"

"I'd gotten it that morning."

"You're joking!"

"No, why?"

Albane was shaken by a salutary laugh, a laugh that made her stomach contract and her legs move nervously, that took her breath away and threatened to suffocate her. When she felt that she was not just going to shed tears but also release mucus, she put her hand over her face, like a gag, and made an effort to calm down.

"Please tell me what's going on before you die," Quentin said jokingly.

He was staring at her with awe: he found her so entertaining, swinging as she did from one mood to another without anyone knowing why, elusive, inconsistent perhaps, but convinced that the center of the world was wherever she happened to be.

"I read the letter because I assumed it was for me," she confessed. "Then when you took it back, I realized it wasn't."

It was Quentin's turn to squirm. The sounds he emitted, halfway between a moo and a growl, were so ugly that the parrots and parakeets, alarmed, fell silent. When Quentin heard his wailing echo through the empty silence of the square, he also stopped, worried.

Albane, on the other hand, had very much enjoyed his hilarity, which was just like his tall frame, his outsized feet, his awkwardness: that of someone who had recently become a giant and was surprised by what was happening to him.

"Actually, I don't know who sent me the note."

"Another little girl in love with you."

"Was it you?"

Albane shuddered. As a matter of fact, why hadn't she taken the initiative and written a note like that? How could she have let some bitch beat her to it? Was she going to confess the truth? If so, she would disappoint Quentin. Above her, the parrots and parakeets resumed their commotion.

"Of course it was me." She turned to him and smiled sweetly, head bowed, almost submissive.

Quentin expressed surprise. "Really?"

"I felt I needed to write to you."

"You sly thing! You throw a jealous tantrum and ask me who the note is for, when it was you who sent it. Girls have such twisted minds . . . "

"Girls? I'm not girls, I'm me."

"All right, but I know what I'm talking about. You really do have a twisted mind."

"Twisted? Is it wrong to say you love somebody?"

"I didn't mean that."

"A twisted mind. Thank you. I open up my heart to you, and you say I have a twisted mind. You and I don't use words the same way."

Quentin fell silent, afraid she was right: they couldn't exchange more than three sentences before they started screaming at each other. Someone should have warned him that there was one vocabulary for girls and another for boys. Then he would have done some research, worked out two separate registers, and wouldn't now be unleashing a storm whenever he used an inappropriate term.

Taking advantage of his silence, Albane checked the plausibility of her lie: Quentin wasn't familiar with her handwriting, and the message contained only expressions she could have used.

"It's neat, actually. We see each other every day, and you still write to me. I like it."

Albane lowered her eyes and assumed an air of modesty. Her lie was having such a positive effect that she was beginning to forget it *was* a lie. Yes, she must have written the note . . .

"It's sometimes easier to tell the truth on paper. When we talk, we're afraid, so we don't always cut to the chase. Whereas when we have a pen in our hand, we're calm and we get straight to the point."

"I'm sure you're right, Albane."

"Besides, it's a lot more romantic, isn't it?"

He looked at her. She was leading him into a fabulous world, a world of delicate feelings, of those poets their teachers were always singing the praises of. Having seen women on television use the word "romantic," he knew that it was one of the key elements of seduction.

He decided to rise to the occasion. Quick to have ideas and to put them into practice, he stood up. "Can you wait here for a few seconds, Albane?"

"But—"

"A few seconds . . . I'll be back soon . . . I swear."

Without waiting for her to agree, he scurried off and disappeared behind the trees. Once he was sure she could not see him, he rushed straight to the florist's.

Xavière greeted him with a quizzical look that suggested his sudden arrival must be a mistake. Undaunted, he asked, "Is it possible to buy just one rose?"

"Yes, it's possible."

"Then I'd like one."

"What color? I'd say red, given your state . . . "

Quentin didn't understand Xavière, much to her delight.

They went to the till, and she told him the price.

Just as he was paying, Orion appeared. "Ah, young Quentin! How you've grown, my boy! It's incredible these days, with the amount they feed you, you all turn into giants. Shall I make up a bouquet for you?"

"You'll have trouble doing it with a single rose," Xavière grunted.

"I'll dress it in some pretty foil."

He took the rose and started working on it, while Xavière shrugged, considering his effort extravagant.

Quentin turned to Orion. "Do you have a card, so that I can write a note?"

"But of course!"

Orion put a card, an envelope, and a pen on the counter.

"Why don't you give him all the cash in the till and your savings while you're about it," Xavière whispered in his ear.

Orion laughed as if she had just said something witty.

Blushing, Quentin scribbled a line and sealed the envelope.

Orion showed him how the red ribbon could hold the note, then wished him a good day.

"Isn't youth beautiful?" he said.

"Yes, beautiful, but broke," Xavière, returning in disgust to the back of the shop. "It makes your mouth water but doesn't feed you."

Quentin ran to the bench, coming to such a clumsy halt that he almost poked Albane's eye out as he handed her the flower. "Here, this is for you!"

Instead of taking the flower, Albane clapped her hands together and emitted a series of high-pitched squeals. Quentin glanced around, afraid he might look ridiculous. Luckily, they could be seen only by the parrots and parakeets, who didn't seem interested in them.

Albane finally accepted the flower as if it were a precious gift. "Thank you."

"I have to go, Albane, or I'll miss my class."

"Bye-bye, Quentin. See you tomorrow. I'm very . . . very . . . very . . . happy."

Quentin blushed, quivered, stamped his feet, and at last made up his mind to leave.

Albane watched his cheerful retreat until he had vanished. Then she looked at the red rose again. It was the first time a boy had given her a flower. She was entering into a wonderful time, her future, where everything would now be as lovely as this.

Grabbing her phone, she typed a message. *Gwen, Q. has given me flowers.* Of course, it was just one flower, but that didn't sound so good in a message. If she said, *Q. has given me a flower*, it might be thought either that Quentin was stingy or that he'd stolen it.

Albane noticed an envelope hanging from the ribbon.

"What a romantic!"

She opened it impatiently and deciphered the boy's rushed handwriting:

I want to sleep with you. Signed: You know who.

10

S he was watching Oxana, who had just discovered the anonymous message in the kitchen. Meg knew she was risking everything: either Oxana would get angry and leave Wim, or she would win him back.

It annoyed her that she couldn't make out was going on in the model's head. She strove to decode her body language but, sitting there on a high stool, with a cup in her hand, Oxana expressed nothing specific.

The telephone rang in Wim's private office, and Meg ran to answer it, shaking off her wild imaginings and going back to being an art dealer's perfect assistant.

As for Oxana, she was rereading the note. The more she thought about it, the more relieved she felt. Wim must have had a very strong relationship with his previous girlfriend, a relationship that was quite likely to resume. She must be very confident in their love to sign the note simply *You know who.*

Oxana got down off the stool, clinging to the refrigerator in order to avoid twisting her ankle, and put the kettle on again.

She was shaking off her sense of guilt. For three months, she had been punishing herself for failing to inspire Wim: he never took the initiative in their lovemaking, he never threw himself on her and whispered that her body drove him crazy, he had never taken her to bed with any ardor. He showed her the kind of respect that, once he had seduced her, caused her concern. She had wondered if she smelled bad or if she was aging fast. Even worse, she had started to question the way she abandoned herself to the delights of love . . .

Since she never stayed with a man long enough, she had never discussed this topic with anyone. Why did her love affairs last such a short time? Until now, she had assumed her breakups were related to geography, to the fact that her job took her to different parts of the world. But now that she had been living with Wim in Brussels for three months, she suspected that this official reason might conceal a more serious cause: Was she a mediocre lover? She suspected that as far as Wim was concerned—Wim who admired her beauty and showed her off like a precious treasure but avoided her in bed—she was second-rate.

This letter provided her with an alternative: Wim's head and heart were elsewhere, he was still involved—or hoping to be involved—with another woman, a woman he might get back together with. She, Oxana, might just be the interim lover.

"Oxana, your taxi will be here in five minutes."

She jumped. Meg was acting as an alarm clock, announcing that it was time to stop dreaming and go to work.

"Tell him I'll be ready in ten minutes."

Meg replied falsely that she would pass on the message, concealing the fact that the taxi would be there in half an hour, time for Oxana to bump into the furniture as she got her clothes together.

On the floor below, Wim was smiling ecstatically at his friend Knud, director of an airline company. "Petra von Tannenbaum?"

"She's been talking about nothing but you since last night."

"I did feel a connection, but I never thought . . . "

"Look, Wim, she couldn't have said it more plainly: 'It's a shame your Wim is tied up with a model because I'd have loved to stay with him while I'm in Brussels.'"

"Wow!"

"She also said, and I swear it's true: 'You should mention it to him anyway.'"

Wim turned scarlet, flattered that he'd caught the attention of a woman who was famous around the world. "You realize of course that if people in the field heard that I was with Petra von Tannenbaum, it'd be—"

"Good publicity?"

"Huge publicity! Berlin, Paris, Milan, New York . . . Everybody's talking about her."

By "everybody," Wim didn't mean the masses—those millions of ordinary beings—but the small, snobbish, elitist modern art set. This narrow clique—a hundred or so individuals in each of the cities mentioned—contained the people who mattered. If he had been introduced to a pop singer who had sold billions of records all over the world, he would have ignored her because she didn't rub shoulders with those kinds of people. For him, fame wasn't a question of universal celebrity, but of the recognition gained within a circle whose members he could list.

Petra von Tannenbaum aroused passion in devotees of the avant-garde because she had reinvented striptease, turning that vulgar, wretched activity, steeped in distress and lust, into an elegant happening. Appearing only in the most select galleries, she demanded a handpicked audience to whom, thanks to the sophisticated lighting provided by some sixty spotlights, she displayed a number of extraordinary tableaux in which she was dressed to start with and naked at the end, although not always—that would have been too predictable.

Equipped with a stunning physique, Petra von Tannenbaum enhanced nature with artifice. Her hair, her makeup, her nails, even the silkiness of her skin and richness of her coloring, everything looked as if it had been retouched by the brush of a great painter. She only ever appeared surrounded by this patina of an old master. Moreover, each scene echoed a famous painting, which she hijacked in an iconoclastic fashion, making the Mona Lisa strip, for instance, and the Winged Victory of Samothrace lift her arms.

"Look, Wim, Petra von Tannenbaum is going to be staying in Brussels for three months. In the next few weeks, she's performing in Antwerp, Ghent, Amsterdam, The Hague, and Cologne. Imagine yourself arm in arm with her at the Maastricht or Basel Fair?"

Wim stamped his feet with enthusiasm. To parade in front of his fellow dealers with a work of art at his side—now that would represent the apex of his career. He slapped himself on the knees: his mind was made up! "Tell Petra von Tannenbaum that I'd be delighted to invite her to dinner tomorrow night. That'll give me time to sort out a few issues."

"Perfect."

"Will she understand?"

"She'll understand."

Wim and Knud gave each other a warm hug.

"How will you deal with Oxana?"

Surprised, Wim gave him a glance that meant: *What an odd question . . .*

Wim went to the gallery, received a few clients, and flicked through magazines while pondering over the situation. Leaving a woman was something he had already done about twenty times. At other times, the separation had happened organically, through boredom or wear and tear, like a leaf falling off a tree in autumn. This time, he had to hasten the breakup.

Should he use the dreariness of their love life as an excuse? That would be the easy option, so why not take advantage of it? He was the victim, after all. No point in admitting to Oxana that his previous sexual relations had been equally appalling. As Knud would put it: "You can't say about a man that he's a bad lay because it takes two to be a bad lay." He would just have to play it by ear. Just as he did when he received a customer . . . Hadn't his brilliant instinct always served him well?

That evening, he had a meal delivered by the best Japanese cook in Brussels, and suggested to Oxana that they eat in the living room, on the couches, while listening to music.

Absently, Oxana hesitated, then exclaimed, "Yes! What a good idea!"

Once again, Wim wondered if Oxana used the short silences she observed to translate the question or search for an answer.

"Oxana, I have something important to tell you."

"I already know, Wim." She had replied with a quiet gravity. Looking him in the eyes, she swept her hair back and continued, "You're in love with another woman."

"What—"

"Much more than you are with me. You're not in love with me, anyway. You think about her when you come to bed, and even when we . . . "

She didn't know the words to describe sexual intimacy, so she made a vague gesture that nearly sent the lampshade flying against the wall.

Wim looked down, embarrassed but also delighted by the way she was interpreting his demeanor. "How did you guess?"

Oxana chose not to mention the yellow letter she had picked out of the trash. "Feminine intuition . . . "

"Are you hurt?"

"No, because now I know why you're not really attracted to me . . . " She smiled tenderly. "You're lucky to experience such passion, Wim."

Wim nodded, aware that the situation required it. Even so, Oxana's words made it clear that she wasn't crazy about him either, and that hurt his pride. He realized at that moment that he barely knew her: he had lived with her for three months, had taken her everywhere, but didn't know anything about her wishes and desires. Curious, he leaned forward. "Oxana, what is it that you want from a man?"

She raised her head, opened her eyes wide, and, with a mixture of sadness and indignation, replied, "That's something I'll only ever tell one person: the love of my life."

She had been as true to her feelings as she could be.

Wim took the blow. He gathered the wooden chopsticks from the two plates. "Would you mind moving out of the apartment tomorrow? Knud's studio apartment is free, if you like."

She looked him up and down. "I can afford a hotel, thank you. Tomorrow's fine. I'm tired tonight."

Without regret, without even sparing him a glance, she went up to the mezzanine.

Wim sat motionless on the couch for ten minutes—a long period of prostration for such an exuberant man—both pleased and vexed that this breakup should have taken place without tears. He had never imagined that he was living with such a solid block of indifference. He wasn't shocked by his own, very male cynicism—he was used to it—but he was bothered by Oxana's. What had she looked for in him? Free accommodation? Company? Once he had come up with the theory that perhaps she had looked for a lover who didn't exist, he put an end to his introspection and bounced back, like one of the springs in the couch, and rubbed his hands: the space was free for Petra von Tannenbaum.

The following day, Meg ordered Oxana's taxi for the last time. Unlike all the other times, she felt quite emotional as she did so, guilty at having caused the model's departure by leaving the yellow letter lying around.

Oxana kissed her, thanked her for taking care of her, and

got in the taxi. The driver was overjoyed at carrying such a beauty.

Wim, meanwhile, was getting ready to dine with Petra von Tannenbaum. What had seemed desirable to him the day before now terrified him. How was he going to suggest that she move in here? And if she threw himself at him, how would he react?

For a moment, he considered seeing Dr. Gemayel again, but then decided not to and vowed to take a few tranquilizers. That should be sufficient to deal with the stress, shouldn't it?

At eight in the evening, he went to pick up Petra von Tannenbaum from the Amigo Hotel. The doorman, the bell-boy, the waiters—they were all agog at this sculpture of a woman: they didn't know who she was, although they found her highly alluring. Some thought she was "a Hollywood actress who's very well-known over there but not yet over here," others that she was "a German countess whose picture was in *Gala* magazine." Nobody imagined that she was a stripper: her sophistication, her elegance, her aristocratic bearing were so much at odds with the image of that profession that nobody would have believed it anyway.

In the restaurant, Petra was charming toward Wim, who negotiated various topics of conversation skillfully but wondered how to breach more intimate questions.

She did so herself, over dessert. Taking out a long cigarette holder, she dug a ruby-red fingernail into Wim's hand. "My dear, my things are ready. We just need to pick them up from the hotel."

"Petra, you bowl me over."

"I know."

"How do you know you'll like it at my place?"

"I've heard all about it. Anyway, I like being with you."

He felt drunk with pride. One thing, though, bothered him. "I worry whether or not you'll like your room . . . "

"My room? I thought it was yours."

Just to underline what she was suggesting, she removed her fingernail and caressed his hand.

Wim turned red.

On the way home, he talked like never before. He talked to conceal his nervousness.

Petra von Tannenbaum let out cries of admiration as she visited the triple loft. Finally, he led her to the private section.

"This'll be perfect," she said, discovering the bedroom.

He bowed his head like an eager servant, then brought up her trunks.

"Use the bathroom before me, Wim. I like to take my time."

Wim obeyed. When he came out, he was clad in an elegant black kimono. Petra gave it an appreciative glance then, holding several toiletry bags, went in and shut the door behind her.

Wim went to have a drink, taking two tranquilizers along with it, and got into bed.

He waited. After half an hour, concerned, he knocked lightly at the door. "Petra, is everything all right?"

"Everything's perfect, my dear."

He waited patiently for her to join him.

She still didn't come out. Thanks to the tranquilizers and the fact that he had been lying down for a long time, he began to feel sleepy. How embarrassing! She was going to come out and find that he had dozed off. He pinched himself, struggling with the wave of well-being that was trying to lull him into sleep.

Another half hour went by and he heard Petra behind the door. "Actually, my dear, I find the light uncomfortable in the evening. Just keep a night light on."

Wim obeyed, and let her know that he had done so.

"I'm coming."

He was expecting a theatrical entrance, like the ones she

usually made. Instead, a shadowy figure slipped into bed next to him.

She laid her head on the pillows as if Wim wasn't there. Once she was settled, he thought it necessary to say, "I'm glad you're here."

"Good. Good. Me, too. Your bedding seems excellent."

He slid a hand toward her, hoping for encouragement. She ignored it, so he grew bolder and grabbed her by the wrist.

She jumped. "Oh!" She turned her magnificent face to look at him. "I forgot to tell you, my dear: I hate sex and never have it."

He stared at her. She wasn't joking. She was stating an important detail, even if it was only a detail.

"You're not angry with me? Thank you."

With that, she turned over and curled up, leaving Wim nothing but the sight of her long, sublime black hair.

He looked up at the ceiling, took a deep breath, then breathed out in relief: he and this woman were going to get along just fine.

11

T he guy's brilliant!"

"And tonight he's really wild!"

Victor was arousing enthusiastic comments around the dance floor. In this bourgeois nightclub frequented by young thirtysomethings, the appearance of a supple, agile, handsome twenty-year-old shaking his hips in such a sexy way, moving in a kind of trance, his eyes half shut, his mouth half open, was making this an evening to remember.

Victor loved dancing. At one with his body, happy with the way it responded to him, he would lose his awkwardness and improvise a thousand moves to the music, unaware of the desires he stirred around him.

"Come on!" he said to the group of people sitting at the table, who had come with him.

The women giggled, tantalized. Already a few of the men were standing up, convinced they would be as sensual as Victor as soon as they started moving about.

Without losing the rhythm, performing a kind of belly dance, Victor approached his female friends and, with a graceful hand gesture, invited them one by one to join him.

Several of them poured onto the dance floor. Victor undulated between the couples, miming someone who wants to appeal to the wife as well as the husband. Everyone graciously entered into the spirit of things.

"He's setting the club on fire."

"What an atmosphere!"

"The owner should pay him."

Victor had decided not to go out with his fellow students because, ever since the arrival of the anonymous message—and especially since its disappearance from the kitchen—he had been scared that one of them, male or female, had amorous designs on him. So he had preferred to join a more mature group, Nathan's friends, in this nightclub he didn't generally frequent. He was causing a sensation not only because he was new, but because he gave the thirtysomethings the illusion that they were his age. Married, some of them with kids, all of them doing well in their careers, they went out to convince themselves that they were free. They were neither young nor old, but old young people.

"Who's this Victor for? Girls or boys?"

"He doesn't go out with anyone."

"You're kidding! He's so cool, he could get anything that moves. And have you seen how relaxed he looks? If he's a virgin, then I'm Joan of Arc."

Tom and Nathan came to join the party at the table, and were immediately buttonholed by the girls.

"You'll be able to tell us. We were wondering if Victor likes men or women."

"Why do you care?" Tom asked, laughing.

"Spare us your lectures," Nathan grunted. "You ask yourself exactly the same question."

"Only when I like a guy."

"You like all of them. You're ecumenical when it comes to sex."

"Stop bickering, you two, and answer us."

Tom and Nathan looked at each other, nonplussed, then shrugged and said, "We don't know."

"What?" the women exclaimed. "Haven't either of you hit on him?"

"What do you take me for, darling?" Nathan said, indignantly. "I'll be married soon. Tom can't wait."

"Why, would marriage make you faithful?" Tom asked, surprised.

"Just talking crap."

"The truth is," Tom continued, "we may not have hit on him, but we have tried to find out what he likes."

"And?"

"Total mystery."

"To be more precise," Nathan said, "he gives the impression he likes everything."

"And we have the feeling he doesn't like anything."

"You boys are crazy: look at how he dances."

They pointed to Victor. His eyes were no longer closed, and he was giving the partners he brushed against the most passionate looks possible.

"So he's a tease," Nathan said irritably. "What does that prove? A tease isn't necessarily a fuck."

"Sometimes it's the opposite," Tom said. "Teases often bolt when it's time to put out. It's the little saints who turn out to be sluts."

"Like Mother Teresa!" Nathan said.

The girls burst out laughing, then studied Victor again.

After a minute, Nathan cried, "Remember, girls, you're attached."

"We can still dream, can't we?"

"And you're ten years older than he is."

"At our age, ten years doesn't matter."

"At his age, it does!"

They glared at him. He had crossed the line between funny and unpleasant.

Tom grabbed him by the hand and led him onto the dance floor.

Behind them, Victor snatched a bottle of vodka, drank straight from it, then offered it to those around him.

"It's always the same," Tom muttered. "As soon as everyone's hooked, he attacks the booze and ends up drunk. That way he avoids the consequences of his provocative behavior."

"Yippee!" Victor cried, dancing even more wildly than before.

He pressed his buttocks against those of the woman next to him, then those of the man. The temperature was rising. Like a will-o'-the-wisp, Victor was shifting from one body to another, erotic, sensual, seductive.

The following day, Victor didn't emerge from under his quilt until eleven. The first thing he did was drag himself to the bathroom, rummage through the medicine cabinet, and take a few pills for his hangover.

It took him ten minutes to drink a bowl of bitter chamomile tea. Then he spent twenty minutes in the shower. The water running over his skin revived him.

At two in the afternoon, finally dressed, he remembered he had to call Tom and Nathan, and then see his uncle.

He phoned the boys and thanked them for bringing him home. They told him jokingly that there would be a wave of suicides in Brussels over the next few days unless he slept with all the men and women he had flirted with the night before.

"You really are a devil!" Tom said.

"I wish!" Victor replied, quite genuinely, and hung up.

It was becoming increasingly imperative for him to leave this city. In order to present his uncle with some specific options, he prepared a load of prospectuses from various universities, even memorizing some of the syllabuses. He needed to give a rational explanation for his desire to leave.

As a feeling of discouragement began creeping over him, he noticed through the windows of his attic apartment some parakeets playfully chasing one another. Feeling the warmth of the sun's rays, he decided to go out for a coffee.

He walked to Place Brugmann, a pleasant spot shaded by

thick chestnut trees and known as Look at Me Square because of a bistro with a terrace where the idle rich liked to be seen. He found a table to one side, next to the bookstore, and sat watching people stroll by.

A woman caught his attention. Slender, staggering on endless legs, she looked like a wounded bird. Having lost a sandal on the pedestrian crossing, she nearly knocked over the sliding panel by leaning on it to tie her strap. Then she spilled the contents of her handbag as she bent down to stroke a poodle, and when she took the last remaining seat outdoors, she managed to upset a jug on the next table.

Victor would have found her comical if he hadn't first found her stunning. Because her perfect body seemed to be in her way, because she constantly looked uncomfortable perched so high up, she gave the impression of being a little girl who had sprouted overnight. Even sitting, she lacked balance, with her head tilted, her legs tangled, and her torso wobbling. All of a sudden, she became radiant, all her flaws creating a jewel box for her noble, refined, intelligent face; her struggle with gravity made her slender neck and the graceful way she held her head seem like a miracle. To Victor, it was as if she were a Greek goddess who had emerged from the stiffness of marble and was attempting the adventure of being human.

He smiled at her. She immediately reciprocated, then, overcome with uncertainty, explored the contents of her handbag, taking out a notebook, scarves, eyedrops, lipsticks, and paper tissues, before she finally found what she was looking for: a pair of glasses she put on her nose. At last she was able to look properly at Victor, who smiled at her again, and realized she didn't know him. All the same, she made a friendly gesture.

Victor remembered the night he had just spent. *Don't start again!*

He thought about his imminent departure.

And not with her! She looks like a nice girl.

So he threw a banknote on the table and left the terrace, making a slight gesture of farewell to the accident-prone girl.

He returned to Place d'Arezzo and rang his uncle's doorbell.

"Victor, my boy!" Joséphine cried, throwing herself in his arms. He wholeheartedly hugged the aunt he adored. He had known her since he was born and had always seen her more as a friend than a relative. Never acting motherly, often behaving more childishly than he did, she demonstrated a deep, unfailing, unsentimental love for him. When he was with her, life seemed almost easy.

"Your uncle's waiting for you in his study." No sooner had she said this than she burst out laughing. "I love saying 'your uncle' when I talk about Baptiste. It's as if I've changed husbands, as if I'm married to an old man. It's so exotic."

"How are you, Joséphine?"

"Good question. Thank you for asking. I'll be able to answer in a few days' time."

"Is something wrong?"

"I'll tell you about it when I can see the wood for the trees." She patted him on the cheek. "And when you look less gloomy and less anxious."

And with this, she took him to Baptiste's study and walked off to the far end of the apartment, singing.

Baptiste hugged Victor.

As his uncle held him, Victor feared he would no longer have the courage to leave. Was Baptiste the only person in the world who spoiled him? Why distance himself from him? Why worry and disappoint him?

They sat down, exchanged a bit of small talk, then Victor took a postcard from his jacket pocket. "Look, my father's written to me. He's in South Africa now."

Baptiste's face clouded over. "Oh, so it's not Australia anymore?"

"He says there's no future in Australia, it's all happening in South Africa."

"I've heard that before."

Baptiste didn't insist, and neither did Victor.

When his mother—Baptiste's sister—had died, Victor was only seven. He didn't know his father, who had left his mother before he was born. But his father refused to allow Baptiste and Joséphine to take Victor in, claimed his paternity, and took the child away with him on his travels. He started involving him in his marvelous adventures which turned out not so marvelous. So many times, he had told his son he was about to make a fortune, because—or so he claimed—he could sense the way the wind was blowing. But reality insisted on thwarting his dreams and he ended up living by his wits. He was a man who thought of himself as a free, bold, intrepid globe-trotter, whereas in fact he was just a loser who ran away from all the places where he had failed.

Victor had quickly caught on to the fact that he was living with an immature adult. He had also noticed that whenever his father found himself in a jam, a discreet check from Baptiste saved them from ending up on the street.

So, at the age of fifteen, Victor had demanded to go to boarding school. Delighted to get rid of someone who kept judging him, his father agreed, even though he criticized his choice, then set off again in search of his fortune in faraway lands. He went to Thailand, where he tried to set up a hen farm, to Greece, where he thought he could make it as a real estate agent, to Madagascar, where he organized safaris, to La Réunion, where he survived as a beach attendant, to Patagonia, where he searched for gold, and, finally, to Australia, from which he attempted to export kangaroo steak.

Victor picked up the postcard again and shook it. "His life weighs no more than a postcard."

Baptiste leaned forward. "Why do you want to leave Brussels?"

Victor withdrew into silence.

Baptiste allowed the silence to grow, until Victor broke it. "Baptiste, please don't ask me to explain."

"You don't owe me any explanations, you owe yourself."

Victor scowled.

"I want to make sure you're not lying to yourself," Baptiste continued, calmly.

"Me too," Victor stammered, suddenly moved.

"What do you mean, you too? You're running away!"

"No."

"You're running away from your problems."

"No, I'm not," Victor said, more faintly.

"You're running away, just like your father."

Victor sat up, angry now. He must never be compared to that idiot.

He took a few steps around the room in order to shake off his anger, then came back, pale-faced, to his uncle.

"Baptiste, you know exactly what it is that makes my life difficult."

"Yes, I do. Why don't you try seeing a psychologist?"

"I'm already seeing one. You have to, in my situation."

"And?"

"And I tell him everything's fine."

"Why?"

"Because nobody can understand me."

"Can you understand yourself?"

Victor's eyes filled with tears. "Shit, you're too smart for me. You always have the last word."

"I'm not afraid of words."

Baptiste opened his arms and Victor rushed into them, weeping.

When he had pulled himself together, he sat down and blew his nose.

"And how are you, Baptiste? Tell me about yourself."

"Oh, no, we're not changing the subject. That trick won't work with me."

Victor laughed painfully.

"You want to leave Brussels," Baptiste resumed, "just as you left Paris and then Lille. Since I know that there are at least twenty universities where you can study Law, I'm getting ready to visit every campus over the next twenty years. In addition, since you're good at languages, I fear your wanderings may soon take us to England or the States, which I would enjoy per se, except that it simply shifts the problem. So, Victor, my boy, you're going to go back home, think about what's driving you to leave, and work out if what's making you leave here is also going to make you leave your next port of call. All right?"

"I love you," Victor whispered.

"At last! Those are the first sensible words I've heard all afternoon."

Baptiste was using humor in order to conceal the emotion that tore at him. Having no children, and feeling vulnerable because Joséphine had just fallen in love with someone else, Victor's declaration was like a dagger through the heart.

The two men looked at each other. All they needed to do was be there, side by side, and know that their feelings for each other were strong and indestructible. Baptiste wished he could say, "You're my son," and Victor, "I wish you were my father," but these words would be suppressed. Between these two reserved men, love would remain silent.

Victor left, his heart more at peace, and decided to walk again. Taking long strides helped reduce his tension. His legs took him to Place Brugmann. Immediately, his eyes sought out the wounded bird on the café terrace.

The accident-prone girl was still there, sipping a mint cordial and soda. Unable to see a free table, he approached and, without hesitation, leaned toward her. "May I keep you company?"

"Well . . . "

"There's no room anywhere else. But that's not the reason I'm asking you."

He winked. She responded with a friendly pout and made a gesture with her hand to indicate the free chair, knocking down the sugar bowl in the process.

"My name's Victor."

"My name's Oxana."

A mother walked past them, holding her baby in her arms. Oxana watched her with a sadness that didn't go unnoticed by Victor.

"You look upset."

"Always, when I see a baby . . . "

"Why?"

She made an evasive gesture.

A minute passed. Perplexed, Oxana studied Victor. "What about you?"

"I also feel like crying when I see a baby."

"Really?"

"I even do it when I'm on my own."

Oxana tried to read his face. She sensed that he was telling the truth.

Moved, they looked away.

Victor discreetly took out his phone and texted his uncle: *I'm staying.*

12

W hen he returned to his apartment that Sunday evening, Hippolyte felt so light he seemed to be walking on air, his eyes half-shut, his face beaming with a luminous serenity.

"Daddy!"

Isis rushed into his arms. He whirled her around in their narrow, cramped hallway.

"Daddy, you smell so good!"

She was so on the mark that he smiled: he smelled either of Patricia or of happiness—weren't they one and the same? He took a couple of steps and stumbled against the table in the cluttered room which served as kitchen, living room, dining room, and bedroom, and where his whole life unfolded. Separately, behind a door, there was only a tiny bathroom as well as a storeroom—an old pantry with a fanlight—which Hippolyte had turned into a bedroom for Isis.

"How was your weekend, you two?" Hippolyte asked Germain and Isis, who had spent it together while Hippolyte was visiting Patricia.

An apron around his waist, a steaming pan in his hand, Germain approached. "Isis has finished her homework, including math—I checked. Around noon, we went to her friend Betty's to watch a cartoon, *Bambi*. In the afternoon, she read while I made dinner."

Hippolyte leaned toward Isis. "Was *Bambi* good?"

"Yes. Germain cried a lot."

Annoyed, Germain clattered the whisk in the soup he was just finishing.

Standing on tiptoe, Isis whispered in her father's ear, "Bambi's mother dies at the beginning of the film. I don't think Germain watched anything after that."

Hippolyte expressed his sympathy, then disappeared into the bathroom to change, eager to spare his only suit.

"By the way," Germain yelped, "I washed and folded your laundry." He pointed to a stack of clothes on a chair.

"Thanks, Germain, you shouldn't have."

"It's OK, I don't mind. I didn't have anything else to do."

Isis stared at Germain, puzzled, wondering how it was possible not to have anything to do; she, Isis, was always doing something, thinking, drawing, singing, reading. She really couldn't fathom adult behavior. In fact, she had to finish her novel before dinner.

"Are you two going to talk?" she asked.

"Excuse me?" Hippolyte asked, coming out of the bathroom.

"I imagine you're going to have a talk now. Right, Germain?"

"Er . . . yes . . . why?"

"I ask so I know if I can carry on reading here or in my room. I think it'd probably be wiser if I made myself scarce."

Without waiting, she grabbed her book and walked around the table. Disconcerted, flabbergasted that a child of ten should say that it would "probably be wiser if I made myself scarce," Hippolyte caught her by the arm as she walked past him.

"What are you reading, sweetheart?"

"*Alice in Wonderland.*"

Naturally, he did not know the story—since childhood, he never imagined it was really possible to enjoy a book. Trying to be kind, he persisted, "What's Wonderland like? Is it nice?"

"It's horrible! There's a rabbit running in all directions, a sly cat, a mad hatter, and there's also a wicked queen with an army of idiotic soldiers. Not exactly Wonderland. More like Nightmareland."

"You don't like it, then?"

"Oh, I love it!"

She blew her father a kiss and went into her room, impatient to return to her monsters.

Hippolyte collapsed onto the sofa bed, blissful.

Germain looked at him. "I assume that since you only just got back, you . . . "

"Yes."

The two men looked at each other.

Germain was genuinely pleased with his friend's success. Through empathy, he received the calm vibes emitted by Hippolyte, the calm of a sated body and an ecstatic soul.

As for Hippolyte, he would have liked to describe to Germain what had happened, only he lacked the vocabulary—the few paltry words he had would have made the story of his amorous odyssey sound trivial. So he simply made a gesture to convey Patricia's feminine curves. His hands caressed her ghost. He sighed with happiness.

Had he had the right words, he would have told how since the previous evening he had quivered every second, how he had savored the emotions—anxiety, temptation, fear, delight, enjoyment, nostalgia. Yes, he had drunk those moments to the full, those delicious, paradoxical, intense moments. Patricia had cast a spell on him. What he had sensed about her from her appearance had been confirmed by the hours he had spent with her: she was not *a* woman but rather *the* woman, the one from whom we come, the one to whom we return, the matrix of love, at the same time mother and lover, the starting point and the point of arrival.

Three years earlier, he had first seen Patricia on Place

d'Arezzo, a queen in a dress whose light fabric gave you a sense of her hips, her belly, her chest; he had been so awestruck at such majesty that he had not dared speak to her, a victim not of a social but of a male complex: next to that imposing oak, he was nothing but a vine shoot, dry, knotty, woven of bones, tendons, and muscles.

Hippolyte believed that weight was a female quality. A mistress had to be large, slow, milky, voluminous. When a friend had said he liked "fat women," Hippolyte had protested: the word "fat" suggested a defect; Hippolyte loved ripeness, fulfillment, harmony; the nasty word "fat" castigated Junoesque figures and took "thin" as an absurd point of reference.

There were two kinds of women: real ones and fake ones. The real ones had triumphant bodies. The fake ones claimed to be female but lacked bellies, thighs, hips, and breasts. It was hard for them to dress: the cloth swayed in the air around them, their clothes didn't provide a space for broad, noble patterns, and they were condemned to plain fabrics and tiny motifs. In addition, the fake ones met a sad end: they showed their age, became wrinkled, laughed less, stooped, and kept a low profile, like cachectic rats.

Whenever he went to Matongé, the black quarter of Brussels, Hippolyte would find himself in a dazzling world: as far as he was concerned, African women, draped in their shimmering boubous, plump, proud, self-confident, cheerful, evoked an image of female supremacy. Seeing their husbands, who were more athletic, more high-strung, more tightly wound, he concluded that a man is always ridiculous compared with a woman; of course, he might be stronger and faster, but what about more beautiful? No. More reassuring? Never. In his eyes, Patricia was an African queen who had somehow ended up in a white skin, on Place d'Arezzo.

Although he condemned female thinness, Hippolyte watched his own weight because the extra pounds don't look good on a man: they add fat without the benefit of splendor or generosity. The proof of that was that, instead of spreading the fat evenly throughout his body, the male stores it all in his belly and looks like an insect with indigestion, becoming uglier, less flexible, less able to breathe easily. Women, on the other hand, swell everywhere, like a brioche in the oven.

So he was unable to tell Germain how dazzled he was by Patricia, how he had made love, slowly, gently, with tenderness. The night had provided them with a carnal extension to their previous emotions: care, respect, gentleness, kindness. For him, sex didn't represent an end in itself, but rather the con- firmation of a relationship. Lovemaking had to be sweet, a sigh that grew into a cry of joy, a gradual ecstasy. He hated taking, conquering, but preferred to melt, to glide. If a woman expected ostentatious passion, male chauvinism, let alone vio- lence, he declined—not that he lacked desire, strength, or stamina; he simply refused to play that game. Didn't Faustina, one of the residents on Place d'Arezzo, once try to seduce him, inviting him to freshen up in her apartment? He had immedi- ately seen what breed she belonged to, the kind that drives the male to act as a predator, the kind that has sex out of sheer exasperation, the kind that expects a man to knead her, to plow her; to resist her insane come-on, he had disgusted her by devoting himself to the dog shit and bird shit he was picking up. He was so glad he had kept himself for Patricia! Climbing on top of that generous queen, he had felt both a man and a child, at once powerful and frail. Had he caught a fleeting glimpse of his mother, who had died when he was five? Had he felt an old sensation, so small on such a large body of flesh? He was certain he had found his place—a place of protection pro- vided by his lover, which he, in turn, had to protect, a sanctu- ary of peace and tenderness.

"You're worse than in love," Germain muttered.

"Maybe . . . "

Germain shook his head, convinced his diagnosis was correct.

Hippolyte looked through his collection for music appropriate to the moment, found the songs of Billie Holiday, and abandoned himself to the languid, drawling voice, as fresh and sharp as an oboe.

When Germain announced that dinner was ready, Isis reappeared.

"Will you introduce me?" she asked as she sat down at her place.

"Who to?"

"Patricia."

It felt surreal to Hippolyte to hear the child utter that name. He looked at Germain and guessed that he hadn't held his tongue. By way of self-justification, Germain shrugged.

"Well?" Isis insisted. "Will you introduce me?"

Hippolyte bit his lip. It hadn't occurred to him; in his eyes, Patricia and Isis belonged to two separate worlds.

"Are you afraid?"

He leaned toward his daughter. "Afraid?"

"Afraid I won't like her."

He shook his head, anxiously. "Now that you mention it: yes."

"Don't worry, I'll be lenient."

As usual, Hippolyte was surprised: how could a ten-year-old say, "I'll be lenient"? Even he, at the age of forty, would have spent a while searching for the right word; this child was beyond him.

"What will you do if I don't like her?" she went on.

Hippolyte considered this for a while, then replied honestly, "I'll . . . I'll see her without you."

Isis pursed her lips. "Then I'd better like her."

Hippolyte and Germain nodded.

"I know what I have to do," Isis concluded.

Hippolyte hung his head. He often had the impression that the roles in this apartment were reversed, that Isis was the parent and he the child.

Germain decided to break the silence. "So, Isis, you don't talk about your boyfriend César anymore."

"He's no longer my boyfriend," Isis said in a sharp tone.

"Why not?"

"I dumped him."

She said this so sternly that both Hippolyte and Germain had to suppress their laughter, sensing it would hurt her.

"I dumped him because I was bored with him. He's not interested in anything, doesn't read anything, he doesn't learn poems or songs, in other words, he has nothing to say."

Someday, Hippolyte thought, *she'll do the same to me, she'll leave me because I disappoint her; it'll break my heart, but I'll have to agree that she's right.*

Their dinner concluded with an apricot tart baked by Germain. Although he lived a hundred yards away, he had gotten into the habit of coming to join the father and daughter without asking if his presence bothered them, subtly imposing himself, replacing Hippolyte in the kitchen, taking care of the laundry and the ironing, checking that Isis did her homework, tidying the tiny apartment. Only the shopping remained the privilege of Hippolyte. All three were now like a family in which Germain played the role of the mother, except that every night at ten he would go back to his own place to sleep, not reappearing until seven the following morning, complete with freshly baked bread.

"It's Sunday, Hippolyte, shall we go bowling?"

Germain was itching to go out. Hippolyte realized he had forced his friend to spend his two days off with a child.

Half an hour later, Germain and Hippolyte were drinking beer on the edge of the long lanes of varnished wood.

Hippolyte's body language continued to express the happiness he owed to Patricia. Fascinated, Germain watched this dumb show without jealousy or resentment, even though he would probably never experience anything like it himself.

They started a game.

Hippolyte took time out to go to the toilet.

When he returned, Germain was being bullied by a group of youngsters who had just arrived.

"I'm going to use him as a ball," the sturdiest one was saying.

"Midget throwing!"

"My favorite game."

"Mustn't damage him too quickly. We should all get a chance to use him."

"Why doesn't he call his family? You don't have a wife we can have some fun with, do you, midget? Brothers, sisters, children? We want the game to last!"

Hippolyte appeared. When he saw him coming, Germain made a negative gesture, begging him not to interfere.

But that only made Hippolyte see red: he leaped into the middle of the group. "Which one's the biggest asshole here, so I can smash his face in?" He grabbed the one who looked like the leader by the shirt collar. "Is it you?"

Without waiting for a reply, he head-butted him. The kid staggered back, stunned.

"Who's next?" Hippolyte asked, grabbing hold of another one.

"We were just having a laugh."

"Oh, really? Were you laughing, Germain?"

A slap sent the second one to the floor. He collared the third one, who tried to justify himself. "What's the big deal? It's normal to poke fun at midgets."

"A midget? Where's the midget? I don't see a midget, I just see my friend Germain."

He slapped the boy. Before he could turn to the others, they had all run off. Hippolyte rubbed his hands and turned to Germain.

"Shall we play, then?"

"Let's play."

Germain was overjoyed. Accustomed to verbal abuse since childhood, he paid little heed to it, because he knew that only cowards picked on a dwarf; still, he was overjoyed that his friend had stood up for him with such rage. What moved him was not getting revenge but Hippolyte's friendship.

They played a long, satisfying, very close game, which Germain narrowly won, then went to the bar for a beer.

"I have the itch," Germain confessed.

"You have the itch? Now? Tonight?"

"Yes. Will you come with me?"

They left the bowling alley and walked to the Gare du Nord. There, they turned off onto streets that were packed with people in spite of the late hour.

Here there were men, just men, strolling past red shop windows where prostitutes in revealing underwear were on display. Acting as if they didn't know that anyone could see them through the glass, they combed their hair, applied make-up, smoothed their thighs, listened to the radio, even danced a little.

"Let's see if my favorite is there," Germain said, sounding like a child on his way to a funfair.

Halfway along the street, Germain stamped his feet and indicated a West Indian woman with huge eyes, wearing pink gingham underwear.

"She's free!"

"I'll wait for you."

Germain rushed to the window and motioned to the woman, who smiled and encouraged him to come in. She closed the door and pulled down the blind.

As was their custom, Hippolyte waited for Germain in the café next door. He had never gone with a prostitute, and had no desire to do so, but didn't stand in judgement on those who did. On the contrary, he thought the world was rather well designed: if these women didn't sell their bodies, how would Germain satisfy his desires? He hated himself so much that, if he had not been able to pay for the services of a consenting woman, he would have lived with his complex until the pain of it became unbearable.

Sitting at a marble table, having another beer, Hippolyte looked sympathetically at the constant coming and going of the clientele. He tried to guess what brought them here: in some cases—old, ugly, or disabled men—their bodies provided the answer; in others, he had to use his imagination. Were they widowers? Single men in a rush? Husbands burdened with wives who hated sex? Individuals who loved to do things their wives found repulsive?

He was studying these people when, just across the street from the café, one of the women pulled up her blind as her client was leaving the booth. That client was Victor, the handsome young man from Place d'Arezzo.

Hippolyte couldn't believe his eyes. He nearly called out to Victor, but stopped himself, assuming he would be embarrassed.

Victor crossed the street, came into the café, and ordered a drink. "Hippolyte!" he cried, equally surprised.

The young man hesitated, then shrugged and came and sat down opposite the gardener. "I can't believe it," he said.

"Neither can I," Hippolyte replied.

There was a moment's pause. Curiosity aroused, Victor cocked his head. "Is it for the same reason?"

"What do you mean?"

"Do you come here for the same reason I do? To avoid . . . "

"To avoid what?"

"I mean so you can be sure that . . . "

Unsure what Victor was talking about, Hippolyte decided to tell him the truth. "I'm here with my friend Germain."

Victor clammed up, and Hippolyte realized too late that now the young man wouldn't reveal the secret of why he was here.

13

Y es, it's a very pretty town house, rather in the French style."

Ève pushed open the double doors and went from room to room, trying not to make the old oak parquet creak, praising the details—the door handles, the molding—caressing the marble mantelpieces with feigned nonchalance.

Rose Bidermann followed her, dressed in a Chanel suit that seemed to have been sewed straight onto her. She liked the space and the light. "I'll put this address on my list. I'm sure that after ten years in London my friend will like this place. May I contact you next time she's here?"

"Of course. But she shouldn't wait too long. Although it's expensive, this kind of property quickly finds a buyer."

"She mentioned she's coming in two weeks' time."

"Well, if I have another client who's interested, I'll let you know immediately."

Rose Bidermann smiled in gratitude.

Ève had been impressed when Madame Zachary Bidermann had contacted her, but even more impressed when she met her: she had the self-assurance of people who have never wanted for anything, are pleasant through upbringing rather than self-interest, and have been dressed by couturiers since they were children. Ève, who had paid with her body and her feelings for every step she had climbed in society, was fascinated by this upper-middle-class matron, a woman in late middle age but still sexy. Rose's classic tweed suit made her look like a Lady Bountiful, but at the same time, this packaging made her curvaceous body seem even more attractive, even slightly obscene. At one point, as they walked past a free-standing mirror, Ève compared their figures and was upset by what she saw: the buxom Rose was both provocative and engaging, steeped in the mystery of femininity, whereas her own aggressive sexuality made her seem closer to a whore. She was suddenly angry with herself for sporting an indecently low neckline, wearing high heels and thigh boots instead of ordinary ones. For a moment, she questioned the wisdom of having such tanned skin, such platinum hair. In Rose, there was no effort to please, and this very modesty made her adorable. Her skin had a natural glow, as did the color of her hair, and her elegance wasn't distracting. With a sigh, Ève realized that she was discovering all this too late.

"Have you been working in real estate long?" Rose asked.

"Six years now, ever since I arrived in Brussels."

Six years earlier, when Philippe—her Roudoudou—had moved to Brussels with his wife and children after three years in Lyons, he had brought her along with his baggage and had found her an apartment and a real estate agency.

"I work in Uccle and Ixelles, specializing in town houses . . . I think I've been inside all the buildings between Avenue Molière and our lovely Place d'Arezzo."

"Really? Then you must know my friends, the Dentremonts."

"Of course," Ève replied without hesitation, out of a desire to shine, even though Philippe Dentremont—her Roudoudou—had forbidden her from admitting to any connection with him whatsoever.

"Oh, that dear Philippe Dentremont," Rose cooed. "Such a flirt, isn't he?"

Embarrassed, Ève simply blinked in agreement.

"I wouldn't like to be in his wife Odile's shoes. She has a lot to forgive him."

"Oh?" Ève said, swallowing.

"Philippe can't resist a pretty woman. He immediately makes a beeline for her. Don't tell me he didn't come on to you?"

"Yes, of course . . . but . . . but I wasn't free, so it stopped there."

"Good for you . . . In his defense, he doesn't choose replicas of his wife. I heard his latest one, Fatima, is a stunning Arab woman. Tunisian . . . When I think that I know and Odile doesn't, I feel embarrassed. You see what I mean?"

Ève almost cried out, "Fatima? Who's Fatima?" but restrained herself, careful not to lose her composure. Shuddering, she walked Rose to the door, exchanged a few pleasantries, and cut their goodbyes short with the excuse that she had to go back into the house and check that all the windows were shut.

Standing outside on the sunny sidewalk, Rose smiled radiantly, promised that her friend would take a look at the house very soon, and walked away.

Ève went down into the kitchen, closed the blinds, and, once shut in, screamed, "The bastard!"

What Rose had just told her was something she already suspected, perhaps even knew, but had avoided thinking about. Of course, she had noticed that Philippe didn't come to see her every day; of course, she had noticed that he avoided certain shops, and that there were restaurants where he was reluctant to be seen with her; of course, he had mysteriously disappeared on several occasions, on the pretext of work commitments. A part of her brain had sensed that these peculiarities were down to the existence of another woman, but her consciousness had refrained from articulating it because she didn't want to be unhappy. And now Rose Bidermann had rubbed her nose in the reality, and it stank.

What should she do?

Meanwhile, strolling beneath the blossoming plane trees, Rose had called her friend Odile Dentremont. "Mission accomplished, my dear: she knows she has a rival."

Odile Dentremont thanked her and took advantage of the opportunity to satisfy her curiosity about her husband's mistress.

"Yes," Rose replied, "very provocative, very much a rich man's 'chick.' She dresses the way all men of that age fantasize about. Poor thing . . . A bit vulgar, yes. Decent, though, I think. She won't be able to live with what she's just heard, and I'm sure she'll get her own back. Yes, out of pride rather than love. After all, you're right, darling: every so often we need to do a bit of housekeeping. His two mistresses, Ève and Fatima, are going to kick Philippe out and he'll come back to you"—Rose nearly said, "with his tail between his legs," but stopped herself at the last moment—"all sheepish and contrite."

To herself, Rose added, "And then he'll start all over again," but Odile said the words instead.

Rose listened, then agreed. "Of course, the only one who waits for him, welcomes him, loves him unconditionally is his wife. You're right, Odile. I'm delighted to have been a part of your stratagem. No need to thank me: it's such fun when a married woman reveals to a mistress that she's being cheated on."

On Saturday morning, Ève decided to go to Knokke-le-Zoute. This name, so odd to foreign ears, actually belongs to the most elegant seaside resort in Belgium, in the far north of the country.

The North Sea is a tired sea, and Knokke-le-Zoute is the place where it comes to rest. The water there discourages all activity. The waves refuse bathers, but timidly lap at the beach—a vast puddle that forces the aspiring swimmer to cover hundreds of yards in order to immerse himself only as far as his shoulders; even here, the water doesn't encourage him, it antagonizes him, its temperature chilling his frolics and the salty wavelets slapping him. For those who prefer walking, the open sea keeps its distance, as insignificant in its presence as it is mean with its colors, its waters merging first with the beige sand, then the gray sky, and finally the bleached blue of the horizon. The North Sea is lazy, and if you didn't see the oil tankers and liners quietly drifting across it, you would think it was indifferent and of no use to humans.

Appearing on the landing stage, Ève caused an immediate sensation. Although Swiss by birth, she had soon grasped how a Belgian seaside resort worked. You don't go into its wild, extensive, infinite part, you parade in the narrow space you pay for, which provides deck chairs, useless parasols, and drinks waiters, and is a kind of spruce little square, all white and blue, facing the shore, where loudspeakers emit pleasant music.

Men and women watched as this stunning pinup arrived, and a waiter chivalrously rushed to find her a place worthy of her beauty. Wearing large round glasses that concealed her eyes, Ève pretended to hesitate, then, looking as if she was obeying the waiter, who was behaving like a knight errant, pointed to the patch where she wanted to lie down. He arranged a chair, laid out towels, raked the sand, placed two small tables so that she could spread out her things, and promised to bring her the fruit cocktail she wanted.

That was how Ève came to be right behind the Dentremont family, which had come to stay in its seaside villa.

Naturally, Philippe Dentremont was the first to notice her—he had probably been watching her since she appeared at the top of the steps, and praying to heaven that she would come no nearer. Nervous and agitated, he pretended to grab some sun lotion in order to throw her a grimace: *What's gotten into you? Are you out of your mind?* Ève responded by removing her T-shirt and revealing her magnificent breasts, which were covered merely by a light square of material kept in place with a string.

Quentin, the family's eldest son, was as quick to notice Ève's arrival as his father, but, unlike the head of the family, his face lit up in a smile. He made no attempt to conceal his joy at seeing her here.

As for the two youngest children, they paid no attention to her, one too busy reading, the other building a sand castle.

Meanwhile, Odile Dentremont lay asleep in the sun, oiled like a sardine.

It was now that Ève pulled a secret weapon from her bag, the weapon that would enable her to obtain everything she wanted: a dog.

An exquisite female Shiba Inu hopped onto the deck chair, a kind of distinguished-looking fox, slim and graceful, her dark eyes delicately highlighted in white, with a coat that was like finery in its mixture of fawn with hints of cream.

Philippe realized that an instrument of war had arrived. He frowned and thrust his chin forward, furious that he could do nothing to stop it.

Ève put a very feminine collar, inlaid with artificial stones, around the neck of the Japanese princess, and set off with her to the water's edge.

The men on the beach only had eyes for her.

Savoring her success, Ève felt pleased that she had persuaded her friend Priscilla to lend her her Shiba Inu in return for looking after her cat and her apartment for the weekend. There is no bait more effective if you want men to start a conversation. It's an accessory that can save you hours.

For the next half hour, so-called swimmers and alleged walkers approached the nymph with the dog. Each time, Ève responded politely but without leading them to believe that they could come on to her. After two or three minutes, she would make it quite clear to them that they would get nothing more from her than this brief chat.

His wife having woken up, it was no longer possible for Philippe Dentremont to go to Ève and order her to leave. Watching helplessly as men buzzed around her, he felt a mixture of jealousy, pride, and anger, unable to fathom why his mistress was inflicting this farce on him.

Ève returned to her spot, her delightful puppet at the end of a leash, and settled on the deck chair in order to abandon herself to the sun's rays. Naturally, her tan was already perfect, as appetizing as gingerbread, stronger, deeper, and more even than anyone else's. Ève was farsighted enough not to go to the beach in order to get a tan but to show off her tan, which had been cosseted over the winter with sun beds, beta-carotene, and tinted lotion. She took out a thick novel—at least five hundred pages, which suggested a regular reader (any less than that and she would have seemed a mere occasional reader)—held it at arm's length above her face, and immersed herself in it.

If she had been on her own, she would have followed the story, since she loved reading, but in public, the bestseller was simply a means to watch what was going on around her.

In front of her, Quentin had stood up and was exposing his newly developed body to the untamed air. Even though he pretended to look right and left but never behind him, Ève knew perfectly well that he was showing himself off to her, that he was thinking only of her. Varying the poses that showed him to his best advantage, he would occasionally stroke his well-formed shoulders, of which he was very proud.

Just to annoy Philippe, who hadn't noticed his son's game, Ève laid down her book and now quite openly gazed at the boy.

Quentin took that as a victory. Eager to show off his strength, he urged his brothers to come and play badminton with him, suggesting they play two against one. A mere thirty feet from her, he was able to give Ève a demonstration of his agility, his reflexes, and his speed.

Philippe hadn't yet grasped what his eldest son was doing, but was horrified to discover that Ève was showing an interest in him. If his wife hadn't been there, he would have made a scene.

Ève felt she had to take things a step farther. She stood up and motioned to the Shiba Inu to accompany her. They both waddled over to the Dentremont children. There, they stopped and watched the game.

Galvanized, Quentin attempted a few glorious returns then, trying to catch an uncatchable ball, risked a dangerous back-flip.

Ève cheered.

He stared at her, his face scarlet. "Would you like to play?"

"I'd love to. Only, who'll look after my little darling?"

Glad of the opportunity to take a break, the two younger brothers offered their services.

"Then take her to the water, I think she might need to have a little pee."

"Of course, Madame."

The two boys set off enthusiastically toward the sea. A match began between Ève and Quentin. This time, he adopted a different ploy: he was trying to lose—not that this was obvious, since Ève, eager to keep her moves harmonious, kept missing her shots.

It didn't matter. Their exchange of mutual complicity proved more intense than their game. Quentin kept making eyes at Ève and she mischievously returned his glances. They liked each other, and made no secret of the fact.

"Phew! I'm going to stop. It's exhausting."

"Are you here for the weekend?"

"Yes, and you?"

He frowned. "I'm here with my parents."

"Your mother's very beautiful."

"Really?"

Although Quentin didn't quite grasp the reason for this comment, she relaxed him by showing that there could be no hostility between his mother and the woman he desired.

"You're a hundred times more beautiful than my mother."

"Now, now!"

"I swear."

"You forget I'm not a hundred times younger than your mother."

"I like real women—not little girls." He made this declaration with a male self-confidence that surprised them both—him because he had never expected to say it, and her because she felt he meant it.

Casting a glance in the direction of the deck chairs, she saw Philippe walking around in circles, at the end of his tether, while Odile was quietly enjoying watching her son act like a man.

Figuring she had done enough, she decided to go back to her deck chair. "I'm going to rest."

"Yes, of course."

"You know, you remind me of a little yellow letter."

"A little yellow letter?"

"Yes. A little yellow letter that you didn't sign." And with this, she gave him such an irresistible smile that he smiled too, which seemed to Ève to confirm her theory.

She went back to her deck chair. At that moment, Philippe walked to the bar, signaling to her to follow him, an invitation she wickedly ignored.

To stir up even more ill feeling within the Dentremont family, she took the anonymous note out of her bag, added her address in Knokke-le-Zoute, and waited for the two younger Dentremonts to bring back her dog. As she thanked them, she gave them the piece of paper and asked them to give it to their brother, which they did without trying to conceal it. Quentin had barely gotten hold of the message when his father appeared.

"Give me that!"

Outraged by his tone of voice, Quentin rose to his full height and looked him coldly up and down. "It's none of your business!"

"Do as you're told. I'm your father!"

"Not for long!" Quentin growled.

Taken aback, Philippe hesitated, surprised and dumbfounded to discover that his son had become someone new, that the boy had turned into a man right there before his eyes.

Quentin was standing up to him, aware of what was happening, intoxicated by this power rising within him, the power to desire a woman, the power to go against his father's wishes.

They stood there for a few seconds, motionless, two males sizing each other up, the elder realizing that he was growing old, the younger that he would soon become the dominant one. At that moment, they were no longer father and son, but rivals.

"What's the matter?" Odile said in a somewhat sleepy voice. "Is there a problem?"

Quentin turned to her. "No, Mom," he gallantly reassured her. "Everything's OK. No problem."

Once again, he had taken over his father's role, while the latter, stunned by the change in situation, exasperated by Ève's presence, wary of arousing his wife's suspicions, shrugged and—temporarily—accepted defeat.

From a distance, Ève had missed nothing of this exchange.

He's ready, she thought, looking at Philippe. *He'll have the nerve to show up at my place, and I'll make sure I get him to explain himself.*

She gathered her things. This time, it was she who signaled to Philippe to join her at the bar. As he walked there, she said goodbye to the three Dentremont boys and took her leave of Odile with a smile.

Philippe was deep into a Bloody Mary by the time she stopped beside him. "Flirting in the kindergarten now?" he growled

"Your son's very handsome. And so young!"

"I forbid you to play that game."

"Forbid me? What right do you have to forbid me?"

"My right as your lover."

"And Fatima's. And lots of other women's."

At the mention of Fatima, Philippe recoiled. Panic flashed in his eyes. "Look, Ève, I can't talk to you this weekend. We have a very busy schedule. I can't get away from my family."

"But we have to talk."

"Ève . . ."

"Maybe I could befriend your wife. Remember how easy it was with your sons."

"Ève, don't use this method!"

"Who's talking to me now? Fatima's lover?"

Put in his place, he lowered his eyes. Here was a self-centered man who always got what he wanted thanks to his money and his frivolous attitude, now revealed as nothing but a coward.

As Ève turned on her heels, she said, "You know Villa Coquillage? My friend Clélia has lent it to me. I'll be waiting."

Relieved, Ève went home and pampered herself in the bathroom for two hours, with a sequence of facial scrub, mask, and massage.

At eight in the evening, she sat down in front of the TV with a dinner tray.

Until ten-thirty, she watched with great interest a show featuring aspiring young singers auditioning blindly before a panel of stars. Identifying with each one of them, she cried a lot, with joy as well as disappointment.

Finally, at eleven, drained from all this empathy, she thought again about her own case and started to worry. She was on the verge of feeling offended.

The doorbell rang.

"At last!"

The sound had restored her self-confidence. What was she going to get out of this heart-to-heart with Philippe? Would he leave Fatima? Would he give her more money? Maybe both . . .

When she opened the door, a shadowy figure slipped inside. "Please close the door, I don't want anybody to see me."

Standing there before her, looking charming, dressed all in white and holding a bunch of tulips, was Quentin.

"I ran away to see you."

14

B etween the two women, orgasm was no longer an end in itself. Shutting themselves in the pastel-colored room with its discreet curtains, and spending hours in each other's arms, naked, relaxed, protected, far from their husbands, children, and social obligations, provided an unexpected, secret, wonderful break.

Whereas in the beginning, desire had been a justification for their embraces, it had now become the quintessence of it all: they didn't need to make love, they needed love—giving it as well as receiving it. It was clear that sensuality had been simply a pretext, which one day had led Xavière to steal a kiss from Séverine and given Séverine permission to draw Xavière into her boudoir. Now, after many caresses, many kisses, many thrills of pleasure, they had become so close that they would sometimes go to bed together in the middle of the day and talk, lightly touch, and share deep silences, without feeling compelled to reach a climax.

Used to seeing sex as a performance, Séverine liked this intimacy: she had to satisfy her husband and also come herself—or at least pretend to. Isn't it the obligation to have an orgasm that poisons relationships between men and woman? They are under pressure to reach it, thus transforming a carefree, pointless moment into a competition that has to be won. Séverine had only ever had sex with François-Maxime in a state of anxiety, and, at the end of every session, had doubted she had lived up to expectations. It didn't really matter to her that she seldom achieved pleasure, but she suspected that she didn't give any either. If she could fake it, then so could he . . . Even though there were obvious signs that he reached a climax, had it been strong? Intense? The word "cramp" kept coming into her mind. As a teenager, she had heard a boy say that for a man, ejaculating was like getting rid of a cramp. The medical nature of this statement had made an impression on her, and she had never stopped thinking about it. When she had given her virginity to François-Maxime, she had, on discovering his tense, hard penis, remembered the word "cramp." Her husband's subsequent thrusting inside her had felt like a convulsion, then his final cry, followed by a collapse and an immediate sleep, had confirmed that the male "got rid" of a pain.

In addition to her concern about sensual pleasure, there was the concern about procreation. François-Maxime had been eager to become a father, the patriarch of a large family, and had made no secret of the fact: before her daughter was born, she thought she might not fulfill his wish, but after Guillaume, the youngest, she had been scared that an accident might inflict another pregnancy on her. Now, watching her offspring grow, she knew she had kept her end of the bargain with François-Maxime. Yet instead of feeling fulfilled, a new fear had come over her: would she continue to attract him? Wouldn't he grow tired of her? Her mature, soon-to-be-sterile body must be less alluring. She assumed that carnal indifference was the fate of old married couples, and every time they made love, she was afraid it might be the last. It was an insidious fear that made things tough for her and kept her from fully abandoning herself . . . And so, in fifteen years, Séverine had never let François-Maxime come near her naked body without trembling.

With Xavière, once she had gotten over the shock—she would never have imagined herself in bed with a woman—she at last felt safe. More sensual than sexual, she was convinced she had met her mate.

It was a different experience for Xavière. Snuggled up against her lover, she was running away from a part of herself and finding another that was quite new. Delightful, attentive, happy, helpful, she had left her grouchy persona far behind. If the local residents had told Séverine how they saw Xavière—a sharp-tongued, tight-fisted pain in the ass—she would have thought they were joking: Xavière showered her with flowers and books, took an interest in the smallest detail about her, joked about everything, and was proving to be the most light-hearted, most cheerful company in the world—that slap across the face aside.

The fact was that, in Séverine's arms, Xavière took a break from herself. She didn't like the person she'd become. Sometimes, she hated herself for it, but often she hated others, especially Orion, who, through his financial ruin, his careless-ness, his pathological negligence, had forced her to become sensible, accountable, responsible for them both. His casual-ness had made her stolid. Yes, he had frozen her in a role. It wasn't a matter of choice. If she had trusted him, they would be on the street by now, or already dead . . . And now she hated this husband who had transformed her into a wicked step-mother . . . In addition, through a kind of perverse force, the more cautious she was, the bolder he became; the more she criticized people, the more he praised them. Unless it was the opposite, each forcing the other to plunge deeper into his or her defects. In short, she didn't like anything about their mar-riage, and yet she strove to keep it alive. Why? Habit. Laziness. Financial self-interest. Reasons that someone in love with love would have considered wicked, but which seemed perfectly good to Xavière.

"Séverine, you know I'm an expert on poison?"

"Are you?" Séverine burst out laughing. It struck her as the

oddest thing to be interested in. "Why, would you have liked
to study chemistry?"

"No."

"Medicine?"

"Pharmacy?"

"No. You see, when you study these subjects, it's because
you want to treat people. In my case, it would be to kill. To kill
Orion."

"You're joking."

"Don't worry, I couldn't do when it came down to it. I'm
like a eunuch in a harem: he knows how it's done but can't do
it himself."

"You wanted to kill Orion?"

"A hundred times, no, a thousand, a million!"

"What stopped you?"

"I must have a conscience. Even so, it always gave me such
a sense of relief to murder him in my thoughts. I pictured him
vomiting, choking, spitting saliva, writhing in excruciating
pain. In the end, it was enough to relax me. They should put it
in the penal code: imagination is the best way to prevent murder."

"Do you hate him?"

"Since I can't kill my husband, I cheat on him."

"I don't like hearing you say that. It's as if you're saying
you're only with me because of him."

Xavière reassured Séverine with a hug. "What about you?
How do you feel about your dashing François-Maxime?"

"He is handsome, isn't he?"

"I must admit he is. At the same time, he's so perfect, so
well-groomed, well-fed, well-dressed, so fit, it makes me
uncomfortable."

"Funny . . . he has the same effect on me. I've always felt
like a complete failure next to him."

Suddenly, Xavière remembered the time and rushed to her

cell phone. "I must leave you, Séverine, I have a doctor's appointment."

"Nothing serious, I hope?"

"Just a regular checkup."

Séverine helped her get dressed, which gave them the opportunity for more caresses.

Xavière went to the chest of drawers, on top of which there was a marron glacé leather handbag. "This is gorgeous!" Without asking for permission, she lifted it, looked it over, even opened it. There was a yellow letter sticking out of the inside pocket. Taken aback, Xavière grabbed it and read it: *Just a note to tell you I love you. Signed: You know who.* Beneath, in unfamiliar handwriting, someone had added, *Me, too.*

"What—"

"It's a gift from François-Maxime."

"Séverine, I received the same note." She turned to Séverine, pale-faced. "You do everything in duplicate: love and mail!"

"I swear it wasn't me," Séverine said indignantly.

"Oh, sure!"

"I swear it on my children, Xavière."

Stopped in her tracks by such a passionate declaration, Xavière accepted her explanation, especially since she suddenly started remembering a few things. Hadn't she seen other people with yellow letters? She focused her mind, and two images came back to her. Quentin Dentremont had produced a similar piece of paper before scribbling a few words to go with his rose, and the gay philosophy teacher, Tom Something, had been reading a letter as he crossed the square and walked past her shop.

She nearly shared her discoveries with Séverine, but realized she was running out of time.

Ten minutes later, she was with Dr. Plassard, her gynecologist, in his office on Avenue Lepoutre, a street lined with chestnut trees.

"So, we weren't supposed to meet for another six months, but you've brought our appointment forward, Xavière. What's going on?"

"Something boring: I've started menopause."

"It's quite possible at your age."

"My periods have stopped, I sometimes feel very tired, and . . . how shall I put it? . . . my nipples are a little sore."

"That's normal. Any urinary problems?"

"Oh, no! Why, does that happen?"

"I'm going to examine you."

For the following fifteen minutes, she decided to relinquish possession of her body. Indifferent, almost absent, she let the gynecologist run the tests and investigations he wanted.

When he told her to get dressed and wait a few minutes, she took advantage of the pause to doze off.

Then Dr. Plassard woke her and asked her to come back into his office and sit down.

"You haven't started the menopause."

"Oh?"

"You're pregnant."

15

S o, no yellow envelope this morning?"
"No. What about you?"
"Me neither."

Mail in hand, Tom brought in the croissants for breakfast—
golden, crisp, and warm. Although he had spent the night at
Nathan's, he had just made a detour to the baker, then to his
own studio apartment, hoping there would be another anonymous letter waiting for him.

Nathan sighed. "We won't find out the truth today."

"Unfortunately not."

The two men were fascinated by this unexplained phenomenon. Once they had managed to convince each other that neither had written the message *Just a note to tell you I love you.
Signed: You know who*, they had tried to figure out who had.
The mystery fueled their imagination, and triggered endless
discussions. Since that day, they had hardly spent a minute
apart.

Taking the croissants, Nathan laid the table. On it, the
china shone with all the colors of the rainbow.

"I have no idea who sent us those letters, but I note that the
main consequence is that you can't tear yourself away from
here."

"Oh, really?" Tom stammered, embarrassed that Nathan
should have noticed it, and dreading in particular that he would
start again on his favorite refrain about their living together.

"My conclusion is that this person wished us well. They

must have known we'd each assume the other one wrote the letter, and that that would bring us closer. Isn't that a clue?"

Tom nodded and started thinking. Did someone wish them well? Surprised, he stopped chewing. "What a strange question! I've never asked myself before. Is there someone on this earth who'd wish us well? I could possibly name those who wish me well—like my sisters—or wish you well—like your parents—but wish *us* well . . . the two of us together?"

Nathan assumed an offended expression, hands on his hips, and aped a black mammy with a drawl, "Wha', M's Scarlett? What yo' talkin' about? Yo' think no one loves yo' n' yo' girl-friend? What yo sayin's mighty sad, M's Scarlett, and it breaks ma heart!"

Tom grabbed him by the arm. "Stop clowning around and think, Nathan: do you know people who really want us to live together?"

"Nobody gives a shit, Tom. Just like we don't give a shit about other couples, gay or not. It's a carousel, and you get on and off as you please. We each of us decide how we're going to be happy in our own way."

"You pretend not to understand: nobody's interested in us as a couple."

"So? Just as long you and I are interested!"

"Doesn't that drive you to despair, the fact that nobody thinks you're my destiny and I'm yours?"

Nathan blinked. "Say that again?"

"What?"

"Say that again, say I'm your destiny and you're mine. It sent shivers down my coccyx."

"Your coccyx?"

"That's where my thoughts lie, at least where you're concerned."

Irresistibly attracted by Nathan's excessive playacting, Tom hurled himself on him and pressed his lips to his.

As soon as he could speak, Nathan continued, "I get the feeling you're seduced by what's worst about me: my vulgarity and all the bullshit I talk."

"I like you in your full glory."

"Whatever! The crazier I am, the more attached you get to me."

"Loving someone means also loving their faults."

"Oh, how lovely: sounds like the title of a song for young girls."

"I knew you'd like it."

This time, it was Nathan, delighted even though he pretended to be annoyed, who initiated the kiss. There always had to be patter between them, sarcastic remarks, ridicule. Banter was their madrigal. Because they feared traditional expressions of love—probably because they feared traditional love—they blossomed when they pretended contempt, mockery, even hatred; every bitchy comment was a gift. The more they teased each other, the more they declared their affection. Their sincerity needed to be clothed in derision to remain authentic.

They rolled onto the couch, locked together, each trying to dominate the other, neither succeeding. They knew they wouldn't make love again—they only just had—but they had a good time pretending.

In the end, they fell on the rug and separated, then lay on their backs, holding hands, staring up at the chandelier.

"I know who wrote those messages," Nathan whispered.

"Who?"

"You won't believe me."

"Yes, I will. Who?"

"God." Nathan sat up, looking grave. "God Himself sent them to us, to confirm us in our love."

Tom also sat up. "So you believe in God, do you?"

"What do know about it?"

"I'm asking you a question."

"Stop there! Just because you've fucked me four hundred times doesn't mean you can get deep into the most private part of me."

"What you're saying is obscene." Tom mocked.

"Damn! And I thought it was really spiritual."

Nathan went and poured himself another coffee, then stated in a professorial tone, "God picked up His quill, dipped it in the ink of compassion, and told us not to wait any longer." He altered his voice to imitate God, trying to summon his deepest cords. "Live together, my children, do not pay two rents but one. This single rent will be the consecration of your union, take my word for it. Tom, my son, give notice to your landlord. Nathan, my daughter, throw away your porn magazines and your array of dildos and make room in your closets for Tom. When you have done what I say, you will be happy, my children, for all the centuries to come."

"Amen," Tom concluded.

Nathan did a double take. "Did I hear right?" He walked up to Tom, his face tense, his limbs rigid. "Did you say, 'Amen?'"

"Yes," Tom replied phlegmatically.

"Did you say that without thinking or because you meant it?"

"What do you think?"

"Tom, I know you're not a Catholic, I know you're not a believer, but do you speak Hebrew?"

"Enough to know that Amen means 'So be it.'"

"So you agree to us living together?"

"If you agree to a misalliance with a nonbeliever."

"I do."

"Amen."

Over the days that followed, Nathan couldn't restrain his joy: instead of walking, he skipped; instead of speaking, he choked in the rush of his own words; instead of laughing, he neighed. Tom was moved at having aroused such emotion in his partner; calm as he looked, he too was delighted.

One night, as they were watching an American TV series in bed, Tom turned to Nathan abruptly. "The anonymous letter was sent by someone who wants to get rid of us."

Nathan switched off the television. "Get rid of us?"

"Yes. An old lover who wants to make sure that you or I are fixed up."

"That's absurd."

"The lover of a lover . . . Someone morbidly jealous who knows how important we were in his boyfriend's life before. So he's trying to push us away."

"That's a twisted theory."

"Human beings are twisted, Nathan. People don't wish other people well, they want what's good for themselves. They're not interested in general well-being, only in their own."

"Translation, please?"

"The person who wrote that letter isn't after our happiness, but his."

So they spent the night talking about past lovers. While they may have started by trying to identify the author of the letters, the exchange became a pretext to discover one another, to talk about themselves and hear each other's stories.

Far from driving them apart, these confidences brought them closer together. They talked about what had seemed their glory in the past, but now struck them as pitiful: the many partners they had had. Because it involves a minority, homosexuality is more defined by sex than heterosexuality: it pushes those who discover that tendency in themselves to seek out skin contact, the meeting of bodies, pure pleasure, the organic, at all costs, and easily neglects the complexity and importance of feelings. Tom and Nathan had at first felt the need to prove to themselves that they were desired and could be desired. To that end, they had had many affairs, some of them lasting no longer than a passing encounter; they had frequented such sex joints as saunas, cellar nightclubs, even public parks, places where conversation is neither useful nor recommended, and where all you need to do is exchange a knowing look for two bodies to come together in the semidarkness. Both had experienced more silent affairs than verbal ones. Nathan had suffered from that: being so exuberant and talkative, he loved conversation and was curious about everything. Tom's sexual urges, mixed with a vague feeling of superiority, had been so important to him that it had taken him longer to find the repetition monotonous. Cultured, thoughtful, passionate about literature, he had such doubts about ever meeting his equal that he approached every boy with disillusioned wariness and no ambition to get to know him. *Make love to him, yes, but conversation, no thanks*, could have been his motto. So Nathan and Tom had experienced many disappointments after sexual pleasure, as soon as their partners, until then reduced merely to skin and cock and sighs, suddenly spoke: discovering an ugly voice, a surprising accent, hearing, after a faultless sensual journey, grammatical errors, flawed syntax, and a poor range of vocabulary; discovering the tastes and interests of a creature whose body they had enjoyed and realizing that, had they known all that, they would never have manifested any desire toward him.

Tom and Nathan hadn't seen these disappointments in the same way. Nathan wanted more from life than a collection of flirtations or brief encounters, and was more inclined toward love than desire. In fact, that was why he had been looking for the romance of his life and, through his impatience, had thought he had found it in two long-term relationships. As for Tom, he hadn't formulated any specific wishes, and had never confused sexual habit with love. Meeting Nathan, and the deep fondness he felt for him, had surprised him.

By dawn, they loved each other more than they had the previous dusk. They no longer needed sex, just to be next to each
other to welcome the day. The anonymous letters had hastened
the deepening of their relationship.

Sharp and shrill, the parrots started squawking, then the
parakeets added their chirping to the discordant symphony.
Their hullaballoo grew with the daylight. Nathan tried imitat-
ing them. He managed after a few approximations, which
both men found entertaining. Then Tom walked naked to the
window.

"I wonder if we haven't made a mistake about the anonymous letters, Nathan. We're assuming we're the only two who
received them."

Nathan got up and, also naked, went to Tom and put his
arms around him. They gazed out at the square, the houses
framing the green lawn like a theater set.

"What if several people here received the same note?"
Nathan said.

"You're right, I hadn't thought of that."

They looked at the birds. Their mediations still had the laziness of dawn in them, moved slowly, lacked elation and energy.
Everything was taking time.

Suddenly, in a tumult of wings, a blacker-than-black crow
sprang out of the gray sky, flew across the square, ruthlessly
chased away the parrots, and settled at the top of a tree. It
cawed, like a prophet of doom cawed, and it was as if miles of
solitude formed around this cruel warning. Stooped, head
tilted, demeanor stern, it studied the surrounding façades. Its
piercing eyes penetrated every house, pitiless, on the lookout
for everyone's weaknesses.

Nathan sensed its hostile examination and shuddered. Tom,
on the other hand, smiled and rubbed the hands resting on his
shoulders.

"Strange . . . Usually, anonymous letters carry insults or

malicious gossip. That's why their author is often referred to as a crow."

Once again, the crow cawed menacingly. "But this is something else," Tom continued gently. "The author is sending words of love, words that provoke love. We aren't dealing with a crow."

"What, then?"

"A dove."

PART THREE
RESPONSES

PRELUDE

The parrots were scratching the feathers of each other's necks and heads, as an invitation to love. Only the younger ones seemed aggressive, their eyes bloodshot, their wings spread like shields, their claws imperious, their cries belligerent, their beaks sharp, ready for a frantic battle, chasing, pursuing one another, stabbing—no doubt hoping to achieve the same pleasurable result.

Because of this springtime of the instincts, there was great confusion in the trees. While Senegalese youyous, cockatiels, African grays, poicephali, budgerigars, and red-rumped parrots spun around the foliage, couples of lovebirds took refuge in the branches, almost motionless so as not to attract attention. A blue-fronted Amazon parrot was building her nest, grumbling at anyone who came close. Some old macaws who, just like balding men, were losing feathers as they aged, and who flew sparingly, creaked whenever a fight between adolescents or the pursuit of a female infringed on their territory. Last but not least, a dignified sulphur-crested cockatoo with a cream-colored coat sat on his thick branch, shrugging at all this excitement, as if none of it concerned him.

It had been fifty years since the Brazilian consul had opened his cages prior to leaving the country, but the birds were still here. If any adventurer among them ever risked a visit to a garden a few streets away, he soon returned to Place d'Arezzo and these fellow creatures he couldn't stand but couldn't do without. How many generations had already succeeded one another in this teeming congregation? No observer had taken the trouble to study it because, at first, all the residents had expected these exotic birds, who were used to captivity, to die out. A few decades later, the fauna still flourished in this jungle. Perhaps some of them had been there from the start, since apparently they can live up to the age of eighty or a hundred.

The vitality of the parrots on Place d'Arezzo both fascinated and inconvenienced the local residents. Even though inner and outer factors—their constant fighting, the hostile environment—conspired to wipe them out, they lived on, chatty, disorganized, and noisy.

What language did they speak, anyway? Their ancestors might have used Portuguese or French, but what was left of that half a century later? What words distorted their shrill cries? Were they saying something? Did it still have a meaning? Or were their desires and urges, their violent energy, just an end in themselves?

D o you mind if I go see Frédéric this afternoon? I feel like making love with him."

Diane had asked her husband the question in the same tone she would have used to inform him that she was going to the hairdresser: a weary tone, almost as if she was annoyed at having to waste her time on such trifles.

"Go ahead, Diane, don't bother about me."

Jean-Noël was relieved: Diane was returning to normal . . . For a few days now—ever since the night at Mille Chandelles—she had been fuming with rage, irritable, idle, wandering aimlessly between the four walls, grabbing every opportunity to rant and rave. Her nitpicking bad humor, even though she was its first victim, proved contagious. The whole apartment was affected by the vibrations of her depression, from the plants that lowered their heads to the dirty windowpanes that had trouble letting the light in, the one most in the firing line being Jean-Noël, whom she picked on from morning till night.

During the elegant orgy, Diane had surprised Jean-Noël by causing a scene. When Zachary Bidermann had started to caress her as she was being served up as zakuski, she had sat up and slapped him hard. Naked, dripping with hors d'oeuvres, she had jumped off the table and gone for him, threatening him and driving him back against the wall with her fists. Not only had she transgressed the swingers' rule, which stipulates a polite dismissal of a partner you don't want, she had also launched into a violent diatribe interspersed with shocking insults such as "pig," "piece of shit," "bastard," "asshole," "pest," "Attila," "despot," "snake," and "murderer," the words tumbling from her mouth like water over Niagara Falls.

The owners of the club had had to intervene, overpower her, and call Jean-Noël to the rescue. Once they had apologized to Zachary Bidermann, they had done their best to recreate a festive atmosphere among the other patrons, who were all shocked.

Shut up in a boudoir with Diane, Jean-Noël had cleaned her up but had been unable to calm her anger.

"What have you got against him?"

"He's a shit, and I hate shits."

"What has he done to you?"

"Nothing to me. And he'll never touch me. But to others . . . "

"Who are you talking about?"

"Oh, leave me alone. It's common knowledge that the son of a bitch throws women away like paper handkerchiefs after he's had his way with them."

"He's a libertine, Diane."

"No kidding."

"Like you and me."

"Shut up, you fool, or I'll smash your face."

Seeing that Diane was no longer in control of herself, Jean-Noël hadn't insisted.

Since they had hurriedly left that catastrophic party, Diane's anger hadn't abated. It simmered, and the slightest mention of Zachary Bidermann, either in the press or on the radio, would incense her even further, turning her into a human torch of hatred.

This caused Jean-Noël to recall a number of puzzling episodes in the past. When they had met, she had demanded to live on Place d'Arezzo, on the pretext that she had dreamed of living there since she was a child, and had forced Jean-Noël to sell his house in Saint-Genest in order to buy the place she had found. Many times, Jean-Noël had caught her staring at the Bidermann town house through the window, as if keeping an eye on it. And, although she never took any interest in what her peers were fascinated by, she never missed an article or a TV program that featured Zachary Bidermann. The morning Jean-Noël had informed her that Bidermann had invited them to a "neighbors' party," she had turned pale, shut herself away, and spent the following week ridiculing the stupid habit of inviting people just because they are brought together by chance. For the date of the famous "neighbors' party," she had managed to arrange a charming weekend in Normandy.

Now that Diane's hatred was out in the open, Jean-Noël thought back to these episodes. What had happened between Zachary Bidermann and Diane? Any other husband's first suspicion would have focused on an adulterous affair but, if you knew Diane, an affair was pretty run of the mill. And anyway, she usually remained on friendly terms with the men she had amused herself with. No, this was something else . . . But what?

Jolting over the uneven cobblestones, Diane was driving her Fiat across Brussels, inexhaustibly angry with the "bunch of idiots" who had clearly won their driving licenses in a lottery.

When she got to the south of the city, close to the fish market, she parked her car, went into a small courtyard, tapped in a number code, and pushed open the door of a studio flat on the ground level.

Frédéric was waiting for her, a wide smile on his face. "Tell me I'm dreaming, my goddess!"

Diane enjoyed the welcome and turned red beneath the dark eyes devouring her. There was a smell of man, and a man's mess all around—stacks of books and records, clothes strewn around, the previous night's TV dinner still on the coffee table.

"I love your apartment, Fred."

"You know you always have the place of honor here, princess."

On the back wall, there was a huge, ten foot by six foot photograph of her lying naked on a bloodstained sheet.

She went to him where he sat in his wheelchair. "I want you," she whispered, biting his ear.

He purred, overcome with pleasure.

Diane stepped back and ordered, "Put on some music."

"What?"

"The kind of crap you like."

"Something to make your ears bleed, O divine one?"

"Precisely."

He pressed the remote control he kept in the right-hand pocket above the wheel, and there was a burst of loud, amplified, deafening metallic sound. Frédéric was a sound engineer, and listened to rock at the volume of a pneumatic drill.

Diane stepped away. In time to the music—or rather, the jagged rhythm of the bass, the only part you could distinguish of that aural magma—she performed a striptease for him.

Intoxicated with happiness, Frédéric watched her, blissful. He was thirty-five, good-looking, with green eyes and large hands—the prototype of the solid, healthy male who attracts girls. Five years earlier, tearing along at a hundred miles an hour, his motorbike had skidded on a wet road, smashed into a concrete wall, and broken his spine. Paralyzed from the waist down, Frédéric couldn't feel his legs and was unable to command them. Strong-willed and courageous, he had done all the physical therapy he could, strengthening his torso, arms, and shoulders, but his lower limbs were still alien to him, condemning him to a wheelchair for the rest of his life.

If Diane had known him before he was disabled, oozing health and the joy of being alive, she might not have paid any attention to him . . . But because a friend had introduced him soon after he left the hospital, she had chosen him as a lover.

"Making love to a paraplegic is amazingly erotic," she was in the habit of telling people, even when they hadn't asked her.

It was she who took charge, deciding the moment, the rhythm, and the moves.

Alerted by a phone call, Frédéric had already taken the medication that would guarantee an erection. It was a precaution he took just to reassure himself, even though Diane knew how to stimulate him. Because she knew he felt nothing from the waist down, she lavished her attention on the sensitive parts of his upper body: his mouth, his ears, his neck, his nipples. She immediately got down to work, clinging to him like a spider to its web.

"Is he sulking?" Frédéric asked, referring to his penis, which she kept concealed from him.

"Not at all."

"Oh, good. He's always sulking at me. Even when I'm excited mentally, he doesn't tell me."

"He's doing what you want, no problem, no need for the vacuum pump today," she said in an admiring tone.

Frédéric soon realized she was right. He noticed peripheral signs of pleasure in the top part of his body: warmth, sweating, an accelerating heartbeat followed by quivers down his torso and the contraction of his abdominal muscles.

Naked on top of him, her legs spread at right angles on the armrests, Diane loved this splendid discomfort, which gave her a baroque mixture of sensations: the energizing cold chrome, the smoothness of the imitation leather, the plastic warming up in contact with their skins, the moist warmth of his penis, which she enjoyed for the both of them.

An expression of euphoria tore across the man's face. Diane moved up and down, swaying like a gymnast of pleasure, allowing this disabled male to feel like a man. Thanks to her, he had rediscovered pleasure, agreeing to forget what he had experienced when he was younger, and rejecting disappointing comparisons. Making a clean break with the past had allowed him to enjoy sex again. Diane was a guardian angel to him, a loving, disinterested angel who expanded his diminished life.

Suddenly, realizing she was about to reach orgasm, Diane clung to the chinning bar she had had fixed to the ceiling.

They kept their eyes fixed on each other, taking advantage of the moment. In this narrow corridor where their eyes met, Frédéric had the fleeting impression that he was normal.

She screamed with pleasure.

Happy, he burst out laughing. "You're a sex genius, Diane."

"Yes, I know!" she replied without false modesty.

She got off the wheelchair and said, with a wink, "Would you like me to . . . " She didn't need to complete the sentence, he knew what she meant. An eserine injection to bring on ejaculation.

Laughing, he shook his head. "No need. I won't feel any-thing more. It was brilliant as it was. I'd rather have you than any shot!"

Satisfied, she lay down on a mattress without getting dressed, while he wheeled himself to the kitchen to get them a drink, maneuvering his chair with the skill and strength of an aggressive motorist.

"I still can't work out if you're a physical or a mental woman," he said, handing her a glass. "Are you the most incred-ible sensualist in the world or is your orgasm intellectual?"

"I gave you credit for being cleverer than that, Fred. You already know the answer."

"Really?"

"If I were nothing but a clam you just needed to touch to make me open, I wouldn't have done all the things I've done."

"So you're the Einstein of the orgasm."

"You could say that."

He didn't dare insist. All she had told him about her adven-tures—the performance aspect, the quest for extreme situations, the worship of the strange and the extraordinary—was, of course, something he took advantage of, but wasn't it a sign of weakness? Did she really need all that playacting to reach a climax? A collector of experiences, Diane quickly exhausted them and so was forced to go farther and farther into the unusual. Frédéric, on the other hand, both in the past and now, never felt compelled to seek novelty. He could enjoy sex a million times in identical ways and not get tired.

"You men just don't understand," she exclaimed. She must have been reading his mind, because she added, "In sex, it's a female characteristic to look for refinement."

"Refinement or perversion?"

"Perversion is a bourgeois term for refinement. We women are more inventive, more romantic, more adventurous, because we're more complex. Possibly because, physically, we can come in three different ways."

"Three?"

She rose to her full height, naked, and stuck her pubis in his face. "Front, middle, and back. Plus the brain. That makes four!"

He sniffed her, rubbed his nose against her skin. Diane was so appetizing that he began to salivate.

"When we're penetrated, there's a boundary between pleasure and pain that only we can determine and possibly shift."

"Really?"

"The proof that sex is a mental thing is that a thrust can be either intolerably painful or deliciously pleasurable. The man may be inside us but it's our brain that holds the handcuffs."

"Is that how you explain that some women don't reach orgasm?"

"It isn't you men who give us the orgasm, it's us. By means of you."

"Don't exaggerate. If the man is hopeless, if he doesn't have stamina, I doubt that—"

"You're just being conceited. I've been known to reach orgasm in thirty seconds."

Having been put in his place, he fell silent.

"Now let's talk about something else, Fred. Tell me what I should be listening to in terms of hard rock and heavy metal. Bring me up-to-date."

This was a field that Frédéric knew thoroughly, and she always loved getting the most informed advice. She made a point of ignoring whatever the public knew, and knowing what it didn't. If anyone mentioned Charlie Chaplin, she would reply Harold Lloyd—not even Buster Keaton. If you brought up Maria Callas, she would respond with Claudia Muzio—not even Renata Tebaldi. If people went into raptures about Balzac, she would mention Xavier Forneret. It was impossible to interest her in what was generally accepted and popular. This taste for swimming against the tide produced in her whole oceans of ignorance, dotted with tiny islands only she and an elite frequented. Never would it have occurred to her that, like any snob, she deprived herself of some masterly works by restricting herself to the marginal. Perhaps in another life, she would have loved Charlie Chaplin's lecherous eccentricity, Callas's tragic sense, the power of Balzac . . . She treated religion in the same way. A long time ago, she had rejected the related monotheisms, Judaism, Christianity, and Islam, in favor of Hindu polytheism and Tibetan spirituality. But ever since Buddhism had been taken up in Europe, she had turned away from it, preferring to study the early Church fathers, with Origen becoming her hero. In truth, there was only one religion she ever practiced: her own originality.

Because Frédéric saw her only occasionally, he was curious: when she wasn't there, if he couldn't love her he could at least try to understand her. After some good musical advice, he changed the subject. "Tell me again about your father."

Diane was taken aback. "What's he got to do with anything?"

"Nothing. You wanted to talk about music, and I want to hear about your father again."

Diane slapped herself on the chest. "I never talk about my father."

"You did tell me about him once."

"That's not likely."

"Yes, you did."

"I don't talk about him even when I'm plastered."

"It depends on what you've been taking. That night, it wasn't booze, it was something more illegal."

"Damn!" She bit her lip, having no memory of what she might have mouthed off about while under the influence of drugs. "What did I tell you?"

"That you never knew your father. That he'd slept with your mother two or three times, and left without acknowledging you. When she contacted him again, he said she was delusional."

"Poor Mommy," Diane said, surprised that these memories should come back into her mind.

"You also told me that, when you were a child, people called you 'the bastard.'"

She hadn't been slapped in the face with that word for decades. She tried to overcome her emotion by bragging, "That's right. The bastard. I admit it. Because bastards are the salt of the earth. Just look at Jesus Christ."

Not taken in by this false self-confidence, Frédéric continued prodding. "Are you avenging your mother by sleeping with lots of men?"

The question was asked so gently that Diane accepted it and took time to think about it. "Maybe . . . I don't know. I think it's more that I'm trying to . . . " It was as if her thoughts were being clarified for the first time. "I'm trying not to get swallowed up by the majority, to remain different, to lay claim to my bastard status." She took another drink. "Conformity rejected me, so now I reject conformity."

"Do you know who your father is?"

It took several seconds before she made up her mind to reply. "Yes."

He nodded. "Does he have a family? Do you have any half brothers or sisters?"

She stood up wearily, feigning indifference. "What's the point in going over all this? Do I dig into your past? Do I ask why you like motorbikes? Or what made you drive at a hundred and twenty miles an hour?"

Again, he fell silent. She had won. He would keep quiet now.

Without waiting, Diane got dressed. Strange how it had suddenly gotten cold.

For several minutes, nothing was said. When she was ready, Diane went and kissed Frédéric on the mouth, more like a friend than a lover.

"Tell me, Diane, you have everything, so what the hell are you doing here with me? Do you feel sorry for me? Do you think you're a high priestess of pleasure come to rescue a lost lamb, a difficult member of your flock? Are you here to practice your erotic cult? Has sex assumed such an important place in your life that you consider it your mission? When it comes down to it, are you the Mother Teresa of fucking?"

No longer considering the consequences, he was pouring out the thoughts he had mulled over a thousand times.

Diane walked to the door, opened it, and froze on the threshold. "You really want to know?"

"Yes."

"Your penis is a bit twisted. It leans to the left. You're the only person I know with that feature, and it gives me some amazing sensations."

And with these words, she left Fred feeling overjoyed, happy for the next three weeks.

I n the game of seduction, it was usually Ève who aroused desire and encouraged a man to come forward.

But that night, in the villa in Knokke-le-Zoute, Quentin had usurped her role. Shy, skittish, willing, disloyal, he was content just to be there, near her, looking wonderful, with his long, well-proportioned body showing unreservedly through his slim-fitting shirt and tight pants, lively then languid, silent, suddenly talkative, his almond-shaped eyes flashing with conflicting emotions, fear, lust, despair, bravado, helplessness.

Ève was thrown by finding herself in the position of her elderly lovers. As performed by Quentin, this act, seeming to give itself while giving nothing, struck her as a little ridiculous. Still, it was effective, since she desired him.

Would she accept his manipulation?

For the last two hours, since he had suddenly appeared in the night, Quentin and Ève had been circling each other, drinking and chatting.

When he had slipped into the hallway, she had liked his audacity, all the more so because she had found the mixture of panic and desire on his face touching. Wondering if she should send him back to his teenage party, she had looked at him for a long time, saying nothing, then decided to let him in. This way, if his father showed up, Quentin would provide another tool with which to annoy, dominate, and tame the lover who was cheating on her.

Now that it was nearly midnight, Philippe must be in the

marriage bed, so she could longer use that excuse. If she was going to keep Quentin with her, it would be for her own sake.

For the time being, she was pretending to ignore the boy's silent plea to remain here, kiss her, hold her in his arms. With enormous effort, she managed to keep the conversation going on various topics, such as his studies, TV series, sports, and favorite songs. At times, she didn't hear his answers, just looked at his full, soft, red lips, marveled at how long his eyelashes were, and stared at the base of his neck, where the skin was so fine it seemed like golden butter.

As for Quentin, he kept giving her intense looks, which vanished as soon as she noticed them, looks that cried out that he idolized her.

When the clock struck twelve, Ève shuddered. So did Quentin. What were they doing together? It was time to get real. They were entering the wild, nonsocial part of the night. The grave tolling of the bell drifted across the village and petered out in the infinity of the sea.

Ève was trembling. She knew that he was expecting her to do everything, that he wouldn't be the one to make the decision. With him there, she had the role of the man.

The room filled with palpable tension. Darkness was again the place that allowed lovers to come together. The silence swarmed with the noise of thoughts, urges, impulses, frustrations.

Ève knew she had to do something, anything, to put an end to this atmosphere of hysterical yearning.

She stared at him. He held her gaze. In his indolence, the boy was crying, "Go on, I'm game!"

But Ève was used to men coming to her, their hands reaching out. She hated having to do it all herself, as if it were some kind of defeat, and she didn't budge.

Did she desire him? Of course. For several reasons. He was not . . . unpleasant, and, by opening her arms to him, she would be taking revenge on his father, who had dared ridicule her by treating her like a thing of no importance. The act would also erase her age, and prove to Philippe that she had a part in the world of youth—his son's world—a long way from his own sixty years. Was it immoral? Asking this question made her feel like an admirable person: to be concerned with decorum when Philippe trampled all over the rules by cheating on both his wife and his mistress! She didn't have to justify herself to a man like that. Which meant she had to take the initiative.

But what would she do with Quentin afterwards? What if he got attached? He would probably follow her around. He certainly wouldn't behave as discreetly as the married men she usually went with . . . Would she be able to . . .

Quentin's large, burning lips suddenly pressed down on hers.

In the morning, a new Ève and a new Quentin welcomed the daylight.

Outside, a white, opaline light bathed the horizon. The sea still seemed asleep, motionless, reluctant to regain its colors.

Quentin emerged from the sheets as if from the waves, eyes half shut, hair disheveled. He looked at her with soft, smoldering, imploring eyes.

Ève answered his entreaty by whispering, "I'm happy."

He growled with pleasure and snuggled up against her.

During the night, she had found and accepted her role as initiator, a position that required a lot of love, not necessarily love for Quentin, but rather love for the human race. Because she believed that the relationship between a man and a woman was sacred, she had dispensed advice, exercised patience, allowed the young man to control his passion and emotion in order to attain the path to their joy. For hours, they had moved together and broken apart, intoxicated with each other, breathless, quivering.

"I'm staying here!" Quentin announced. "I'm not going back home!"

"All right. Me, neither!"

This rebellion against the timetable sealed their adventure: Quentin informed his parents that he would be returning to Brussels with a friend, so they needn't worry. More discreetly, Ève canceled her appointments—with the agency, female friends, lovers—and switched off her cell phone so that she could ignore Philippe's calls.

The days to come belonged to them, and they were delighted by that. They were on vacation from their ordinary lives, aware that they were venturing on an enchanted interlude.

Fearing to meet familiar people outside, they idled within the walls that had housed their encounter. Quentin walked around the rooms wearing only boxer shorts—something an older man would have never risked—his chest chiseled with newfound muscles. There were times when he struck Ève as so perfect and so aware of being perfect that she felt as if she was touching not a lover, but a rival.

And yet he moved her deeply. After every kiss, his face would throb, as if quivering inside. When they made love, his orgasm overwhelmed him and he couldn't help crying out in awestruck surprise. In discovering sensuality, he was refreshing Ève's sensations after all the years when habit had dulled the beneficial violence of pleasure in her.

Whenever she walked past a mirror, she noticed a new seriousness in her face. Previously, the practice of lying had fixed her features in a perpetual smile, but now that she was keeping less watch on herself, she had shed this mask.

On Monday, knowing that the Brussels residents they wished to avoid had left the resort, they went out. They strolled by the water, cycled out into the green, flat countryside, had drinks on café terraces, played mini golf, and did all the clichéd things people did in romantic movies, Quentin for the first time, and Ève with a new genuineness. Usually, she would display the outward signs of a love affair more than she actually felt them, without cynicism but with determination: so strong was her need to believe in what she was doing, it could even be said that she displayed those outward signs with sincerity. But there was always a degree of calculation in these romantic scenes: the men would pay for everything, not to mention buying her lots of gifts. It was not enough to keep her, they had to spoil her too. With Quentin, she was experiencing a previously unknown pleasure: that of taking out her purse at the end of a meal, paying for a waffle, a cocktail, an ice-cream cone. Whenever she did so, she felt stronger, more loving. Quentin accepted the situation quite naturally, more naturally than she ever had in her entire life, because he didn't keep count, whereas she had always added everything up in her kind so that she could measure the men's commitment.

All the same, when, on impulse, she tried to buy him some clothes, he got angry. Believing she had hurt his male pride, she tried to justify herself, but stopped when she realized that, for Quentin, the purchase of clothes was something a mother did.

Who cared? Even Quentin's occasional brusqueness had charm. Being somewhat unsure of himself, he dared to give her the kind of imploring looks no man ever would. Whenever he took her, he was ardent, feverish, both tremulous and passionate, so astonished by the feelings he was experiencing and those he aroused that he seemed to be shot through with a thousand different emotions.

They had decided they would have three days of happiness. On the second, Ève changed. The more Quentin bloomed, the deeper she sank into her thoughts. She was a woman everyone thought as happy as a lark, but her carefree demeanor was merely a façade. She was constantly obsessed with her security and her future; the lark concealed a squirrel.

On the third day, she plunged into gloom. The more successful their shared moments, the sadder she became. At around noon, she understood what was happening: in spending time with Quentin, she had realized that she was getting old. It wasn't something she saw in his eyes, or in anybody else's. She herself sensed her lack of enthusiasm, the fact that her joy was a response to Quentin's, rather than an instigator of it. She had always been the nymphet, the spirited, slightly crazy girl, and now here she was, the wise, thoughtful, experienced one. In the course of a conversation, he boasted that he was having an affair with "a mature woman." She nearly strangled him. Nobody had ever considered her "a mature woman" before. What would tomorrow bring? If Quentin wished to continue this relationship, in six months, a year, three at the most, he would leave her for a girl his own age. She studied her face in the mirror: if this affair were to continue, she would be a pathetic woman, fearing and expecting her downfall. She might think she was spring, but he was hurrying her to her autumn. Only pride could shield her from decay.

It was best to break up, to break up as soon as possible. This fling had to be curtailed. Three days were enough for Ève. Any more would depress her.

If she rejected Quentin, she would become young again—or at least, a child in comparison with her aged lovers. If she rejected him, she would go back to being a woman who used men, not a woman who kept a prince. If she rejected him, she would become the center of her own life again.

At five o'clock, when they returned from a cycling trip along the canals, she stopped him from fantasizing about their evening.

"Go, Quentin. Go back to Brussels. Now you know how to act like a man with a woman. The world is your oyster."

"When are we going to see each other again?"

"Never."

Taken aback, he frowned so much it was if he was trying to

stop a cap from being blown off by the wind, and blinked, convinced she was joking.

She took his warm hand, so smooth and impatient. "Forget my phone number. I won't say hello if I see you in the street, I won't answer if you speak to me, and I'll leave you waiting outside if you knock at my door. We'll never touch again, Quentin. From now on, you'll keep a nice place in your mind where I'll be one of your memories, your first memory of a woman . . . and you . . . you'll be one of my memories too . . . " She was surprised to feel her eyes fill with tears. "One of my most beautiful memories . . . " she said.

Her voice broke. How dreadful! She had to fight against the emotion! No heartache! Not here! She felt sorry for herself, for her lost youth, for this unknown, frightening period of maturity that lay before her. Compelled by the gun pointed at her head, the woman sentenced to death was moving forward along the path leading to her destruction.

She threw herself into his arms, so that she could sob without his seeing her. He clasped her to his hollow young chest, stroked her face with his huge hands, surprised by this searing pain. Who had ever cried for him before? Albane, but not like this. She had never sought refuge in her tormentor's arms.

His chest swelled with pride. Holding this woman to comfort her, he was taking another step in his initiation into manhood and, although Ève's vulnerability upset him, it also filled him with pride.

As for the separation, he didn't believe it.

The doorbell rang.

The taxi Ève had ordered had arrived to pick up its customer. Quentin couldn't accept the fact that she had made up her mind. But he kept quiet.

Ève kissed him one last time, and escorted him majestically to the door. Distraught, intimidated, Quentin let himself be led. The cab set off.

Once she was alone, and the door was closed, Ève stood frozen, overwhelmed by a pain she was only too familiar with: the obligation not to admit to anyone the things she wanted to scream.

A minute later, pulling herself together, she sighed with satisfaction. She had just escaped a huge danger, an unknown force that could have defeated her, a mysterious force that would have led her to favor Quentin's happiness over her own, an intolerable force that would have made her forget about herself, a generous force that would have destroyed her interests instead of strengthening them.

A strange force that, had she not vanquished it immediately, she could have given its rightful name: love.

The miracle hadn't been hard work . . .

The three lovers had embraced, touched, caressed, penetrated one another. A leg stroked a rump, an arm slipped into the mêlée, two mouths joined together until a third came to seal them, flesh touched nameless flesh, skin lost its identity but dispensed the ecstasy it could provide with a generosity that was boundless.

At first, even though Baptiste watched Joséphine kiss her female lover without embarrassment, he shuddered when he felt his wife's eyes following his own lovemaking with Isabelle and held back, not sure whether or not to continue, feeling disapproval moving through the clear zones of civilized consciousness to express an instinctive possessiveness, the product of the primitive brain. Joséphine found it painful to see her man in the arms of a lover, even when that lover was hers. Aware of the contradiction, she called on her own will, ordering it to remedy her reflexes and endure the scene. As a result, it was Joséphine who sometimes directed Baptiste's moves in relation to Isabelle, just to convince herself that the situation wasn't out of her control. The three of them clung together, forming an ever more homogeneous trio with every hour that passed.

In the morning, they felt as if the universe had changed. They had left a shrunken, petty world, a maze of prejudices and prohibitions, and entered another, broader, brighter, more open world.

They made love again, gently, weakly, the way you hum a song you've previously sung at the top of your voice—more than anything else, it was an excuse to stay in bed.

The women fell fast asleep in each other's arms.

Isabelle lay in the middle, a sign that she belonged to the two of them.

He slid toward her, pressed his nose against her wrist, and breathed in deeply, going from her elbow up to her armpit, and lingering in the soft hollow of her neck, storing her scent, ordering his brain to keep its imprint, to associate it forever with sensuality. Much to his surprise, he already wanted Isabelle to be a part of his future.

Sated with pleasure, but still hungry, he got impetuously out of bed. Satisfaction had advantageously replaced sleep. He hadn't made love several times in one night for a long time, and had almost forgotten it was possible—living with the same woman for fifteen years, you are so lulled by the rhythm of conjugal life that you lose the sense of urgency. This past night had reminded him that desire doesn't end with orgasm but outlives it and even continues to affirm itself beyond its own strength.

Still, the freshness Baptiste felt this morning was due to an essential lightening: he had shed the burden of jealousy. His intellect had always shunned such insecurity, but now it had vanished completely.

He walked to his computer, using his *Encyclopedia of Love* as an excuse to switch it on, found the entry on *Fidelity*, and quickly improvised:

Is there anything more foolish than the kind of fidelity that frustrates us? True fidelity consists in the following promise: I will give you as much tomorrow as today. That's love! It certainly isn't: I will give only to you and no longer give to others. Is parsimonious love, miserly love, love that excludes, still love? What kind of inconsistency is it that demands that loyalty should amputate us? How has society linked commitment to chastity outside the couple? After all, there's no connection between constancy and abstinence. There are spouses who end up not having sex anymore: is that fidelity? There are spouses who end up hating and despising each other: is that fidelity? I think infidelity comes down to forgetting your oath to love your spouse for the rest of your life. But I still love Joséphine as I did, and I also love Isabelle. It's different. Isn't it an aberration to reduce love to a couple?

He got up and went to the window, which looked out on Place d'Arezzo. A parrot was courting a pretty, multicolored female macaw, while a lawn-green parakeet watched.

Why do we confuse love and reproduction? Of course, you need a male and a female to reproduce. But we are not just reproducing animals. Outside procreation, why is a couple necessary? Why has it been established as a unique model?

Absurd!

Baptiste walked back to his desk and switched off his computer, knowing he wouldn't publish what he had just written, then went to the kitchen to prepare a gargantuan breakfast. It was important to lay the table, warm the croissants, make scrambled eggs and pancakes. After a night that had gratified his manhood to such an extent, he didn't want to seem like a male chauvinist to his two lovers. He felt it was an essential expression of his feminine side to stand over the stove for a bit.

The trio blossomed. Every night was as dazzling as the first. During the day, Isabelle and Joséphine were together in the hours when Isabelle wasn't working. At last engrossed in his *Encyclopedia of Love*, Baptiste wrote about various topics—*caress, kiss, Don Juan syndrome*—with new authority.

Isabelle and he were slowly getting used to one another. Whenever Joséphine was absent, they would feel terribly shy, becoming aware of the gap between their sexual intimacy and a psychological intimacy as untouched as fresh snow. They didn't know each other's backstory. Although you could guess Baptiste's sensitivity from his books, he had characteristics—times when he was reserved, or cheerful, or had qualms about something—that Isabelle hadn't suspected.

As they got to know each other, Joséphine became worried. Although it was she herself who had wanted this threesome, she had trouble accepting it, realizing that this experience took away her exclusive rights to Baptiste, and to Isabelle. She feared that, by making everything common property, she would lose everything. She was overcome with doubts, some-times painful ones: if Isabelle and Baptiste were away from her for an hour, she thought they would leave without her; if they lingered in bed after she had gotten up, she imagined them taking advantage of her absence and would go back without warning, a questioning look on her face.

A burst of enthusiasm when she boasted about this incred-ible success—an actual threesome—would be followed by unjustified fits of anger.

Baptiste suggested they talk about it. "The three of us won't be able to live together unless we use our intelligence. We have to speak out, Joséphine, we have to say when we feel frus-trated, unhappy, or sad."

When he said this, Joséphine rushed into his arms. "I'm sorry, Baptiste, I'm sorry. I've ruined what existed before, I've ruined the great love the two of us had."

"Don't talk that way," Baptiste said, struggling with his own emotions. "Our love is still there, only in a different form."

"I've destroyed everything!"

"Let's be constructive. Even though there are three of us now, we still have our couple. Isabelle is fully aware that she's the additional element. As a matter of fact, I don't know how she stands it."

"You and I are for life, Baptiste."

"And this is the proof."

They kissed, and were soon joined by Isabelle. Joséphine recovered that playful, insolent mood of hers, which they all needed so much.

One evening, as the three of them were making dinner and chatting, Baptiste was just putting a tray of lasagne in the oven when he suddenly remembered something. "My God! The lecture!"

Joséphine dropped her knife. "I forgot to remind you." She rushed to get her diary. "It's in twenty minutes, at the Centre des Congrès."

"Tell them you're sick," Isabelle suggested.

"I'd sooner drop dead!" Baptiste cried.

Joséphine grabbed Isabelle's hand to stop her. "Baptiste never cancels. It would make him sicker to miss an event than to go there with flu, or even dying."

He had already gone into the bedroom to change, while Joséphine called a taxi.

"Would you like us to come with you?" Isabelle asked.

Baptiste was about to answer yes, but before he could, Joséphine said, "Oh, no, we'll only get in his way. Besides, frankly, after fifteen years, I know all the questions, all the answers, all the stories he's going to tell. What a bore!"

"You're so clever, why don't you go instead of me?" Baptiste growled, struggling with his cuff links.

Joséphine burst out laughing. "Don't panic. You'll be perfect."

When he got to the venue, Baptiste walked in through the stage door but saw no one, called out in the deserted corridors, then decided to go up to the lobby on the upper floor. There, he spotted some movement. No sooner did they see him than the organizers rushed to him, nervous and agitated. *They're going to tell me they haven't sold a single ticket*, Baptiste thought, relieved at the thought that he could leave again.

On the contrary, they laughed, already tipsy, and told him that it was a full house, and that no lecture had attracted such a large audience in ten years. Not only were there eight hundred people in the auditorium, but television screens had been placed in two adjacent rooms, since a total of one thousand two hundred people had bought tickets to see and hear Baptiste.

He felt like running away: he hadn't prepared anything.

"Do you happen to have an office where I can be alone for a while?"

"What? Aren't you going to have a drink with us?"

Baptiste looked at the merry, blotchy-faced mayor, who was kindly handing him a glass, and nearly told him that if he stepped onstage in his state, there would be no audience at all next time.

"Later . . . " he muttered, with a conspiratorial smile that seemed to suggest that all kinds of madness would be possible after the event.

Having paid tribute to the general good mood, he was taken to a room where he could prepare.

What is the purpose of literature? said the program.

Baptiste folded a piece of paper in two, and scribbled on it. Like a pianist who jots down the chords on which he is going to improvise, he established the points he was planning to tackle. An author addressing a crowd is more like a jazz musician than classical composer: instead of writing a text and performing it, he must create a unique experience for the audience by taking risks, digressing, landing back on his feet, grabbing whatever formula pops up, and letting the emotion of the moment color an idea before bouncing back with a change of tone or rhythm. It wasn't out of disrespect but, rather, respect for the public, that Baptiste never wrote out his lectures. In the past, every time he had handed in a prepared speech, it had lost all life when he had read it in a drone on the stage, his nose glued to the page, dull and devoid of presence. As a reader, he didn't touch people's hearts: they had the impression that the real Baptiste had stayed at home and sent his twin brother, who was less lively, less sparkling, and just stammered his words in his place. Baptiste had drawn the conclusion that he was a poor interpreter of himself.

On the other hand, when, taken by surprise or having misplaced his papers, he had had to improvise, he had brought the house down. For a writer, to speak the way he writes isn't about reading a prewritten text, but finding in front of an audience the same inventive boldness he has when he's alone, demonstrating a mind in action. What he has to show is the fire, not the cold object; the work process, not the result.

That Saturday evening, Baptiste knew he had to have the self-assurance to show himself off in his workshop. That was where the difficulty lay: recently, he had acquired confidence in his ability to seduce and to give and receive pleasure, but he had neglected his second job—that of the writer who speaks on behalf of the writer who writes.

They came to get him. He walked into the auditorium to wild applause.

He was immediately encouraged by the faces focused on him. He soared on the wings of inspiration, moving between naïveté and high culture—neither his naïveté nor his culture was fake, although both were part of the act.

An hour later, the audience gave him an ovation, and he was led into the lobby for a book signing.

Several people in the field kept him company around his table: representatives from his publishing house, a bookseller, and Faustina, the publicist he liked as a character out of fiction but wasn't drawn to, because he always expected her to go too far and replace humor with nastiness, witty remarks with malicious gossip.

As he signed his initials in the books, Faustina and her colleagues showed him such attentive, even exaggerated politeness that he detected a hint of pity.

What's so pathetic about me? Was my lecture ridiculous?

Everybody was fussing over him, making sure he was fine, offering him food, drink, cigarettes, whatever he wanted. The bookseller kept complimenting him on the power he exercised over the women whose books he signed.

"You really can seduce anyone you like, Monsieur Monier."

"They're crazy about him," Faustina added.

"Here's a man who couldn't stay single even for a couple of days."

"Actually, I have a friend," Faustina continued, "probably one of the most beautiful women I know—and rich and intelligent to boot—whose dream is to meet you, Baptiste. You're the only man she desires. Shall I introduce you? No strings attached . . . "

"Stop bothering Monsieur Monier, Faustina. He knows what he wants. All he has to do is click his fingers and the women will come running."

Baptiste suddenly realized what was going on: they thought Joséphine was cheating on him. She and Isabelle must have been smooching on the streets, and a rumor had started. He looked at the people around him as, lips pursed, they leaned over him with expressions of commiseration.

Now I know how people look at a deceived husband, he thought, struggling not to burst into a fit of the giggles.

A week later, in the middle of the afternoon, the doorbell rang.

Baptiste went to open the door and was surprised to find Joséphine and Isabelle on the landing. "What's the matter? Don't you have your keys?"

Joséphine pointed at the large number of bags and suitcases cluttering the landing as far as the staircase. "We have to ask your permission for something."

Her submissive tone suggested a little girl begging her parents to allow her to go out.

"What?"

Joséphine indicated Isabelle, who was leaning against the wall, looking ravaged, not knowing whether to smile or cry. "She's moved out."

Baptiste was worried that Isabelle might have been physically abused. "Did you have a row? Did he insult you? Did he throw you out?"

Isabelle came closer and said in a breathless, trembling voice, "My husband doesn't know yet. I've left a letter on the kitchen table. He'll find it when he comes home tonight." She didn't dare touch Baptiste, even though she wanted to. "I can't bear to keep living there," she stammered. "It's not my place anymore. I . . . "

She couldn't finish her sentence, and Joséphine completed it for her. "She'd like to live with us. Is that all right with you?"

Baptiste was surprised by the way the scene was unfolding. Was it the writer in him who was astonished? Wondering more about the form than the content, he pointed to the bags. "I get the impression you've both already made your decision without me."

"Not at all," Joséphine protested indignantly. "That's why I rang the bell. To ask you to welcome Isabelle, not to force her on you."

"What were you planning to do if I refused?"

"I'd put all the stuff in the basement and we'd look for a studio apartment nearby."

"I won't live with my husband anymore," Isabelle said firmly.

Baptiste shook his head. "It's just that . . . forget about my answer . . . I find the way this is being done lacks . . . "

"Lacks what?" Joséphine exclaimed.

"Romance."

The two women burst out laughing. Shocked, Baptiste took a step back.

"No, Baptiste, don't be offended. We're laughing because we were sure you were going to say that."

Trying to be serious, Isabelle said, "It's true, Joséphine predicted your reaction."

Joséphine pointed her index finger at Baptiste. "I remember when I proposed to you: I was wearing a shower cap—you hate shower caps—and polishing my nails—and you can't stand cotton wool between the toes. You were so shocked that I should choose a moment when I looked such a fright, you didn't even reply." Sardonically, she turned to Isabelle. "His lordship is actually quite sentimental in real life. He may seek out unconventional situations for his books, but he expects his life to be like a Hollywood B movie."

"Have you finished making fun of me, Joséphine?"

Baptiste's putting a stop to his wife's chatter made her realize she had veered away from the main subject.

He turned to Isabelle. "Isabelle, I'm delighted that you're coming to live with us. I've been hoping you would since that first evening. You've only waited—

"A week!" she cried, rushing into his arms.

Joséphine also came up to him and whispered in his ear, "I'm so proud of you, my Baptiste. You're the freest man I've ever met."

"I'm not free, since I'm your slave."

"That's exactly what I meant."

They picked up the bags and swept into the apartment, trying to figure out how to reorganize it so as to live there as a threesome.

4

L ying on a reclining bed, Victor watched as his blood flowed into various glass tubes. The nurse worked skillfully, taking a series of samples while keeping a benevolent eye on Victor.

"I'm not hurting you, am I?"

"No, not at all, thank you. I'm used to it."

The nurse nodded, affected by what she had guessed on seeing which tests had been ordered.

Victor moved his eyes away from his forearm and took a more thorough look around the room. Since he was a child, he had seen so many places like this one, painted in bright colors, lit by fluorescent lights, furnished with white closets and cork noticeboards with cheerful postcards from patients to the medical staff pinned to them. Paradoxically he felt at home in these dens of treatment because they had been the only points of stability in his life during the years when he had followed his father from one misbegotten venture to another. He found hospitals reassuring. He loved the smooth linoleum floors, the waiting rooms with their vases of plastic flowers, the low tables covered in ancient magazines, the smell of disinfectant, the sound of wooden-soled shoes. He was particularly fond of the all-pervading femaleness of the place. Deprived of his mother at an early age, he had seen the nurses, auxiliaries, psychologists, and social workers as the women in his life.

"That's done," the nurse said, pressing a cotton wool pad to the vein. "You can see Dr. Morin now."

He thanked the two women and headed for the cubicles where the medical consultations took place.

Professor Morin, a little man with coal-black eyebrows and a permanent smile on his garnet-colored lips, asked him to sit down. "Good news, Victor: your results are excellent. Although the virus is still present, it's stopped reproducing. We've managed to trap it in spite of its many mutations. It may not have disappeared, but we've attacked it so much, it's stunned." The doctor was as excited as if he was playing a video game. "This diminution of the virus in your body is more important to me than your immune defenses, which are stable anyway, and at a sufficient level. Your triglyceride level is good. Your liver's perfect. No cholesterol." He was rubbing his hands.

Victor knew that the doctor was a good, brilliant man, devoted to treating people, but he couldn't resist a dig. "So you're telling me that I'm a sick man in perfect health?"

The doctor gave him a kindly look. "For as long as we're unable to eliminate the AIDS virus, we'll make every effort to allow you to live with it. It's not a total victory, only half a victory, but it'll ensure that you can lead a more or less normal life."

"It's the 'more or less' bit I'm tired of."

"What is it you're feeling? Are you getting side effects? Are you unable to tolerate the treatment anymore?"

"No, I can tolerate it."

"You just can't stand taking it anymore?"

"No, that's not it either."

"Then tell me what it is."

How could you explain something obvious? Infected with AIDS in his mother's womb, Victor had been an HIV-positive baby, an HIV-positive child, and an HIV-positive teenager. Although, thanks to medical progress, he had become an HIV-positive adult, the earlier training hadn't helped: whenever he approached a woman, he suffered worse than ever. Of course, he did make love using condoms, but he had discovered that lovers are quick to forget all about caution and start flirting with danger. As soon as that kind of passionate intimacy arose, Victor was horrified. He was too honest to lie, or conceal his condition, so he would disclose his illness, which was tantamount to saying, "I'm not your future. We'll never be able to do without a rubber barrier between us. You'll be constantly afraid and so will I. And I'll never be the father of your children." He had put a stop to so many relationships that had begun well that he had ended up pushing girls away before the affair even started. Anything possible became impossible. At the age of twenty, he had shut himself off from love.

"I'm rotten inside, so my life is rotten. I can't commit anymore."

"Are you in love?"

Victor looked up, surprised by the relevance of the question. Yes, he was in love with Oxana, he hadn't been able to resist that feeling, and they had been having sex for the last few days. "I keep wondering when I'll have the courage to leave her."

"Before you get to that point, tell her you're HIV-positive."

"What's the point? She'll leave. I'd rather get in first."

"Is it a matter of pride?"

"It's so as not to be hurt. And I don't want to be seen that way."

"What way?"

"As a sick person."

"There's no dishonor in being sick. Just as there's no merit in having good health. If your mother was still alive, would you make her ashamed of having caught a virus?"

"No."

"Do you think your girlfriend will blame you for having caught the same virus while you were just an embryo?"

"All right, so 'shame' isn't the right word. But she'll dump me."

"How do you know that?"

"From experience."

"You're talking about the past. This is the future."

"Same thing."

"Prove it to me."

Victor sat there open mouthed. Dr. Morin had never before ventured beyond clinical results.

"I insist. Prove to me she's unable to value you for what you are. Prove to me that your chronic condition will suddenly make her think of you as ugly, stupid, nasty, a pariah. Prove to me that love doesn't exist."

Victor stood up and slammed his fist on the desk. "Do you enjoy this? Coming out with all these beautiful words and noble feelings? Great fun, isn't it?" He turned to the wall, kicked it, and struck it with the flat of his hands, over and over, ever more violently, unable to calm down. Then, exhausted, his lips quivering with anger, he repeated the doctor's words, "Prove to me that love doesn't exist! Bullshit! Easy to say when you aren't sick!"

"How do you know?"

"What?"

"That I'm not sick."

The answer stopped Victor in his tracks. He hesitated, his hand raised in midair, swayed, tried to keep his balance, moaned, and fell on the consultation couch.

"What a fool!"

The doctor went to him and patted him on the shoulder. "Don't worry, I'm used to people speaking to me as if I were behind the counter at the Social Security office, as if I wasn't human anymore. Be brave, Victor. Tell the woman you love what you have."

For a whole week after this conversation, although Victor didn't follow the doctor's advice, he did try, whenever he was with Oxana, to accustom himself to the thought that he would eventually. At times, the truth felt like a death sentence, at others, a prelude to happiness.

Since they had fallen in love at first sight on Place Brugmann, Oxana and Victor had made rapid progress. Although she had kept a suite in a hotel, she never left his apartment, indulging in all the delights of discovery. As well as pleasure, what she felt was surprise: it was the first time she hadn't resisted a man's advances but had given herself to him that same night. Usually, she would waver and procrastinate, out of a mixture of caution and dignity, but above all to test her own desire. With Victor, she had had a strange premonition that if she didn't agree to his holding her in his arms a few hours after they had met, it would never happen. There was a kind of tension in him, filled with urgency and impatience, a nervous voracity that had nothing to do with the usual male selfishness or lust.

Never had she been as happy as she was in his small attic room that reminded her of her grandparents' attic in Lviv, where she had felt protected, sheltered from the sky by its roof, from people by its height, and from reality by dreams. Sitting cross-legged on the bed, carefree and relaxed, she read novels she found on the shelf. What better way to enter a stranger's world than through his library? Jules Verne, whom she had never read, rubbed shoulders with Conrad, Stevenson, Monier, and Hemingway. These titles struck her as a boy's choices, echoes of the globe trotting Victor she could see in the various photographs placed here and there, such manly choices that when she opened the books, she felt as though she was breathing in her lover's smell, a blend of leather and freshly-cut grass.

Victor was delighted that Oxana had moved in of her own free will. Watching her sitting happily on the bed, engrossed in a book, her soft hair held in place by a tortoiseshell clasp, filled him with joy. He hadn't experienced such a feeling of fulfillment since he was eight years old and had watched the kitten Baptiste had bought him offer its downy, innocently white belly to the light.

Victor thought of Oxana as a barbarian goddess with the power to consume time. When he was with her, the past no longer existed, nor did the future: intense and radiant, she focused everything on the present. Because he couldn't detach himself from her, or take a critical distance, he forgot about his previous affairs and didn't think about tomorrow. At most, it was the next half hour that concerned him, as he wondered what he would cook or which movie they would go to see.

Sharing a student's life made Oxana discover that she was young. She was the same age as Victor: twenty. But having been a model for many years, and being accustomed to earning money and navigating a tough profession, she had lost her freshness, and not only because she collected much older lovers. Often, when faced with the difficulties of her job, she felt worn and discouraged. And, even worse, when, at casting sessions, she saw fifteen-year-olds in whose eyes she was old, she thought about retiring. Victor had given her back her freshness with his passion, his admiration, his brotherly simplicity, and especially because he was taking a long course, certain that once he had qualified, the world would be his oyster. So that's what youth was: waiting at the start of the track, ready to run.

"What could I do after modeling?" she asked him one day.

"You're asking a question only you know the answer to. What do you love?"

"Besides you?"

"Besides me."

"You."

"And?"

"You."

He leaped out of his chair onto the bed—which wasn't much of a leap—and smothered her in kisses. "I want an answer, Oxana."

"Let's see, what skills do I have? I speak several languages. Translator?"

"Would you like that?"

"I could do it."

"Oxana, you're dodging the question: what do you want to do? Do you think I study law because I can? No, I do it in order to be involved in humanitarian actions or in international criminal justice. What matters is to *want* to do something; then you try to live up to it."

Until now, Oxana had always believed that you lived by your wits. Right now, she was making a living by selling her beauty, tomorrow she would get by by marketing her linguistic abilities. Living was about surviving, nothing else. Listening to Victor describing his ambition to be a lawyer in the service of noble causes, she realized that you could give your life a meaning.

Victor still hadn't been able to tell Oxana the truth, but it struck him that introducing her to his uncle might help him get there. The more involved he became, the more he would be forced to be truthful.

He told Oxana what he concealed from his fellow students, that he was related to Baptiste Monier, the famous writer. As she had just read several of his novels, she was very impressed and got him to repeat it several times.

"I mean, honestly, Oxana, do you think I'm a liar?"

"No, I'm sorry. I just realized I'd always thought a great writer was a dead writer."

"As far as I'm concerned, Baptiste is first and foremost my uncle. When I was a teenager, I even refused to read his books. Because everyone had access to his books, I felt he belonged to me more if I didn't read them."

Victor arrived at Baptiste's house without warning. A blonde woman with a radiant smile opened the door, which threw him. "Er . . . hello, I'm Victor, Baptiste's—"

"Victor, the famous Victor Baptiste so often talks about?"

"Er . . . "

Joséphine appeared, looking cheerful, kissed him, and put her arm around the blonde woman's waist. "This is Isabelle. And she isn't our new housekeeper."

Both women laughed. Victor felt as if he was with two teenage girls out for a good time. Sensing his embarrassment, and vaguely ashamed of their own superficiality, Joséphine and Isabelle called Baptiste to their rescue.

He appeared, looking very relaxed. His face lit up when he saw his nephew. "A surprise visit! The kind the writer hates but the uncle loves. Come in, Victor, I have lots of news."

"Me too," Victor replied, infected by the reigning good mood.

They went to Baptiste's study, and he cried out to no one in particular, "Go to the market without me, girls, I'm staying with Victor."

Victor raised an eyebrow at the word "girls," which he had never before heard from his uncle's mouth. What was going on in this household?

Baptiste cheerfully described to his nephew the sentimental revolution he and Joséphine were living through with Isabelle. It was the first time he had told the story, and he was delighted that it should be his nephew he was telling it to. Victor's amused and delighted reaction brought confirmation of his own happiness.

His heart pounding, Victor was discovering new aspects of his uncle—his vigor, his imagination, his sensuality—which pleased him because he had tended to see Baptiste as an intimidating statue, an effigy of intelligence, talent, and authority. Glimpsing beneath the marble the bashful lover of

Joséphine and the new lover of Isabelle made him seem more approachable.

All of a sudden, he had no difficulty telling him that he loved Oxana, and wanted to introduce her.

Nothing could have thrilled Baptiste more, and he declared that they would wait no longer. "I'm taking you all out to dinner tonight. All right?"

"All right."

This innocence and enthusiasm overwhelmed Victor who, not daring to disturb his routine, tended to exclude from his daily life anything improvised, any immediate pleasure, any spontaneous plans. Hugging his uncle, he felt that, now that he was in his stride, he would hesitate no longer to tell Oxana about being HIV-positive.

It was a lovely evening. Exceptional, in fact. For everyone involved, it marked a first time: the first time Victor and Oxana were introduced as a couple, the first time Baptiste, Joséphine, and Isabelle paraded their threesome. Each enjoyed being there, in the company of the others. Affection, the only reason to get together, circulated between them, like a strong wind of love bearing confidences, emotions, deep sighs, hysterical laughter.

Overwhelmed by the fact that these people were offering to be her new family, Oxana had constant tears in her eyes. She had no idea it was possible to feel so comfortable, so close to others. At times, she was stung by a touch of nostalgia, remembering her Ukrainian childhood with her loving grandparents, before there were money worries and her parents forced her to live with them in their tiny Khrushchev-era apartment on the outskirts of Kiev.

As for Isabelle, she was overcome by the way the two young people looked at her: they accepted her, didn't judge her, didn't treat her like a dangerous parasite. Since, for now, within her own family she met with nothing but hostility, this conviviality encouraged and soothed her.

At the end of the meal, they chatted so much that it took them a while to notice that the restaurant was empty, that the waiters had cleared the tables, and that the owner was yawning behind the till.

Baptiste paid the check. They went for a stroll, with the threesome walking the couple back to Place d'Arezzo.

Over the blue-tinted square, amid the phlox and the purple rhododendrons, hung a soft, liquid silence filled with a sweet scent given off by the jasmine a street vendor had put down on the bench beside her as she gazed up at the moon. You could only hear tiny, fluid movements from the parrots and para-keets, the fluttering of wings, the caress of feathers, as if the peace of the stars had also spread to the wild fauna.

"Will you believe me," Baptiste said in a low voice, "if I tell you that in the tree facing my window there are two male cock-atiels who look after a female?"

They smiled and tried—in vain—to see them. Nature, they all thought, was definitely a lot more imaginative than human society.

They parted happily.

The following day, Victor had an international law exam at the university, so he left Oxana early, spent the morning revis-ing in the library, had a sandwich, then took the exam in the afternoon in a windowless auditorium lit with fluorescent lights and smelling of tangerines and old, damp carpet.

At last, at seven in the evening, he returned to Place d'Arezzo and went up to the attic apartment. This time, he was going to admit his state of health to Oxana. Since the night before, he had felt ready, certain that their relationship would not only survive the truth but be strengthened by it.

When he walked in, he saw that the apartment was empty. All trace of Oxana—clothes, bags, suitcases—had vanished.

A yellow sheet of paper was waiting for him on the bed.

I'm sorry, I've never loved anybody as much as you. I'm leaving.

He couldn't believe what he was reading, and looked around for proof that he was having a bad dream.

Without thinking straight, he went downstairs four steps at a time, ran through the streets to his uncle's, and rang the bell impatiently.

Pale-faced, Baptiste opened the door. Victor rushed in. "Help me, Oxana's gone!"

Baptiste's eyebrows lifted. He seemed to be looking for something on the floor.

Victor waved the yellow letter, and Baptiste read it.

So far, he hadn't said a word, but now he raised his head and hesitantly placed a hand on Victor's shoulder. "Joséphine has gone too."

5

"Oh, shit, not that idiot again!"

"Who is he?"

"Patrick Breton-Mollignon, editor of the newspaper *Le Matin*. He's been coming on to me for years."

Just as Faustina was saying this, the man in question got out of his car and waved at her eagerly as she walked down the street with her lover. Taking her by the elbow, Dany tried to turn the corner in order to avoid this unwelcome encounter, but she resisted.

"He's going to approach you," Dany grunted.

Patrick Breton-Mollignon hurried to catch up with them. He was tall and oddly-proportioned, his ungainly trot suggesting a camel walking on uneven ground.

"Tell him to go to hell," Dany said in a low voice.

Instead of obeying, Faustina freed her arm and turned to the man, feigning delighted surprise. "Hello, Patrick! How lovely to see you!"

"I didn't think you'd noticed me," he said, trying to catch his breath.

Dany watched with contempt as this ridiculous individual attempted to walk faster, which was obviously a strain on his heart.

Faustina threw her arms around him. Clumsily, he banged his chin against her forehead before he could get to her cheek.

"My dear Patrick, this is Maître Daniel Davon."

"Well, everybody knows Maître Davon," Patrick Breton-

Mollignon replied, proffering a limp, moist hand. "You're about to have a book published, aren't you?

"Excuse me?" Dany replied.

"We're definitely talking about it very seriously," Faustina exclaimed.

"Is it about the Mehdi Martin case?"

"We're not allowed to say anything," she added.

"So it is about the Mehdi Martin case. Well done, maître. I really must see the interesting bits, Faustina. I'll publish them in the paper."

"We can talk about it later . . . "

"Maître Dany Davon and Mehdi Martin, that's dynamite. I'm counting on you, Faustina, OK?"

Faustina lowered her eyes, assumed the expression of a schoolgirl about to swear an oath for the first time in her life. "I give you my word, Patrick."

"Wonderful." He turned to Dany "You do know you're in the hands of the best with her?"

"The best what?" Dany asked, an amused glint in his eyes.

Faustina stifled a laugh.

Patrick Breton-Mollignon seemed unaware of their mocking complicity. "The best publicist. Faustina operates at such a high level, she's left the competition way behind."

Faustina felt obliged to protest. "Don't listen to him, Maître Davon, he's only saying that to flatter me."

Dany raised an eyebrow at the formality of her address.

Turning his back on Dany, Patrick Breton-Mollignon moved closer to Faustina, his manner seductive and insistent, as if the other man wasn't there anymore. "When can I invite you to lunch?"

"I'll check my diary and call you."

"You always say that."

"When you get a call from me, you'll realize I've often told you the truth."

Having said that, she rose on tiptoe, planted a light kiss on his cheek, then walked off in the direction of her building, followed by Dany.

"Explain to me why you allow that drooling oaf to hit on you."

"He edits the most important daily paper in the country."

"He wants to fuck you."

"That's natural, isn't it?"

"And you encourage him."

"For as long as he runs *Le Matin*, he has a right to hope. I have to make a living."

"How do I know you haven't already—"

"Oh, no, please. He's so bad in bed, do you know what they call him in the business? The boiled leek."

Reassured, Dany smiled and raised his chin. "Definitely not the man for you."

"How conceited you are!"

Even so, she agreed, and they went up to her apartment.

It was five o'clock. Faustina played the accomplished housewife by squeezing some fruit in order to make them a tropical cocktail. "I'm concocting something to match the parrots on the square."

Dany was lost in thought, and it didn't occur to him to help her. "He flirted with you right in front of me, as if I wasn't even there."

"Let's just say as if you weren't my lover."

"The thought didn't even cross his mind. Does he think you're a saint who's above earthly appetites?"

She burst out laughing.

"What then?" he insisted.

"I don't think he imagines for a moment that I could go out with a man of mixed race."

Dany winced. He stood up and started striding up and down the corridor, like a man working off excess energy, then rubbed his chin and came back toward her. "Are you sleeping with a man of mixed race?"

"More often than not, yes." She tried to underline her words with a caress, but he pushed it away.

"Do you think of me as a man of mixed race?"

Aware of his growing aggressiveness, she tried to put an end to it. "Dany, you're missing the point. I'm trying to tell you that idiot Patrick Breton-Mollignon is a racist since he can't imagine us being together, and you're getting at me."

"Yes, I'm getting at you. I don't give a damn about Patrick Breton-Mollignon. He's a racist, but I'm just finding out that you are too."

"Me?"

"Yes, you. You sleep with a man of mixed race."

"Am I having a bad dream? Surely, if I sleep with a man of mixed race, that must mean I'm not a racist."

"Wrong. You should say, 'I sleep with you' and not 'I sleep with a man of mixed race.'"

"So you're not a man of mixed race, then?"

He raised his hand, ready to strike her. His face was distorted in a grimace, and he was grinding his teeth. He dropped his hand and walked away.

For a moment, Faustina glimpsed two ways of getting herself out of this situation: the first, the gentle one, was to try to understand why he hated the mention of his being of mixed race, what buried pain explained his anger, what childhood traumas came rushing back into his consciousness as soon as someone saw only his physical appearance; the other option, the offensive one, consisted in demolishing his argument.

He interrupted her as she hesitated. "Is that what you say to yourself when you're in my arms: I'm screwing a man of mixed race?"

Faustina was taken aback because that was literally, word for word, what she had said to herself on that first evening as she was marveling at her discovery of Dany's body. If she were to admit that, he would be furious.

"So what should I say: that I'm screwing Santa Claus?"

"You're so coarse."

"Coarse maybe, but not a racist! You're out of your mind, Dany. If I'd turned you down, you would have accused me of being a racist. I reciprocated and you say I'm a racist anyway. What was I supposed to do? Sleep with you without realizing you're of mixed race? Sorry if I'm not that kind of idiot."

"You really don't get it."

"And what do you think when you sleep with me? I'm screwing a blonde?"

Dany stood there with his mouth open for a second, as she had done earlier. She deduced that she had hit the target.

"Tell me the truth, Maître Dany Davon: have you had any black lovers?"

"I forbid you—"

"Answer me."

"I—"

"No black ones? How about lovers of mixed race?"

"You—"

"No point in lying, because the ones you've already mentioned were white. You sleep only with white women."

"Yes."

"So then you're a racist."

"It's not the same thing. In Europe, everybody's white. There's nothing unusual about it. It's the norm."

"Really? Oh, but I thought that, when it came to sex, you weren't into the norm. So it's all right to try something a bit out of the ordinary as long as it's with white women, is it? You want to know something? You're the full-blown racist, you're the one who hates black and mixed-race people. At least I can assure you I haven't gone for men with prejudices. You can't."

"I'm within my rights to like white women."

"Is it because you like them, or because they make you forget you're of mixed race?"

Although Faustina might have been pleased with her answer for the moment, she regretted it almost immediately: her words were like a bombshell in their effect on Dany. He screamed, his features twisted with exasperation, and began hitting at everything around him. Vases, dishes, the telephone, the TV set, framed photographs, everything was hurled to the floor. He barely caught his breath before lunging into the next room where he swept the books off the shelves and stamped on them. Clinging to the wall, Faustina yelled at him to stop, knowing that if she went any closer, he would kill her.

Suddenly, running out of things to hit, he froze, his legs apart, his chest heaving, his hands open, ready to strike again. He stared at her with bloodshot eyes.

At first, she held his gaze, then, aware that she had to respect the archaic code of submission, she lowered her eyes.

He groaned, looking more human again, and left the apartment, slamming the door as he did so.

Once she was sure she was alone—and safe—Faustina sat down on the floor and allowed herself to weep; she didn't know what she was crying over but her tears gave her a comforting feeling of ordinariness.

For the next four hours, she threw away whatever Dany had smashed and tidied whatever had escaped the massacre. The more she erased the marks of violence, the better she felt. She gave up trying to understand what had been behind that fit of rage. A "psychopath"—that was all Dany was. A psychopath, which meant he was "not to be associated with," and also meant it was "pointless trying to understand what's beyond understanding"; he joined a gallery of monsters, like Hitler, Genghis Khan, Stalin, possibly Mehdi Martin, the serial killer defended by Maître Davon—they were both crazy, so it was no wonder they got along!

Her affair with Dany was over. Good. She'd started to get bored anyway . . . Of course, it was nice to fuck passionately for hours on end, in eighteen thousand different positions. Even so, repetition was boring. Especially since they had gone so over the top that she'd already had vaginitis twice. She had felt flattered the first time, as if she had been decorated for valor on the battlefield: the inflammation of the mucous membranes was a kind of a trophy, the proof that she had been brave in the battle of love. But the required abstinence had complicated their lives over the following days, so that she and Dany wanted to bite each other when they couldn't make love. As a result, a second case of vaginitis had led her to take an unplanned, prudent trip to her mother's. As she vacuumed up the pieces of glass from the gaps in the floorboards, she realized she had endangered her health. As for the swingers' clubs, she hadn't enjoyed them for very long. That had always been her problem: she quickly tired of people and activities.

She was startled by the sound of a key in the lock. A shadowy figure slipped into the corridor. Dany stood before her. She froze.

"I'm sorry," he said in a low voice.

She didn't react.

"Faustina, I'm sorry. My anger wasn't aimed you, you took the brunt for the others."

"What others?"

"Those who only see me as a man of mixed race."

The long silence that followed brought a fragile peace. Faustina sensed that Dany was being sincere: he was suffering, he was ashamed.

She wondered if she too was suffering and realized that she was more than anything annoyed at having spent four hours tidying up.

"I beg you, Faustina, forgive me. I'll replace everything I smashed. And more. Please . . . "

She looked at his full lips, his fine features, his firm skin, his very white eyeballs. A powerful wave rose within her, which she took for forgiveness and which must have contained a certain amount of desire. She opened her arms, and he immediately took refuge in them.

As long as he doesn't cry. I hate men who snivel.

She giggled: Dany's skillful fingers were already trying to take off her skirt.

The following day, Faustina demanded that Dany come to the party she was organizing in her apartment. "You'll see, you'll like my friends: they're all gays."

"Excuse me?"

"That's right, I don't know why, all my friends are gays. They're sure to love you."

In truth, she knew perfectly well why her friends were men who liked men: it allowed her to hold court. In their eyes, she was the woman, the temptress, the seductress they wanted not to possess, but to be.

Her mother had taught her about this power early on. "After fifty, sweetheart, you're a woman only in the eyes of homosexuals. As far as heterosexuals are concerned, you become a cast-off." Faustina hadn't waited that long to exalt her femininity, and had made friends with the gay men life pushed her way. She enjoyed talking about men as coarsely as they did, had the freedom of knowing they admired her without desiring her, and liked the fact that she was relieved of her sometimes difficult role of sex object: with them, she could laugh and joke without any ulterior motive.

Dany looked worried. "Are you sure you want me to stay?"

"Absolutely. Are you scared they'll eat you up like a delicacy? It's what's going to happen, you know. Don't worry:

they'll look at you, sniff around, listen, but they won't leap on you."

"You're a real bitch," he exclaimed, laughing.

"I know. It's part of my charm."

When those Faustina referred to as "the boys" arrived, Dany felt comfortable. The remarks they made were funny, bitchy, sometimes hilarious; he was flattered by the lingering looks they gave him. Caressing him, serving him first, boasting of his legal exploits, Faustina treated him like a king, and the eight other guests approved of his privileged status.

Tom and Nathan brought up the subject that was most on their minds: the obscure business of the anonymous letters. "We've discovered four anonymous letters," Tom said. "Our two, and then when we talked to the florist, who has to be the most malicious woman in Brussels—"

"In the world, my dear, in the world," Nathan corrected.

"—we discovered two more: the one Xavière received and the one—she found out by chance through his wife—received by that degenerate aristocrat at Number 6."

"If that one's straight, then I'm the Queen of Spain."

"That's not the point, Nathan!"

"It is the point. To be snubbed by a pervert who's always got his hand on his zipper, ready to open it, I mean, that's rich!"

"Anyway," Tom continued, "it's always the same modus operandi: a yellow envelope, a yellow sheet of paper, an identical message: *Just a note to tell you I love you. Signed: You know who.*"

Faustina gave a start. "I got one, too!"

Her words created a stir. She rushed into her bedroom and, after a few curses that echoed around the apartment, returned with the paper.

Tom and Nathan were delighted: their theory of an eccentric

writing love letters to the residents of the square was confirmed.

"What was your reaction to the letter?"

"Do I need to tell you?" Faustina replied, the color draining from her face.

"Yes, you do. It's vital to the investigation."

She turned sheepishly toward Dany. "I thought he'd sent it."

Dany came closer and read the note. "It's not my handwriting."

"We believe you, Dany," Tom said. "Especially as there's no reason for you to have sent us this."

"Which is a shame, really," Nathan said. "I'd have loved it."

Faustina gave him a little slap on the head. "Hands off my man, you."

"Don' hit me, massa, don' hit me," Nathan moaned, putting on his *Gone with the Wind* voice.

This sent a wave of embarrassment through the group. In exercising his sardonic imagination, Nathan had dispensed with political correctness to the point of forgetting that putting on a slave voice in the presence of a man of mixed race wasn't exactly tactful. Faustina feared the worst.

Rising above it, Dany chose to ignore the incident, grabbed the sheet of paper, and turned it over and over. "I'm afraid I can't help you there, my friends, since I've never dealt with a poison pen case."

"Oh, but this person's no crow, he's a dove, a Cupid. These letters are messages of affection, not hatred."

"Well, one thing I can guarantee is that he or she is left-handed. Look at the way the T's are crossed . . . from right to left."

"The Cupid is left-handed!"

"Let's think," Dany said. "The writer of a poison pen letter is usually someone who's frustrated, dissatisfied, marginalized."

"That narrows it down," Faustina said.

"He often has a physical deformity."

"I can't think of anyone like that around here."

Tom looked at her. "Did receiving the message have consequences?"

"You're joking! Of course not."

"You thought Dany had written it. That brought the two of you together."

"We were already together. Let's say it made him take root—not in my heart, since I don't have one, but in my life."

"It was the same for Nathan and me, it had a positive effect. We haven't been apart since."

"I'm even picking out wedding dresses," Nathan said. "Cream, of course, I wouldn't dare white."

They considered this. Faustina formulated out loud what everyone else was thinking. "It's rather embarrassing to think that a stranger wishes me well. It makes me feel uncomfortable."

They changed the subject, and the merry tone of the evening returned.

The party broke up at around eleven. To avoid having to hug the eight "boys," who had been waiting just for that, Dany waved goodbye to them and took refuge in the bedroom, claiming that he had an urgent phone call to make.

Faustina escorted her guests to the door, and they congratulated her on her choice. Hips wiggling, eyes sparkling, she received their compliments as if she had created Dany's beauty, then, with a few excessive sighs, she confirmed that what they hadn't seen was definitely worth seeing.

"You bitch," Nathan said. "My one consolation is that you at least can satisfy him. When I see these women who cling to stunning men and then just frustrate them, I feel like murdering them."

"Calm down, Nathan," Tom said. "Let's leave Vaginitis to our friend Faustina."

"Oh, I love the nickname," Nathan chuckled.

"Shut up," Faustina muttered, trying to stop herself laughing.

"When you called him that, Faustina, I laughed all day. And now that's what I call him in my head. Several times tonight I nearly said, 'A bit more wine, Vaginitis?' or, 'Would you like more sausage, Vaginitis?'"

They laughed. Faustina frowned and put her index finger on her lips. "Come on, boys, go home and don't be good."

"Have a good night with Vaginitis, darling."

As she closed the door, she heard them going into hysterics on the stairs. That was why she loved Tom and Nathan: they shared her fierce, dirty sense of humor.

She returned to the living room, where Dany, grim-faced, was collecting his things.

"What's wrong?" Faustina asked anxiously.

"I heard everything."

"What?"

"'Vaginitis.'"

She shuddered. "Come on," she stammered. "It's rather flattering. It suggests your . . . your skills . . . You know, it matters to them . . . "

Dany walked past her without so much as a glance, threw his key into the bowl in the hallway, and left. "Goodbye. You have no respect for me."

6

D oes your G-spot work OK?"
Holding to her chest a dish she was torturing with a
linen cloth on the pretext of drying it, Marcelle came
out of the kitchen to talk to Mademoiselle Beauvert about
what was preoccupying her.

"I ask because I had a G-spot before it was even discovered. I was a pioneer. I was seventeen when I found it, and that was at a time before anyone was talking about it. Incredible, isn't it?"

Refusing to encourage the confidence, Mademoiselle Beauvert didn't reply.

Rubbing the dish with renewed energy, Marcelle went on, "I guess I can't really take credit: I was just made that way. As soon as you get inside me, I'm off." She nodded her head several times, to make sure, amid her memories, that she was telling the truth. "Every time, bam! Hold on to your hat!" Pleased with herself, she nodded again, looked up, and was surprised by her employer's silence. "What about your G-spot, Mademoiselle?"

"Marcelle, this kind of conversation—"

"All right, I get it. The G-spot isn't your thing. There are women like you. Plenty. Apparently, the majority. Poor things . . . We're not all the same in that department. Still, you have certain advantages I don't."

"Like what?"

"Money, education, class."

"Thank you, Marcelle."

"Yes, frankly, you've been spoiled. Because, actually, apart from being attractive to men and having a G-spot, I haven't been dealt a good hand."

Mademoiselle Beauvert looked at Marcelle with a mixture of irritation and commiseration: how could this squat, surly creature with all the grace of a boar attract men? She clearly appealed to them, there was no doubt about it, because lovers came and went with the regularity of a metronome, and she hardly ever spent more than a month on her own. But Mademoiselle Beauvert idealized love, and the kind of union she admired was between a handsome male and a beautiful female. Any other bond seemed weird, intolerable, possibly even obscene. If every male toad could find his female toad, then we weren't humans anymore, just animals.

Nature had probably invented different kinds of attraction to ensure that couples should form and perpetuate the human race. Yes, there must be invisible factors, smells, enzymes, molecules—chemical phenomena, in other words—floating in the air to induce a reasonable-looking man to leap on a mole like Marcelle. It was this invisible aura that Mademoiselle Beauvert lacked. So much the better! Ever since she had been aware of existing, she hadn't seen herself as a wife or a mother, but rather as a "daughter of," an appendage of her beloved parents. The premonition she had had when she was young that she would avoid affairs of the flesh had been confirmed.

She had been spared the brutishness of it all. As far as she was concerned, this indifference to carnal torments meant that she lived in a healthy atmosphere uninfected by lust. Her body too was pure, and her soul wonderfully free. She didn't experience stupid heartbreaks or constant frustration, she dressed as she pleased, and she was the only person to touch her skin, except for hairdressers, physical therapists, manicurists—professionals who were there to make you feel good. Better still, unlike other women of her age, she wasn't aware of getting old, and the cessation of her periods had meant nothing more than the end of unnecessary pain. As for her wrinkles and slightly pasty complexion, nobody had commented on them—not even she.

Every now and again, she was convinced that her good cheer and her energy were linked to the preservation of her virginity. She had noticed the same innocent joy in some nuns. It wasn't true that sex made women feel fulfilled. As for motherhood, it just exhausted them, nothing else.

"How was your weekend in Geneva?"

Mademoiselle Beauvert smiled. "Wonderful . . . "

"Is it fun in Geneva?"

"John came with me."

"John?"

"John."

"Oh, you mean your boyfriend, the one who's very close to Obama?"

"He's the only one I have, Marcelle."

"I wish I was in your shoes. All these weekends all over the place, in big cities . . . I've always dreamed of going to Rome, Moscow, Istanbul."

"It'll happen, Marcelle."

"With what money, Mademoiselle? With what money? How much did your ticket to Geneva cost, for instance?"

A cruel idea crossed Mademoiselle Beauvert's mind, one that she couldn't resist. "Two hundred and forty-two euros."

"Two hundred and forty-two euros? Really? That's incredible. It's exactly the amount I gave my son to make me a night table! The way things are going, I'm not going to see Geneva, or my bedside table, or my two hundred and forty-two euros!"

"When's your boy getting married?"

"They're getting engaged first, Mademoiselle. The Peperdicks insist. Those people are old-school."

They're stalling, Mademoiselle Beauvert thought. *They clearly don't like it that their daughter is marrying a concierge's son.*

Marcelle chuckled. "Funny, really, that I'll be married before him."

"Excuse me?"

"My Afghan's asked me to marry him." With an unexpectedly girlish gesture, she raised her hands to her flushed cheeks.

Mademoiselle Beauvert froze. No, she wasn't going to allow such a mistake to be made! She owed it to herself to intervene. At first, she tried to circumvent the obstacle. "At least wait for your son to be married."

"No way. I think it'll be much nicer to go to my son's wedding on the arm of my Afghan. I'll look less like a poor, lonely woman . . . " It struck Marcelle that she might have wounded her employer. "Oh, I'm sorry, Mademoiselle Beauvert, I don't mean you, nobody thinks you're alone, you have such class, and besides you could go to the wedding with Obama's buddy, your black boyfriend who plays the saxophone."

"He's not black and he plays the piano." Mademoiselle Beauvert made an imperious gesture to stop her replying. "I hope you haven't said yes to his proposal."

"Why would I say no?"

"You didn't marry the other ones."

"None of them asked me, but my Afghan can't wait."

"And haven't you wondered why?"

Disconcerted, Marcelle felt silent.

Mademoiselle Beauvert rose to her full height, filled with the importance of what she was about to say. "Hasn't it occurred to you that your Afghan might be after something?"

"After what? I don't have anything."

"You have one thing he values."

"A roof over my head?"

"A nationality. He'll get it by marrying you, and then he'll have the right to remain here."

"Of course, why not?"

"My dear Marcelle, you're so naïve. Aren't you worried he's marrying you to escape his country of origin, to stop being illegal, to put an end to his uncertain status, to obtain a residence permit?"

"I don't like what you're saying."

"I'm saying it because I'm fond of you, Marcelle. But I can assure you that I won't be the only one coming to the same conclusion: as soon as your banns are published, Social Services will come here to Place d'Arezzo and start investigating."

"What?"

"In every town hall in Brussels, there are civil servants looking out for sham marriages."

"A sham marriage? You're joking! My Afghan and I haven't waited to get married before—"

"A sham marriage doesn't mean an unconsummated marriage, but a marriage contracted just to obtain papers. The investigators will want to know if your Afghan has paid you to marry him."

"Paid me? No, I'm the one paying for everything, he doesn't have a cent."

"They'll wonder about his motives. Remember he's twenty years younger than you. That doesn't exactly suggest he's genuine."

"Excuse me?"

"I'm telling you what other people will think, not what I think, because I know you attract lots of men. Let me give you a hint of your immediate future: Social Services are going to pour dirt on your relationship, depict your partner as a crook and you as a fool."

"My God!"

"It'll be painful, Marcelle. You're strong. But he has nobody apart from you."

"My Afghan—"

The doorbell rang.

The two women froze, unable to switch their attention immediately.

The doorbell rang again.

Marcelle grimaced. "All right, I'll get the door. It's time for me to go to Madame Martel's, anyway." She handed Mademoiselle Beauvert the earthenware dish. "Here. I'll carry on tomorrow."

As usual, she was abandoning the apartment halfway through her chores.

A few moments later, she admitted Ève to the living room. "Here's your visitor, Mademoiselle."

"Thank you, Marcelle, I'll see you tomorrow."

Marcelle looked Ève up and down, noting the perfect tan, the slender waist, the impressive cleavage. Nostrils flared, senses on the alert, ready for a fight, she was weighing up a rival. Then she saw the six-inch heels, gave them a look of contempt, shrugged, and left the room.

"What a nice apartment!" Ève exclaimed.

"Before you look around, let me explain my situation." Mademoiselle Beauvert hesitated before continuing. There was an emotion stirring inside her, making her feel vulnerable. She walked over to Copernicus and took him out of his cage. The parrot gratefully rubbed himself against her. His tenderness restored her courage. "I've met a man and we've fallen in love."

"That's wonderful!" Ève said, meaning it.

"Only, he lives in Boston, so I have to part with all I have here. The furniture, the apartment . . . It's a pity, but I'm prepared to take the risk!"

"You're quite right."

The parrot started squawking, "Sergio! Sergio!"

Mademoiselle Beauvert leaned toward him and whispered, "No, darling, not Sergio." She raised her head. "How much do you think I would get?" she asked anxiously.

"For what?"

"My apartment. You're a realtor, right?"

"You live in the golden triangle of Brussels, where the price per square foot is at its highest. Plus, you overlook Place d'Arezzo."

"How much?" Mademoiselle Beauvert insisted.

"Let me look around and I'll tell you."

"Go ahead. I'll wait here."

Mademoiselle Beauvert's heart wasn't in it; good as she was at pretending, she could no longer summon up the energy. This past weekend, which she claimed she had spent abroad like all the others, she had gone to the casino in Liège, sixty miles away, and lost an astronomical sum. Her inheritance had been swallowed by her gambling debts, and she didn't have a cent left, no securities portfolio, no life insurance, no cash savings, no gold in a safe—nothing! As for her jewels, she had pledged them long ago. Now her banker was refusing a loan. All she had left was this apartment and its contents. If she didn't do something quickly, the bailiffs would come in, seize her furniture, and auction it all off.

While Ève was valuing the property, Mademoiselle Beauvert, the parrot on her shoulder, returned to her writing desk and took the form from the Ministry of the Interior she had filled in that morning and now only had to sign in order to be banned from all the casinos in the country.

I don't care, I'll go to Lille, a voice inside her whispered.

The thought frightened her. Would she never stop? Would a demon drive her to lose more in an attempt to win?

She signed quickly, as if her life depended on it, slipped the letter into an envelope, and sealed it. She would mail it on the way out. This decision relaxed her temporarily, like the way you feel when you have an infection and have just swallowed your first antibiotic pill.

The parrot leaped onto her desk and came toward her,

dancing from leg to leg, then suddenly lowered his wings and regurgitated his seeds into the palm of her hand.

"No, Copernicus, no. You mustn't give me your meal. Even if I have nothing left, my darling . . . "

She rubbed the bird's belly with her index finger, and he, eyes aflame, offered himself to her, emitting sharp trills.

Ève came back and announced that, in her opinion, the property could sell for a million euros.

Mademoiselle Beauvert froze: one million euros was the sum she owed. What would she live on?

"Banco!" she cried.

It was the word she always used when she was very scared.

7

L udo was aware of the ambush as soon as he walked into the room: four young women with heady perfumes and arched backs, sitting on the edge of the couch, drinking tea, and talking with the slowness imparted by a clear, sunny afternoon.

"Ludo, my dear!"

Claudine feigned astonishment—even though she had urged him to arrive at 5:15 sharp. With a brief gesture, she motioned him to come in and turned back to her guests, eager that they should take advantage of this surprise. "This is my son, Ludovic."

The women stood up, awkwardly. Introductions were made, and they smiled and pecked each other on the cheek— except for Ludo and his mother—to show that they were young and relaxed. When Ludo accepted the cup of Darjeeling, the redhead cried, "Ah, at last, a man who drinks tea!"

"With my mother, it's impossible to escape the ritual."

This amused the women, although Claudine gave her son a dirty look, knowing full well what he was alluding to: for years now, she had been joining all kinds of clubs and associations with the sole aim of meeting young women she could then introduce to her son at a supposedly impromptu tea party. How many activities had she already tried out, even though she had no talent for handicraft? Cross-stitching, painting on silk, crocheting, pottery, mosaics, marquetry, origami, and flower arranging had been followed by sportier practices, such as yoga, bodybuilding, African dance, Pilates, and aqua gym, not forgetting language courses—she only ever chose languages with a future, Chinese, Russian, Portuguese, Korean, thinking they would provide her with more dynamic characters. Having noticed her son's chronic solitude, she had seen it as her duty to find the perfect woman for him and introduce them. At first, she had chosen carefully, subjecting her recruits to a thorough investigation. Over time, her energy sapped by a series of failures, she had become less selective and would just round up all the pleasant single women she could find.

"How did you all meet?" Ludovic asked.

"Guess," one of them said.

"Are you a rock band?"

The women laughed.

"A troupe of acrobats?"

They laughed again.

"A church choir?"

They all made reproachful faces.

"We attend the same bum and tum classes," Claudine explained.

Ludovic nodded respectfully, refraining from commenting on the effect of those classes on the behinds displayed around him. Thinking he knew one of them, a splendid peroxide blonde, he leaned toward her and asked if they had met before. When Ève told him she lived on Place d'Arezzo, Ludo realized who she was and decided to take revenge on his mother.

Within a second, he had changed completely. As if rooted to the spot, he focused his eyes and conversation on this one woman, paying no further attention to the others. Although the guests were at first amused by Ludo's interest in Ève, they soon felt humiliated by his attitude, Ludo having become deaf and blind to their presence.

Claudine, though, was overjoyed: after so many years, she

had finally succeeded! Ludo was falling in love. Her maternal heart throbbed with so much emotion that she stopped talking to her three other guests, who, feeling as if they were merely window dressing, cleared their throats and exchanged weary looks.

As for Ève, she was nonchalant and pensive, seemingly quite unaware of anything. Free despite being monopolized by Ludo, replying sparingly to his volley of questions, she was daydreaming and only pretending to be there. Not only was she not interested in the young man, she didn't even realize the stir she was causing and responded to his flirting out of mere politeness.

It was she who, getting a text message on her phone, suddenly stood up, blushing, and said that she had an appointment. Relieved, the three other young women got up in unison, showered Claudine with thanks, and escaped as quickly as they could.

Alone with her son, Claudine was unable to hold back for more than thirty seconds. Blushing with happiness, she cried, "Tell me if I've gone mad, but I have a feeling you like Ève."

Ludo shrugged. "How can any man resist her? Anyone would fall head over heels in love with her."

"What has she got that the others haven't?"

"Mom, I'm ashamed of you. Didn't you see her? Didn't you hear her husky voice? Didn't you notice her modesty, her simplicity? Didn't you grasp that she goes to all the best plays and concerts in town? She isn't a woman, she's a pearl, a treasure."

"I've never seen you so bowled over."

Ludo nearly lost it at this point and had to adjust a lampshade so that he could turn away. But then he continued teasing his mother. "There's no point in dreaming. A woman like that isn't interested in a man like me."

"Why not?" Claudine cried indignantly.

"Did you see her? And have you seen me? We're like Beauty and the Beast."

"I forbid you to speak like that about my son. Life isn't just about beauty. There's also—"

"What? I'm not Croesus, and I'm not Einstein."

"Stop putting yourself down. If that young woman had wanted to, she would already have married Croesus or Einstein. And yet she's single."

"And how does that make me more desirable?"

"It means there's still a possibility."

"You're out of your mind."

Claudine was excited by the challenge. She wanted to prove to her son that, having introduced him to the love of his life, she was going to make sure he married her.

To put the finishing touches to his performance, he said, "Look, Mom, if I thought for a fraction of a second that it was possible for me to marry that woman, I'd say yes without the slightest hesitation."

Claudine rubbed her hands, like a woman congratulating herself on sealing a successful business deal.

By the door, just as he was leaving, Ludo frowned. "It might be a good idea to get some information about her . . . "

"I'll take care of it, darling."

"I think . . . who was it? . . . someone told me about Ève . . . Who could it have been? . . . let's see . . . Oh, that's right, it was your friend Xavière!"

"Xavière the florist?"

"Yes."

"You're right. Xavière knows everything about everybody. I'll call her right away."

"Thanks, Mom."

"It's so rare to hear you thank me, darling."

"I needed the opportunity. Now I'm counting on you. Promise?"

"Promise! Your Mom will sort out your girlfriend."

Ludo left with a show of joy, like a man in love who wants to dance. In truth, he was joyful because he'd so enjoyed the trick he'd played on his mother.

Back in his apartment, he couldn't resist the temptation to check if Fiordiligi had written to him.

A message had arrived an hour earlier:

> Our relationship is so perfect and so complete that I don't want to break it up. Why take the risk of seeing each other when we get along so well?

He typed:

> Dear Soul Mate, you have so many faults, you are so seductively awkward, that I long to meet you.

Much to his surprise, she replied immediately:

> You might not like me.

Amused, he decided to start a conversation:

> What do you know about my taste in looks? What do I know about them myself?

> I'm sure you love blondes.

Ludovic smiled, thinking about the act he'd put on to Ève in front of his mother.

> Real ones or fake ones?

> Fake ones, those who think they ought to have been blonde.

Dear Fiordiligi, why not come out with it and say I like sluts?

You'd be the first man not to like them!

He thought this over for a few seconds.

Fiordiligi, do you look like a slut?

The reply arrived, as quick as lightning:

No.

How would you describe your style?

Old lady.

What do you mean?

People wonder where I buy my shapeless sweaters, my pleated skirts, my embroidered jerseys, and my printed blouses.

Grungy old lady, then?

Yes. What about you?

Non-grungy old man.

The thick sweater and loose jeans type?

Add spotless but overlarge boxers.

I love it.

Why?

It's amazing at a time when men are as vain as women. It's not sexually correct.

I don't think I'm trying to be rebellious or to stand out from the crowd. Basically, I just don't care.

Stop showing off, you're driving me crazy. What about shoes?

The same style since I was fifteen, solid, round suede shoes with crepe soles. I keep several specimens in reserve. The day they stop manufacturing them, I'll cut off my legs. What about you?

A closet full of colored pumps. My feet are the only part of me I see all day long, so I look after them and dress them with care.

Iron tips on the soles so as not to damage them?

Of course. I love the sound they make. I feel like the school supervisor who screams at the kids. It fuels my sadism.

Stop it, Fiordiligi, you're getting me excited. I love your style: at ease with your own absurdity. It's so attractive!

All right, I'm going to leave you now, you naughty boy. I have better things to do than please you.

Ludovic looked at his watch and decided to go to the pool. He loved swimming—one of his few healthy habits. Even though he practiced on a regular basis, he didn't have the physique of a swimmer, far from it. He still looked like a piece of cardboard, with no muscle emerging from under his white skin. It didn't matter. All he needed to do to protect himself from sarcastic remarks was to keep this activity more secret than if he was indulging in something shameful and go to the pool at times when he didn't risk bumping into anyone.

At this time of day, when the building was only open to schoolchildren, he would keep to the lane reserved for regulars.

Once he had shut himself in the locker room, he smiled at the fresh, stimulating, unerotic smell of bleach. He slipped on his dark blue swimming trunks, which were neither tight nor revealing, and went into the shower room, where he liked the white tiles, the overheated air, the sugary scents of shampoo. It was a place where the atmosphere wavered between the clinical and the cosmetic.

Finally, he came out into the pool area, taking care to avoid the footbath, a microbe-breeding puddle he found disgusting. He looked at the kids splashing each other.

The heated water created condensation beneath a dome that dispersed the sounds like hollow echoes, as if words and cries were diffracted by the steam.

The head swimming instructor, a man with chiseled pectorals, gave him an unfriendly look. Never having understood the reason for his recurrent hostility, Ludo had concluded that it was an expression of the hatred felt by the handsome for the ugly, the champion for the loser. The instructor was certainly athletic, with his broad shoulders, his narrow hips, and his prominent spindle-shaped muscles from the tibia to the trapezium. At the same time, what Ludo found fascinating was the man's gait: although slim, he would trudge along in tight wooden sandals, swinging one shoulder, then the other, leaning on his left leg before transferring his weight to the right, like a giant exhausted after some marathon or other. Seeing him move so slowly, majestically, and awkwardly, you felt he was making an effort better suited to a heavier, thicker, larger body than his, carrying around a huge, invisible carcass that impaired his movements.

Ludo entered the water and moved to the accessible narrow lane. In order to avoid the kids, he tried to go quickly, but couldn't. He suddenly grasped why the instructor moved the way he did: he walked on dry land as if he was in the water, pushing the air aside like heavy liquid.

Ludovic put on his cap and goggles and, confident that he now looked like a fly, began doing his lengths. He swam without style, but he always swam for a long time.

Today, though, he found it impossible to go beyond that five-minute point after which the heart muscle adapts to continuous effort; his heartbeat was irregular, refusing to adopt a steady rhythm. Accustomed to such rebellion, Ludo decided to come out, breathe, and start all over again once he had caught his breath.

He heaved himself up the ladder, recovering bar by bar the pounds the water had relieved him of. Light as a jellyfish in the pool, he weighed his full one hundred and eighty pounds on the tiled floor.

Absentmindedly, he walked in the direction of the small pool. A thin, bony father with muscles like ropes was dealing with his little girl. She hated water, but he didn't seem to care. Because she screamed at the slightest splash, and cried when forced to go further into the water, the father lost his patience and slapped her.

Stunned, she stopped crying.

Feeling he had taken an important step, her father pushed her back down into the water. She started screaming again. He gave her two loud slaps. This time, in a state of shock, the child fell silent.

When she recovered, she moaned, and received four slaps.

The scene verged on the absurd: the slaps would mechanically eliminate the sobs. The man just kept hitting her, as if he had forgotten there was a human being taking the blows.

Ludo made up his mind to intervene. He opened his mouth, but no sound came out. He ordered his body to get up: nothing moved. The walls spun, and he collapsed and rolled on the floor. Even when he came to a stop, he was unable to move or make a sound.

He could no longer hear clearly what was going on, whether or not the man was still hitting the child, or if his actions had triggered a response. Everything had suddenly frozen. Ludo was receiving blurred visual sensations—shapeless colors—and even more blurred perceptions of sound—a kind of cathedral acoustic that blurred the origin of the echo.

How long did this paralysis last?

They were shouting at him . . . hands were touching him . . . there was an insistent rumbling, which grew sharper and finally became words. "Monsieur? Monsieur? Are you all right, monsieur?"

He realized that his dizzy spell had been noticed, and that he was being taken care of.

They laid him on his back: he saw the face of the instructor, who was the one asking him questions. Ludo lay there, eyes wide open, unable to reply.

They put a blanket over his body. Firefighters arrived. They slid him onto a stretcher and carried him to a room away from the pools. There, he had the impression he was regaining his hearing. They placed a mask over his face and told him to take a deep breath. The dose of oxygen refreshed him, and his muscles relaxed. Life was returning. He smiled.

He was told to keep breathing deeply. The rescuers stood aside.

Ludo heard the instructor talking to the firefighters. "He fainted as he got out of the water."

"Does he come here regularly?"

"The pedophile? Yes, he's a regular. He's a lousy swimmer, but he can swim for a long time."

"Why do you call him the pedophile?"

"My colleagues and I call him that because he only ever comes at the same time as the schoolkids."

"Has he ever . . . ?"

"No, never. Still, you must admit it's a bit odd to pick the time when children are in the pool and making a hell of a racket. I can't help thinking . . . Anyway, we keep an eye on him. That's why I immediately noticed he wasn't feeling well . . . "

Lying on the stretcher, drugged by the shot of oxygen, Ludo felt like laughing. Now he knew why the instructors always gave him those stern, inquisitive looks when he got close to the pools: they thought he was a pedophile! Him! He never even looked at children. He considered himself a child who had grown up by mistake.

The firefighters turned to him. "Monsieur, can you hear us? Blink if you can hear us."

Ludovic obediently blinked.

"Can you talk?"

Ludovic thought it was an illusion, but he heard himself say, in a battered voice, "No, I . . . Yes."

"What happened, monsieur?"

His eyes filled with tears. Ludovic suddenly saw the picture of the little girl being hit by her father, his reaction, his powerlessness. No, he wouldn't answer the question.

"Could I have . . . a little bit of oxygen?"

The firefighters exchanged dubious glances, worried they might be dealing with a drug addict, even if only an oxygen addict; one of them took the gas cylinder, put the mask on Ludo, and gave him a dose.

A feeling of bliss swept over Ludovic, a sense of utter

contentment, followed by an epiphany: the reason his life was a disaster was because of his childhood.

Like the little girl, he had been beaten as a child. An adult had used violence against him, and he hadn't understood why. There was just one certainty: whenever his father appeared, there were blows. After the beating came the worst part: the kisses of remorse. Having slapped him until he had bruises, his father would feel so guilty, he would smother him in kisses. Ludovic as he was now was descended from that child. The reason he couldn't bear being touched was because his father had connected physical contact with violence. And since his mother never touched him, he doubted that a body could be anything but a place that was brutally invaded by other people's moods and bad habits. His parents had stifled him, and hadn't helped him to bloom.

Ludo wept and at the same time burst out laughing: he was a hopeless case. The firefighters saw this paradox as the effect of the oxygen, and decided to leave.

Ludovic slowly returned home. He felt a happy kind of weariness.

On the way, he discovered from his phone that his mother had called him some twenty times. He listened to the lengthy message she had made up her mind to leave:

"Ludo, since you're not picking up, I shan't use kid gloves, I'm going to tell you the truth. Too bad if it hurts. I'm sorry to have to tell you this, but you must never again give that woman any thought. I forbid you to see her. You see, Ludo, there's a limit. I spoke to Xavière: this Ève is a . . . how shall I put it? . . . she's a . . . I'm just repeating Xavière's words . . . she's a whore! There, I've said it. She's a kept woman. Kept by rich lovers, and she has lots of them. I didn't believe it at first, but then Xavière provided details. Yes, you're right, the woman's charming, but we know how she uses her charms! So there it is, Ludo: don't even say hello to her if you see her. And to think that I introduced her to you! It gives me the shivers . . . In any case, from what I gathered, you're not old enough or rich enough for her. So spare yourself the heartache. I hope you're not angry with me, darling. Call me. I'm still your mom."

Ludo smiled. His plan had worked out just as he'd expected. His mother was feeling guilty for introducing her son to the devil, a remorse that would eat away at her for two or three weeks and put introductions to other potential girlfriends on the back burner. At least that was something . . .

Back home, almost without thinking, he sat down at his desk and wrote:

Dear Fiordiligi, we must say goodbye. My case remains hopeless. I was prepared to commit to you because I knew we would never meet. I knew I would raise the temperature then vanish into the digital ether. What I love about the Internet is its immateriality. And yet what pains me in my own life is my immateriality.

Please let's break off all contact. My only strengths lie in my mind. I experience feelings through books. I experience sex on a screen. Yes, even my memories of love don't belong to me, they're other people's memories. I'll never leave this virtual prison.

What is a lie? The truth we wish for, the reality we don't experience. There's nothing more genuine than my deception. When I said I wanted us to meet by a lake, I knew that would never happen, and yet I longed for it deeply. When I imagined a life with you, I was summoning up an impossibility that appealed to me. In other words, the Ludovic who made promises was the perfect Ludovic. The one who will never keep his promises is the real Ludovic. Our correspondence was nurtured by my desire for the best. What is more moral than mystification, since it involves an ideal?

There is nothing more generous than a lie. Nothing more petty than reality.

Alas, I realize that what is best about me will always be ethereal. Something keeps me trapped in my mediocrity—the past, no doubt. I can't seem to overcome my victim status—the victim of a father's violence, the victim of a mother's tactlessness.

Dear Fiordiligi, I shall stop this lament now. Rereading what I've just written, I feel as if I'm presenting myself as a martyr, when in fact I'm nothing but a loser.

Having said that, wouldn't it be even worse not to justify oneself?

Forgive me. Goodbye.

Ludo pressed *send* without any sense of relief. He felt nothing anymore.

Exhausted, he went into the kitchen, took out the most harmful foods he could find—chips and chocolate—and started munching them alternately, washing it all down with a slightly acid soda.

When he came back into the living room, he saw from the window blinking on his screen that Fiordiligi had already replied. He read out loud:

Ludo, dear, I got your message and realized how unhappy your father and I made you. I'm getting in my car and I'll be right over.

The blood drained from Ludo's face. "Mother?"

8

O n Place d'Arezzo, Tom and Nathan headed for the Bidermanns' town house. There seemed to be a flurry of activity there: limousines dropping off visitors, others picking up those who were leaving, the whole thing coordinated by diligent chauffeurs in black suits and a regal-looking employee at the top of the steps. The two men gazed at the solemn façade blending brickwork and stone with pompous regularity, the ostentatiously ornate wrought-iron balconies, the gutters embellished with animal gargoyles; from the sidewalk, they caught a glimpse, through the tall windows, of chandeliers, woodwork, gilding, even the top parts of the frames of monumental paintings, and were astonished to realize that ceilings in themselves could testify to the wealth inside. A poor person's ceiling, in comparison, was white and bare, with a lightbulb hanging at the end of a twisted wire . . .

Feeling suddenly intimidated, they hesitated. Nathan leaned toward Tom. "I'm not going there. They'll think we're Jehovah's Witnesses."

Tom looked at Nathan's outfit: plum-colored pants, pointed shoes, a fuchsia-colored imitation lizardskin jacket. "No, I don't think they will."

Nathan turned his back on the building and murmured very quickly, "Here or anywhere else, can you imagine ringing someone's bell and asking if they've received an anonymous letter?" In his hands, he had the yellow sheets of papers that had been sent to them.

"They may be pleased to find out they weren't the only ones," Tom replied.

"Pleased? You think so? When everybody interpreted the message in their own way, when everybody changed their lives after getting that letter?"

"Don't exaggerate."

"I'm not, Tom. Just look at us: we haven't been apart since, first because each of us thought the note came from the other one, and then because, once we realized our mistake, we decided to discover who it was from."

"If it's enriched our lives, there's nothing to regret."

"But who's to say it's been the same for our neighbors? A message like that could lead to a disaster."

"A love letter? I don't see how—"

"A love letter can be intolerable when you don't want it."

"Everybody wants love."

"Bullshit! Lots of people shy away from love. They live more easily without it. Most of the time, although they might agree to receive it, they don't particularly want to give it. Love can be destabilizing, a breach in the wall of selfishness, the fall of a citadel, the death of a regime: there's another being who's more important than you! What a disaster! That breach could let in altruism and change the inner balance."

"You're crazy!"

"Do you want proof that love is intolerable?"

"Go on."

"Well, there's the story of a nice young man, unmarried, who gives up his job as a carpenter in order to travel around and tell people that God loves them and that they should love one another. And this guy practices what he preaches: he heals lepers, he gives their sight back to the blind, he brings his pal Lazarus back to life, he stops a wretched woman from being stoned to death because she slept with another bearded guy who wasn't her husband, and a lot more besides. Miracles, parables, all kinds of good acts, they're all on Jesus's program. And what does he get for it? He's only thirty-three when they arrest him because they can't stand any more of him, they give him a bogus trial, then nail him to a plank of wood. Quite a reward! Not surprising there aren't many people who want to follow in his footsteps. You'd have to be a saint to play at being Jesus after that."

"What are you trying to prove, Brother Nathan?"

"That love is like dynamite, it's revolutionary. That people who talk about love seem like terrorists in a society ruled by the Internet and governed by fear. That the anonymous letter couldn't have brought only happiness. We aren't living in a fairy tale!"

Tom put calming hands on Nathan's shoulders. "You're talking crazy because you're scared to ring Zachary Bidermann's doorbell."

"You ring."

"I'm scared too."

"There you are!" Nathan clicked his fingers, as if Tom's admission of defeat meant his own victory.

The door opened and a woman came out, wearing a severe-looking off-white pantsuit. Tom's face lit up. "We're saved!" He rushed to greet the newcomer at the bottom of the steps. "Madame Singer, what a surprise!"

She looked at Tom and smiled. "Monsieur Berger! I'd forgotten you live on Place d'Arezzo."

"The most amazing place in the world, if you ask me. Madame Singer, this is perfect timing, because I'm conducting an investigation. Only, I wouldn't like to bother Monsieur Bidermann. Perhaps you could help me?"

She frowned, ready to defend her boss. "Yes?"

"All right. Several people who live here have received anonymous letters. We need to determine who they were sent to, so that we can investigate further and find out who wrote them." He held out the two yellow letters. "Have Monsieur Bidermann or Madame Bidermann received anything like this?"

Madame Singer reluctantly took the papers and glanced at them skeptically. A grimace of disapproval crossed her face. "I don't deal with Madame's mail," she said, returning the letters. "I think Monsieur Bidermann did receive a similar envelope. I didn't read what was in it, but I noticed the ludicrous color. He didn't say anything to me about it."

"Thank you, Madame Singer. You've been really helpful."

She nodded, sorry that she had divulged an element of her professional life. "Even so, I think that message is harmless enough."

A couple of yards behind Tom, Nathan, who had been listening to the conversation, couldn't help saying, "That's what everyone thinks at first!"

Surprised to see him suddenly pop up, Madame Singer looked at his outfit, sighed, and walked off resolutely. "Have a good day, gentlemen."

Amused, Nathan walked up to Tom. "The sergeant major's a dyke, isn't she? If she isn't a dyke, then I'm Saint Bernadette. How do you know her?"

"I taught three of her children at high school. Go back to your cave, Bernadette."

"Let's not get sidetracked. We have confirmation of another anonymous letter. Let's go ask Marcelle."

"Marcelle?"

"The concierge at Number 18."

Tom was surprised by this sudden spurt of energy. "You didn't dare ring Zachary Bidermann's bell, and now you're going to bother a concierge? That's social contempt."

Nathan shrugged as they walked toward the building. "First, it's a concierge's job to be bothered. Second, the Arezzo dragon doesn't talk, she barks, and bites before thinking. If you had a clearer idea of the aggressive mastiff concealed under those unbelievable print dresses, you'd realize that right now I'm demonstrating remarkable courage in order to advance our investigation. Now, Tom, shut up and put on your crash helmet: I'm going to introduce you to Marcelle."

They walked into the lobby and knocked on the glass door, which was hidden by a pleated curtain.

"Hello, Marcelle, it's Nathan."

The door creaked and Marcelle appeared, looking haggard. Her eyelids were swollen, and she was holding a damp handkerchief. She glanced at Nathan, recognized him, came out of her lodge, and burst into tears.

"He's gone."

"Who's gone, Marcelle?"

"My Afghan."

As she sobbed on Nathan's jacket, he explained silently to Tom, with gestures and grimaces, that the Afghan wasn't a dog but a hairy individual who slept with the concierge. Tom found it very hard to stop himself from laughing at Nathan's obscene miming.

After a few sobs, Marcelle pulled away and looked at the two friends as if they had always been her confidants. "We were so happy, me and my Afghan. It's true he did damn all. He wanted us to stay together, and so did I—I just needed to sort out the question of my night table. It's been hunky-dory recently. He proposed marriage, I was about to say yes, when all of a sudden, he disappears."

"Without an explanation?"

"An explanation? He left me a note. 'Thank you,' he'll remember me as an 'angel' and one of the 'kindest' people he's ever met." She pointed an accusing finger, challenging them. "'Kind'—do you think that's the right word when you're leaving your . . . girlfriend?"

"No, 'kind' . . . isn't very kind. Nor is 'angel,' for that matter."

"Ah, Monsieur Nathan, you understand me. You just don't say to a woman you've been . . . well, you know what I mean, even if it's not your kind of thing . . . you don't say to your lover . . . "

Her eyes glistened at "lover." This time, she'd found the right word.

" . . . You don't say to your lover, 'Thank you, you've been very kind.' No, not to your lover."

Nathan recoiled with a shudder. "Marcelle," he butted in, "you've got it wrong."

"Excuse me?"

"Don't forget that your . . . your . . . what was his name again?"

"Ghuncha Gul," she whispered, wiping away a tear.

"Your Ghuncha Gul didn't speak French very well. So what he wrote to you probably got lost in translation. I'm sure that in Afghan you don't—"

"There's no such language as Afghan, he spoke Pashtun," Marcelle corrected him, which proved to Tom that she knew a lot more than she seemed to.

"In Pashtun," Nathan continued authoritatively, "these words don't have the same connotations, Marcelle. 'Thank you' and 'kind' might be delightful in Pashtun. They might be the most beautiful words in the language. As for 'angel,' that speaks for itself."

Marcelle stopped and thought this over, tempted by the idea. She was suffering less now. There was a gleam in her eyes. "Come in and have a drink," she commanded.

Tom was about to protest, but Nathan interrupted him. "We'd be delighted."

They walked into the lodge, which was cluttered with knickknacks.

"Sit wherever you like," she cried, indicating the only couch, a two-seater. She took a sticky bottle from a cupboard.

"Would you like some Guignolet? That's all I have, anyway. It's cherry liqueur." Without waiting for an answer, she filled some glasses and sat down opposite them on a stool she had miraculously pulled out from under the table.

"Cheers, then!"

"Cheers!"

"What shall we drink to?"

"Let's drink to the old saying, Marcelle."

"What old saying?"

"There are plenty more fish in the sea."

It seemed to Tom that Nathan had gone too far this time, but to his surprise, far from taking offense, Marcelle burst into a big, fat laugh.

"You exaggerate, Monsieur Nathan. Plenty more Afghans in my bed! He's so funny!"

She closed her eyes, doubled up with laughter on her three-legged stool, sipping her fortified wine.

Nathan took advantage of this to nudge Tom with his elbow: he indicated, with a movement of his eyes, a yellow envelope on the shelf where Marcelle kept her infrequent mail.

A few glasses later, they left the lodge, exhausted.

Nathan suggested they continue their investigation upstairs, especially since he knew several people by sight, among them a charming, quite funny old girl, Mademoiselle something . . . what was it again?

At that moment, three men approached and knocked brusquely on the concierge's door. "Which floor is Mademoiselle Beauvert on?"

"Third," Marcelle replied.

"Is she in?"

"Yes."

Marcelle closed her door and the men went up the stairs.

As they disappeared, Nathan whispered in Tom's ear, "This doesn't look good."

"What do you mean?"

"I recognized the leader of those three goons: he's a bailiff my firm used to collect a debt. I don't know what poor Mademoiselle Beauvert has done."

"Don't be so dramatic. A bailiff could simply be delivering a court document."

"Not when there are several of them. That's more likely to be an eviction or an inventory."

Prudently, they left, as if it was dangerous to remain in a building where a tragedy was about to unfold.

Having crossed the street, they decided to remain under the trees for a while. The conversation between Nathan and Marcelle had exhausted Tom: the way they jumped from pathos to bawdiness was quite disconcerting. He needed a dose of silence.

Instead, they had to suffer the racket being made by the parrots. What was going on in the branches? The macaws and cockatoos weren't talking but screaming. A tempest of sounds tore through the branches, sharp, piercing, strident, a tumultuous din that assaulted their ears.

And yet, paradoxically, this confusion gave them a sense of well-being, because it was so healthy, so alive, so joyous, so shambolic. The cacophony created harmony. Just as seeing a bird that's more colorful than a rainbow gives you a feeling of joy, the bright, sharp sounds of these birds conveyed a sense of glee.

When they had calmed down, Tom summed up the situation. "So that's you, me, Victor, the florist, the aristocrat, Zachary Bidermann, and the concierge. Seven people received this note. What do they all have in common? They live on Place d'Arezzo. First clue: somewhere in this area, there's someone who wishes his or her neighbors well. Second clue:

this person is good, kind, and generous, which rather narrows down the field of investigation."

"It wipes out the field completely. People like that don't exist."

"Who was it who mentioned Jesus Christ and the saints earlier?"

Nathan looked at him. "All right, let's say it was a dove, a Cupid who wrote to us. How do we find him?"

Just then, a man who looked about twenty-five came strolling easily and nimbly along the path, singing joyfully to himself. Tom and Nathan interrupted their conversation until he had gone.

"Tempting," Nathan said. "Where did he spring from?"

"Cheerful, too," Tom agreed.

They breathed. Nathan turned to his lover. "Tell me, Tom Berger, you look as hot as a French fry stall. Am I to deduce that when I start living with you, you'll cheat on me?"

"Or maybe you'll cheat on me, Nathan Sinclair, because, if you noticed, I wasn't the one who was struck dumb when that cutie appeared."

"OK. Only, I'll set a condition: do whatever you like but be discreet and never tell me about it."

"I promise."

"I promise too."

Silence.

Tom gently took Nathan's hand. "You know, Nathan, I'd rather not cheat on you."

Nathan looked at him, moved. "That's a lovely declaration. I like it." Misty-eyed, he smiled at the parrots. "It's what we should say at a wedding. Instead of making promises we can't keep, we should just say, 'I'd rather not cheat on you.'" He raised Tom's hand to his mouth and kissed it. "Why do people cheat on each other so much, Tom?"

"The real question is: why are people obliged to make promises they can't keep? Why go against human nature?

Why do men and women imagine they're something they're not?"

"It's about a sense of the ideal. We aren't animals. At least I'm not."

"You're confusing a sense of the ideal with the negation of biology. Just like the parrots and parakeets over our heads, we're driven by impulses that are stronger than us, and more numerous than we'd like, into directions they—not we—choose. Infidelity is natural, whereas we stop being natural the moment we take a vow of frustration."

"It doesn't matter. I'd rather not cheat on you."

"Neither would I, Nathan."

They sighed with relief.

Three people emerged from Avenue Molière onto the square. Tom squeezed Nathan's hand. "Do you see what I see?"

The gardeners, Hippolyte and Germain, followed by Isis, were bringing their equipment onto the square. Nathan thought that Tom was pointing out Hippolyte. "Please, give me a break! You whisper words of love, and a second later you get excited by the first stud that comes along."

"I don't mean him, you idiot!"

"What? You're not eyeing up the handsomest guy in Brussels?"

"No, I'm talking about our investigation."

Nathan made a sign to indicate that he couldn't quite follow.

"Would you agree that those gardeners often come to this square, and that they're part of the area?"

Nathan turned to look at the two men, who were lining up their tools on the lawn while Isis sat on a bench, engrossed in her book. It was a scene he had witnessed dozens of times over the past few years, so he nodded.

"And do you remember what Dany Davon said when we

were at Faustina's? That writers of anonymous letters are individuals who are alienated from society because they're different, sometimes deformed."

"The dwarf?"

"Exactly."

They looked at Germain in a new light. He was smiling as he raked the gravel.

"How shall we go about it?" Tom said.

"Elementary, my dear Watson: the sandbox method."

"Meaning?"

"The child. A female friend assured me that's how you come on to attractive fathers in parks. You make sure your kids are playing together, then you casually start a conversation."

"Brilliant. Have you brought any children with you?"

Nathan got to his feet. "You forget I'm still very much a child."

Nathan walked up to Isis and perfectly naturally began talking to her. Since he had read and loved Kipling's *Just So Stories*, which she was finishing, they started a discussion of the book.

Hippolyte and Germain, having noticed the scene, waved to Nathan and carried on working.

Tom was seething with impatience. Why hadn't he followed Nathan? At this point, it would be difficult for him to join in, especially since he could sometimes feel the gardener's puzzled eyes on the back of his neck. The gardener probably hadn't liked the way he'd flirted with him the other day.

As for Nathan, he was laughing with Isis about the "Bi-Colored-Python-Rock-Snake."

Suddenly, Isis interrupted him. "Why is your friend over there? Did you have an argument?"

"No."

"Tell Tom to join us."

Nathan was startled. "You know his name?"

"Of course. And yours too, Nathan."

"What? That's incredible."

"My name's Isis."

Nathan gave a military salute. "Delighted to meet you, Mademoiselle Isis. How do you know all this?"

"Oh, it's Germain," she replied. "He doesn't talk to anyone, but he knows everybody."

Nathan sank deeper into the bench. His suspicions were confirmed. "Does Germain like coming to Place d'Arezzo?"

"He says it's the most magical place in the world."

"Really?"

"I think so too. What about you?"

"I share your enthusiasm, Mademoiselle Isis." Nathan scratched his head. It seemed to him that a whole lot of clues were emerging. "Could Germain name all the people who live here?"

"I'm sure he could."

Nathan was close to his goal. Risking everything, he took the yellow letters out of his pocket. "Tell me, have you ever seen Germain with a letter or a paper like this?"

The little girl frowned and grew pale. This obviously brought back memories for her.

Nathan gently insisted. "They're wonderful letters, you know. Magical letters that make lots of people happy. Have you ever seen Germain with one of them?"

The child raised her head and looked at Nathan. "Daddy got one."

"Your daddy's the handsome gentleman over there, right?"

She nodded. "He got one, and so did his girlfriend. They didn't speak to each other and it's because of the letters that they met. So I guess my daddy's very happy now."

Nathan nearly cried out for joy. After the clues, he had just discovered the motive: the man had used this trick to make his best friend happy! Germain the dwarf was the Cupid!

9

Paralyzed, Xavière stared at the gynecologist, so astounded that she couldn't think clearly.

Dr. Plassard stood up, came and placed himself in front of her, put one buttock down on the desk, leaned forward, and took her hand. "Come on, cheer up."

He was surprised by how cold Xavière's palm was. All the blood seemed to have drained from her face.

At last, her eyelids fluttered. "That's absurd."

"I'm sure of it: you're pregnant."

Xavière slowly shook her head.

"Xavière," he joked, "you're not going to tell me you've stopped having sexual relations?"

"No, I do still have them."

"There you are, then!"

"With a woman." She looked up at him, suddenly childlike and touchingly helpless. "Is it possible with a woman?"

"Listen, you may be having a relationship with a woman, but you have made love with a man."

"Never! I don't desire men anymore."

"What about your husband?"

"Orion? Oh, no, we haven't done it in a long time. Ten years. It'd disgust me. That's why I no longer use contraception. No point protecting myself from an ectoplasm."

"Well, it isn't an ectoplasm you have in your womb, it's an embryo."

"No!" She sat up straight and gave him a withering look.

"It's impossible, unless you can get pregnant by sitting on a toilet seat or drinking from someone else's glass."

Xavière was denying it with such assurance that the gynecologist was shaken. "Would you like a second opinion? Would you like me to send you to see a colleague of mine?"

"No."

"Xavière, you're refusing to face facts."

"No."

"I tell you you're pregnant, but you don't want to listen because you're convinced I'm making a mistake."

"It's obvious you got it all wrong."

"Well, if you're so sure of yourself, go to see my colleague to make sure I'm talking nonsense."

"All right, I will. And I hope you'll feel ashamed of yourself!"

Dr. Plassard went back to his seat, grabbed a sheet of paper, scribbled an address, and handed it to her. "Please be aware I'm not upset."

"This was all I needed. I come about menopause and I leave pregnant. Talk about customer service!"

Three days later, the second gynecologist confirmed the opinion of the first. This time, Xavière accepted the verdict. As he saw her out, the doctor advised her to go back to his colleague Plassard.

"You can tell him whether or not you want to keep the child. But don't delay. You don't have much time left to make the decision."

These words totally threw Xavière. Once the door had closed behind her, she stood there on the landing, unable to breathe. *The child?* She placed her hand on her belly . . . With that expression, her pregnancy stopped being a sickness, a series of dizzy spells and feelings of discomfort, and became something much worse, something insane: there was a human being inside her. She didn't just have a bellyache, she was carrying a baby.

The very thought of it struck her as intolerable. She retraced her steps and hammered on the door with her fists.

The doctor's secretary opened up, astonished by this racket.

"I want it taken out immediately!" Xavière screamed.

"I beg your pardon, madame?"

Trying to force her way in, Xavière started scratching the secretary, who was barring the entrance; fortunately, the gynecologist, alerted by the noise, arrived immediately and grabbed Xavière by the shoulder.

"Follow me."

Too late: she threw up on the waiting room carpet.

Once back in the consulting room, she screamed, as if a complete stranger had suddenly taken up residence inside her, "You have to take it out! I can't bear the thought of this thing squatting in me!"

"We'll do whatever you decide, madame, but in the meantime you won't get rid of it by throwing up."

She scratched her abdomen. "This little alien is going to get bigger and make itself at home, it's going to tear my skin, pull my guts to pieces. If it isn't flushed away, I'm going to crack." She brought her face threateningly close to the doctor's. "Where did it come from? I haven't slept with any men."

"Yes, my colleague did mention that on the telephone, so I did a bit of checking. Reproducing without a male is called parthenogenesis."

"Oh!"

"It only occurs in plants and reptiles, not in mammals. Except perhaps—although some scientists dispute this—in female rabbits."

"Female rabbits? That's nice, thanks very much."

The doctor tried to regain her attention. "Do you mind telling me why you've never had children before?"

"Children are like television: not compulsory. None of us are forced to ruin our lives."

"I'm trying to understand you."

Xavière started sobbing. "What's happening to me?"

"Don't worry. Your body is undergoing hormonal changes that affect your emotional state. Cry as much as you like, but then try to explain, if you can."

In a whining tone, a handkerchief in her hand, Xavière began her story. In spite of her tears, there was anger in her eyes. "I never wanted children because I suffered too much when I was a child. I had a strict family, and I was bored. It seemed to me that if I also brought a baby into the world, I'd be condemning it to the same torture, and it'd be just as impatient to come of age and leave as I was."

"You may be wrong, but you're perfectly entitled to think that way."

Surprised by how indulgently he was treating her, Xavière sniffed, encouraged. "I married a man who's useless and irresponsible."

"In other words, a man you were sure wouldn't make a father."

Xavière had never explained her choice of Orion with such clarity. She nodded pensively.

"Do the two of you often have sexual relations?" the doctor asked.

"I haven't had sex with him in years."

"That makes sense. If he's no longer a lover, there's no chance he'll become a father."

"I've cheated on him with women."

"Another way to protect yourself against pregnancy."

She raised an eyebrow. The doctor's insight opened new perspectives, even though she found it hard to bear the fact that in such a short time a stranger could read her so accurately.

"Basically," he insisted, "you couldn't wait for the

menopause, could you? There was still a woman in you who was able to have children, and you wanted to see the back of her."

Xavière's eyes misted over again. She couldn't get over how well this man could see through her. She had surrounded her-self with barbed wire—her sharp tongue, her sarcasm, her cyn-icism, her contempt for Orion, her double life with Séverine—to such an extent that nobody knew who she really was.

"May I go on?" the gynecologist asked, aware of her intense emotion. "What you're telling me," he resumed in a softer voice, "indicates that you're going to ask for a termination of your pregnancy. In principle, I suggest that before you do that, you imagine the opposite, just imagine it . . . Something has clicked inside you, which has made this birth possible—because what's happening in your womb is already a birth. That means that an intimate part of you has rebelled against the dictates of your conscious mind, that a secret part of you longs to attempt the adventure you've always refused. Think, madame, and listen to the whole of yourself. You have the opportunity to change, to free yourself of your fears, to accom-plish your destiny. This birth could be the chance for a rebirth."

For a moment, she absorbed this speech, then shrugged. "So I have a baby that comes from God knows where, the child of God knows who, and I call him Jesus Christ. Is that the plan?" She gathered her things and, as she left the room, said, "I'm going back to your colleague to arrange for an abortion."

That afternoon, like the two previous ones, Xavière was due to see Séverine. Until now, she had done so with pleasure, because she had been in denial about her pregnancy; this time, she dreaded seeing her again.

Lingering in the shop, she surreptitiously observed Orion, his grotesque figure—swollen abdomen over thin legs—his contorted torso, and, above all, that drunkard's face with the puffy eyes and the skin covered in red blotches as if dipped in wine. He was busy doing his work, running from the shop to the storeroom, from the flowerpots to the rolls of paper, expending a hundred times more energy than his activities necessitated. For a moment, he noticed her watching him and winked at her: she lowered her head angrily. Did he have to inflict his unbearable good humor on her in addition to his ugliness?

The vibration of her cell phone interrupted these dark thoughts. *I miss you. Come. I'm waiting. Séverine.* Xavière merely replied: *Can't.*

She spotted Patricia crossing the street and murmured without realizing it, "If I had legs like hers, I'd never wear skirts."

"Come now, Xavière," Orion retorted. "She can wear whatever she likes."

"There should be a law to stop people who have a physical defect from inflicting the sight of it on others. Actually, I'm stupid, there already is a law: indecent assault. When Patricia exhibits those hams of hers, I call it indecent assault."

The art dealer Wim emerged from his house and, before getting into his car, waved cordially at Xavière, whom he glimpsed behind her window.

"What an oily type that one is! Why's he always smiling? Does he think he's irresistible or what?"

"He's just in a good mood a lot of the time."

"He's a fool. If I had teeth as gray as his, I wouldn't smile that much."

"You don't smile much anyway."

Xavière refrained from reacting to Orion's remark, but thought: *You'll pay for that, my good man.*

At that moment a young woman looked in. "Isn't Madame Dumont still here?"

"No, she paid for her flowers and left."

"Which direction did she go?"

Annoyed that a mere passerby, who wouldn't even buy anything, should turn her shop into an information bureau, Xavière replied, "You just have to follow her smell."

"I beg your pardon?"

"You can't miss it. Does she stink because she has dogs?"

Stunned, the young woman stood there in the doorway for a moment, then beat a hasty retreat.

The cell phone in Xavière's pocket vibrated again. *If something's wrong, let's talk about it. Séverine.*

Suppressing a sigh of exasperation, Xavière imagined herself lying naked in Séverine's arms, explaining what had happened to her, and, to her relief, being listened to and understood. Why not? If Séverine was her lover, why couldn't she also be her best friend?

Claiming she had an urgent errand to run, she left the shop and hurried to Number 6 Place d'Arezzo.

"Is something wrong?" Séverine asked as she closed the door behind her.

It suddenly occurred to Xavière how far-fetched what she was about to say would seem: she had to convince her friend that she hadn't slept with a man but had nevertheless fallen pregnant.

By way of reply, she pressed her lips to Séverine's, as if placing a gag over her mouth. Then she demanded, by the insistence of her gestures, that they go up to the bedroom. Although surprised by such fervor, Séverine acquiesced.

As soon as they were upstairs, Xavière made violent love to her, like a warrior raping a woman during a raid. Her eyes focused elsewhere, she crossed the border between caresses and blows. Séverine accepted it all, and even came more quickly than usual. Was it to avoid this whole thing going on too long?

Xavière looked at her tenderly. "You liked that!"

"Since it's a game."

"How do you know it is?"

"You were supposed to be telling me about your problems."

"I don't have any problems. But I'm worried about a friend of mine who does."

"One of your exes?" Séverine asked, unable to suppress a touch of jealousy.

Xavière grimaced. "A friend—not an ex—who's the same age as me has gotten herself accidentally pregnant." She avoided adding "for the first time," because that would have made it obvious that she was talking about herself. "She doesn't know what to do."

"What to do?"

"In other words, whether to keep the child or have an abortion."

Séverine shuddered. "As a Catholic, I'm opposed to abortion. But in this particular case, I'd advise it."

"Why?" Xavière exclaimed.

"Having a child at the age of forty-five? Apart from the fact that it's risky for the mother, there's a good chance the child might be born with a defect. And your friend also needs to think of the future: she'll be pushing seventy when her child is twenty. That's no fun for her or the child."

What an idiot, Xavière thought. *I'd never noticed before how stupid she is.* But she tried to control her animosity in order not to give herself away.

"Is that what I should tell my friend? 'You're too old, have an abortion, you won't be able to have a normal child. And even if you do, the child will blame you later.' Wouldn't it be easier if I just told her to kill herself?"

"Xavière, don't fly off the handle: you asked for my advice."

"Well, you gave me your advice. And I think your advice is stupid."

Séverine's eyes misted over, and her lips quivered. "That's hurtful," she said.

Xavière exploded. "Oh, that takes the biscuit! You talk crap and expect me to console you? This is like a bad dream."

"I . . . I . . . I don't know what's gotten into you. I don't know who you are anymore."

"There it is, then! You don't know who I am, and I don't know who you are. Goodbye!"

"And good riddance," Xavière muttered to herself as she crossed Place d'Arezzo.

Back in her shop, she went over the discussion: even though she herself had been thinking about abortion, Severine's reasons for advising it were so different from hers that she'd been unable to stand the suggestion. The main reason she didn't want a child was because of her own childhood, and secondly, because she didn't know whose kid it was. But old age, or the risk of deformity—no, she wouldn't listen to that kind of argument. Worse still, it made her want to give birth just to prove to silly women like Séverine, dumb conformists who'd had their children young, that she too could produce a beautiful baby and bring it up. Honestly!

Orion came back from the storeroom, his hair—or rather the crown of hair that went from one ear to the other—completely disheveled.

Disconcerted to see her staring at him, he winked at her.

She turned away. *My God, how can I live with this?*

All at once, she walked back toward him. "Orion, when was the last time we made love?"

He chuckled. "Don't you remember?"

"No, I definitely don't remember."

"Two and a half months ago, after the party at the Durand-Debourgs'."

He lowered his eyes modestly. Realizing that he was telling the truth, Xavière shuddered: all she could recall was the beginning of that party, which had in fact been quite successful.

"Where did we do it?"

"Same place as usual."

"Same place as usual? Where's that, Orion?"

"In the car. Before we got home."

Xavière looked at him openmouthed. "Me?"

"Oh, yes."

"Me with you?"

He nodded in delight.

"Oh, my God!" she sighed. "I don't remember a damned thing!"

"Not surprising. You were drunk."

"I may have drunk a little but—"

"For years now, we've only ever made love when you've been drunk."

"What?"

"I love it when you're like that. You're so funny, so relaxed, so sweet. The way you were when we first met."

That evening, Xavière set off for Knokke-le-Zoute. The flatness of Flanders struck her as interminable.

She hadn't said a word to Orion about her condition, informing him simply that she was going to take a little break by the sea and wanted him to mind the store. But then he never decided anything, either for her or for himself.

The sun was setting as she entered her fisherman's cottage. There, on two narrow floors, she had the impression of being better housed, better protected than in Brussels. The house was a refuge that represented her true identity. Decorated by her, these three rooms, with their red gingham, their ribbons, their fringes, their porcelain animals, the thick romantic novels on the white-leaded wooden shelves, revealed a charming femininity, a delicacy, a tenderness—in other words, qualities usually well buried beneath the icy persona that Xavière presented to the world. The place was a secret, the official reason—the one she told Orion—being that she didn't want anybody to know their lifestyle, the unofficial one being that she had no desire for anyone to pay her a visit there. Recently, she had made an exception for Séverine when the latter had been able to get away for two days.

In the refrigerator, she managed to find a few things to eat, and was surprised by her own appetite. Then she just had time to climb the narrow staircase leading to the former attic that had become her bedroom before sinking into sleep.

The next day, as soon as she went out, the salt-laden wind cooled her face and she saw life differently. What was she complaining about? She had what she wanted, she could do whatever she liked. Although this surge of optimism surprised her, she accepted it.

Her basket in her hand, she did her shopping in a new way: whereas she usually counted every cent coming out of her purse, she now spent extravagantly, increasing the quantities, buying enough food for two. Even though she realized it, she continued, carried away by a kind of intoxication.

At two o'clock, she felt the pressing need to eat waffles at Marie Siska, a pleasure she usually denied herself because she was afraid of seeing people she knew there, who would be sure to ask her what she was doing in Knokke. But it was a Tuesday, and everyone would be working in Brussels; she could allow herself this treat without too much of a risk.

Out of caution, however, she avoided the terrace and jammed herself behind the upright piano at the far end of the room with the large windows.

As she ate her waffles, she saw a pleasant-looking couple arrive.

They sat down on the terrace, with their backs to her, but as the man leaned over and kissed the woman, she made out their profiles and recognized Quentin Dentremont and Ève. At first, she thought that her imagination was playing a trick on her, but then she realized that it was indeed them.

Her first reflex was to be indignant—"She's getting them from kindergarten now!"—the second to think of the gossip she could spread from her shop about the cougar of Place d'Arezzo. Curiously, these sarcastic thoughts were drowned out by a wave of positivity. After all, what was wrong with it? They looked happy. Very happy. They exuded joy. Why should she criticize? Was she going to censure them on the pretext that when Quentin was forty, he would be living with a woman of sixty? No, that was the kind of stupid thing Séverine would have said, with her conventional view of age.

"What a drag she is!"

Without meaning to, Xavière had cursed out loud. The things that had attracted her in Séverine now repelled her: her willowy quality, which she had taken for evanescence, her sadness, which had proved to be a rich woman's indifference.

This anger reassured Xavière after the bursts of amiability she had lately been experiencing. She knew what was causing them: the enemy child inside her was changing her, messing with her hormones.

Going back to the fisherman's cottage, she noted that Séverine had left some dozen messages, but she made no attempt to read them.

At five o'clock, a storm broke out, which filled Xavière with enthusiasm because she loved huddling in the warmth when the elements were unleashed, feeling no fear, only the relief of knowing herself protected, enjoying her four walls and her roof as if they were the most fabulous inventions on earth.

This was how she would organize the rest of the day: reading Jane Austen, and then having a meal. In fact, it turned out differently: she dozed off and nibbled at food between her naps. What did it matter, as long as she was enjoying herself?

Outside, the wind and rain were increasing, making the beams creak. The whole cottage was groaning. From time to time, to amuse herself, Xavière imagined it was going to yield to the storm.

Night had fallen, and the storm, ever more violent, tore her away from her reading. It was a lot more romantic, more unpredictable than her novel. After each flash of lightning, she counted the seconds in order to determine how far away the lightning would fall. Whereas, at the beginning of her calculations, the lightning had hit the ground some two and a half miles away, it couldn't be more than three hundred yards now. The center of the depression had moved to Knokke-le-Zoute.

Xavière was just reassuring herself one last time, recalling that the neighboring church had a lightning conductor on its belfry, when a different noise made her jump.

She stood up, trembling.

The noise resumed, more urgent now. A knocking sound.

She went to the door and pressed her ear to it. This time, she could clearly hear the knocker hitting the wood.

She opened the door. There in the darkness stood Séverine, in her raincoat, buffeted by the wind.

"Can I come in?"

"No."

Séverine thought it was a joke and moved forward into the doorway.

Xavière pushed her back roughly, out into the rain and wind beneath the threatening sky.

"What? Aren't you going to let me in?"

"Did I invite you?"

"What's gotten into you, Xavière? With what's happening between us—"

"What is happening between us?"

"We love each other."

"Oh, really?"

Shocked, Séverine stared at her. Xavière, impassive, sheltering behind a shield of indifference, was denying her all access.

"Don't you love me anymore?" Séverine stammered.

"I never loved you, you idiot!"

Xavière slammed the door in her face.

10

At first, François-Maxime presented Séverine's absence as unimportant. When he told the children in the evening, over dinner, he had almost believed his own explanation.

"Your mother has gone to take a break. She didn't tell you because she didn't want to worry you."

"When is she coming back?"

"Soon."

"Is she sick?"

"No, just tired."

"Is she tired because of us?" Guillaume asked.

"That's precisely why she sneaked out, my boy: she was afraid one of you would ask that."

"So it's true, then: she *is* tired because of us."

"No, it isn't true. If you'd said that, she would have stayed just to prove it to you."

"I hope she'll be back soon."

When he had gotten home at six o'clock, surprised not to find his wife in the house, François-Maxime had dialed her number and left an innocuous message on her answerphone. Then, going up to take a shower, he had discovered a note on the chest of drawers in their bedroom.

I'm sorry, I'm getting away for a while. I can't stand it anymore.

That had puzzled him even more, and ever since, he had been calling her anxiously every ten minutes, cursing the recorded message in which Séverine's indolent voice suggested he leave his message after the tone.

Once the children were in bed, he contacted the people they were closest to and asked if she had taken refuge with them: a delicate exercise, because he was determined to obtain the information without admitting that she had run away. His inquiries proved fruitless.

At midnight, judging it indecent to disturb people at that hour, he took refuge in the living room to think. Séverine was suffering from depression, that was becoming clear. Her constant melancholy, her inability to make up her mind about anything, her almost generalized indifference showed that she had lost the one thing that keeps a person going: desire. Why hadn't he realized it earlier? Why hadn't he intervened?

Consulting his address book, he thought about what professional to send her to the very next day. A psychiatrist or a psychotherapist? In view of the conversation they'd had the other night, during which she had told him the story about her father, psychotherapy seemed the more sensible course. But that might drag on, like all psychological treatments . . . In order for her condition to improve quickly, it might be better to turn to a psychiatrist, who would prescribe medication. The ideal would be a psychiatrist/psychotherapist who would combine the qualities of a sprinter with those of a long-distance runner. François-Maxime vowed that at eight o'clock the following day he would contact Varnier, his colleague at the bank, a notorious hypochondriac who, in his state of constant anxiety, knew the best specialists for every disease.

Returning to his bedroom, he didn't bother to undress, just threw himself down on the bedspread without turning it down. Not sharing his bed with Séverine made sleep seem hostile; he hadn't often slept alone since they'd been living in this house.

For a long time, he stared up at the dark ceiling, illuminated briefly by distant flashes of lightning. The storm was moving away from Brussels in a northwesterly direction, leaving only a trail of dull, monotonous rain.

Should he blame himself for his own inadequacies? Of course, he should have paid more attention, devoted more time to Séverine, less to his work or his children. But although he was ready to criticize himself, he considered himself a good husband—all the more so in that he had a secret, his furtive sexual encounters with passing men. If he hadn't had those clandestine pleasures, he would have succumbed to the tedious routines of married love, like many husbands. As it was, returning to the marriage bed after assuaging his forbidden desires, he had to be perfect for her.

He suddenly sat up. Could it be that Séverine had discovered his secret? His heart started racing. But then he lay down again. No, it was impossible! He took too many precautions. And if anybody had told Séverine, she would have dismissed that person out of hand.

That meant it was a bout of depression.

From time to time, he relaxed his vigilance and dozed off. Each time he woke, he felt bad about it: he mustn't give in to exhaustion, he had to wait for her.

Letting his mind wander, he thought over what she had revealed to him about her transvestite father. How could she have hidden it from him for so long? He wondered if their whole relationship wasn't made up of enigmas, if both of them hadn't built it on silences rather than words. What would have happened if he had immediately admitted to her that he desired men more than women, or if she had confessed the difficulty she had in trusting anybody?

He sat up again. That was the source of her depression: she didn't trust him. Wrongly, because he loved her and took care of her. Rightly, because she was with a husband who had one whole side that was unknown to her. Did she sense it? Did it cause her pain?

At six in the morning, his cell phone vibrated. He grabbed hold of it. Séverine had just sent him a message: *Forgive me.*

Immediately, he dialed her number, got her voicemail, and tapped in an answer: *I have nothing to forgive you. I love you.*

In writing *I love you*, he had tears in his eyes because it was something he rarely said to her, and also because an intuition told him that he was saying it too late.

He waited for a reply. An hour later, disappointed, he got up, determined to see to the children.

After his shower, breakfast, and checking the satchels, he drove them to school; unlike the other days, he didn't feel in the mood to go riding in the wood.

He returned home thinking that he would stay there waiting for Séverine, dealing with business by telephone or e-mail.

As he parked on Place d'Arezzo, he saw two police officers climbing the steps in front of his house. He dashed out of his car and called out to them, "Are you here to see me, gentlemen?"

The older of the two turned. "François-Maxime de Couvigny?"

"That's right."

"Married to Séverine de Couvigny, maiden name Villemin?"

"Yes, of course."

"We have some bad news for you, monsieur. At 6:30 this morning, your wife threw herself off a tower. She's dead."

For a long time, François-Maxime was prostrate with grief. He couldn't think about anything, all he did was relive the scene: Séverine climbing the spiral staircase, reaching the seventh floor of the parking garage, the one that ended in a terrace; taking care to lock her car, plunging her key into the pocket of her raincoat, then climbing onto the parapet.

Had she hesitated? Surely not. When you stop to think, you don't jump. She had looked down to make sure there was nobody on the sidewalk where she was going to land, then had let herself fall into the void.

François-Maxime was told that she had died instantaneously on impact.

It's better that way.

He started reliving the scene on a loop. Nothing else occupied his consciousness. He was no longer himself but Séverine, trying to understand her last moments of lucidity.

Near to him sat Varnier, his number two at the bank. Because François-Maxime, on learning the horrible news, had had but one reflex: to inform his office that he wouldn't be coming in to work. His colleague had come running to help him, and was now keeping him company in the locked bedroom.

Varnier grabbed his phone, frowned, and left the room.

He came back with a woman in her forties, with a gentle, open face. "François-Maxime, I'd like to introduce Marie-Jeanne Simon, a psychiatrist specializing in traumas. As I was saying, the children must be told."

François-Maxime emerged from his lethargy and said, in a panic, "I can't! I can't!"

The woman came to him and put her hand on his shoulder. "It's quite natural, Monsieur Couvigny. Nobody brings children into this world expecting to tell them that their mother has died."

"Will you . . . tell them . . . how she died?"

"When it comes to something as important as this, there's nothing worse than lying. Your children have a right to know. They'll rebuild their lives better on the basis of truth than on a fairy tale."

"Are they back?"

"They're having their afternoon snack in the kitchen. I've

just seen them: they're wondering what's going on, they sense the tension, they're asking for you."

"Please go to them, I beg you. I'll be along later."

When she left the room, François-Maxime listened out for every noise: footsteps on the stairs, the sliding of the door, the babble of the children, then, suddenly, silence. She must be talking to them. Was she? What was she telling them?

In a state of anguish, he was about to rush downstairs to interrupt the drama when he heard the children's cries of grief.

He put his hands over his ears, pressing his skull as if to crush it.

Varnier returned, pale-faced. "There, it's done," he said in a low voice. François-Maxime turned his head away. A cold silence reigned now over the house. The cries of the children, though, continued to echo in his mind.

"Séverine, why did you do it?"

Moved, Varnier approached, ready to blurt out anything that might bring him solace, but François-Maxime motioned to him to keep away.

"I'll pull myself together before I see the children. Please go."

Respectfully, Varnier withdrew and closed the door.

François-Maxime walked around in circles, hoping that stretching his legs would clear his mind.

In vain . . .

Idle, exhausted, he stared at Séverine's closet, half opened it and looked through her things. Everything seemed to deny that she was gone. Her lily of the valley scent was still there, her silk scarves, her cashmere sweaters, her fine cotton blouses. He lightly touched these objects, and doing so eased his pain.

He opened the wardrobe and, without thinking, took out an ecru dress. Stroking it, sniffing it, he decided to lay it out over the bedspread. Then he took out another, and laid it out by the side of the first. Then another, and another . . .

Now, on the bed, four Séverines lay waiting for him, docile, abandoned.

Opening the closet again, he came across his favorite of her evening dresses, a refined mixture of black silk and velvet panne. Séverine had worn it for important occasions. Taking it off its hanger, he held it against himself.

Looking at himself in the stand-alone mirror, he remembered happy moments with his wife on his arm, when he had felt so carefree and so proud of her.

He heard a tear-laden voice behind him: "Daddy?"

François-Maxime turned. There stood Guillaume, red-eyed, who for a moment had imagined he had seen the figure of the mother he was mourning.

11

All of a sudden, silence fell, and a wave of impatience swept through the gathering.

The three hundred participants turned their heads: through the main entrance, which was flooded with light, Séverine's coffin entered the church, borne by four men in dark suits. The oak casket did not seem to weigh on their shoulders. Accompanying their advance, the organ played a Bach chorale, grave and measured and profound, full of the attentive respect that is owed to life as to death, music that distilled both sadness and its resolution: hope. Gentle yet voluminous, the flutelike sounds wove a meditative emotion in the air.

Hippolyte bowed his head, unable to bear the thought that a woman lay within those planks of wood. To his right, his daughter Isis, her light blue eyes wide open, followed the ceremony with fascination, watching the slow march of the pallbearers as it merged with the music. In the same row, Germain, who really wished he wasn't there, had withdrawn into himself; if circumstances hadn't conspired against him, he would have been somewhere else, in one of the city parks, his arms bare, his head in the sun, looking after the hedges; now he had to suffer the colder shade of this place, to see hundreds of flowers murdered, thrown in sprays on the altar.

At first, Hippolyte had wanted to go to the ceremony alone. Learning that a woman, a mother, whom he had seen for years, frail, melancholy, but very polite—she had always waved at him in greeting—had killed herself had come as a shock. How could you take your own life when you had four children? Because of Isis, he would never kill himself. Out of love and a sense of responsibility. In formulating the impossibility of this, he had realized just how desperate Séverine must have been. She must have entered a zone of pain where even her affection for her own family ceased to matter. Imagining that despair had unsettled him. In attending the funeral, he was not only bearing witness to his sympathy for her, but also trying to prove to her that she had been wrong: human beings loved each other, helped each other, he trusted in their solidarity. It didn't matter to him if he didn't understand, what he wanted was to reassure himself. It was essential to him to prove that Séverine had been wrong to think she was alone in the world. After all, the church was full.

In order to be here, he had taken half a day off. As if by chance, that morning Isis had told him that, as the teachers in her school were on strike, she wouldn't be going to classes. Immediately, he had called Germain, who was taking a professional development course on the other side of town and therefore couldn't take care of Isis. He had had to resign himself to the fact that he would be taking his daughter to the funeral.

During the ride on the streetcar, he had feared tackling the subject. Did Isis know what death was? So far, she hadn't lost anyone near and dear to her. But from the height of her ten years, she dominated the situation.

"What did that lady on Place d'Arezzo die of? Was she old?"

"No."

"Had she been sick?"

"I don't know."

"Did she die in her armchair or in her bed?"

"I don't know. What matters is that we pay her a last tribute."

"Will she realize?"

"I don't know."

Hippolyte cursed himself: all he could think of to say to his daughter was "I don't know," either because he didn't know the answer, or because he was hiding the truth. *She'd be right to take me for an idiot.*

After due thought, Isis concluded, "When it comes down to it, it doesn't really matter if she realizes or not. The most important thing is that we do it."

On the square outside the church, Germain had joined them at the last moment and suggested to Hippolyte that he take Isis somewhere else. Too late: the girl was intrigued by now and had insisted on attending the ceremony. So, in the end, Germain had shuffled in after them.

The four pallbearers put the casket down by the altar, then placed a photograph of Séverine on the lid.

"Oh, it's her!" Isis exclaimed in astonishment.

Hippolyte realized that his daughter had started shaking. "Are you going to be all right, sweetheart?"

Her cheeks pale, she whispered, "I knew her. I . . . " She turned to her father, her nostrils pinched with sorrow. "Why?"

"Everyone dies eventually, sweetheart."

"Why?"

Her voice was so imploring that Hippolyte felt he could no longer reply just "I don't know." In a panic, he looked to Germain for support, but the dwarf was engrossed in contemplating his shoes.

The priest now spoke up, monopolizing everyone's attention.

The service began. Now Hippolyte no longer feared that Isis should hear some unpleasant details: the representative of a Church that condemned suicide would almost certainly pretend to be unaware of the exact circumstances of the death.

Hippolyte relaxed and looked around him: hundreds of

strangers, of course, but also the inhabitants of Place d'Arezzo had gathered.

There was the impeccable Mademoiselle Beauvert, stiff-necked and red-eyed; the pinup from the realtor's, her face camouflaged by round dark glasses; Ludovic and his mother, thrilling at every dramatic word uttered by the priest; Rose Bidermann, calm and attentive, giving luster to the ceremony, responding to the greetings that everyone addressed to her. Farther away, in a corner, he recognized Baptiste Monier, without his wife, in the company of a blonde woman. Closer to the front, the concierge Marcelle was pulling paper handkerchiefs from her bag, taking a kind of fierce pleasure in weeping. The engineer Jean-Noël Fanon had come with his rarely-seen wife Diane, who was wearing a tight-fitting black tailored suit and openly yawning. The gallery owner Wim remained for a few minutes, looked at his watch, slipped a note to his assistant, a pleasant Flemish woman, then slipped out, looking like a man who cannot possibly miss an important meeting. The ones who surprised him were the florists, Orion and Xavière: she, usually so unemotional, seemed to be in the grip of a profound grief; her features drawn, her eyes glassy, her skin grayer than cardboard, she was biting her lip like a woman trying to stop herself screaming; Orion, usually so carefree, was fully aware of her state and was supporting her by the arm.

Hippolyte looked everywhere for Patricia, but couldn't see her. Turning to the other side, to the right of Isis and Germain, he saw her in his row. She was watching him. Without thinking, they smiled at each other. For a split second, they forgot where they were and why.

A young girl stood up and walked to the microphone, facing the crowd: it was Gwendoline, the oldest of the four motherless children. There was a hint of appehension in the silence.

She stood at the microphone, a handwritten sheet of paper in her hand. The audience held its breath.

Isis seized her father's wrist anxiously and murmured, "If you died, Daddy, I think I would die too."

Overcome with emotion, Hippolyte leaned down and clasped her to him.

Gwendoline began her speech in a clear, determined, courageous voice. On behalf of her brother and sisters, she talked about the mother who had just left them, a wonderful, gentle mother, always there, always willing to help; she talked about her love, which was serene and never burdensome. As she said farewell to her beloved mother, her voice grew firmer and the audience wept. The bravery of this teenager touched everyone, making Séverine's death even more cruel and incomprehensible, her sudden departure inexplicable. Then Gwendoline dared to venture on more sensitive terrain. Turning to face the casket, she took her mother to task:

"Why did you so rarely talk to us about yourself? Why didn't you tell us your sorrows, the secrets that made you suffer? Why did you try to spare us to the point of neglecting yourself? Why did you suppose that we wouldn't understand? Why did you think that we would have loved you less if we'd known how fragile you were? Why, Mommy, why?"

Her voice broke. In response to these questions, the silence grew deeper, disturbed only by a little sniffing. Gwendoline stared at the casket, the mute photograph, and waited for an answer that would never come.

Hippolyte felt a strong pressure against his leg: Isis had seized it in her arms and, her head buried in the folds of his pants, was weeping bitterly.

He couldn't help turning his head toward Patricia, who was watching the child, visibly moved. Their tear-blurred eyes met: at that moment, he knew that Patricia was ready to love Isis.

On his left, a nudge of the elbow threw him. Tom and Nathan, who were late, were trying to take their place in the row, apologizing as they did so.

Hippolyte gave them a kindly smile and invited his neighbours to shift up. Raising her head, Isis was pleased to see these familiar, friendly faces.

The ceremony continued.

Isis, demanding that her father lean down, whispered in his ear, "She killed herself, didn't she?"

Reassured that he no longer had to lie, Hippolyte murmured "Yes, she did."

"How?"

Now that he had started, Hippolyte saw no more reason to hesitate. "She threw herself off a tall building."

Isis looked at him openmouthed.

The priest announced that they would now hold communion. Nathan abandoned Tom to go to the altar. Hippolyte hesitated. Although a believer, he was not a regular churchgoer, and he wondered if he should go up. When he saw Patricia step out into the aisle, he entrusted Isis to Germain and made up his mind to join the line of communicants.

Patricia followed him, almost pressed up against him. They said nothing, didn't try to look at each other, content just to be close. Because they were thinking about their relationship, they were unaware of the buzz around them: the people present were determining who was Catholic and who wasn't. In a country like Belgium, split down the middle, not by French speakers and Flemish speakers but by the line separating Christians from atheists, who took or didn't take communion would be a subject of conversation for months to come. The priest being assisted by a deacon, the line divided into two on the last steps. In a daze, Hippolyte and Patricia suddenly found themselves side by side in front of the choir, each facing a clergyman holding out the host. Together they bowed. Together they accepted the offering. Together they received the blessing. These seconds gave them an intense and, for both of them, premonitory sensation; forgetting the context, they saw nothing but the glittering stained-glass windows, the virginal lilies, the huge gilded crucifix, and, borne on the powerful chords of the organ, they had the impression that they were rehearsing their own wedding.

They went back to their seats, eyes lowered, hearts pounding, holding the round host on their tongues, full of that glimpsed promise.

A soprano approached the organist and a sublime song rose up into the vault: *Laudate*. Mozart's aria gave thanks; it blessed the Lord for giving us this life, so fragile and so precious, expressed the ecstasy of having this chance, mingled with the tender light that bathed the building.

Hippolyte no longer felt sad, but genuinely joyful, joyful at being here, joyful at having his daughter, his friend, and his future wife beside him. Did he need to come to a funeral to realize it? He remembered a strange sentence he had heard during his childhood: *One must die so that the other may live.* Looking again at the photograph on the casket, he seemed to notice a new expression on the face captured on the glossy paper; it now had a goodness, a kind of all-pervasive tenderness; Séverine had become his good angel, the guardian of his love.

On the left, a noise startled everyone. Xavière had felt faint, her husband hadn't been in time to stop her, and she had fallen between the pews.

Nathan muttered between his teeth, in such a way as to be audible to his neighbors, "What's she trying to make us swallow? That she has a heart? What nerve! Ladies and gentlemen, the wickedest woman in Brussels has pretended to faint."

Tom stopped him with a slap. Too late. Some, including Hippolyte, had heard and expressed their own surprise: Xavière was indeed the last person anybody would have thought likely to swoon.

Orion was fluttering over her, in a panic, powerless to do

anything. Nobody went to his aid. All at once, Dr. Plassard elbowed his way through.

"We have to take her out and let her breathe."

He took hold of Xavière by the armpits and undertook to drag her outside. In trying to help him, Orion kept bumping into things, overturning chairs and prayer books.

"What's the matter with her, doctor?" he asked. "Why did she faint?"

"She's pregnant, you fool!"

Orion froze openmouthed in the middle of the aisle. Tom, Nathan, Hippolyte, and Germain looked at each other in astonishment. Nobody dared to believe what they had just heard. Orion broke into a run to catch up with the doctor and Xavière, who had already gone out through the main door.

"What a couple!" Nathan murmured. "The kindest man in the world lives with the wickedest woman."

"Orion might have been the Cupid."

"You're right, he might have been."

At that moment, they turned toward Germain, who bowed his head.

The priest resumed the service and launched into a speech that did indeed imply that the dead woman had killed herself.

Isis stroked her father's hand. "Will you introduce Patricia to me?"

"What? Today?"

"Daddy, stop hiding." And to underline her comment, she pointed to the casket. "Life is short."

Once again, Hippolyte wondered how a child of ten could come out with such a statement and nodded. "Later."

Another piece of music started. The four men in black reappeared, lifted the casket, and headed calmly and solemnly for the exit, followed by the family.

Walking in front, holding his son Guillaume by the hand, François-Maxime looked the very picture of grief. Eyes fixed, staring into the distance, he advanced like an automaton, summoning up all his energy to make the gestures the ceremony demanded. For the first time, Hippolyte felt a surge of sympathy for the aristocrat whose arrogant perfection usually made his blood run cold.

As for the three girls, they followed, hypnotized, the box containing their mother, refusing to admit that she was about to leave them once again.

Isis tugged at her father's hand. "Daddy, what can we do for them?"

Hippolyte almost replied, "I don't know," then heard himself say, "We can pray, sweetheart. Sometimes we just have to accept the fact that we suffer and other people suffer too."

While he himself was trying to fully grasp what he had just said, Isis looked at him and nodded, reassured.

"Are you planning to go to the cemetery?" Tom whispered to Hippolyte and Germain.

"No."

"Neither are we," Nathan said. "We are just going to leave a note on the register of condolences."

He pointed to a large open book on a lectern standing at the far end of the church.

The group got to the book before the rest of the crowd.

"Go ahead," Tom said to Germain.

The dwarf seized the pen in his right hand and wrote a few words.

Tom stepped back and whispered in Nathan's ear, "Forget about him. He's right-handed."

"You're joking!"

"Take a look."

Nathan confirmed that Tom was telling the truth, but couldn't resign himself. "He's trying to throw us off the scent." He went up to Hippolyte and asked in a low voice, "Is your friend usually right-handed?"

"There's nobody more right-handed than he is. His left hand is like a hook."

Tom and Nathan looked at each other, infuriated: their theory that Germain had written the anonymous letters had come crashing down!

Patricia appeared at that moment and knelt down in front of Isis. The child looked intensely at the adult. Patricia felt intimidated, and started shaking, but Isis took her hand.

"Hello, I'm Isis."

"I'm Patricia."

"We're the two women in Daddy's life, aren't we?"

12

H ello, Albane."
"Well, well, Quentin, you're still alive. I thought you were dead."

This morning, the parrots were agitated and noisy, screeching like saws attacking hard wood. The low sky, in which a storm was brewing, brought an occasional flight of swallows, eager to land on the square but bouncing back in swarms before they could touch the ground, fearful of the reaction of the cockatoos, although they didn't resign themselves to leave immediately.

"Can I sit down next to you?"

"The bench doesn't belong to me."

"Is that a yes?"

Every now and again, the muffled but fierce beating of wings bore witness to the sexual and territorial wars that were being waged in the branches.

"Please forgive me, Albane."

"For what?"

"For not coming to see you lately. You got my note, I hope, the one where I said not to worry, that I wasn't sick, that I'd soon be back?"

" . . . "

"Were you . . . Were you here, these last few days?"

"Yes."

"Waiting for me?"

A parakeet rose angrily into the air and flew around the square crying out his rage.

Albane was hesitating between crying and losing her temper. She opted for a third solution: sarcasm. "You'd have liked it, wouldn't you, me waiting around like an idiot when you didn't come?"

"Albane . . . "

"Well, I did come here, but only because I'm used to it, not for you. Why should I wait for you? We aren't married. We aren't engaged. We aren't even together."

"We are together. At least, we were . . . "

"What does that mean to you, being together? Disappearing without letting me know where you are? Coming back like a stranger greeting a stranger? You and I will never understand each other."

Quentin was surprised. However morose, unfair, touchy, and irritating she was, Albane still attracted him. He should have left, called her a pain in the neck—which she was—especially as he would never get from her what he had gotten from Ève, but there he stayed, awkward, weighed down with his new secrets, hypnotized by that pretty, animated face, knowing that he was going to say the wrong things again and cause further misunderstandings.

Confident that he was listening to her, Albane launched into her lament. "I don't know who you are, Quentin Dentremont. The other day, your last note said, 'I'd like to sleep with you,' and then on Saturday, at Knokke-le-Zoute, you ran away when Servane and I arrived at the party."

"I didn't run away because of you."

"Oh, come on! You were the only reason I went to Knokke. I felt so humiliated! You made me lose face. In Knokke, just like in Brussels, people know we're together. I was the laughingstock of the party."

"Albane, I swear I wasn't trying to avoid you. It was just that . . . I had to be somewhere else."

"Where?"

" . . . "

"Who with?"

" . . . "

The parrots fell silent as a huge unidentified bird passed slowly and threateningly over the square with a terrifying drone.

"Don't you have anything to tell me, Quentin Dentremont?"

"I have nothing against you, Albane, I don't think anything bad about you. On the contrary."

The helicopter disappeared westward, behind the rooftops, and the parrots resumed their arguments at a lower volume.

"You have nothing against me? I must be dreaming. You behave like a pig and you tell me you have nothing against me? The world has turned upside down . . . What a nerve!"

Quentin grabbed her by the wrist. "I love you, Albane."

She felt like crying for help. Now that she was finally receiving the words she had longed to hear, she shook her head, dismissing them. That declaration disgusted her. There was no question of accepting his love. Quentin was bringing her nothing but torment.

"That's bullshit!"

"I swear it, Albane."

"Why didn't you tell me before?"

"Because, before, I wasn't mature."

"What's matured you since Saturday?"

"If I told you, you wouldn't understand."

"I'm stupid, is that it?"

"No, you're young and you're a girl."

Albane tore herself from his embrace, turned to face him head-on, her brow furrowed, eyes popping out of their sockets. "Oh yes, much better to be sixteen and a boy!"

"No."

"Frankly, this is an eye-opener. I never knew you were such a pompous male chauvinist."

"Albane, it's not what I meant to say!"

"That's just it! You don't want to say anything, and when you do say something it's not what you mean. 'Pompous male chauvinist,' no, that's way off the mark. I should add 'moron.'"

The angrier Albane became, the calmer Quentin felt. He was so touched by her rage that he felt like laughing. He could feel his heart melt in the face of such fury. His passion was growing.

"Albane, the reason I left . . . was to come back a better person. I know who I am now."

"You're making a fool of me!"

"Not at all."

"You needed to leave in order to come back a better person! And I'm supposed to just accept that? Do I really want a guy who invites me to a party seventy miles from where I live and then runs away when I get there? It's one thing being in love, but I'm not going to be made a fool of, and I'm not going to be a victim, oh, no!"

Quentin burst out laughing, as if he were watching a comedy act. Sure of himself, certain of his feelings, more in love than ever, he didn't realize that Albane thought he was just being cynical.

"So now you're laughing?"

Looking at her tortured face, he laughed even more, laughed until he couldn't breathe. How cute she looked when she was angry! He was amused by her rage the way we are sometimes amused by a child moaning about something or a household pet unable to comprehend a situation: he was laughing with genuine tenderness.

"You are a real monster!"

When tears welled up in Albane's eyes, Quentin saw them only as the culmination of the comic scene he had been watching: he had no idea that he was humiliating the girl.

"Goodbye! I never want to see you again!"

With a furious stamping of her feet, she walked off without turning around. Quentin hit himself in the stomach to tone down his hilarity and called after her, "Come back, Albane, I love you!"

"Liar!"

"I've never loved you so much!"

"Too late!"

"Albane, I swear I love you!"

"Fuck off, you bastard!

Her last words were like a slap in the face. Albane wasn't usually vulgar. Shocked, he gave up the idea of running after her and sat for a few moments longer on the bench.

She disappeared from sight.

His laughter returned. Now it was a laugh of relief. What a wonderful thing! How happy he was to discover both Albane's depth of feeling and the extent of his own affection for her! Since the episode with Ève, he had dreaded the thought of seeing her again; but his reunion with her had confirmed to him that he had matured and that she was dearer to him than anyone else . . . Had this discovery given him such satisfaction that he had disregarded her distress and neglected to see how upset she was?

Three parakeets pursued a cockatoo through the tree trunks, brushing against Quentin as they did so, making him lower his head.

I love you. Too late. Why didn't you tell me before? The words echoed in his head. Even though he was too happy to dwell at length on the subject, it struck Quentin that in love everybody utters the same phrases, but seldom at the right time. Life is a mediocre writer: the words are there, and so are the feelings, but in wrong order. Someone ought to write the story and make sure it's worked out properly. We ought to hear the words "I love you" at the moment we need them, "I want you" should reach ears ready to receive them, deserts should be crossed together, oases discovered simultaneously, instead of expecting what doesn't come and getting what we weren't expecting. A harmonious love story is basically a story well told, in which time and circumstances have conspired together to produce the desired effect.

Quentin rubbed his hands, trying to let calm take root in him. True, he had made a hash of his reunion with Albane, but tomorrow was another day. He would make up for it. He would make up with her. Hadn't they done nothing but quarrel from the start?

From now on, confidence would nourish him, the confidence of a man in love, the confidence of a body that, at last knowing physical love, no longer prevented him from thinking clearly. Quentin counted on time to do the rest.

A limp noise on his left caught him by surprise. A putty-colored lump of bird shit had just landed on his shoulder.

He looked up and yelled, "That's it, go on, shit on me!"

There was a sniggering sound from the branches.

"Bunch of idiots!"

With the help of a handkerchief, he cleaned the blue threads of his sweater, which had quickly absorbed the dropping.

"A good thing it didn't happen earlier," he muttered to himself.

At this thought, he started laughing again.

Perched on a nearby branch, a red macaw, surprised, squawked something at him.

Quentin nodded. "Thanks for waiting, guys. And at least it was me, not her. Because you know something? The girl you saw just now, well, I can tell you this: one day, she's going to be my wife."

One leg in the air, the macaw tilted its head to the right, motionless, intrigued.

13

Is happiness bearable? Sluggish and satiated, Patricia rubbed her nose on her bare arms, which still had Hippolyte's smell on them. She closed her eyes, freeing the sensations trapped in that scent; she felt Hippolyte's hands running over her shoulders, gentle hands so used to flowers that they caressed her like a petal; she tasted the sweet, salty sweat she had gathered, like dew, from his feverish neck as he penetrated her; she lightly touched Hippolyte's silky cock with her lips, then kneaded his powerful, dappled buttocks with her palms; she heard again his rich, intoxicating voice accompanying their lovemaking, because, when he made love, Hippolyte talked, a phenomenon she hadn't encountered before. Patricia had let herself be overwhelmed, body and soul, by her Apollo, agreeing to give herself to him whenever he wanted, however he wanted, for as long as he wanted. He would often worry about her passivity and ask her guiltily to dictate her preferences; she would reply without a shade of hypocrisy that she had no preferences, except a preference for him. Far from wanting to be in control, she would abandon herself; that was the way for her to reach the heights. Giving herself was not the same as forgetting herself, it was finding herself at last in the other person's eyes.

Hippolyte had just left her to go home. Breathing in the gentle night air that bathed Place d'Arezzo, Patricia wondered if her happiness wasn't too intense. She wished she could die, there and then, on a high, because there was no guarantee that tomorrow would be as good as today. If she passed away tonight, her life would have been a success, and she would leave this world in glory. Why wait for impending decay?

Ah, the ambiguity of satisfaction . . . Contentment is both victory and surrender: it represents the fulfillment of desire but also its death. Having reached the apex of sexual pleasure, drunk with sensuality, worn out by orgasms, Patricia felt as if she would never want to make love again. She was tingling all over. She kept quivering, probably as a way to revive Hippolyte's imprint on her flesh.

In a flash, she thought of his navel, like a little lock on his hard, slim belly, a lock she so wanted to open so that she could penetrate him entirely, curl up inside him . . .

When it came down to it, she was going to live. First, because the power of inertia, weak as it was, stopped her from doing anything dangerous. And second because—she remembered—pleasure didn't kill desire: she would want Hippolyte again. *My problem is that I can't just accept happiness. I think too much, whereas being happy consists in not thinking anymore.*

Indulgently, she sighed with joy and went back into the apartment.

Albane had come back an hour earlier—two or three hours before the time she'd said she would! Patricia had shuddered when she'd heard the bolts pulled back on the front door: Hippolyte was still there, his head resting on her shoulder, and she had been scared her daughter would knock on her bedroom door, but, luckily, the girl had shut herself in her own room. So Patricia had asked Hippolyte to leave quietly, then had changed into something less provocative. Now she was lounging in a hostess gown, as if she had spent a normal evening.

Walking down the corridor, she heard unusual noises behind Albane's door. "Are you all right, darling?"

Albane did not reply; the noises continued.

"Albane, what's the matter? Albane . . . "

Patricia pressed her ear to the wooden door. A kind of shrill moan came from the room. She knocked. "Albane, open the door, please."

No reaction. She grabbed the handle. To her surprise, it turned, and the door opened. What was going on? Normally, Albane locked herself in.

Patricia saw Albane writhing with pain on the bed, her hands clutching her stomach. Rushing to her, she saw that her daughter wasn't bleeding but, with her face sallow and her eyes close, was clearly feeling faint.

"Don't fall asleep, my darling, hang in there, Mommy's here. I'm calling the doctor."

Twenty minutes later, Dr. Gemayel came out of the room where he had just spoken with Albane and given her an injection.

Anxiously, Patricia approached Gemayel. "Well?"

"Let's go somewhere private, Patricia."

They went to the living room and sat down. Patricia had switched on only the night-lights, so the room had a gloomy atmosphere, and the only bright light came from the square with the parrots.

"Your daughter tried to kill herself."

"What?"

"Don't worry, there are two pieces of good news. First, she didn't succeed, and second, she didn't mean to succeed, or she would have locked her door and used a different method."

"What did she do?"

Dr. Gemayel stood up and helped himself to a drink, because Patricia was so distraught, she had forgotten to be a hostess. He drank a large glass of water and turned to her. "Suicide by Nutella."

"Excuse me?"

"Albane ate fifteen jars of Nutella and somehow managed not to throw up. As a result, she has really bad indigestion. She won't be spending time in the grave, but on the toilet seat." He helped himself to another drink.

"That's . . . that's ridiculous," Patricia said in a choked voice, trying to make sense of the situation.

"Definitely ridiculous, but not stupid. Your daughter's an intelligent young woman, Patricia. She wanted to attract attention. No point in endangering her life for that. I've known people who drank bleach, or liquid for unblocking sinks, and didn't recover. Amateurism doesn't always preclude success. In the case of Albane, she failed in her suicide attempt beautifully, let's give her that."

"Who is she calling for help?"

"She didn't tell me."

"Me?"

"She mentioned she was having romantic difficulties."

"Oh, so it's an unhappy love affair . . . " For a reason she couldn't fathom, Patricia's cheeks turned red and feverish, and her heart started racing.

"Unless the unhappy love affair is a cover for other problems," Dr. Gemayel continued. "Albane is clearly trying to tell us something. What do you think of her boyfriend? Or her ex-boyfriend?"

Patricia rubbed her forehead, annoyed at the fact that she couldn't remember. "Well . . . I don't really know . . . Albane has a new boyfriend every couple of months. I must confess I've stopped paying attention."

"Maybe that's the problem."

Panicking now, Patricia realized she had been neglecting Albane. Yes, for several weeks now, obsessed with Hippolyte, she had been colossally selfish, speaking to her daughter only to make sure she wouldn't be around when Hippolyte came over, listening to her talk about her boyfriend only in order to replace him with the image of Hippolyte.

"Oh, my God . . . "

A sense of guilt rose inside her. Her daughter had tried to kill herself, and she hadn't noticed a thing. She burst into tears.

Dr. Gemayel rushed to her. "Now, now, Patricia, don't get me wrong. I didn't say it was your fault."

Patricia plunged into a pit of despair. There it was, the answer to her earlier question: while she might be able to bear her happiness, her daughter wasn't. She had no right to happiness. Did that mean she had to give up Hippolyte?

The following day, she went back to being an attentive, devoted mother, and dedicated herself to caring for the sick girl. Albane made no protest at being looked after, which was a good sign, she thought. Still, Patricia sensed that she was expecting some kind of gesture.

"What is it you want, my darling?"

"Nothing."

"I think you want something."

Her daughter stared at her, surprised by how perceptive she was.

"Is it something I can give you?"

Albane took time to think in order to answer honestly. "You can help me."

"How?"

"You could tell Quentin what I did."

A silence ensued. Patricia placed a kiss on her daughter's forehead and murmured, "Was it because of him?"

Albane bowed her head as a sign of the affirmative.

Patricia took a deep breath. Maybe she wouldn't have to dump Hippolyte after all. "Do you love him?"

"Yes."

"Do you know why you love him?"

"No."

"When you know why you love someone, it means you don't love him."

Albane raised an eyebrow, surprised by her mother's expertise on the subject.

"My darling, I'm going to take advantage of our time together to tell you the truth about what's going on with me."

"Is there something going on with you?"

"To say the least."

And so Patricia told her daughter about her relationship with Hippolyte. Without going into details, she didn't conceal the fact that they were lovers, nor that they couldn't live without each other. Albane was so astonished, she forgot to be sarcastic; she was discovering a new woman behind the one she had condemned, a woman who was impish and alive, a woman of flesh and blood. Although Albane didn't realize it, this transformation restored hope to her. If, past forty and in a state of physical neglect, even Patricia aroused love, then there was a future for her too, one that didn't involve suicide.

In the end, Albane was pleased with her mother's adventure. She didn't criticize her choice of the municipal gardener; on the contrary, the fact that her mother had secured this handsome specimen all the women had their eyes on was a real feather in her cap. Carried away by her story and her daughter's attention, Patricia grew ever more excited, making no attempt to conceal the passion that man had aroused in her. At first, Albane replaced Hippolyte with Quentin. Then, as Patricia talked about how mature he was, levelheaded yet ardent, experienced as well as enthusiastic, Albane had to admit to herself that her teenage love for another teenager was mission impossible: neither she nor Quentin could ever overcome their moods, their impatience, their tempers.

"Will you introduce me?"

"I'll call him." Patricia stood up and went to the door, but stopped. "Forgive me. I've been selfish again, telling you all this. There was something you wanted me to do first: speak to Quentin."

Albane bit her lip, hesitated, then said, smiling, "Actually, no."

Patricia took the smile for a sign of recovery. Had her daughter given up hope? And therefore given up suffering?

Two days later, Hippolyte rang the doorbell, ready for the introduction.

Once more, Patricia ordered Albane to come out of her room—she had already told her six times in the past hour—and went to let him in. As far as she was concerned, this meeting made their relationship official: since, at their age, you introduced your boyfriend to your children rather than your parents, she was hereby proving to Hippolyte that she was ready to commit.

As was his custom, he had brought her some splendid flowers: this time, white orchids with fuchsia hearts, bought from Xavière at great expense.

Patricia embraced him, alarmed as soon as she heard her daughter's steps behind her. Albane appeared in a miniskirt, high heels, and an almost transparent blouse that revealed her young, slim, perfect torso. As she drew closer, it became noticeable that she was wearing heavy makeup: eyes highlighted with kohl, crimson lipstick. Here and there, she had applied glitter to her golden skin, drawing attention to her cheeks, neck, breasts, and thighs.

Patricia had never seen her daughter like this, transformed into a vamp.

"Good evening," Albane murmured, making up for her daring outfit with an embarrassed demeanor.

Surprised, Hippolyte smiled and kissed her warmly on the cheek. She giggled as he hugged her.

Patricia decided not to make any criticisms: it was important for this encounter to be a success.

They went to the living room and sat down. Patricia and

Hippolyte, so used to being alone in the apartment, felt as if they were parading their affection in public; their informality, their expressions, their gestures suddenly seemed suspect, planned. In front of this teenager, they were performing their intimacy rather than living it. Albane, however, didn't seem to notice their unease; chatty, taking part in the conversation, helping her mother more than expected during the aperitif and then during the meal, she was trying to hog the attention. Before long, Patricia and Hippolyte decided to keep quiet and listen to her wit and eloquence.

Uneasily, Patricia was discovering Albane's sex appeal, noticing for the first time how long her legs were, how pretty her figure, and especially how bold she was in her attempts to charm Hippolyte.

Restrain yourself, Patricia, she thought. *Your daughter tried to kill herself a few days ago, and now look how happy she is in front of your lover. She may be dressed like a whore and behaving appallingly, but you've only got yourself to blame for that. Just put up with it this evening, you can set her right in the weeks to come.*

As for Hippolyte, the more the evening wore on, the more petrified he was. There was no doubt that Albane was flirting with him. He had to feign naïveté to reject her advances.

After dessert, Albane took advantage of her mother taking the dishes back to the kitchen to suddenly move her chair right up against his.

Pretending to notice the time, he exclaimed that he had promised Germain to relieve him of his nursemaid role before midnight.

"What a shame!" Albane purred. "Isis is so lucky. And what a mysterious name, Isis. Did you pick it?"

"Yes."

"I'd have liked to be called Isis."

"Albane's a lovely name."

"Really?"

"Really."

"And does it suit me?"

He didn't know how she had done it, but her mouth was three inches from his. Albane was so carried away by her desire to seduce that she'd lost all control.

Hippolyte rushed to the cloakroom in the hall, thanked the two women for the evening, and during the final hug grabbed Albane by the shoulders to stop her from clinging to him.

"I'll see you to the elevator," Patricia said.

Tipsy, drunk on herself, Albane spun on the spot several times, picked at the strawberries on the table, then, realizing her mother hadn't come back, went to the door to see what was happening on the landing.

Half in and half out of the elevator, Hippolyte and Patricia were talking in low voices.

"I can't stay, Patricia, the situation's getting unhealthy."

"I'm so sorry. I never imagined she'd behave like that. You have to understand, the girl never had a father. She probably sees you as a surrogate father who—"

"No, Patricia. Not as a father. Sorry, but she didn't look at me the way you look at a father. You're deluding yourself."

"I can't believe she—"

"It doesn't matter, Patricia. It's just a childish whim, and it's not going to come between us. We'll see each other without her until she's more mature. She's just a little girl who thinks she's acting like a woman because she's climbed up on high heels, a kid convinced that applying foundation by the shovel-ful will hide her acne, a virgin who believes she'll become an adult if she rubs herself against a man."

"I'm devastated."

"Watch out. She considers you her rival."

"My God!"

"Put her in her place, Patricia. It's the best thing you can do for her. Keep telling her she's fifteen, that she's spouting non-sense when she talks just for the sake of it, that she'll never attract anyone if she acts that way."

Albane didn't listen to anything more. She ran to her room and looked around for something to break. Except that she cared about her things . . . Best to take it out on herself! She didn't have sleeping pills, or any kind of medication. What could she take? Oh, yes, bleach! Her mother had made the mistake of saying, "Thank God you didn't drink bleach."

She rushed into the kitchen, grabbed the bottle, and opened it. The smell was revolting. No, she'd never be able to drink that. Too toxic.

What, then?

She heard the front door close and knew that Patricia would be coming in to give her grief. There was only one thing to do: run away.

She unbolted the back door which led to the spiral staircase and ran out, while upstairs her mother called for her in every room.

Once she was on the street, she strove to put a distance between herself and this neighborhood where everybody knew her.

She crossed Place d'Arezzo, where there was a constant to and fro of cars outside the Bidermann residence, scene of a large party, and turned onto Avenue Molière. In the chilly air, she felt as if she was walking through the night naked; the strip of material that acted as miniskirt and her thin, open blouse suddenly felt insubstantial.

When she got to the end of the Chaussée d'Alsemberg, on the edge of a less exclusive area, a car honked. She turned. As it drove past, four men inside, clearly in a good mood, indicated by their gestures that they thought she was a real stunner. Amused, she considered her outfit in a different light. She may have been shivering from the cold, but she was beautiful. These men were telling her that unequivocally. Hippolyte was an idiot!

A dark red station wagon slowed down and honked. A bunch of twenty-year-olds, beaming and tipsy, yelled obscenities at her and she was delighted. Normally, she would have been scared, but tonight, after Hippolyte's contemptuous insults, any tribute to her looks was fine by her.

She moved toward a half-wooded park that led down to the neighborhood around the station. Forgetting the dangerous aura of the place, she went in and walked under the oak trees, treading on the damp grass.

At first, she didn't see the shadowy figures, only the tree trunks. Then she noticed that the trees were moving and smiled, realizing that they were men. Another hundred yards, and she would reach the lighted boulevard where the streetcars ran.

Suddenly, three men loomed up.

"Hello, darling, aren't you scared of you who might bump into?"

A hand grabbed her buttocks. Another, her thighs. Another, her breasts.

Albane screamed.

"Look at this bitch. Goes around practically naked, in a skirt up to her pussy and a blouse no bigger than a handkerchief, and now she acts all innocent."

"Let go of me."

A powerful hand was clamped over her mouth, stopping her from screaming.

14

T he doctor brought the long, thin, sharp needle close to Wim's skull. Within a second, Wim predicted that the syringe would pierce his forehead as easily as butter, reach his brain, and rummage around in its membranes. The horror of it! The poison would wreck his neurons, and he would lose his faculties, be reduced to living like a vegetable . . .

"Please don't move," the dermatologist said. "Trust me. I do this procedure several times a day and nobody has ever died."

Too late to turn back! Wim closed his eyes, determined to confront this operation like a man. After all, lots of women went through it. Clenching his jaws, he felt the steel going into the crease between his eyebrows. The cold of it went through him. *My God, when I think that this substance paralyses the muscles and I'm being injected with it.* He felt wretched, life was humiliating him: not only had he been landed with a very average physique, but he had to fight to keep it average. The Botox wasn't going to make him handsome, only prevent decay. Did he have to spend a fortune, endure this pain, just to keep a face he hated? The pain was getting worse, and he felt like weeping . . .

"Maybe if you breathed?"

Wim swallowed air and noticed that his discomfort came mainly from his having held his breath at the sight of the needle. He concentrated now on his breathing, making sure it was regular, and this distraction made him feel better.

"There you are," the dermatologist concluded. "The blockage of your muscles should last at least six months. Now let's see what I can boost."

Wim decided to go with the flow: this torturer's job consisted in preserving or arranging faces.

Ever since he was a teenager, Wim had been dismayed by his physical appearance. His childhood had been happy and carefree, but by the age of fifteen he was looking in the mirror and examining what was happening to him: things were growing in all directions and in no apparent order, with hairs appearing here and not there, developing in an arbitrary way he couldn't control. Several times, he had sat down at his desk to draw, with anatomical examples for comparison, the body and face he desired, hoping that by defining them, concentrating on them, he would force nature to obey. All in vain! By the time he was seventeen, he had been forced to consider his face and figure as definitive; disappointed, he had concluded that he would never go very far with that: he would have to be clever, or else . . . So he had developed the intelligence and energy of the ill-favored, becoming lively, friendly, cultivated, funny, full of stories and anecdotes that he told in order to dazzle—giving the word its precise meaning: to stop the other person from seeing.

Ever since he had become involved in the modern art world, he had regretted the fact that he was average rather than ugly. The ugly can be remarkable, it attracts attention, disgust, enthusiasm, rejection, in other words, emotion. In art as in life, the ugly is the one challenger of the beautiful, David against Goliath, the antihero turned hero. On an impulse, Wim had thought of getting himself scarified: deep cuts, horrible scars, would have made his face unforgettable. But making some trials with tracing paper placed over his photograph, he had concluded that he would be more likely to look like an accident victim than someone who was fascinatingly ugly. Slashing the canvas of a Sunday painter didn't turn it into a masterpiece.

The doctor was now pricking his face in order to firm up the flesh in various places.

"Don't forget to apply arnica cream if you don't want lots of bruises."

"All right, doctor."

Although Wim had no desire to see the result, the doctor handed him a mirror. "There, what do you think?"

Wim didn't recognize himself. He had been replaced by his mother. The cosmetic procedure had made him look even more like that good, ordinary Flemish woman whom he had no desire to resemble.

He ventured a slight criticism. "It's smooth and round, but maybe a little too . . . "

"Young."

"Feminine?"

The doctor took away the mirror and examined Wim thoroughly. After some thirty seconds of silence, he concluded, "Not at all!"

"It's all right, then."

Wim was lying, and knew the doctor was too, but he didn't insist, aware that, without a strong dose of hypocrisy, there would be no social life.

Meg was waiting for him at the gallery, having already solved two thirds of the problems the business was encountering. Out of habit, he looked through her work then congratulated her.

"You're a real pearl, Meg."

Touched, she lowered her head, quivering with embarrassment. To regain her composure, she took a package from her handbag and extracted a tube, which she held out to Wim. "Here you are. I knew you had an appointment with Dr. Pelly, so I thought you might need arnica."

He took the tube, disconcerted by so much thoughtfulness.

"Thank you, Meg. You really are incredible. You're the woman I ought to marry." He got pensively to his feet and repeated as he left the room, "Yes, I often tell myself that. You're the woman I ought to marry."

Then, without turning, he disappeared to join some customers who were looking at paintings by Rothko.

Meg sat there on her chair, downcast. Those last words had crucified her: the reason he had uttered them so innocently was because he considered the idea far-fetched! There had to be nothing equivocal between them for him to risk saying it. Why was the thought of marrying her so grotesque? What did she have that discouraged love?

After wasting several hours with customers who couldn't make up their minds, Wim strolled unhurriedly back to Place d'Arezzo. He was in no great hurry to see Petra von Tannenbaum, who was proving to be somewhat boring company outside public occasions. She spent her days looking after herself—her body by practicing gymnastics, her diet by eating seeds, her skin by using all kinds of treatments and creams, her clothes by bullying a theatrical costume designer—and if she had any time left over, she would cut out photographs and articles from newspapers and stick them in exercise books like a lovestruck teenager; as her own biggest fan, she collected everything she could find about herself.

As for her conversation, it didn't last beyond two or three meals together. Wim knew by now what she allowed people to know about her; for the rest, she experienced nothing and was interested in nothing. He was so talkative, so loquacious, that he sometimes had the impression of addressing only silence, because she really didn't listen to him.

The only moments they shared were when they went out together in public. At a cocktail party, a first night, a reception, a private viewing, the two of them were so charismatic, they inevitably attracted attention and gossip, however rude or skeptical it might be. Like conspirators, they greedily savored the rumors they provoked.

Entering the loft, Wim saw a yellow envelope bearing his name on the marble work surface in the kitchen. Inside it was a cutting from a newspaper.

He unfolded the sheet of paper, and the headline was like a blow to his solar plexus: *Premature ejaculation: should we try to remedy it?*

Anxiously, he looked around. Who was playing this nasty trick on him? He turned the envelope over and over, remembered having seen it before, and realized that it had been reused. Someone had come into his apartment and laid a trap for him . . .

Meg? But how could she know? She never came into his private sphere; she was the perfect assistant because she always showed respect and discretion. A member of the domestic staff? The Filipino men employed in the kitchen and the Filipino women who did the housework didn't understand French, and communicated only in English. Petra, then? Petra was unaware of that intimate fact about him, since he and she had never slept together; not only did she not like sex, she didn't give a damn about other people.

Irritably, he looked at the sub-headlines that interspersed the article: *80% of men under eighteen suffer from premature ejaculation . . . Not a physical deformation . . . Medication is no help . . . Controlling the emotions . . . Persuading your husband he has a problem . . .*

The page came from a women's magazine, which disturbed him even more. Meg? Petra? Impossible.

His eyes skimmed over the article: *"The premature ejaculator often releases his seed less than a minute after penetration, being unable to delay it."* Less than a minute, yes, that was it.

He heard footsteps and quickly stuffed the paper into his pocket. Petra appeared, holding a box.

"Oh, there you are, darling. I was just coming to mix my creatine."

She put two spoonfuls of powder in a glass, added water, and stirred it with a silver spoon.

Wim realized that he had left the envelope open on the marble surface. She also noticed it.

"Oh," she said, "you saw the article I cut out for you."

He turned white.

Knocking the spoon against the glass, she continued without looking at him, "Oh, yes, I heard from a girlfriend in London that this was your problem. The model Policy, do you remember? Very beautiful, yes. Very talkative. Especially when she has a glass in her hand. No, don't be angry at her, poor thing, it's thanks to her that we're here today, because that was what first drew my attention to you." She drank her concoction, grimaced, then emitted a slight burp. "That kind of thing doesn't bother me, for obvious reasons. But I told myself that, for you, it must be a real problem."

Wim turned red, unable to answer.

"Yes, as you say," she went on, "it's kind of me." She burped again. "I really can't take this creatine anymore. I can't wait to go to New York, they say there's a new mixture there that has a similar effect on the muscle structure, but without this horrible taste. I read all about it in bodybuilders' blogs."

In normal circumstances, if he hadn't been humiliated, Wim would have been amused by the scene: the sophisticated Petra von Tannenbaum poring over sporting tips from pumped-up musclemen.

At last she looked at him. "Anyway, darling, this is just to say that I can keep a secret. I hope you can too." At last, she was coming to the point. "I'll have left you with the memory of a torrid partner. And when I think of you, I'll suppose that . . . you were amazing. Do we agree?"

Petra suggested to Wim that she never mention his sexual

difficulties if he, in return, remained silent about her indifference to sex.

"Agreed, Petra. It's what I would have said even if you hadn't shown me that article."

"Yes, you'd probably have said it boastfully. I prefer it should be out of fear."

With that, she left the room.

For the second time that day, Wim found life absurd and interminable. So much effort to hide the sordid reality . . .

That Saturday night, Petra von Tannenbaum was due to perform at the Petrodossian Gallery in front of an audience of the most fashionable people in Brussels.

Stage fright made her horrid; she screamed in several languages at the Filipino staff, called Meg a fat, stupid cow when the latter couldn't get the organizers of the event on the phone, and insulted Wim with sharp, scathing, repetitive cruelty.

They took the blows without responding, as fatalistically as people awaiting the end of a storm.

At last, the props were sent to the gallery and Petra, locked in the bathroom that constituted her temple, finished her preparations.

When Wim suggested giving her a lift to the venue, she merely murmured, "Don't behave like an old husband. I'll get there on my own, if Meg manages to find me a taxi." She turned suddenly and looked him in the eyes. "On the other hand, I would like you to join me in the wings as soon as the show is over and behave like a jealous lover, I give you permission for that. It's the best way for me to get rid of unwelcome admirers."

Wim nodded, not knowing if he should hate or admire the way Petra had of assigning tasks like an army officer.

He left the mezzanine and joined Meg in the loft. "You know about the taxi?"

"Oh, yes, it was ordered three days ago. I've already called back at least four times to make sure it'll be here on time."

"Thanks, Meg."

"Would you like a glass of whiskey? A fifteen-year-old Lagavulin?"

"I think I need it."

She brought in the drink. "On the rocks, the way you like it."

"Thanks. You're the woman I ought to have married."

Meg made no attempt to decipher from Wim's inscrutable face what was hidden behind that last nuance: "I ought to have." How much longer could she hold out, being at the side of a man she loved but didn't love her, a man who was constantly mentioning their desirable but impossible marriage?

As was her habit, when her morale has been sapped, she went and took shelter in the toilet.

At seven o'clock, Petra burst on them like a bomb, took out her anger on Wim, Meg, the organizers, and this "shitty Belgium" with its "stupid public," wondered one last time why she was making so much effort to satisfy people who were ungrateful and devoid of taste, then, slamming the door, went down to get her taxi.

Left alone, Wim and Meg looked at each other like two camel drivers after a sandstorm has passed.

"Another glass of whiskey?" Meg suggested.

"Absolutely," Wim replied.

Sipping the amber liquid that tasted of peat and smoke, they discussed the affairs of the gallery, some of their customers, and a new artist whose work they had discovered and were trying to promote. For both of them, there was nothing more pleasant than this relaxed conversation about what constituted their everyday life. Wim really didn't want to leave, and Meg had to point out the time on her watch.

"Don't miss the show."

Wim sighed and got laboriously to his feet, with none of his usual liveliness.

"And don't forget your keys."

"I won't, Meg."

"I'll switch off the lights."

"Thank you, Meg, thank you for everything."

He grabbed his keys and walked out.

Meg checked all three floors, closed the shutters, switched on the alarm system, and got ready to leave.

Her keys had disappeared. In a panic, she looked in her pockets and her bag, then, for fear of setting off the alarm, blocked the antitheft system, and began a systematic search for her keys.

Alas, Wim had taken them by mistake.

She had no way of getting out. Of course, she could simply slam the door shut behind her, but how could she take that risk when art worth several million euros was hanging on the walls? No, she would have to wait for Wim and Petra to get back. Grabbing the bottle of Scotch, she poured herself another glass, not a Parisienne's portion this time, no, the portion of a true Flemish woman.

After all, what difference did it make if she stayed here? Nobody was waiting for her.

Petra von Tannenbaum's show had delighted the exclusive Brussels audience.

"Nothing vulgar about it at all!"

"A revolution in the genre!"

"Female beauty, but with a hint of irony just beneath the surface, and, underlying it all, a sense of kitsch."

Hearing these conventional comments, Wim kept drinking. During the performance, he had come to the realization that he couldn't stand Petra anymore; even her statuesque figure had stopped fascinating him: he knew all the work that went into forming those curves, he sensed the sweat beneath her powdered skin, he was aware of her efforts to keep her stomach ideally flat and her insides on the inside.

As expected, he played the guard dog outside the dressing room, filtering those who came to pay their respects by glaring at them in a hostile manner. Since this comedy would help his reputation as a man for whom everything always went right, he performed it to perfection.

Boredom only kicked in when he found himself alone again in his car with Petra. The latter, relaxed after the success of the show, was in a talkative mood, which was quite unusual for her.

"Darling, at what age do you think I should quit? Thirty-eight, that's what I've decided."

"You'll still be gorgeous at the age of thirty-eight."

"That's what I mean: I'll quit when I'm at the height of my beauty. I won't tolerate any image of myself diminished. It's unbearable enough to see photographs of my childhood or my teenage years show up here and there."

"What will you do when you quit?"

"What a question! When I quit, I quit. That's it. The ultimate farewell!"

"I don't understand."

"I'll kill myself, darling."

"Petra!"

"But of course! In order to be complete, my legend requires a tragic ending."

"You are joking, I hope?"

"Not a bit of it. Only death will transfer my life into a destiny."

"Why don't you just wait to die?"

"I'll never agree to decay, not after the sacrifices I've forced myself to make. At the age of thirty-eight, I'll kill myself, it's been decided for a long time."

"Petra, I beg you to—"

"Look at poor Greta Garbo: she was smart enough to quit movies when she was perfect, but then she chickened out and carried on living. Have you seen the photographs taken by paparazzi outside her building in New York, with her sublime face ravaged by time? The shame of it! But *I'll* have the courage."

Wim fell silent. Petra irritated him so much that he almost regretted she wasn't already thirty-eight so that he could get rid of her.

"Don't worry, darling, I'll have published my memoirs first. Just to stop people saying whatever they like. And I think I shall write a few very friendly lines about you."

"Thank you, Petra. I'm touched."

She gave a slight grimace. His answer wasn't the one she'd expected. "What about you?" she asked. "Will you write your memoirs one day?"

"Of course, Petra. When a man has met an artist like you, the publishers demand that he write his memoirs. Have no fear."

"Thank you," she concluded in a satisfied tone.

The car reached Place d'Arezzo, which was congested thanks to a reception being held at the Bidermanns'. Women in long dresses and men in tuxedos were entering the fully lit town house, from which the sounds of a string orchestra emerged. Out of politeness, Wim thought he should explain the purpose of this event to the indifferent Petra. "Our neighbor, the European Commissioner for Competition Zachary Bidermann, a world-renowned economist, is going to be appointed Prime Minister of Belgium."

"Oh, yes, I know all about that."

Wim suppressed an exclamation of surprise. Did she follow current affairs? Had he misjudged her, thinking she only read articles about herself?

"Are you invited, darling?"

"No."

"Why not?"

"I have no desire to take sides politically."

"Phone them, I'd like to go."

Petra had given him this order as if telling a taxi driver an address.

"I'm sorry, Petra," he replied irritably, "I'm not in the habit of begging for invitations."

"You're pathetic, darling."

Wim didn't react to the insult. The sense of well-being brought on by the many drinks he'd had lessened his anger toward Petra.

Once they were back in the apartment, she put on a sumptuous ostrich feather coat and announced, "I'm going to that reception."

"Without an invitation?"

"I don't think they'll turn me away. The fact is, I haven't been invited anywhere for years now, but I've been received everywhere. Naturally, you're not coming?"

"Naturally," Wim replied.

She shrugged and walked out the door.

Wim went to the window and amused himself watching her as she crossed the square. Arrogant and regal, like a queen in exile, she climbed the steps, talked with the servants, and went inside.

"Just stay there," Wim muttered.

Feeling happy, he looked for the Lagavulin, but couldn't find it. What he did find was a bottle of Jameson. He poured himself a full glass and put on a Duke Ellington disc.

An hour later, drunk but feeling carefree, he went up to the mezzanine and threw himself on his bed.

He struck a body. Startled, he lit the bedside lamp and discovered Meg, drunk and fast asleep on the comforter.

Amused, he gazed down at her. Her plump, smooth pink

flesh demanded to be caressed. He sniffed her hair, which had the heady aroma of sour apples. To his surprise, he realized that he felt like making love.

He stood up, determined to go down to the loft and sleep on the couch. Meg turned over, opened her eyes, and saw him.

"I drank too much," she said, smiling.

"Same here," Wim replied cheerfully.

She seized his head in both hands and, without thinking, brought it close to hers and kissed him.

Amused, he abandoned himself to this kiss. Their bodies touched.

When they looked at each other, they burst out laughing. In their minds, disinhibited by the alcohol, they weren't doing anything serious or important, they were just playing a nice game. Besides, they got along so well . . .

Caressing all the while, and constantly bursting into laughter, Wim undressed Meg, then undressed himself. Then he lay down on top of Meg and cuddled her.

Just as slowly, he entered her. She abandoned herself.

Wim started making love to her. Never before had he had this feeling; whereas he usually came too quickly, now he was transformed into a supple animal, undulating in the other person's body, varying the positions to increase the pleasure.

Meg let herself be manipulated, delighted to discover such a good lover.

After twenty minutes of these sweet embraces, she felt a great warmth flood through her. "I . . . I'm going to come."

Wim neither slowed down nor speeded up, he merely continued, subtly and inexorably, the movement that was making her so happy.

She screamed with pleasure and clasped him to her, exhausted but radiant.

Wim left her body. For the first time, he was a male pleasuring a female. Even though he had serviced a woman and her orgasm, he felt powerful. This was the supreme power: the power to hold back.

"Make me come," he whispered.

So Meg got down on all fours and helped her lord and master to achieve climax.

15

The show broke the ratings record—something the channel immediately realized from the number of e-mails and phone calls flooding in during the live broadcast—because Zachary Bidermann, besides being viewed by the nation as the man who could stem the crisis, had a gift for holding the public's attention. When he was on, whether you were illiterate or had a degree in Economics, you didn't switch channels.

He was reassuring. Not so much through what he said but through his body language. Sturdy, well-built, broad-shouldered, with a thick neck, Zachary looked like a powerful, huddled animal, ready to pounce. He kept his strong, muscular hands, capable of anything—grabbing and breaking, caressing and strangling—close to his chest, guardians of their master, ready to intervene, to seethe with indignation as he commented on figures or put forward solutions. His neck suggested strength: broad, solid, lined with visible veins, a chimney sending energy from the torso to the brain. His eyes, reduced to half-moons by heavy eyelids, were hypnotic, thanks to their ocean blue color turning to steel-gray; motionless, then looking in a different direction without anyone noticing them move, the pupils followed their own rhythm, indifferent to external prompts. Although his hair was immaculately white, his black eyebrows testified to the fact that his youth and vigor were still intact. As for his mouth, it either drooped cynically or rose at the corners, producing a cruel, even voracious smile, like a wolf's chops. A laughing Zachary was different from a reasoning Zachary, and the contrast was fascinating. He was a living paradox, a top-level intellectual hidden inside the body of a beast.

In spite of herself, the interviewer had fallen for his charms. Even though, coached by her journalist colleagues in the editorial offices, she had geared herself up to be combative, during the debate itself she couldn't stop herself from drinking in her interviewee's words; at times, when he complimented her on a question, she even blushed. There was a kind of erotic tension between them, a tension she endured and he controlled. And the e-mails coming in showed that it wasn't just the interviewer's desires that were being aroused by Zachary Bidermann, to judge from the number of passionate declarations of love.

What was the appeal of the man? He was neither ugly nor handsome, so what spell did he cast? In the case of the interviewer, he showed her that he never forgot she was a woman, even in the middle of a debate, even at the height of a fierce exchange of views; there were features in his face that said, "I can't wait for this cerebral interaction to be over, because we have better things to do together." Even though he was addressing her educated consciousness, he stirred her primitive brain, the part that still yearns for the instinctual, that searches for the strong, protective adult whose semen will bear fruit, the chief who will guarantee food, safety, dependency. Beneath the tailor-made three-piece suit, beneath a rational discussion of economics, there was a Neanderthal male addressing a Cro-Magnon female.

Men saw him as a chief rather than a rival, a natural leader. Without the usual shilly-shallying of a politician, and without any show of false modesty, Zachary Bidermann exerted his influence, the commander a defenseless era needed.

Léo Adolf and his Party associates, who were in the studio

audience, were pleased with the show: there was no doubt that it would allow them to put forward Zachary Bidermann as the head of a so-called "technical" government to deal with the crisis. Not everyone was happy with the choice, but after his performance tonight there would be only a few naysayers left.

There were thirty seconds to go: the interviewer came to the topic on everybody's mind.

"Monsieur Bidermann, your expertise is beyond question, and there's talk of you taking over the highest position in the country. What's your reaction to that?"

"The only thing I've ever wanted over the last fifty years is to serve my country and Europe."

"So are you ready?"

"Since last night."

"Excuse me?"

"Last night, I got my wife Rose's permission. She gave me the go-ahead to devote my time and energy to serving the nation."

"Won't she be jealous?"

"She promised to be patient, but for her sake, and your sake, and all our sakes, I'd better succeed quickly."

The interviewer smiled, delighted that the program was ending on a personal note, paying tribute to wives, which gave the show a human dimension. When the credits started rolling, accompanied by percussive music, she thanked him profusely.

"Well done! You were wonderful."

"Thanks to you, mademoiselle."

They were both thinking of their own interests, which, for the time being, coincided: a brilliant guest meant a brilliant show.

As she got up from her stool, and before the audience rushed to ask for autographs, the interviewer switched off her microphone and whispered in his ear, "I'm a great friend of Carmen Bix."

It was her way of implying that she knew everything about his torrid relationship with the Spanish woman. He took in the message, narrowed his eyes, and said in a velvety voice, "You choose your friends well, mademoiselle."

At that moment, the interviewer understood why this man was so seductive: what made him handsome was that he thought women were beautiful.

That evening, Rose Bidermann had organized a reception in Place d'Arezzo, to celebrate her husband's progress to power. As far as his supporters were concerned, Belgium's most-watched TV program was already a political triumph for Zachary Bidermann: in the days that followed, he would step onto the national stage as prime minister.

In the hallway of their town house, Rose beamed as she welcomed her first guests. She'd always believed that one day she would stand here proudly on the arm of the most powerful man in the country. When she had fallen in love with Zachary, her passion had been genuine, but also served her stated ambitions: this brilliant economist would take her to the very top.

Rose was one of those women who find power erotic.

She believed that a man had to excel at all things: authority, money, culture, intelligence, sex. Those who had known Zachary in the past described him as exceptionally gifted but an amateur, even lazy; at the time, he didn't exploit his talents because he was too fond of living. She had changed him. Because she had seen him as a superman, he had tried hard to become one. Since Rose, thanks to her or because of her, he had been obsessed with success. He wanted the best, because he hoped to live up to the way she saw him. On occasion, nothing pleased Rose more than an old friend of Zachary's commenting on the progress he had made and congratulating her on her influence on him. Nevertheless, she hardly suspected the collateral damage of their mutual ambition.

Since she could only see him as the best—the best econo-mist, the best politician, the best statesman—the idler had been replaced by a workaholic, the hedonist by a distinguished official. With pressure had come compulsion. Zachary was plagued by an all-pervasive fear of not living up to expectation. Several times a day, in the midst of his activities, he would plunge into depression; it wasn't fatigue he felt, it was anxiety. The only way he could fight it was with orgasms. Pleasure wiped out his dark thoughts, the sensual waves spreading through his body calmed him. At first, Rose had sufficed for his pressing needs; but as his capacity for work and success grew, his sexual requirements increased. His meteoric rise had led him to adultery, to frequenting prostitutes, and, sometimes, to making sudden passes at any representative of the fair sex.

Rose was not only unaware of this obsession, she denied it if anyone so much as hinted at it. How could a husband who made love to her so often—once or twice a day—be leading a double life? In addition, her faith in destiny made her trust Zachary; because he hadn't made any mistakes in his race to power, she imagined him to be inexhaustibly virtuous. And so the most cheated-on wife in Brussels displayed the radiant serenity of a woman who believes she is the one and only . . .

The reception rooms of the town house were becoming more crowded by the minute. European commissioners, tech-nocrats, ministers, and would-be ministers pressed in, so that later they could say, "I was there."

Rose and Zachary had given up standing in the hallway to welcome everyone. Letting the staff direct the new arrivals, they circulated, separately, from group to group.

"What the hell are you doing here?" Zachary said in a low voice to a sixty-year-old man in a checkered cap and a tweed hunting suit, with a nose that showed the effects of alcohol.

"Surprised to see Dédé?"

Zachary Bidermann grimaced.

Dédé from Antwerp managed several brothels in Belgium. He pointed to Rose, who was laughing with Léo Adolf some distance from them. "Look at that, I never knew your lady was so buxom! Congratulations, old man: you've ticked all the right boxes, haven't you?"

"What the hell are you doing here?"

"I've come for a drink because, believe it or not, I'm soon going to be the buddy of the Prime Minister."

"Don't go bragging about it."

"Come on, you know Dédé. If you're not discreet in my line of work, you won't last long. No, I dropped by because I was thinking . . . Now that you're taking the top job, maybe you could help to ease my tax problems."

"Really?"

"Let me tell you. They're asking for four—"

Zachary put a hand on his shoulder. "Look, Dédé, let's be quite clear about this, man-to-man. The fact that I know you is neither here nor there. I'm not going to help you. In fact, I won't help anybody. In a few days' time, I won't be me anymore, I'll be the Prime Minister. Impartial and without a blemish."

"Fine words . . . "

"Dédé, you're the first to say politics is rotten."

"Of course, but—"

"You've had my final word on this, I won't change my mind. But I'll still come to your establishments and pay without haggling over the price, because you've got some terrific girls. That's my only promise to you."

Dédé, who cried easily, became misty-eyed and, suddenly full of admiration, stammered, "You're a great guy, Zachary."

He seized his hand and shook it. Dédé couldn't have thanked him more if he had actually helped him. He, the king of wheeler-dealers, the prince of cheats, slippery as an eel, was fascinated by the image of an incorruptible man: he felt as if he was on friendly terms with King Solomon.

As he walked away, Zachary smiled at the thought that, if the elections were brought forward, he would at least get the vote of the greatest crook in Belgium.

He greeted his neighbor, the widower François-Maxime de Couvigny, who stood there looking tense and drawn, spoke to him for a few seconds about the recapitalization of the banks, then approached another group.

He gave a sweeping glance around to see if his famous neighbor, the writer Baptiste Monier, had snubbed him as usual. Zachary was shocked at the way Monier kept himself to himself and rejected social life. Why was such an internationally renowned novelist always stuck at home? Why didn't he have any friends? The worst of it was that in a few decades, Zachary Bidermann and all the politicians here would be forgotten, but people would still be reading Baptiste Monier, who would by then be considered a true witness of his century, even though he hadn't seen anything of it.

He was sighing when a man he didn't know came up to him. "Good evening, Monsieur Bidermann. Sylvain Gomez."

"Have we met?"

"Yes, at Mille Chandelles."

Zachary didn't flinch at the mention of the swingers' club. "Did my wife invite you?"

"I took the liberty of coming. I'd like to speak with you."

"Gladly. Give me five minutes."

Casually, Zachary walked away, isolated himself for a moment in a room closed to the guests, called his loyal Singer, and conferred with her.

Affably, he returned to the hallway, where Sylvain Gomez was waiting for him. "Shall we adjourn to my office, monsieur?"

Unfazed, Sylvain Gomez followed Zachary to his office, which overlooked the square with the birds. Tonight, the usual chorus of parrots and parakeets was drowned by the hubbub of the reception.

Zachary Bidermann sat down behind his solid desk and waited for the man to speak.

Embarrassed by the silence, Gomez cleared his throat and began, "You must be wondering why I'm bothering you."

Zachary Bidermann continued to stare at him without answering.

"I was at Mille Chandelles the other night, and inadvertently took a few pictures."

The word "inadvertently" sounded a false note: the owners of Mille Chandelles demanded that you leave any recording device at the entrance, it being the rule in such places to respect everyone's anonymity. Clearly, the man had cheated.

"I have some photographs of you. Would you like to see them?"

Zachary remained impassive.

Gomez persisted, scrolling through the snapshots on the screen of his cell phone. "Don't you like souvenirs?"

"I prefer my own."

Zachary's metallic voice had resounded, clear and abrupt in the large room.

The man grinned. "Let's see, who would be interested in these photographs? Your wife, perhaps?"

Zachary said nothing.

"Your friends in the Party? Or your political enemies? You've got lots of those."

Zachary looked up wearily at the ceiling.

Disconcerted, the man grew resentful. "Or the press? Yes, the press loves that kind of scoop."

Slowly, Zachary drank the aperitif he was holding.

"You're not exactly helping me," the man growled. "You should ask me how much."

Immediately, Zachary's voice echoed without conviction, "How much?"

"Ten thousand."

"Is that all?"

"For now."

"Oh, that's reassuring."

The man was nervous and uneasy. The conversation wasn't going according to plan.

Zachary leaned forward. "I'm going to offer you something better than that." He held out a bowl of peanuts. "I'm going to offer you a peanut."

"Excuse me?"

"A peanut for your photographs. Then you won't have come all the way here for nothing."

The man stood up, humiliated, and took a couple of steps around the chair, then, finding new inspiration, sneered in exasperation, "You don't seem to realize the kind of tsunami I can unleash."

"And neither do you, monsieur. You keep this up, and as early as tomorrow morning, Monsieur Sylvain Gomez, you'll be subjected to a tax audit on all four of your companies: Lafina, Poliori, Les Bastonnes, and Découverte asiatique. In addition, I'll take the liberty of calling my friend Meyer, the Finance Minister of Luxembourg, just to check if you have any accounts there, a favor he won't hesitate to grant, believe me. Then, if I don't find any morsels there, I'll call my contacts in Switzerland, Panama, the Cayman Islands. You'd be amazed at how many friends one has when one's a European commissioner for competition, there's really no need to become prime minister."

Gomez had turned pale with fright. "But . . . that's blackmail."

"Who started it?"

"You don't scare me," Gomez said, trying to brazen it out.

"Oh, really?"

"No. Because you seem to think I'm dishonest."

"I don't think. I have proof."

Because Zachary had brought up the possibility of blackmail, Gomez concluded that Zachary was already in possession of compromising information.

He swallowed and sat back down. "All right, I'll stop with the photography."

"Excellent idea, you don't have a talent for it. Are you sure you wouldn't like a peanut?"

Zachary Bidermann stood up and ordered Gomez to leave the room with him. "I shan't see you out: you can find your own way."

The man slipped away.

With a confident stride, Zachary Bidermann returned to his guests, sneaking Rose a passing kiss.

Léo Adolf detached himself from the group he was talking with and caught Zachary by the arm. "A great success tonight, a success that sweeps away any remaining hesitations. I've spoken with the heads of the various groupings in Parliament and they've agreed to provide you with a coalition majority. All we need now is for poor Vanserbrock to resign, which will happen in the next couple of days. So basically, starting tomorrow, we're going to set in motion the procedure that will make you prime minister. Congratulations."

"Thank you."

Léo Adolf suddenly dropped his voice and led Zachary into a quiet corner. "Politicians have such a damaged reputation nowadays that we're taking a big risk. A leader must be seen to be beyond reproach. Even when he is, people will be as quick to hate him as to love him. We've got the life expectancy of a paper handkerchief. I don't think there'll be one idiot left to take the job twenty years from now."

"What are you getting at?"

"You're our last hope, Zachary. If you fail, the political class will be rejected. But if you stumble before you've succeeded, that'll be even worse. All trust will disappear."

"'Stumble?'"

"Swear to me that your behavior will be exemplary. I am, of course, referring to women."

Zachary burst out laughing. "I swear."

"You say it very easily, but I know how hard it is to change."

Zachary felt a painful little contraction in his heart. "How do you know? Maybe my flitting around is just an expression of unfulfilled ambition. Now that I won't be denied power as much as I was before, it may be that I'll give up on these compensations."

Leo was sure this was all just talk on the part of Zachary, but he chose to be prudent and refrain from insisting: after all, if there was one chance in a million that Zachary believed in what he was saying, Léo wouldn't be the one to disabuse him. "Even if you do change, Zachary, there may be charges that can be dredged up from the past."

"You're really paranoid!"

"In other words, Zachary, how well could you stand up to blackmail?"

The way I did ten minutes ago, Zachary thought. Out loud, he said reassuringly, "Well, I've managed up until now."

"The higher you climb, the more of a target you are."

"The higher the target, the harder it is to reach."

"I wish I could share your optimism."

"It's because you don't share it, my dear Léo, that they want to give me this position, not you."

Léo took it on the chin, in a spirit of fair play. The two men had been running side by side in the political race for twenty-five years, often in opposition, sometimes as allies, always keeping an eye on each other. A camaraderie of rivals had developed between them: they loved their country, they were building Europe, they frequented the same people among the powerful and the powerless. Throughout their careers, whenever one of them experienced a failure, he would think about the failures the other man had overcome; when they had a victory, they remembered how fragile it was. Both now in their sixties, different as they were, they felt a sense of brotherhood, the brotherhood of a generation that had navigated the same dangers together.

Léo was conciliatory by nature, whereas Zachary was an attacker. The former excelled in analysis and synthesis, the latter in inventiveness. One managed while the other created. In these chaotic times, men like Léo Adolf weren't enough: the nation needed more than an administrator, it needed a visionary, an artist, someone positive and optimistic who offered people a future.

"All right, now you'd better go and flatter Costener, Zachary, it'll oil the wheels."

"Your wish is my command, Monsignor."

Zachary resumed his journey from guest to guest, polite, approachable, both casual and regal. Outwardly, he acted with ease, but deep inside him his usual depression was coming on. His conversation with Léo had made the prospect of power concrete, and that was starting to eat away at him. He might have played scenes from a comedy with Dédé from Antwerp and Gomez, but now they were giving him the leading role in a tragedy: the country's finances. Would he be able to get the necessary measures through? He would have to convince everyone, from cleaning ladies in Hainaut to Flemish parliamentarians. Wasn't that impossible?

He felt a strong urge for sex. Rose? She wouldn't leave her guests. He looked for Dédé and found him by the stock of champagne.

"Dédé, do you have any supplies with you?"

"What do you need?"

"The minimum."

"A blow job?"

"Yes."

"Sorry, Zachary, I didn't bring anyone. Have a look around. At this kind of party, there's no shortage of whores, if you ask me."

Zachary climbed one step and looked over his guests. Too bad it was only men who waved at him, eager to congratulate the hero of the day.

His migraine was getting worse. At that moment, a waitress scurried past him on her way down to the cellar to fetch more bottles of champagne. She was short, blonde, and placid-looking, the perfect victim, a bird without wings.

Without thinking, he followed her. When he got down there within the cool brick walls, the rotting mushroom smell reminded him of the muggy atmosphere of a sauna and excited him. He sped after the waitress between the rows of bottles.

There, he grabbed her and forced a kiss on her. She struggled but he used his strength. When she managed to move back a little, she realized it was the master of the house and panicked even more.

"Don't scream, my dear, just give me pleasure."

Maintaining his grip, he took her hand and placed it on his crotch. Blinking, the girl understood.

"You're willing to give me pleasure, aren't you?"

He was holding her so tight that she thought it best to give in if she didn't want to be strangled.

Lowering herself, she opened Zachary's zipper and obeyed.

Seven minutes later, relieved, Zachary thanked the waitress. He put his clothes back on and went back up the stairs to the reception rooms.

Exhausted and disgusted, the girl was still huddled there, wanting to sob.

A shadowy figure emerged from a corner of the cellar and approached her. Somebody had witnessed the scene. A tall, elegant woman with a face like a Madonna leaned over the girl.

"I got lost looking for the toilets and saw everything. We're going to report him."

"No, madame, I'll lose my job."

"Ignoring this is out of the question."

"Please, madame, I don't want any hassle. If you say anything, I'll deny it."

The woman slowly nodded, then gave her a handkerchief. "Here, wipe yourself."

At around midnight, the party was still in full swing, the string orchestra was playing more modern, more rhythmical pieces, and some of the guests had started dancing.

Zachary Bidermann was talking with everyone. He was in a cheerful mood, and more brilliant than ever. The press photographers flashed their cameras as soon as he stood next to a famous person.

Suddenly, Zachary demanded that Rose be included. They struck a cheerful, amorous pose, which was applauded by the guests.

In the midst of the ovation, three police officers burst in. "Excuse us, ladies and gentlemen, we've received a call about an assault."

Petra von Tannenbaum appeared from behind a screen. "I made the call."

Everyone looked with surprise at this magnificent creature nobody had noticed: in marked contrast to her extreme sophistication, the straps of her dress were torn and her hair was inexplicably disheveled.

Trembling, she pointed a finger at Zachary. "He's the one who raped me."

A shudder went through the assembled guests.

She took a handkerchief from her reticule and added, with a sob, "I have proof."

PART FOUR
DIES IRAE

That night, a night when a tense heat weighed over the city and would disappear only with a thunderstorm, the parrots spoke their mother tongue, the one that is still a mystery to men. Their lively chatter built footbridges of sound between branches, threw creepers from tree to tree, recreating a jungle on the square, from the majestic nest occupied by the macaw to the huge boat of twigs where several families of small green parakeets resided. The hullabaloo added to the fog inside the brains of the humans.

We may train parrots to say whatever we want, but parrots actually say what they want. What is a speaking parrot trying to explain? What is a silent parrot trying to express?

When civilization shuts parrots in cages, we can view them as acoustic monkeys—unless, that is, we view monkeys as acrobatic parrots.

Let us stop seeing them with human eyes.

They babble, cackle, prattle, then, all of a sudden, they observe a minute's silence. The hubbub resumes and, here and there, there are fragments of French, Portuguese, Italian. Are they reproducing echoes of our sentences without understanding them, or are they revealing their exceptional skills? Perfect linguists with sharp ears, they might be double agents, able to handle the language of men as well as that of birds. What makes us so sure that we are superior to them, we featherless bipeds with no lexical duplicity?

When they speak our language, are they addressing only us

or are they conducting a conversation among themselves? Perhaps they are spying on the acts of humans, reporting on them, criticizing them, circulating malicious gossip about them . . .

The more time you spent on Place d'Arezzo, the more convinced you were that you were entering a zone of mystery. Even the name of the square bordered on the surreal, paying homage as it did to the Benedictine monk Guido of Arezzo, who invented the system of musical notation to dispel the fog of oral transmission. "He who performs without understanding is nothing but an animal," he said. In music, Guido of Arezzo was a killer of parrots. Repetition wasn't enough. He wanted to put an end to imitation and allow us to analyze, note down, write. So, around the year 1000, he named the notes *do, re, mi, fa, sol, la* . . .

By what irony of fate did parrots and parakeets decide to move into this particular square?

That night, there were as many humans as birds. The atmosphere felt explosive. There was a feeling that something was about to happen.

"But what?" an African gray parrot kept crying. "But what?"

As soon as she heard the screams, Diane knew it was no game. Around her, beyond the trees and the lawns, the city rustled with an ever-changing cacophony that the residents took for silence. And yet the cry for help cut through the night.

In spite of the darkness, in spite of her high-heeled thigh boots, which made it hard for her to run, in spite of the uneven ground—stumps, clods, roots—that the clearing set up as an obstacle, she rushed to the spot from where the screams had come.

Amid the chestnut trees, she made out three large shadowy figures crouching over a girl lying on the ground. The victim was struggling with all her might, but being hit seemed to excite the men even more as they indulged their pleasure. One was holding the head of their prey, trying to gag her with his arm, which she was wildly fending off. It was a battle. A smell of blood and sex hung in the air. Diane immediately saw the gravity of the situation. A fight has to have an outcome, and this one could well be a fight to the death.

Without hesitation, she charged at the rapists. Only the one holding the girl's head saw her, but he barely had time to cry out before Diane brutally kicked the others on the backs of their necks. Caught by surprise, they rolled onto their sides in pain, and Diane now aimed for their genitals. They screamed and crawled away into the grass, moaning.

Then the one who was left was bitten by the girl, bellowed,

and pulled his hand away, which gave Diane a chance to deliver a hook to his nose.

The three men lying on the ground, astounded that they were being attacked by a woman on her own, got ready to attack out of male pride.

But then the sound of a siren came from the boulevard below, and without thinking they stood up and scurried off.

They were absorbed by the night.

The siren stopped.

Diane's heart wouldn't slow down. All she wanted was to keep fighting.

Her fierce excitement was interrupted by the victim's moans.

Diane bent over her and recognized Albane. Her legs bruised, her lips bleeding, her body shaking, the girl was crying, shielding her private parts with one hand and hiding her face with the other.

Diane had the good sense not to return her straight to her mother.

In spite of all the guests flooding Place d'Arezzo to attend the Bidermanns' party, she managed to park her car on Rue Molière and sneak Albane up to her own apartment, concealed under a tartan rug. Jean-Noël wouldn't disturb them: he was on a business trip to Stuttgart.

Once indoors, she helped the girl to pull herself together.

Albane stood in the hot shower, unable to move, at once distraught and convalescent, as if the water might cleanse her of what had happened, wipe the memory of her attackers from her skin, restore her lost purity. In that humid atmosphere, she was also able to cry.

On the other side of the door, Diane was worried. The girl had locked herself in—which was only natural—and Diane was afraid she might do something fatal. Although she had hastily removed anything sharp—razor, scissors—she knew that the resourcefulness of a desperate person should never be underestimated.

What reassured her was hearing Albane's regular sobs: they proved she was still alive.

An hour later, the shower stopped.

"Are you all right?" Diane asked. "Do you want a hot drink?"

She heard a weak "yes."

Albane appeared, wrapped in a robe, a towel tied around her head like a turban, which reassured Diane: if the girl was concerned with her hair, that meant she wasn't planning to leave this world.

They sat in the kitchen, where Diane prepared a hot toddy with a liberal amount of rum.

Albane told her about her ordeal. It wasn't easy for her. She had to break off her story several times out of anger and amazement. At other times, she was choked with hiccups.

Diane listened, then asked for details. She thought it vital that Albane put her attack into words, if not to overcome it, then at least to tame it, to remove it from that terrifying violence and put it into the order of language.

By her second glass of toddy, Albane had finished.

She felt a dumb kind of relief, verging on lethargy: she had put everything into words, but hadn't rid herself of the horror. Images and sensations kept coming back to her, tearing at her flesh.

"Do you want a doctor?"

"I don't know."

"We'll talk about it with your mother."

At the mention of her mother, Albane lost heart and collapsed.

"What's the matter?" Diane exclaimed.

"Mommy . . . She'll be so upset when she finds out . . . Oh . . . "

Diane propped the girl up and tried to reason with her. "Albane, be clear about this. She won't be any more upset than you are."

"Yes, she will."

Diane realized the girl meant what she said. To her great surprise, this realization took her back decades, to when she herself was a little girl trying to shield her mother from life's hardships. A loving child faces her own pain, but refuses to torment her parents. She put this recollection away into the drawer where she kept long-dead feelings and took Albane into her dressing room. Since the girl couldn't wear her torn outfit again, she had to be clothed before she returned home.

Albane stopped being a martyr and spent a few moments marveling at what she saw. Since the capricious, versatile Diane liked playing different scenes, there was everything and its opposite in her wardrobe: leather and tweed, angora and latex, a business suit alongside a sexy nurse's uniform, a hippie tunic next to a lamé shift. The wardrobe was like the costume department of a theater, the storeroom of a quick-change artist rather than the closet of a respectable Brussels resident.

Diane chose a pair of jeans and a loose-fitting sweater, then, holding Albane's hand, took her to her mother's.

Half an hour later, leaving Patricia's apartment, she felt a sadness akin to helplessness, which had been triggered by Albane's question: "What were you doing there?" Naturally, Diane couldn't tell the truth, so had improvised on the theme of "I was driving around, stopped to smoke a cigarette, and rolled down the window." Mother and daughter had swallowed the lie, exclaiming, "Thank goodness!"

But Diane hadn't gone out to smoke. She had been hanging around the park in Forest, an area with a dangerous reputation, because, her husband being away tonight, she was hoping for an encounter. The truth was, she had been there to experience

the very act that had befallen Albane—but of her own free
will! Could she ever admit that? Could she even hear herself
say it? She could barely understand it herself . . .

She suddenly felt worn. Compared with Albane, she realized she had experienced everything, tried everything,
exhausted everything. Her search for something new, extreme,
and dangerous had led her to a critical point of humanity—or
inhumanity—in which she practiced universal irony. In her
cynicism, she found entertainment in what scared other people. Could she still feel anything? Hadn't she dulled her emotions? Even violence no longer seemed like aggression, but
more like a game, since she would immediately turn it into a
staged scene. Every event became a ritual, and she an extra in
the ritual.

*I am my own surveillance camera. I become the night watch-
man who enjoys watching me on the screen in strange situations.
In a way, I no longer live but watch myself live.*

Who was she, this woman who spent more time outside
than inside herself?

As she crossed Place d'Arezzo, Diane noticed a different
kind of agitation. Whereas earlier she had sensed a cheerful
impatience in the guests rushing to the party, there was now a
tension: the music flooding out of the windows had stopped,
and on the square everything had come to a standstill.

She saw the large door of the town house open and police
officers emerge with Zachary Bidermann.

Diane thought she was hallucinating: the proud, haughty
Zachary Bidermann, escorted by four police officers, looked
like a suspect being taken into custody. He was rolling his eyes
in outrage and keeping pace with those leading him. They
finally pushed his head down and bundled him into a white car
with blinding blue revolving lights. Anyone would have
thought he was a criminal!

Rose appeared at the top of the steps, her face haggard, holding a handkerchief, supported by a few close people, among them Léo Adolf, Chairman of the European Commission.

Diane might have been stunned by the sight of Zachary, but that of Rose overcame her completely. Looking away, almost hiding, she ran off past the trees until she got home.

The following day, at dawn, she heard through the media about the scandal that had occurred on Place d'Arezzo.

At around noon, returning from Stuttgart, Jean-Noël found her glued to the TV screen. She pointed to a platter of cold meat she had prepared for him and carried on watching. He barely managed to exchange a few words with her, and they were only about the events unfolding.

"Poor woman," Diane exclaimed.

"Let's not exaggerate," Jean-Noël grunted. "Sure, she was forced to give him a blow job, but she'll get over it."

"I meant Rose."

"Rose?"

"Rose Bidermann, that bastard's wife. She's the one who's suffering the most right now."

"Oh?"

"Now that she knows he's been cheating on her, what she's refused to admit for years is going to come crashing down on her head. People have been talking since this morning, and all sorts of details are coming in about his sexual obsessions. The press are going to town on it and digging up lots of witnesses."

"Honestly, Diane, are you shocked?"

"What?"

"A compulsive sex drive like that—"

"You wouldn't understand," she muttered, turning up the volume.

That morning, Diane woke, heard the whistling and chirping of the parakeets on the square, and decided it was time to act.

Today, she would do what she had never attempted in the past few years.

She got ready, doing her hair and applying her makeup as if going to a prestigious evening, then dialed the number she had obtained years earlier.

A curt voice answered. "Zachary Bidermann's office, Madame Singer speaking."

"I'd like to make an appointment with Rose Bidermann."

There was an irritable silence, then the voice said, "Who's speaking and what is it concerning?"

"This is Diane Fanon."

"Does Madame know you?"

"No."

"What is this in connection with?"

"I have something to reveal to her."

A weary groan preceded Singer's reply. "Look, madame, we're receiving revelations from women by the truckload. Mistresses, lovers, exes, the ones still to come, the ones who were forced, the ones who hesitate, and the ones who would quite like to—believe me, that's all I'm getting on the phone. Can we have some common decency, please? Madame Bidermann isn't remotely interested in your revelations, and I don't understand how you can have the gall to try. Learn to respect other people's grief, madame."

"But I do respect it! I love Rose."

"What do you mean? You just said she didn't know you."

"Look, I don't want to tell her anything about Zachary Bidermann, it's something else I want to talk to her about."

"What?"

Diane hesitated. Would she utter the words she had been avoiding for years? She resorted to a subterfuge. "Tell her I want to talk to her about . . . Zouzou."

"Zouzou?"

"Zouzou. Tell her—"

"I don't understand."

"She'll understand."

Diane dictated her phone number and hung up.

Her heart was pounding fit to burst. She felt as if she had just committed the riskiest, most indecent act of her existence. Unwilling to leave, she lingered by the phone, waiting for the return call.

Luckily for her nerves, it came soon. A few minutes later, Madame Singer suggested an appointment at five that afternoon.

Diane presented herself solemnly at the front door, ignoring the reporters and photographers camped out on the sidewalk. She kept her head down, ignoring their questions, focusing on her objective.

She gave her name and the butler invited her to slip inside, careful to prevent an indiscreet snapshot, and led her up to the main floor. Here Rose Bidermann was waiting for her, standing in the middle of a room blooming with peonies. Her hair neatly done, prettily made up, dressed in light colors, with a resonant voice and a smile on her lips, she behaved magnificently, her grace and ease contradicting the tragedy that had befallen her.

Diane accepted her invitation to sit down, the cup of tea, and the macarons, and they exchanged a few platitudes about the splendid weather. Then she pulled herself together and said, clearly, "Does the name Zouzou mean anything to you?"

Rose tensed, then smiled. "Yes. It was my father's name. I mean his nickname. To those who knew him well. Basically just my mother and me."

"It was my father's nickname too. Also to those who knew him well. In other words, my mother and me."

There was silence. Rose wanted to make sure that she understood—or rather, that it wasn't a misunderstanding. "In my father's case," she said, "Zouzou was a rather odd diminutive of Samuel. Unusual, isn't it?"

"Yes, unusual. The same for mine."

There was silence again. Rose looked confused. "Who was your father?"

"Samuel van Eckart, just like yours."

Rose lost her composure.

Diane took a photograph from her bag and held it out to her. "This is the only picture I have of him with Mom. He broke up with her soon afterwards. As for me, I saw him only two or three times because he didn't acknowledge me. He'd occasionally send money or gifts, and sometimes did us the favor of a quick visit to ease his conscience. I wasn't allowed to call him 'Daddy' under any circumstance."

Rose grabbed the snapshot. "That's definitely my father."

"With my mother."

"How can you prove—?"

"I can't. My honesty is all I have. And my mother's. In other words, some very fragile elements that your father held in contempt."

Rose felt the emotion rising in Diane. She no longer knew what to think or how to react.

Diane continued, "Oh, and there's also this . . . "

She bared her right shoulder and indicated a mole at the top of her arm. "He had this. I do too. What about you?"

Rose turned pale. In reply, she slowly pulled down her blouse and showed the same mole in the same place.

Diane's eyes filled with tears and she started breathing heavily. "So Mom wasn't lying . . . Poor Mom . . . " She curled up in her armchair and within a few seconds became again the little girl who had wept as she wondered about her identity.

Rose went over to her, hand outstretched, hesitant about comforting this stranger. She stood in front of her, overwhelmed with sadness at discovering another new lie, not by her husband this time but by the other important man in her life: her father.

Although sunk deep in her own pain, Diane raised her head and saw Rose standing there biting her lip and looking totally helpless.

"Why?" Rose asked. "Why now? Why not before?"

"Because I didn't need you. But with all that you're going through now, I thought perhaps you might need me."

"You?"

"A sister."

Rose stammered in amazement. Usually, she was the one in charge, the one who took care of others and fixed things. And now a stranger who claimed to be her younger sister wanted to help her . . .

Diane opened her arms and Rose, lost and weary, threw herself into them, letting the grief pour out of her, the grief of a woman who had been cheated, betrayed, humiliated, mocked—the woman she was and refused to be.

When she returned home that evening, Jean-Noël waved a black and gold card at her by way of greeting, his eyes glowing with desire. "My darling, I have an invitation to Tea for Ten, where they're holding a swingers' party. You know, the one that has a Turkish bath with steps where you can do anything you like."

Diane looked at Jean-Noël and put a hand on his shoulder. "Listen, Jean-Noël, that's very sweet of you, but I'm fed up with sucking endless cock. How about going to bed, just the two of us?"

A man's downfall. What could be more fascinating? François-Maxime hadn't left the living room where the TV, permanently switched on, was endlessly broadcasting items about Zachary Bidermann. Both the main channels and the news channels were devoting their airtime to the incident on Place d'Arezzo. Endless news flashes, eyewitness reports, and discussions, trying to fill the void created by that explosion, to wipe out the feeling of stupefaction that had overwhelmed the citizens. The political eagle had been brought down in full flight: whereas the previous week Zachary Bidermann had been about to accede to supreme power, now he had been arrested, questioned by the police, kept in custody for twenty-four hours, and finally charged. In a few hours, a single thing having broken his rise, he had plunged to the bottom of the social ladder, farther than the bottom, because everyone was talking about him, his crime not benefiting from any anonymity. Excessive honor had been replaced with excessive indignity.

François-Maxime had been at the reception when the alleged rape had taken place and the victim had pointed out her attacker to the police. He was fascinated by the case. His interest didn't derive solely from the fact that it involved his neighbor, but rather from a more basic closeness: François-Maxime projected his own downfall on Zachary Bidermann's.

In a few seconds, he had lost his status, his happiness, his balance: Séverine's suicide had made him a widower, responsible for four orphans. Beyond what had happened to him, the worst could still take place: the reality of his vices might be detected, his furtive encounters in male pickup areas, where his body wordlessly sought contact with identical bodies. How would his bank, financial circles, his children, his family react to a revelation like that?

For a moment, he envied Séverine for having left with her secrets intact: at least she wasn't running any more risks. Death was still less painful than dishonor.

Much to his surprise, he discovered that he wasn't the only one in the house to remain glued to the news; the cook, the cleaners, the handyman, all the staff seemed to be spending all their time in front of a screen, a radio, the Internet: Zachary Bidermann was the focus of everyone's attention.

Why are they so interested? They don't have anything to lose . . .

François-Maxime assumed there was an element of social revenge: the powerless feel pleasure at the fall of a powerful man.

That morning, waiting in his car for the children to come out so that he could drive them to school, he saw Marcelle, the concierge from the next building, come striding toward him.

"Did you see what happened to Monsieur Bidermann?"

"I was there."

"What? You saw the rape?"

"No, I was at the reception, I saw the arrest."

"Do you think he's guilty?"

"I have no idea. There are lots of things that point to it."

"Poor man! It's a frame-up."

"That's also a valid theory."

"I haven't slept a wink all night, monsieur. I watched television so much, it made me feel dizzy."

François-Maxime, having no desire to get on intimate terms with such a gossip, refrained from admitting that he was the same. "Why?" he asked in a less firm voice.

"Ruin, monsieur, ruin. What a fall! I told myself it could happen to me."

He bit his lip, conscious that he mustn't be sarcastic. She was right, anybody could fall, from a greater or lesser height . . . "Why, do you have something to hide?"

"I have nothing to hide!" Marcelle bellowed.

"Well, then?"

"Not everybody has something to hide, but everybody has something to lose."

And with this, she turned to bawl out a man walking his dog who hadn't taken the trouble to collect his animal's excrement from the sidewalk. "That's it, do just as you like! Do I take a leak outside your front door? Get out of here, you disgust me!"

As if François-Maxime had never existed, she kept on at the man even as he tried to apologize.

François-Maxime's son and daughters came hurtling down the front steps and into the car. In the old days, Séverine would have waved to them from the door; that was something they all remembered and had to make an effort to forget.

They were driving in silence when Gwendoline, the eldest, said, "Daddy, I've thought a lot about Mommy. I think I know what happened."

François-Maxime threw an anxious glance at the rearview mirror, then encouraged her to continue.

"Mommy had an incurable disease, and she knew it."

"Who told you that?"

"I guessed."

"Tell me more, sweetheart."

"She found out she wouldn't get better, so she made the first move to avoid further pain. She was thinking about us before anything else."

"About us?"

"She didn't want us to suffer from watching her suffer."

They all fell silent, thinking this over. The car stopped at a red light.

"I like what you said, Gwendoline," François-Maxime said calmly. "It's not only plausible, it's very like her."

"Yes," Guillaume said, moved. The two younger girls muttered in agreement. The car moved forward again.

François-Maxime let the idea sink in. At least this theory had the advantage of being more comforting than others: Séverine hadn't given up on life, it was life that had given up on her. Why deny it? Didn't harmony matter more than truth?

He dropped the children at school, gave them big, solemn hugs, as if he wanted to imprint his affection on their bodies, then got back in the car.

Normally, he would go to the bank. Or rather, no: normally, he would go the wood before going to the bank . . .

Would he do so today? He scratched the back of his neck. When it came down to it, he didn't feel like it. Not at all. He didn't want to feel a horse between his thighs. And he didn't want some young man's embraces.

He shook his head. Wasn't it precisely because he didn't want it that he should do it? It might help him to recover . . .

Recover from what?

Disconcerted, he sat there for a moment, his hands on the wheel, wracking his brain to figure out what it was he wanted . . .

Nothing.

He set off, hoping that the car itself would direct him.

He drove for a while and parked on the edge of the wood. No way of getting to the stables from here. So he wouldn't ride today. He had to continue on foot.

François-Maxime abandoned his car and, advancing beneath the trunks, came to the paths where individuals wandered up and down before disappearing, in couples or in groups, into the trees.

He stopped. All at once, this merry-go-round struck him

as ridiculous. Worse still, it disgusted him. In this constant stream of men on their own, he no longer saw appetite or pleasure, only sexual misery, forced anonymity, small, fleeting orgasms, frustration, dissatisfaction. They were just unfortunate people who wanted to maintain their wretched condition, sick people drinking from a poisoned well, just enough to continue being sick, not enough to die of it. Nobody was happy here. Bodies tensed beneath supposed caresses whose aim was not to last, but rather to cease. They rushed to climax, a frantic race from foreplay to ejaculation. Sperm flowed, of course, but with a cry and a grimace, merely in order to rid themselves of desire, not to achieve an apotheosis. How ugly they seemed today, these solitary hunters, with their stooped shoulders and shifty eyes, their hands in their pockets, not looking at the eyes of the other walkers, only at their groins.

A young man approached, stopped, fixed his eyes on François-Maxime, and pouted at him.

François-Maxime spat.

The young man recoiled, incredulous.

"Faggot!" François-Maxime snarled through clenched teeth.

Then he turned on his heels and strode back to his car.

Over! It's all over! I'll never come back here again! It's all too sordid.

His sudden temper had made him forget the thousand times he had left the undergrowth smiling, filled with a new energy, feeling happier, more virile, more seductive. If anyone had reminded him of that, he would have denied it.

He drove to the bank. Seeing the way the guards saluted him, the respect his employees showed him, the obsequious demeanor of the executives, he came back to life. *A banker and a boss, yes, I'm still that.*

Entering his office, he allowed himself time to converse

with his secretary, who was nervous, torn between her usual behavior and the behavior expected of her in the circumstances. He spoke to her tenderly of his children, the plans he had for his next vacation with them.

At his request, his colleagues joined him and they settled down to the problems of the moment.

Around midday, as the meeting was drawing to an end, they couldn't help bringing up the Bidermann scandal. They all enjoyed making comments, which were more revealing of themselves than of the case itself. Some spoke from the point of view of the broken marriage, others from that of the broken career, some suggested a conspiracy, one colleague remarked on the madness to which power leads, another sought to establish a link between libido and politics.

Varnier waited for the final remark before concluding, "What a mess!"

"Yes. What a mess!"

The ambiguity of that phrase summed it up for all of them, with nobody prepared to specify if the "mess" meant Bidermann's shattered ambitions, the violence inflicted on a woman, or how impossible it was going to be for the nation to find a better leader.

Varnier tapped François-Maxime on the shoulder. "Since you're here, why don't you join me in interviewing the trader we've been sent from Paris? I'm seeing him in five minutes."

"All right," he replied, anxious to avoid solitude.

Once seated in the paneled room reserved for prestigious customers, François-Maxime and Varnier asked for the applicant to be sent in.

As soon as he entered, François-Maxime raised an eyebrow. The man, who was in his thirties, was clearly homosexual. The signs were unmistakable. His suit had neither the usual cut nor the usual sobriety, his tie had a huge, almost obscene knot, his pointed shoes screamed originality. François-Maxime hated him at first sight, all the more so as the trader made it obvious, from the way he looked at him, that he was attracted to him. This casualness was the last straw, and François-Maxime decided to keep quiet and watch.

Varnier conducted the interview. The young man responded brilliantly to the questions; nothing that was thrown at him seemed to faze him. He was so competent that he even taught his interviewer a thing or two. Admiringly, Varnier ended up abandoning the usual neutral attitude; he thanked him warmly and told him that they would be sure to call him very soon.

Turning to François-Maxime, he asked him if he had anything to add.

François-Maxime pointed to the ring on the young man's finger. "What's that?"

"My wedding ring," the trader replied, unperturbed.

"Are you married?"

"Yes."

"Do you have any children?"

"That might be difficult," the trader declared with a nonchalant smile. "My husband's name is Charles."

François-Maxime sank further into his chair.

Immediately, the young man looked straight at him. "Is that a problem?"

"I find your tone aggressive."

"Reassure me and it won't be. Is it a problem?"

"Of course it isn't!" Varnier exclaimed.

The trader nodded, but indicated François-Maxime. "I was talking to Monsieur de Couvigny."

Finding the applicant's attitude really distasteful, François-Maxime got to his feet. "We are a family business, monsieur."

"I have a family too, monsieur."

"Not like ours."

The trader absorbed this, and stood up, dignified. He

shook Varnier's hand. "I'm pleased to have met you, but, since I'm sure I'll have no difficulty finding a job, I must tell you—and I'm really sorry about this—that I prefer to be part of a company that takes me as I am. Forgive me if I've wasted your time."

Then, without a word or a look at François-Maxime, he left the room.

"Good riddance!" François-Maxime cried when the door had closed.

Varnier shuddered. "Please, I never want to see that again."

"What?"

"A performance like that."

"What are you talking about?"

"That kind of homophobia."

"You think I'm homophobic? That guy's no homo, he's just a caricature."

"Shut up, François-Maxime! I feel ashamed. He was the best candidate we've interviewed, it was really hard for me to persuade him to come to Brussels, and you just wipe your hands of him. Your excuse is that you've just suffered a terrible loss. For that reason, and that reason alone, I'll forgive you."

Varnier slammed the door.

François-Maxime sat there in the middle of the oak-paneled room. Varnier hadn't got it wrong: he couldn't stand homosexuals anymore, didn't want to meet them, and wished he could wipe them out.

Seeing his children again at dinner cheered him. When he was with them, he no longer questioned himself; he could listen to them, talk to them, play his role as a father.

The meal continued on its untroubled way, lively and full of energy. His son and daughters amused themselves talking about their day, and exchanging information about the new James Bond they were planning to see on the big screen. Over dessert, François-Maxime promised to take them to the movies on Saturday night.

He accompanied each of them to his or her room, chatted at the foot of the bed, then, dismissing the domestics, went to the living room, where the television immediately started churning out news of the Bidermann affair.

Attention had now shifted to the victim, Petra von Tannenbaum, described as a "contemporary artist" who "performed" in the most fashionable galleries—clearly, a zealous press attaché had distributed the information. She was depicted as a well-balanced, self-confident woman who had transformed her body into a work of art, or rather into the instrument of works of art: the performances that she gave.

Intrigued, François-Maxime examined the few images of her that kept passing on a loop. The woman's evident sophistication attracted him. Not sexually, but in another way . . . It struck him that she was right, that artifice constituted an aim, or rather, a refuge. Strange thoughts sprang up in him. For an hour, he had the feeling he was forgetting his grief and his troubles, fascinated as he was by Petra von Tannenbaum.

When the endless replaying of the identical clips and comments started to wear him down, he went to his bedroom.

The room was filled with Séverine's things.

Mechanically, François-Maxime sat down on her seat by the dressing table, where every evening she would sit and methodically take off her jewelry and loosen her hair.

He looked at himself in the mirror, grabbed the brush, and used it. This gesture filled him with an exquisite calm. Enchanted, he sat down and opened the drawers containing her makeup.

Touched by the smell of lily of the valley that reminded him of Séverine, he applied foundation cream to his cheeks. Strange . . . he and she had almost identical complexions.

Carried away by his experiment, he put on powder, mascara, and eyebrow pencil, finally choosing a lipstick for himself.

Looking at the result in the mirror, he thought he looked ridiculous. Above all, he found himself neither handsome nor beautiful: he was no longer a man, but wasn't a woman. Nevertheless, he took a genuine pleasure in gazing at himself, as if he were escaping a danger, a threat . . .

Standing up, he opened the wardrobe and chose from among Séverine's dresses the one that suited him. Completing the transformation, he put on stockings and high-heeled shoes—here, the choice was limited to those she had bought in the United States, getting the size wrong.

He looked at himself in the stand-up mirror. What did he look like? A woman? No. A transvestite. He shrugged. Well, why not?

Taking a few steps around the room, he evaluated his body sheathed in a dress on high heels: neither the balance nor the sensations was anything like what he was familiar with.

He looked at the clock on the mantelpiece. Thirty minutes after midnight . . .

Carrying his shoes in his hand, he descended the stairs, taking care not to make any noise, walked out through the front door, put his shoes back on, and set off into the night.

For a hundred yards, he didn't meet any of his neighbors. When he saw a friend of Séverine's coming out of a house, he ran under a tree; once the danger was past, he hailed a passing taxi and told the driver to take him to the Flemish quarter in the lower town, where the chances of meeting people he knew were minimal.

The following nights, he continued his quest for transformation. After midnight, he would do his hair, call a driver, and plunge into the Flemish speaking quarters. His nocturnal wanderings had no aim other than to take him away from himself. He never let a man approach, let alone hit on him; nor did he allow any woman to start up a conversation. He didn't want sex, he had no desire to shine, he just wanted to be. To be different. To leave the character of François-Maxime de Couvigny magnificently ensconced on Place d'Arezzo, to abandon the weeping widower, the devoted father, the efficient banker, and be content with an imprecise identity, to exist because he was walking on high heels, to feel the lace on his thighs or the thin straps on his collarbone. He offered to the air a face protected by cream that was even, beige, smooth, perfect, thick, and gave him a sense of perfection.

Frequenting the all-night stores, the french-fry stalls, the bars, talking briefly with the traders, he discovered the people of the night, who were different and open to difference. Now it no longer seemed to him that Brussels comprised two cities, the French-speaking and the Flemish-speaking, but four, since on top of these two the day city and the night city were superimposed. Overwhelmed with joy, he discovered a Chinese supermarket open until two in the morning, where he could hang out as an ordinary customer, examining the underwear, the cosmetics, the hygienic articles.

Before each escape, the time he spent in front of the mirror became a time of passionate involvement. He had become an expert at makeup, and loved to use it, like a Japanese Noh actor, adding, at the last moment, imperfections that produced an illusion of naturalness: blush on the cheeks, shading on the temples, marks on the bridge of the nose. Painting someone else on his face gave him a feeling of serenity.

One Friday night, at one in the morning, he was walking up a cobbled street. At the end of the street, a group of revelers was coming out of a bar. He slowed down to avoid them, then continued on his way, his progress made difficult by the uneven ground.

As he passed the bar, another man came running out after the others, crying, "Hey, wait for me!"

François-Maxime found himself face-to-face with the trader he had interviewed not long before.

The young man stopped in astonishment, thought for a moment, hesitated. The light from the street lamp was falling directly on them and its orange glow accentuated every feature, every contour of their faces, almost clinically. The man recognized the banker who had mistreated him.

"It . . . It . . . It isn't true!"

A snigger hovered over his lips, invaded his eyes, his face, his body . . . The trader was screaming with laughter.

François-Maxime stood there frozen, unable to react.

The trader was holding his stomach, bent double, trying to control his breathing, savouring his discovery.

François-Maxime tore himself away and started running. Alas, running on high-heeled shoes wasn't something he was in the habit of doing, and he twisted his ankles several times, which merely increased the hilarity of the man watching him from a distance. At last, he turned several corners and disappeared from his sight, escaping his mockery.

He hailed a taxi and returned home. Even though humiliated, he felt a curious relief: he knew that this excursion had been the last one; he would no longer resort to cross-dressing; he had exhausted its pleasures as well as the need for it. Chilling but effective, the trader's infernal sneering had cured him.

When the taxi dropped him on Place d'Arezzo, he had the impression that a shadowy figure was moving on the roof of his house. He thought he was dreaming, but then again glimpsed the figure between the chimney pots. At that moment, a man appeared, walking his dog, and François-Maxime hurriedly rushed into the house rather than take the risk of being identified. He ran up to his room, took off his clothes, hastily removed his makeup with a hot towel, put on a man's robe, armed himself with a golf club, and went up to the attic. There was no doubt about it, someone was trying to break in through the roof.

When he opened the skylight, the cold air hit him in the face. He couldn't see anything abnormal. Either he had been the victim of a mirage, or the man had fled.

Pensively, he went back downstairs, visited every room to make sure no intruder was hiding there, half-opened the doors to all the children's rooms, then, reassured, went back to his own.

The days resumed their normal form, and so did the nights. In the evening, François-Maxime would devote himself to his children, then go to bed, forcing himself to read a novel until sleep overcame him.

One morning, a letter from Niger made his heart beat faster. Niamey? Wasn't that the town where Séverine's sister had moved twenty years earlier, when their family had broken up? Through the diplomatic service, he had attempted to inform her of the death.

The letter was indeed from Ségolène. He read it immediately:

> *Dear François-Maxime,*
>
> *I hope you don't mind me saying "dear." I want to thank you for contacting me and for taking care of my sister's children, who have nobody but you now.*
>
> *I'll be brief. If I went into details, this letter would become a novel.*
>
> *I loved my sister Séverine. I've just been crying for a long time after learning of her tragic death. Although I hadn't seen her for many years, it wasn't because of her, but rather because of the context with which she was associated, in other words, my parents. I won't go on about the sense of guilt that exists side by side with the grief because 1) it's obvious 2) I feel no remorse.*

I fled my family a long time ago. Why? I wanted to save my life. Clearly I did the right thing, because my sister has just lost hers. Our family is cursed. The reason I'm writing to you is that I want it to cease.

I have no memory of being taught to speak when we were children, whereas I remember perfectly well being taught to keep silent. We weren't supposed to express our feelings or ask others to explain theirs, we weren't supposed to ask indiscreet questions, let alone give answers to them. In short, I grew up with my parents, my brother, and my sister, like a cow in a cowshed.

Our family wasn't comprised of love but of silences. Learning of Séverine's tragic end, I thought I should tell you that.

Be vigilant, François-Maxime, because what happened in the past has just happened again, and may yet happen in the future.

Our grandmother on our father's side threw herself out of a window. I only discovered that recently, I don't know if my sister knew it. Did she consciously copy her? Or had she stored deep in her mind a memory transmitted through some channel other than words?

Yes, our grandmother threw herself off a building, just like Séverine. She was unhappy. She was a pretty woman, and she preferred women to men. Her husband discovered it, and threatened to have her institutionalized. She preferred to kill herself.

Our father loved his mother, who died when he was seven. How do I know he loved her? When he died, we found lots of photographs of her in his room; he even kept one in his wallet. It seems my father felt terrible about her death and never got over it.

Did Séverine tell you? Our family split apart when our elder brother Pierre discovered that our father was a transvestite. Oh, he didn't sell his body, no, he dressed up in women's clothes and paraded through the streets. At the time, this news destroyed us, put an end to whatever harmony we had. Because it revealed a monster beneath the outward shell of a father we feared and worshipped. Because it demonstrated that nobody knew anybody in our household. Because it said loud and clear that everybody was lying. I left France with Boubakar, my boyfriend then, my husband now.

Although I don't regret getting away, I regret that I didn't try to understand. Why did our father dress as a woman? I've been putting together the threads and I realize my father was trying to find his mother again, to rejoin her through her clothes, her hairstyles, her accessories, her femininity; my father still loved his dead mother; if he couldn't bring her back to life, at least he could get closer to her. It was pathetic, ridiculous, tender, beautiful, desperate. And we didn't understand it. Did he understand it himself? You can't cure yourself of yourself.

After our father died, then our mother and our brother, I refused the inheritance. I advised Séverine to do the same. If she had followed my advice, we would have been close sisters, and she probably wouldn't be dead now . . . She agreed to shoulder the burden. I remain convinced that she didn't just inherit the family money but also the family fate. In getting those millions, she also got the problems, the silences, our curse.

Traumas repeat themselves, François-Maxime, especially when we're unaware of them. We inherit what we don't know. Silence kills.

That day, François-Maxime merely pretended to do his work; in reality he couldn't stop thinking about Séverine, or about his children.

At midnight, he was still thinking about them, sitting on the balcony, looking out over Place d'Arezzo, where the parrots and parakeets, quiet at last, were sleeping.

Suddenly, a hurried takeoff broke the peace. In a cacophony of feathers and screeching, the birds perched on the highest branches flew up in a panic, scared by something opposite them.

Trying to see what was going on, François-Maxime leaned forward and looked up at the top of his house.

Once again, a shadowy figure was visible between the chimney pots.

This time, François-Maxime rushed up to the top floor and came out onto the roof less than a minute after the commotion.

Beneath the gray moon, Guillaume watched in astonishment as his father emerged from the skylight. In his fright, he almost slipped and had to hold on to a TV antenna.

"Daddy?"

"Guillaume, sweetheart, what are you doing here?"

The boy was surprised to hear "sweetheart" instead of being bawled out. Seeing his son on the edge of the void, François-Maxime immediately realized what was going on: the child was trying to get to know his mother better, to resemble his mother, maybe even to see his mother again. He was flirting with oblivion, caressing suicide.

He ran to the boy and hugged him in his arms. "Come, Guillaume. You have to talk to me."

"Aren't you with the lady?"

"What lady?"

"The one who's taken Mommy's place. The one who comes to see you at night."

François-Maxime smiled, painfully. "Come, sweetheart. I have to talk to you too. Nobody's perfect."

And, with his child in his arms, François-Maxime climbed back down the stepladder to the cluttered attic, vowing that

he would never again hide from his son the complexity of
human beings, not Severine's, and not his own, even if it
meant losing his pride or the ideal image of himself that he
had fabricated.

J oséphine's absence devastated both Isabelle and Baptiste, in her case because she didn't know her very well, in his because he knew her all too well.

During those last days, which had been so happy, Isabelle had never suspected that Joséphine could leave; on the contrary, galvanized by the novelty of it, she had cheerfully organized their life as a threesome, arranged the apartment so that they each had their own space, planned their next vacation. True, in the middle of this whirlwind of activity, Joséphine would occasionally demonstrate hints of irritation or melancholy, which Isabelle had attributed to her uncompromising, excessive, theatrical temperament. Everything she felt, Joséphine expressed in an emphatic way—quite unlike the reserved Baptiste. A badly presented dish would ruin her appetite even if she had come to the table feeling really hungry; an unpleasant smell would make her leave a department store in a huff; a grammatical mistake would make her lose track of the meaning of a speech; a regional accent would transform the speaker into an irresistible comic; a pimple, a rash, a hair on a face made her recoil. As far as she was concerned, details mattered as much as the overall picture, if not more. With her love of the absolute, her perfectionism, she couldn't help being disappointed by reality. Either enthusiastic or exasperated, she alternated between appetite and anger, displaying an unceasing intensity that enchanted her camp followers and prevented most people from appreciating her. This extreme sensitivity, which deprived her of so many pleasures, was sometimes an affliction. As the first person to suffer from her moods, she would turn to Baptiste, her guide, her sage, wanting to absorb some of his moderation, hoping he would help her get things into proportion—but this, too, she demanded so frantically that she would fly into a temper if he took too long about it. Sweet Isabelle had been so in love with that tempestuous nature that she had been unaware of the depths of suffering it concealed.

Baptiste, though, had had an inkling of the coming crisis. Since that first night, he had known he was being spied on, watched, judged. Although Joséphine had been delighted that he had welcomed Isabelle, she had later been surprised by it, then suspicious. How could her husband accept the unacceptable; had he welcomed Isabelle into their household because he was bored with their relationship? Was it out of love for her, or out of weariness? At times she saw in their threesome the triumph of love, at other times its betrayal. Although she gave herself the right to love two people at the same time, she didn't grant it to the same extent to her man. Baptiste had sensed this dilemma in the way Joséphine had looked at him, sometimes withdrawing from the moments the three of them shared and taking up a position as a spectator, an examiner, a judge, a prosecutor. Recently, she had even gotten into the habit of bursting into rooms, as if hoping to catch the truth unawares; if Baptiste and Isabelle so much as decided something without her, she would withdraw, morosely; if she got up before them, she would lose her temper if they lingered in bed after she had made them breakfast. The moments when Baptiste and Isabelle were working separately, she took as a personal offense. Even in the past, Joséphine had attacked Baptiste's activities: "I get bored when you're writing, Baptiste. I feel as if I've stopped existing."

With the years, though, she had learned to attenuate that

jealousy, to consider these hours of creation not as a scandalously selfish passion or a punishment being inflicted on her, but as the basis of their life, the vocation she served by relieving the artist of additional worries. Deep down, she had found her place in her husband's writing.

Isabelle's arrival had upset that balance, he knew. Now, there were two spheres outside Joséphine's control: Baptiste at his desk, and Baptiste with Isabelle. It was too much for a woman who, in spite of her pleasure-loving character, had little respect for herself.

So she had renewed contact with her old demons, those that Baptiste had fought against: her self-hatred, the certainty of her own emptiness, the metaphysical dismay that led her to doubt that she had a good reason to remain on earth. Joséphine, so alive, so forthright, so brazen, so feared, considered herself useless. Even though she appeared to be a shining sun, she saw herself as grayer than the moon. In her own eyes, she had no value, only the importance that other people gave her. Only Baptiste's unconditional love had given her substance; now that he was suddenly infatuated with another woman, her fragile, painfully acquired self-confidence had been destroyed.

The evening they discovered that Joséphine had gone, Baptiste and Isabelle remained together in the living room, talking, combining their anxieties. In spite of Isabelle's questions, Baptiste kept silent about his analysis of the situation, not to retain any kind of superiority, but rather out of a sense of hope: the hope that he was wrong and that Isabelle might see things differently.

"Did she give you any reason to think she wanted to leave?" he asked her.

"I didn't pay any attention at the time. She kept saying, 'When it comes down to it, you and Baptiste are having so much fun together you'd be better off without me!' I found that so absurd, I didn't reply. What about you?"

"Well, she's always so careful with her words in front of me . . . On the other hand I did notice some hostility, several times, in fact."

"Hostility?"

"She was angry with me."

"Why?"

"I guess for accepting you. Feeling desire for you, attachment toward you."

"But it's what she wanted!"

"Oh, Joséphine's a bundle of contradictions. No, what worries me . . . "

"Yes?"

"Is that she left in order to think . . . There's nothing more harmful to her than thinking."

"Baptiste! That's horrible!"

"I swear I say it without any kind of contempt. Joséphine thinking means Joséphine alone, with no one to turn to, despising herself. If she doesn't feel a human presence, if she isn't aware of a safeguard, she gets a little crazy and can easily go over the edge. That's what scares me."

At that moment, the doorbell rang. They gave a start, thinking that Joséphine had returned.

It was Victor, looking stricken, who had come to tell them that Oxana had vanished.

Once they had shared the young man's pain and told him of their own, Baptiste and Isabelle found themselves alone again, worried at having to spend a night of doubts and questioning.

"Do you realize, Isabelle? Just the other night, the five of us were having dinner together, happy, drunk, invincible, and now both Oxana and Joséphine have run away. How fragile happiness is!"

Isabelle got energetically to her feet. "Let's not be complacent, Baptiste! Let's not wallow in tragedy. You have to find the solution."

"Me?"

"Yes, you."

"Why not you?"

"If only I could! But you've known Joséphine for fifteen years, you must know where she's gone."

"I don't!"

"Baptiste, you've always boasted of the human soul thanks to your work as a writer, so for God's sake use your brain! Sit down at your desk and search!"

Too surprised to protest, Baptiste obeyed. The thing Isabelle was ordering him to do was something Joséphine would never have allowed herself. He almost told her that, in order to complain, but didn't.

"In the meantime, I'm going to the bedroom to rest," Isabelle said.

"Oh, I see!"

"Just to show you that I trust you." As sweet now as she had been commanding before, she tenderly kissed the back of his neck. He smiled, shrugged, and switched on his computer.

This is absurd, he thought. *There isn't anything here that can help me. Why go through with this ritual?*

After a few minutes, the computer, the chair, the desk played their roles: aids to concentration, they allowed him to set in motion those mental capabilities previously impaired by anxiety. As if Joséphine were a fictional character, he gathered information, sensations, images relating to her. Little by little, things started to come together. Because a novelist loves his characters—that intimate cohabitation, that risk he takes of opening the doors and letting the character come in and draw substance from what he has accumulated, can indeed be called love—he went beyond the passivity of his own memories and called his imagination to the rescue. What would the heroine Joséphine do in such a situation?

She wouldn't go to her parents because, even though she

worshipped them, going back would be tantamount to regressing. She wouldn't go to any of her female friends either, because she had so far kept their threesome a secret. Would she just set off aimlessly? She didn't like relying on chance, at least not for long, because it accentuated her feeling of not being in control. Would she book a hotel in a large city, a noisy bustling capital, where she could keep boredom at bay? This hypothesis gave him food for thought . . . Yes, she might well be capable of taking refuge in one of the cities she loved: St. Petersburg, Amsterdam, Istanbul . . . But since they had discovered them together, plunging into their shared past would be upsetting to her. There had to be another option . . . Baptiste was getting close to the truth, he could see it as if it were a figure in the distance, and was trying to hail it, to make it see him, but couldn't quite manage it. Somewhere there was a solution—he was convinced of it—the facts were just waiting for him to grasp them.

Isabelle was right: his investigation into Josephine was like the writing of a novel. The story was there at the back of his mind, he just had to summon it up. There was nothing to invent, everything to discover. Baptiste didn't claim to be a creator, just a patient archeologist digging up hidden treasures.

To help his consciousness descend into the most protected parts of his mind, he had recourse to his usual ploys: music and cigars.

Lying down on a couch, he put on Mozart's C minor Mass. He didn't want to listen to it—he knew it by heart—he wanted to let his mind wander beside it, roam in its choral expanses, throb with its strings, fly on the wings of its song. The work was merely meant to be a springboard for his reverie.

But Mozart had entered the room and sat down by his bedside, and was now talking to him, forceful, intense, passionate, voluble, varied. Baptiste was following the composer's ideas, not his own. To break the spell, he leaped to his feet and went to change the disc, looking for a steadier, less engrossing piece that wouldn't stop him thinking freely. Schubert, with his repetitions, his restraint, his divine longueurs, struck him as perfect; as the arabesques of the Arpeggione Sonata rang out, Baptiste lit a big cigar.

Watching the wreaths of smoke curl up into the air, warming himself with the rounded, capricious melodies, he started thinking again. Where had the character named Joséphine gone to take refuge?

Once again, an answer was stirring deep inside him, but he could make out neither the features nor the form. All the same, he knew that he would soon formulate it.

At last, the combination of the music and the tobacco produced the desired effect: he felt a sudden, almost violent need to sleep, like a blow to the head. *Don't resist it.*

He dozed off.

A few moments later, he woke up, brandishing the idea like a diver emerging with the coveted pearl: Joséphine was in Ireland!

He ran to the bedroom, where he had no need to disturb Isabelle's rest: she was already packing.

"What are you doing?" Baptiste exclaimed.

"Packing our bags."

"Why?"

"To go to the place you're about to tell me."

He smiled, dazzled by so much optimism. "Josephine is in Cork in Ireland. In a boardinghouse."

The plane was a direct flight to Cork. Isabelle was about to set foot for the first time in the land of the shamrock. She was in an emotional state, totally focused on her objective: to win Joséphine back. As for Baptiste, the nearer they got, the more confident he felt.

"None of my characters has ever lied to me. I've never been

deceived by a character. I've sometimes deceived myself by stopping halfway, not going far enough to meet him, making do with seeing him only from a distance." Over the North Sea, he explained to Isabelle all about "proof through sleep," one of his credos as a writer: in his opinion, going to sleep led to the truth. He always had to go down that corridor. As soon as he detected the existence of a character, as soon as he started to hear him, he would go to sleep for a few minutes in order to wake up next to him. Ever since his beginnings as a novelist, the god Hypnos had taken Baptiste by the hand, leading him away from factual reality and toward the essential truths contained in his imagination.

"Joséphine is in Cork, getting bored. As soon as I reach the truth, I know I'm right."

The plane reached the Emerald Isle and started flying along the coast, its round contours made smooth by millennia of winds emerging from the waves to caress the land.

They were hit by occasional turbulence. Below them, the vast hostile sea, a uniform, almost violent blue, rumbled and prowled around the cliffs, as if determined not to spare the rocks.

"Look, there are the first flocks in Ireland, flocks of clouds."

As the plane began its descent into Cork, green replaced blue, uncovering hills crisscrossed with low walls, brown stone manor houses clinging to promontories, gray mountains in the distance.

"Now tell me how you guessed that we were supposed to come here," Isabelle said, eyes closed, trying to ignore the turbulence.

"When Joséphine and I first met, I fell in love with her, but refused to admit it. I thought I was in love with just one thing: my freedom. I made Joséphine suffer. She gave herself to me entirely, unreservedly, but I would leave and come back, determined to prove to myself that nothing bound me to her, that I was still my own master. Frankly, a major relationship didn't figure in my life plan, I'd imagined myself flitting from woman to woman, having lots of affairs. The plural, I was obsessed by the plural, and refused the singular. But Joséphine had realized from the start that this was it, we had to be together. Every time I was with her, I felt the same, but every time I forced myself to leave, hoping to rid myself of that dependency. Settle down? Never! One morning, Joséphine disappeared. Although we weren't living together, we'd gone as a couple to stay with some friends on the Greek coast for three weeks. After five days of total happiness, Joséphine vanished into thin air."

"Were you worried?"

"She'd taken the precaution of leaving a note to stop us thinking she'd drowned or something bad like that. That was when I understood."

"What?"

"How much she meant to me. I loved her more than my freedom. I was planning to go back to Paris, but then she sent me a telegram telling me she'd send me her address soon if I was interested. It was one of the most unpleasant moments of my life: I'd made up my mind, I knew how much I loved her, and I couldn't tell her. At last, the address arrived, and I took a plane for Cork."

A smile lit up her face.

"She was waiting for me in the house of an Irish family with six children and a lot of sheep."

"Why there?"

"There's no why with Joséphine, you just have to take it or leave it."

The plane touched down, hesitated, reared up again, then embraced the runway.

"Thank you for bringing me," Isabelle said in a low voice.

"What do you mean?"

"You're proving your love for me by taking me into the heart of your relationship with Joséphine."

As if in confirmation of this, Baptiste kissed her passionately. A true kiss, long, vibrant, endless. The stewardess was touched, assuming they were on their honeymoon. How could she ever have imagined that the reason these two lovers were embracing with such force was because they were about to throw themselves into the arms of another woman?

At the airport, Baptiste decided to rent a car. "It'd be too complicated to go by taxi, I couldn't give the driver an exact address. But I think I could find the way once we get to the harbor."

Isabelle agreed.

Baptiste looked down at his feet in embarrassment. "Can you drive?"

"If you want."

"Oh, no, it's not that . . . It's just that I don't have a license."

"Did you fail the test?"

He blushed in annoyance. "No, I'm not stupid! The fact is, I never took it."

Amused, Isabelle put her arms around his neck and covered him in kisses. The more time she spent with him, the more complex she found Baptiste, the solid Baptiste, the unshakable Baptiste, the respected writer—almost as complex as that multifaceted diamond Joséphine. Just when you thought he was rational, he turned mystical. When you had determined that he was a responsible adult, he turned into a big child.

"You have to understand," he said by way of self-justification, "I'm too easily distracted. Instead of looking at the road and the signs, I think about my characters, or else I watch the movement of the telegraph wires because I like the way they curve."

She hugged him—this little boy who dreamed up stories

when he was in a car—put her license down on the counter, and chose a red racing car.

They set off for Cork. In spite of having to drive on the left, Isabelle was a confident driver.

The farther they advanced, the more Baptiste noticed how much Ireland had changed since his youth. Roads, industrial buildings, warehouses . . . A kind of ugly prosperity had invaded the once rural landscape. Although he was pleased that the country had cast off the poverty in which it had stagnated for centuries, he wondered if he hadn't made a mistake . . . Since the world had changed, maybe he had too? In which case, so had Joséphine, and they had traveled hundreds of miles on a mere intuition.

They reached Cork, a city cut in half by a river, and came out onto the harbor. Isabelle was amazed at the low, colorful houses press closed together. Their riot of color was surprising: it could have been tropical, and it wasn't; it could have been vulgar, and it wasn't; it could have been kitsch, and it was picturesque and charming. The hues of the housefronts—Cadillac pink, lagoon blue, pagoda red, fluorescent green, soda orange—weren't too garish because the drizzle, the clouds, the atmosphere of the ocean muted them, giving them a matte varnish like the opaque layers on an old master painting.

They stopped on Saint Patrick's Bridge with its three arches, and Baptiste searched his memory. He then suggested several contradictory directions. Like all people who don't drive, he had an idiotic, useless, crazed memory for places, relying on details like plants, posters, shopwindows, all elements that had disappeared.

Isabelle was so aware of his unhappiness about his own failings that she didn't lose patience. At last, he recognized a terracotta Virgin Mary at a crossroads, and they left the city and set off across country.

All at once, a dazzling light illumined the landscape, like a second dawn rising in the middle of the day, as if to signal the end of their worries; the sky cleared, and the few clouds were reduced now to a painter's brushstrokes, making the blue even more intense.

They drove along paths lined with moss-laden little walls and dilapidated fences. At a point where two paths crossed, they spotted a rustic sign.

"Murphy's Bed and Breakfast! That's it!"

Baptiste was jubilant!

The cars set off along a stony track surrounded by sheep.

Joséphine was sitting on a rock in front of the farmhouse with its purple shutters. She looked crestfallen. When she heard the noise of the engine, she got to her feet and quickly stood up on tiptoe to try to see what was inside the red car.

The car came to a halt.

Baptiste got out, followed by Isabelle.

Joséphine smiled at them.

Without moving, they looked at one another for a long time, eyes full of love. Above them, seagulls circled cheerfully. Blushing with emotion, Joséphine bowed her head and said in that grumpy street urchin tone of hers, "Well, you took you time. I thought you'd never get here."

Then, laughing, she threw herself into their arms.

A few minutes later, they were in her room: she'd had to persuade the farmer's wife, Mrs. Murphy, a rough woman as broad she was tall, to allow her to bring her guests here.

Joséphine lay down on her narrow single bed, and they lay down on either side. The springs protested.

At the risk of shocking, Baptiste told Joséphine that he could only love Isabelle when she, Joséphine, was around, and provided she continued to love him. In this way, he was putting his wife back in the center of this adventure.

"I would never have been drawn to Isabelle without you.

You led me to her. The fact that we now get along so well, that we love each other, won't wipe that out." He turned to Isabelle. "Isabelle is ours, Joséphine, both of us. She's part of us."

"You're like two drops of water on a windowpane," Isabelle said in a low voice. "The Joséphine drop and the Baptiste drop. A long time ago, the two drops joined to become one. Nobody can ever separate you. I can't imagine loving one of you without the other."

Joséphine looked at them, saw they were sincere, gave up trying to protest, and took them both by the arm.

"Take me away with you, right now. None of the fundamentalist Catholics in this place will ever be able to understand what we're doing. We're in the ninth century here, just after Saint Patrick converted the Celts."

"You're exaggerating."

"Not a bit of it. A depraved Irishman is an Irishman abroad. Look at Oscar Wilde."

"Or else a drunken Irishman?" Baptiste suggested.

"No, that's a happy Irishman."

Laughing, she took out a bottle of whiskey hidden under her bed, locked the door, threw herself on the bed, and hugged Baptiste and Isabelle to her.

T ell me something, Ludo, do you prefer boys?"
Claudine stepped back, folded her arms, and looked her son's face over.

Ludovic let the smoke well up slowly from his throat and narrowed his eyes. "I've been expecting that question. Given all my failures, I've wondered myself."

"There's nothing terrible about it. People don't despise gays anymore."

He shook his head. "I know there's nothing terrible about it. Nobody makes fun of a gay man who's comfortable in his own skin, but they make fun of me."

"What do you mean? Everybody loves you!"

"Well, people like me well enough, the way they like a child. But when they remember that I'm twenty-six and am just as alone as a panther in a circus, they laugh."

"Ludo, don't dodge my question. Is the reason you have problems with women simply that you like men?"

"Simply?" He took out another cigarette, thought about it, and put it down, giving up on the idea of lighting it: he had something important to say. "You know Tom, the philosophy teacher who has a studio apartment opposite?"

"Who doesn't?"

"Do you think he's handsome?"

"Yes. He's lost to us women, but he is very handsome."

"Well, I also think he's handsome."

"You see!" Claudine was trembling with joy. Once again,

she'd be able to help out her Ludovic. From that moment on, her destiny became clear: she would become the wonderful mother of a perfect, happy, fulfilled homosexual, she would be proud of him and would stand up to the whole world. Of course, that meant giving up on having grandchildren . . . Never mind! Ludovic before everything!

Ludovic raised an eyebrow at the enthusiasm on Claudine's face. "Tom has a theory: there are no straight men, there are just men who haven't been laid in the right way; according to him, the whole world is gay. So, one evening when I was doubting myself, I convinced myself that he was the solution to my problems."

"And what happened?"

"For five weeks, I went on a diet, just to lose the spare tire around my belly. It was easy, I ate nothing but seeds."

"Seeds?"

"I felt like a hen, but it worked. Strange when you think about it, that the food that fattens poultry makes human beings slimmer. Anyway, looking at myself after a month in the farmyard, I thought I was, if not magnificent, at least passable. So I invited Tom over, gave him something to drink, then told him I'd been wondering if I wasn't gay. Being a sex maniac who fucks several times a day and reacts to the slightest compliment, he immediately jumped on me and we went into the bedroom. And when we were there . . . "

"Yes?"

He sighed. "I got the giggles. Terrible giggles. Every time he touched me, I thought it was a joke and I giggled. And when he undressed, I thought it was . . . ridiculous. I . . . I . . . He was quite upset."

Claudine bowed her head sadly. "You're hopeless."

Ludovic was amused at her defeated air. "Sorry, Mother, but I'm not gay. I didn't think you'd be so disappointed."

Claudine got up from her armchair, her temples reddening. "So what are you, then?"

He shrugged. How could he answer a question like that? Do we ever know what we are? We are what we do—except that he did nothing.

Claudine started pacing up and down the room, muttering, "Frankly, I have no luck with you."

This comment didn't go down well with Ludo. "Sorry for existing."

"You don't make things easy for me, Ludovic."

"Tell me what business that is of yours. My private life is my concern. I advise you not to interfere and to stay in your place, Fiordiligi!"

At the mention of her Internet handle, Claudine assumed an outraged expression. "I was expecting you'd bring that up!"

"How perceptive of you! You don't think you went a bit too far there?"

"I—"

"Answering a personal ad from her son, is that the act of a mother? It's monstrous!"

"It was out of love, Ludo."

"That's what I mean: your love is monstrous, you think it gives you rights. You think you can interfere in my private life and control everything. Don't you realize? I thought I was communicating with a woman, and I was writing to my own mother."

"I'm a woman!" she cried.

He looked at her in alarm. She caught his gaze and held it. Such a lack of awareness was too much for Ludovic's patience; he couldn't hold back anymore. "Has it never occurred to you how hard it's been for me to become a normal adult with a mother like you?"

"What?"

"A mother who never defended me when my father beat me—of course, he beat you too—a mother who ever since has been clinging to me to the point of stifling me."

"I 'cling' to you?"

"I'll never forgive you for flirting with me on the Internet."

"Hold on! We didn't get very far."

"But how did you know that when you started?"

"With you," she sneered "I know everything from the start."

"What if that hadn't been the case, what if I'd really fallen in love? Maybe I was already in love, but I didn't have time to find out because I was soon brought down to earth."

"That shows I respect you. As soon as I realized you were getting attached, I revealed my identity. That's proof, isn't it!"

"This has to be a bad dream! You're boasting about stopping when you shouldn't even have started?"

"I needed to know."

"To know what?"

"Who you are."

"No mother knows who her son really is, especially in bed. You just have to be like all the others and ignore him. That's the only way to establish a healthy relationship between a son and a mother."

"A healthy relationship . . . A healthy relationship . . . You certainly aren't afraid of words! Monsieur goes on about a 'healthy' relationship when at the age of twenty-six he still isn't capable of having a girlfriend!"

"Of course, talking about my girlfriends, either it's my mother who introduces them to me, or it's my mother who takes their place. Isn't that so, Fiordiligi?"

"When are you going to stop blaming me for that?"

"Never, Fiordiligi."

"Don't you ever make a mistake?"

"Yes, but I try not to deceive other people, Fiordiligi."

"Stop it, Ludo."

"No, Fiordiligi."

"Ludo, I'm not going to beat about the bush: if you keep repeating that name, Fiordiligi, you'll never see me again."

"Fiordiligi! Fiordiligi! Fiordiligi!"

It was as if he'd been overcome by a fit of madness. He started walking around the apartment, yelling that name in an increasingly hoarse voice.

Claudine picked up her handbag, ran to the hall way, and slammed the door.

At that sound, Ludovic stopped yelling. The silence that fell was like a reward. He was intrigued by one thing, though: he didn't hear the elevator.

He tiptoed to the door, making sure the floorboards didn't creak. As discreetly as possible, he put his eye to the spyhole and looked out at the landing. Claudine was standing just outside the door, motionless, listening.

"Fiordiligi! Fiordiligi! Fiordiligi!" he roared.

Furious, Claudine kicked the door, grunted something indistinct, and ran off down the stairs.

The scene had aroused a new state in Ludovic, a kind of unease that he decided to call relief. Intellectually, he had been right to denounce his mother's abuses. Emotionally, he wasn't pleased at having chased her away, and his hands trembled.

He devoted himself to his work. Just so as not to think about Claudine! The cultural magazine he had created still demanded hours of editing.

In the afternoon, writing an article on the American minimalists, he remembered his story about Tom. Of course, he'd invented the whole thing, but it struck him as significant. In telling it, he'd convinced himself that it would have happened like that. Should he try it all the same? Should he force himself to experience what he had no desire to experience, since he already knew the outcome?

"I'm tired of establishing how useless I am. From now on I accept it fully."

He saw again his mother pestering him to sleep with girls or men.

"What an obsessive! Is it such a burden to her to be a widow?"

For the first time, he realized that the pressure came from outside, not from him. Endlessly, since he was twenty, people had been demanding that he develop a sex life—his pals first of all, then, because he got on better with girls, his female friends, his mother, strangers. His entourage was obsessed with it, whereas he never thought about it.

Meekly, he had listened to their advice with goodwill, then had tried his luck in the market of physical relations. Would he have ventured there without their assistance? Surely not. In fact, Ludovic felt neither the need nor the desire for sex.

In order to relax, he opened a bar of white chocolate and switched on the television.

"Again?"

Zachary Bidermann's face had just appeared on the screen. Psychologists, sociologists, sexologists, and political analysts were discussing his case and sexual addiction in general.

"As far as I'm concerned, it's as exotic as an item about gazelles in Ethiopia!" Ludovic exclaimed, both irritated and interested.

A psychologist explained that the individual seeks sensations of pleasure because they liberate endorphins. Or the opposite, retorted a neurologist. But all the assembled experts were in agreement on the vital role played by sex.

Ludo felt like cutting in with, "What if we don't have a libido?"

The more he listened to them, the more he realized how alienated he felt from the society of his time, where sex was not only obligatory, but had to be successful.

Success in sex, he thought. *What a strange idea! Objection, gentlemen: success in life outside sex, can you imagine that?*

Happiness, balance, helpfulness to others or to oneself, was that impossible without rubbing your genitals against someone else's?

Ludo switched off the TV. In performing no sexual activity at all, he had the impression he wasn't only in the minority, he was a shameful person; he was pointed at with the finger of infamy, was blamed for lacking testosterone.

If my balls had been crushed in an accident, people would at least feel sorry for me.

Yes, he would have been forgiven his physical disability. He would even have been forgiven his perversion.

Sexual perversion is reassuring. People understand it.

Twisted sexuality was still sexuality. People tolerated the urges that threw one body onto another, whatever the result.

Yes, if I collected whips or old socks, my mother would be able to hold her head up high in society. She would even prefer it if I screwed goats or ran after cows. The indulgent mother of a zoophilist, yes, she'd be ready to become that! She would lead a campaign. She'd go to see the king and get him to open his stables once a year. But the way I am, no!

His mother was a good example of the tawdriness of the era, a time that put sex above everything. In other centuries, the case of Ludovic would have been less problematic: he could have taken refuge in a religious order, he could have claimed to be practicing abstinence.

Abstinence? What a laugh! You can only practice abstinence if you've been fucking all your life.

The absence of desire, though, the peace of the body—nobody admitted that. Asexuality was only a problem in a time of frenetic sex.

He switched the TV back on just as one of the political

analysts was venturing a theory about the link between the appetite for power and the appetite for sex.

"Oh, shut up!"

He ran to the kitchen and took from the cupboards the things he ought to avoid eating: wafers, walnut cookies, cereal bars, white chocolate. A calorific feast that he accompanied with a tub of banana yogurt. He didn't like eating—he always ate quickly—what he liked was feeling so sated that he wanted either to throw up or to sleep.

Passing the mirror, he glanced at himself.

"A little more effort, Ludo, and you'll finally be unfuckable."

He smiled, and even underlined his words with a wink.

Suddenly, he froze. He had only just realized what he had said.

With his unhealthy eating habits and his terrible clothes, he'd been abusing himself in order to put himself out of the game, to withdraw from the race the others wanted him to take part in. He'd been trying to justify his amorous failures by demonstrating that he couldn't inspire love. He'd been destroying himself to gain peace.

He examined himself again in the mirror. The fact was, he had no real desire to mess himself up, he was perfectly ready to value himself, especially as, in all other aspects of life, he showed refined tastes. Only the pressure of this sex-obsessed world had led him to twist himself out of shape.

He sat down on his favorite cushion and put on Debussy's *Sirènes*, a sensual piece of music in which a wordless woman's chorus mingled with the waves of the orchestra, an interweaving of sounds as fascinating and sophisticated as cigarette smoke on a summer evening.

Even his deepest tastes justified his living apart; classical music isolated him, since listening to it attentively necessitated solitude and silence. That was something he couldn't and wouldn't change. It was too late for that anyway. The rest, however, mistreating his body, making it ugly or ordinary . . . Yes, he could free himself of these constraints.

The doorbell rang. He jumped, suddenly remembering that he had made an appointment with Tiffany.

She came in and put her arms around his neck, trembling like a leaf. "Oh, Ludo, I'm so pleased to see you!"

"You've had problems with your man!"

Tiffany rushed to an armchair, and while gobbling down Ludo's little snack, told him about the difficulties she had been encountering with her boyfriend. Ludo listened to these confidences, encouraging her, giving a piece of advice here, clarifying a point there.

Then she started repeating herself, and he took advantage of this to think about his mother. He had never before rejected her like this, but then she had never before committed such an offense. The more he thought about it, the more unforgivable her interference in his love life seemed.

Tiffany, tired of stewing in her own problems, dismissed the subject and talked about the troubles their mutual friends were facing.

"Pat and Jean are over, can you imagine?"

"I know. I heard that Pat had gotten together with Paul."

"That's already in the past."

"So it goes. And how's Graziella?"

"She's leaving Aldo. Rudy and Laetitia are splitting up."

"Even them?" Ludovic said, surprised.

He realized that Tiffany had eaten all the cakes he had put on the coffee table. There, he'd started his diet!

"By the way, Tiffany, I wanted to tell you that I'm OK."

"What do you mean?"

"I mean I'm OK."

She made an incredulous face. "All right . . . "

"So there's no point in your friends and you continuing to think of me as sick."

"Ludo?"

"What's a problem for you isn't a problem for me."

"What are you talking about?"

"I'm talking about sex. I'm just not sexual."

She suppressed a smile, then pretended to be looking for inspiration on the ceiling. "As it happens, I thought of you the other day when I saw on the Internet that there's a new group called the 'asexuals.' They're trying to get themselves recognized."

"I don't give a damn. Pointless, I won't become any more normal by finding people who are just like me. I don't feel the need to belong to a herd."

"We must all have a place in society."

"I have a place, and it doesn't need to be normal. And besides, the place I occupy is mine, and I'm keeping it." He leaned forward. "I'm not so sure I'm isolated, you know. What are the great friendships if not asexual relationships? What is father love, mother love, filial love, if not an asexual relationship? The only kinds of love there are that work don't involve sex. Everyone, without making too much effort, can be a son, a brother, a friend, a father. Rarely all at the same time. And yet the world persists with sexual love, even though it has a tendency to fizzle out. I'm going to tell you something in confidence: the woman I prefer in my life is the one with whom I've never had and will never have sexual relations."

"Who is she?"

He said nothing and went to the window looking out on Place d'Arezzo.

Tiffany came up to him.

He shivered. "You feel sorry for me, is that it?"

"I feel touched by you. And you often amuse me."

"Yes, but you also feel sorry for me . . . Actually, I prefer compassion to love, it only commits the person who feels sorry."

"Don't you want to be like other people?"

He thought about this for a long time. "No."

She nodded and sighed admiringly, "You're lucky. I wonder if you aren't the strongest of us."

At that moment, through the window, Ludo saw Zachary Bidermann getting out of a black limousine, having just been released from custody, and being assailed by photographers, curious onlookers, and angry feminists, all in the grip of a fever they couldn't control. Around them, surprised by this flurry of human excitement, parrots and parakeets flew nosily about the square.

"Maybe I am," Ludovic murmured phlegmatically.

Then he moved away from the window, went to the computer, and gently typed in the following words:

Fiordiligi, are you still there?

D amn!"
Disappointed, Tom closed the book of condolences. The words and signatures entered in its tall pages during Séverine's funeral were of no help to him in his investigation.

"Well?" the priest asked.

Around them, the room where children were taught catechism was decorated with bright, cheerful drawings that almost diverted attention from the dust, the dilapidated walls, and the sparse light struggling to penetrate the dirty windows.

"There's no evidence," Tom said. "None of the handwriting here matches the handwriting in the anonymous letters. As for my two leads, one holds up, the other doesn't."

"Which one doesn't?"

"The writer, Baptiste Monier. For a while, I thought he might be playing some kind of intellectual game, provoking the residents of the square just to see their reactions. I had the idea that each of the letters might be the first sentence of a chapter. An experimental novel."

"Sounds like fun. And?"

"He's right-handed, so it can't be him."

"Maybe he's ambidextrous."

Tom scratched his head, admitting he'd probably come to a hasty conclusion.

The priest noticed a piece of green chalk on the platform, picked it up, and put it back in the groove of the blackboard.

Then he picked up the book of condolences. "What about your other lead, Tom?"

"It's Orion, the florist, the nicest man in Brussels, married to the nastiest woman in the universe."

The priest smiled. "That's the way it works: only a gentle soul ever gets together with a bitch."

"Why?"

"Because he's the only one who doesn't know how hard it's going to be."

"It feels a bit weird hearing you, a priest, call someone a bitch. It doesn't sound very charitable."

"Why is it that atheists enjoy lecturing us about charity, generosity, and piety? Is it something you all lack?"

"No. I'm just taking the opportunity to tell you that I understand your system, and I don't think you really believe in it."

"In order to forgive, the subject must first have something for which he or she needs to be forgiven. Xavière seems to be an eminently forgivable person."

"And I reject the idea that an individual should be reduced to a thing, a character trait. In my opinion, there's no such thing as a bitch, or a gentle soul, or, for that matter, a saint or an asshole."

"What about Zachary Bidermann?"

"He's a perfect example. He acted like an asshole the other night, but he isn't an asshole."

"You refuse to judge him?"

"I judge an act, not the man. A man is more than what he might say or do."

"You deny the existence of vice and virtue. And yet through habit, repetition, or temperament, an individual acquires a second nature and behaves either 'generally well' or 'generally badly.'"

"All right. But he can still shift, like sand. Show me a saint today, and I'll prove to you that he may well sin tomorrow. The same applies to a villain: he may behave well."

"I see what you mean. So you, Tom, are not a homosexual?"

"No more than you're a priest."

"Excuse me?"

"It so happens that right now, you have the role of a priest—"

"The vocation."

"—but you haven't always been a priest, and maybe won't continue to be one. Even now, you aren't a priest every second of the day."

"Is that so?"

"You aren't a priest when you shit, when you eat, when you think about your mother, when you see a woman walk by that you like."

"Yes, I am!"

"No! You're a man who likes her, instinctively, and then the priest intervenes and tells the man to restrain himself and throw his desire in the garbage. The same for me, I can't be reduced to a homosexual even though I sleep with men. When I think, when I teach, when I listen to music, when I talk to you, none of that has anything to do with my preferences in bed."

"I'm not accusing you of anything, Tom."

"What's that got to do with it? We were talking about Orion."

"You're right, we were talking about Orion."

"He's still my principal hypothesis because he omitted to sign the book of condolences. This is a man who greets everybody as if they were an absolute marvel, a man who wishes well of the whole world. He's actually Christlike, this Orion. What do you think, Mr. Priest?"

"I wouldn't wish him to be Christlike, because then he'd come to a bad end, but he's certainly evangelical. He gives love to everybody."

"Which is quite disturbing."

"Yes, it is. People wonder what he's after, what his ulterior motive is. But he doesn't have one. It's just disinterested love, pure love."

"Consequently, they treat him like an idiot."

"Idiocy is what cynics ascribe to the pure."

Tom nodded his approval of this definition. He licked his lips, then looked at the priest. "Tell me, do you ever get carried away like this when you preach?"

"Sometimes."

"I should come, for that if nothing else."

"You'd be very welcome."

Tom stood up and kissed the priest on the cheek. "Thank you for the book of condolences. I'll carry on with my investigation."

The priest gave a thin smile. "It's natural I should help you, since you're looking for Jesus."

Tom burst out laughing. "Now please don't try selling me your wares."

They left the classroom, walked down some rickety stairs, between walls covered in pious images, then opened a dilapidated door and came out at street level.

Outside the presbytery, Tom gave the priest an affectionate wave. "See you at Mom's on Saturday morning?"

"Don't forget it's her birthday this time."

"Shit! Already?"

"Tom, why can't you ever remember Mom's birthday?"

Tom made a gesture of powerlessness, then turned the corner. He and his brother had never prioritized the same things.

As he reached Place d'Arezzo, he saw Madame Singer, looking like a sergeant major in her khaki outfit, lashing out at a reporter who was crawling up onto a branch, scaring the parrots and parakeets as he did so, in order to get his lens closer to the Bidermanns' town house.

Being a coward, Tom decided to get out of her way before she called him over to help her. Instead of going home, he took refuge in Nathan's building.

He went up to the sixth floor, used his key, and entered the apartment, which was unusually silent. Normally there would be music spreading through the rooms, or else Nathan singing from wherever he was. And yet he must be home: his keys were in the bowl by the door.

"Nathan?"

The silence absorbed his call.

Rather than worry, Tom went straight to the bathroom. There was no noise from the shower. The room, with its tiled walls, was empty.

He went to the bedroom and opened the door. There, he just had time to catch a glimpse of a shoulder diving under the comforter. Nathan's head popped out from the other end of the mattress.

"Oh, it's you . . . " he stammered uncomfortably. "I . . . I wasn't expecting you so soon."

He gave Tom an apologetic grin to express his remorse, but Tom wasn't looking at him, he was staring at the shape of the body hiding under the sheets.

He suddenly felt a coldness spreading through him. Should he move? Should he say something? He knew exactly what was happening.

"OK. Bye."

His abrupt tone expressed all the contempt he felt for the two men in the bed. He turned on his heels and walked out.

He trudged wearily down the stairs. Only one word echoed in his head: Nathan. The name that up until now had evoked only happiness now meant cowardice and betrayal.

He left the building and went over to a bench on Place d'Arezzo, just opposite the front door. From there, he'd be able to see the man escape.

He sat down, hands deep in his jacket pockets, and stared straight ahead. What would he do? Smash his face? What would be the point in that? It wouldn't change anything. Nathan was the guilty party. His lover, whoever he was, hadn't betrayed anybody, hadn't been performing a belly dance for him for three years, trying to persuade him to move in.

He looked at the time.

One minute. Only one minute had passed since he had rushed out onto the square, and already it felt like an eternity. How long would he have to wait? Would those pigs upstairs resume their fornicating? Would they dare? If they did, he might as well go back up and set the place on fire.

The door moved and a man stuck his nose out. He was still finishing getting dressed, in a hurry to get away. He looked right and left, making sure that his rival wasn't waiting to beat him up.

Tom gave a start.

The fugitive didn't think to look in front of him, onto the square, and so wasn't aware that the man he feared was right there. He disappeared down Rue Molière. Tom remained on the bench, frozen. He knew the guy. He had a Greek name . . . Nikkos! That's right, it was Nikkos. He had slept with him the month before.

Embarrassed, Tom looked at his hands. Should he laugh or be angry? Here he was, blaming Nathan for doing what he himself had done a few weeks earlier.

Tom couldn't be angry for very long. Not that he was unaware of anger, but he hated it and took care to get rid of it. Was there anything more stupid than anger? It rebels against the world and, through its intensity alone, hopes to change it. Then it hits out, insulting reality without altering it. Anger is a form of powerlessness that believes itself to be strong.

He wiped the palms of his hands on his jeans, tried to force himself to laugh, but failed. He was disgusted by this whole business.

Of course, Nikkos wasn't any kind of danger. He might be a pretty boy, but he fucked in a boring way, overexcited, impatient, jerky, rushed, and he grunted a lot. Once was enough. Maybe once was too often . . . Besides, Nikkos never tried to take root or see a fleeting lover again, he always ran away once it was over. From what Tom had gathered, he liked encounters, but didn't like people.

Come on, laugh about it! It's no big deal!

He was finding it hard to overcome his sadness. The problem wasn't Nikkos, but Nathan. Nathan was always suggesting they live together, always talking to him about love, and probably loved Tom as much as Tom loved him. So why, then, did he take advantage of a free moment to get his rocks off with a stranger?

Nathan appeared on the sidewalk opposite, dressed in black, which didn't suit him, making him look too solemn. Avoiding a car that zoomed past, he came toward Tom.

"Are you angry with me?"

Tom shrugged and looked away, furious. "No, I'm thrilled."

"I'm sorry, Tom, I wasn't expecting you. We weren't supposed to meet until tonight, because of the schoolwork you have to grade."

"What are you sorry for? Doing what you did? Or getting your timetable wrong?"

Nathan assumed an outraged expression and hit the air with his hands. "Is this you, Tom, the guy who can't keep his zipper closed, the horniest man in Brussels, preaching chastity? I can't believe it! OK, I admit it wasn't pleasant for you to catch me like that, and I repeat, I wish I could have spared you, but I'm not going to pretend I'm ashamed of having done it."

Tom wanted to retaliate in an equally outraged tone but, either because of Nathan's comical indignation or because of what he was really thinking, he felt the onset of laughter.

"What?" Nathan grunted, fearing he looked ridiculous.

"Was it worth it, at least?"

"Not really."

"Oh?" Tom was increasingly struggling to keep a straight face.

Nathan raised his eyes to heaven and said in a harsh tone, "Anyway, thanks to your entrance, we didn't even go all the way."

"You didn't miss anything," Tom murmured, fighting to ward off another spasm. "With Nikkos, you just get the sound track to a porn movie, but nothing else."

"What?"

"I promise."

"You know Nikkos?"

"Same as you."

At the sight of Nathan's bulging eyes, hilarity gained the upper hand and broke through the dam: Tom exploded with laughter.

Thrown at first, Nathan began to understand what Tom was implying. He sat down next to him and, slowly, by fits and starts, also started laughing. Soon, the two men were doubled up.

Once they had finally managed to stop, Nathan turned to Tom. "And you call this a fit of jealousy?"

They immediately burst into a further fit of the giggles. After this scene, they knew this was the most fun they could ever have, sitting side by side, fellow conspirators, laughing until their bellies hurt.

Catching his breath, Nathan took hold of Tom's arm. "I love you, you know."

"I know."

Nathan pursed his lips. "You do realize you were supposed to answer, 'Me too?'"

"I'll tell you when it comes naturally."

"And is that still likely?"

"Anything can happen."

"Are we still together?"

"We're still together."

Tom sat up straight on the bench. "But there's one thing that does end here: living together."

"Oh, no!"

"I was about to end my lease, move my books, go through all that hassle, in order to expose myself to . . . what I just saw."

"You *are* angry with me, Tom!"

"I fully admit that it's hard to resist temptation—I'm the first one to give in to it—but there is one temptation I'm going to resist, trust me, and that's the temptation to live with you. Why do you want us to live together, Nathan, when you cherish your freedom and I cherish mine? The ideal arrangement to keep that freedom isn't a shared closet, it's separate homes. You want to have it all: the butter, the butter dish, and the milkman's ass! If it's natural to have flings here and there, then the only way to bear it is for the other person not to know. I'll love you more if I don't catch you between the sheets with another man—or a boy! I'll love you more if, when I'm in a foul mood, I can shut myself in my own apartment. I'll love you more if I can decide to sleep at your place. I'll love you more if I can invite you to come and sleep at mine. I'll love you more if I can avoid you when you want to be with someone else. I'll love you more if you don't find me in the place of the one you desire. I'll love you more if you aren't an obligation. I'll love you more if you aren't a habit. I'll love you more if you remain my choice. I'll love you more if I can prefer you. I'll love you more if you allow me to love you the way I want to love you. Our love is much too important for me to let it be ruined by living together."

Moved, Nathan nodded. Tom patted his cheek. Nathan blushed.

"So we part in order not to break up, right?"

"That's right. I won't live with you because I want our relationship to last."

Tom leaned slowly, very slowly, toward Nathan, and pressed his warm lips to his. Up in the branches, there was a beating of wings, like a burst of applause.

When the kiss was over, and Nathan was finally able to catch his breath, he looked at his lover, intoxicated by his scent and his desire for him. "When all's said and done, Tom, contrary to appearances, of the two of us you're the romantic one."

"Romanticism is the wisdom of the hot-blooded."

6

When Patricia was left alone in the empty apartment, without either Hippolyte, who had judged it wise to leave, or her daughter, who had run out by the back stairs, she wandered dejectedly from room to room, hearing the cheerful interjections rising up from Place d'Arezzo, looking at the mess around her, counting the cost of that disastrous party . . . There was no doubt that she was the evening's greatest loser. Her daughter was gone, and so was her boyfriend.

There was clearing up to be done, dishes to be scrubbed.

But she was so discouraged, she simply collapsed into an armchair. With one finger, she switched off the lights and let the semidarkness overwhelm her.

Her life was falling apart. From the way Albane had behaved, it was clear that she wouldn't be able to keep Hippolyte. Until now, they had met only in secret, in this apartment or in the discreet café in the Marolles. It was as if they had been living on a desert island. Well, now their Robinson Crusoe days were over! They were back in the big wide world, with its dangers and its ugly competitiveness. Albane had given her a foretaste of what would happen: women wouldn't be able to stop themselves from coming on to Hippolyte, whether deliberately or not.

So that was what awaited her. Uncertainty, struggle, betrayal. Not to mention ridicule: the handsome Hippolyte and Patricia the fat lump. The times she'd heard people say of someone, "What a guy like that is doing with such an ugly woman is beyond me!" Had she ever said it herself? Of course she had.

As for Hippolyte . . . For the moment, he was playing at being the gallant knight faithful to his lady, and rejecting an underage Messalina. But, in a month or a year, how would he react to a grown-up woman who was bolder than Albane?

She couldn't keep a treasure like him in her arms forever.

She breathed out.

That very second, something broke within her. It was over. She had lost all trust. In herself and in Hippolyte. In others and in society. Her illusions were crumbling.

To put herself out of her misery, she went to the bathroom. When she saw herself in the mirror, she thought for a moment that she didn't look too bad: her hairstyle matched her face nicely. This flash of satisfaction was something she both liked and disliked. What was the point? There comes a moment when a woman must choose between her face and her body. Fat had preserved her face, keeping it round, firm, and without wrinkles, but down below, Patricia had become enormous. And to think of all the work she had put in over the past few weeks. She'd been as busy as someone training for the decathlon. If you couldn't see it in the mirror, it ought at least to be visible on the display screen of the scales. She stepped onto the scales. What? It must be a mistake. The needle must have jammed. Impossible. She had lost only three and a half pounds.

Flying into a rage, she started hitting her body, striking her stomach, arms, and thighs. What was this cellulite doing here? She had never invited it!

The sound of an altercation came from the street. Afraid Albane might be involved, she rushed to the living room window. Two young men wearing tracksuits were having a row with a couple in dinner suits over a parking space, each claiming it as their own. The young people, as agitated as they were foul-mouthed, were yelling, while the posh couple kept asking them to be quiet.

Fearing that violence was about to gain the upper hand, Patricia intervened. "Is there a problem? Do you want me to call the police?"

The society couple looked up, and the two young people turned their anger on her. "The police? What have the police got to do with it? This is our space. We always park here."

"Parking spaces don't belong to anybody," she replied.

"Look, old lady, why don't you just fuck off and leave us alone? Wrinkled hags like you should be in bed at this time of night."

"It's all right, madame," the posh man said to ease the tension. "We'll park a little farther on."

Patricia withdrew and took refuge in her living room. Old lady? That was all she needed. They just had to take one look at her, and they called her old? Fat maybe . . . but old?

She shuddered. So she had grown old! Here was the reason for her unease, this was what she had been feeling all evening. Albane in a miniskirt, Albane made up to the point of being indecent, Albane purring when a man looked at her, Albane transformed into a sex object: Albane had been communicating the fact that she, her mother, had to withdraw, drop out of the race, because she was fit only for the scrap heap.

Her heart started beating faster. She put a hand on her chest. Everything was clear now: even though she and Hippolyte were the same age, he was so attractive that it was possible for Albane and Hippolyte to get together, whereas it was highly unlikely that any male friend of Albane would come on to her, Patricia. Her time had run out.

An image flashed in front of her: the golden light striking the white flowers on the coffin at Séverine's funeral. Peace. Rest at last.

There was no time to waste.

She rushed to her room, got up on a stool, and rummaged through the top of her wardrobe. There, she found the box she was looking for, took it down, and opened it. In it were several bottles of Veronal pills. They had been there for years. The barbiturate had been prescribed by Dr. Gemayel when she had turned forty, to help her get to sleep; except that Patricia didn't give two hoots about sleeping at night because she preferred to read. She had bought the pills and put them there, just in case.

It was as if she had fixed an appointment with herself years in advance. If she took an excessive amount of the drug, she would fall asleep and never wake up again. A perfect death, without suffering and without any damage to her body. She wouldn't inflict on others a terrible sight that would traumatize them. It would be a clean death.

But she mustn't wait! If you stopped to think about that kind of thing, you were screwed.

She went into the kitchen, took the pills from their packaging, and lined them up carefully on the table. Then she poured a large glass of water and grabbed the first pill.

The doorbell rang.

She hesitated. Should she answer or not? There was never any peace here. Who was it at this time of night? It must be a mistake.

The doorbell rang again.

What if it was the two young guys from the square, coming up to murder her?

Who cares, Patricia? You're in the process of committing suicide. In a few minutes, you're going to fall asleep. So why should you care?

She lifted a pill to her tongue.

The doorbell rang again, more steadily and for a longer time.

You can't even die in peace these days. All right, I'll deal with it, then carry on.

Silently, she went to the door and looked through the spy-hole. She was surprised to see a neighbor, one of those you didn't see much of, the engineer's wife, what was her name again?

Just then, she heard a voice say, "Mommy, please open up."

Albane? Looking more carefully through the distorting lens of the spyhole, she saw an oddly-dressed young girl at the end of the landing . . . Albane?

She opened the door.

Her daughter threw herself into her arms. Diane asked if she could come in with her. In a few words, since Albane had started sobbing again, she explained what had happened.

The following morning, when Patricia saw the kitchen table covered in white pills arranged in rows, she felt ashamed. How could she have been so thoughtless, so irresponsible as to want to leave? Albane was still here, and she really needed her. *Imagine if she'd come in here after being violently raped and found your dead body?* Shamefacedly realizing the selfishness of suicide, she threw the pills in the trash.

Dr. Gemayel arrived at nine in the morning, after Patricia had left him a voicemail message at dawn, reporting the drama. As soon as he appeared on the landing, dark-skinned, cleanly shaven, dashing, with his phlegmatic Lebanese virility, she wondered if she wasn't making a mistake by bringing in a man to see her daughter. But she felt calmer when she saw the relieved expression on Albane's face when he entered her room: Dr. Gemayel was their doctor first and foremost, and only secondly a man.

He was with her for a long time. To him, being a doctor was about more than just medicine, and his activities comprised more than diagnosing and prescribing. He also liked to listen, to understand, to reassure, to get the patient thinking about his or her future. At once a humanist and a scientist, he believed that to provide care was to form a relationship with the person.

In his opinion, this bond was as important as pharmaceuticals, and had to be kept up in all circumstances, even if the treatment failed.

At the end of the consultation, he asked to speak to Patricia.

"The injuries are more emotional than physical. Albane must be helped to regain confidence in herself and in other people. At her age, that's crucial."

"Don't worry, I'm here."

"Your presence is essential, absolutely essential, but not necessarily sufficient. Albane will be too embarrassed to tell you everything."

"Yes, I know."

"We have to stop her from withdrawing into herself and seeing sex as violence."

"I'll help her."

"I have no doubt of your good intentions. Forgive this intrusion into your private life, but what's your situation at the moment?"

"What situation?"

"Men, sex. Are you single?"

"Yes . . . No . . . Actually, I'm in a relationship. We're considering living together."

"Does Albane like your future partner?"

"Er . . . yes."

Patricia closed her eyes, thinking she should have replied, "A bit too much, actually." As she thought this, she realized that none of this would have happened—Albane's running away, the rape—if she hadn't introduced Hippolyte to her daughter. She turned pale.

Dr. Gemayel was watching her, aware of her conflicting thoughts. He took out his notepad. "I'm going to refer you to a colleague of mine. She's a trauma expert." He scribbled her details on a prescription sheet. "Marie-Jeanne Simon. Please call her. In a case such as this, it's the family as a unit that needs to be treated, not just the person involved. Sometimes, those close to the victim are as affected by the trauma as the actual victim."

The Bidermann affair made Patricia's situation even more complicated. When it was revealed in the media that there had been a rape in the Ixelles area of Brussels the previous night, Patricia thought, *Why aren't they mentioning my daughter's rape?* The more attention the case got, the more the hype weighed on her: didn't they realize that Albane had suffered far worse violence than Zachary Bidermann had inflicted on one of his guests? The conjunction of the two events was a cruel one. Every mention of the case was like a knife through her heart. Crime was everywhere. Inside the apartment, the assault on Albane hovered in the air and was constantly in her thoughts, and then, as soon as she switched on the television or the radio, the assault committed by Biderman would come flooding in as well; outside, the square was monopolized by journalists, TV vans, photographers, and voyeurs. Rape had taken over the world.

In a state of shock, Patricia was losing control of her thoughts. Whenever Albane mentioned her attackers, Patricia would superimpose Zachary Bidermann's face on those shadowy figures, seeing three of him bending over her daughter's humiliated body. Whenever she heard the news, she imagined Albane at the Bidermanns' dramatic party. The boundaries between personal history and collective history were becoming porous, Patricia felt as if the horror of it all was pursuing her; the world was growing dark.

She no longer knew how to deal with Hippolyte. Should she tell him what had happened to Albane—that would mean accepting him once and for all as part of the family's private life—or keep him at a distance until Albane felt better?

He was hassling her over the phone, wanting to see her. At first, she had managed to make up credible excuses, but Hippolyte had sensed her resistance and asked for an explanation. "Is it because of your daughter?"

"Yes, it's because of her."

"Tell me."

"Soon."

Patricia felt responsible. Her relationship with Hippolyte had begun like a dream but turned into a nightmare, especially since she couldn't help making a causal connection between Hippolyte and her daughter's rape: if Albane hadn't dressed up like a provocative whore in order to excite him, she would never have met and aroused those three bastards!

Madame Simon took to coming every morning. Patricia would exchange a few words with her, but remained on her guard. Although she had obeyed Dr. Gemayel by consulting her, she felt that the psychiatrist was usurping her role as a mother. Albane shouldn't be confiding in a stranger, but in her, Patricia! She had carried her in her womb, raised her, educated her, comforted her after the death of her father; when this shrink put the case behind her, she would forget all about it, while Patricia would still be here, taking care of Albane until her dying breath. That was unfair! Besides, what was this woman hearing from her daughter's lips? Every time she left the girl's bedroom, Patricia would give her a sideways glance, frantic at the thought that she might have just been told about her mistakes or faults; with each passing day, this intruder must be coming to the conclusion that most of the daughter's problems came from the mother.

When Madame Simon suggested they talk, Patricia struggled with the impulse to run away. She couldn't have felt more humiliated if she'd been handcuffed.

Madame Simon sat across from her. "Albane is intelligent and brave."

You don't need an advanced diploma to work that one out, Patricia thought defensively.

"She'll get back on track. You're here for her, and that's good, I congratulate you, but, in the present circumstances, she's suffering a lot from the absence of a father."

Does she think I'm going to resurrect him? Did she study medicine or did I?

"It might be good if there were a male figure taking part in the process of recovery. I don't think she'll be able to heal fully in an all-female household. What she needs is the presence of a kind man, a figure that would counterbalance the aggressive ones. Don't you have a partner?"

"I . . . I have a boyfriend," Patricia stammered, "but we don't live together."

"Do you trust him?"

"Yes."

"Has he behaved in an ambiguous way toward your daughter?"

"No, never. I have no doubt on that point."

"What do you have doubts about?"

Here we go, the viper's sizing me up, as if I were her prey.

"I doubt I can start a new life with him."

"Don't you love him enough?"

"Oh, yes, I do!"

"What about him?"

"The same, I think."

"What is it, then?"

"I don't know how beneficial it would be to start a new life, to upset the current balance."

"Allow me to express a few doubts concerning the 'current balance.' You live alone, almost like a recluse, with a daughter who until recently thought you had given up on sex. It may be a cocoon, but it's an unhealthy, regressive, unrealistic cocoon. For Albane, having a happy mother who's pleased to be with her partner would be excellent medicine. Besides, she needs a father figure to whom she can show affection."

Patricia frowned: should she tell this psychiatrist that Albane had tried to seduce Hippolyte? No, that would be disloyal.

"See you tomorrow, madame."

The psychiatrist got up and left.

Is that all?

Disapproving in her heart of hearts, Patricia obeyed the prescription. She arranged to meet Hippolyte in their usual café in the Marolles and told him what had happened to Albane.

As she told the painful story, Patricia felt every detail of the rape in her flesh and her soul. She choked, struggled, cried, screamed. Upset, Hippolyte had to cradle her in his arms for a long time before she pulled herself together.

When she returned home that afternoon, she announced to Albane that Hippolyte would be joining them that evening.

"Good," Albane muttered, and went back to her room.

Patricia was terrified by this acquiescence. She was so used to Albane being morose that her amiability aroused her suspicion. Would the horror start all over again?

Still, Albane showed up to the second meal with Hippolyte dressed plainly, in fact, even more modestly than usual. She behaved pleasantly, didn't do anything untoward, and Hippolyte genuinely enjoyed getting to know her and talking with her.

Even so, Patricia couldn't stop worrying. Every time she went to the kitchen to clear a dish or bring in the next one, she would stop once she was out of sight and listen to make sure that the tone or the subject of the conversation hadn't changed.

At ten o'clock, Albane said goodnight to the two adults and retired to her room. Patricia and Hippolyte chatted quietly, then Hippolyte said, "I can stay tonight, if you like. Germain has offered to look after Isis."

Patricia was surprised to hear mention of Isis. Accustomed to meeting Hippolyte on his own, she often forgot that he was raising a daughter, so seldom did he speak of her. In any case, he never mentioned her as a problem. *Men and women really are different. His daughter isn't a major issue in his life.* Hippolyte's casual attitude when it came to Isis irritated her so much, she had to stop herself at the last moment from calling him an unfit father.

He came and put his arms around her; she finally stopped thinking, and allowed herself to be led to the bedroom.

When, after several kisses and slow caresses, he gently tried to undress her, she panicked and stopped him. "I can't."

"Don't you want to?"

"I can't!"

He looked at her uncomprehendingly

She tried to explain. "It's because of . . . "

"Because of Albane?"

"Because of Albane."

"Because she's here?"

"That's right. I'm not used to it."

"Don't you think you should be getting used to it?"

Patricia shuddered even more. Searching for a solution, she improvised. "You're right, we should be getting used to it . . . So I suggest you prove that you're ready to share your life with mine."

"Great."

"Let's spend the night together and not make love."

He looked at her for a long time, then, his face lit up with affection, he agreed enthusiastically.

Patricia also pretended to be happy. It didn't matter that Albane was sleeping down the corridor. The truth was, she didn't feel like sex. After what her daughter had been through, she found the thought of a man, even Hippolyte, intruding on her body intolerable. Yes, tonight she hated men, fornication, that torture passed off as sensuality, and couldn't fathom how she could ever have enjoyed it.

She woke in the morning to realize that Hippolyte was already up and that there was an appetizing smell of toast in the apartment.

She went to the kitchen and stopped halfway: there was laughter coming from there, frivolous, conspiratorial giggling that expressed the happiness of being together rather than the reaction to a joke.

Albane and Hippolyte had their backs to her, but she could see them perfectly well. They were having coffee. Their laid-back manner, their casualness, their relaxed body language had the kind of informality that usually develops after months of acquaintance. She saw Hippolyte raise his hand to Albane's cheek and almost tenderly wipe away a crumb.

"Out!" she screamed.

They both jumped.

"Out!"

They turned to see Patricia's face twisted in anger.

"Out, Hippolyte! It's over between us. You're never to set foot in this apartment again. You hear me? Never!"

The scene had lasted no longer than half an hour, but Patricia couldn't stop going over it. Yes, in spite of Hippolyte's protests, in spite of Albane's incomprehension, she had rejected her lover and broken up with him for good.

When he had demanded an explanation, she had replied that he already had an explanation, all he had to do was look into himself.

At that moment, Hippolyte's face had altered. His skin had turned gray, and the light had gone out of his eyes. He had even lost a few inches in height, and had left, dejected, without saying a word.

Ever since, Albane and Patricia had barely spoken. They stuck to practical exchanges of no more than a few words. Patricia, on the other hand, had called Dr. Gemayel to her aid twice. The first time was because she had vaginal mycosis. The second time, because she had suddenly felt weak and fainted. The doctor had referred her for a blood test, to make sure it wasn't anemia.

On the third morning after the breakup, Madame Simon asked Patricia to have another talk.

This time, I'm telling her everything—too bad.

The psychiatrist looked at Patricia, at the apartment, sighed, then stared again at Patricia.

"I'm going to be brutally honest."

"With everything else I'm going through . . . "

"With everything else you're going through? That's an interesting statement. Have you recently been the victim of violence?"

"Are you joking?"

"Not at all."

Patricia's mouth fell open.

The psychiatrist persevered. "I'd really like to know what violence you've been victim of."

Patricia nearly lost her temper, but restrained herself. *Not in front of a psychiatrist. Calm down.*

"Who do you think you're talking to, Madame Simon?" she asked, so levelheadedly that it felt like a victory.

"I'm talking to the victim's mother, not the actual victim."

Patricia gave a start.

"You're putting yourself in your daughter's place," the psychiatrist continued in her calm, even voice. "Listening to you, anyone would think you were the one who was assaulted, you were the one suffering physically, you were the one who'll never make love again."

What? How does she know?

"I think you're a very good person, Patricia, but you lack emotional maturity. I know that from Albane: you're more your daughter's daughter than your daughter's mother."

"I beg your pardon?"

"You vegetate in this apartment, doing nothing except reading, you have no social life outside these walls, you expect too much from your interaction with your daughter. She's the one who tells you about the outside world, she's the one who forces you to fight against letting yourself go, who sometimes makes you wash, look after yourself, go to the hairdresser. Was it also she who had to force you to meet a man?"

"What? That's not true!"

"Didn't you meet Hippolyte after a scene with Albane that convinced you you couldn't bury yourself like this anymore?"

"It had nothing to do with it. I'd been admiring Hippolyte for three years, then I received a message from him, a letter full of affection, which triggered things between us."

"Really? I think the real trigger was your daughter, your daughter who, like a mother, told you it was time to grow up and fly the nest."

Patricia fell silent, confused and dismayed.

"Please, Patricia, you must keep growing. It's asking a lot of Albane to drag this baggage with her: a mother like a child, and then a rape. If you love her, Patricia, think of her. You, too, must heal! And that will speed up your daughter's recovery."

As usual when she considered the interview to be over, Madame Simon stood up and left without another word. All those outlandish ideas! A bagful of theories had just been hurled at her, each stranger than the other. She—like a child? She had never considered herself that way. That was just silly . . .

She got unsteadily to her feet. It had been quite a shock . . . *This trauma specialist is pretty traumatic herself, isn't she? What kind of healer is that? Oh, right, you treat like with like . . . Just been punched? Here's another punch to stop you thinking about the first one.*

She went to the kitchen and instinctively opened the food drawer. No. She wasn't hungry. She'd lost her appetite. If she got punched like that every day, she was sure to lose weight. Depression is perfect for shedding the pounds. Almost as good as cancer.

She started to cry silently, placidly, without sobbing. Tears falling like blood.

When she returned to the living room, she automatically looked out the window at the square.

Hippolyte was working on the square with Germain. He had his back to her. Intentionally, no doubt. Around them, people were bustling, still preoccupied with the Bidermann affair. What a mess it all was!

She looked at Germain. That's what she must have looked like next to Hippolyte. Like a reject, a cripple. Just as grotesque. She quite liked Germain, but found it odd that Hippolyte should like him. As odd as the fact that he should love her. Well, Hippolyte was odd, which explained everything.

Exhausted, she went back to the kitchen, automatically again, just as she always had in the past, when the slightest anxiety would lead her to raid the fridge. She opened it. There was nothing left. Bare shelves. Obviously, since she'd stopped going shopping. To feed Albane and herself, she ordered take-out Chinese, or sometimes Japanese. It was so extreme it encouraged you to diet. She had gone off food.

She left the kitchen. Should she go and have a talk with Albane? Why not?

At that very moment, as she crossed the hallway, she was aware of a figure moving on the landing. Somebody on the other side was sliding a letter under the door.

It was on yellow paper, like the previous time, and the handwriting looked exactly the same.

7

I t had probably been the worst night of her life. Sitting naked on her bed, her legs folded against her chest, her hands clutching her knees, Faustina was reflecting on what had happened.

A man who for months had claimed to be in love with her, who had raved about how seductive she was, who had agreed to be rebuffed twenty times, so consumed was he by desire, this same man, once he had reached the Grail, once she had opened her arms to him, had been content to lie there, hurrying through foreplay and climaxing sluggishly after a number of limp, repetitive, boring, brief, passionless thrusts. He had then given her a conspiratorial, supposedly smoldering look, as if he had taken her up to seventh heaven. Worse still: he had fallen asleep, exhausted, like an athlete at the end of an Olympic event. In fact, nine hours later, he was still snoring. What an achievement!

Faustina rubbed her chin against her left knee. This fiasco should have made her angry, yet she felt satisfied. She who loved torrid encounters, tempestuous sex, multiple orgasms, hadn't been disturbed by this little venture into the calm waters of ordinary sex; she might even have liked it. The serenity she felt as she woke was a new sensation.

She got up without disturbing Patrick Breton-Mollignon, who, taking up two-thirds of the mattress, had requisitioned most of the pillows to make his sleep more comfortable. Surprised that the director of *Le Matin* hadn't been hassled by his colleagues on the phone since daybreak, she leaned over the night table and saw that he had switched off his cell phone. Should she feel flattered that he had prioritized her, or laugh at a man to whom such an ordinary night represented something exceptional?

Going to the window, she checked that onlookers and photographers were still milling about outside the Bidermann residence. There they stood, in small, scattered groups. She sighed, happy that the excitement hadn't subsided, that she lived in a strategic spot that was the center of media attention.

She noticed Patricia down below, striding into the building. "Oh, my God, I nearly forgot!"

Panicking, she quickly covered up, gathered her hair in a rubber band, closed the doors to the bedroom, and ran to meet Patricia on the doorstep to stop the bell from waking Patrick Breton-Mollignon.

After the ritual kisses, she led Patricia into the living room. Patricia, looking very tense in a somewhat severe purple dress, took some materials out of her canvas bag. "Here are your files." Patricia spread the handwritten dossiers on the coffee table.

"Don't you want to add any comments?"

"There's no time," Patricia grumbled. "You'll find everything you need on those sheets. Have you prepared the money?"

Faustina handed her an open envelope containing bills. "So, have you been following the story?"

"What story?"

"Our distinguished neighbor, that pig Zachary Bidermann."

"I think it's disgusting."

"So do I."

"What I find even more disgusting is people who talk about it."

"Why?"

"All they do is talk about him, what's happening to him, his fall, his thwarted hopes, his broken career. But it's that woman that something terrible happened to. She was raped!"

"Yes, of course . . . "

"'Of course'? You're barking like the rest of the hounds, Faustina. You're more interested in the executioner than in the victim. Where you see the tragedy of a powerful man, I see the drama of a woman."

"Are you joking? He's the one who's well-known. The country wanted him to be prime minister. Whereas she—"

"What about female solidarity, Faustina?"

"No, thanks! I stopped believing in that a long time ago. Female solidarity? The worst stabs in the back I've ever received have always been from women."

"Maybe you asked for them . . . Let's drop the subject, before I get angry."

Angry, her mind on other things, Patricia stood up and walked quickly to the door.

"Patricia, aren't you forgetting something?" Faustina called after her in an abrupt tone.

"What?"

"The next books you have to review for me." Faustina indicated a stack of six new publications on an armchair.

"Oh, you're right," Patricia mumbled. "I did forget something." She retraced her steps, and stood rooted to the spot. "I forgot to tell you. I quit."

"What?"

"I'm not going to read instead of you anymore."

Automatically, Faustina corrected her, "To read for me."

"Precisely. You can manage on your own from now on."

"On my own? I won't have the time."

"Neither will I." Patricia turned and grabbed the door handle.

Faustina rushed to stop her. "What's wrong with you?"

Patricia looked down at the floor, struggling with her emotions.

"Problems?" Faustina asked in a gentler tone.

"That's my business."

"I'm your friend, Patricia."

Patricia shrugged. "You were my undeclared employer, but never my friend, definitely not."

"Well, thanks for that."

"Besides, I wouldn't say a word even to a real friend. So, here's the information that concerns you: I'll no longer be reading novels or nonfiction in your place."

"What if I gave you a raise?"

"It's over! I've said it clearly, there's no going back."

"Look here, Patricia, you come and announce this so suddenly, after years of collaboration! What am I supposed to do?"

"You'll just have to learn to read. Here, look, on your embroidered robe: you can start by revising the alphabet." She went out onto the landing.

Faustina caught her by the arm. "I've never seen you like this, Patricia!"

Patricia's eyes misted over. "Me neither. Goodbye."

Patricia escaped to the stairs.

Faustina went back inside, furious. If that cow dropped her like this, how was she going to present books she hadn't even leafed through to journalists? How would she make writers she entertained believe she had loved their most recent work? Not only would her own work suffer, her income would too, since she was in the habit of reselling these dossiers at an exorbitant price to a famous Parisian literary journalist, who, like her, preferred to talk about books rather than read them.

She went to the kitchen and made breakfast. Funny how she liked the ritual! She found it reassuring, it helped her fight a sense of emptiness before the day monopolized all her attention.

As she was finishing making the scrambled eggs, Patrick Breton-Mollignon appeared, a towel tied around his hips, looking nondescript with his hollow chest disrupted by a few sparse long hairs, his hunched shoulders, his soft, falsely-slim belly. Fleetingly, she thought about how Dany would look in the same towel, or even others who had preceded him . . . There was no comparison: Patrick Breton-Mollignon was her most mediocre suitor.

"Good morning, my darling, how are you?" she asked, slipping easily into a maternal tone.

"Wonderfully well. I'm happy."

Poor thing. He has no idea how pathetic he is.

She slid a hand over his cheek. "You have every reason to be."

Patrick Breton-Mollignon's eyes glistened with pride: with her words, Faustina was awarding him the good lover medal. "Really? Did you enjoy it?"

Don't dig or you'll discover the truth, my pet.

"I loved it, Patrick. It was so . . . "

Awful? Boring?

" . . . disconcerting."

"Disconcerting?"

Why does he insist? He's so vain. Does he really think he made the earth move?

"Disconcerting that you and I should have done it . . . "

Is that enough for him? Probably not.

" . . . and done it so well."

She planted a kiss on his cheek. He purred with pleasure.

Joyfully, she laid the table and they talked cheerfully about the various people they knew.

Faustina had seldom felt so good. Not owing any pleasure to a man she had been to bed with, despising him gave rise to new gestures and words. Her pity for this disastrous stud aroused a commiserative kindness in her and made her not pretend tenderness, but actually feel it.

Compared with him, she was freer than ever: he could leave, and she wouldn't be sorry; he could stay, and it wouldn't bother her. When it came down to it, she couldn't care less.

So when, at the end of breakfast, he asked her to marry him, she accepted without hesitation.

The news traveled very fast, since Patrick Breton-Mollignon knew lots of people and spread the information unreservedly, savoring his upcoming marriage as a victory over previous women—not many, admittedly—who had rejected him, and a victory over men—there were many more of those—who looked lustfully at Faustina.

She, on the other hand, imparted the information more economically, not even telling Nathan, Tom, or her other gay friends, knowing only too well that they would immediately quiz her about Patrick's physical performance. Would they understand that she was agreeing to marry him only because he was awful in bed?

One afternoon, her nose stuck in a hefty romantic tome whose author she would soon be accompanying on a media tour, she had a sudden revelation: Patricia was right!

She grabbed the phone. "Patrick? Do you want to get one over on your competitors on the Zachary Bidermann story? Sell more papers? Beat your record? Be taken up by the world's media?"

"Do I even need to answer that? Do you have a scoop?"

"No, a piece of advice. Take it as a wedding gift."

"Tell me quickly!"

"Focus on the victim."

Her suggestion was greeted by silence. It was followed by a scream. "You're fucking brilliant!"

When Patrick Breton-Mollignon and Faustina saw Petra

von Tannenbaum walk into the editorial office of *Le Matin*, looking regal with her raven-black hair and eagle eyes, they immediately felt uneasy. This victim didn't look like a victim.

Now there's poor casting, Faustina thought.

Petra sat down elegantly in the armchair she was offered and took out a cigarette holder. "It was high time," she said icily.

"High time for what, madame?"

"That someone took an interest in me."

Patrick agreed and announced his paper's intention to devote two entire pages to her.

"Two?" she murmured in a disgusted tone.

"At least two," he corrected himself.

She put the folder she had under her arm on the table. "Here's my file, with all the principal elements of my life. With regard to photographs, you have the names of agencies to contact at the back."

"Can you tell us what happened?"

Petra told her story. Her thoughts, her choice of words: everything upset Patrick and Faustina. The more she spoke about the rape, the more unpleasantly Petra came across. Before she had even finished, they'd lost any desire to listen to her.

They exchanged looks of despair. They were facing a real professional problem: the wronged party, the person you were supposed to feel sorry for, provoked revulsion.

Patrick made a sign to Faustina to intervene. She waited for Petra's final, categorical statements about the rudeness of the Belgian police, then said, "I looked at your official website— which is truly magnificent, as you are—but it lacks biographical details."

"A work of art should remain mysterious and incomprehensible. I am a work of art."

"But here, in this awful business, you're more the plaything of a loathsome character. That's what may attract the sympathy of a very large audience."

Petra didn't understand, but the mention of a "very large audience" grabbed her attention.

"Is your name really Petra von Tannenbaum or is that just your stage name?"

Petra stiffened. "It's my real name."

"Since when?"

"Since I married Gustav von Tannenbaum, who died a year after we were married."

"And your maiden name?"

"I won't allow you to—"

"Trust us."

Petra von Tannenbaum shrugged, looked away, and said, "Smith. Nicole Smith. I'm an American."

"Where from?"

"Texas."

"Really? You're not a German aristocrat?"

"Yes, I am, I became one by marriage."

"That's a terrific story, you know. An ordinary American girl who becomes a sophisticated aristocrat, a widow, an artist . . . I'm sorry, there are romantic elements here, the public will be interested."

"Really? Then why aren't the media interested in me?"

Faustina stood up. "I'll tell you why, Petra von Tannenbaum. May I be so bold as to give you some advice?" Not waiting for a reply, Faustina got into her stride. "Don't push yourself forward. Don't be so authoritative. Stop boasting about your career—it's up to others to do that. Act simple. Don't smoke with a cigarette holder, smoke rough, unfiltered cigarettes and puff at them like a woman who's disoriented. Dress simply, you want to give people the impression that, even in a sweater, you can't help being the height of elegance. Wear light, almost invisible makeup, so that nobody thinks you've prepared yourself for the cameras. Give the impression you're always scared, as if every man who comes near you now might be a potential rapist. Don't look people straight in the eye. Loosen your neck, look down at the carpet, appear wounded. Then you'll make the headlines and the public will adore you."

Patrick was petrified, fearing Petra von Tannenbaum's reaction. Pale and tense, she had listened with evident annoyance. Her eyes, more fixed than those of a bird of prey, gave off an unbearably cruel glow.

"You're perfect," Petra von Tannenbaum finally said, uncrossing her legs. "I want to hire you for my PR. What do you charge per month?"

Nobody knew where Faustina disappeared to on Saturday mornings.

Officially, she went running in the Bois de la Cambre. Come rain or come shine, she would set off. Anyone who asked to go with her was turned down. Nobody had ever seen her there. Anyone wishing to investigate her would have noticed that she returned with a sports bag in which no piece of clothing carried the slightest trace of dampness.

Faustina parked her car outside the Résidence des Cèdres. She greeted the manageress, and an obese nurse took her up to the third floor, to room 201.

"How is she?" Faustina asked.

"There's been no improvement."

"Has she spoken in the last few days?"

"Not a word, from what we've seen." She opened the door. "I'll leave you to it as usual, shall I?"

Faustina walked in tentatively, suddenly much slower than usual, less noisy, less imposing.

"Hi, Mom, how are you?"

The old lady huddled in an armchair by the window,

unaware of there being anyone else in the room, kept on staring at a tree in the grounds.

"How has your week been?"

Faustina knew perfectly well that her mother wouldn't
answer, but she acted as if everything was normal. What else
could she do? Sit down and say nothing? In that case, she
might as well not come.

Standing in front of her mother, Faustina started on her
weekly report; her babbling was typical Faustina—cheeky and
comical—but her unusually gentle voice and overarticulation
showed that she was knowingly putting on an act. In this way,
she announced her decision to marry Patrick Breton-Mollignon.

The old lady, who had a permanent smile on her face, wasn't
listening or looking at her.

"I'm telling you I'm getting married and you're not reacting?"

She looked closely at the worn face and felt that if she
insisted, she would start feeling sorry for herself, a woman
announcing her wedding to a mother who was indifferent.

Faustina dragged a chair to the window and sat down
opposite her. "Shall we sing something?"

The Alzheimer's had deleted most of the patient's memories: her daughter, her husband, her brothers, her sister, her
parents. It would have been easy to say that she was just a vegetable if it wasn't for the fact that singing sometimes, fleetingly,
still linked her to humanity.

Faustina hummed:

Quand il me prend dans ses bras,
Il me parle tout bas,
Je vois la vie en rose . . .[1]

---

[1] When he takes me in his arms, he talks to me softly, and I see life
through rose-tinted glasses.

The worn eyelids, the lashes covered in pollen dust, reacted a little. Her mother sensed the presence of music. Faustina continued, and little by little the old lady started to mumble, venturing a word here, a sentence there, like a traveler hesitant to board a train.

Faustina finished the song then started singing *La Mer*. The patient immediately joined in.

La mer
Qu'on voit danser le long des golfes clairs
A des reflets d'argent
La mer
Bergère d'azur infinie.[2]

As they uttered these lines, Faustina had the impression that her mother's expression somehow underlined the words, her eyes seeming to say, "You hear that? That's so refined," just as she had in the past.

They yelled out the end together. Faustina was pleased. Since her mother had always loved singing, she felt as if she'd entertained her.

She was about to leave when the old lady, of her own accord, started a new song:

C'était un gamin, un gosse de Paris,
Pour famille il n'avait qu'sa mère
Une pauvre fille aux grands yeux rougis
Par les chagrins et la misère . . .[3]

The frail voice, as thin as her fingers, was droning out an old tune, *Les Roses blanches*.

[2] The sea we see dancing along the bright gulfs has silver glints; the sea, infinite shepherdess of the blue.
[3] He was a boy, a child of Paris; his only family was his mother, a poor girl with big eyes reddened by sorrow and poverty.

Faustina dreaded this song so much, she stiffened. When she had heard it in the past, coming from her beloved mother's mouth, at an age when her soul was totally unaware of mockery and cynicism, she had cried, saddened by the pathetic tale. Ever since, whenever she heard it, a strange phenomenon would take place: although she heard it with the ears of the present, her heart was still the heart she'd had in the past.

C'est aujourd'hui dimanche, tiens ma jolie maman,
Voici des roses blanches, toi qui les aimes tant.
Va quand je serai grand, j'achèterai au marchand
Toutes ses roses blanches, pour toi jolie maman.[4]

In spite of herself, she was touched by the words, which took her back to a time of love and innocence. She turned away and bit her lip. She found this emotion unbearable, because the pain of it brought a dead woman back to life, another Faustina, a Faustina of yesteryear, a Faustina who no longer existed or who was slumbering beneath layers of cruel, humiliating, hurtful experiences. Should this Faustina be awakened?

Au printemps dernier, le destin brutal,
Vint frapper la blonde ouvrière.
Elle tomba malade et pour l'hôpital,
Le gamin vit partir sa mère.[5]

Faustina was shaking . . . Had she been right to become hardened? The present-day Faustina would laugh out loud at this melodrama, find it totally stupid and idiotic. But the child she had been was reborn with this song, and made her realize

[4] Today is Sunday, pretty Mommy, here are white roses, which you love so much; when I'm grown up I'll buy all the white roses from the seller for you, pretty Mommy.
[5] Last spring, a brutal fate struck the blonde working girl. She fell sick, and the boy saw his mother leave for the hospital.

the defensiveness in her sarcasm, the distress concealed beneath her insensitive self-confidence. What if she was wrong? Wouldn't it be better to accept her feelings?

> *Puis à l'hôpital il vint en courant,*
> *Pour offrir les fleurs à sa mère*
> *Mais en la voyant, une infirmière*
> *Tout bas lui dit, "Tu n'as plus de maman."*[6]

Faustina looked at her mother. Was she aware of what she was singing? The words followed phonetically, correctly, like pure music, but did they still have a meaning?

The old woman's voice, reduced to a thread, quavered. Her eyes with their dull corneas reddened. Yes, she knew what she was saying . . .

> *Et le gamin s'agenouillant dit,*
> *Devant le petit lit blanc:*
> *"C'est aujourd'hui dimanche, tiens ma jolie maman,*
> *Voici des roses blanches, toi qui les aimais tant.*
> *Et quand tu t'en iras, au grand jardin là-bas,*
> *Toutes ces roses blanches, tu les emporteras."*[7]

The old woman ended her song looking into her daughter's eyes, holding her hands in hers. Faustina was smiling and crying. From the confused place where her consciousness had lost its way, her mother was sending her a message: "I know you're my child, and that you bring me white roses; your visits are all I have left; thank you for these beautiful recollections of you: I'll take them with me when I die."

---

[6] He ran to the hospital to give his mother the flowers, but seeing him, a nurse said in a low voice, "Your mother is no more."

[7] And the boy knelt by the little white bed and said: "Today is Sunday, pretty Mommy, here are white roses, which you love so much; when you go to the big garden up in the sky, you'll take all these white roses with you."

When the nurse who came to fetch her saw Faustina so transfigured, so blissfully happy, and at the same time so desperately unhappy, she was moved. "You're a good daughter, you know. If only everybody was like you . . . "

Faustina got back to her apartment to find Patrick waiting for her, a diary in his hand: he wanted to fix a date for the wedding.

It was becoming concrete now. They agreed on September 4th, and Faustina danced around the room, delighted. Flattered as he was by her joy, Patrick tried to moderate her fervor. "Don't get too excited, organizing a wedding is exhausting."

"How do you know, Bluebeard? From experience?" She indicated the desk, where Patrick's computer was blinking, besieged by urgent messages. "You get on with work, Mr. Editor-in-Chief. Meanwhile, I'll tell a few girlfriends."

He sat down, and she went into her bedroom. As she was about to share her joy with her girlfriends, a message stopped her in her tracks.

Congratulations, my little bitch. I hear you've got your claws on a large morsel (I'm referring to the position, of course). Dany.

Her cheeks burning, she replied, cheerfully:

Thanks for your congratulations. I accept them.

A few seconds later, another message arrived.
I love married women. Especially frustrated ones, which is going to be your case.
She keyed in a response. *I intend to be free.*
Free for what?

Free to do whatever I like.

Like screwing me, for instance?

She bit her lip, took a furtive look around, and replied, *Why not?*

She waited anxiously for a new message to appear. It took a full minute to arrive.

As I said, I love married women. They're the worst kind of bitches.

I wouldn't know. I've never cheated on a husband.

Meet me at the Blue Moon in twenty minutes.

She burst out laughing. What a cheek! He really had gall, did Dany. Why was it they'd broken up?

OK.

She quickly changed her underwear, slipped a bottle of perfume into her bag, and went into the living room.

Facing the window that looked out on the noisy, excited parrots, Patrick was working, hunched over his computer, the very image of the conscientious workaholic.

"Will you be much longer, darling?"

Without looking up, he muttered, "Another two hours at least."

He could have looked up at me. I'm not a servant. Honestly, if he'd looked up, I might not have gone.

"Then I might as well go out and run some errands." She ran to him and stroked his shoulder. "I love you, darling."

At this, he looked up. *At last!* He screwed up his eyes, grabbed her hand, and said solemnly, "I'm a happy man."

She nodded, dying to laugh but managing to restrain herself. "You are, darling, you are. You're the happiest of all of us."

8

When the bus charged onto Place d'Arezzo, like a marble launched at high speed, Mademoiselle Beauvert huddled in her seat, hand over her face, heart pounding. Would she be able to see without being seen?

She had taken public transportation just so that she could get a glimpse of her old apartment, and revisit her native neighborhood. Fortunately, there were only two passengers on the bus—herself and a woman asleep in the back row—so there was nobody to be surprised by her unusual behavior.

Peering through her fingers as the bus drove around the circular garden, Mademoiselle Beauvert saw the Bidermann town house, outside which photographers idled, smoking, hoping to snatch a furtive shot. She then tried to catch a glimpse of the Couvignys, either the father or the children, to see how grief had transformed them. But in vain! When they drove past her own building, she quickly turned away on seeing Marcelle's huge form taking out the garbage pails. As she did so, she discovered on the other side, under the trees, the council gardener, a dwarf, and a little girl playing bowls. *What a nerve!* she thought. *So our taxes go on their amusements.* No sooner had she formulated that thought than she came up with two counterarguments: firstly, she was venting her own bitterness because she found it intolerable that anyone should be happy without her; secondly, the municipal gardener was a handsome man. Why hadn't she noticed that before?

In a cacophony of trembling steel, the bus fled Place

d'Arezzo and continued on its way, plunging into darker neighborhoods with gray, smoky façades.

Mademoiselle Beauvert waited a while, then sat up straight. One more change of buses and she'd be home! Having mastered the bus, streetcar, and subway routes, she had become the queen of connections, her brain superimposing maps without difficulty and devising the most ingenious journeys. Her recent poverty offered her so many new activities that she had no time for boredom. Traveling for a few cents and eating for three euros stimulated her mind. Each day brought her incredible challenges: doing her hair by herself, dyeing it herself, looking spruce without a makeup budget, making sure her clothes were clean without expensive dry cleaning, economizing on water, gas, electricity. Her obsession with numbers was still with her, but this time they no longer corresponded to casino chips or roulette pockets but were written down in the small notepad she always had with her and in which she gathered sums, subtractions, rules of three, as well as ideas for improving her daily life without increasing her bills. Sometimes, she felt a kind of intoxication in discovering ways to save, an intoxication that recalled the ecstasies of the past; as she had before, she was savoring the joy of the struggle, not against chance now, but against necessity.

Mademoiselle Beauvert got off at her stop, in Madou.

Madou! If anyone had told me in the old days . . . But she wasn't complaining, she was enjoying it. For decades, she had imagined Madou as a complete abstraction, a non-place she certainly had no wish to get to know. First of all, what language was the name of that shabby Brussels neighborhood? "Madou" was neither Flemish nor French . . . And it was nothing but a cluster of streets down which no normal person would have a reason to walk. Why would the Ixelles middle classes do their shopping in a Turkish grocery or a North African supermarket? And now Mademoiselle Beauvert was living in this maze, finding her bearings, and delighting every day in her new habits.

This wasn't a decline, it was a rebirth. For as long as she had everything, she hadn't realized the value of anything. Nowadays, the purchase of any item led to a debate. Did she really need it? Could she find something cheaper? What would she have to cut back on in order to afford it? So, for example, a bath mat made of synthetic fur with a white rubber base had occupied her thoughts for several days. It was ugly, true, but it cost only a few euros and, being nonskid, would stop her from slipping on the wet tiled floor of her tiny shower. Of course it wouldn't be an object of admiration if anyone visited her apartment, but firstly, she never invited anyone, secondly, she had nothing worth showing visitors, and finally, breaking her hips was beyond her means. She had been ecstatic when she bought that blue mat at the Sezer minimarket and now would gaze in satisfaction at it not only whenever she washed herself, but sometimes even during the day, for the sheer pleasure of it, the way you say hello to the household pet standing behind the door.

She walked into No. 5 Rue Bakmir, down the green and yellow corridor, across the courtyard, and into her studio apartment. Her few square feet enclosed her bedroom, dining room, and kitchen. Soon, as promised, the carpenter from No. 9 would give her his leftover paint, which she intended to use to rid her walls of the marks of posters and prints that previous tenants had hung on them.

When he heard the lock, Copernicus woke, shook himself, and cried excitedly, "Hello, Madame, hello!"

"Hello, Copernicus, dear."

Besides her clothes, the parrot and his cage were the only survivors of the bailiffs' raid. Like his mistress, the bird didn't seem to be suffering too much from the move, and enjoyed spending more time with her.

Mademoiselle Beauvert unbolted the cage and freed the macaw, who rubbed himself against her. She stroked his beak, tail and belly. He welcomed her attention with wild, feverish, passionate joy, and a kind of melodious cooing emerged from his throat.

"We're happy here, Copernicus, aren't we?"

In reply, he nibbled her arm affectionately.

With the bird on her shoulder, she sat on her narrow bed and thought about the trip she had just taken. What was the point? Why go back there? Actually, it hadn't had much effect on her. She hadn't felt the least bit homesick, or been sorry she had left. Of course, it was nicer, a thousand times nicer than here. But those years on Place d'Arezzo were marked by her chronic sickness, her gambling frenzy, her night escapades, her secret weekend expeditions. She had spent far more energy fleeing her large apartment on the square with the parrots than living in it.

Her neighbor knocked on the window.

"Mademoiselle Beauvert?"

"Coming! Coming!"

She adjusted her pleated skirt, made sure there wasn't anything lying around, and opened the door, with Copernicus against her cheek.

"So, shall I leave them with you?"

The neighbor, who had rings under her eyes, indicated seven eight-year-old children gathered behind her.

"Of course! You got them all together? Shall we do as arranged?"

"The mothers all agree, Mademoiselle Beauvert."

"Come in, my darlings."

Casting wary looks at the bird, the children rushed into the apartment, sat down around the table, and laid out their books and exercise books on the oilcloth.

The neighbor put two trays and a pan on the sink. "Here

we are: yufka-based böreks as a starter, some lamb skewers to be warmed up, and sütlaç for dessert."

"Rice pudding? I love that. And Copernicus does even more."

Mademoiselle Beauvert thanked her neighbor, who left, and turned to the little ones. "What do you have to do for homework this evening?"

The children reported their teacher's demands, and Mademoiselle Beauvert helped them with their exercises. When she had moved here, she had, quite by chance, explained to a schoolboy from the building how to do his subtractions. Delighted with her kindly manner and the clarity of her explanations, the child had returned the following day with his little cousin, who had subsequently told her neighbors in the building. And so, in an almost natural manner, Mademoiselle had arranged an exchange: in return for helping out with schoolwork she would get meals. These mothers were already feeding large families, so an extra helping was no big deal, whereas it was very important for them that a real, French-speaking Belgian, so refined and educated, should ensure the success of their offspring. They had accepted enthusiastically.

Mademoiselle Beauvert had used this exchange as an excuse to justify her task, but the fact was that day by day she was getting more and more pleasure from looking after the children of immigrants. She was discovering not only how useful the information she had learned by heart was, but also how precious. Her excellent French and her accurate arithmetic had become a treasure she was able to transmit and impart. The attentive, eager, even admiring looks in the children's eyes gave her an unexpected thrill.

When a little girl asked her about Copernicus, she told her that she used to live in a wonderful square where parrots flew, all kinds of parrots, as well as green parakeets. People lived in the houses, parrots lived in the trees, and they all watched each other. The little girl giggled, and none of the children believed her. She insisted, saying it was in right here in Brussels, not much more than a mile away. They obstinately shook their heads. They believed—just as she had done previously—that there was more than a border, more than a mountain, more than a desert between Madou and Uccle, and that they belonged to two separate worlds. No resident from here ever went there, or vice versa. What did people want? she thought. Reality or dreams? Whatever they found most convenient.

They started on revision. As she spoke to the group, Copernicus, still perched on her, also listened alertly. Every so often, like a schoolboy taking notes, he would repeat a word enthusiastically—"Subjunctive!" or "Rule of three!"—and the children would burst out laughing. Mademoiselle Beauvert was proud of him because he followed the lesson and entertained the kids. On the other hand, she was surprised to observe that, whenever she started talking to a single child, he would shuffle to express his annoyance.

It happened when she leaned over plump, frizzy-haired Abdul and made him revise his irregular verbs. In spite of her attentive, gentle manner, the boy kept hesitating and making mistakes.

"Brrr! Brrr!" Copernicus screeched after the tenth mistake.

Even as she stroked the dunce's head, Mademoiselle Beauvert profited from this intervention to say, "You see, Abdul, even Copernicus can tell you're not concentrating."

"He doesn't like me," the boy grunted, frowning at the bird.

"He doesn't like it when you make mistakes. If this carries on, he's going to give you the answers."

"I dare him to!" Abdul cried, throwing back his head.

Copernicus didn't like the child's sudden, aggressive move. He spread his wings, rose an inch or two in the air, and went straight for the boy with his beak.

Abdul screamed, which excited Copernicus even more, making him peck more and faster.

The seven children all started yelling. Suppressing her astonishment, Mademoiselle Beauvert tried to control the commotion. "Quiet! You're making him even more annoyed! Quiet! Copernicus, stop it! I said, stop it! Copernicus! Copernicus!"

The more she called the bird, the more he attacked Abdul.

Scared of becoming the next victims, the girls jumped up from their seats, pushed open the door, and ran out into the courtyard.

Abdul's cousin grabbed his ruler and tried to hit the bird. Angrily, Mademoiselle Beauvert stopped him. "I forbid you!"

"But Mademoiselle—"

"Copernicus will stop of his own accord. Copernicus! Copernicus!"

But the bird wouldn't let go of his prey. By now, Abdul was moaning instead of defending himself. Mademoiselle Beauvert decided to throw herself into the fray and, without breaking the bird's wings, try to separate him from the child. "Copernicus!"

Suddenly, the parrot let go of his prey, gave Mademoiselle Beauvert a fierce look, and, with a burst of energy, went out through the open door into the courtyard and flew away.

Panic-stricken, she rushed after him.

"Copernicus!"

By the time she got out into the courtyard, all she could see was a flash of color quickly rising to the gutters and the roofs. The bird vanished into the blue.

"Copernicus!"

Her voice faded into the empty sky.

Mademoiselle Beauvert's eyes filled with tears. The sound of crying behind her brought her back down to earth. She went back inside and saw the scratches, bites, and bruises on the boy's face.

"My God!"

She let out this cry not so much because she felt sorry for the child—he'd recover soon enough—as because her pet had gone and she suspected that this advantageous exchange was at an end.

In the hours that followed, Mademoiselle Beauvert was partly able to salvage the situation: the mothers didn't break off the deal—firstly because Abdul had a terrible reputation, and secondly because the source of the danger, the parrot, had disappeared.

But after these negotiations, when she found herself alone, at midnight, in her tiny apartment, she felt completely helpless. In losing Copernicus, she had lost both her old life and her new one; nothing seemed bearable to her anymore—neither the fact that she had disposed of everything she owned in order to pay off her absurd gambling debts nor the fact that she was stuck forever in a few square feet at the far end of a courtyard that stank of doner kebab. Her loneliness struck her as pathetic, and her poverty permanent . . .

For the first time in her life, Mademoiselle Beauvert felt sorry for herself. She had failed at everything. That night, not only did she not sleep a wink, but she experienced every second of every minute of every hour, as if she were attached to some kind of lethal drip. On the dark, dirty walls with their old grease stains, she saw her future, and it was an abyss. She was condemned to a dungeon. A dungeon? If she were in prison, she would still have the hope that she might be released. But there was no release, no commuted sentence possible here. All she could do was endure it until she died.

At about four o'clock in the morning, she rebelled against the despair that was crushing her. Why was she thinking her life was over just because a bird no longer occupied a cage at the foot of her bed? Ridiculous! A wild animal she had bought for next to nothing five years earlier wasn't her salvation! *Goodbye, you stupid bird! Just stop thinking about that macaw! That's an order!*

But when despair comes crashing down on someone, it doesn't do things by halves, it completely suffocates that person. Mademoiselle Beauvert was shaking, hoping with each breath that she could just die, convinced that day would never break.

In the morning, light came in shyly from the courtyard through her tinted windows. For a moment, a pink glow cast a soft aura over a sprig of lily of the valley that one of the children had left for her. Mademoiselle Beauvert sat up, slapped her thighs, and made up her mind to find Copernicus.

From seven o'clock onward, she tramped the streets of the neighborhood, calling the bird, listening twenty times at every tree, beating the sparse bushes, looking at every window, every gutter, every gable, every eave.

Hearing her call out that name, the neighbors asked her the reason for her panic, and she told them. Some helped her, for a while anyway, while others asked her to be quiet. Then some shopkeepers, growing tired of her constant yelling, started to insult her. Never mind! She persisted. No complaints or gibes could stop her. As for being ridiculed, she couldn't care less.

By noon, she had to face facts: there was no trace of Copernicus.

Queasy, exhausted, upset, she couldn't have swallowed a thing even though her stomach was knotted with hunger. If she ate, she would be betraying Copernicus for a second time. Because there could be no doubt now, she was guilty! The day before, by taking Abdul's side, she had offended the bird. In trying to detach the parrot from the child, it had been Copernicus she had attacked, and, unable to bear her betrayal, brokenhearted, he had fled.

There was nothing accidental about that terrible episode:

she had behaved badly toward an animal who had put his trust in her. She deserved the sadness she was feeling. When she thought of the sadness *he* must be feeling . . . She cursed herself: how could she have given the bird so much pain! If he was sulking, shivering with cold, risking his life by becoming the prey of cats or aggressive humans, then it was all her fault. What was he going through now? Was he getting anything to eat?

At about two in the afternoon, she suddenly had an idea: she should speak to a specialist in order to analyze Copernicus's behavior.

She checked how much money she had left in her wallet. Five euros? Not enough to pay for a visit to a vet . . . Maybe she could get around him by explaining that . . . No, it was impossible! She didn't know any vets, and she couldn't take the risk of having to pay for a consultation, especially as she looked like a wealthy dowager.

Suddenly she stood up, determined. She would go to a pet shop that sold parrots and ask the staff for information.

She remembered seeing, during one of her streetcar journeys, a shop devoted to exotic animals—snakes, birds, spiders, lizards, iguanas—so she worked out the route and set off.

On Quai de Mariemont, by the gray, meager canal, she passed warehouses that had been turned into studios and boutiques. Worried she might not find the shop, she walked for twenty minutes until she saw *Le Monde Perdu* written in Gothic lettering.

In the dark shop, she walked past glass cages that she avoided looking at, letting herself be guided by the smell of bird droppings to the section dedicated to parakeets and parrots.

No sooner had she entered the room than the sounds gave her a familiar feeling. The cries and the shuffling and the swishing of wings took her back to Place d'Arezzo and close to Copernicus.

She spotted a sales assistant in a dark T-shirt, complete with tongue piercing, as skinny as a heron. She fed him the story she had concocted: she wanted to buy a macaw, but before going ahead she wanted to find out about their personality. The young man gave her some commonsense advice, then suggested she look at the animals in the cages. In the very first one, she saw a parrot regurgitating his food and remembered that Copernicus had been doing that lately.

"This one's vomiting. Is he in poor health?"

"No, madame. He's bringing up his food for the female in the next cage. He's courting her. He's giving her what belongs to him to show her that he likes her."

"Oh!" Mademoiselle Beauvert exclaimed, disconcerted. "Could he ever do that with a human?"

"Not usually. If he did, it'd mean that he considered the human as his mate, as the person he loved and wanted to make love to."

Mademoiselle Beauvert swallowed with difficulty: the assistant was shedding an unexpected light on Copernicus's behavior. "My God . . . That's serious."

"Yes and no," the young man said nonchalantly. "On the one hand, it establishes a strong bond between the parrot and his owner. On the other hand, the human can prevent confusion by refusing to behave in a certain way, especially by avoiding certain kinds of contact."

"What do you mean?"

"You can look away when the bird dances about. Turn your back on him when he talks."

"Oh . . . And what else?"

"You especially mustn't touch the parrot's intimate parts, even if he asks you to."

"Intimate parts?"

"His belly, his tail."

Mademoiselle Beauvert choked when she thought of the

thousands of times she had stroked Copernicus's belly and tail with her finger. "What about his beak?" she asked anxiously, aware that Copernicus was particularly responsive to being touched there.

"The beak too, of course. It's a very erogenous zone."

Mademoiselle Beauvert shuddered from top to toe. She had thought she was leading as chaste a life as possible, and now she suddenly discovered that not only had she been sharing her apartment with a parrot in love, but that her stroking him encouraged him and even constituted a kind of sex life for him. She swallowed painfully. "Tell me . . . a parrot doesn't always behave like that, does he? . . . I mean . . . before."

"It starts in adolescence."

"And when does adolescence start?"

"It depends on the size. In small species, at eighteen months. In the case of large macaws, for example, hormones don't start to kick in until the age of five or thereabouts."

Mademoiselle Beauvert closed her eyes: five years old, Copernicus's age!

"It's natural," the young man said, "because they live longer. Up to the age of fifty, or even eighty in captivity. So what have you decided, Madame?"

"Mademoiselle," she replied automatically. "One more question: is there a mating season?"

"It's now, as you saw with the vomiting cockatoo. Males and females are trying to reproduce. Well?"

"I'm very tempted," she replied, turning red. "I'll give it some thought and call you."

"As you wish."

Mademoiselle Beauvert continued to play the part of an undecided customer, pretending to be interested in various specimens, then, taking advantage of another customer coming in, brushed past the cages and discreetly fled.

As soon as she was back out on the Quai, exposed to the

scorching sun, she rubbed her forehead. She suddenly had a thought: what if Copernicus had gone back to Place d'Arezzo in search of a female?

She didn't know quite what to make of the idea. On the one hand, the theory offered a solution—and thus, a glimmer of hope—and removed all misunderstanding between herself and Copernicus. On the other hand, it suggested that Copernicus no longer loved her and was looking for a female of his own species.

As she thought this through, Mademoiselle Beauvert lectured herself. *Of course he must look for a female. I'm not his female, I'm his mistress.*

Immediately, she realized the ambiguity of the word "mistress."

No, I'm his . . . his owner.

This word sounded equally inappropriate and unpleasant, for a different reason this time. *Owner!* Could you own a living creature? By what obscene logic could she consider Copernicus, a jungle bird that had been born free, as her property? Besides, the bailiffs had left him to her precisely because he was a companion as opposed to a belonging. Otherwise, those vultures wouldn't have thought twice. She shuddered at the thought of their selling Copernicus in an auction. That made her wonder about their behavior. Had they shown kindness, unexpected pity, in leaving him to her? But pity for whom? Her or the bird?

She shrugged. A parrot like Copernicus was invaluable, beyond price.

Back in her apartment, she quickly worked out a plan. Since this time she couldn't hide on Place d'Arezzo, she would have to look very elegant. Not for Copernicus, but for her former neighbors.

She got to Place d'Arezzo at four o'clock, looking quite

dapper and concealing the fact that she was out of breath from getting off the bus a stop early and walking the rest of the way.

Head high, she first looked up at her old windows, then at the roof, then at the neighboring balconies. No Copernicus.

As she was continuing with her search, the one person she wanted to avoid appeared: Marcelle. Even more broad-backed than before, her head sunk in her shoulders, arms glued to her body, she was rubbing her eyes uncertainly. "But . . . but . . . "

Mademoiselle Beauvert forced a laugh. "Yes, Marcelle, I'm passing through Brussels. I had a few things to sort out with my lawyer and at the bank. Well, you know what it's like."

Marcelle nodded, her jaw clenched: no, she didn't know what it was like for rich people, and she'd never met a lawyer in her life.

"How are you, Marcelle?"

"Have you come to see me?"

"Of course. I'd like to hear your news."

"My news? I don't have any. At least not any good news. You know my Afghan left, don't you?"

"Yes, Marcelle, I was on the continent when it happened." She mentally congratulated herself for having unearthed that term, "the continent."

"Well, that's it. There's nothing else."

"Nothing?"

"Nothing!"

"That's not like you, Marcelle."

"I don't have to be like me anymore." She threw a dirty look into the street and then, turning back to Mademoiselle Beauvert, asked in a curt tone, just to be polite, "How about you? How's life in New York?"

"Boston, Marcelle."

"Oh, that's right. Is it going well?"

"John and I are . . . very happy."

Marcelle refrained from saying, "Damn," again, and merely sighed.

At that moment, a fight broke out in the branches. Three parakeets were chasing after an African gray parrot.

Mademoiselle Beauvert watched them with growing anxiety. "I'm going to tell you the truth, Marcelle."

"The truth about what, Mademoiselle?"

"Have you seen Copernicus?"

"Excuse me?"

"When I was leaving for Boston, there was a . . . a false maneuver at the airport. Copernicus's cage opened on the tarmac. My parrot has disappeared."

"So he's not living with you in the States?"

"No. It's for the best really, because, unlike me, John doesn't like animals very much. Well, never mind that."

"I do understand, you know. Mind you, when it comes to dogs . . . Well, at least they obey. I've had two that—"

"I know, Marcelle, I know. Copernicus probably wanted to come back to where he'd grown up and always lived. Place d'Arezzo."

"Yes, that makes sense."

"It does, doesn't it?" Mademoiselle Beauvert exclaimed, a powerful sense of hope surging within her.

"But I can't say I've seen him."

"Oh!"

Since, thanks to her lie, Mademoiselle Beauvert could now examine the trees with impunity, she went out onto the square and cried at the top of her voice, "Copernicus? Copernicus! Copernicus, are you there?"

Marcelle let her shout for five minutes, then went up to her with a sympathetic expression on her face. "I feel sorry for you. Mademoiselle Beauvert. Your Copernicus isn't here. I would have seen him. And, frankly, I doubt he'll have survived at the airport. It's a well-known fact that birds get sucked up by the plane engines. Whoops, and in they go! Do forgive me, but your Copernicus has probably ended up like a slice of pâté."

"You've never liked him!" Mademoiselle Beauvert was so angry, she couldn't restrain her words. She was hurt by the casual way Marcelle had evoked Copernicus's possible demise. She looked at her and congratulated herself on having put up with her for so many years: not only was she a mediocre cleaner, but her conversation was depressing. "What about your son?" she asked in a honeyed voice, certain that the mention of him would hurt Marcelle.

"We've had a falling-out."

"Why?"

"It all went horribly wrong."

"What did?"

"The thing with his fiancée. What a pain in the ass! A real little vixen!"

Mademoiselle Beauvert was delighted by what she was hearing. "What happened, my poor Marcelle?"

"He decided to introduce her to me on 'neutral territory,' as he called it. A strange expression, to start with. As if we were at war! Anyway, we met in the tearoom of a big hotel. Right from the start, I didn't like the face the stupid girl made when she saw me, Mademoiselle. What did she expect? That I'd look like my son? I'm a woman, so it's different anyway, and on top of everything else, I'd gotten all dressed up. I was wearing a hat."

"A hat?"

"Yes."

"You, Marcelle?"

"Oh, I'd taken on board what you'd told me . . . that we were from different worlds, the Peperdicks and me. So I bought myself this hat from Inno. With a veil."

"A veil?"

"Yes, it's very fashionable."

"A black veil?"

"Oh, no, a white one. I'm not in mourning."

"And what happened?"

"Because I thought the girl was a bit shy, I made her comfortable by talking instead of her. It's only natural, with age and experience you have more things to say. It was a friendly conversation. I was very pleased. In the evening, my son called me and insulted me. He said I had no business saying what I'd said."

"Like what, for instance?"

"Everything. He called it 'despicable.' I remember the word because I'd never heard it before. 'Despicable.' I've looked it up in a dictionary since. But I understood what he meant from his tone, anyway."

"Be specific, Marcelle. What did he accuse you of?"

"The girl had hay fever, so we talked about health. My son couldn't stand the fact that I told her about my prolapse. But a prolapse is painful. Then I told her about my treatment for constipation. You know perfectly well, Mademoiselle Beauvert, that I've always had these problems. It's because of my left colon."

"Your left colon?"

"Yes, my left colon is too long. That's the way it is! It's too long, so it gets blocked."

"Thank goodness it's not your right one!"

"Anyway, now my son's gotten on his high horse and doesn't want to see me again. Too bad! I'll punish him, I won't go to his wedding!"

"And what about your two hundred and forty-two euros?"

"My two hundred and forty-two euros?"

"For your night table."

"He gave them back to me."

For over five minutes, Marcelle wept, her nose in a handkerchief that was too small. Mademoiselle Beauvert took her over to a bench, sat down with her, and gave her comforting pats on the shoulder, all the while searching the branches. Alas, even though she twisted her neck in every direction, Copernicus was nowhere to be seen.

After a decent interval, she kissed Marcelle, promised she would come back on her next "trip to the continent," then walked away with a light, coquettish step.

Half a mile farther on, dripping with sweat because of the heat and her frayed nerves, she got on a bus that would take her back to Madou.

As soon as she was in her neighborhood, she slowed down and her mood darkened. A kind of emollient liquid spread through her. Twice, she stopped and leaned in a doorway, felling so weak she was afraid she would faint.

As she paused outside the Abuzer sandwich shop, a man came running up to her. "Mademoiselle Beauvert!"

She stared wide-eyed at the dark-skinned man smiling at her from ear to ear.

"Mademoiselle Beauvert, it's such a pleasure to see you."

She looked around for someone to help but could only see other, equally hairy men, and muttered anxiously, "Who are you?"

"Don't you recognize me? I used to live in the same building as you."

"As me?"

"On Place d'Arezzo."

"You?"

"Yes. I was staying with Madame Marcelle."

"Oh, yes!"

She suddenly recognized the man the concierge had always referred to as "my Afghan."

Nervously, he said something in an unfamiliar language to a woman and three small children who were on the other side of the street. "Let me introduce my wife and children. They were finally able to join me here." He added with a radiant, conspiratorial smile, "A family reunion!"

With forced politeness, Mademoiselle Beauvert shook hands with each of them. Intimidated, the Afghan's wife and children greeted her as obsequiously as if she were the Queen of England, which made her resolve to continue the conversation. "So how are you, my dear . . . " She couldn't remember his name. "Have you found a job?"

"Yes, I've found a position as an interpreter."

"That's wonderful. I didn't know you spoke French."

"French, English, Arabic, and Pashtun."

"Yes, yes, of course," Mademoiselle Beauvert nodded, wondering why Marcelle had claimed the contrary.

Since his family didn't understand French, the man was able to ask the question that had led him to approach Mademoiselle Beauvert. "And how is Marcelle?"

"Marcelle? What can I say? She's getting ready for her son's wedding. He's marrying one the richest heiresses in the country, you know."

"I'm very happy for her. Marcelle is a generous woman. She offered me hospitality. Of course, she has her faults, she tries to ignore the passing of time, she refuses to believe that a lady her age should give up on certain things. Apart from that, she's very kind. Thanks to her, I had a roof over my head, food, and time to look for a job. An angel. Marcelle is an angel."

"You haven't seen her again?"

He blushed, embarrassed. "No, Madame, I can't. Because of what I've just told you, because of the things she imagines . . . She never accepted, even for a minute, the fact that I was married, that I love my wife, that I was faithful to her and waiting for her to come here." He turned scarlet, embarrassed to be talking about this. "But she's a kind woman, very kind. I owe her my life, and my family's life."

Since his face betrayed his emotion, he tried to avoid his

family's inquisitive looks, quickly blurted out a goodbye, and set off again down the street in a flurry of waving.

Mademoiselle Beauvert thought about Marcelle and him for a few minutes. Which of them was twisting the truth? Marcelle? The Afghan? Or both? She would never know. Perhaps neither of them knew themselves, given the extent to which people tell each other the truth as they wish it to be, as opposed to how it is.

She dismissed these concerns and carried on walking. None of this would give her back her parrot. She had destroyed her one love affair through her own stupidity. The only living creature that had loved her, in a pure, surprising, disinterested way, had fled into a hostile world. And all because of her! She sighed and stopped to catch her breath once again, then continued shuffling along, holding on to the walls.

She felt swallowed up when she reached No. 5 Rue Bakmir. The prospect of shutting herself in her dark, damp single room made her shudder. Brushing her hand over the letterboxes, she noticed that she had a stack of mail: knowing it contained bad news, she ignored it.

She went into the courtyard, got out her key, shoulders stooped, neck aching, and inserted it in the old keyhole that had been forced so many times.

"Sergio!"

She gave a start.

From out of the sky behind her, a shrill voice repeated enthusiastically, "Sergio! Sergio! Sergio!"

"Copernicus!"

Before she could turn around, the parrot landed on her shoulder. "Hello, Madame."

He rubbed her cheek; tears in her eyes, Mademoiselle Beauvert let herself be made a fuss of. Then she asked him to sit on her fingers—which he did with a little waddle, as voluble as a jazz musician—and opened the door to her apartment.

"Come in, darling. We're going to have a nice evening."

They looked into each other's eyes. She thought she saw a flame in the bird's black pupils, a flame that made her blush, warmed her, and disturbed her. She smiled. He cocked his head.

In return, she gave him a kiss. When her lips brushed his beak, he quivered. Then she gently held him to her chest, thinking about what the bird seller had told her: a large macaw like Copernicus could live for fifty years.

She closed the door behind them. They would grow old together. And, with a bit of luck, she would go at the same time as him . . .

9

A woman with a parrot is a common motif in painting."
Wim was commenting on a huge acrylic canvas by a
New York painter to a number of potential buyers who
had flocked to his loft. The painting showed a beautiful naked
girl surrounded by a flock of parrots; even though it was ten
feet by six and a half, the painting simulated a rough sketch, a
drawing with thick lines that had then been filled in using pri-
mary colors.

"A naked, lascivious woman holding a parrot, don't you
recall? The bird in its multicolored plumage always looks at
the white flesh with desire."

The visitors expressed astonishment.

"Remember the Tiepolo," he went on, "where a lovely
young girl places the bird on her bare chest. There's Delacroix,
with his odalisque caressing a green and red parrot. Courbet,
of course, looking forward to *The Origin of the World* with his
Woman with a Parrot in 1866. In the same year, Manet, in an
allusion to Courbet, shows his mistress with a parrot, but this
time, the lover remains chaste, dressed in a robe, which is quite
humorous, because the parrot symbolizes eroticism and the
exotic. Since then, the theme has been treated many times:
Renoir, Vallotton, Frida Kahlo. Here, Bob John, a young artist
from Manhattan, a rising star, has given his own twist to this
inspiring scene."

"I understand exotic," a female customer in a silk suit cut
in. "But why erotic?"

"The parrot seems to be saying something, like the lover. It comes out with recognizable words, but what is it actually trying to say? The sound appears to matter more than the meaning. What language are parrots talking beneath the French, English, Spanish words they use? What's their intention? What are they implying? The answer that painters give is: desire."

"I'd never thought of that."

"A parrot, like a man, presents a semblance of civilization. On the surface, the bird composes sentences; in reality, it wants to consummate. Beneath the babble, its natural wildness is expressed, becoming almost threatening, whatever the sophisticated forms it takes."

"Funny you should be telling us this so close to this square with its parrots," the woman in the suit exclaimed. "Recent events seem to have proved you right about their erotic magnetism."

"I beg your pardon?" Wim asked.

"Zachary Bidermann," she said wickedly. "He does live here, doesn't he? He must have fallen under the spell of the parrots!"

"A good spell or an evil spell?" her husband asked.

"Both. Sex is a razor's edge."

"As long as it's not blunt!"

Everybody laughed at the husband's quip. He was a big, smug, ruddy-faced man, who thought of himself as a great joker. Wim, who hated the kind of live wire who only listened to what you said in order to twist it his way, turned away irritably and threw Meg a look of distress, a look she understood.

"Wim!" she cried out. "Phone call for you from Dubai!"

"I'll be right there."

Being redolent of fortunes in petrodollars, the word "Dubai" made an impression on the customers; Wim merely had to add an elegant "Excuse me," and they looked at him admiringly and let him go.

He got to his office and wearily pushed open the door. "Thank you, Meg. There are days when I really can't stand my profession."

"Why?"

"They're only here because of the Bidermann scandal, because of the address, so that they can look at Place d'Arezzo from my windows. They won't buy anything. There's no point making an effort."

"Would you like me to take over?"

"That'd be very kind of you. But don't overdo it, Meg: they're not going to dig into their pockets."

Resolutely, Meg strode back to the group. She didn't have Wim's eloquence, but she was precise and well-informed and could talk intelligently about works of art.

Remaining in his office, Wim relaxed and skimmed through an auction catalogue in order to distract himself. Since the night of the Bidermann reception, he had grown uncertain as to what direction his life was taking.

After that pleasant night they had spent together, he and Meg had greeted the day with surprise. Or rather, Wim had been surprised to wake up beside his assistant, who lay rolled up in the sheets, naked, her head sunk into the pillow, fast asleep. Because of his hangover, it had taken him a while to remember the previous evening. When he had finally put the situation into specific words—*I had sex with my assistant*—he had panicked. *What on earth got into me? Not only is she not my kind of woman, but I'll never find a better assistant.*

During the night, alcohol had clearly excused everything, but how was he to think about what had happened now that the intoxication had worn off? Drunkenness and the removal of inhibitions had probably been good reasons to make love, but sobriety reminded him of good reasons not to have made it. *How could I have had sex with that Flemish pudding? I'm not attracted to her. Worse still, I don't even think of her as a woman. If I can sleep with that, I'm done for. There are limits. Below a certain level, it's really not for me.*

Wim had gotten up, taken a shower, shaved, brushed his hair, then had concluded, once his image had been restored, that he would never refer to that episode again, but would speak and act as if nothing had happened. He didn't yet know to what extent Meg was going to help him with this denial . . .

Meg had slept so soundly that she didn't open her eyes until quite some time later. When she sat up in a deserted bedroom she didn't recognize, she felt a pang of fear. From outside on Place d'Arezzo there was a clamor of loud voices. She went to the window and saw onlookers, police officers, photographers, reporters. Her instinctive reaction was to move back against the wall in order not to be seen. When she realized that they probably hadn't come for her, she peered through the window again.

The movements of various groups were converging on the Bidermanns' town house.

A throng of women was screaming, "Bastard! Bastard! Bastard!"

To their right, a group of railroad workers held up a banner proclaiming a strange message: *You won't fuck Belgium.*

Scratching her head, she was lost for a few moments, searched for the TV set, sat down in front of it, and switched it on.

Within a few seconds, she had learned all about the scandal that had provoked these gatherings. Shocked and dismayed, her head in a vise, she pondered on this first news of the day; accustomed to the fact that nothing unusual ever happened to her, she didn't wonder about how she had spent the night, remembering only that she had been stuck here the previous evening and had started drinking to kill time.

She gathered her clothes, went to the bathroom, cleaned her teeth energetically, and tried to eliminate the leftover smells of alcohol that made her mouth feel like cardboard. It wasn't until she was in the shower that sensations connected with Wim rose to the surface! Wim kissing her. Wim sliding into her. Wim kneading her buttocks. Wim bringing her to orgasm, smiling, attentive, looking down into her face. She froze. Had she dreamt it? Was she taking her desires for reality? It was quite unlikely that . . .

But the images kept coming back into her brain, unbelievable but strong. What on earth had happened?

And anyway, where was Wim? If he hadn't been lying asleep next to her, that meant he hadn't been in the room. The reason she had gotten up alone was because she'd slept alone. Were what she interpreted as memories merely fantasies?

Dazed and embarrassed, as uncertain in her gestures as in her thoughts, she found it hard to get dressed, to make herself look more or less normal.

Once she had done so, she trembled at the thought of leaving the room. When she joined Wim downstairs, she would learn the truth. Either he would throw himself amorously on her and they were indeed lovers, as her tormented brain suggested, or he would treat her as he usually did, and she had imagined everything. What would be the best outcome? She dreaded both.

She descended the stairs, immediately becoming aware of loud voices.

Wim and Petra von Tannenbaum were having an argument.

"No, I know you only too well," Wim sneered.

"How dare you?"

"You made up that story, Petra, just to get yourself talked about."

"To get myself talked about? Do I need to be raped in order to get myself talked about? People were talking about me before, as far as I know."

"But not enough. Nothing will ever satisfy your narcissism,

no amount of fame will ever be enough for you, Petra, I've understood that perfectly well. It doesn't bother me. But this time you've acted badly. You've attacked a man who's world-famous and respected, and who ought to be prime minister in this period of crisis! You're causing irreparable damage. And that disgusts me."

"He forced himself on me!"

"I don't believe that for a second."

"What would you need as proof?"

"Real evidence."

"Don't worry, there will be. Even if it's only the analysis of the handkerchief—"

"Oh, sure!"

"Why won't you believe that I could be a victim?"

"You, a victim? You're the universal predator."

"I don't give a damn about what you think. Anyway, I'm not asking you to feel sympathy for me, I'm just asking to stay in this apartment."

"Out of the question."

Meg gave a start when she heard these words. Was he doing this so that she could take Petra's place? Then that meant they really had . . .

Petra stood up and pointed her finger angrily at Wim. "All right then, if you insist, I'll go outside, throw myself weeping in front of the reporters and photographers swarming out there on the square, and tell them my boyfriend, the famous gallery owner, has just thrown me out, like the worst male chauvinist there is."

Wim recoiled as if he had been hit. "You bitch! You wouldn't do that, would you?"

"And you wouldn't do it either, darling: throw me out now."

There was a silence. Although Wim had quit smoking years ago, he lit a cigarette. "OK, stay."

Without thanking him, Petra sat down, satisfied. She let a minute ago by, then said, "Of course, I have no desire to share your room anymore. After what I've been through . . . "

"What are you talking about?"

"My rape, you idiot. Put me on my own in another part of the apartment. That way I'll see as little of you as possible."

"On that point, we're in agreement," Wim concluded, getting to his feet.

It was then that he saw Meg standing in the corridor with her arms down by her sides. "Meg, you're just in time. Tell the staff to put Madame von Tannenbaum downstairs; explain to them how to arrange things so that she can do whatever she likes there and doesn't need to come upstairs."

"OK."

"And if you don't mind going to the kitchen, I could really do with a strong coffee. After the night I've had . . . Or rather, after the night Madame von Tannenbaum has given us."

Petra shrugged contemptuously.

These words removed any last doubt from Meg's mind: she must have dreamed it all.

Life resumed—to all appearances, just as before. Meg, an exceptionally devoted and considerate assistant, continued to help Wim; never once did she risk a familiar gesture, a conspiratorial smile, or a lingering look that would have suggested that she had been intimate with her boss. And with good reason, if her supposed memories were nothing but fantasies.

As for Wim, he would have died under torture rather than admit what had happened. A relationship with Meg didn't suit his personality. As an art dealer, he didn't merely sell beauty, he cultivated it, he surrounded himself with it, and was merciless toward any lack of taste. To show himself in public with an ugly duckling would not only have been a professional blunder—how can you choose paintings if you can't choose a woman?—it would have negated all his efforts. A beautiful apartment, a beautiful car, a beautiful woman, a beautiful gallery: everything had to match, everything had to be in harmony. A single mistake, and the whole house of cards would come crashing down. Beneath his behavior as a refined aesthete, behind his sophisticated culture, lay an unprepossessing child's naïve belief that by surrounding himself with beauty he could suppress his own ugliness, or even acquire beauty by a process of osmosis. It was an age-old reflex, close to religious cannibalism, which had led him, when he was very young, to eat the same dishes as the fashionable people he met; today, all that remained of that magical practice was a negative version: in a restaurant, he would refuse to choose a dish ordered by an obese neighbor. Similarly, as much to forget his nondescript appearance as to believe that he looked better than he did, he had condemned himself to flirt only with gorgeous women, even if they were trivial, even if they were stupid, or even if they were hateful like Petra von Tannenbaum.

If only he could erase his night with Meg from his memory, or even just stop thinking about it! But there was one thing about that night that kept niggling at him, stopping him from achieving this state of indifference: he had loved making love with her, he had shown himself to be a patient lover, only too delighted to wait until she had reached orgasm. Whenever he thought about it, he would look for explanations that excluded his partner: the alcohol, the unexpectedness of it all. But there was one simple explanation that clinched it: he didn't find Meg attractive. That was why he had taken so long to come, that was why he had amused himself with all kinds of foreplay . . . The way to avoid coming too quickly was to sleep with a woman he didn't find attractive!

He reflected on this theory, especially as a memory from his schooldays gave it a further degree of credibility: whenever he had translated from Latin at school, he only shone if the text was particularly difficult. If the teacher gave the class an easy passage from Cicero, his grade would be only average; whereas if it was a piece by Livy, or some thorny verses by Lucretius, Wim would triumph over the pitfalls and be top of the class. Why shouldn't it be that way in love? Could his possibly be a unique case of a split between desire and orgasm?

One afternoon, in the gallery, seeing an unattractive American woman come in, wearing Bermuda shorts, very short and with very white skin, he decided to prove the correctness of his theory. He walked her from painting to painting, sticking close to her, almost smothering her, flirting with her shamelessly. At first, she didn't catch on to what he was up to, but when she did she blushed, torn between embarrassment and pleasure. As he showed her out, he gave her his business card and told her that nothing would please him more than to spend an evening with her. Remaining circumspect even though she was tempted, she let him get as close to her as possible before delicately taking his card. At that very moment, Meg walked past and gave them a look of complete astonishment. Wim's face fell. From his reaction, the American woman immediately assumed that Meg was his wife.

"You son of a bitch!" she exclaimed.

Furiously, she pushed Wim away and threw the card on the floor as violently as if she had spat on it.

Wim stood motionless, watching her walk . . . Too bad the scene had finished as abruptly as it did. He wouldn't have been able to go any further anyway in his attempt to prove his hypothesis that he was only a good lover when he was with a woman who didn't attract him.

Meg's questioning look had disturbed him. It had been like an arrow to his heart, and he had felt wretched and, above all, guilty. What on earth was going on?

After three days of investigation, it was confirmed that the

DNA found on Petra von Tannenbaum's handkerchief was Zachary Bidermann's.

When they heard this on the radio, Wim and Meg happened to be together. They were silent for a long time. That Petra could have been the victim of a sexual predator still astounded them. However much they blamed themselves for their doubts, however much they forced themselves to consider her anew as an abused woman, they couldn't manage to feel the slightest compassion.

When Petra appeared, looking victorious, Wim said, "I'm sorry I didn't listen to you, Petra. I've been hateful. I've behaved in a way I reprimand in other men: I denied rape. I beg you to forgive me."

"That's all right."

Wim was surprised by such magnanimity. To help him understand the reason, Meg, her head bent over her computer, said aloud, "It's all over the Internet."

"Yes, isn't it?" Petra cried, proudly. "And there's a two-page interview with me in *Le Matin*."

"Two pages? That's amazing!"

Almost joyful, Petra was about to go back down to her apartment.

"Petra, are you comfortable in the apartment we set up for you downstairs?"

"Oh, yes, darling, very comfortable," she replied, adding in a decidedly friendly vein, "and you know, darling, you can carry on sleeping with the maid, it doesn't bother me."

She pointed to Meg behind Wim's back, and at her appalled reaction, which she found ludicrous, she burst out laughing and left the room. Wim gulped, his neck burning. He didn't dare to turn around.

As for Meg, she had the impression she suddenly weighed a ton. So her sensual dreams of Wim were memories, alcohol-influenced memories, certainly, but traces of an actual event.

But as she stood there trembling, all she could find to say was: "I'm not the maid!"

That day, Meg and Wim tried to avoid each other, which was mission impossible, since their daily life led them to share everything. They therefore tried not to talk or to look at one another.

By the end of the day, this avoidance had created the inverse effect of the one desired: no longer addressing either words or looks to one another took up so much energy that each thought only of the other, felt the other as a mass of light and volume whose presence occupied all the space.

At seven o'clock, Meg assumed that her deliverance was at hand, since she was about to leave. Since Wim had taken refuge in the kitchen, she dragged herself there to say goodbye.

On the table was a bottle of whiskey and two glasses. Wim sat waiting, his head resting on his left hand.

She understood, and in a voice distorted by emotion, asked, "Would you like a drink?"

"I'd love one," Wim replied in a toneless voice.

Now, as the days and nights succeeded one another, Meg and Wim were never apart. At night they were lovers, by day mere colleagues. An airtight border separated their night existence from their daily existence. In order to cross the border, they had recourse to two methods: whiskey at dusk, sleep in the morning. Through these airlocks, Meg, the fountain of sensuality, became once again the zealous colleague, and Wim, the expert in pleasure, the owner of the gallery.

One day, when it was nearly seven and he was looking for a bottle of bourbon, Wim almost broke the rule by saying, "Do we have to become alcoholics to continue our affair, Meg?" but immediately he stopped himself, showed Meg that he regretted his words, and resumed the role that was appropriate to the hour.

Petra von Tannenbaum continued with interviews and, occupied by her excess of fame, was totally indifferent to them. Her one demand was that from time to time she be allowed to accompany Wim to premieres and private viewings, determined as she was to perpetuate the idea that they were living together.

Meg didn't take umbrage, treating Petra with professionalism, never letting the slightest jealousy show through, not protesting when her rival monopolized Wim, and not demanding her place on his arm.

While in his mind he was grateful to Meg for being so understanding, Wim was nevertheless surprised by it. One evening, after only one glass of whiskey, and without waiting for the state of intoxication that allowed them to behave as lovers, he turned to her, his forehead creased with worry, and asked, "Does Petra being here bother you, Meg?"

"Not in the slightest."

"Really?"

"Really. As long as you can bear her, I'll bear her. When I'm with you, I don't need a conventional life."

He truly admired her. She was an extraordinary woman. What a pity he couldn't display her in society!

As she poured herself a second glass of whiskey, Meg added, "Poor Petra, when all's said and done, I feel sorry for her."

"That's crazy, Meg! There's no reason to feel sorry for Petra."

As far as Wim was concerned, in this case Meg's humanism verged on stupidity. You could invent stories about Petra, you could find her sublime, exciting, unique, poisonous, irritating, hateful, a pain in the ass, but you couldn't feel sorry for her.

He shook his head in denial.

"Oh, but there is!" Meg insisted. "I've seen the medications she's obliged to take."

"Petra?"

"Haven't you noticed all the stuff she hides in her makeup cases? There isn't just foundation in there."

"Meg, don't tell me you've looked through her things?"

"Yes. Are you angry with me?"

"Not at all."

"The morning after our second night together, I admit I couldn't help picking up the bottle of liquid she'd injected into herself with a syringe. It was a good idea, because since then I've understood her better. My brother's a doctor, and when I asked him, he told me what it was. What a tragedy!"

"I beg your pardon?"

"She had the operation, but she still has to take hormones. For the rest of her life, I suppose. When you know that, it's easier to stand her behavior, her desire to be the most beautiful, to shine in everybody's eyes, and especially her rejection of sex."

"What are you talking about?"

"Didn't you know? Petra von Tannenbaum was born a man."

10

She had found a husband, although he wasn't hers. Nevertheless, she clung to him as if he were her property. No other woman was going to steal him from her.

When she got back from Knokke-le-Zoute, Ève decided that she had to go to war, to destroy her rival in order to get Philippe back.

That morning, a crucial battle was about to be played out. She therefore got up in a cheerful mood.

"Barbouille! Where are you, Barbouille?"

The cat had climbed down off the bed and now sat on the ledge of the open window. Going to her, Ève grasped the reason. Because of the many local citizens as well as tourists now visiting Place d'Arezzo, the parrots and parakeets, considering themselves invaded, were reluctant to come down onto the cluttered lawns and so had annexed the higher territories, the balconies or gutters of the buildings. As a wise hunter, Barbouille had noticed this and was hoping she might be lucky and catch one of these detested birds. That was why, as soon as she got up, she had installed herself on the window ledge, on the lookout for parrots.

Ève leaned out and looked at the front steps of the Bidermanns' town house, where Zachary and Rose were arguing with reporters.

"How ugly he is, that Zachary Bidermann! Don't you think so, Barbouille?"

Ève meant it. Even though none of her elderly lovers were

stunningly attractive, it seemed to her that she could never fall for someone like Zachary Bidermann. She was a commonsensical Swiss girl from a farming family, and to such people the impossible had no attraction; when she had realized, years earlier, that Zachary collected women but didn't give them anything but his company, she had put him in the category of "without interest, to be avoided."

She lifted her cat and carried her into the bathroom. "Who's the pretty one? You or me?"

The cat struggled and protested—she had better things to do with her time—but Ève kept hold of her and looked at the two of them in the mirror.

Although neither wore any clothes, the cat looked dressed while Ève was the naked one, with her smooth, hairless golden skin and gorgeous curves; the feline, on the other hand, with her fur in disarray and her tail flicking angrily, looked like a society lady who has hastily put on a coat.

"You're the pretty one, darling. Nobody has eyes as precious as yours."

In spite of the compliments, the cat struggled, let out a sharp growl, managed to spring out of Ève's arms onto the floor, and slid, tail erect, along the walls, furious at having wasted her time, getting back as quickly as possible to her lookout post on the window ledge.

Ève placed the tall panels of glass in the right position around her. The little that a woman knows about her appearance, she learns not from mirrors, but from the words of men. Gazing at herself surrounded by mirrors, twisting in order to see her profile or her back, Ève was trying to connect what she saw with what she had heard. Her well-rounded ass . . . her irresistible rump . . . the hollow of her lower back . . . her slender torso . . . her breasts that stayed up without support . . . What she herself most admired didn't always provoke comment; for instance, she was very fond of her feet, but not a single man seemed to have noticed them, and the most they noted with surprise when she pointed them out was that they were "quite small." Poor men! They really lacked the vocabulary to describe female beauty.

She went closer to a round enlarging mirror next to the washbasin and gazed at her long lashes, like those of a china doll.

"Better hurry up, girl, you only have an hour."

She went as fast as she could, although doing things quickly wasn't in her nature, especially since the time she devoted to getting ready was the time she cherished most of all.

Dressed in a light beige suede pantsuit bought in Saint-Tropez, she jumped in her car and drove to the café in the Galerie de la Reine, where her meeting was due to take place.

Staking out Philippe had brought her the contact details of the famous Fatima, his most recent mistress, the one Rose Bidermann had told her about. She had called her the previous evening, introduced herself as "Sonia, a friend of Philippe Dentremont," and had suggested they meet in a public place "with peaceful intentions, for your good, my good, and his, I beg you to believe me."

Ève sat down at the far end of the room, between the old Art Deco posters advertising long forgotten liqueurs and the dessert cart. She kept on her dark glasses, just to accentuate the storybook flavor of the encounter.

Fatima didn't show any hesitation. As soon as she entered the room, she spotted Ève and came toward her.

Ève cursed inside. Fatima looked great, with ebony hair, ardent eyes, a noble bearing, and a peach-like complexion. Should she be upset or pleased?

"Good morning, Fatima, I'm Sonia."

"Good morning," Fatima replied, without any effort to be friendly, and sat opposite her.

"What are you drinking?" Ève asked.

"Fresh lemon juice."

"Oh, that gives me heartburn."

Fatima shrugged, as if to say she didn't care.

Everything's going well, Ève thought. *She thinks I'm stupid.*

When the drink came, Fatima dipped her lips in her glass, then looked straight at Ève. "What am I doing here?"

Ève took off her dark glasses and put them down on the table. "I haven't told Philippe I was seeing you. I wanted to meet you because I know we won't change him, and this isn't the first time I've had to share him with another woman."

"I beg your pardon?"

"I mean, another woman apart from his wife."

Fatima's eyes had filled with rage.

"I've been Philippe's mistress for years," Ève continued with studied nonchalance.

"What about now?"

"Where do you think he goes every other day at about six o'clock? Do you believe him when he says he works or joins his family?"

Fatima couldn't speak.

"First of all, Philippe hardly ever sees his family—his relationship with Quentin, his eldest son, leaves a lot to be desired—and secondly, Philippe works very little. He's a shareholder in the company created by his father, the multinational we all know. He lives off his private income, even though he tries to convince the world that he's still an entrepreneur."

Ève was enjoying saying all this in a honeyed voice, first of all because it was the truth, then because she liked making fun of Philippe.

Aghast, Fatima stared down at her glass, around which her hands had tensed.

"So basically, don't worry. If you want to hold onto Philippe, which I quite understand, you have to accept him as he is. But what he is, he won't reveal to us. I'm here to help you."

Fatima shuddered. She felt like running away.

Without further ado, Ève went on, "Does he ever talk to you about his wife?"

"No. He told me she was a dull and fat."

"On the contrary, Odile is stunning and, even though he cheats on her, he's still crazy about her! The power she has over him is incredible. And what about me? Has he ever mentioned me?"

"Never!"

"Sonia?"

"Never."

"Or Ève?"

"Who's Ève?"

"You see what he's like! Secretive, underhand . . . He can't help himself! But he's a good man, a generous man. I've had proof of that a hundred times. You just have to see the way he behaves with the children."

"What children?"

"Our children."

"Your children?"

"The children we've had together."

"I beg your pardon?"

"We have a boy and a girl. Thelma and Louis."

Immediately, Ève realized how casual she was being about inventing names, but it was obvious that Fatima, who was getting angrier with every passing moment, wouldn't even pick up on it.

Determined to deal the final blow, she took a photograph from her bag. "Look at my little darlings."

She held out a snapshot showing her and Philippe with two children aged three and five.

"They look like him, don't they? He has strong genes, does Philippe, Dentremont genes."

The blood drained from Fatima's face. She started cursing in Arabic.

Ève let her lose control then grabbed her arm. "I'm not jealous, Fatima. You can see him, you can have children with him, just doesn't bother me. If need be, demand that he gives them a sufficient sum of money. It took me years. A real battle. He refused to start with, for fear of putting his legitimate children at a disadvantage. In any case, there'd be no point in my children, or yours, competing for the inheritance because, first of all, it won't happen for another twenty years, maybe thirty—as long as possible, I hope—and secondly, how many children will there be, demanding their share? If we don't take precautions now, we'll have to be content with scraps when the time comes. I finally managed to get him to open me a bank account in Switzerland and put money in it."

Fatima got to her feet. "I'm leaving the son of a bitch!"

"Oh no, Fatima! Don't do that! He'll be so sorry to see you go!"

"I'm leaving the son of a bitch, He never told me anything. For the past six months, he's been saying he's going to leave his wife."

Ève looked genuinely upset. "Did he tell you that? No, that's not good. He'll never do it."

"When I think I was planning to come off the pill! What an idiot!"

"Don't blame yourself, Fatima!"

"Why don't you just shut up? I'm not like you. I don't share. Either he's mine, or he goes. I'm going to have it out with him tonight."

"Fatima!"

She was already leaving the café, in a hurry to admonish the man who had betrayed her.

Ève sighed and took out her compact; as she opened it, she saw herself in the mirror and winked.

"Poor Fatima, she really doesn't measure up. Too neurotic."

When she got home, she sat down with a nice thick novel on the new couch she had been bought by Philippe Dentremont. In an excellent move, she asked the cat, who ventured onto her belly, "Do you know this book by Bob, darling?"

The cat miaowed somewhat irritably.

"It's the kind of beach novel I like. I don't have the beach, but I have the novel."

She knew she'd have a quiet evening, because Philippe was seeing Fatima. Even though she was interested in what she was reading, she couldn't help imagining the scene: Fatima must be a real fury when she lost her temper, Philippe was going to suffer, to receive blows, have things thrown at him, be called names, and he wouldn't understand a damned thing of what she was talking about—Sonia, the mistress with two children, the others. Ève chuckled with satisfaction. Hurting Philippe gave her joy.

The amorality of her conduct didn't even occur to her. She was so self-absorbed that she never judged herself. Generally speaking, her conscience knew no guilt because it lived in the moment.

At around eight o'clock, Philippe called. His tone was sullen. "I've just left work," he said quickly. "Can I drop by?"

"Oh, Roudoudou, that makes me so happy!"

When he appeared, wild-eyed, hair disheveled, exhausted by Fatima's violent attack, he could not have imagined that sweet Ève, lying on her couch, her cat on her belly, a book in her hands, might have the slightest share of responsibility in the disaster he had just endured.

"How wonderful, my Roudoudou, to get an impromptu visit!"

"It was pure chance. I had a meeting that didn't last as long as expected."

"Come here and kiss me."

Preoccupied, he obeyed and lightly brushed her forehead with his lips.

Ève noted this coldness, but was unperturbed. "I love the book I've been reading while I was waiting for you."

"Who's it by?"

"Bob Bob, the American writer."

As he picked up the book, Philippe Dentremont reflected that Ève had lousy taste in literature, but he pursued this thought no further because a sheet of yellow paper stuck between two of the pages stopped him dead.

On the letter, someone had written by hand: *Just a note to say I love you. Signed: You know who.*

He grimaced. Ève was delighted to see that her ploy was producing the desired effect. Philippe could only desire a woman desired by others. The lust of strangers and competition between males constituted the most effective spurs to his appetite.

"What's this?"

"Oh, that note . . . Is that where it ended up?"

"Ève, what is it?"

"I got it this morning. Flattering, isn't it?"

"Who's it from?"

"That's what I've been wondering. Maybe it's the start of a beautiful romance . . . "

To silence her, he kissed her on the mouth.

11

To find Oxana: Victor had never before wanted anything as much as he wanted that.

She had left the hotel where she had stored her bags while she was staying with Victor: neither the receptionists nor the porters nor the doormen could tell him where she had gone; they had seen her get in a taxi but hadn't heard the address she had given the driver, so had no idea if she had gone to the station, the airport, or a new residence.

Stubbornly and systematically, Victor had drawn up a list of hotels in Brussels, phoned the receptionists, and asked to speak to Oxana Kourlova; each time the switchboard operator replied in an assured voice, "One second, monsieur, I'll put you through," he had hoped he would reach her; but each time, they came back and told him that unfortunately no one of that name was currently staying in the establishment. Although he explored all categories of accommodation, from five-star hotels to youth hostels, by way of bed-and-breakfasts and furnished apartments, he didn't find her.

In spite of this failure, he didn't give up. He went to see his uncle Baptiste and explained the situation.

"Just as I was ready, for the first time in my life, to tell a woman the truth about my condition, she vanishes into thin air."

"Why did she leave?"

"I have no idea."

"Did you quarrel?"

"No."

"Did you have a difference of opinion about something?"

"No, none."

"Did she blame you for anything?"

"Not that I recall."

"What about you?"

"Me neither."

"Did you ask her for something she couldn't give you?"

When his nephew shook his head, Baptiste's eyes shone wickedly.

Victor, his nerves on edge, was offended. "Anyone would think you found this funny."

"I have the feeling I understand the situation."

"What do you mean?"

"I'll tell you later. In the meantime, we're going to find this Ukrainian girl of yours. You know Isabelle works in the media? I'm going to suggest she call Oxana's agent for a photograph."

"Brilliant! But what if Oxana isn't in Brussels anymore?"

"Something tells me she's still here."

"Baptiste, stop acting as if you're a clairvoyant."

"I have experience, Victor."

"Experience of finding missing models?"

"Especially Ukrainian models."

"Are you joking?"

"Don't forget I'm a novelist. So I've lived a hundred lives."

"In your imagination."

"What difference does that make?"

"You think a novel is reality."

"No, I think reality is like a novel."

"Life is dull."

"Life is much more inventive than any writer. If you want proof of that, just look at this threesome it's given me at the age of forty."

"Maybe, but you don't learn about life through imagination."

"How else do you learn about it? If you're informed by your experience, you'll never know much; but thanks to stories, confidences, daydreams, virtual journeys, you begin to find your way through the maze."

"I reject your theory."

"You're talking only about yourself, Victor. You use your imagination. Apart from the moments when you're absorbed in reading, your prophecies have merely served to worry you, to fear the worst, to bring on the end of your relationships."

"All right, I give in. Let's get back to Oxana."

Baptiste burst out laughing. "Don't force yourself. I'll help you even if you don't agree with me."

The very next day, Victor got a call from Baptiste confirming that Oxana was still in Belgium.

"I'm hoping to set up a preliminary interview with a press photographer from the newspaper, and that photographer will be you. Agreed?"

"Agreed."

"Where?"

"The greenhouses at Laeken."

Victor had come out with the name without thinking, simply because he'd read that morning that the royal greenhouses, in accordance with a tradition established a century earlier, were opening their doors to the public for three weeks.

"A good idea," Baptiste concluded, "and above all very credible."

When, two days later, Victor made his way through that transparent city of glass and iron, he had a strange feeling of familiarity; not that he was at all accustomed to these gigantic palm trees, these giant ferns, these camellias, these azaleas, nor did the mingled scent of cinnamon and lemon geraniums recall anything either.

Taking advantage of the fact that he was ten minutes early,

he sat down on a bench, looked up at the graceful dome that protected trees and columns from the sky, and at last realized the source of his impression: the sounds! He was hearing the birds from Place d'Arezzo . . . Amused, he started searching, but couldn't see any parrots or parakeets; letting himself be guided by the cries, he followed a path that led to . . . a loudspeaker. When the greenhouses were open to the public, the gardeners played a recorded sound track to enhance the visitors' experience.

He sat down again.

Oxana appeared, frail but regal, dressed in light linen.

She was looking for a photographer and didn't notice Victor.

He gazed at her, heart pounding, mouth dry. He had never been so much in love.

"Here I am, Oxana."

She stumbled, stopped dead, twisted her legs hesitating on the direction to take, flapped her arms, then froze and turned pale. "Please, Victor, go away."

Without waiting for his reaction, she sped away. In spite of the visitors and the guards, Victor raised his voice. "Don't go!"

"I have an appointment."

"I'm your appointment."

She carried on along the gallery joining two of the greenhouses. He caught up with her and stood in her way. "Oxana, I'm your appointment. It was Baptiste who put the call through to your agent so that we could meet here."

"That's not very honest."

He bowed his head. "I wanted to see you again. And I was afraid you wouldn't come if you knew it was me."

"You were right. I wouldn't have come."

"So I was right to be dishonest."

Oxana was shaking. She kept repeating the words honest, dishonest, then stopped and moaned in discouragement.

Victor pointed to the white wrought-iron chairs, sat down, and gestured to her to join him. Wearily, she obeyed.

He took her hand. She quickly pulled it away, as if his fingers were burning her.

"I love you, Oxana."

She shivered, then, breathless, deeply moved, said, "And I love you too, Victor."

"Well, then?"

"Well, what?"

"You love me, and you run away?"

She shook her head, searched for her thoughts, her words, took a deep breath, gave up, and bowed her head. "It's better if we part soon! In a year, in a month, I wouldn't have had the courage to leave."

"Oxana! Why?"

She went limp, as if she no longer cared what she looked like. She bit her lip and scratched at the chair she was sitting on. Victor looked straight ahead and waited: it was better to be patient than to insist.

Japanese tourists passed at a measured pace, followed by a noisy Italian couple. A guard warned some small children not to touch the petals of the azaleas.

Oxana broke her silence. "I'm going to tell you the truth."

"Why didn't you tell me the truth before?"

"I still hoped . . . Because once I tell you, it'll be over between us."

Victor wavered. Oxana was expressing herself with such sad resolution, such firmness, that he feared the worst. He wished he could turn the clock back. What if she was right?

She sensed that he was hesitating. "Are you sure you want to hear this?"

At that moment, what he most wanted was to run away, to flee the Laeken greenhouses, to avoid facing up to reality. But he sensed that Oxana, now that she had made up her mind to speak, would have been disappointed by his change of heart. For her sake, rather than for his, he urged her to continue.

She sighed. "I am a bad woman, a failure."

"I don't believe a word of it."

"I left because I'll never be able to give you what you have a right to hope for."

"I'm sorry? All I want is to love you. And for you to love me a little."

"Yes, it always starts like that . . . But then . . . "

"Then?"

"Then you make plans for the future, you decide to live together, to get married—"

"Are you already married?" he cut in, convinced that he had guessed the reason for the departure.

In spite of the gravity of the situation, she let out a brief laugh. "Oh, no! No danger of that. I don't run the risk of big—bigamy . . . No, bigamy means two wives for one man . . . How do you say two husbands for one woman?"

"Biandry, logically, but that doesn't exist. The reality is even more male chauvinist than the vocabulary."

They smiled at each other; for a split second, the complicity between them had been reborn.

Frightened by this renewal, Oxana turned her head away to avoid looking at Victor, stared down at the gravel path, and frowned "You get married," she continued, "and you start dreaming about a family. That's why I'm leaving, Victor."

"You can't have children?"

"I can't have children."

Victor didn't react.

Oxana turned to him and said, "I can't."

He still didn't react.

"I'm sterile." Tears welled in Oxana's eyes. "Victor, do you understand what I'm saying? I have a malformation of the uterus that prevents me from keeping a fetus. On top of that, there's an infection that I got when I was about fifteen that . . . No, it's too disgusting! Why should I humiliate myself by telling you all this? I don't have to give you my medical record or justify myself. I want you, you want me, so I have to leave. I'm not a gift for a man."

Openmouthed with emotion, Victor slowly turned his head toward her and exclaimed, "That's wonderful!"

Startled, Oxana raised her head.

"It's wonderful," he repeated, and burst out laughing.

Oxana leaped out of her chair. "In addition to everything else, you're making fun of me?"

Anger had turned her face pale: stamping her feet, jaw tensed, fists clenched, she looked at this boy she had the misfortune to love and blamed herself for not having grasped before now that he was a monster. Without thinking, she slapped him. Once. Twice. Three times.

Victor stood up, pulled Oxana to him to stop her getting away, entwined his hands with hers, moved his lips forward, and stifled her anger with a kiss. When he broke away, he said in a low voice, "Now it's my turn to tell you the truth." His sensual mouth brushing against Oxana's right ear, he admitted, "I'm no gift for a woman either."

"You, Victor?"

"Just listen."

Without shilly-shallying or beating about the bush, in simple words and short sentences, he told her what he had been hiding from everybody: how his mother had been infected with the AIDS virus at the age of twenty and died five years later, how he was born HIV-positive, how he survived thanks to drugs that had gradually brought the disease under control. In full flow now, he told her about his bitter adolescence, when he had realized that he could never get close to anyone without endangering that person. He told her that he was in mourning, not only for his mother, but for the dream of getting married and starting a family.

"Collège Saint-Michel, don't scatter, stay together, and don't disturb other people!"

A sonorous voice had interrupted his confession. Victor and Oxana saw some thirty schoolchildren come into the greenhouse and move in their direction in a disorderly formation, trampling the gravel, as noisy as a herd of buffalo. Behind them came a female teacher, who was shouting herself hoarse but whose instructions were inversely proportionate to their effectiveness: the more she yelled, the less the children obeyed her.

"Collège Saint-Michel! Discipline, please! Don't make me regret organizing this study trip! Collège Saint-Michel, quiet please!"

Some pupils trod on Oxana and Victor's feet, others came to a halt in front of them and looked them up and down as if they were part of the attractions.

Prudently, Oxana sat down again and Victor joined her. In order not to attract comments, they sat three feet apart, silent, frozen, like two hikers waiting for a rain shower to end.

When the group had finally gone, Victor, without looking at Oxana or touching her, continued his story.

But something had broken. Trust perhaps, or the feeling of urgency. How could he have allowed himself to be carried away by that surge of optimism? The farther he got with his confidences, the more Oxana escaped him. Each word pushed her away, each word increased the distance. Soon what had always happened would happen again: the truth would kill his relationship. How could he ever have imagined that he would escape his curse?

He stopped.

Above them, the sharp cry of a bird reached them through the big panels of glass.

Victor shivered. His skin was hot, but his heart was getting colder. He knew now how the scene was going to play out: because she was a good person, Oxana would thank him, sympathize, urge him to open up even more, promise that she would keep this friendship between them and help him as much as she could—in other words, she would flee.

He sat there, head bowed, ears burning, hands shaking although he still managed to hide it. *Why doesn't she hurry up about it? Why doesn't she just dump me? There's no point waiting too long.*

He looked up, turned to her, and saw that her face was streaming with tears. His first reaction was to console her, but he held back, conscious that she was mourning their lost love. So he remained stiff and dignified, even though the emotion was wearing him down.

Oxana took a handkerchief from her bag and wiped her eyes.

What a grotesque existence! Victor thought. *We talk about our failed lives, our dying feelings, and it all boils down to noses full of mucus, eyes running, convulsive shakes. We're merely bodies that shake until death delivers us.* Overcome with sadness, he thought about his mother—something he usually avoided—her grave in Père-Lachaise, and what her body must have become. His mother, at least, was delivered from suffering. *Rest in peace.* Maybe her corpse was smiling, happy to feel nothing anymore. *Rest in peace.* What a salutary program! To die, yes, to die quickly. He felt an acid taste fill his mouth, provoking a spasm. He coughed. Oh, yes, to fall, to collapse here once and for all and have done with it. Just as the weight of his head was drawing him down to the ground, he became aware that Oxana was holding him back. *Yes, nurse . . . Women are all a bit like nurses, aren't they?* Flooded as he was with a desperate self-contempt, he nevertheless let her pull him up.

She raised his head and forced him to look at her. "I love you, Victor, and I don't want any other man but you."

Half an hour later, outside the city of glass, the biology teacher was summing up for her class from the Collège Saint-Michel what they had learned during the morning.

"Thanks to science and technology, favorable environments, individuals, forms, even new species are created. Today, in plants, animals, or humans, life is served as never before. The more we know, the more we can do. So what's the lesson of today? Have the botanists gotten in ahead of the geneticists? Today we have in vitro fertilization, but maybe that's because we already knew about grafting plants."

"All the same, mademoiselle, basically it's disgusting."

"What's disgusting, my boy?"

"Well . . . how plants are fertilized . . . How children are made . . . "

The group laughed, as much with embarrassment and mockery as with approval.

"That's right," the teenager with the round glasses insisted. "It's disgusting. Basically."

The children again let out a big mocking laugh.

The teacher took the boy's side. "Your friend is right. All flowers grow on manure; only, a lot of people forget that."

At that moment, the children from Saint-Michel, busy gathering up their notes from where they had scattered them over the lawn, saw the couple they had disturbed in the greenhouse pass by. Victor and Oxana advanced calmly, majestically, arms entwined, looking supple, beautiful, radiant.

For the girls, who were thirteen and already thinking about boys, they presented a dazzling picture of the ideal. Seeing them, they nudged each other and fell silent, out of respect, as they came closer. Who would ever have suspected that these two physically superb individuals considered themselves handicapped? The girls thought they saw swans; Victor and Oxana thought of themselves as ugly ducklings, failures, inadequates. Only their awareness of their own misery had made them strong. Devoid of arrogance, they knew they were vulnerable, wounded, infinitely mortal, and it was in the idea of death, together with the difficulty of living, that their love had been sealed.

12

Oh, no, I hate the countryside."
The customer couldn't believe her ears: a florist who hated fields and meadows?

"The countryside is repulsive!" Xavière went on. "There's earth everywhere, and earth, apart from being ugly, becomes dust when it's hot, and mud if it rains. What a gift! And then the smells . . . Mold and animal droppings! Nothing but filth decomposing, just like that, in the open air, ready to attack your nostrils. I tell you, you just have to set me down in front of a 'magnificent' view and all I want to do is scream, 'Flush the toilet!' Not to mention the wind, the mosquitoes, the wasps, the bats, the spiders, the horseflies. An American soldier gets more peace among the Taliban in Afghanistan than I do in the country: it's war!"

"But nature, Xavière, the flora . . . "

"There, you said it: the flora! Here in my shop, I have flowers; in the countryside, they have flora. What does that mean, flora? It means things springing up just anywhere. Does it satisfy your critical sense, seeing dandelions scattered all over a field? Do you find poppies growing in a ditch a pleasant sight? Have you ever managed to make a bouquet out of wildflowers? Any pleasure you get from them lasts about twenty minutes. Even before you've put them in water, they're weary, they droop, they lose their color. The fact is, they've come to your home to die. It's false advertising. 'Wildflowers': it sounds so sturdy, so robust, 'a product of the soil.' It's marketing,

madame, because wildflowers are worthless, they're like nothing else, they only survive in a field! Even calling a wildflower
a flower is a lie. It's just a measly little petal with a stalk and a
few leaves, all the parts you don't want. It's as if I gave you the
trunk and branches of an apple tree to eat instead of the fruit.
You'd get upset, and you'd be right!"

"Xavière, from what you say, the flowers you have here
weren't invented by nature."

"Precisely! They don't come from the country, they come
from a nursery. That's the whole difference. I don't sell you
things you can pick up from the ground, I sell you works of art,
products of human genius, jewels that have been shaped and
polished over the centuries by intelligent, determined, and
patient craftsmen. Getting beautiful flowers takes more than
bending down. Just as it takes more than gathering stalks to
make a flower arrangement."

"Of course."

"So go fill your vases with primroses or violets, they're just
dwarves that'll barely fill a saucer. Make sprays of thistles, why
don't you? Oh, God, it's so tiring to preach in the wilderness!
People have lost their sense of the value of things. Civilization
has gone downhill. I'm going to retire, and then you can all go
gathering dandelions on the square, insipid little yellow dandelions covered in parrot droppings. You don't deserve any
better, any of you!"

"Xavière, I never thought I was going to put you in this
state by offering to take you to the country."

"My state? You don't know anything about my state."

"Well, I know that Orion has health problems . . .
Alzheimer's, so I've heard?"

"Alzheimer's is nothing, compared with . . . I'm sorry,
Madame Riclouet, I'm not feeling well."

Feeling a weight on her bladder, Xavière went into the back
room, relieved herself, then, instead of going back to the shop,

sat down in a sagging armchair, preferring to stay there. *What a stupid profession! Throwing pearls before swine, no thanks!*

The customer stood there in the middle of the shop, with nobody to look after her: Xavière had disappeared, and Orion was out making deliveries. She hesitated between waiting and leaving, looked longingly at the flowers she had been going to buy before Xavière had launched into her diatribe, and called out, "Are you all right, Xavière?"

There was no answer.

"Xavière, I really need a bouquet, I'm visiting with some friends."

A haughty voice cried from the back room, "Come back in half an hour, Orion will be here then!"

The lady nodded, not so sure she wanted to repeat the experience: every time she came into the shop, she had the impression she was risking her life. If only a competitor would set up shop in the neighborhood!

Hearing the chime signal the customer's departure, Xavière heaved a sigh of relief. Too bad about the money she'd lost, but she wouldn't prostitute herself for a few euros. With any luck, Madame Riclouet would bump into Orion, who, with his constant willingness to help, would serve her and recover the sale.

"What an idiot he is too!"

Xavière was feeling better. She was getting over Séverine's death through her anger. She might have collapsed with grief during the funeral, but that sadness hadn't lasted.

When she had heard of the suicide, Xavière had been knocked for six. Never having imagined before that Séverine might hate her life so much, she had realized for the first time the extent of the despair eating away at the woman. Then she had wondered about her own share of responsibility: if she hadn't rejected her that stormy night, would she have thrown herself off a high building? Her response to this question was a complex one. Even if Séverine hadn't killed herself immediately, she would have done so later. It was inconceivable to Xavière that disappointment in love could have been the only thing driving her to suicide; if that had been the case, Séverine would have left her a message. So Xavière exonerated herself. *I wasn't the reason for her unhappiness, no, I was her balm, her remedy, with me she was fine.* But even after settling things with her own conscience—like all human beings—Xavière had found it hard to cope with the emotion of it all. Was it due to hormonal changes? The circumstances? She had felt an intense compassion for her dead friend, a terrible nostalgia, and it was when her affliction was at its height that she had fainted on the day of the funeral.

Giving in to unhappiness, though, was alien to Xavière, who had an active, enterprising temperament. So she had soon replaced tears with spite, a constant irritation that she cultivated toward everything and everybody. Nothing found favor in her eyes these days; this indignant rage erased her melancholy and reinvigorated her.

The child was growing in her. She could say "the child," because she was certain now that there was a living being in her belly. Sometimes, in fact, when nobody was watching, she would warm it with her hands, at other times she would talk to it. When she indulged in these contacts, she didn't feel as if she was a madwoman conversing with her own belly, but rather as if she had acquired some kind of calm wisdom. Very strange!

Officially, she hadn't decided anything yet, since events— Séverine's suicide, the Bidermann affair—had prevented her from worrying about herself. In the middle of this maelstrom, the legal date for abortion had passed; this deadline seemed to her merely a second stroke of fate, the first being the arrival of a fetus. Regarding this pregnancy, she continued to show real apathy. Wasn't that what gestation was: a test of passivity?

The chime rang. Someone was coming into the shop. She

didn't react. *I'm too tired.* She even held her breath in order to avoid being heard.

"Is there anybody here? Hello? Is there anybody here?"

The determination in that flat voice suggested an individual capable of coming into the back room, so there was no point hiding anymore.

She sighed and went into the shop. "Yes, what can I do for you?"

The man, who was short and broad and wore a stained raincoat, looked her up and down smugly. "Hello, madame. I'm a journalist for *La Gazette européenne* and *Le Quotidien des Ardennes.* I wanted—"

"A bouquet?"

"Er . . . no . . . I wanted to ask you if—"

"No point, monsieur, I sell flowers, not gossip."

"Please. Just some information."

"Why should I give it to you?"

"Because you're a kind person."

With his unctuous voice and his pouting mouth, he was trying to win her over. She looked at him contemptuously. *Kind*: that was definitely not the word to use when speaking to her. There was an amused gleam in her eyes that he took for consent.

"I'm listening," she said.

"Was Monsieur Bidermann a customer of yours?"

"His wife, Rose Bidermann, loves gorgeous bouquets. It's not surprising she has the name of a flower."

"No, indeed. What about him? Did you ever see him?"

"From time to time."

"And?"

"I didn't like him to come in here. It was because of him that I had to dismiss a number of female assistants. They claimed he'd forced them to do things . . . Well, you know what I mean . . . "

"What? In here? That's incredible!" The journalist's eyes opened wide in astonishment. He was overjoyed at the thought of having a monumental scoop.

"Yes, right here among the flowerpots."

"Incredible!"

"I didn't believe them at the time."

"Do you regret that now?"

"To be honest, I was more jealous than anything else. Because I thought he came here just for me. The two of us used to do it in the cold room. I don't know why, but he was excited by the cold room, with all those bulbs and sprays around. Strange, really. Men don't usually perform very well in the cold, but with him it was quite the opposite."

"Incredible! Incredible!" The journalist was all agog at this revelation.

"Any more questions?" Xavière asked, smiling affably. "Was I *kind* enough? Is that stupid enough for your rag? If you like, I can make up other stories. How about the way he tied my husband with leather straps or sodomized my young clerk, for example?"

Realizing that she'd taken him for a ride, the journalist turned pale.

She opened the door and with her hand indicated the way out. He passed in front of her, assuming an offended air.

"Incredible, isn't it?" she murmured as he brushed against her.

Sheepishly, he went back to the group of reporters and photographers milling about on Place d'Arezzo.

From their large dark nests built between the branches, the parrots and parakeets seemed to stand aloof, entrenched in the heights. This suspicious influx of unknown onlookers prevented them from descending onto the grass as often as they had before, and, like Xavière, they hoped the Bidermann affair would soon stop polluting their habitat.

Remaining in the doorway, slightly back from the street, she put her hands on her belly, massaged it gently, and whispered, "You see the kind of world you're coming into? Do you find it tempting? I warn you, ninety-nine percent of the people in it are idiots. Of the one percent that are left, there are autistic geniuses you don't associate with, artists you'll never meet . . . and your mommy."

She was astonished that she had uttered that word. Did it suit her? Coming out like that, without anyone around to hear, it suited her well enough.

"Yes. There will be Mommy. Just you and me, surrounded by all these imbeciles. We'll have a good laugh."

She felt like laughing now, but instead tears welled in her eyes.

"Damned hormones! You'd better come out of there soon, kiddo, because Mommy would like to be able to curse in peace without whining like some fan of sappy music. By the way, do you like westerns?"

Nathan crossed the street and came running toward the shop.

"Can I talk to you, Xavière?"

If it had been anyone else, she would have replied, "No, I sell flowers," but she granted a special status to Nathan. She felt, if not friendship, at least a benevolent sympathy toward him, partly because he wasn't like the others and she liked his extravagant dress sense, and partly because he was scathing about people—the only way he could bear mankind was to make fun of it. If she'd been a man, she would probably have behaved just like him. So they often scoffed at their contemporaries as they passionately discussed flowers and the best way to put them together.

She pointed to Nathan's legs, which were clad in some kind of scaly material. "I love it! What are your pants made of, Nathan? Snakeskin or crocodile?"

616 - ERIC-EMMANUEL SCHMITT

"Plastic, darling. I don't want animals to be killed just to make me look sexier. On the other hand, I don't mind men being exploited to dig oil wells or the planet being trashed to create synthetic fabrics."

She closed the door behind them. The calm of the shop contrasted admirably with the noise of the street and they felt as if the roses and the lilies were enclosing them in a kind of perfumed silence.

"Xavière, I'm not going to beat about the bush, I've come about Orion."

"Oh, my God, poor Orion!" Xavière exclaimed, surprised that her wretched husband could retain anybody's attention.

"Yes, Orion. I think it's him."

"What do you mean?"

"He's the writer of the anonymous letters."

Xavière raised an eyebrow. With all that had happened recently, she had forgotten all about the letters. "What makes you say that, Nathan?"

"First of all, this shop seems to me the ideal place to plot something like this. It's a vantage point. From here, you know everybody."

"That's true of me too. That must make me a suspect."

"Secondly, it has to be someone who's full of kindness."

"I'm not a suspect anymore."

"Precisely. But Orion does suffer from that affliction."

"You could say that," she grunted.

"Does he feel goodwill toward everybody?"

"I'm afraid he's quite capable of it. He has no sense of discrimination."

"Do you think he actually loves everybody?"

"Who knows? He's kind to everybody as soon as he meets them. Maybe if he saw someone killing me in front of his eyes—"

"I think we'll spare ourselves that experiment."

"Please."

"So if Orion loves everybody, that throws a new light on the situation! These letters aren't a ploy intended to lead people to the love of their life. The signature 'you know who' doesn't refer to different people. He's writing the messages in his own name. And the fact that they're all the same means that he feels a sense of fraternity with everyone. When it comes down to it, these letters are like the times when he says hello to you as he's crossing the road without looking."

"Like a dog. That's what I always tell him, that he's as stupid as a dog. And you know what he replies? That the dog is man's best friend."

"Another confession!"

"You really have to be as stupid as a dog to be a friend to man."

"To cut a long story short, Xavière, I have every reason to believe it's Orion. All the clues point to him. There's just one thing missing."

"What's that?"

"If you answer yes, we have the proof."

"What is it?"

"Is Orion left-handed?"

"Yes, he is!"

They looked at each other triumphantly.

"What do we do now?" Xavière asked.

"Will you talk to him?"

"Leave it to me."

"I have to go now, I'm late."

Nathan turned to leave, but Xavière held him back by the arm. "How's Tom?"

"That's a good question. Thank you for not asking it."

He walked tensely away, avoiding the onlookers and the reporters.

Xavière thought over Nathan's last words with a certain pleasure. So Tom and he were going through a few problems.

She was pleased. From time to time, the idea had occurred to her that only gay couples stood the test of time; learning that they went through ups and downs just like everybody else reassured her.

As she walked through the shop, she noticed that the peonies were wilting.

They won't even have lasted three days. What a waste!

She had opened the wrong shop, it would have been better to choose an activity that didn't demand fresh produce. For example, she would have loved to have a pharmacy, that way she could keep up to date with everyone's ailments.

She returned to the half-darkness of the back room, collapsed into the armchair, and started thinking.

One must die so that the other may live. Those words had been haunting her for a week. Séverine's death told her that she had to bring this child into the world. It was the only way to give any meaning to what had happened. Of course that seemed stupid, complicated, hateful, but also obvious. It was as if her lover's death had given her the solution.

The chime rang out, and Xavière heard Orion's voice along with that of Madame Riclouet. *So he did pick her up, she'll get her bouquet after all.*

The customer Xavière had abandoned was at last able to buy her flowers and left again.

Orion, his hair sticking up around his ears, approached his wife. "How are you feeling?"

"I don't know."

He looked at her, wet his lips several times, scratched the back of his neck, looked away, and said, "I don't understand why you don't talk to me about it."

"About what?"

"You're pregnant."

"No, I'm not. How do you know?"

"The doctor told me when you fainted in church."

Xavière sighed, hoping he would think she was sighing with irritation, when it was actually relief. "All right, it's true, I'm pregnant. But what business is it of yours?"

He gave a start, looked around him for imaginary witnesses to the fact that he had heard correctly. "It's our child!"

She sat up, cut to the quick. "*Our* child?" Anger was rising inside her. She had only just accepted this child as her own, and now they were already trying to take it away from her. "How do you know it's yours?"

"We made it together, Xavière, in the car."

"I was drunk."

"That makes no difference."

"How do you know this child isn't someone else's? Don't you think I might have a lover?"

He looked at her and gave her a kindly smile. "Do you have a lover, Xavière?"

At that moment, she thought of Séverine—her soft honey-colored skin, her smooth shoulders, her neck that turned red when she left kisses on it—and she burst into tears and fell back in the armchair.

"No, I don't have a lover," she managed to say through her sobs.

He ran to comfort her. "It's all right, darling, it's all right."

He cradled her for a long time against him, which she allowed him to do because she felt genuine peace, mourning Séverine in his arms. It seemed to her that everything was returning to normal. *His ugly and he's stupid, but he's here, he's always here,* she thought with tender contempt.

He brought her a paper handkerchief, and she wiped her eyes.

He remained there, kneeling in front of her, attentive, anxious to do the right thing.

Feeling calmer now, she said, "Do you . . . do you want to be a father?"

"I'm sure I'm quite inadequate," Orion replied. "But the world is made up of inadequate people."

"That's what I think."

"What about you? Do you feel ready to be a mother?"

What did being a mother mean? Did you have to put abnegation, self-sacrifice, and love in the mix? None of that was for her. At least it hadn't been so far.

"Listen, Orion, why not? I was starting to get a bit bored. It was either a child or a dog."

"Oh, a dog is good," Orion said, totally serious. "I like dogs a lot. And dogs love me. I've always dreamed of having a dog. Ever since I was a kid. More often than having a son or daughter. Oh yes, much more. When it comes down to it, I'd be game for a dog. What do you think?"

"It's going to be a child, you idiot, not a dog."

Orion burst out laughing, and so did Xavière—in spite of her willful reluctance.

He disappeared into the cold room and came back with two bottles of champagne. "Let's celebrate! The happy event will only be official with the first glass of champagne."

Xavière stopped him. "No, Orion. A question first."

"All right."

"I want you to tell me the truth and nothing but the truth."

"I swear."

"Did you send those anonymous letters?"

"What anonymous letters?"

"The truth, Orion! The anonymous letters we received here on Place d'Arezzo, written on yellow paper and saying something like 'Just a note to tell you I love you, signed: You know who.'"

"That's awful, I didn't receive one."

"Stop playacting, Orion. Was it you?"

Stunned, he raised his hand as if taking an oath in court. "I swear it wasn't."

"What? It wasn't you?"

"The child is mine, not the anonymous letters."

Xavière lowered her head, disconcerted.

He was surprised. "You seem disappointed."

"Yes. It was stupid, but it was a great idea all the same. And it caused a hell of a stir in the neighborhood. A pity!"

Orion devoted himself again to his task: uncorking a bottle.

Taking advantage of his attention being elsewhere, Xavière put her hands on her belly, stroked the bulge with both palms and murmured, "You hear that, kiddo? You mustn't idolize your father too much. Quite apart from the fact that he took sixty years to make you, he's not used to doing anything out of the ordinary. One last thing: he's an alcoholic and we conceived you when we were both plastered. Will you come all the same?"

Orion turned, thinking she was talking to him. "What was that, Xavière?"

"Nothing, just daydreaming . . . "

13

Albane!"
His cry had the sharp, nasal quality of the parrots and parakeets bustling about in the trees.

"Albane!"

He couldn't help it. Emotion made his voice ugly, quite apart from the fact that it had recently broken and he had consequently lost all control over it.

"Albane!"

The fear of not being heard made his cries even shriller, so that they blended with the screeching of the parrots and were lost in the middle of all that cacophony. It was like one of those nightmares in which the dreamer, in spite of running as fast as he can, is caught by a monstrous giant moving in slow motion. Quentin realized that, even though he was shouting at the top of his lungs, Albane wouldn't hear him.

So he leaped off the bench and waved his arms.

Dragged abruptly from her daydream, Albane saw him, gave a start, took fright at first, then recognized him and smiled slightly.

Hesitantly, she decided to cross the street and go to him.

As if it was the most natural thing in the world, he returned to the bench to welcome her.

"So you still come here?" she asked.

Her disconcerted tone suggested that she was surprised Quentin hadn't noticed the changes in the world: a war had broken out.

"Of course. Every day. I've been waiting for you because you stopped answering my notes."

Albane remembered that she hadn't answered his messages. It wasn't that she didn't care—on the contrary, whenever his name came up, it warmed her heart—but she kept telling herself that she would call him as soon as she felt better. Had she really been down for so long?

"What happened?"

She looked at him. He looked worried, sensibly worried. He had no idea what she had gone through . . . Luckily!

Seeing those clear blue eyes, which knew nothing about her ordeal, she felt lighter. At home, neither her mother nor Hippolyte nor Dr. Gemayel nor Marie-Jeanne Simon, the psychiatrist specializing in trauma, could ever look at her innocently.

"I've been ill," she said.

"Seriously ill?" Now he did look alarmed.

She had better reassure him as quickly as possible, she didn't want him to feel sorry for her. "No, it wasn't a physical problem."

"What, then?"

"It was a girl thing. Not important. It's fine now."

She was astonished by what she was saying. This urge to spare Quentin—or spare herself in his eyes—sounded a new note that seemed at once shocking and comforting.

At the mention of a "girl thing," Quentin lowered his eyes. He wouldn't investigate further: he was a young male and knew that women belonged not just to a different sex than men, but to a different species. Boys had to respect a "girl thing." In recent years, he had realized that their bodies contained very special equipment, organs that bothered them, hurt them, stopped them from going swimming, and exempted them from classes without anyone objecting. As far as Quentin was concerned, there was no need to veil women: even naked, they remained shrouded in mystery.

He sighed and rubbed his hands. "Phew! At least it wasn't something I did to upset you!"

Albane looked at him tenderly. He was so harmless, so delicate. How could he ever do anything to upset her? True, he related everything to himself, and yet she found his attentive, devoted egocentricity touching. In a parallel life, she could have loved him.

In relation to him, Albane had two lives that were difficult to reconcile, the old and the new. In the old, arguing with Quentin, annoying him, picking on him, flirting with him had been really important to her; in the new one, which had started with the assault, she found herself confronted with a childlike, inexperienced boy.

Would she manage to find a third life, in which, although hardened by the rape, she would still find within herself a fresh inclination to listen to such a boy and look at him?

"You know," he said, "you can be honest. It's better that way. If you don't give a damn about me, then just tell me."

"What's gotten into you?"

"I've been waiting for you all these days, while you—"

"Hey, let me remind you that in the past it was always me waiting for you!"

The argument hit home, and he bowed his head. "Precisely. When you wait, you have time to think. And I need to know if . . . if I'm right to wait, if you care about me a little."

She quivered with pleasure. "Of course I do."

He looked up, delighted. "Do you really?"

"Yes, really." Albane smiled. This endless, pointless chatter felt so good! She felt alive again.

Quentin grabbed her hand. She was surprised that his palms should be so warm and soft; she felt that her own hands were still cold and clammy, no more pleasant to touch than a goldfish. Well, as long as he didn't notice . . .

"I'm going away, Albane," he announced in a measured, serious voice. "I'm going to London."

It took Albane's breath away.

"I leave Brussels at the end of June," he went on. "For two years."

"Why?"

He looked at her, saw how defeated she looked, how she trembled, and he wavered. Should he tell her the reason? Admit that it was because of her? He chose instead to serve up the official version, the one that had convinced his family. "I want to complete my studies at the International Lycée in London, and get a European Baccalaureate, which is recognized everywhere. And I also need to practice my English."

"Oh?"

"Plus, I'm finding it harder and harder to get along with my father."

A few weeks earlier, Albane would have joined in with a sarcastic tirade against parents and said some disparaging things about her own mother, but she remained silent.

"He can't see what I'm becoming. He insists on treating me like a child."

Albane glanced at him. His father must not be paying attention, because Quentin, in a way that was both sudden and obvious, had become a man: his body was so much stronger, his eyes were filled with confidence, and his voice had at last broken. She found him quite impressive.

As for Quentin, he was concealing his true motive. He was taking refuge in London because she'd said she wouldn't make love until she was sixteen and a half. He wouldn't have the patience to mope around, waiting for her; if he stayed, he would turn hysterical, obnoxious, even violent maybe . . . From a distance, he would be able to bear the situation. It wouldn't matter if he amused himself with superficial girls or women to assuage his impatience. Only she mattered. He would return when she was ready.

Albane shook her head, staring into space. Why was life

snatching away from her the only person who made her glow with happiness?

The parrots were fluttering about energetically, busy taking grains and seeds to their babies, who were opening their eyes to life.

They sat on the bench like two castaways. Sex was tossing them around like corks borne on the swell, and they moved to its rhythm, not according to their own strengths or desires. For Albane, it had gone wrong; for Quentin, it had gone right. Still, they were aspiring to something else, hoping for a different relationship than the one they had had. Even though they had some trouble formulating this hope, they nevertheless felt it deeply and already knew who to place it in: what Quentin was expecting from Albane was that love could merge with pleasure; what Albane was expecting from Quentin was that love should be a consensual encounter.

"Do you have to go away?" she asked in a low voice.

She was revealing a great deal of herself with these words, and Quentin realized it.

"If I leave, Albane, it doesn't mean we won't be friends anymore. On the contrary. You're my best pal. I have every intention of talking to you every day and writing to you every day."

"Is that true?"

"I can't see how I could forget you. You're the only thing I'm going to miss about this place."

Albane was tempted to run away. So much kindness, so much passion disconcerted her after these bitter days when she had shriveled at the thought that she would never love anybody again, and would never allow anybody to love her. She had imagined that she could protect herself behind a thick wall of indifference, but Quentin had just made two breaches in it, first by making her sad at his departure, and, second, by showing her how much he cared for her. What should she do? Continue to feel, to let her heart beat faster? Or shut herself away from emotion?

He pointed skyward. "Look at those two birds, Albane, there on the edge of the nest, above the street lamp. Can you see them? They're lovebirds. They're called that because the male and female get together when they're young and form a couple that lasts till the end of their lives."

"Is that possible?"

"Among birds, yes."

She sighed. So did he.

"Among humans, the love of children and teenagers is downplayed. Adults always put on that clever, superior air, hear you without listening, and look without seeing. 'It won't last,' they say."

"So?"

"So the parents of lovebirds aren't like that. Which is why lovebirds form lasting couples."

"What are you trying to say?"

"That my mother and father aren't lovebirds. My father has been cheating on my mother forever, my mother has been cheating on my father for a little while, after being hurt by him. What's stopping them from splitting up is the children and their commonly held property. If I told them . . . " He broke off. He had turned red, and his heart was pounding. He hesitated to continue: his words committed him so much, they risked making him ridiculous. "If one of their children were to say that he's met the love of his life, they'd shrug. Because they no longer believe in love. And yet it seems to me that sometimes, being in love isn't a state but an insight, an intuition about what is going to happen. Even if you're young, you're old when you love, because you've seen the future, you've already experienced it."

Albane looked at him without understanding. He rummaged through his bag, pulled out a book, and waved it. "Here, look, I found a passage in this book by Baptiste Monier, you know, the local writer?"

"Local writer? You're joking! According to my teacher, he's translated all over the world."

"'Love at first sight is as mysterious in art as it is in love. It has nothing to do with a first time, because what you find often proves to have been there already. It is not so much a discovery as a revelation. A revelation of what? Neither of the past nor of the present. A revelation of the future . . . Love at first sight is a kind of premonition . . . Time folds and twists, and in a split second the future appears. We travel through time. We access not the memory of yesterday but the memory of tomorrow. "Here's the great love of my years to come." That's love at first sight: discovering that we have something powerful, intense, and wonderful to share with someone. When you sent me your letter, I received the assurance that we would have a long and happy relationship, that for my whole life you would be with me, following me, guiding me, confiding in me, entertaining me, comforting me. Did I get it right? I'm counting on you.'"

Quentin put the book down on his lap. Albane looked at his endlessly long hands respectfully stroking the pages.

There was a moment of hesitation between them. Every word in the text triggered strange echoes. The letter mentioned in the text could have been the unsigned message Quentin thought he had received from Albane. The delayed love at first sight could have been this thunderbolt that had struck these two children who had known each other since infancy. The assurance of a joint destiny could have been Albane's stubbornness, or Quentin's new decision. They let their thoughts murmur and fell silent, charged with emotion.

Quentin gently closed the book and put it back into his backpack. He started speaking again as if Albane wasn't there, addressing the tree trunks bursting out of the soil. "Imagine that I'm in love with you . . . That would mean I've seen from the start that we're meant to spend our lives together, that I've already seen the children we'll have, that I've guessed what you'll be like when you're a bit older, even when you're elderly, and that I was attracted by that."

Albane quivered. "You've imagined me when I'm older?" She liked the idea because, in the past few days, she had thought a hundred times that she was going to die.

"Yes."

"And what's your conclusion?"

"That you'll always be attractive."

"Not if I look like my mother."

"Your mother's very attractive."

"She's fat!"

"It suits her."

Albane was dumbfounded. Was he another one who thought her mother was presentable? Men were strange!

At that moment, Victor and Oxana crossed the square, their arms around each other. Victor was talking animatedly and Oxana, with joy in her eyes, seemed to be drinking in his every word like nectar. Albane sighed. To be like that one day, maybe . . . You fall in love the way you become a painter or a musician, by imitation. If you see a Renoir, you buy brushes; if you hear Mozart, you learn music; if you glimpse the splendor of love, you want to embody it yourself.

Quentin gave a start. "My bus!"

"Already?"

"Yes, I'm going to miss it."

He jumped down, closed his bag, and put it on his back. He smiled at Albane, waved at her, and set off at a quick pace. After ten steps, he ran back, looking anxious. "You did say you wouldn't make love until you're sixteen and a half, right?"

Sixteen and a half felt too soon to Albane, but she didn't want to contradict herself. "Yes," she confirmed, bowing her head.

"So that's in a year and a half?"

Will I manage it in a year and a half? she thought. *Oh, I hope I can. I'll probably have healed by then.*

"Yes, a year and a half."

"In that case," he said gently, "will you wait for me?"

14

ENCYCLOPEDIA OF LOVE
by Baptiste Monier
Extracts

Caress. 1. Light touch applied to a person's skin, sometimes voluntary, sometimes involuntary—the voluntary kind lasts longer, but the involuntary kind may have major repercussions. 2. Problem between two naked people when their two skins do not feel the same thing.

Flirtation. 1. State of indecision between a man and a woman who wonder if they might not to be able to do better elsewhere. 2. Habit of people who are lacking in self-confidence.

Kiss. 1. Exploration of a person's oral cavity with the intention of undressing him/her. 2. Common practice among homeless bipeds, frequently performed in cars, in doorways, and on benches. 3. Act forbidden in certain professions such as prostitution (or tax auditing).

Love. 1. Problem between human beings that some take for a solution. 2. Selfishness that achieves a temporary balance with another person's selfishness. 3. Unusual ability to take an interest in another person while losing one's own self-interest. 4. Subject of novels.

Masturbation. 1. Most common form of human sexuality, making it possible to dispense with other people and their complications. 2. Method of thinking about another person while touching one's own body. 3. Preparation used by some people in order not to be overexcited when they arrive for a date. 4. Common practice among women making love with men who are in a hurry. 5. Teenage occupation.

Passion. 1. Persistent illusion about another person, accompanied by numerous signs of affection. 2. Mental illness with no known remedy; generally, the victim of passion, once cured, has no idea what happened to him/her.

Penetration. 1. (For a man) Result of several dinners out, a few evenings at the theater, and frequent visits to the florist's. 2. (For a woman) Way of rewarding a man who has told her repeatedly that she is beautiful. 3. (Medical) Practice entailing many risks (diseases, children, etc.). 4. (Rare) Highest expression of love.

Penis. 1. Male sexual organ whose size varies depending on the emotional state of the man. 2. True seat of the brain in some males.

Pregnancy. 1. Method by which a woman keeps her husband at a distance by asserting her superiority over him. 2. Pleasant period during which a woman, unusually, is encouraged to put on weight. 3. Means by which a couple can say goodbye to irresponsibility. 4. First sign of joys to come. 5. First sign of problems to come.

Provocation. 1. (In a woman) Discreet way of finding out if a man likes her. 2. (In a man) Indiscreet way of making sure that a woman likes him.

Reproduction. 1. Ulterior motive underlying sexual relations in very religious people. 2. Anxiety in sexually liberated people. 3. (Common) Contraceptive accident.

Sperm. 1. Liquid of which 99.99% has no use. 2. Sign of impending exhaustion in a man. 3. Secretion sometimes accompanied by the use of coarse vocabulary. 4. Compromising stain on material, resulting in disasters at home or at work. 5. (Archaic) Man's seed, which, by linking up with the ovum, makes it possible to have children: this usage is practically obsolete.

Tenderness. 1. Kind of loving that is neither sexual nor genital. Suitable for friendships and family relationships. 2. Replacement for sex in elderly people. 3. Form of sainthood.

Underwear. 1. (In a woman) Erotic adornment intended to excite the male. 2. (In a man) Anti-erotic adornment designed to be removed quickly. 3. (Gerontological) Hygienic protection.

Vagina. 1. Inner female part, a genuine object of obsession in men. 2. Reward sometimes given to a deserving penis. 3. Area that is mysterious and terrifying to homosexuals. 4. Area of endless play for lesbians.

15

T he birds made a contribution to the upkeep of the square by scattering a daily dose of fertilizer on the ground.

Hippolyte loved coming to Place d'Arezzo, not only because he was taking care of a garden threatened by urban pollution, but also because he always felt as if he had gone on a journey; watching the parrots, listening to their hullaballoo, admiring their huge, dark nests made up of modified twigs, as compact, watertight and solidly built as Noah's Ark, he would escape Brussels, its asphalt and its bricks, and come to a world that was untouched, colorful, lemon-scented, talkative, as young as the Earth and as immutable, showing by its refreshing persistence that it didn't give a damn for human civilizations. Whenever he caught a glimpse of a parrot's round head, its dark, startled eye, its lack of interest in the activities of the city, he felt relief; so there were other creatures that lived as he did, absorbed in the present moment, with little concern for what preoccupied sophisticated minds.

He had no interest in the Bidermann affair, for instance. That a man should have forced himself on a woman was, unfortunately, a commonplace act of violence. They should pity the victim, punish the culprit, then stop talking about it. Why couldn't the media let go of the subject? Why were people clamoring for more details? Anyone would think they had discovered evil for the first time . . . *I'm not clever enough, I must be missing something.*

Whenever there was something he didn't understand, Hippolyte would lash out at himself, blaming his own short-comings; he always lent credibility to his contemporaries, society, the universe. Any stupidity or absurdity could only be coming from him. He lived with the conviction that everything had a meaning, and if the meaning escaped him, then it was because of his wretched head, not because something was meaningless. Naturally, the world was so much more complex than him that his little mind couldn't grasp its structure or its details.

"I'm happy."

The thought of his happiness had emerged all by itself from his mouth. Startled, he propped his chin on the handle of his shovel.

"Strange to be happy when . . . "

Yes, he had just been rejected by Patricia, Patricia whom he loved, Patricia with whom he had dreamed of spending his days and his nights, and yet this morning, holding his tools, in the process of spreading bird shit, he felt really happy. Was that normal?

He went up to Germain. "Tell me, Germain, are you happy?"

"Of course," the dwarf replied. He wiped his forehead and looked up at his colleague's face. "Why do you ask?"

"Because I'm happy too, and I find it strange."

Germain was amused by this feeling of surprise. "What do you mean?"

"I should be sad, gloomy, downhearted, lacking in appetite. I miss Patricia, you know. All I want is to have her back again but, in spite of that, I feel good. My soul is at peace."

"Maybe you have no soul!"

Germain had meant it as a joke, but Hippolyte took it seriously. "Maybe . . . Do animals have souls? Do parrots and para-keets have them?"

"Most people say they don't."

"That's what it is, then . . . No wonder animals are my friends. I'm like them. Every morning is a new day."

He left Germain and went back to work. No wonder Patricia had left him. How could an intelligent woman be crazy about such a boring man?

He had to mow the lawn now. He hesitated, partly because there were lots of people on the sidewalk, drawn here by the Bidermann affair, and partly because he liked to push the machine bare-chested but didn't want Patricia to see him like this. If it was all over between them, he didn't want to feel again the way he had felt so many times on this square, knowing that not only was he being warmed by the rays of the sun but also being caressed by her eyes.

And indeed, the back of his neck was burning, as though she was there. He didn't dare turn to see if she was spying on him through her window.

"You couldn't mow instead of me, could you, Germain?"

"You're kidding. You know the handles are too high."

He had stupidly hoped that Germain wouldn't remember that. Keeping his T-shirt on, he started the motor and pulled the machine. He had only just begun when Xavière appeared, brows knitted in fury.

"Do you have to make all that noise, Hippolyte? You're stopping my flowers from growing."

Hippolyte was scared of Xavière; the delight this woman took in annoying her contemporaries was one of the mysteries he couldn't fathom. He immediately stopped the noise. "I have to, madame, otherwise the grass will take over everything."

"You call this grass, these few hairs chasing after one another? It looks more like my husband's skull than a lawn."

Hippolyte glanced at the lawn and had to admit she was right. "It's because people walk over it."

"Yes, everybody wanders around this square, and once

they've trampled the grass, they wipe their shit-stained shoes on the sidewalk outside my house. This area is becoming shit on toast. I'm going to write to the mayor."

"I have to mow, madame, I have my instructions."

He started the motor again.

She glared at him. "You would have followed any order during the war, wouldn't you?"

"Excuse me?"

"Never mind, I know what I'm talking about."

Before starting on a first strip, Hippolyte turned down the noise of the engine to ask a question. "Is it true there are flowers that stop growing if it's noisy?"

"Of course. Why do you think they play Mozart to grapes in the Bordeaux vineyards?"

Hippolyte shook his head in admiration and got down to work, full of new ideas.

As for Xavière, she smiled, delighted with what she had said; every time she spoke to Hippolyte, she loved to make up new nonsense. *Is there such a thing as immanent justice? In his case it's easy to believe: he's as stupid as he is decorative.*

By the time Hippolyte got home, Isis was back from school. She eagerly told him what she had learned that day and pulled out a list from her exercise book. "Daddy, our teacher told us to buy a calibrated ruler, a compass, and a set square. We're going to learn geometry. Brilliant, isn't it? Can you take me to the stationery shop, please?"

Hippolyte shuddered. There were two kinds of shops he hated: bookshops and stationers', because he felt out of place in them. Worse still, he felt like an impostor. He could never find what he had come to buy and would end up having to show his shopping list to the assistants, who would either spout something incomprehensible that made him even more confused, or treat him with condescension.

Germain came out from behind the oven. "I'll go. Do you mind, Isis?"

"No, that's great! Shall we walk or take the streetcar?"

"We'll walk."

"How long will you be?" Hippolyte asked, feeling defeated.

"To get to the end of Avenue Louise and back? At least an hour and a half. More likely two hours."

Once he was on his own, Hippolyte sighed. He had to use this time fruitfully. Between a girlfriend—ex-girlfriend—who devoured novels, and a daughter who couldn't get enough of them, he felt like such a snotty-nosed kid that he had decided to make up for the lost years and become a reader. So he forced himself to spend hours over books whose titles he had noticed in Patricia's apartment.

He had a shower—a tribute to the books: he never touched them unless he was clean, well shaved, and scented—put on some boxer shorts, and lay down on the bed.

Without hesitation, he grabbed, from among his ten books, the slimmest one, which was by Baptiste Monier. When she had recommended it to him, Patricia had whispered, "When you begin a story by Monier, you can't stop, you have to read to the end. He takes you by the hand and leads you. Trust him, he won't let go of you."

He opened it, hoping for the miracle. *"When I was thirteen, I smashed my piggy bank and went to visit whores."* He looked around, embarrassed. Such language! Honestly, was this literature? *"Whores."* Couldn't they have used a nicer word? And it's so unrealistic! At thirteen, you can't yet . . . Oh, actually, yes, you can . . . A little bit, anyway . . . And who was speaking? Where was it taking place? When? It would probably be mentioned later, but he'd rather know now, so that he could decide if he wanted to continue or not. He turned the book over and examined the cover. The publisher should have specified if it was a true story or if it was made up. Or if it had any true facts in it. Hippolyte was quite willing to make an effort, but what was the point if it was the product of the author's imagination?

Annoyed, he put the book down on his stomach. For the time being, he seemed doomed to disappointment. He had only just finished a mystery novel that had made him angry. He'd liked the crime at the beginning, but the investigation had dragged on: the identity of the murderer was revealed only at the end, even though the writer clearly knew who it was from the start and had concealed it for two hundred pages. That was just cheating! Even worse, she had misled Hippolyte with red herrings. If he ever had the chance to meet this Agatha Christie, he would tell her exactly what he thought of her manners: when you know something, you come out and say it!

As for the romantic novel he had tried, *La Princesse de Clèves*, he had found that long-winded too. When it came down to it, what was it all about? Some kind of Lady Diana falls in love with an aristocrat but, because she's married, she doesn't allow herself to see him, so she languishes and dies. Talk about unrealistic! Yes, there were some interesting things in the details. In the details! But you weren't going to tell him that literature was just about details!

The doorbell rang.

Thinking it was Germain or a neighbor, he went to open the door in his boxer shorts.

Patricia was standing on the landing, red-faced, out of breath, stamping her feet. "Oh!" she exclaimed, seeing him practically naked.

He didn't have time to express either surprise or joy. She suddenly turned pale, swayed, and tried to hold on to the door frame. Then her eyes rolled back and she collapsed.

Hippolyte was quick-witted enough to catch her before her knees or head hit the floor. He carried her in his arms as far as the bed, laid her down, and opened the window to let the air in, then dabbed her cheeks with a towel soaked in cold water.

Patricia opened her eyes, saw him, and seemed reassured.

"It's all right, I'm here," Hippolyte murmured.

She blinked affirmatively.

He gave her something to drink and helped her to sit up against the pillows. She was struggling to regain her strength.

"Are you sick?"

She fanned herself before replying, and the delay worried him.

"I'll call an ambulance. We're going to Emergency."

"No!" she said firmly.

He froze.

"I'm going to be all right. It's—"

"The emotion?" Hippolyte whispered, remembering their first encounter, when he had passed out on Patricia's landing.

"Maybe . . . but mostly the dieting."

Then Patricia told him everything, her hang-ups, her mood swings, her occasional weakness, her fits of temper when, to stop hating herself, she hated the whole world. He found out about the sacrifices she had imposed on herself since they had met, the way she was endangering her health.

"I wanted to tell you the truth, Hippolyte. It's not because of you that I'm breaking up with you, but because of me."

"I love you just as you are, Patricia."

"Stop it! Don't say that! I can't bear anyone to say that! I feel as if I'm being given charity, or if I'm a madwoman they're trying to calm down."

"Patricia, I love you the way you are. I don't want you to be any different."

"You have blinkers on!"

"No, I can see perfectly well."

Hippolyte explained his passion for her. Since he lacked the gift of eloquence, he expressed his adoration using his fingers and hands and eyes as well as words; even his chest, against which she had huddled, spoke, through its warmth, of his determination. This time, Patricia let herself be taken into Hippolyte's world. What could be more graceful than a plump woman's wrist? No bones, no tendons, just silky skin. You marvel at the fact that it can also be functional, that, according to doctors, it's still a joint. The thighs must be the promise of a secret: if they're skinny and far apart, they become sticks to move the skeleton, whereas when they're wide and overflowing, when they conceal what is between them, they invite caresses, kisses, myriad tender attentions designed to open them. A woman must always be something of a mother, of a nurturer, a large, powerful queen bee who would crush the half-starved males around her if she didn't inspire their devotion.

Cradled by this litany, Patricia quivered, abandoning herself more with every passing minute. When she felt him grow hard against her hip, she panicked. "Hippolyte, I haven't come to make up!"

In reply, he stroked her arms.

"Hippolyte, even if I believe you, even if you're being sincere, I have a problem being with you."

He froze. What was it? Money? No, not with Patricia . . . She was about to tell him that she thought he was stupid. She had already alluded to that when they had broken up, saying, "Look deep inside yourself and you'll understand why I'm leaving you."

"You know, I've started reading," he suddenly exclaimed.

"Really?"

"Yes. The books you told me about."

"Don't change the subject, Hippolyte."

She felt behind her back that he had lost his erection.

"My worry, if I stayed with you . . . How can I explain it? . . . Well, I guess I don't like being seen as a slut."

"Excuse me?"

"A horny woman, a woman who thinks only about fuck-ing."

"Patricia, mind your language!"

She looked at him tenderly: she often forgot how easily shocked he could be. His sensitivity to words was exquisite. This strapping lad would be incapable of singing a bawdy song, which was something Patricia did at dinner parties as soon as she'd had a few drinks.

She made an effort to be more specific. "When people see us, they'll think I'm with you because you're handsome."

"I'm not handsome."

"Yes, you are. And I know it."

"All right, let's say I am. What of it?"

"I'm not the kind of woman who lives with an Apollo."

"I really don't understand."

"Because I'm plain."

"I've just told you you're stunning, Patricia. And I'd very much like to be seen with you on my arm, because that would be a way of saying to all the other guys, 'Look at this wonder! Well, I'm the one who bagged her!'"

"This is me you're talking about?"

"Yes, of course it's you."

"I really don't understand."

He kissed her neck. She blushed and tried to protest. "Hippolyte, we're not together."

"Yes, we are. It's what you came to tell me."

He gently slipped beneath her and smiled. She felt their hunger return, hers as well as his.

They made love. The narrow bed forced them to be even gentler than usual.

For Hippolyte, this was the apotheosis of his relationship with Patricia. She had come to see him here, in a poor neigh-borhood, in this tiny studio apartment where the clutter had removed any desire for decoration, a place that did nothing to conceal his true condition, in this bed he had never dared invite a woman into, and not for a second, with either with a look or a word, had she judged or belittled him.

As for Patricia, she had come to hear what she had already guessed: that he loved her in a totally lucid way, and wanted her as she was. For someone who had so little love for herself, there was something dizzying about this revelation, and she shook constantly as she reached her climax.

As if drunk, they rested after their lovemaking, staring up at the cracked ceiling, which seemed to them as sumptuous as the fresco of a Venetian palazzo.

"What gave you the courage to come here?" Hippolyte asked.

"Your letter, of course."

"My letter?"

"The yellow letter telling me you'd wait for me all your life and that I was blind not to see your love. Like last time, you signed it 'You know who.'"

He slowly sat up. He felt sure enough of himself and of her to reveal the truth. "Patricia, I didn't write that letter. Or the previous one."

"What?"

"I swear. Those two letters have played a decisive role, they've brought us together, but I want you to know that I wasn't the one who wrote them."

Patricia leaned pensively on her elbow. "Then . . . " She gave a little laugh. "Then it was him."

Hippolyte frowned. "Excuse me?"

"He's the one who writes them. I thought he was simply your messenger when I saw him run off down the street the other day after the message was slipped under my door."

"Who?"

"Germain, of course. He didn't just deliver the letter, he wrote it."

I'm sad about leaving you, Singer."

Sitting embarrassed on the edge of his desk, Zachary Bidermann looked down at his stubby hands and saw that brown age spots were beginning to appear. He hid them behind his back.

"Yes, Singer, we're to part after working together for twenty years."

Concealing her emotion, Madame Singer turned to look at Place d'Arezzo. Through the open windows, she could see couples of adult parrots stooping tenderly over their offspring.

Throughout her life, she had dreaded this scene, the moment when she would have to part company with the great man. Some days, she had imagined herself organizing a magnificent party to celebrate his retirement; on other days, she had pictured a very simple, dignified, respectful ceremony; at yet other times, tearful farewells. Instead of which, it was happening at dawn, behind closed doors, and he was letting her go for financial reasons, with only the indifferent birds as witnesses.

"I have very much valued your devotion, your energy, and your professionalism."

Right, my stupidity! Madame Singer thought. *I never imagined he was lying to me, or that he pounced on anything that moved.* Discovering that her boss, who had always behaved so well to her, had had all those women was upsetting to Singer, both as a secretary and as a woman. She couldn't help thinking that he had cheated on her as well as his wife: not only had he concealed the truth from her, but he had acted toward her with a decency that verged on the insulting. The laughter of those to whom, outraged by the journalists' accusations after the arrest, she had stated that she knew no man more respectful than her employer still echoed in her ears. Oh, yes, she understood that laughter all too well. It meant that she wasn't the kind of woman a man could desire.

In full flow now, Zachary Bidermann continued to talk in his deep, slightly guttural, seductive voice about all they had accomplished together. Singer shuddered. Who was this talking to her? The intellectual she had admired for twenty years? Or the pleasure-seeking, violent, contemptuous libertine who used women shamelessly? She couldn't imagine the two coexisting, let alone that these two contrasting beings could together constitute the truth about Zachary Bidermann.

Guessing what was upsetting her, Zachary cut the meeting short and walked her to the door, taking care not to touch her; ever since this story had exploded, he, who used to be so tactile, had been making sure he didn't grab an arm, seize a shoulder, or stroke a cheek, rather like a teacher suspected of being a pedophile.

Luckily, the phone rang on his desk, which allowed him to cut the goodbyes short. Singer disappeared down the hallway and Zachary ran to the telephone. Unused to picking it up himself, he answered, breathless, "Yes?"

"Bidermann? It's Léo Adolf."

"Good morning, Léo."

"Er . . . I was just calling to ask where you can be reached in case—"

"In case what? I have no more responsibilities! You made me resign from my post as European Competition Commissioner, I've been expelled from the Party, and I've been kindly informed that I'm no longer a member of any of the boards I used to sit on. And I haven't even had my trial yet! So let me repeat the question, Léo: in case what?"

"The thing is, Zachary, decades of political work can't just be dismissed like that."

"Yes, they can. That's exactly what's happened to me."

"Or decades of political friendship . . . "

There was a pause. Zachary Bidermann was so disgusted, he couldn't summon up the energy to respond. What was the point of speaking if you weren't being heard?

Léo Adolf was surprised. "Hello? Hello? Zachary, are you still there?"

"I don't know. Why are you calling me?"

"You and Rose are separating. I've been told you're moving out. I wanted to—"

"Are you ashamed?"

"Excuse me?"

"Are you ashamed of dumping me?"

"Are you out of your mind? Ashamed? If anybody should be ashamed, it's you, not me! I didn't rape anyone. I didn't discredit the political class. I didn't fuel people's hatred toward their leaders. I didn't sabotage my country. You've landed us in the shit, Zachary, first because we had high expectations of you, both for Europe and as the leader of Belgium, and second because we're suspected—we, your political friends—of having covered up your shenanigans. God only knows how many times I warned you. And now the media are looking for the next politician to denounce, anyone who's abused his power to steal from the cash box, screw women, perhaps even screw whole countries."

"Stop your whining, Léo! You're making no sense. You've turned me into a scapegoat, and I'm paying for all of you, so you don't have to worry. It's as if you've acquired five years of virtue by pointing the finger at vice. Who profits from this business? By blackening me, you've cleaned yourselves up and come out white as snow. And you dare complain? And to me?"

"You need treatment, Zachary. I don't think you realize you committed a crime. You raped a woman! While your own wife was just a few yards away, throwing a party in your honor, you forced yourself on a poor woman! For heaven's sake, stop acting the victim! You're the aggressor."

Zachary Bidermann shrugged. He hated this version of the facts.

Taking his silence for an act of contrition, Léo Adolf assumed he had got through to Zachary and softened his tone. "What are you going to do for the next few weeks?"

"Give lectures. Several universities around the world consider me to be an expert on the world economy. They don't think the tribulations of my penis affect my intellectual abilities. Fortunate, don't you think?"

Actually, Zachary was lying. Several universities had cancelled his lectures, either because the teaching staff had demanded it, or because groups of students—female students, especially—had protested, with banners held high, that they refused to listen to a pervert. In an attempt to counter this campaign, Zachary had written an article entitled *The Puritans and their Extermination Camps*, in which he denounced the confusion of competence with conventional morality. In his opinion, American puritan ideology was trying to standardize the planet, impose its own model of bland morality, and only promote standard individuals to important positions. "And yet," Zachary Bidermann wrote, "the world's history is bursting with libertines who were an asset to their people and puritans who destroyed them. Who would you choose, the chaste Hitler or the free Churchill? There is nothing to indicate that intelligence, a sense of responsibility, an ability to make brilliant hypotheses are the exclusive prerogative of good fathers who are faithful to their wives. On the contrary . . . Before this

scandal besmirched my name, millions of people went to sleep at night believing I was a good economist; overnight I became incompetent. Where's the connection? You don't have to share my lifestyle, you may even disapprove of some of my excesses, but you cannot kill the whole man, his career, his studies, his thoughts, his expertise because of one detail. The attitude of my critics is reminiscent of the worst days in History, when Nazis would condemn music because it had been composed by Jews, burn Jewish literature, Jewish philosophy, Jewish science, and then despoil Jews of their wealth. These racists considered just one element of a man: his Jewishness, which was enough to condemn the rest of him. Unfortunately, we know how far this rejection went: since a Jew must no longer breathe or reproduce, it was off to the death camps with them! These days, pouting and putting their hands on their hearts, protesting their virtuous intentions, puritans engage in the same kind of extermination! Whether a Nazi or a puritan, a fascist is still a fascist. The devil is good at changing his appearance . . . "
Alas, this virulent piece only succeeded in alienating his remaining bastions of support: Jewish associations, which immediately denounced the connection Zachary made between the Holocaust and his personal troubles. As a result, contrary to what he claimed, Zachary had been asked to deliver his analyses only by the rejects of the system, the extremists of Right and Left, people whose spokesperson he would never have wanted to be in the past . . .

"Where are you going to live?" Léo Adolf asked.

"I have a villa in the Ardennes. I inherited it from my father."

"Alone?"

"For the time being."

"Give me your contact details."

"I don't have them handy," Zachary Bidermann lied. "I'll send them to you."

Léo Adolf pretended to believe him.

"I'll see you soon, I hope, Zachary. And please, from now on, whatever you decide to do, keep a low profile. Remember the proverb 'The nail that sticks out will be hammered down.'"

Zachary sighed and hung up, regretting that one of the most unpleasant aspects of his new situation was that everybody seemed to think it their right to give him advice on how he should behave. Then he quickly thought over what he still had to do this morning: the files from his office having already been packed by Singer, all that remained for him was to make sure that the servants on the private floor had finished putting his clothes into protective covers and to gather his own personal effects.

So he went up into his bedroom, where open cupboards revealed empty shelves. Rose was out. Zachary couldn't work out whether she was being tactful to ease his departure, or whether it was yet another sign of her indifference to him.

In the bathroom his wife had assigned him, he pulled out his belongings: razor, creams, shampoos . . . He tore out a hair that was protruding from his ear, then urinated.

Surrounded by mirrors, he saw his reflection, an elderly, overweight man with his penis in his hands. Was this the man who had set off a media storm? How absurd! He held his penis in his palm and examined it: it was wrinkled, amorphous, with purplish skin. Was this what that had destroyed his ambitions? This misshapen thing? This appendage that had ceased to be functional? For a moment, he felt so wretched that he pressed his forehead against the tiled wall to avoid swaying.

He hadn't used his cock for weeks. In police custody, he had refrained from touching it, fearing he would substantiate the erotic obsession he was accused of. On his release, he hadn't dared either pleasure himself or call a prostitute. Even within the four walls of the bathroom, he felt as if eyes or cameras were watching him, or as if a female judge might leap out at any moment, wag her finger, and shout, "It's him! Look what the pig is doing!" The pressure of fear had replaced sexual pressure. As for Rose, she hadn't wanted him anywhere near her and had exiled him to a guest room, the smallest one there was, right up in the attic. When he had begged her forgiveness, she had looked away. Rose loved him as a winner, not as a penitent or a casualty. Besides, since that woman Diane—who was she, anyway?—had come between them, Rose and Zachary had been living like strangers under the same roof, on different floors, aware that they must avoid each other.

He heard someone clearing their throat outside the door. Zachary buttoned himself up and came out. It was the butler, who informed him that "a young lady" wanted to see him.

Surprised, Zachary demanded to know her name.

"You won't know it. But she told me she was sure you would recognize her."

Zachary tried to decipher the butler's thoughts beneath his deadpan expression: he must be imagining it was one of his mistresses. Was he wrong?

"Ask her to wait in my former office, Benoît, I'm coming down."

Inscrutable as he was, the butler blinked at the mention of the "former office," which suggested that Zachary's departure was imminent.

Zachary put his last few things in a bag and, five minutes later, went downstairs.

As he walked in, a young woman stood up, clutching her hands to her stomach, shoulders slumped, as if crushed by the protocol of this mansion.

"Mademoiselle?"

Embarrassed, she tilted her head to one side and stared at him with dark-ringed eyes. He recognized her: it was the waitress he had followed down to the cellar on that fatal evening.

She knew he had placed her.

They looked at each other, both standing motionless, trying to get used to each other, then Zachary regained his composure, asked her to sit down, and walked behind his desk, fiddling with his cell phone.

She sat down, placed her bag on her lap, her body tense and contained, as if she was waiting on an uncomfortable seat for a bus. At last she took the initiative. "I've been following it all on TV."

"You have?"

"I saw that woman who claims that . . . At first, I didn't know why she was doing that, because nothing happened to her, she was just hiding in a corner, watching. I even thought at first she'd intervened out of a concern for justice. Then I worked it out. She's an artist, an ambitious woman, she took advantage of the situation to get everybody talking about her. Now she's famous. I hate her."

She spoke monotonously, in a flat, thin, pitchless voice, with no particular emphasis or passion in her words. It was as if she was reciting a shopping list, not referring to a terrible event that had marked her deeply.

As a way of encouraging her, Zachary Bidermann smiled.

"I've been thinking," she went on. "If you like, I'll tell the police it was me."

"You'd do that?"

"I'll do even better than that. I'll tell them she stole my handkerchief. And especially that you and I, when we . . . did it, we agreed. That I consented."

She had uttered these words looking down at her shoes. She was forcing herself to speak a text she had prepared. Had she trained herself to go through with a scene that went against her self-effacing nature?

"Why would you do that?"

She raised her head and looked at a spot next to him. "For money, of course."

He nodded. "Everything belongs to my wife. I don't have all that much money."

"But you have more than me!" She had lost her reticence. Poverty, trying to make ends meet, bare cupboards and closets, lack of secure accommodation: none of that was abstract. Her cry came from a place of genuine pain.

"How much?" Zachary murmured.

She swallowed and made every effort to be brave and, this time, look him straight in the eye. "One million euros."

He nodded again. One million euros? It was possible . . . He looked her up and down briefly. Was there someone putting her up to this? A boyfriend? A brother? Someone who had advised her to come here, someone who'd made her rehearse this scene? Or was she here on her own initiative?

Never mind. She was giving him the opportunity to get rid of his adversary, Petra von Tannenbaum, who would be seen for the liar she had always been. If the girl denied it had been rape, then he would come out of the trial with his head held high, his rights restored.

That was certainly worth one million euros.

But what would he have left afterwards? Not a penny. As for his positions, as European Competition Commissioner and as Rose's husband, he would never recover them. Not to mention the jackpot of being prime minister . . . Politically, he was dead. "I refuse," he declared.

Startled, she bit her lip, leaned forward, and murmured, "If you want, I can do it for less."

"One million euros or less, I won't pay."

"But—"

"It's my final word."

She looked around nervously. "So what I suggest isn't acceptable to you?"

"It doesn't matter."

"What do you mean, it doesn't matter?"

"It doesn't."

She stood up and cried feverishly, "Well, too bad. I'll go anyway and tell them what really happened. I want the truth to come out. Why does everyone always have to take everything from me? You who . . . and that German woman who's playing at being a victim instead of me. I'm going to report both of you, the liar and the bastard."

"You'll be making a lot of effort for nothing. Nobody will believe you."

"Why not?"

"Because if the first accuser can be proved to be a liar, it'll be easy to say so's the second one."

"Really?"

"It'll be a walkover for an experienced lawyer. Especially since I've recorded our conversation on my phone . . . " He brandished his cell phone. "All I have to do is produce the beginning of the tape, where you offer to state for money that it was you, not Petra von Tannenbaum. You'll look like a blackmailer."

"That's disgusting!" the young woman shouted.

Zachary Bidermann didn't reply.

She looked around for a way to hold back the emotion that was overwhelming her. She was shaking, her eyes had turned red, and her teeth were chattering. "So they've taken everything from me, I've been made to do something I didn't want to, I've been forced to do disgusting stuff just because I'm a lousy servant, my life is stolen from me, even my problems, nobody wants to give me a cent . . . and they won't even listen to me when I tell the truth? Well, I guess I'm worth nothing. Nothing at all. Nobody gives a shit about my life, about what I feel or say . . . " She looked up at Zachary Bidermann with tear-filled eyes. "It's ugly!" She swallowed the snot that was choking her. "Life's really ugly!"

On an abrupt impulse, she picked up her bag and almost ran out of the room.

Zachary Bidermann went to the window. The girl was crossing Place d'Arezzo, her shoulders hunched, her face buried in a handkerchief, her cheap bag flapping about on her arm, small, awkward, graceless, a victim of everything, her birth, her poverty, society, men . . .

He suddenly panicked. Patches of heat radiated through his body. What was the matter with him? With a trembling hand, he wiped the sweat from his forehead. Was he about to faint? Was he having a heart attack?

He sat at his desk, drank a glass of cold water, and tried to steady his breathing.

Yes, he was getting better. His body wasn't letting him down. He breathed.

His mind was filled with the image of the young woman, all-consuming, obsessive. "It's disgusting!" she had cried. "They've taken everything from me."

For the first time, Zachary Bidermann realized he had raped a woman. Yes, she was his prey and he the hunter. He had used her like an insignificant object, just so that he could soothe an itch that was ruining his evening. Forcing her to touch his cock, to make him come, hadn't seemed monstrous to him at the time—it had given him pleasure—even though he knew the act didn't correspond to any desire or logic in the young woman's life. *I'm a bastard!* He was becoming aware of his crime. Before, he had thought only about himself, his flattering idea of himself. Before, he had attacked his accusers, not imagining for a second that he could have committed a bad act himself, not he, not the brilliant Zachary, not the genius Zachary, not the pleasure-seeker the weaker sex liked so much.

His throat was constricted with anguish. He took a breath of air, undid his tie and his top button. He needed air. He needed to escape himself, to flee this intolerable sense of guilt. He wandered around his office as if floating, empty, poor, disgusted, sick. Reality was no longer bearable.

"Benoît, I'm going out for a stroll. I'll be back."

He had to leave this grand town house where he had strutted for years, even up to a few seconds earlier. He unbolted the door and hurtled down the stairs.

The air was like a slap in the face. Zachary suddenly felt scared, scared of the city, of the cars, of the noisy motorcycles, of the silent bicycles. Was he familiar with these sidewalks? He felt like a newborn baby. Everything surprised and frightened him. He had lost his bearings.

He who had never seen danger now saw it everywhere. Inside him as well as outside. What could he do? He was terrified, shaking more than a leaf.

Walk! Yes, walk to clear his head.

He walked quickly. Crossing the street, he looked up, startled, at a blue macaw who was defending his nest from an aggressive crow. At that split second, he didn't see the truck charging at full speed onto Place d'Arezzo, and fell headlong beneath its five tons of steel.

POSTLUDE
LUX PERPETUA

On the brightest day of the year, the summer solstice, the residents of Place d'Arezzo were in the habit of organizing a "neighborhood party." Under the trees, amid the blooming rhododendrons, each person would bring his or her own choice of food or drink. Some would bring pies, pizzas, cakes, or salads, others punch, wine, fruit juice, or beer. They would set up folding tables, open canvas chairs, plug in a stereo in this makeshift, open-air living room, and, lulled by a melodious sunset, the local residents would take the place of the birds and watch the theater provided by the façades from the vantage point of the parrots.

The arrangement of the houses, though, was reflected, unchanged in the arrangement of the people: the villas on one side and the apartment blocks on the other. The rich toasted with the rich, the less well-off with the less well-off, the young kept to the young. Social classes, cliques with shared interests, and age-related communities would be reproduced on the grass.

There were those who stuck to their group, like Quentin with his pals, and Albane with her girlfriends—a habit from childhood—in the secret hope of joining other groups later. Some came in couples, like Victor and Oxana, who were inseparable now. Some kept to themselves, like Baptiste, Joséphine, and Isabelle, who were roaring with laughter over a bottle of Burgundy, forming a cluster it would have been difficult to break up. They were probably trying to avoid Faustina and

Patrick Breton-Mollignon, who were coming closer and look-ing for an excuse to interrupt them. Zachary Bidermann's death had changed Rose's habits: in previous years, she had sent a crate of champagne accompanied by a note excusing her absence. This time, though, she was mixing with the throng, in the company of Diane, who introduced her husband Jean-Noël. Ève had joined Ludo and Claudine on a sunbed, where they were sharing not just space but a joint. A little farther on, Philippe Dentremont, his wife Odile at his side, watched them with a mixture of disapproval and envy. On the central path, François-Maxime de Couvigny had organized a game of bowls with his children, and had been joined by Patricia and Hippolyte. Wim had only dropped by for five minutes, volu-ble, eager to please, apologizing a hundred times for being unable to stay, leaving behind, as his ambassador, the smiling Meg with boxes of chocolates that she offered everyone, mak-ing sure she also helped herself to them. As for Tom and Nathan, they had decided to contribute by setting up a barbe-cue: and here was Nathan handing Marcelle a grilled merguez sausage with the comment, "Sausages are my specialty." Already flushed from the punch, Marcelle shed a little tear at the thought that Mademoiselle Beauvert was not among them this year, although she was lucky enough to be living in Washington, with Obama.

A little earlier, Xavière and Orion had created a sensation. To everyone's surprise, they had crossed the square, proud, regal, she with her protuberant belly clothed in a maternity dress, he as attentive as a fly buzzing around her: anyone would have thought they had invented pregnancy. Once they had created their effect, Xavière had feigned dizziness so that they could go home.

On a bench to one side, the dwarf Germain and lilac-eyed Isis were talking in hushed tones.

"Why did you ask me to take a letter to Patricia?"

"Well, as you saw, it worked a treat. Thanks to the letter, Daddy and Patricia are together again."

"What was in the letter?"

"Part of my novel."

"What novel?"

"The one I'm writing."

"Really? How far are you with it? I never see you writing it. Which exercise book are you using?"

"I'm not writing it in an exercise book."

"In what, then?"

She indicated the world around then, the façades, the guests, then said, "I'm not exactly writing it, actually. I only thought of the beginning. Then I stopped because I got scared."

"Scared of what?"

"Of the characters. They don't do what I expected. They act in their own way. They're strange. I don't understand them."

"Why not?"

"They get a love letter and aren't pleased. None of them react the same way." Isis looked up at the parrots and parakeets and sighed. "It's a pity. I just wanted them to be happy."

"How do you know they're not? For them, happiness isn't the same thing as it is for you. I think there are as many different kinds of happiness as there are people." He stood up solemnly, like an acrobat about to perform a circus trick. "Look." The dwarf Germain approached Isis, stood up on tiptoe, and gave her a delicate kiss on the forehead. Then he made an authoritative gesture. "Your turn, now."

Amused, Isis jumped off the bench and placed a kiss in the middle of Germain's forehead.

"You agree that it's the same action, don't you?" he said.

"Yes."

"The same kiss?"

"Yes."

"Except that they're different for you and me."

"Of course. It was your idea, and I did as I was told."

"Not just that. Which did you prefer—the one you gave me or the one I gave you?"

"The first one, the one you gave me. I was surprised. I thought it was kind, and I was delighted. What about you?"

"The first one too, but for a different reason. For me, giving you a kiss is more important that getting one because of the way I look, because of my history . . . Do you understand now why you're having so much trouble with your love story? In spite of appearances, given the same action, nobody feels or expects exactly the same thing."

Isis nodded gravely, grabbed her bag, took out sheets of yellow letter paper, and threw them into the square garbage can.

"What are you doing?" Germain exclaimed.

"I've had enough of my novel."

About the Author

Eric-Emmanuel Schmitt is one of Europe's most popular and acclaimed authors and playwrights. His many novels and story collections include *The Most Beautiful Book in the World* (Europa, 2009), *Oscar & the Lady in Pink,* and *Monsieur Ibrahim and the Flowers of the Koran.* A keen music lover, Schmitt has also translated into French *The Marriage of Figaro* and *Don Giovanni* from the original Italian. In 2001, he was awarded the French Academy's Grand Prix du Théâtre. Schmitt divides his time between Paris, France, and Belgium.